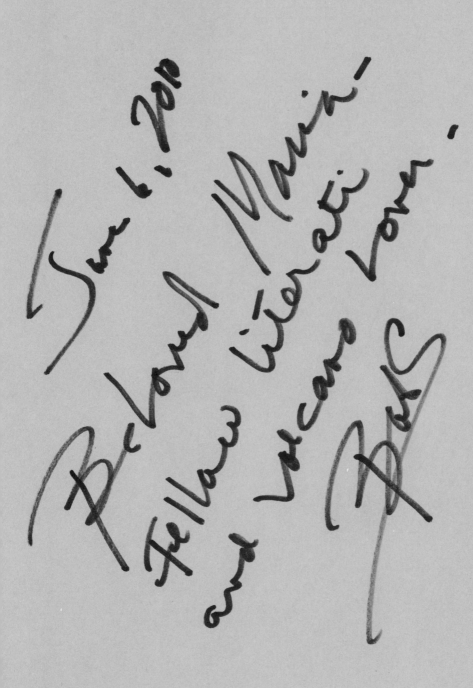

June 6, 2010

Beloved Maria —

Fellow literati

and welcome home —

Bob

SWIMMING IN THE VOLCANO

SWIMMING IN THE VOLCANO

A NOVEL

Bob Shacochis

Charles Scribner's Sons
New York

Maxwell Macmillan Canada
Toronto

Maxwell Macmillan International
New York Oxford Singapore Sydney

Charles Scribner's Sons
Macmillan Publishing Company
866 Third Avenue
New York, NY 10022

Maxwell Macmillan Canada, Inc.
1200 Eglinton Avenue East
Suite 200
Don Mills, Ontario M3C 3N1

Macmillan Publishing Company is part of the Maxwell Communication Group of Companies.

Excerpts from the following work have appeared in *Intro, Vogue, GQ, Outside,* and *Clockwatch Review.*

The author wishes to express his gratitude to the Florida Arts Council and the American Academy and Institute of Arts and Letters for their generous and timely support.

The author gratefully acknowledges permission to reprint excerpts from the following works:

Heather McHugh, "Have or Love" and "The Ghost" from *To the Quick,* copyright 1987 by Heather McHugh.

Julian Evans, *Transit of Venus: Travels in the Pacific,* Copyright © 1992 by Julian Evans. Reprinted by permission of Pantheon Books.

The Never-Ending by Andrew Hudgins. Copyright © 1991 by Andrew Hudgins. Reprinted by permission of Houghton Mifflin Co. All rights reserved.

Library of Congress Cataloging-in Publication Data
Shacochis, Bob.
    Swimming in the volcano : a novel / Bob Shacochis.
       p. cm.
    ISBN 0-684-19260-8
    I. Title.
    PS3569.H284S94   1993
    813'.54—dc20   92-37116   CIP

10 9 8 7 6 5 4 3 2 1

Printed in the United States of America

Author's Note

The trilevel presentation of an imaginary West Indian dialect (provincial, standardized provincial, standard) is an intentional—and, the writer hopes, comprehensible—act of bridging between popular and conventional usage.

SWIMMING IN THE VOLCANO

Prologue

September 1976

On the northern end of the Caribbean island of St. Catherine, there is an active volcano, Mount Soufrière. Dormant since its last eruption in 1902, its massive crater had collected a brown hot lake of tropical rains, and magma formed a fiery island within the lake in a gradual reawakening not many years ago. La Soufrière, as if aware of her accelerating metamorphosis from beauty to beast, had been increasingly moody, an unpredictable and worrisome neighbor to the island's citizens. The government of St. Catherine responded by establishing a monitoring station, and the Ministry of Agriculture was prompted to send a man up Soufrière, the forest ranger Godfred Ballantyne, on a weekly basis to check the equipment housed on the volcano's rim.

Several months after the American economist Mitchell Wilson had been assigned to the ministry, he expressed an interest in seeing the volcano himself, and the chief agricultural officer arranged for Ballantyne to take the American up the mountain with him.

From the outskirts of Queenstown, the capital at the bottom of the island, they drove recklessly northward for over thirty miles, the Land Rover straining on a broken roadway of switchbacks and climbs, the flank of the volcano and its cloud-smothered peak sometimes in sight, rising glorious from the monotonous spread of jungle and surrounded by her court, the lesser mountains of the north. They stopped once, flagged to the roadside at Camell by apologetic national police, confident men, vain in their uniforms, leopard fatigues and burgundy berets. Their papers were examined and returned by the officer in charge, who joked with the forest ranger Ballantyne, talking to him as if he were a medical doctor assigned La Soufrière as a patient, and acknowledged his white passenger with a perfunctory salute.

Two hours out from the city, they turned inland until the dirt road they bounced over ended in a breezy plantation of coconut palms. Wheel tracks flattened the underbrush ahead, two pale compressed lines that burrowed from sight within yards, and Ballantyne downshifted into their channel and drove ahead until the right front wheel slammed into an unseen hole. Wilson's hand flew up to keep himself from banging into the windshield.

"Ahlright," Ballantyne said, and decisively set the emergency brake on the incline. Even after he had removed the key and pocketed it, the engine continued to stutter before it died with a pop. The fumes of the overheated engine filled the cab of the Rover, stinging Wilson's eyes and increasing the nausea he felt from the ride which was like being on a rowboat in open water. Ballantyne laid a hand on the white man's shoulder. When he realized the hand had no message to deliver, Wilson looked at it sideways, puzzled.

Ballantyne was an iron-muscled man, not large but stoutly built, possessing a rugger player's body best suited for pushing through walls of opponents. He leaned across the seat to make a show of scrutinizing the shoes on Wilson's feet. Then the ranger took his hand away and sat back, one thick arm draped on the steering wheel, still looking at Wilson, sizing him up, the white man becoming embarrassed by the close attention paid him, Ballantyne's sober eyes so clearly focused on his basic worth.

"What are we doing?"

"You cy-ahn run?" the ranger asked plainly. He glanced at his gold wristwatch.

From where they were in the palms the path to the volcano's summit rose more than four thousand feet in six miles, sometimes at a grade equal to a stepladder's, through lowland jungle, strands of bamboo and waist-high begonia, tropical rain forest, high elevation scrub, devil cane and grasses canyoned by old lava flows, then fields of perpetually glistening ferns before the cinder wasteland of the crown. Wilson thought the man was joking.

Ballantyne smiled, and his smile was a subtle transformation that domesticated him. "You believe so?" he said. He bounded out of the Rover and was running before Wilson could say another word.

In the first hour of their ascent Wilson was able to stay with him. The second hour, as the slope became more slippery and precarious, the ranger would be out of sight for long intervals, his head eventually visible, bobbing through the flora several hundred yards up the trail. The weather changed from steamy to temperate, then chilled blasts of wind caught them as they came out of the forest onto the austere scarps and ridges where nothing tall could grow. For the final half hour he could see Ballantyne far ahead of him when the clouds permitted, loping across the dark lava and through the scrub onto the ugly cone, going up and up and up.

Wilson's clothes were clinging wet from sweat and sudden rain-showers by the time he reached the top, twenty minutes behind Ballantyne. The quick swirl of clouds provided minimum visibility—he knew that they were at elevation primarily because Ballantyne was no longer running, he had stopped and was waiting for him, his back sheltered against an outcropping of twisted rock to escape the cold gusts. Wilson sat down next to him, huddling into the same rift, feeling not so much in the tropics as in the Scottish highlands in April. The flood of mist rolled by at arm's length in front of them, swift and horizontal.

From his haversack the forest ranger rummaged out two sugar apples. As he bit into one with large teeth, he offered the other to Wilson. Because he was disoriented and beginning to wear down, Wilson's gaze lingered stupidly on the open bag in the dirt, seeing but not registering its remaining contents. The apple remained in front of him in the air, its skin vividly saffron in the black man's grip, the only color at the top of La Soufrière. Ballantyne raised his eyebrows and shrugged, dropping the fruit into Wilson's lap. Wilson picked it up and nibbled at its sweetness as they waited together in the dripping rocks with no thoughts to share, until the cloud they were inside of passed along so that they might have a view of what was below.

In time, as if the light around them came from candles surging with a fresh draft, the gloom brightened and the nimbostratus that was on the mountain began to drag off the far rim and tear into pieces, first a white edge of sunlight, then a distant patch of milky blue that was both sea and sky, next the circling shape of the burnt crown, and then, as though a lid had been pried and removed, the immense bore of the volcano's crater, shattering any sense of human proportion.

To Wilson, the scale seemed borrowed from another world—a fantasy land of fire giants, a geography more dreamlike and therefore more threatening than it actually appeared or was. The light spilled into the huge bowl and they could see across the span of the vent almost a mile to the sheer walls of the opposite side. There was no slope, only a raw precipice of rock that dropped straight for hundreds of feet to the surface of a doomed lake. The interior island appeared

3

incongruous, inappropriate and trashy, as if somehow an old coal barge had been abandoned here in the eye of disaster, the cargo still smoldering in the hold, latent, a glowing seedbed that would one day blossom with a ferocity that no one could imagine. Gliding down into the crater, a frigate bird rocketed skyward as it encountered the thermals above the island.

They were standing on the east rim. Looking down underneath the ceiling of staggered cumulus that had replaced the mist, Wilson could turn and see the ocean on all but the southern horizon. From here, he understood how manageable a country became when one looked down on it from a great height, and he understood that coming to St. Catherine from the United States produced the same effect in his thinking.

The wind began to blow again, throwing a sandy ash into their faces. They jogged along the rock-strewn edge of the cavity to the southwest rim where a small concrete blockhouse contained sensor instruments. Wilson felt exhilarated. The earth had become grotesquely exaggerated, and although there was no danger, it seemed that if by chance he were to lose his footing on this crest above the green jungles and the smoky hole, only the most extreme of fates awaited his fall, glory or perdition, lightness or darkness. There would be nothing halfway about the consequence.

Ballantyne continued running past the turnoff trail that cut across a rough knoll to the monitoring station. Eighteen months ago someone had mashed up the instruments soon after they were installed by a group of scientists from four nations, but no one outside the ministry was supposed to know this, though, of course, everyone did. The vandalism, pointless as it was, was easy for Wilson to imagine. The islanders seemed to have an unlimited capacity for petty rage as well as ecstasy, the schizophrenic fevers of the tropics.

Ballantyne's job, readjusted to this circumstance, was to measure the height of the water in the lake and record its temperature. Wilson didn't see how anybody could get down to the floor of the crater without rapelling gear. But there was a vague path stepped into the wall where the rim dipped and flattened in the southwest quadrant. It was very steep, yet passable, the ranger said, so down they went.

Soufrière was the name given to the mountain by the French when they came ashore three centuries ago. The word meant sulfur and Wilson inhaled strong sour puffs of it. The trail plunged, tightly traversing unsettled rock and crumbling soil, jagging around brittle igneous fingers of stone, and it demanded more strength and concentration than the running had. From their new vantage point Wilson saw that underneath a fractured crust, the top of the island was a furnace of orange cinders. They reached bottom, standing on a shelf of piled ellipsoidal rock that was younger than they were. *Ground zero.* Wilson tried to visualize the mountain shuddering and dancing, heaving up in one convulsion that would deafen everything of lesser existence and shake the island to its prehistoric foundation. Its single thunderous message would be delivered in supernatural fires, a heat that was both the end and the beginning, the destruction, as much the creation, of the world—but it was impossible to imagine such an event. The problem again was one of proportion, and of elemental propensity. Human beings controlled their own affairs. Mountains did not explode. No other logic led to the future.

Ballantyne checked the water level. Despite a constant replenishment by storms, the level had been receding at the rate of two inches per week for several months, which Ballantyne took for a sign that the core was heating up. That such a phenomenon was being understood in simple schoolroom fashion impressed Wilson. The forestry ranger stooped on the incline of the shore with what looked like a meat thermometer to take a reading. Ninety-two degrees Fahrenheit. He sat down in the coarse, spurlike gravel, unlaced and removed his dusty boots, peeled his socks, and then stripped completely, finally pulling off his wristwatch and setting it atop his shirt. Ballantyne was going out to the base of the inner island for another reading, its nearest point about a hundred-yard swim from where they were. He approached the water cautiously but then threw himself in, executing a dive that placed the impact fully on his chest, his head remaining doglike above the surface. Wilson removed his own clothes and went with him.

The water, the color of murky old tea, smelled foul and felt oily and dense, hard to stay afloat in, currentless but not calm. Wilson had not realized he was exerting himself beyond his limits. Water came into his mouth, a bitter mustard taste, and he gagged and spit it back out. Breaststroking through the spa of the lake's warmth, he began to experience vertigo, his muscles growing weightless. He frightened himself into clawing ahead the last few yards to where Ballantyne rested belly-deep on the black tailings of the island. The rocks were all small; none appeared too heavy to lift, and each had precise edges, as if it had been broken by prisoners with sledgehammers, a tableau still seen in St. Catherine's quarries. The rubble rose in an abrupt bank twenty-five feet above them.

"Should we be out here?" Wilson gasped, trying to control his breathing. It was apparent to him that there must be some risk in swimming out to the island, for Ballantyne's movements, slow and careful and alert, were the physical clichés of impending trouble.

Ballantyne wagged a finger, dismissing any breach of faith in his judgment. "Only watch you doan slip into La Soufrière's arse," he said, holding the thermometer underwater with his other hand. He told Wilson not to try to climb on the island, to move with eyes in his feet along the pitch of the slanting bottom so he wouldn't start a slide that would bury them together, poaching their bodies like fish in a kettle. The right side of his body was submerged up to his shoulder, invisible directly below the surface. Ballantyne suggested to Wilson that he stick his hand down into the rocks as he was doing, and Wilson wiggled his fingers into a cleft until the tips were scalded.

Cookin nice, no?

They paddled back, worked themselves into the discomfort of their wet clothes, and started out of the crater after Ballantyne had made notations in his logbook. The forest ranger hopped ahead of him from foothold to foothold like a young ram. Using his hands with almost every step, his boots searching for traction through the surface layer of lapilli, Wilson crawled tenuously up the side, thinking this must be what it feels like to be stuck halfway up a skyscraper. His last energy shivered out of him with each fresh gust of wind. Ballantyne was waiting for him at the top but began to run again as Wilson pulled himself out of the hole. After several feeble strides Wilson halted, his exhaustion absolute, without even the desire to go on. Ballantyne saw him lie down in the cinders and trotted back.

"What the hell are you running for? I can't do it."

Ballantyne hovered over him, a flat silhouette against the blue wash, as laconic as a god. "I'm in trainin," he said. "You see?"

Wilson stared up, trying to comprehend this notion through his light-headedness. He felt out in space, claustrophobic as a lost diver from the lack of oxygen. He closed his eyes, willing the dizziness to subside.

"For what?" he finally asked.

"What you mean *fah what*? Fah de day when she blow. When La Soufrière blow."

Part I

Forgiveness is based on the fact that there is no adequate form of revenge.

CHARLES NEWMAN

Chapter 1

Start here, on Mount Windsor, locally known as Ooah Mountain, where the brakes went out on *Miss Defy*, Isaac's taxi, on the way to pick up Johnnie at the airport. Isaac stomped the floor pedal at that bleak moment of discovery as if it were attached to a bass drum, and he turned to look at Mitchell for solace, his eyes glazed with a fear that was altogether theological in depth.

"Serious mahl-function takin place, Wilson."

They had just crested the mountain in the old Comet and there was no going back. The Comet, a mostly red vehicle, had survived more than a half-dozen owners known to Isaac, and, having been imported from Newark long ago, a variety of climates and the traffic of two distinct worlds and automotive practices. If there was a limit to the Comet's tenacity, an inevitable challenge to its lifespan, this seemed to be it. They had only begun the two-mile descent toward Brandon Vale and the airport when the brake pedal squirted fluid down onto Isaac's ankle the first time he tapped it—a viscous, chocolaty coconut oil which a mechanic friend of Isaac's assured him had the correct hydraulic properties and could be substituted for the real stuff, no longer available on the island for a reason nobody even bothered to analyze. Section by section, level by level, the two-lane road turned to admire itself as it somersaulted down the mountain, a crooked series of highway acrobatics, dodges, and loops, uncoiling from the jungled chute at the summit, downward along unforgiving cliffs that dropped into the sea and, at a lesser height, into the muck of mangrove swamps.

It was immediately clear to Mitchell that Isaac was determined to take the Comet all the way to the bottom, race death down Ooah Mountain and live for years off the legend safe on the bar stools of St. Catherine. As the car picked up speed toward the first unfriendly curve, Mitchell vaulted into the backseat and crouched on the floor, throwing empty Ju-C bottles out the window so they wouldn't crystallize in his face as they did in his imagination, salting his flesh during the impending crash. From his position behind the seat he coached Isaac, warning him to downshift.

"No no, mahn. De engine buhn right up."

"This won't do," Mitchell complained. "This won't do." He thought Isaac should put the car into the mountainside, the sooner the better. Isaac gave him a quick look of scorn over his shoulder.

"You pay fah repair? Eh?" Isaac sadly shook his head as they began to enter the turn. "I ain goin do it," he said.

Isaac loved the Comet dearly and it would have been pointless to hold this refusal against him. Besides, the roadway was lined with concreted drainage ditches, three feet across and two deep, which meant the Comet would have to sacrifice at least an axle and an oil pan before it could plow into the hard cushion of the embankment. Running off the road was a dire option, and yet, somewhere ahead, it was their fate, waiting for them to appear on the scene.

Then too, the car had been manufactured in the United States and there was a magic in that fact that Isaac clung to and believed in. By owning the Comet outright after a year of humping bananas off other people's land, Isaac owned a part of the optimisms of the north, the guarantees of competency, the possibility that if he treated the car with responsible care, one day he'd find himself summoned to the Comet's homeland, no point in fretting over the details of how this would happen, except maybe with a few expenses paid, and there he would be introduced to the opportunity for the unlimited advancement he had mentally prepared himself for. This Isaac believed in absolutely. This was credo, this was gospel, prophecy, everything, and he would not fail in its pursuit. This was manifest destiny trickling south. It had happened to his cousin Robbie, the weaver, and to his brother-in-law Larris, the musician. It had happened to Mr. McPherson, the boat captain, and to countless others. If you behaved yourself and kept ready, it would happen the same to you. People who didn't behave had lost faith, committing the blasphemy of despair. They had excommunicated themselves from this ladder of salvation and were condemned to circling the island forever, circling, circling—big wheels on a small track.

So Isaac had puttied in the galaxy of rust holes on the fenders, sanded the blemishes day after day until they were as smooth as the inner lip of a conch shell. The original paint job had faded into a chalky brick color, unmatchable, and the Comet's northern prudence relinquished itself to an island style. The fenders and hubcaps were brushstroked with housepaint, a yellow enamel, glossy as buttercups. Glued to the upper trim of the front and rear windows, a fringe of red and green pompons produced a peculiar bedroom effect within the otherwise businesslike interior of the car, which doubled as a taxi only when Isaac was in the mood. Cracks in the vinyl seats were duct-taped together. On each door the Scuffletown sign painter calligraphed the name, all capital letters in flowing script, that Isaac had chosen for the car in honor of some oblique but universal political sentiment. *Miss Defy.* Her maintenance was as near to perfect as Isaac had a right to insist upon, given his low resources, and the collection of spare and spent parts he kept in the trunk rose or fell like an economic indicator for the entire island.

Mounted up front, a fourthhand radio-cassette player broadcasted continuous pulsation into the atmosphere. As crucial to the operation of Isaac's Comet as the hand-cut gaskets on the engine block and the sparks in the cylinders, the unit had been mailed down from Brooklyn by the émigré cousin Robbie, said to now be rich enough to petition for generosity. Isaac had installed it directly after retrieving the package from the Customshouse—labeled *Broken! Don't Work!* for a reduction on the duty tax. He had an arrangement with an eight-year-old nephew, who in exchange for driving lessons slept nightly in *Miss Defy* so that the music and everything else that was the Comet's identity would stay put, his own for the time being, protected from the sticky and ravenous fingers of Scuffletown.

Only two hours earlier they had ended a long night of rum sweetened with Isaac's ananci stories, island fairy tales and convoluted nonsensical narratives about an ancient feud between a donkey and a monkey. Mitchell had ridden the bed like a carnival horror, spinning and bumping through the remaining minutes of the night while Johnnie, it seemed, gazed down upon his agony with the beatific face of a Madonna. Isaac had wobbled out to the Comet parked up the slope on the roadside, rejecting the spare room, fallen unconscious on the front seat with the driver's door open, the shoes on his feet only inches away from any traffic that passed. When the alarm clock sounded on the stage of Mitchell's nightmares, he showered and dressed and went to rouse Isaac, cradled in *Miss Defy,* his hands tucked securely into the top of his pants, his head hanging off the seat, his mouth frozen open and his remarkably pink tongue sagging out like a thick slice of bologna. Mitchell woke him by clicking on the radio: one station, one brave volume, and more and more for the

11

past week, an old song, the "Edison Banks Calypso," pleading with young Mr. Banks to return from his studies at Gray's Inn, to finish his lawyering degree and come home and pick up the torch of justice once more. The song playfully warned of the danger of becoming a student-for-life, and urged him to come back to the throne of his love on the island of St. Catherine, calling across the sea, penetrating his self-exile, asking for him to recognize the ripeness of the time, the early hours of a new day, an age for poets, heroes, patriots. He had indeed harkened to the song and come home to have his life rattled and his head beaten for two years of mobilizing the opposition against Delwyn Pepper, who had sodomized the nation for almost a decade, and in the end Banks had won an election that everyone predicted would be bloody but was not, at the price of an unsavory coalition of factions. The song debuted four years ago and was earning a lot of replay on the government station to celebrate the first anniversary of Banks' tenure as prime minister, and the invisible successes of the new ruling party, the People's Evolutionary Alliance of St. Catherine. Now, rolling down the mountain in *Miss Defy*, the song was requested again, the jockey announced with transparent enthusiasm, and its chorus blared into Mitchell's skull from out of the door speaker,

> Come take de swell from me lil boy's belly
> Take de cruel hand from me lil gy-url's skirt
> Lift de sufferin, strike ol' massa
> Save me heart from dis hurt,

farty, stuttering horns and rapid patois distorted by volume into a palpable electronic throb, a continuous threat of audio-aneurism, blending somewhere under his chin with the awful sound of tires losing traction. A wave of centrifugal thrust rose and rose and receded the length of his prone body as they made the curve and swung out onto the next short straightaway. Mitchell raised his head above the seat and remarked that this was it, that they were dead, that these were their last quick moments on earth, and would Isaac please turn off the radio so God could hear their prayers. Isaac swabbed perspiration from above his haunted eyes with a rag he kept handy for cleaning the windshield.

Mitchell pounded his shoulder, yelling at him to downshift.

"I know, I know," Isaac said, becoming annoyed. "Sit back, Wilson."

The car speeded toward a full stop against a red rectangle of cut rock, the severe curve to the left dipping and dropping out of sight like a river spilling over a waterfall, the bottom third of the curve horseshoeing a lethal distance directly below them. Isaac squeezed the emergency brake and they smelled it melt away. He tried to steer, both of them awed by the velocity with which the Comet was entering the turn.

"Downshift," Mitchell whispered, leaning across the seat to Isaac's ear. "Downshift, downshift."

Isaac chopped the transmission out of gear but couldn't force it back in, jamming the shifter forward until third gear began to stink like industrial fire and reproduce the noise of a crosscut saw chewing into sheet metal. Mitchell heard teeth fly off inside the housing, hot bullets ricocheting deep inside the Comet's gut. Finally the gear nudged into place and Isaac, loathe to do anything without his customary smoothness, had to let the clutch spring back before it was too late. Mitchell shot forward across the seat and into the dashboard, his nose squashed. Blood gushed down onto the white cotton shirt he had yesterday paid a matronly neighbor the going rate of fifty cents to wash and iron in preparation for his unsolicited reunion with Johnnie. The drive train reduced revolutions with a siren's whine while the body of the car pitched onward, obeying the laws of nature. Isaac negotiated the curve with increasing expertise, downshifting again to twenty miles an hour, and flowed the Comet cleanly through a slalom of S-turns, but as the car regained momentum, it became necessary to climb back through the gears.

"Sorry, Mitchie bwoy. You okay, nuh?"

Mitchell slumped back behind the seat, licking warm blood from the fountain in his nose, wanting to wreck right now and get it over with, arrive at the airport in an ambulance (though he had never seen one on the island), collect Johnnie, plead her onto the gurney next to him, commence the nursing process without delay, submit to the truce of medical crisis under which old animosities could be justifiably ignored. The force of still another radical hook in the road packed him into a smaller and smaller space against the base of the car door. Again Isaac was grinding the transmission into third gear, a hellish racket that did not result in the anticipated roar of rpms. The clutch engaged, the engine idled in a terrible calm. What was once third gear Mitchell supposed had been lathed down to a sprocketless hub. Isaac bullied his way into second, a gear not made for the speed they had accumulated. The Comet bucked as though it were launching missiles, the cylinders howled with abuse, smoke filtered through under the dashboard, and the machinery, now a field experiment in the process of fission, blew up. The exhaust manifold gave an explosive belch and went silent. Mitchell looked up and saw Isaac with his jaw clenched. Angry tears appeared in his eyes, and he shouted.

"*Miss Defy! Miss Defy!* You weak obsocky bitch, how you mash up so!"

With half the mountain to go they were freewheeling and bitterly terrified. The radio continued to play, however; the music and its partisan melodies gave Isaac a poor reason to hope for the best. They rolled faster and faster, a steel trap of locomotion and churning rhythms, down the hill. The Crab Hole Bar flashed by: a smear of pastels, gray planking supporting a rusted zinc roof, a line of disinterested fellows on broken chairs in a dirt yard, laundry draped over pigeon pea bushes, a little boy in a tee shirt but no pants having a handless pee, the thick flora again, more pedestrians as the mountain was frequently residential at this lesser elevation. People hopped off the road into the homicidal gutters of the Crown agents, shooed by Isaac's hornblowing. *Miss Defy* screeched around a blind bend into the path of an oncoming sedan; Isaac fought heroically to regain his legal portion of the thoroughfare. Crouching back onto the floor in an unheroic position himself, Mitchell discovered that the trash he had been tossing around on, one of the plastic shopping bags, had ripped open to dispense hundreds of individually wrapped, multicolored prophylactics. At the sight of them he felt extremely sorry for himself, thinking, God, they're going to pluck these out of my mangled corpse after we smash. Sister Vera will come and nag over my body about family planning and wastefulness.

Every male in St. Catherine beyond the age of eleven had been accosted by Sister Vera from the Ministry of Health and People's Welfare. Some foreign-aid deal, annotated by many strange complexities, had stuck her with an entire freighterload of rubbers which she personally distributed by the bucketful. In this way she was herself the recipient of a variety of insults and slander—cradle robber, barren puppet, "whore of the empire's executioner," one left-wing mimeograph called her—and the government didn't concern itself with her mission as long as she got rid of the condoms before the time came to renegotiate this particular aid package into something more appealing, like video equipment or an armored personnel carrier.

It was no mystery then that Isaac had been induced to carry a year's supply of rubbers in the backseat of the Comet. Sister Vera was assiduous, arguing that his fares could help themselves from the bag even though Isaac swore to her over and over that he would never wear such a smothering device himself, that he was spiritually opposed to the practice. He held a peculiar scientific belief relating to this matter. Isaac believed that the actual spirits—he called them angels—of his father, his grandfather, his great-grandfather, and so on, resided in the realm of his penis. It was understood by him that his ancestors were down there, every last one of them but too many to know by name, reduced to something approximating molecular waterbugs in the pool of his seed, yet whole and autonomous and accessible. Mitchell had even seen Isaac mumbling to his dick as if it were a microphone into the netherworld. To Isaac, this was science—an old old old one, true, but recently confirmed in his opinion by what he had read of the study of genetics. He loved newspapers from the States and considered tabloids the highest source of encouraging information. In fact, in a Florida sheet he had read that his special ability to talk with the deceased was a common and legitimate exercise, now studied inside machines and under microscopes at major universities.

Mitchell had met both Isaac and Sister Vera within minutes of his arrival on the island eight months previously. The nondenominational Sister, dressed like a meter maid, advanced on him as he waited for his gear to be lugged out of Customs by a mafia of porters. Perhaps the sight of his footlocker had provoked her—a white man moving in to bombard the local ovaries with blue-eyed imperial genes. She swooped down on him, lecturing with the fierce rhetoric of a victim, as though he were to be held accountable for every birth on the island in the past year, and urged him to accept her handout. Infrequent weeks of whirlwind missions—a deficit symposium in Rome, a consultation with the Export Office in Kathmandu—were the extent of his travel abroad; Mitchell did not yet know how to say no (and mean it) in a foreign country without excessive anxiety and a scarlet rash of guilt. Sister Vera's only clear affiliation seemed to be the cult of contraception, but she had a deft talent for intimidation, her success at it rivaling the most orthodox harangues of the greater religions. She gave him the usual, shoved it into his arms, a shopping bag containing one gross of loose condoms, and when she left he opened the mouth of the sack and stared at them wistfully. They were little time bombs of copulation, in such quantity they could only be of use to the tireless libertines that undoubtedly roamed Sister Vera's dreams.

Isaac too had been alerted by the footlocker and wandered over to offer *Miss Defy* for hire. Mitchell's first impression was that he was too chummy, too upbeat, a potential nuisance, and he dismissed him regardless, because someone from the Ministry of Agriculture was supposed to meet the flight, to be there with Mitchell's official welcome. Isaac grinned as if he knew better and strolled off in the direction of the airport bar, greeting everyone as his brother and sister. He was wearing the ugliest shirt Mitchell had ever seen, a synthetic made from petroleum, splashes of gray, yellow, and bright red, like smeared viscera. Parked on his trunk, Mitchell finished reading the *Miami Herald;* both the crowd and his optimism began to thin out. Where's my official welcome and my official driver, Mitchell complained to that part of himself that he also considered official.

After refreshing himself at the bar, Isaac came back for him, prescient to the altered expectations of official white men. Mitchell looked at his slick pointed sideburns and his half-cocked grin, saying to himself this better work out, and stood up. Isaac took him to Rosehill Plantation, a hotel and guesthouse where Mitchell checked in until he found quarters of his own. Isaac took half his payment that day in the form of several rounds of Guiness stout at Rosehill's beach bar, a strategic spot to examine the rise and fall of quality in female tourists. Women in bikinis would walk by and he would nudge Mitchell and say, *Oh oh, look de bubbies!* or *Cheese on!*, and tug at the knees of his khaki trousers. Down at the tideline an island boy and his younger brother played with a handful of their own certified prophylactics. The older boy filled one long green sheath with sand until it bulged obscenely and used it as a weapon to club the other boy in the head. Mutual entertainment developed into a one-sided beating. The casing finally burst, showering the little one with the powdered coral of the beach. The victim cried like a professional, a virtuoso crier. Their huge mother fired admonitions at them from where she floated in the lagoon, a battleship in a hot-pink leotard, and Mitchell thought, surveying the mountains and the sea, what a magnificent land I have come to.

In the months Mitchell had lived and worked on St. Catherine, he mailed two postcards, inscribing them with typical postcard language, to Johnnie in Hawaii. He had kept in random touch with her over the years since they had separated, the nature of the touch sometimes forlorn, sometimes smart-alecky, sometimes lonely, and the most prevalent tone was that of friendship, a seasoned song of tacit forgiveness and never, he hoped, anything but realistic. She had telegrammed back a shocking message just days ago: *I want to see you. Will arrive in St. Catherine a.m., 3/30/77. Surprised? Your friend, Johanna.*

He hissed those words under his breath, *your friend,* his fingers digging mindlessly into the clear plastic packets of prophylactics. His sinuses felt as though Styrofoam cubes had been brutally inserted into their cavities. When did she start calling herself Johanna anyway? *My fucking friend,* he cursed on the floor of the Comet. My friend, my private merchant of love and treachery, a southern belle with a slow white fire thrumming in her veins the last he saw her.

Isaac's prelude of honking ended with a sharp bang into something distressingly solid. There was a nauseating sensation of uncontrolled coupling and then a swaying release. He lay on the horn again; there was another, more violent bang. Mitchell emerged from behind the seat only high enough to see what had happened and was disheartened. The Comet was boxed in by a steady flow of traffic chugging up Ooah Mountain and a frightened lady driver ahead of them going down too slow for the Comet's independent rate of descent. They had rammed her, she had defensively and stupidly applied the brakes after they had disengaged, and *Miss Defy* struck her a second time, losing a few miles per hour from the impact and a moderate rise in the road, and the woman ahead, panicking, accelerated out of sight.

At twenty miles per hour they approached a curve requesting ten. Rummy sweat dribbled off Isaac's forehead and obscured his vision. Entering the turn, Isaac cranked the wheel, his elbows flapping, and the Comet responded as if the asphalt had turned to ice. The traction gone, *Miss Defy* rotated gracefully around the bend of the parabola and whipped full circle back into the straightaway, steady again, just like you see in the movies, Mitchell gasping and shrunken but Isaac far in rapture over his accomplishment.

"I nevah see such as daht before, mahn," he said, marveling at the stunt.

In the abbreviated distance ahead, the driver of the car they had crumped swerved half off the road, perpendicular into the entrance of a dirt drive. She exited her vehicle, a late-model Morris, shiny black, with imposing fury. She was a sizable woman and burly, her bosom swinging underneath a yellow blouse, and she charged into the road to flag them down and give Isaac a thrashing. The bumper on the rear of her Morris had an experimental shape to it, the taillights ceased to exist—small damage all told. Isaac was helpless to obey her directions. He took his hands off the wheel and raised them level with his ears as *Miss Defy* rolled past, not merely to advertise his innocence, but to express his exasperation at being the object of this person's wrath. Since he had knocked into her without malice or intent, he seemed to be saying with his shrugging gesture, she herself might take a moment to consider that he was only a poor man about to be crushed by a destiny he could no longer persuade.

The gesture was sincere but ill-timed. Like a horse with a plan of its own, the Comet veered radically to the left, pulled by wheels last aligned in another era. There were no drainage ditches here, the shoulders too abrupt, the slope too precipitous, to collect water. *Miss Defy* catapulted off the surface of the earth, nothing in sight for a brief eternity but a blue horizon scratched with clouds. They completed their arc and nosed downward, hopping back onto rough ground, their jaws slamming shut, the tops of their heads denting the inside of the roof, making stars explode behind their eyes. Isaac hung courageously to the wheel as they plunged. *Mercy, mercy, mercy,* he croaked, his first surrender to fatalism. They rumbled through dry brush, the Comet an ocher dust storm lashed by branches and spiky shoots. There were noises to fear—something substantial ripped from the undercarriage and the thumping of a tire burst into shreds. Scrub hens bounced off the windshield and iguanas skated across the plane of the hood. Isaac resembled a captain at the helm in high seas. They regained the pavement by dozing through a low rock wall, circumventing two impossible curves above in the road by the grace of this route. Through a final turn, *Miss Defy* boomeranged sloppily and was expelled off the black tongue of the mountain onto the flat shorn vale of the airstrip, leaking an inauspicious trail of prophylactics from a gash in the floorboard. Isaac guided the car into a newly planted cane field and they rolled peacefully for fifty feet until it died in the dirt. The whole episode had seemed unreal in a gross, cheap way.

Mitchell asked Isaac if he was okay. He looked sleepyheaded, overcome with lassitude, as if he wanted to dream backward through the catastrophe and nullify it. He closed his eyes and held the side of his skull; lazy blood seeped through the spaces between his fingers.

"Wha?" Isaac said, rocking with pain. "Me ear bust in twos."

Without much conviction, he affirmed his well-being and then complained further of a sprained ankle, a wrenched knee, and a sore chest from being hammered into the steering column. With sighing despondency he turned off the radio and dismantled it, even yanking the speakers from their door mounts, the silence as sad as taps played at a memorial service. A lot of noise remained in Mitchell's own ears, a high-volume residue of calypso, brain-shaking, accompanied by the distant rasp of waves on the beach at the edge of the coastal plain. Mitchell wobbled out of the back of the Comet and stood with his hands thrust into his pockets, trying to think of what he could say to Isaac that would not sound like eulogy. Nothing but the bleakest remarks came to mind. Isaac, without *Miss Defy*, owned nothing. He sat like a deposed carnival king in his chariot, the strips of pompons from off the windows draped over his shoulders like a tawdry royal stole.

They walked away from the car as if they never had any business with it, as if the misfortune it represented, the perils and the fear, had been sustained by others. The Comet was something done with, *finish up,* that national litany Mitchell heard whenever he turned a corner, like the brake fluid in the weird island garages, *finish up,* like potatoes or milk or soap in the markets, *finish up,* like schoolbooks for the children, like the phone service that only went to one out of every four customers who wanted it, like the Carib Indians and the secret language of their women, like slavery, like the old regime of crooks and thugs Edison Banks had disposed of or co-opted so shrewdly, like the plantations and the plantocracy and the sugar industry and last night's bottle of strong rum and like a thousand other pieces of junk pushed off the narrow roads of St. Catherine into the embrace of the bush, the Comet *Miss Defy* had joined the chorus of this collective destiny, had run itself into the ground and was now for all time *finish up,* bequeathed to scavengers, jerry-riggers, scrap revivalists, trash hobbyists, bugs, birds, lizards, rain, sun, moon, and myth.

"Coconut oil," Isaac mused. He refused self-pity. "Why I believe daht shit, Wilson?"

Chapter 2

The LIAT desk had not yet opened although there was laughter and short-wave radio garble coming through the closed door behind the ticket counter, nor was the Customs staging area preparing for operation as it should have been, because Johnnie's flight was scheduled to arrive momentarily. The souvenir stand, purveyor of inexpertly screened tee shirts, coconut shell ashtrays, and conch shell lamps, was still locked up, as was the Batik Boutique, a mystery shop which Mitchell couldn't recall ever seeing open. In fact, the Brandon Vale airport had all the charm and credibility of a foreclosed and abandoned warehouse. It was a venue of pathos and prayers, a wretched place for passengers concerned with their welfare. At one end of the long flat salmon-colored complex stood the control tower, an edifice modeled along the lines of a prison fortification. On the opposite end of the building, constructed as an entrepreneurial afterthought, a hand-hewn timber and thatched roof parasite living off the sluggish metabolism of the terminal, was a bar, and the bar was open for business.

Saconi was in there at one of the tables, blithe and ambivalent in the diffused natural light. His companion of choice, a Michoacán acoustic guitar inside a tattered cardboard case, was propped on the seat next to him, and an uncapped bottle of reputable scotch, a rudiment of inspiration, stood centered on the varnished plywood of the table. A master lyricist and a performer both hostile and seductive to the legions of his audience, Saconi had composed the "Edison Banks Calypso"—not for money alone—and was therefore much in favor these days, even though his current single lectured the coalition for acting like a jackass with a head at each end, its two mouths both straining to reach the same mango hanging from a branch. He had recorded in Trinidad, Port of Spain, the New York of the lower

Caribbean, toured up and down the islands, and received occasional airplay for his albums as far away as Toronto and London. He was a celebrity and a hero of upliftment. The success he had earned was as much a source of boasting as it was of envious disdain for the people of St. Catherine, his people, and his relative worldliness was tolerated the same way illiterates will tolerate a friend who reads books. Because of his lover, a doughnut-hipped Peace Corps volunteer known as Big Sally, Saconi was familiar with the tribe of expatriates on the island, and chronically skeptical of the more transitory community of foreign professionals—the consultants, bankers, multinational representatives, mafiosi, political sightseers, aid administrators and pirates, the army of surrogate invaders who believed they could float St. Catherine into some nirvanic backwater of their own influence.

When they shambled in, Saconi looked them up and down and snorted. Isaac limped and carried his radio equipment, stiff wires dangling from its housing like chicken feet. One of his ears was split and raw. Mitchell had a bib of drying blood on the front of his shirt.

"Who strike de fust blow?"

Saconi's speaking voice itself was laden with cushiony music. He had a marimba for vocal chords, producing syllables lubricated with a range of tonal inflections governed by West African rhythms. Mitchell loved to listen to him, despite his attitude which was often ironic, curried enough to divide the meek from the sportsmen.

"Satan," Isaac answered miserably. Saconi pointed his finger at Mitchell.

"Don't look at me," Mitchell protested.

"What, you not Satan? I hear some talk Satan is a backra mahn, you know. God, Lucifer—all dem big shots is backra, white like you."

Mitchell was never certain, on the several occasions they had been together, how much racial conviction lay behind the musician's wit. Saconi expressed himself with a tooth-hidden smile, a mock severity to the intelligence of his eyes, and a taunting posture that could turn willowy and fettled without notice.

"Admit it, Wilson. Somehow you twistin up dis poor fella Isaac's life. You born into it, eh?"

"Offer us a seat," Mitchell said. "All we expect is a small act of decency and a drink to calm us down."

They could skip wisecracks across the opaque depths of their histories, ridicule the swirl of centuries at their backs, but the other hand was perpetually occupied with more serious work, dismissing the fence of distance between races and cultures that made any search for brotherhood too arduous for pastime. Most attempts of this sort were charades, performances in masquerade. Mitchell was by nature cautious with people although the island seemed to contradict this tendency in him. Isaac he knew was trustworthy on all accounts, as a friend without an agenda of need or expectation. Saconi he wasn't sure about.

"A blameless white guy," the musician said to Isaac. "Imagine daht."

Isaac's spirit was overburdened and he couldn't be enticed to play. "*Miss Defy* finish up," he reported sadly. "Ooah Mountain mash she." He told the story of what had occurred as if it were a natural phenomenon, not mechanical failing or human error. Saconi let him moon a little longer over the bottle of scotch before he waved him on it with a grousing air of obligation.

"Take heart, bruddah," said the composer Saconi. "*Miss Defy* nevah finish so. Calypso redeem she to you."

"Cy-ahnt drive a fuckin song," Isaac said. Restitution in any form was a rarity on St. Catherine though its promise was as common as sunrise. He grimaced with the bottle to his mouth, drank, and gave it back with a smack of appreciation.

"Mitchell," Saconi said, "you must import womahn? De shelves not stocked to suit you, bruddah?" He poured himself another inch of whiskey, the gold rings on his fingers tapping the glass, restless percussion.

Johnnie's coming burned Mitchell's stomach and crowded his thoughts. He had no idea of the implications of her visit; he couldn't have been more nonplussed if Jacqueline Onassis had sent him a note on personal stationery saying prepare the spare room and cancel all appointments. He repeated what he had rehearsed over and over again to himself. "She's an old friend. Somebody I used to know." She was probably just stopping over on the way to the Vatican to kiss the Pope's knuckles, off to southern Africa to photograph beasts, en route to Bangkok to teach English as a second language . . . answering a siren call, fueled by an exotic cause, a process in which he would appear spliced in for a ten-second cameo, a minor, fleeting effect.

"Friend," said Saconi, inflecting the word so that its content was erotic.

"I haven't seen her in years."

"You ain discovah a nice black Catherinian picky-head puss? Wha? And I tell myself you is a skinsmahn, Wilson? Dese gy-url here love to cook and sweep and suck, bwoy. You missin out."

Mitchell felt overly soreheaded but smiled back at Saconi idiotically, trying to maintain goodwill. They had been standing around the table like two rubes with the sense knocked out of them. Mitchell pulled out a chair, stepped in front of it, squatted to sit down. Saconi extended his leg and kicked the chair away. Like scales set to mismatched weights, relationships that traversed cultural grooves took some adjustment before they balanced effectively. Often it took Mitchell a second to figure out the exchange factor on what was taking place around him.

"Excuse me," he said, "this isn't my country. I don't know when somebody's being an asshole."

Instead of an apology, Saconi lectured them. "You two fellas lookin bummy, you know. If you sit with a famous guy like me you muss wash you face. Look de snotty bloodstring hangin out you nose, Mitchell, and dut on you cheek, and hair all stickied wit some kinda shit. And Isaac, what a razzy sight him is, wit tree and leaf in he locks, and busted pants, and like some goat chew on he ear. Christ, mahn—wash up, sit down, take a civilized drink like gentlemens, nuh?, not scamps. What de womahn feel, Mitchell, when she see such a messy guy like you wit dis ragboy Isaac to greet she?"

"We too ugly to sit wit Saconi," Isaac said, sagging with resignation. He plucked a twig from his electrocuted hair and glared at it, seeing evidence of disgrace, dissipation, ruination. "Me life comin straight reverse to naught." Had the Lord decided to take everything away from him today? Suffering the antiprogress of his fortune, he deposited the last relics of *Miss Defy* on the table and turned away, and together he and Mitchell shuffled back into the terminal to the bathroom, another of the airport's idiosyncratic constructions, for it was obvious the architect who designed it had never worked with big spaces before and felt licensed to be extravagant with areas usually assigned more economically. The janitor's broom closet, for instance, was larger than the janitor's one-room shack where he lived with wife and babies on the slope of Zion Hill, and although its installations were conventional—two urinals, a pair of toilet stalls, one sink—the lavatory was vast enough for a square dance. It had a hallowed atmosphere which it certainly didn't deserve.

Mitchell bowed over the sink, his eyes closed, to wash his face and mustache, hawking up globs of blood from the top of his throat. When he opened his eyes again he was staring at a pinkish whirlpool running into the drain. Straddling one of the urinals, Isaac was mumbling, ostensibly engaged in more ancestral dialogue, putting in requests for a return to favor and maybe an Impala convertible like the one Kingsley, the potentate of agriculture and natural affairs and Mitchell's boss, drove around, the envy of every motorist and dream motorist on the island. To console Isaac was pointless. The man seemed to Mitchell a veteran of adversity, someone who knew how to roll and spring and rise again, groping for the bright side of squalid circumstance, however elusive. He had developed his own system for outlasting loss, setback, and failure—the island quotients provided by x, y, and z, fill in the blanks with whatever imperial power or local politician, economy, and dates best applied to the list of current grievances.

Initially Mitchell had been wary of Isaac's queer habit, this dick chatter that was close to shamanism, an alien form of eccentricity that he couldn't accept with any seriousness.

"It's the wackiest thing I've ever heard," Mitchell had declared the first month on St. Catherine, when Saconi's girlfriend Sally tried to explain Isaac's preoccupation with genitalia—his own and everybody else's.

"Well, you don't understand," she had retorted with a passion that caused her to jerk. "Isaac's one of the few souls on this anchored melodrama who has made peace with the past. He accepts what's there, puts it behind him, and goes on. You might think that's simple but it's exactly the opposite. He just doesn't have a big problem with history . . . not like some people I know," she added, shifting her eyes in Saconi's direction. He was across the room at the kitchen table strumming his guitar, his eyes half-lidded, not interested in their game of backgammon.

Mitchell was still cynical. "It's all an elaborate euphemism for a style of masturbation," he pontificated, "and a ruse to heat up the ladies."

"You just don't understand, man," Big Sally insisted. "For a Catherinian, Isaac is a man of the future."

The public water always tasted stale, disflavored with brackishness. It had a not-quite-transparent look to it, as if it had been filtered through moldy bread crusts, and it harbored flecks and types of mote-sized growth. Mitchell swallowed some accidentally as he rinsed his mouth but forced it back up before the microbes could celebrate a new host. He had suffered bouts of dysentery off and on the first six weeks, planning his movements around the availability of a toilet. Isaac meanwhile had hung up the hotline to his ghosts, buttoned his trousers back in place, flexing his shoulders. Since the world had not been made right it was his duty to make himself right for the world.

There was no mirror in the room, which was a blessing in the aftermath of a night of alcohol and a morning of injury and fear. A metal paper towel dispenser hung crooked on the wall, empty, but its chromed surface allowed a blurry reflection pocked by an archipelago of brown oxidation. Mitchell combed his sun-bleached hair with his fingers and examined the tumescent smear of his nose, broken again, he knew from experience. Leprous blotches of rust scarred his cheeks and forehead yet the radiance of his health could not be obscured. He was as robust as a sailor and he knew it, knew, for what it was worth, that for the first time in his adult life he had passed some physical frontier within himself and his appearance was markedly different than it had been before he left the States. What might Johnnie say after such a long hiatus, looking upon this transformation? You look swell, Mitchell, I had no idea you were going to grow up into a man, I guess I should have stuck around? He caught himself lingering over the dispenser in a mild narcissistic crush and jumped away. Not Johnnie alone was coming for a visit, but an unwanted accomplice— she was bringing his adolescence with her.

As Mitchell turned in circles looking for something to dry himself on, Isaac took his place, positioning himself in front of the useless fixture to rummage through the depths of his hair for remnants of Ooah Mountain. His fingers probed what was ordinarily a neat helmet of stubby coils that resembled six-inch sections of hemp rope, like a clown's wig, the tips orange from sea-bathing, protruding from his scalp. Their wild ride in *Miss Defy* though had tangled everything up, a composition that made Mitchell think of cheap, wind-torn macramé, something that Johnnie, bearer of ill-chosen gifts, might have disappointed him with on a Christmas past. Mitchell started to wipe his hands on his shirt but stopped, repulsed by its filthy, stained condition, and decided to get rid of it. Life on St. Catherine required the daily challenge of mundane improvisation. Everyone but the richest seemed circumscribed by a life-style of scouting, foraging, camping out, wiping backsides with banana leaves, newspaper.

No sooner had he removed his shirt than the door to the bathroom inched open and in tottered one of the legion of dispossessed, a fuzz-headed elder in mud-caked laceless shoes, decomposing pants with a purply sheen like the casing of a fly, a frayed nylon cord belt cinched above his imperceptible hips, an undertaker's black frock coat hanging like old drapery off his shoulders, a piece of clothing that must have been distributed by one of the churches on the island long ago. The abandoned wardrobe of a far-off community. Three quarters of the populated planet existed on what the remaining quarter threw into the trash. Five-gallon plastic buckets, ideal for toting water; deformed bicycles, ideal transportation; the last war's guns, no longer fashionable but still fine for spreading influence—there was no telling what an intrepid scavenger might resurrect from the junkbin of affluence, including, for the trained eye, the dross of once-valuable ideas. The bin was full of tossed-away ideologies, remaindered polemics: determining which ideas had mileage left on them was an acquired skill for the scavenging elite. But the man who approached Mitchell in the bathroom was not to be counted among them. He clearly was of the lowest sort, a human form of flypaper or spiderweb, a disciple of passive acquisition and thus a perfect candidate for meaningless charity.

Mitchell gave him his shirt.

Full of apprehension, Mitchell watched this cotton-headed fossil make a beeline for him, sliding his clunker shoes along the rough concrete floor. His right hand ascended with quivering effort, the glossy, weathered palm extended with mendacious authority. A feeling of susceptibility heightened until Mitchell was conscious only of being stripped and exposed, of being subtracted from himself, of nakedness, of naked immobilizing whiteness. The air resonated with the strain of the man's breathing, the drag of his shoes. There was no undershirt beneath the coat, only a bare sepia chest white-capped by curlets of stiff hair, a bonescape of ribs like a series of stalled waves threatening to collapse into the recess of his abdomen, wild currents of muscle running under his loose skin to tie the body together. Through the yellowed ruff of beard, the lips of the man pursed with an incomprehensible verdict, a mouth shaped not by hunger but by an indifference to it. His trajectory toward Mitchell seemed fixed, prearranged, and as Mitchell looked into his watery eyes and down at the arthritic cup of his fingers, he felt blinded by the disgusting surge of pity, the unknown and unknowable interiors that the old man confronted him with. Knowing how absurd it was to do this, Mitchell gave him the shirt and again with a practiced sense of movement, the old man clutched it, offering no change of expression, and headed back out, inscrutably satisfied. The spell he had created would not dissolve until Isaac, who had monitored the incident with a severe patience, spoke a gentle command.

"Move on, grahnpoppi," he said, following after him. "Move on. Give back de shurt." He laid a hand on the old man's shoulder.

The thought of having the shirt returned confused Mitchell, made him unhappy. "Let him have it," he said. "If he wants it he can have it. I can't wear it anymore."

Isaac looked at Mitchell with disapproval but finally shrugged, taking his hand away; the old man released like a wound-up toy. Mitchell felt like he had become someone who needed to be protected from his own caprice. This was sublime ridiculousness, to give away a blood-soiled shirt to a walking corpse. A stick of animated carrion. Hang a shirt on decrepitude and nothing whatsoever in the world changed.

The old man disappeared out the door, a zombie come and gone. Mitchell dismissed a moment of petty guilt—why not give him a few coins if you were going to give him anything. Throw a dollar down the fathomless hole, into a need so pure it had no earthly solution, abstracting into the untouchable. You could talk about it but you couldn't change it, any more than you could fill a bottle with oil that had already been filled with water. But then, to do something so meaningless and farcical as give him a rag of a shirt, take it right off your back?

"What was that, man? Obeah?" He counterfeited a laugh. "That old man had some kind of hold on me. You know?"

"Nah," Isaac said. "Him just a poor dutty mahn wit he hand put out." Now that Isaac had washed his ear, Mitchell could see that it might need stitching. He asked again if Isaac were all right. "Not so good," Isaac had to admit. "Daht ride knock some language in me ear I nevah esperience. Like ten womens whistlin and clickin tongue." Mitchell wouldn't acknowledge this connection with yet another world. Access to one was more than enough for anybody. They were at the door and Isaac swung it open: an acrid stink seeped in behind the throb of Mitchell's nose.

"What smells funny?"

Isaac sniffed around, testing the air for himself. "Smell like some dy-amn religion buhnin gungee stick," he said.

The souvenir stall had raised its grated door, doggedly anticipating customers, the collection of foreign currency. Incoming flights were customarily late; newcomers disembarked frazzled, wary, and discomposed. Some first-timers were doomed from the start, as if they were traveling under the weight of anesthesia—the couples from Liberty, Missouri, from York, Pennsylvania, from Coos Bay, Oregon, on an unmeditated leap out onto the globe, victims of Fireman's Ball raffles and travel agents that never should have been listened to, excursion packages and the defensive lies of their friends who went to some of these places aboard a cruise liner and adored it. Dwayne and Jean, Bill and Helen, about to step off into the five most appalling days of their lives, on vacation in the Third World.

Mitchell walked under the grating sheepishly, aware of the impropriety of his shirtlessness. The people of St. Catherine expected their guests to honor a code of respectability. The code was straightforward and universally known, not unlike the standard Mitchell was raised by in Virginia: a sound appearance is a great comfort to everyone's nerves, particularly when among scoundrels. A tastefully dressed crook with a shine to his wing tips, a pederast who drives to the Fairfax Hunt in a Jaguar and spreads an eighteenth-century carpet on the lawn for lunch at the rail—these were citizens one could depend on not to disturb the public peace, wholly preferable to a state's attorney who purchased suits off the rack at Woodies and licked gravy from his butter knife. Whatever backroom tendencies you pursued which might bring shame down upon your house and loved ones, appoint yourself handsomely with the proper weaves, exude a delicate fragrance, make reference to your forefathers and investment strategies, stay out of the penitentiary and let heaven be your judge since nobody on earth was qualified for the position. The manners of the Virginia countryside, whether you were born under their influence or not, sugared the surface of human affairs in a land with few bridges between those who had access to the Almighty's benevolence and those who could not be considered chosen except by the heel of the Almighty's boot. The code was in fact a colonial vestige, which is why Mitchell found it so easily recognizable in St. Catherine, and obeyed its arcane formalities. In the puddle of island society, he had a professional reputation to sponsor, no matter how young and green he was, and without his consent or conscious complicity, a racial illusion to uphold. Despite his desire to subvert this mentality, he was made to understand that white men, who supposedly had the world in their pocket, were expected to look as if they deserved it. Bad packaging just upset needlessly; it was interpreted as flaunting, or mockery, or parody, and oppressed peoples had a volatile sensitivity in its presence, as if any sign of slackness or weakness were an incitement. Who could say how much law and order had been eroded by soup stains, a careless buttoning, an inept shave. It reminded him of nothing so much as the social diplomacies and trivial appraisals of family reunions, and of schooldays.

The demands of his office were not as staggering to the spirit, though he was still assigned an image to pantomime through: to perform as the answer man, the specialist from the North, rattle off stats like baseball esoterica, confirm the intelligence of people already in place so they could get some respect, perhaps, from their own. Finally, not to dishonor the managerial class by looking like anybody could crash its party. At least at the ministry you accomplished something, if only an honest intention; the womb that expelled you and the soil you landed on were no longer considered trump, as everyone tried their very best to be modern.

Violation or not, he wasn't going to make Johnnie edgy walking around like Tarzan. The clerk inside the cramped souvenir shop, a woman with black harlequin spectacles, her hair tortured straight and shellacked into a rain-forest look, made no attempt to conceal the affront of his nakedness upon the harmony of her morning. She suffered such a low class of customer unwillingly, offering not service but an arctic freeze. The tee shirts Mitchell fingered through were all size Small and he was afraid to ask her if there were any others in stock. She thrust her hips in aggravation against the counter behind which she ruled, making cowrie shell necklaces and black coral jewelry hop in their displays. He took a shirt, threw money on the glass of the countertop, and hurried for the door.

"Oh my my my," the saleslady bawled. "You come back, eh?"

The sight of dollars transformed her into a calm ally of commerce. Harpooned by the sharpness of her command, he stood by as she licked a pencil point with her tongue and painstakingly added and subtracted figures on a tiny gray pad, boxing her scratches into one corner of the paper. Mitchell reclothed himself. The arms of the tee shirt barely rounded the curve of his shoulders, the hem hung an inch above his navel. He was made inflated, musclebound and awkward by the shirt, a burlesque act. A bizarre logo expanded across his pectorals, a yellow and brownish Brahman bull, the colors blended along their borders into a rancid green so that the animal, stretched into a lethargic dragon, looked as though it had been dredged from a slime pond. *Without the farmer the world can't spin,* read the slogan ballooning underneath the beast. *St. Catherine Agricultural Exposition 1977.* The shoplady conquered the mathematics of the sales tax. He was due small change, which she counted twice and shoved at him, and provided a receipt without his asking: *Mr. White. Porchis one shurt. $9.35EC.* The virtue of financial transaction was its power to rocket above other failures to communicate.

According to Isaac, someone was cooking blackfish in the terminal. Blackfish was what the islanders had named pilot whales. The fishermen from the leeward side succeeded in wrestling to shore about two dozen of the whales every season. Mitchell had seen some hauled up on the beach at Kensington, resembling the burned fuselages of DC-3s. The aroma punched into you from miles away when the fishermen heated the flesh to collect one of the world's superior oils, used to lubricate aeronautical instruments. It wasn't blackfish frying though. Somewhere nearby plastic or chemicals had caught fire, the fumes stirring the bumblebees that inhabited Mitchell's broken nose. A creeping haze had entered the air, irritating their eyes and depositing a metallic taste on Mitchell's tongue. The plane should have been down by now.

Saconi came out from the bar, strolling along with guitar and case, bottle of scotch and glass of it, a smile held just short of arrogance. He could advertise easygoing better than most. Here's the juice, he seemed to say, cakewalking now that he had spotted the two of them. Here's the tune and the juice, the light and the sound, the music and its maker, *me,* the only guy around this duncey place with the means to an intelligent end. He halted in midstep as he encountered the gathering bank of smoke, surveyed the atmosphere and continued toward them, an expression on his face that said, I will rescue you . . . if I must.

"You fellas on a rahm-*page,*" he snorted. "Wha de hell you mash up now to get dis stink?"

Outside the wide rows of windows facing the airfield, a fire engine rolled out of a machine shed down the runway toward the terminal, overloaded with a crew of saviors in street clothes or yellow slickers, clinging tenuously to the running boards. The truck stopped opposite the exterior entrance of the LIAT station. The men hopped to the tarmac and unraveled a rust-stained intestine of hose. Within the terminal, the door behind the ticket counter slammed open and employees scuttled out under a billow of marbled smoke that exited as they did, choking and tugging at their nicely knotted blue neckties. Within seconds water squirted everywhere. A crowd materialized, coming in off the roads, to make commentary and observe the firemen break up equipment in a frenzy of service, and before long the airline's operational center was hammered, axed, foamed, and otherwise destroyed. Three stories were quick to circulate, embellished at will with as much creativity as news releases from the Government Information Office. Conservatives advocated number one: technology being the serpent that it was, the hardware in the ops room mysteriously burst into flame, a sign from the very guts of the island that St. Catherine was bounding pell-mell into the mistakes of the nuclear age. Old gods and new gods were jostling each other in the corridors that led to the future. A second version was supported by more progressive witnesses to the event: obeying the logic of a civil visionary, a disgruntled employee, fearing that the island's aviation systems lagged far below contemporary standards, exploded the antiquated equipment with a bomb manufactured from components smuggled ashore from Cuba-Florida-Israel-Argentina-Bulgaria, confident that what he had ruined in the ensuing conflagration would be replaced, expeditiously and with a clamor of pledges for more to come, with the most up-to-date do-flicky and gittimas, a flock of foreign agencies competing for this right.

The less dramatic rumor in consideration was the more plausible (though Mitchell didn't wish to diminish the credibility of the former two). For months, they heard from one of the kids who lifted luggage on and off planes, the radio operator had been tossing the greasy paper wrappers from his lunchtime roti behind the short-wave unit where they had collected between the wall and the radio housing. The trash had achieved a high enough level finally to settle against exposed tubes, and as the operator switched on the set and talked to the plane en route, the paper had combusted with a *woof*, the flames disposing of the link between ground and sky as if it were a fantasy anyway. The wiring at the airport was centralized and the entire circuit, a jam of hot veins and copper branchings that ended in question marks, sizzled and blew, causing an outage in the tower as well. Before he lost contact with the pilot, the radioman was able to relay a temporary instruction: Maintain altitude and position until further notice. No one could be bothered by an arrival at the moment.

Mitchell didn't look for sense in that rationale. On his cheeks were tears steamed out of their ducts by the toxic atmosphere. Hot and cold tears, drops of luckless outrage and the smooth beads of the melancholy he fought, and behind them pooling up, tears of desperate laughter. What wretchedness was this of a morning, to be borne down the slopes of Ooah Mountain in a brakeless vehicle, to have his nose accordianed into a plump oozing throb, to helplessly watch a bum spirit away his shirt, to have his old sweetheart pinwheeling above the ocean while the pilot read the newspaper and a team of controllers and kibitzers couldn't start their backup generator, or find replacements for their battery-pacs? Why was Johnnie coming here anyway? She had not given him time to say no to the idea, which is what, given the chance, he would have said.

*   *   *

"Mistah Foreign Fuckin Aid," Saconi said, hearing how Mitchell came by the slime-haloed steer on his front, "give de shurt off he back to a needy mahn. Real grahss root movement, bwoy."

"It wasn't like that," Mitchell replied, wishing he weren't so ginger around Saconi's clever mouth.

They sat along a concrete bench on the deck of the terminal's roof. Isaac wanted to stay below and view the fiasco to its finish, but they had coaxed him away from the unwholesome black clouds and an abundance of deputized firemen who had taken advantage of the situation to be pushy. A society that did not plug its culture into television preserved in its citizens a fresh and invigorating appreciation of catastrophe down to the cruelest detail, for catastrophe, if it didn't include you, was a windfall of entertainment. Isaac had to admit that the inferno of the LIAT office was a dull event after all, though an appreciated diversion from his own troubles. So they retreated to the bar for plastic cups of ice, then to the rooftop for the visceral sense of being above mundane concerns, Isaac weak on the stairs with further loss. Saconi had left the car stereo and speakers unattended. Now they were gone, thieved (naturally, compulsively, instinctively), and the musician made no attempt to assume responsibility.

The view from the roof had all of geography's headlines—the possessive, sheltering sea; the mountains with their illusion of a spectacular land mass—and, abstracted as Mitchell stared at the blank strip of possibility that was the runway, he measured the vicissitudes of this strange way of life on St. Catherine, a communal life that was definitely predisposed to fakery and magic-in-the-night, to blood-drawing sight gags and all seductive forms of low comedy, this against the reliability of the land, rich and giving and embracing after centuries of abuse. Nothing formed as strong a bond for the people discarded here by empires—not history, not politics, not religion—as the intimate resource of the land on which they were once no more than two-legged oxen. He looked at the houses built on Ooah Mountain and Zion Hill, like cotton patches of color sewn into the human poverty of the lush slopes, banana and cocoa plantations threading the hollows and crests, the blue-green range of peaks to the north, their jungles a thick sponge for the nurturing radiance of the early sun, and told himself that all you had to do was get a little leverage on your troubles and woes and paradise could almost happen.

Then he thought, *this stupid island.*

Saconi uncased his instrument and picked a sequence of notes, snapped and then sustained on the metal strings, boingy sounds that suggested flying fish careening over the waves in Los Muertos

Channel. Isaac fretted and sucked whiskey, the bottle slanted into his mouth. The scotch sparkled and flashed in its chamber, a liquid ano-dyne. He took a long therapeutic swallow and put ice cubes in his mouth, crushing them between large molars. Mitchell filled his cup halfway and then passed the bottle to Saconi, who topped off his own cup and routed the bottle back to Isaac. Saconi started playing again, strangling a country-and-western tune, oleaginous and distantly familiar, out of the guitar. They passed the bottle a fourth and fifth time, an eighth and ninth time, and Isaac finished it off, scowling at the bottom.

Then Isaac jerked up from the bench and wobbled until he found his equilibrium, his muscles operating on the faintest neural mes-sages. In front of them, a parapet of arabesque cinderblocks laid waist-high along the roof's edge prevented drunks and children from stepping off into space. Isaac went to it to spit down on the world and purge his nostrils, which he did with a fair amount of wet noises. Afterward he cocked his skinny hips and rested on his elbows, reviewing what he could see of his nation.

"Look aht daht foolishness, bwoy," he said after a while. There was no encouragement to the words so Mitchell didn't consider it a rec-ommendation. Saconi glanced up absently, involved with music. The alcohol began to soften Mitchell's physical perspective, made him feel loose as water, drifting, and the effort to keep himself awake culmi-nated in the idea of standing up. He braced himself on invisible sup-ports until he thought it wise to go forward, and once alongside Isaac, peered beyond the line of the roof with a dimwitted fascina-tion. He asked what was going on, but it was plain to see. On the tar-mac below the fire truck had caught fire, its hood raised like a shout and its engine undergoing a shower from its own hose.

"Is this a special day or something?"

"Nah."

"Day of Judgment?"

"Same as ahlways, mahn."

"Murphy's Day?"

"Moiphy?"

"Yeah, you know. Murphy's Law—everything goes wrong."

Isaac corrected him, stone-eyed and somber. "We is Pollimen Tree."

"Oh," Mitchell said, nodding his head uncertainly. "What kind of tree?"

"Pollimen Tree. Daht's de best we mahnage as yet."

Mitchell pondered this insight, baffled; perhaps it contained a truth or ideology he had missed. Pollimen Tree, he said over and over to himself, until it evolved into *parliamentary* and he expected it to reveal some cornerpiece of knowledge, but its syllables grew meaningless and reverted back to nonsense.

"This place is the shits," Mitchell announced vacantly.

Saconi stopped playing, his hand muffling the strings, and lifted his head. "I'll write daht song," he said, giving Mitchell an unfriendly wink. "It will be about you, Mistah Good Guy."

"Hey, why don't you fuck off." The scotch went toxic in his veins. "You're always riding my ass, Saconi. What the hell do you want from me anyway?"

"Yeah, yeah, Wilson. Want some of daht yankee humor, bruddah."

"Today it's being tested."

"Oh ho. I see, I see. Wilson, hear now, what you believe a good humor fah in de fust place?"

Regret made Saconi's weak grin sadly honest. He pivoted around so he could lie down on the bench, hugging his guitar—this is how he would look when they laid him to rest in his coffin. He pumped his groin into the soundbox and smacked a sharp cord, singing like a cowboy in a mournful tremolo. "A-we ahll issa slapstick, enna you-ahll issa big stick'—how de next line go, Mitch?"

"Oh me," Saconi sighed when Mitchell shunned his invitation to sport along. He put aside his instrument and sat straight up. "Doan be vexed, Mitchie, eh?" To press his appeal he joined them at the wall, creating a mopey trio, three dogs in the pound.

"Your wisecracks—" Mitchell said, and clamped his mouth tight before he could say *are unfair.*

"Look, tek no offense, mahn. Rudeness have a big mahket in dis place. Is my life, ya know, to twist straight and straighten twist."

"Rudeness, teefin, devilment, mash up," Isaac added, graduating his misfortune to general conditions.

Their collective mood had found its cellar, a malaise like a ladder they had descended rung by rung. Mitchell wished to make some definitive statement on his own behalf, explain why he had come to St. Catherine, how he should be treated during his tenure. Justification whirled down toward his lips like an insect that flew too randomly to anticipate and capture. "Uh, uh," he heard himself grunt. The danger was to say anything trite but he lacked the facility to say anything more complex than a footman's proclamations. He was too high, his brain too hazed. He felt like cartoon footage, the Saturday-night evolution of Kurtz . . . go ashore, get ripped and hazardous with the locals.

"I am a guest," he proclaimed, "of the frigging queen."

"True," Isaac said, intent on studying the sky to the south for sight of the incoming plane. In his concentration he resembled a black tomcat willing a sparrow out of a tree. "We ahll in de same leaky boat."

"Queen finish up, mahn. You too late. People runnin queenless now."

"Same boat," Isaac affirmed. He nodded out to sea, a plane there sinking out of the blue through blades of sunlight, a bright angel of glass.

"Is the plane on fire too?"

"Nah."

Mitchell felt queasy. The plane's wings flared violent white, twin furnaces in the tropic heat.

"You happy now?"

"No."

The last time he had seen Johnnie, five years ago in the mountains of Virginia, she wore a navy blue pea coat which she kept on all day as she lay on the couch in his apartment, a used syringe thrown down on the carpet, recovering from an abortion—her second, to the best of his knowledge. He remained on campus, in the arts and sciences library, until late at night, reading the same three or four sentences in a botany textbook again and again, but they guarded a meaning that was indecipherable. He was home for half an hour, hadn't opened his mouth and neither had Johnnie, when she got up from the couch where she had been picking at imaginary blemishes and said, I think I'll just leave, all right?, and she did. But he had never answered her, had never said all right, go. The day before he had told her, "I spend three bucks a week on Trojans because the pill makes you water-logged and puffy. How'd you get pregnant?" She said she didn't know, and kept saying it until she had convinced herself it was true. He wouldn't have even known about it if he hadn't answered the phone, the clinic wanting to confirm her appointment.

The plane banked east to north into its landing pattern and glided onto the runway, raising an assembly of cattle egrets from the guinea grass as it touched. The birds scattered and flapped like snow-white handkerchiefs thrown into the air, fluttering in the propwash. The machine shimmered through watery heat waves the length of the pale concrete, losing its shape, melting and re-forming, not entirely real to Mitchell, given its alleged cargo of one old girlfriend well educated in betrayal. The roar from the engines faded, crescendoed, diminished, the pilot taxiing down from the end of the strip, the biggest noise on the island and Johnnie embedded therein, closing her magazine, checking her makeup, if she ever ended her pretense against the stuff, replacing the gum in her mouth with a new stick to clear the taste of tobacco if she still smoked—the woman he had once loved flying back into his life for a reason he could not say, and did not want to think about. The plane inched up to the terminal, scaring him.

Mitchell knew they must look predatory on the spread of the low roof. The sound of the propellers whining increased his agitation, but when the noise stopped so did his courage, a hasty resolve to grant reconciliation only as a diplomatic favor. Maybe if he just cut his heart out and tossed it down to her she'd get back on the plane and leave, he thought. A ground crew idled over to chopblock the landing gear and manhandle the luggage. The hatch in the cabin was lowered, folding stairs released from inside, and a stewardess in a lime-green pantsuit descended like the Queen of Sheba, patting her blown hair back into its cone. She was professionally discreet in her acknowledgment of the smoldering fire truck, the charcoaled entrance to the airline's ops room only thirty yards away, offering her attendant's aloof vision of a world in good order, a world safe and sane.

"Long time since I jook daht gy-url," said Saconi, and Mitchell, who had been ruminating in his own language over an identical fact in regard to Johnnie, felt enlisted into a larger conspiracy. "She know how to play special," Saconi concluded, "but she doan know how to *be* special."

In the hatchway behind the stewardess stood a man dressed like a dentist in white knit trousers and a powder-blue shirt-jac, the clinical style of the modern West Indian man of affairs. His name was Vincent Archibol, and he was mesmerizingly handsome, to the degree of glamor. He clambered down the steps as if he were hurrying to take ownership of the island, swinging a briefcase in his hand, his neck encircled by a braid of gold.

"Hail de conquerin hero," Saconi said.

Vincent Archibol was one of Edison Banks' oldest friends and followers, another architect of the coalition, the beneficiary of PEP's successful maneuvering to combine the foreign and diplomatic portfolios, thus depriving Kingsley of a voice abroad. Archibol now served St. Catherine as her ambassador to the United Nations, where he enjoyed firsthand the courtship of the continents, and ranted selectively against their hegemony. Mitchell had not been introduced to him as he had the other bulls of state, though he had encountered his reputation for progressive action often enough. Archibol and

Banks were the darlings of the new generation of patriots on the island.

There was a sudden renewal of Isaac's distress. "Oh yeeiii yi yiii," he whimpered miserably. "Look de shitty luck God givin me today. Look, look," he instructed, covering his eyes with one hand and pointing with the other at a woman advancing out onto the tarmac to embrace the homecoming ambassador. Archibol was shoved backward from the thrust of her bosom. They gave each other a brisk and publicly conscious dose of affection. Mitchell didn't recognize her face, but he remembered the square-shouldered heft of the woman, the nightmarish breasts, and the yellow blouse from the roadside of Ooah Mountain.

"Why you cryin so?" Saconi challenged Isaac. "You lucky, bwoy, she ain marry you."

"Isaac ran into her car this morning up on the mountain."

"Isaac smash Archibol's wife?" Saconi asked, his eyes signaling mischief. "Hey," he hollered crudely down at the couple as they were passing into the building through the Customs gate, "Am-bahssa-mahn, you muss keep daht womahn from behavin so reckless when you away, nuh?"

Archibol disappeared with ministerial imperiousness through the entrance, but his wife paused a step, craning her neck to look up, her hand in a salute to shade her eyes, her heavy slick red lips pursed in an expression of such censorship that her very essence seemed to be intolerance, and the capacity to make that intolerance effective against all violations, real or imagined. Isaac, horrified, ducked behind the ornamental wall and slugged Saconi in the thigh. Mitchell watched Archibol's wife march after her husband.

"Why you do daht? Why you play de fool, Saconi?" Isaac railed. "Why you behave so bumby-head? Why you so smahtass, eh? Why you want to fuck me up?"

Saconi threw up his hands. "What she cy-ahn do, mahn? She ain see us, besides. Juss have a bit of fun, ya know."

"She ain have to see us, she juss smell we, like tiger," Isaac said, back on his feet and shaking with anger. Mitchell had never seen him lose his temper before, and Isaac was different as a shouter, more like one of the crowd, alien and potent. "You set me on de run," Isaac said, stabbing the musician's chest with his finger. "I ain limin about fah she to kick me ass when Customs finish."

"Tek it easy," said Saconi, making a grudging effort to calm him down. "Tek it easy."

Isaac snickered; his face glazed with woodenness. "Easy ain de way it come." Saconi's insolence had reminded the former owner of *Miss Defy* how little of anything he could afford, including protection from power. "Sorry, Mitchie," he said, close to defeat, "I goin go. I gone now," and though Mitchell reached out to pacify him, to do or say something to stop his fugitivisim before it got started, Isaac was, as he said, gone.

Saconi was not inclined to acts of contrition. "Craziness get in him," Saconi said. "Him hit'n run and he worry? Hah, you jokin, mahn. Hit'n run, daht's de fuckin national anthem here, in dis place, in dis time. Ain no one give a shit."

Passengers continued to disembark, the majority of them Catherinians rebounding home, sharing the same bright countenance, relief or triumph—ain no place like dis sweet island, they were saying, or, I only comin back to let you see I mek sometin of meself, eh? Look de Rolex, mahn. Check it out. A few white faces like china masks bobbed in the flow, come to conduct odd business, seek expensive pleasures, practice Edwardian statecraft, force a broadening of the democratic horizon. Mitchell wished them all good and speedy purchase as he searched for Johnnie in the herd. Maybe she wasn't coming after all, maybe in the midst of some induced state this was her idea of a memorable prank, her cracked sense of humor reaching out to Mitchell to arouse the vestige of romance that shadowed his heart, gathering a line of data for future use: obsession plus love decreases at such and such a rate per year of separation, squared by distance, until even the strongest of previous attachments have achieved a certain entropic quantity, a formulaic numbness, a death. Tilled soil erodes, doesn't it? she had asked him one day, smoking a joint and thumbing through one of his sourcebooks. Today's gardens are tomorrow's deserts. He could picture her back in Hawaii, giggling as only a girl who refused to be serious could giggle, as she tried to guess whether or not he took her telegram at face value. He was sorrier than he should have been that she was not on the flight, but then there she was, incredibly there she was, and he gazed upon her with all the unstudied intensity of a fellow who had just been shipped a mail-order bride, a tingling in his heels, ready to leave, to bolt. Now it was beginning, he thought, the sequel to the original production: Kids Fucking Up. This was the new show—no rehearsals, no script, only old times and unacquainted adults in an extemporaneous staging, amateurs' manqué with a fragile morale, everything handicapped by the blunt disaster of their last co-starring performance. A role like this, a role that returned ex-lovers and secret sorrows into the lights, could only punish its players, and punishment would be its only merit.

There she was, maneuvering through the dim background into the open hatch, enormous straw bags looped over each slender arm. Mitchell asked himself why he should believe the sight of her and answered, believe, believe, in the grasp of an undisciplined reality, believe whatever you see. He asked himself without joy, what does this mean? what does this mean? what does this mean? until his throat constricted and he repulsed what felt like a chemical release of sentimentality. Is this anybody I know? he wondered: the same woman who jilted a beau from the Naval Academy to take up with him during their senior year in high school, burning the cadet's photograph, like an effigy of a boring future, in front of him in the ashtray of her Volkswagen and, to underscore her change of heart, slipping her panties off from under her skirt without being asked; the same one who skipped thirty-one days of class with him throughout the autumn and early winter in favor of a mutual curriculum of sensual studies, first dry-humping in the basement of her parents' split-level, cocooned in cheap incense and the music of a new San Francisco, her pelvis drubbing his crotch with such fury that he suspected her passion was abnormal, that most girls weren't like this or they'd all be locked away; the same woman who once fretted about if other girls got as wet as she did, the same one who asked him to masturbate for her so she could inspect this male novelty at close range, the same person who one afternoon announced, This is the day I want you to make love to me for real but first you have to stop looking like you're about to take an exam, and when he entered her she hid her face in his shoulder and sobbed, with pain, he supposed, although he heard something else that he had never heard before, and when he tried to withdraw out of confusion she said, No, it's all right, leave it there, I've got to get used to it inside me. Then afterward she cried with strained happiness about what-it-meant while he lay beside her with her pillow over his head, the pillow she slept on each night alone in her room, the queen of his imagination, and he trembled like a bad dog because he had gotten so deep into her world, as if he had been issued a temporary visa into a forbidden country, and the pleasure of being admitted into that foreign place astounded him, and he said to her what everybody says, and meant it with gratitude and great conviction, and she said what anybody would say who thought they had fallen in love forever—completing the first stage of a process that now seemed like the biggest prank in all creation, for how could the sacred and precious and sublime collapse so inevitably into the sophomoric, with such a premonition, a prescience that lit the darkness like a flare, that it would do it again and again throughout the course of a life, until complacency ruled.

Sure, I knew her, Mitchell thought, you bet, but she had gone away. She had dropped out of her second year at Sweet Briar to come live with him in Charlottesville while he studied for a degree that tried to absurdly navigate the crosscurrents of his father's bureaucratic expectations and his own generation's retreat to the land. She left seventeen months later. When her letters started to arrive in the mail, he answered back like a dutiful brother, keeping in touch, wishing her happiness on her birthdays, peace with each new year she welcomed without him, finally comfortable with a ritual of civility, and here she was again, back before him, not an answered prayer, coming down the stairs with big straw bags filled with the objects that were necessary to her on her journey, her sandaled feet reading each step carefully under the obstruction of her load, her legs concealed to the middle of her calves by a loose skirt made from blue jeans. She lagged to hitch the bigger bag over her shoulder, her breasts outlined perfectly during this readjustment under her sleeveless olive jersey. Before she continued she looked quickly around, smiling with unwarranted reciprocity as if she were aware of someone she had not yet identified paying her attention. Wave, Mitchell told himself, but his hand stayed where it was. They were nothing more than two people about to meet for the first time after years of hearing anecdotes of each other from friends in common. Any other view was pointless, since she had not traveled this far, had she, to resurrect old pain or start new fires.

"Which one yours?" Saconi asked.

Mitchell did not want to debate the issue of possession with Saconi. The one that was his was the one neither of them could see, a girl with a Raphaelite luxuriance of hair, on her back in a Virginia pasture, shouting out at the October sky that the world was changing just about as fast as she could ask it to. But her caramel hair was lighter than Mitchell recalled, and drastically shorter, banded into a cool ponytail. She wore a white sun visor, a red lightning bolt emblazoned on the bill, and aviator sunglasses, so that there really wasn't much visible of her face except her mouth, set with lines of determination, the scrolled upper lip and the fat, pouty lower one closed tight over a tongue he heard rehearsing lines and lies that he wished she would swallow.

"Come, Wilson. We goin serenade dis gy-url."

Saconi exploded into performance, wildly strumming the guitar strings with a beat only roosters could dance to, yapping a frantic calypso in the whiny Methedrine voice some of the island talent had copied from the mainland to the south. It was so ridiculous Mitchell shook his head and reluctantly smiled.

"Come on, Wilson. Come, come."

"She's not worth it."

"Come, mahn. Come."

Saconi accelerated the tempo; the music earned its right to obedience through sheer aggression. Mitchell's feet, aided by a lingering alcoholic freedom, moved on their own into a shortened two-step, and he was married to the cadence before he knew it. St. Catherine, he thought, you are wicked, wicked, to deny a man his self-pity. Johnnie saw them and waved excitedly, her hand restricted though by the bag on her arm. She stopped to appreciate the scene on the roof. Her mouth cracked open and she nodded her head as if she had foreseen just such a reception: spreeing, singing, fine-looking men and a bath of sunlight to herald the wonder of entry into a different kingdom, these fetching arrangements on the other side of leavetaking.

"God," Mitchell had to admit, "I love airports."

Chapter 3

They went back down into the charry murk of the terminal, the floor spotted with puddles and tracked grime. In the happy crowd assembled outside the glassed-in Customs area, Mitchell found Tillman Hyde, the proprietor of Rosehill Plantation. Tillman had inherited the tourist resort from his late father, an advertising executive turned addict of exotic speculations, and Tillman, in the absence of any other commitment besides late nights and unproductive days as a clubhound in Manhattan, had decided to manage the place himself hands-on against the advice of family lawyers and bankers, who had a constitutional aversion to the idea of one loser operating another. They did not foresee that Tillman's personality, a tranquility they had judged vagrant, would conform so successfully with the requirements of the job, the obstacles to conducting ordinary business that no reasonable person should have to tolerate.

"I don't suppose you hire out, do you?" Tillman said, his eyes running over Mitchell. "St. Catherine must be getting to you. You look very local this morning."

Tillman had current information on the airport vaudeville. The tower crew, mad at everybody, had insisted on hot-wiring their back-up generator to the battery of the fire truck. The cables were attached carelessly to their posts and the battery blew up. One man was trundled away to the hospital, his face sprayed with acid. A belated inspection of the old generator's spark plugs revealed they were corroded beyond use; a new set was procured. Another triumph in the day-by-day siege of technology upon the collective wit. The plane was invited down from its holding pattern over Los Muertos Channel.

Tillman was at the airport to collect his latest arrivals, among them the newest recruit in a seemingly inexhaustible supply of girls he had dated in New York City. He pointed her out to Mitchell and Saconi, a mere wafer of womanhood, blond hair and a face shaped like a strawberry. She was at Johnnie's side, sharing confidential laughter, jitterbugging, not ashamed of her energy or the excitement of being a newcomer. She was one of the first to claim her luggage and escape through the queue, dashing into Tillman's arms to bestow a genuine kiss, one of her legs raised like a flamingo's while she delivered it. "What a flight," she exclaimed. Her voice was sharp with urban assertiveness. She whirled around, her hair elevating with girlish flair off the slopes of her cheeks. "It was strictly the twilight zone. We could see the pilot fall asleep reading the newspaper. What's going on here anyway? Is there a war?" You could tell from the eagerness of her smile that a war would be just the thing. Her name was Adrian. She was the publicist for a syndicate of galleries in Soho, an impresario of special events. Dressed in Eddie Bauer sportswear, safari garb from the young boy's rack, she looked lifted from the pages of *Seventeen,* Miss Global Frolic, her lips with an acrylic shine, her skin unblemished but for the splatter of butterscotch freckles on each pink cheek and brow, altogether too cute for the world outside of vanity magazines and so, Mitchell surmised, a woman who saw pampering as an inalienable right.

"Are you two meeting somebody?" Tillman asked, looking from Saconi to Mitchell.

"His girlfriend," Adrian volunteered. "I met her on the plane."

"I didn't know you had a girlfriend," said Tillman.

"I don't."

Adrian's eyes widened. "Oh, terrific," she said tartly. "That's news to Johanna."

"Sounds like you're in for some fun," Tillman grinned, tugging Adrian backward. He picked up her canvas suitcase and directed her toward a group of pale and weary North Americans filing through the Customs door.

"Wait and meet her," Mitchell said. He wanted them there as insulation against the rising goose bumps, the dwindling oxygen, the cool agony and the deadpan heart that were the messengers of Johnnie's imminence. But Tillman's flock was waiting, they had to go, and Saconi begged off too to catch a charter flight to Cotton Island where the Princess kept him on retainer to entertain at her playpen for terminal bloodlines and her pukka friends. He swaggered off to the airport's only gate where an official was taking down the number 1 and replacing it with the number 2. No baggage but his guitar in a scuffed case. Whatever the musician needed, Princess' staff would provide and Saconi didn't want to underuse the privilege. People stepped into his way for a word, island women turned their heads brazenly, called to him, *eh, eh, tek me where you goin, mahn, sing babysweet fah me.* Mitchell turned back to his own object of private fame, *femme vital* and *femme fatale,* the love that had slipped through his fingers, the celebrity of his one great personal disaster.

What Mitchell watched through the glass wall was all too familiar: Johnnie dicking around, the exclusive style of behavior as if her timing, like Greenwich's, set the pace for everyone else, oblivious not to people but to what was most practical. Not a gal for shortcuts or even direct routes. He saw her squat like a coolie, draping her skirt between her legs, and tear through one of the handbags looking for her passport. Finally she lurched away from the luggage queue, swinging gear onto a processing table to be inspected by a rigid agent. Mitchell groaned when he saw her old backpack, utilitarian relic of hippie days. Where did she think she was? The Appalachian trail? You could feel the creepy gratitude of the customs officer as he shed his boredom and upended the pack, letting its contents rain out. Johnnie's shoulders tightened and flinched under the loathsome and darkly violating caress of the procedure. The man scattered the pile of her clothes like a deck of tarot cards, pawing through it for signs of her fortune. He rubbed the black material of a bra between thumb and forefinger. He opened a pill bottle and inhaled its aroma. He unzipped her cosmetic bag and emptied it as if it were filled with jewels. When he selected her blue diaphragm case and was about to unclasp it, she snatched it out of his hands before he understood how to pry the clamshell edges open.

In shock, Mitchell prayed for her to put it back down.

What was she trying to do, the naif, in a land she had never been before and probably never imagined, painting herself a target for a man who ached to put his two-hour special training in the hideaways of the body to use, and here was Johnnie offering him an invitation to the full range of secret spots, not just physical access but unrestricted license to interiors, the attics and cellars of her identity. The Tourist Board needed more truth in advertising, a poster with a guy like this one with hammerhead eyes, his handsome braided tunic and officer's cap, his grin studded with a gold tooth, a speculum in his breast pocket underneath a colorful row of bogus medals of honor, his left hand drawing a chalky surgical glove down over his upraised right hand, the fingers juxtaposed with the immaculate sails of a yacht, an umbrella of palm trees, a bikinied woman about to enter the perilous sea. Regardless of the undertow of danger, Johnnie would not give back the diaphragm case. Not only would she not return it, she shook it like a safe pass in the man's deadly humorless face. Her protest, inaudible through the glass barrier, made Mitchell so angry that he thought, whatever she got she deserved. But people in St. Catherine, even uniformed homicidals on the civil payroll, weren't so simple, or at least you could say that their simplicity came with a tradition of ingenuity. They loved big mouths and big wind, they admired fights and fighters for the honesty of expression as long as no one pulled punches, as long as passions were ignited, and the fighter, especially the one who represented the rightful cause, was as blind and defenseless as Johnnie. A crab confronting the fisherman, a slave back-talking a master, the island romance with futility.

The agent's face became a small nova of pleasure and he accepted Johnnie's tantrum as his light amusement for the day. He obviously enjoyed her show of fury and checked his fellow officers and even the head porter to see if they appreciated that he was the inspiration for this little white fuckable, beatable treasure of foolish defiance. Johnnie twisted an arm behind her to point randomly into the terminal, apparently giving Mitchell's name as a counterbalance of authority. Mitchell saw the villain shift his eyes beyond her, scanning the crowd behind the sheet of grease-smeared window to locate the man she claimed as patron. Mitchell dropped his head, a lesser St. Peter, denying the challenge to be held accountable because of the outlandish judgment of this woman.

Her passport was returned and the agent advanced down the table, automatically clearing the next three passengers in line, Johnnie forgotten except in mockery. She restuffed her belongings into the backpack with sharp jabs, ramming her clothes into its mouth, hoisted her straw bags to the crooks of her elbows and reared up, tempestuous, her lips still moving and not likely in thanks. The exit door kicked open.

"What a complete bastard," she said with reckless disregard that he might hear her. Her hip blocked the door's return swing and she muscled through unassisted, hung with possessions. "I've had it with men like that. They can go screw themselves because they're not screwing me." She turned her head toward Mitchell, her mouth exasperated. "Can't you help," she said, a demanding boldness in her voice that didn't match the picture he had of her, the private composition, the image that had nothing to do with other people, or the chess game of social issues, or the public performances. In private, the Johnnie that Mitchell knew had been trapped in the flux of ambivalence for who was right and what was wrong. That Johnnie never learned to scream, never participated in confrontation, walked away from fire as if she were doused in gasoline.

A bag slipped off her arm and pooched to the floor. She stayed where she was and tried to come to some conclusion about Mitchell's immobility, the few yards of one kind of distance that remained between them. "That other cocksucker only gave me two weeks," she said. "The guidebook says I'm entitled to three months." Implicit in the way she stood there, in the agitated way she spoke, in the matter-of-fact manner she was trying to uphold, was the expanding reality of her decision to come this way, back to Mitchell. Maybe she realized how tough she was playing it because she untensed, dropped the aggression of her shoulders, and reversed the lines of her mouth into a shy smile. "Hello," she said and laughed self-consciously, shaking her head. "Are you ready for me?"

"It can be changed," Mitchell croaked, breaking out from his severe daze. She gave him a puzzled look and he said, "Your visa, I'll take it to the Immigration Office later on today," but when he reached for her passport she inserted it back into the handbag. Mitchell grabbed the other tote but wouldn't let himself touch her, sure something would go spontaneously wrong if he touched her so readily. And wasn't two weeks enough anyway? Three months took the form of cruel and unusual punishment, and what about the Sierra backpack and the two piddly grassmat handbags? What was she, a gypsy? Three months on an aspirin and a change of underwear?

"Improper border behavior," Mitchell advised coldly. "You don't grab things out of a customs officer's hand."

"Perhaps," she said. She smiled in a way he knew too well—a suck on the lemon of irony. She raised her arms and flopped them against her sides. "I didn't know what else to do. I have five grams of coke taped to my diaphragm."

He stood staring at her, stunned by her audacity.

She knew all the admonishments, all the sermons. She threw herself at him to cut short any scolding, kissing him on the cheek, her lips a sticky press, her arms around him, her hands remembering his back.

"Look at you," she said, "you look so good, and so-o serious." Her head tilted back to really take him in for the first time. Her sunglasses disturb me, was all Mitchell could think. "So how have you been, Mitch?" The hug he traded with her was feeble. I can't see you, he thought. You can be anybody. Maybe there was no Johnnie anymore, maybe nobody lasted unless you stayed glued to their side.

"So what have you been up to?" Her voice sped nervously along. "You have dirt in your hair, in case you didn't know. And what's with this shirt?" Her fingernails grazed the exposed inch of his stomach. "Your banjo here looks pretty. A little skinny maybe. Tight. Hard. I've been associating with slobs."

Mitchell had forgotten she chattered a lot, this inflated gaiety, whenever she was hyper or high. Whatever she read she was easily persuaded by. One month a Buddhist, the next a disciple of Ram Dass, a stretch of infernal depression instigated by Camus. Virginia Woolf and primal therapy. It had been difficult to keep his equilibrium with her as she exchanged one sensibility for another, a honeybee in well-pollinated gardens of thought. That was five years ago and more. He hated this reunion, hated everything about it.

"You smell like whiskey."

"Mmm."

What on earth was she now, what trend or fad was she fastening on? She never made mention of her constant realignment of interests in any of her occasional letters, periodic updates of the trivial. Weather's splendid out here, I'm doing fantastic, met a guy, moved to Montana, met another guy, I'm learning how to sail, moved to Honolulu, moved to the North Shore, moved to Maui, here's the new address, come visit.

"Don't you smile now that you work for somebody's government?"

"I can smile."

"Let's see you."

Mitchell bared his teeth.

She did write that her mother drank herself to death a year ago. Her father was a child psychiatrist, now in Chicago. Was that right, Chicago? Minneapolis? Johnnie had nicknamed him Doctor Lick, the man who gave tongue to all hurt, all the hurt little boys and girls.

He felt bad, making her jittery like this, but he couldn't locate what it was he should be doing. All the lost days, like a stream vanishing underground, but resurfacing (to borrow from the current political rhetoric in fashion on St. Catherine) in this place, in this time. Unforgivable?—no, not quite that. Forgiveness might be efficacious, but it wouldn't make a dent in the mystery of the deprivation, those irrecoverable days. They were terrifying, they were *ours minus us*, he said to himself.

"You really haven't said anything," she moaned, and though he couldn't see he could hear the incipient tears. "I thought you'd be glad to see me."

Mitchell had to clear his throat to speak. "Yes, I am," he rasped.

She had a pack of cigarettes in her hands, fumbling with the wrapper, and she stooped to rake through one of the bags for a book of matches. He gazed down at the two hemispheres of her hair framed by the band of her sun visor, the brown undertones and wisps of blond, trying to recall the duties of each side of the brain. As much as one half of her favored him, the other half always had a way, an argument, a design, to undo it.

"I'm sorry." Her words strained through the constriction of her throat. She had stopped searching for a light but stayed down in her penitent's crouch. "I didn't think it would be this hard. Stupid me."

His head wagged no no no. "I'm a little drunk," he blurted out.

"You're being a shit."

When she said that, Mitchell knew he could afford to smile. He recovered enough sense to open the door and bail out, let the masochism of his memory plunge ahead without him, without hope. He now had the headache he had labored to earn but smiled through its stabbing pulse at Johnnie, who had stood up and taken the unlit cigarette from her mouth. It disappeared in her hand and both hands dived into pockets sewn near the waist of her skirt, her arms compressing her breasts, the nipples perked the shape of limpet shells under the cotton, rocking on her flat heels looking pleased and *there*. Mitchell had nothing to say, again, to this pleasure of hers. It was all so easy, yet he couldn't stop himself from feeling inflamed and clogged.

She nudged up against him, took his wrist, let her hand glide into his and grabbed when he wouldn't. Her breath smelled of tobacco and peppermint. "Are you all right? You're shaking."

"Let's just go."

He hoisted the inciteful backpack by its straps and carried it that way. Walking through the terminal by his side she rotated her attention this way and that, perplexed by the unusual aspects of the Brandon Vale International Airport, a facility decorated in calamity and breakdown.

"What happened here? We saw the smoke from the air and thought you were all murdering each other." She surveyed the black pools, the stone-faced locals, filth tracked all over the tiles, the soot on the walls, the chopped-up LIAT station wetly smoldering.

"This is how we do things here," Mitchell said. "Welcome to the muddle."

❖ ❖ ❖

In the taxi she took her sandals off, the skin on her ankles branded with red stripes, her toes puffy from the heat. She gave him little room on the seat, hogging the middle. Mitchell leaned forward both to feel less confined and to ask the driver if he had seen Isaac.

"Yeah, I see him. He mek a quick skip up Zion Hill. Look like he chasin a fella."

"Drive up that way, would you."

Johnnie coaxed Mitchell back next to her and held his arm as though she thought he might run away. "Don't get mad," she said. "I actually thought you were trying to punish me there for a while."

"I don't know," he answered wearily. "Maybe I was."

She brought her knees up flat onto the seat and turned at the waist, facing him with her body, using its confident language. Her anxiety was no longer there, she had made a decision to be calm. "I thought you had forgiven me," she said, and although it was a dramatic line to say she said it quietly, plainly.

He watched the roadside, the vendors caged in their booths with a stock of beer and weird West Indian soda. "I thought I had too," he said, and wondered if he would have to do it again, or could, now that it must be true.

Up Zion Hill and at the crest, Isaac was nowhere to be seen. The driver doubled back and headed for Howard Bay. The escapade had come to an end; Isaac would be home in Scuffletown by now, crawling in his bed like a refugee to be saved by sleep, hurrying to lose consciousness.

They motored back down the hill across the cane-green meadows of Brandon Vale. Mitchell didn't care to look in the direction of *Miss Defy* foundered and lamed forever in the fields that would be harvested to sweeten wealthier parts of the world. The driver shifted into a lower gear as they began to climb Ooah Mountain, the engine a wounded wheeze. Johnnie stared thoughtfully out the window, the sun visor on her lap, the scented breeze fragmenting the strands of hair that had loosened from her ponytail. A gangly man pedaled up the grade on a thirdhand bicycle, a load of cassava root netted to his back, his heaving grunts briefly audible to them over the grind of the car.

Johnnie sat away from the window, retaking the center of the seat. Mitchell reached up and put her sunglasses on the crown of her head. Here she was then, complete, more of her than he ever had the chance to know. The unhealthiness of her eyes was another shock, the token repair of eyeliner and mascara, the red mist of exhaustion that travel alone could not account for. Her eyes didn't look young anymore, they were years ahead of her, waiting for the rest to catch up. There was still a power in their green and hazel depths though, its source not so much a feminine quality as it once was, the innocence or freshness they had once expressed, but something else, something greater that had been severely challenged without breaking, and something fractured and sadly resigned, an inner life in which Mitchell did not want to be enrolled. She had rubbed blush on her cheekbones but it was wearing thin in the heat. Underneath, her color was faintly jaundiced, not right for a woman just arrived from the beaches of Hawaii. Her eyes darted back and forth trying to interpret what he saw in them.

"You've stayed beautiful," he said. And she had, even if it was a beauty under transition, perhaps a beauty about to rupture. She rested her forehead against his shoulder. He thought by now she had been granted ample time to practice an answer, and he needed to hear it, shrugging so she was forced to raise her head, look at him. She knew what was coming.

"Yesterday you were thousands of miles away, in another life. Why are you here?"

Johnnie didn't falter or drop her eyes. "Will you believe what I say?"

"Okay . . . why not."

She had a two-minute presentation worked out, an overview. She talked about people coming into each others' lives, and people hopping out of each others' lives, and good timing, and bad timing, and off timing. Mitchell didn't know what she meant and said so.

"I want to be with you again—if you'll let me."

He was slow to react to her revelation, the only possibility he had dismissed outright. He heard himself chuckling, but the sound was rich with contempt and menace. She observed the changes in his face with alarm. All these festering urges—to push her out of the car, to bury himself in the curve of her neck and weep, to fling her into bed in a rage of domination and then order her back in the air. Mitchell squirmed; blades of fever took short looping slices at his nervous system. He stared out the window, sighed, looked back steadily into her road-worn eyes.

"You know, I don't find this stuff funny anymore."

"Now I don't know what *you* mean," Johnnie answered softly.

His voice rose. "You experienced a moment of overwhelming affection for me, right?, like a mystical vision, is that right?, and you had to drop everything and run to my side. Do I have it straight?"

His words ended in a harsh whisper. The taxi banked into a hairpin turn that squeezed them together, the pressure from her increasing by her own will. He pushed her off with his elbow.

"Johnnie, I've got a headache, a brain-buster, and I think, on top of that, I broke my nose this morning. I'm going to lie down here. I'm going to close my eyes for a minute. Don't say anything, all right."

Mitchell started to slump down, falling away in the opposite direction from her but Johnnie caught both of his arms and bent him around, cradling his head into her lap, flipping the visor onto the floor. She stroked his hair tenuously, as if afraid of being told not to. Mitchell inhaled the laundered fragrance of her skirt, felt the pack of muscles on her thighs beneath the denim. He was no longer incited or unsound, and hadn't the energy or the zeal left for further righteousness. As she massaged his temples, he discovered himself wondering if she were wearing panties. She used to disdain the habit and the implication of underclothes. What had she thought, that their purpose led to another hopeless middle-class trap. No, of course not, it was just a feeling she liked, a tiny, private freedom. He felt ridiculous thinking about it now, in complicity with the customs agent, the wonderful shades of her lingerie shaken out on the examination table.

One thing Mitchell had not forgotten about Johnnie though. Like a candidate for higher office, amassing loyalties, Johnnie had always overpromised her love.

Chapter 4

Isaac was talking to the dead but couldn't get their attention: his father Crissy Knowles; his father's father, Samson Knowles; that one's father, Cedric Knowles; and that one's father, Alfonzo Knowles; and the next in line, Parnell Forbes; and the next, Etson Bynoe, and his father Aubrey Bynoe; and the Creole *filibustier,* Gireaux; and then the half-breed Maroon named Biabou; back and back through a clan of patriarchs to the one they called Anselm, the name lacerated on the eggplant skin of his shoulder by an English slave trader, down through the blood of the centuries to this one who had crossed the waters from Guinea and mixed his seed with the wild Indians. Behind this father there were no others, only a mythical homeland, a vast incorporeal voice unintelligible to Isaac though he addressed it as Yah-weh, and understood it as an ancient ended world once ruled with the strict cruel wisdom of the warrior-princes who were the sons of Cain.

Isaac was muttering to them about pollution, the bad luck that was somehow draining into the stream of his tolerable life, muttering that he, their good son, should have been forewarned, but the dead were playing a raucous game of dominoes under the shade of a *bwa homme,* a man tree, puffing away on their clay pipes and tossing back pitties of strong rum. They didn't want to be distracted—never did, it seemed. Isaac converted his conversation to the living, then—Fitzroy Roberts, Basil Trent, Noel Charles, Stuffy Paine, and the rest of the fellows who drove the taxis parked along the circle drive servicing the air terminal—but they weren't listening either. Plane juss reach, they shrugged, and since it was not possible for him to pay a fare or for them to accept his payment, he couldn't buy or beg their time away from chauffeuring tourists.

Then one of the dead lifted his lacy white head from the action of the domino board and said, *Look alive, bwoy.* This was one of their jokes, and they cackled hilariously when they used it. *Stop lookin dead like we, look alive now. You missin sometin up de road, nuh? Shoo. Hurry.*

Isaac scanned beyond the airport compound, along the road that led toward Zion Hill and down into Queenstown. The thoroughfare was populated as always with its flanks of cyclists and foot traffic, its opposing currents of jitneys and lorries, vans and passenger cars trailing plumes of raw exhaust. Look close, he advised himself, and soon he saw what he thought he was supposed to see, a monkey of a boy scampering onto the hill a step faster than everybody else, dodging the slower walkers. Swinging in the boy's grip, unmistakably, was a flat, square boxy object—the radio from *Miss Defy.* Readin you loud and clear, Isaac thanked his tribe of domino-slapping ancestors, and took off across the parking zones and the untended lawn, in pursuit of the boy before this day of losing things got any further out of his control. General runaway. General blowup.

Anselm: it was his arms, in a cane roller.

Parnell Forbes: one eye pricked out, with an acacia thorn.

Cedric: died of the everything-drop-off disease.

Samson Knowles: beaten back into infancy with a brass trumpet, having offended its Scottish owner, a member of the Fort George Queen's Regimental Band.

A knee was stiff and an ankle swollen but Isaac paid no mind to their steady broadcast of pain, the pain was nothing compared to the satisfaction of getting back what was yours. Yours was yours—simple, simple, and people had no right to lift it. He was halfway there, and then halfway through the remaining distance, when he began to get signals that something was wrong. To ease his anxiety, he forced himself to go a little faster, his lope bouncy from his hobbling knee. The boy slowed to a shamble and joined a queue of other boys and girls, and Isaac approached near enough to see his mistake. Here was no thief but a schoolboy late for the bus stop, carrying his noon meal along in a rusty tin lunchbox. He watched the bus come, the boy climb aboard.

Missin sometin up de road, sonny.

Hush, he answered back. You prankin me now. Fulla prank.

A car swerved in behind the bus, hit its brakes, then began to reverse along the shoulder, scattering pedestrians to one side or the other. Isaac hadn't really thought about what the car was doing until it halted just short of him, and only then did he recognize its mangled posterior. The horn beeped once to summon him, an arm with a gold watchband snaked out the driver's window and motioned Isaac to come around to the front. He wasn't in any shape to win a footrace down through the yards so there was nothing he could do about it. He limped up to the window and bent over, down level with the driver. Archibol glanced over at his frown-faced wife and she sucked her teeth, like a backward kiss, in confirmation, turning to look straight ahead, presumably at Isaac's own sorrowfully finite future. Isaac, his eyes on the dried-out disk of an old squashed crapaud in the gravel and grass tufts under the car, tried to behave himself and not make things worse by being cheeky or undignified.

"I know you, eh?" Archibol asked in a voice that had traveled off the island, north, and been influenced. "You Crissy Knowles' boy?"

Isaac scuffed the dirt with his good foot. "Me brakes give out, sah. I ain have no control. Me very own auto and livelihood mash up, come to a pile of junk."

"Get in," Archibol directed. "Come." The minister reached behind him to unlock the rear door of the sedan. Full of resignation, Isaac obeyed. There was some comfort to sitting down in the air conditioning, getting the weight off his legs. Before they could even return to the roadway, the woman furiously cranked her window open.

"Smell daht bwoy, Archie," she complained. "Him ahll drunk-up."

They drove up and over the crown of Zion Hill and down fast into town, through the blackened stone arch of the gate of the central police station, and parked on its cobbled parade ground. Archibol was committed to relieving himself of the distraction of Isaac as quickly as possible. A man arrives home from overseas where he has been conducting the serious business of his nation and is in no time at all ensnared by the trivial business bogging down the lives of common citizens. A fellow bang into the car and race off, his wife tells him. What does he care, he has more important things on his mind, but still he is only a man and his wife is upset. He's tired from his long journey, he's fretting about the maneuvering between his comrades since he's been gone. He doesn't want to think about such a small thing as an automobile, he wants to forget the whole business, the damage is only superficial and now the automobile looks like any other automobile on the potholed roads and dirt tracks of St. Catherine, so quit making this damn big fuss, woman, *fah Cyrise sake!* There were more compelling and fateful matters to concern himself with—he'd been summoned back from New York by the PM but not for reasons as yet explained. Quit making such a stupid fuss, eh?—but this was part of coming home, pretending sympathy and partnership in the meaningless obsessions of his spoiled wife, entering within the walls of her domestic kingdom where he was willing to let her reign with only occasional ritual challenges to her petty rule. It was nothing to him, except for such frivolous moments as this, their annoyance a mere tithe, a tax he must of necessity pay for sex, a home, a family. She insisted he stop on the road away from the airport and so he stopped, and now all he wished was for Crissy Knowles' oldest boy Isaac to come along to the police station and file an accident report so that his wife could be assured her vengeance—submitting a proper damage claim to the insurers, an act which would eventually bring about purpose and pleasure for her, given the plodding mishandling of such claims. He felt exactly as though he were providing her with a privileged position of employment—an opportunity to engage in long and fruitful harassment, bullying a chain of clerks and agents who would have no recourse but to listen to her caterwauls, and strive to please her.

Since Archibol had trained himself to see past the difficulty of any moment to its profits, he felt, by the time he had parked the sedan, gracious enough to open the back door for Isaac, and to walk according to the measure of the young man's lethargic pace, rather than nudge him forward though the grand fortress doors of the station. He was being conciliatory, he had found a clever way to make his wife a gift—but even this reversal of the minister's mood couldn't allay Isaac's fears. He balked at the threshold to the station, the voices of the dead in his ears, counting off licks: *One, fah freeness. Two, fah freshness.* Three for all-around *chupidness.* On the botsy, on the headside, cross the knackers and over the knees.

To guide him forward, Archibol touched Isaac's elbow, and Isaac recoiled.

"You ain bring me to jail, sah?" he said, planting his feet. "Was de brakes fail, ya know." Archibol himself spent a rare smile on this comedy and explained to Isaac the reason he must file a report.

"Is just formality, mahn," he said. "Relax, eh?"

The public reception room was not a welcoming sight. Its concrete floor was coarse and cracked. Two framed photographic portraits—one of the Queen, the other of Edison Banks—broke the bare monotony of the limestone walls, disregarded shrines. Two wooden benches, unoccupied, their surface polished by human friction, repeated the corner made by their adjacent walls. A doorway at the back of the room opened into a corridor, lined with austere offices. Against the far wall, facing out, was a metal desk, painted gray, and there sat the duty officer, pencil in hand, doodling on the front page of a copy of the *Crier.* As he saw the minister approach, he stood, coming to attention, and remained rigid while Archibol ignored him to chat with Isaac as if they had stepped into a pub, two old friends having a drink.

"I knew Crissy, ya know."

"Mm hmm."

Isaac had not had much opportunity to know his father except as dead—a murdered and martyred man, too fresh in the grave, too mad with his enemies, who remained among the living.

"Yes, I knew Crissy," reminisced Minister Archibol with self-importance. "Mahn, is true, but time fly, eh? Twenty years come and go since Crissy raise me up in de cutters union." With each word, the minister's language undressed itself until he was speaking the singsongy patois of his boyhood in the countryside—and of the campaign trail, too. "Me jussa bwoy bahck den, not so old ahs you. Crissy and Kingsley runnin de cane fields in dem days, eh? carryin on hell fah massa. When Crissy die, fust I tell meself, world come to end today. But world juss begin when Crissy tek de bullet from de white fella's gun, nuh? Crissy cotch de bullet daht set we free."

"Mm hmm," said Isaac, morosely.

Isaac had never been one to talk much about his father—what was there for him to say on a subject so readily converted into cheap fuel for mouthy politicians. When the first union of cane cutters had formed, illegally, on St. Catherine, Crissy Knowles had been one of the organizers, more inspiring to his mates than inspired by the role of leadership, and Joshua Kingsley had been their first elected union boss. Delwyn Pepper, nascent tyrant, was voted treasurer. Crissy Knowles was in the forefront of the union's struggle to be recognized, and when it came time to strike against the old families who owned the sugar plantations, Crissy led it. Crissy knew the stakes—he cut in the fields for a living. Kingsley and Pepper had never whacked a stalk of cane in their lives, except to have their pictures taken. When the strike busters mobbed the scene, Crissy's was the first head bloodied. For men like Kingsley and Pepper, men with no prospects, men who used their mouth the way others used their muscle, the union was a stepping stone to power, leverage against the colonial status quo, and when they were enfranchised into the affairs of the administrated state as unequal partners, it was Crissy who remained behind in the union, a fella who spent the day in the field with the rest of the workers. When England decided it had exhausted its interest in St. Catherine, a withered consort whose time had come to be retired from the payroll, Kingsley and Pepper matched up against the candidates of the old planters in the island's first elections for self-government, and it was Crissy they easily convinced to execute their most unsavory business, Crissy who talked the laborers into a season-long strike that starved them, Crissy who shepherded gangs of toughs against the Dominicans imported to harvest the cane. And finally it was Crissy, persuaded by God knows what argument, who had taken a thirty-pound crate of dynamite up to Jack Dawes Estate, packed it under the boilers of the island's only sugar refinery, and lit the fuse. The explosion tore out the last stubborn roots of the island's planter class, and a night watchman's bullet was the end of Crissy, and the end of what had since been called the Sugar War. Kingsley and Pepper had conveniently placed themselves in Trinidad for the fiery climax. They came back to bury Crissy Knowles a hero, but until this growing season cane had not been planted on St. Catherine for twenty years, for twenty years St. Catherine had sweetened her tea and cake with outside sugar, the cane cutters sat on their stoops for twenty years, sitting in darkness, and for twenty years Isaac Knowles had heard them curse his father's legacy of ruination, for twenty years he had listened to the big shots continue to drum his father's bones on the treasure chests of their venality, using Crissy the way preachers used Jesus, to stay in business.

Except through two images he had managed to preserve from his childhood, Isaac did not know Crissy Knowles as a man who had existed on the surface of the world. The first was of his mother peeling long green tongues of aloe, the gel glimmering in the lantern light of their wattle hut in the bush near the Jack Dawes Estate, her hands emulsifying it with a dribble of goat's milk, kneading and massaging the ointment into his father's forearms, shaped and colored like two legs of smoked mutton, but cratered with old scorpion bites and crosshatched with the paper-thin lines of the cane leaves, where the hard blades had sliced his skin. Nice, nice, Crissy would murmur as his wife worked on him. Then she'd pull off his pants to rub his legs, and he would sit down to his dinner in his sweaty underpants, at peace with himself, for the moment, in his rage against the old families.

The other image was of his father brought home that night that concluded the Sugar War, carried like a slain panther by four awkward disciples, four co-conspirators less brave and therefore still alive, one man to each arm, one to each leg, Crissy's rump bouncing on the dirt, his head lolling back impossibly far, scraping the dirt, rolling loosely with the steps of the men, and the worst of it, his father's tongue, extending horrifically out a gash in the side of his face to the ground, coated with blood and blackened by the soil it had dragged through, as though his father's dying effort had been to taste the earth. That is what Isaac knew and remembered of his father—an earth-eating animal whose flesh had been butchered by the knifelike slashes of the sweet harvest. As far as Isaac could determine, Crissy in his grave, the one absolute victim of the conflict, was a spirit divided, spending one half of eternity enamored of his own pride, the other half suffocating in a coffin of remorse.

Isaac leaned wearily on his arm against the edge of the desk in the vestibule of stone and mustiness, indifferent to Archibol's strange effort to patronize him. He had endured twenty years of his father's erstwhile mates, now the leaders of an independent nation, making irregular pilgrimage to pay their respects to Crissy Knowles' widow. In the early years they came knocking at the wattle hut in Jack Dawes and, when Crissy's pension checks stopped because the government—these same men—decided it would no longer fund a defunct union, they knocked at the clapboard house in the slum of Scuffletown, donated to his mother by a source unknown to Isaac. He and his brothers had grown up with the politicians petting the tops of their heads for good fortune. They would press a warm shilling into Isaac's hand and tell him, Keep awake in school, *bwoy*, this poor place going need your brain someday, and then they would saunter out into the yard to stand and speak to the people who had gathered there to see the notable men, native sons who had learned to talk back to the world. These men would finish their speeches and leave, as they always left, leaving Crissy's wife and boys to fend for themselves.

"Is a nation*ahl dis*grace," Archibol proclaimed, causing his wife to blink, smirking at his pointless oratory, "we fellas in Government House ain ahs yet move to put up a site, eh? like dem statue figure of de mahn Columbus, to honor Crissy properly." Spurred by his inspiration, he realized that a small relationship with Crissy Knowles' oldest son would not be a useless thing, even though the martyred union boss was a shopworn symbol for the conservatives and the Banks faction had so far ignored him.

"Is ahn idea in dis day, in dis time, nuh?" he said, his head nodding to solicit Isaac's approval. Isaac stared right through him, mimicking the nod, and Archibol assumed he had won his loyalty. Out of habit, he clapped Isaac on the shoulder, shook his unwilling hand, and forgot about him.

"Come," he said, rapping his knuckles on the desk to rouse the duty officer, "where de affidavy?"

The duty officer's heels popped together, as he had been trained to pop them for all of ministerial rank, and he emerged from his dullness.

"Sah?"

"Fah accident report, nuh? Bring it."

A ledger was produced from within the desk, its pages blue-ruled, like a composition book. Its used portion bore the painstaking handwritten accounts of yesterday's cruel involvements between the people of Queenstown, incriminations as old as slavery or as modern as packaged milk, the brawling feuds and larcenies, sexual assaults and drunken rampages that were the community's malformed and inarticulate self-expressions of justice. The duty officer took his chair, licked the tip of his ballpoint pen and remained poised, head down, waiting for the minister to begin his statement. But Archibol glared at his wristwatch and deferred to his wife, who had stood off to the side throughout, contributing a look of universal disapproval to the proceeding.

Archibol clucked impatiently at his wife. "Speak to de mahn," he said. He tapped the glass of his watch, already late for an appointment with the prime minister. "I walkin meself down to Government House to see Eddy."

The St. Catherine Crier

March 29, 1977

Low & Behold
by Epictetus

Eppy: Well, gents, another noisy week at Government House since we last adjourned our curbside choir. The hullabaloo brings to mind an observation offered years ago by a famous lady, to wit: No good deed shall go unpunished.

Beau of the Bawl: I for one am not surprised a woman said that since they are the ones who ensure its truth.

Sir Cease-All: The sentiment of a bachelor and card player. As for myself, you'll never find me lacking in my admiration for the fairer sex.

Beau: I hear it's the speed of your admiration that falls short, heh-heh.

Joe Pittance: As I see it, fellers, the lady's wisdom points right on target to the politicians, those keen at keeping poor St. Catherine in the bushes.

Sir C: There you have it. Why, look at this boy Banks trying to fill the shoes of PM. Not to insinuate the worst, but I thought only the communistic philosophy allowed that it was fine and dandy to go around the countryside uprooting families and turning them off the land. First the planters, and now the peasants themselves must go! The people have placed their hopes and dreams in his trust and he has shown them his backside. There's a fine reward for a good deed, and now perhaps you shall tell me we shouldn't expect so much from a hot and sweaty youth who borrows his ideas from the academy rather than the workshop of experience.

Joe: No no no. There are some ministers we would have no trouble naming who have begun to bite the hand that fed them, like they looking to smash up the Coalition, and bring old Pepper back to ruin us.

Beau: Coalition my foot! That's what we are calling it now when cats decide they are better off with the rats and divvy the cheese between them. Shenanigans filled up Government House this time, fellers, not votes.

Eppy: It's never an easy job to steer our beloved ship but I for one can't make heads or tails out of this land reform business. Who is doing what, and why, is what I want to know. Surely we each agree that fallow or under-used land is of no help to the economic situation. For as anyone will tell you, you can't call it dancing if all you are moving is your feet.

Beau: Is dancing all right, Eppy—straight into a potter's grave. A rat by any other name would smell as bad, but go ahead and put a fancy title to it like Agrarian Reform or PLDP. Mum, come to the window, is Agrarian Reform coming down the street. Well, poor Mum looking left and right but ain't see a thing but pests. PLDP?—all that is the PM's push to Kingsley's shove, eh?

Sir C: I believe you speak of the practice whereby the political inclination of a parish is physically manipulated. If that were all it was, I would say that is the same old game of dominoes, but the persecution of innocents will not go unheeded if the programme is carried forth.

Joe: With all due respect for your record of service, Sir C, the masses have had to do the best they can without a Robin Hood of their own. For their sake and for the good of the nation, the old estates which are now in the public domain must be reorganized and made to turn a profit as they did in the old days.

Beau: I am hoping that our boys have a plan to do this without a return to the old ways.

Sir C: You know that on all issues I share the view of God, the Queen, and of course the underdog.

Beau: Make heads or tails of that without getting a headpain and a tailache.

Joe: More for St. Catherine is more for all.

Beau: More for government is less for all.

Eppy: As they say, gents, A Naked Freeman is Nobler than a Gilded Slave. Let our little group set a standard for the rest. Practice patience and with-hold judgment until we know more about the scheme. By the way, have you noticed the PM's anniversary present to the Police?

Sir C: Well, it makes me very sad to see our men stripped of their smart white jackets and navy trousers with red stripe. How many young boys grew up longing for such distinction? Now they are required to dress as common troopers.

Beau: Battledress is all the rage now for traffic patrol. Just look at

Dominica they playing Marine over there. Straight army fantasy, boy. Barbados the same thing, Jamaica, Trinidad.

Joe: Modern times is what you're seeing in the force these days. The old uniforms left over from the colonial bygone had to go. I say cheers and best of luck.

Eppy: Enough about appearance, as long as the force continues to do a very good job let them wear whatever pleases them. I might add before we part: the *Royal Tropic* shall call at the island this Wednesday for the first time in two years. Congrats to Mr. Dexter Brisbane of Tourism and Trade for bringing the *RT* back to us after the unfortunate assault on several of her passengers by scoundrels who weren't thrown into prison quick enough to suit me. Let's all be down at the wharves to welcome the ship when she comes in. Once again, it's time to show the world we are the friendliest folks in the Caribbean. Until next week then, *Clarior E Tenebris.*

Chapter 5

Lloyd Peters stood restlessly to his feet, straightening the square tail of his linen bush jacket, and sat back down, aware that it was his role to lead the men in the room to certain conclusions, his role to make points of views inevitable, to establish clear lines of direction, like a magnetic compass, and then herd his comrades to a common path, thus giving the prime minister the opportunity to make decisions in an atmosphere of consensus, if not factuality. He must do this because Eddy was a bit of a dreamer, a disappointed Utopian for as long as Peters had known him, until now, because throughout the past year he had watched the most subtle of transformations occurring in Eddy Banks: the whole, imposing presence of the prime minister these days was of a disappointment in the process of recovery. Eddy was healing himself, had begun to believe in the gift of his power, yet still his capabilities remained fragile, and in need of orchestration.

Not all of the men present in the private quarters of Edison Banks' office understood this fragility; or, in understanding, appreciated the barrier it implied at this critical juncture in their reinvention of the world. They were the ones who had set the roots in the thin soil of St. Catherine, organizing the study group that had hardened and crystallized into the People's Evolutionary Party, each of the founding members of PEP now a chief minister or advisor, within the circle, to the government, and they were intent on clarifying the ambiguous nature of what was out there beyond the circle, what mutation might have erupted to deform the dream, what conspiratorial viruses may yet infect it, other than their own. Unlike Grenada, on St. Catherine fate and Eddy Banks had allowed a window for rational change; its own alliance of opposition parties did in fact manage to constitutionally defeat the old regime, and thus embarked on a delicate, factionalized stewardship of the nation which—and Peters did not have to persuade anybody on this point—was the most push-and-shove way to achieve nothing, to achieve less than nothing, like harnessing a donkey at each end of the wagon of reform, each driver lashing the dickens out of his own ass, striving to get down the road. PEAS—the ruling alliance—was a classic coalition of conflicting interests, united in a common hatred but divided by irreconcilable ambition. Yet this did not disturb the young men of PEP, the People's Evolutionary Party, not at all; they had expected just such a conflict, and had anticipated managing whatever attitudes or selfish aspirations, whatever regressive manipulations, sought to inhibit the forwardness of their programs, especially land reform, the modernization of agriculture on the admittedly backward island. All that Edison Banks required of their efforts was that there be a beauty to them, an inspiring elegance of execution, so that they could say, when the struggle was over and won, that they had done no more than to provide their foes with a rope to hang themselves with, and were blameless in the hearts of the people, and could not be held accountable in the more severe scrutiny of their real and lasting enemies.

Lloyd Peters—the former civics teacher at St. John's; a Boston-trained lawyer and now, by choice, minister of information—had educated Banks in this aesthetic, but the youthful Banks had allowed his own immaturity to color it—which was not intellectual immaturity but moral naïveté—and now, as prime minister, he placed an unfortunate faith in love and forgiveness, and it was Lloyd Peters' mandate not to dissuade him from this faith, not likely at any rate, but to protect him from its consequence. There were occasions when Peters looked at his former student—Banks' piercing visage of a gaunt nobleman, like a reproduction of an El Greco Moor, the crescents of inanimate flesh that drooped from the bridge of his nose to below the flat sockets of his lugubrious owl eyes, giving the impression of someone often overtaken by bouts of melancholic insomnia—and thought of him as a romantic anachronism, a monarch from a golden age, so contrary to the blunt West Africanness of an Archibol or a Kingsley, the minister of agriculture, or Peters himself, as polished and lacquered as Guinea totems. Eddy acted as if he had lost a world he never had, thought Peters.

Nevertheless—and it was not a masquerade but a separate self—in crowds or addressing parliament, the prime minister was, as a man of the people, a charismatic lion; an object of veneration and source of national pride. He was not the distant, preoccupied man known to his closest associates, nor was his mind perpetually inhabited by matters of state, or circumscribed by the images of power. He could be lighthearted and teasing, yet impervious to social niceties, never shaking a hand or asking after wives and kids, but he was famous for showing up unannounced at the wattle huts of villagers with a sack of groceries in his arms—*For the children, a little something, eh?* he'd say—and then sit to share their country dinners of dasheen and gristle. For superficial gestures and synthetic contact he showed little tolerance, but he would come to his work at Government House from his modest two-bed up the hill in Cunningham's, the middle-class suburb where he was raised, riding the crowded lorries with the laborers, grinning attentively at his constituents, not quite knowing what to say to them but more interested in listening anyway, joining the good-natured laughter that rolled with their criticisms, a son or brother who awoke their loyalty, and their ribbing would turn away from *pal-o-tics* or *pol-i-tricks* to life's more vital topics, women and cricket and sailing and fishing, farming, building, the art and science of normalcy, the dream that they carried to consummate the greatness of Edison Banks.

They agreed on goals—the coalition was a marriage of convenience, a hybrid fruit meant to bloom only once, briefly, for display, for *color*, and then be promptly discarded, and a more prolific and pure variety grafted to its roots. Unhouse Kingsley, they all agreed: it was both as simple and as complicated as that, for once you invited the devil to your table, he would eat and eat and eat, and always call for more, and could not be discouraged or dislodged by mere force alone. Shove his face into his own shit, they were learning, and he will devour it, smacking his lips.

They agreed on goals, but on the path they had chosen, they were running out of solid ground: parliament, the courts, the constitution, so defiled by the former government. Rule of law. Unlike their opposition, they were young men, they had no time to waste, they had waited a year, and a year was plenty, a year was enough. A year without change, some of them argued, was *too much.* They agreed on ends but not on means, yet now the resistance of those among them most unwilling to risk bolder actions, to risk *risk* itself, had begun to waver, a change of atmosphere for which Lloyd Peters gave himself credit. They were less reluctant to try things out, test the limits, make things up—like this gerrymandering so artfully introduced, at Peters' suggestion, into the land reform program—as they go along. But Kingsley had not taken their bait, he had not dug in his heels and reacted predictably when they shoved his face into his own shit and began, without his knowledge or consent, to shuffle the peasant communities squatting on the government estates and relocate them irrationally (but temporarily, insisted Banks) on unsuitable lands. Dispossess the peasantry. Blame it on Kingsley, the minister given authority over these affairs.

They didn't expect the scheme to work, but that, too, was part of its beauty. It was a constitutional issue and would be tossed up through the courts, yet by then it would be too late. Kingsley's constituency would be decimated. Better still, Kingsley's own frustrations and impatience would accelerate his demise, he would make a mistake, invite disaster, and then anything was possible. What might he do? Who knew, who could say? They would welcome resistance in any of its forms, but Joshua Kingsley had said nothing and done nothing to undermine himself. He continued doing as he had done since the beginning—dragging his ass—mouthing his allegiance to the land reform program insofar as it achieved the restoration of the sugar industry—and this to the dismay of his ministry's own experts.

Sugar was his phoenix, all he secretly cared about. If he could have that, Kingsley believed, he could have everything. He, himself, would be restored.

Lloyd Peters was not going to let him have it—which is not to say he disagreed with the minister of agriculture about the power of sugar, because the Achilles heel of every revolution was the economy, and to make a strong economy the masses needed discipline, they needed organization, needed control and structure.

They needed sugar. And, if not sugar, they needed hell, as they had never known it, to focus their hearts and minds, but he could not say these things as yet to the men assembled in the room. The triumph of their compromise still rang in their ears. No one was actually prepared to say the word *revolution*—the one word in their vocabulary softened by success. *No,* they found themselves forced to say to the world, *we are not a revolution, we are a coalition.*

No, Peters was determined to make them admit, *we are who we dreamed we are, we are the revo, and we have come.*

Like shaking a box of bees, Lloyd Peters had encouraged Basil Hamilton, the minister of public works, to propose; had himself put those words into the man's mouth so that he could weigh them, as if for the first time, when Basil spoke. Hamilton sat now between the prime minister and Foreign Minister Archibol, sharing the couch with them; it was Basil's infatuation with naive grassroots reform that excited him, and he was already positioned in the shadows to assume Joshua Kingsley's important portfolio, should the coalition ever dissolve—*when* it dissolved—in order to remake itself into the lean, firm, and efficient industry of truth in action they always meant it to be.

But in the stagecraft of dethronement, Kingsley had not taken the bait, had not even blinked. Trapped into administering a reform program he did not wholly advocate and could not as a politician survive, he neither protested the unauthorized relocations nor acknowledged their existence and thereby admit that the process was out of his control, the power and influence of his office stolen. Why didn't he resist, why didn't he resign, why didn't he have the sense to remove his fat sow self from the road so the future could pass around? This wasn't like Kingsley, and they didn't know what to think. Perhaps they were missing something. Perhaps they were wrong to wait for a response, since they knew it would come, the bees would sting, sooner or later, the way they were pressing the old man. *Joshua throwin old womens out they house and home,* people were saying, and not a peep heard from the old bastard.

Lloyd Peters licked his purple lips. "Troublesome rumors, nuh?" he said enticingly, and the council began. It became for him a matter of momentum, to preserve the endgame from the dilution of indecision. The issue of dismissal was raised again, and again rejected: Joshua must be finessed into a position of impotency, said Banks, not martyred only to be resurrected by a reactionary opposition.

Peters looked toward Selwyn Walker, hoping he would speak. Walker had been a less than average student at St. John's, the captain of the soccer team, cocky and popular, fearless. He had attended the study group simply because, in Peters' opinion, he had a keen nose for winning—he had smelled conflict in the group's makeshift kitchen, and it had whetted his appetite. Now it so happened he was the only one of four lieutenant commanders on the National Police Force indoctrinated into PEP objectives from the beginning, the one officer of significant rank who had been cruelly beaten by his fellow members of the force during the days of opposition to Pepper, and you do not question the loyalty of such a man, you simply destroy him if he turns on you. What he lacked, Peters believed, in intellectual capacity he compensated for in hubris and bravery, and in the less glamorous skills of logistics, but Peters was convinced the man was not sophisticated to the degree that he would relish a theory, hold the structure of it in his mind like an architect his building, a surgeon his anatomical branchings; not interested in the immaterial skeletons of theory on which all creation hung, yet he was deft—or at least not clumsy—with strategy, and his tactical instincts were of real value, here at the vanguard of a new St. Catherine. If there was a problem with Walker, Peters had to concede, it was that the man, like Banks, but from an opposite pole, was tempted by disillusionment, counting the endless moments it sometimes seemed to take for the gears of change to spin. Unknown to everybody but the men in the room, Selwyn Walker was, in the coming months, to inaugurate the formation of a national defense guard, to counteract the imbalance of the national police, whose commandant remained strapped by corruption and blood to Kingsley and the conservative members of the coalition, Pepper's old cohorts, who had betrayed him but not yet and never would be satisfied with Edison Banks and his club of supercilious schoolboys.

Selwyn Walker's steel-rimmed spectacles magnified the flickering energy in his eyes, eyes gone prematurely weak after his beatings by Pepper's men; they scouted his superiors' nuances like a radar imager, mused Peters, watching the light spark in diamonds on the lenses. Walker looked a bit like a towering black Gandhi, the ascetic severity of his face mocked by an unfortunate pair of jug ears. Walker's head was shaved, in military fashion, and Peters focused on its dark, icy gleam, wondering if the shaving, the deliberate baldness, represented some sort of . . . what? Again the word immaturity came to mind. Archibol spoke, making some damn speech clouded by righteousness and vanity, and Peters said to himself, *Save it for them damn fools in New York.* "We are not afraid, we are confident," Archibol was saying.

Last Friday, the Agricultural Credit Union in Comfort, a town in the interior, below the wilds of Soufrière, had been robbed, and that same night, Peters had seen Selwyn Walker at the bar of the Admiralty Club in Churchill Bay, and they had spoken, only briefly, about the robbery, and what some people perceived as increasing lawlessness in certain parts of the island associated with the oppostion.

Suppose, Selwyn, Peters had said in a casual voice, *there was a force up north.*

Force?

Suppose, for the sake of argument, man, the true perpetrators of this crime are our enemies. That these crimes are political crimes. This banditry. This lawlessness.

Just hooligans and rastas, eh?

All crimes are political crimes when they are committed within the context of the economic violence of imperialism, true?

True, true.

Suppose there is a force, and that force is against us.

Walker had exhaled air out of his nose—a disdainful snort. *That would not be smart.*

Imagine Delwyn Pepper, up so in New York, washing his hands of our business. Eh? He would ever do that? Ever? Eh?

Not smart.

Imagine Kingsley, Pepper's right hand, telling the man, "Don't come to me with your money and tricks." Eh? Kingsley?

Not smart at all.

All I am saying is, we could not stand by, or we would be lost, eh?

Selwyn Walker said nothing more on the subject, but he met Peters' eyes, and his look was thoughtful.

I believe I know how to make you say what it is you must say, Lloyd Peters told Walker in his mind, then as now, studying him across the room where he sat in his straight-backed chair, facing the prime minister's Queen Anne sofa and boxed in a sunbeam, having no aversion to the broiling morning light of the tropics. Kingsley is not merely a master of our own trickery, but a *force* within us, a necessary side of our own personality, not to be uprooted by games, nor withered by our posturing and improvisation. You will say it, Selwyn, and we will send Archibol back to New York, believing it, *defending* us with the credibility of an outraged heart, and Hamilton out into the streets, believing it, sowing that belief among the masses, and you and they will make it true.

"You are spoilin for a fight, eh, Selwyn?" Peters said, half jokingly, and then immediately changed his manner, reciting in all seriousness what Banks had made clear, time after time, that nonviolence was the signature of the noblest cause, and of the men dedicated to that cause.

"And Archibol is right," Banks added, unsmiling. "We have nothing to fear."

"But that is not natural," complained Selwyn Walker, closing his eyes and slowly opening them, as if he would sigh. "That is not positive. That is cowardly, under the circumstances."

"True and not true," declared Banks. "Nonviolence is an act of supreme faith, and supreme intelligence. You will see. The masses will see. Only God would know otherwise."

Lloyd Peters wanted to know. "What circumstances, Selwyn?"

The lieutenant commander tightened his lips and appeared agitated, grim. *Joshua Kingsley is wiser than all God-foolishness,* Selwyn Walker said to himself, bursting with an anger he would not permit himself to express out loud. *I can say this, because Joshua Kingsley is the rot and filth that ignorant men name the devil. I am the man who does know. Because I am the man who must stand in front of him and take his bullet, I am the man who does know. Because I am the man you will ask to cut out his tongue, and slay his bad children, I am the man who does know. Because, Eddy, I am your emissary to Hell and its horrors, I know.*

"Tell us," said Lloyd Peters. "*What* circumstances?"

Banks shifted his gaze to Peters as if he finally realized where all this murky talk was leading. "Tell us, Selwyn," he said.

Selwyn Walker glanced at Edison Banks with impenetrable composure, rejecting his own misgivings, the qualms he felt in answering—the answer or the lie he had just heard the prime minister solicit, to legitimize their hard business. But once he opened his mouth, there would be no falsehood, now or ever, only a revelation gathered from something not unlike a time capsule, but sent backward from the near future to its point of conception in reality. He was not a liar, he was a visionary, a priest of the seen and the unseen.

He told them he had received reports that had caused him grave concern. Reports that alleged that Joshua Kingsley had men up north—agents, traitors—in the mountains, in the forests behind La Soufrière. They were organizing, they were . . . up to no good. He was unprepared for their skepticism, especially Lloyd Peters', but then he felt that their doubts comforted him, minimizing his anxiety.

"But, dis a fahntasy, mahn," guffawed Peters.

"Folks talkin shit," said Archibol.

Walker conceded he could offer only circumstantial, inconclusive evidence, at the moment, but that he would fail in his duty to them if he did not express his suspicion. A reliable source had eluded him, although certain other prospects had yet to be properly investigated. He paused to gauge the impact of these qualifications, but rather than an air of foreboding descending into the room there was satisfaction, glad relief; his message was welcomed. *You see, I was right,* Selwyn Walker told himself. He had not been summoned here today to be cheated, to condone girlish intrigues, but to be anointed and sent forth. He took his hands from the armrests of his chair and placed them atop his knees, since his legs jittered, betraying his excitement.

Lloyd Peters advised him to check and double check the information, before reporting back to them, or initiating a response. We must remember, he cautioned, the virtue of our cause.

Within the depths of Edison Banks' eyes there seemed to be an intellect in danger of being exhausted by its own singular abilities, yet unhurried and clinically objective nonetheless. His elbow was on the sofa's arm, his neatly bearded chin in the palm of his slender hand, as he listened and agreed and voiced his reservations.

"But patiently, no? Don't be bloody, Selwyn."

Because if you are bloody you will lure Pepper back into it, from the North, and he will bring the North with him. Don't be bloody, Selwyn, or our children will starve. Don't be bloody, Selwyn, or we must live with Americans or Cubans or Russians in our homes. Don't be artless, Selwyn—the rise of one art and the fall of another takes time. Every procedure has its art; every art has its careful science. Collect the evidence, detain the guilty, let the people judge for themselves, and the coalition will split apart without unseemly artifice, and the world itself will smile because we are not savages, and no one will be against us, even if they are not with us, and there will be no guns to put away, because what is most difficult is to resist the temptation not to put away the lightning of democracy which is the justice of the gun, but this is a storm we cannot live with, and that is why we have worn our masks of coalition for so long, and dissimulated ourselves, and brought this unwholesome pressure gradually to bear upon our people, and exposed them to these confusions, so that finally a small discretion—and not wrath, and not vengeance, and not chaos—could make us free. Don't be bloody, Selwyn. It is a game of blood and history—*true and not true.* But I will not look upon the blood of my people, and you will not show it to me, because you will be loving— however you have loved your people and your nation, you must now show them both a greater love, a love transcendent and pure—and you will be clever, I trust you will be clever, Selwyn. We are not clowns, our country is not a comedy, although many wish to see it that way; we are not Hamlets, our country is not a tragedy, although many people want to see it that way too.

Lloyd Peters marveled at Selwyn Walker as he rose and saluted, loose on his feet, as though he had drunk from the bottle of Pinch— which no one had bothered with except Archibol—on the marble-topped table between the sofa and chairs. He seemed inspirited, this man, this *chrysalis.* What a beauty he might come to be, a steel-winged insect, a deadly ornament of the night. And into that same night, he would eventually disappear.

"Don't be bloody, Selwyn," Banks urged a last time, as if to thwart such an outcome he must say it over and over again. "We are not savages."

We are not yet men, Walker thought, and blithely reassured the room. *Have faith in the unseen: It need not be God, to be powerful.*

They stood up with him, relaxed, moving on to small talk.

BOB SHACOCHIS

Archibol complained about some stupid business with his wife and car involving one of the sons of Crissy Knowles.

The trouble with us, Selwyn Walker thought, thinking of his colleagues as he left Government House to return to downtown headquarters—Edison Banks and his old schoolmates from form days at St. John's Apostolic—*we moving too slowly. Developing too slowly. As if we had no cause at all. As if class still in session.* He had studied with them at St. John's, and studied *of* them, and learned that *schooltalk cheap, bwoy,* learned that all philosophy was school dress-up and never dirtied itself in the world, until someone fed up with this nonsense came along and stripped it of its shoes and fancy pants and threw it out onto the streets to fight and shit and bleed. That was the true test for ideas, the application, when they forfeited the daydreamy security that gave them license in the schoolhouse. Then philosophy risked becoming something less than ideology, and something greater, something factual and historic for the schoolbooks and the schoolboys to feast on, and that is why he, Selwyn Walker, did not follow Eddy Banks and Archibol and Lloyd Peters to schools in London and Toronto and Boston, but took his higher education among the masses, wearing the royal colonial uniform of authority, a tool of power, because he knew he was destined to be the flesh of their schoolboys' daydream, the muscle and arm of their theories and here, now, finally, in this day and time, the mask would be lifted for all to see that his face was not the *booj* face of the monkey.

The booj world! Babylon, eh, as it is known to warriors, the filthy, spewing, white-hot engine of destruction, the petit bourgeoisie. White people—free market slavemarket. The States, eh?, hegemony like cancer. Booj TV and booj music and booj film—we are the stinking black and rich crude oil of booj culture and booj economy, and these were the days, *now,* of uprising and naked freedom and throwing off the curse. Because look to our warrior brothers, look to Cuba, look to Vietnam, Cambodia, Ethiopia, Angola; look to Guyana, look to Trinidad and Jamaica, and look to us. Because if you win an election in a puddle like St. Catherine, all you can hope to become is a booj pet, and still must beg for scraps, and the booj massa say democracy is a fine mess, everybody come to its table, but this was a lie that sent men to their graves, and St. Catherine cry to move ahead, and democracy ain no help and ain hold we together no more, mahn.

Archibol told him, and Banks and Peters told him, *Dem booj fellas ain concerned by we,* and he wanted them to care, because you can't fight an enemy who doesn't care. So you must show your face at their

door, bloody and bloodthirsty and raving. Then they will care. *Then.*
Then they will size you up. Then they will confront the truth of
nature and of the world as it has become, which is the truth of the
atom—the smallest of the small, where the greatest power lay coiled.
That was the lesson of David, true?, that strength is a matter of perfect proportions, and with this knowledge David was well armed to
challenge the Goliath, who was an aberration of form, and a perversi-
ty of growth. A cancer. Then they will see that the world that once
was, but had become dead and remote, will pass this way again alive
and beautiful, like a bird of light. Then they will understand, there is
no feud that is not ancient, and holy. Then they will learn, there is no
greater booj sin than to love us only like a father. We, who are not
children, have conceived a future inside the darkness, and thus were
our own fathers, fathering a new life forth from nightfall and shadow,
like the sun, and made ourselves complete, like a cycle, like an atom.
Because that is what complete means, to be the father of oneself. To
know that the booj world cannot swallow what is complete without
choking, that the booj world cannot rule completeness, only that
which is open and unformed and split, like the sex of women.

The trouble with us, Selwyn Walker pondered. *The trouble with us.*

He went through the arched gate, across the courtyard, into the
public entrance, and there on a bench against the wall, his elbows on
his knees and his head hung low, was a youth, who caught his eye,
and he passed through the room throwing knifelike glances at the fellow, trying to recall how he might know him, and when he reached
the hall entrance that led to the administrative offices of the national
police force, he stopped and went back to the duty officer and asked
why that boy was here. Then he remembered, and then he went and
shook the fellow by the shoulder.

"Here now, you Crissy Knowles' bwoy, eh?" The fellow answered
by saying it wasn't his fault, what had happened, let him make his
report and leave, why must he wait so, and Selwyn Walker said,
"Come with me." He put a hand on the boy's shoulder blade and
steered him toward the hall, whistling fragments of a calypso, which
to those who knew him meant Selwyn Walker was having a good day.
St. Catherine would crawl out of the ditch of forgottenness where it
had lain stunned and suffering for centuries, and begin anew, and
because of this, he had been called upon to reveal his true self to the
world, and nothing less could gratify him.

Chapter 6

"I had to get away." Johnnie snapped her fingers. "You know, like that. Fast. There was a problem."

There was always a problem, Mitchell thought. He pictured her this way: Looking over her bare shoulder for a pair of murderous oriental eyes as she flagged a taxi on King Kamehameha Boulevard. She tosses a large bill at the hack—from a purse bloated with gems, bank notes—when they reach the airport and doesn't wait for change. Inside the terminal the ticket agent informs her sternly that her flight is now boarding. She rips into the sky for six hours of first-class coddling, served Dom Pérignon and sashimi, a preview of the life awaiting her when she hits the mainland. Real lurkabout idiocy. Surfers in over their heads. Come on, he wanted to say, who are you trying to bamboozle.

Her eyes canvassed the tiny bathroom she had stepped in to inspect on her tour of the house Isaac had helped Mitchell locate. It was the first suitable place he had been shown after two weeks of Isaac's benign attempts to hustle him into one-window rooms in the homes of people so drastically different from Mitchell they might as well have been extraterrestrial, folks Isaac claimed were his aunts or uncles or cousins, their quick servility and outsized hope at once uncomfortable and taxing, llama eyes begging Isaac in his role as agent for the windfall of a boarder. Half-finished neighborhoods piled with rubbish and grazed by scrawny livestock, biblical provincialism amid the urban sprawl on the hills above the government houses and harbor. The houses and compounds were brushed ineffectively with watery paints, their lots defined by a guesswork of decrepit fencing—branches, broken lumber, upended bicycle frames and metal sheeting and chicken wire all tied together. Unpaved streets waited for the tar promised them, breadfruit trees grew from ground as bare as a parking lot, fruit dropped rotten and fly-blown. Sullen girls walked barefoot from the public spigot with water buckets balanced on their heads. Somewhere nearby a child was always bawling, and boys played soccer with a wounded ball, their arguments like birds rioting over scraps of bread. Roosters crowed, transistor radios were turned full volume to occupy the minutes of the unemployed. It was initially hard to make Isaac understand that the environment was too negative and psychologically remote to hang his hat on without making big changes in what he, Mitchell, was. It required cellular adaptations in thought and nerve fiber. Forget it, he told Isaac. This won't work. It was beyond Mitchell's power to assimilate that deep, that far into a cultural and racial antipode. He desired a modest house outside the city in proximity to the spectacular fascinations of the water, private enough to forget that the people of St. Catherine had trouble tending to their own domestic affairs though they had a handy expertise for the affairs of others. When Isaac eventually admitted he could not wear down Mitchell's resolve nor convince him how well attended a bwana he'd be, how any one of Isaac's relatives would make it a point of personal honor to ensure that Mitchell's stay on the island be gilded with security and service and lovely cooking, the two of them drove out to this cottage overlooking the blue ear of Howard Bay. Isaac reluctantly recalled the place had been vacant for almost a year. Mitchell rented it from the half-sister of the owner, a schoolteacher gone to Toronto with her three children.

Mitchell reclined against the doorframe, swallowing a Percodan, and then buttoned the khaki workshirt he had substituted for his souvenir of the Agri-Exposition. Johnnie made an ugly face.

"These are disgusting. What do you do, reuse your Q-tips?" She pointed at the cotton swabs in the ceramic mug on the tank of the toilet, their tips a yellowish sprout of mold, the spores of another tropical ubiquity flourishing in the air.

He wondered how long he could survive her presence until the state of unease within him broke, before the abnormality and strange novelty of her reappearance dissolved into the commonplace, the quotidian and habitual. What were your options when an erstwhile love returned? Was she to be regarded as a ghost, a courtesan, lost lamb, misunderstood goddess? Was she an alien, a close friend, a person to be treated as a bad business partner, with mistrust and the tacit entente that compensation was expected? Someone you thanked heaven for sending back? Let her deflect him away from what he most wanted to know, it didn't matter. She had arrived, closing the door in on herself, not slamming it behind as she bounded out, killing the clock, and he had her at his leisure. She picked up one of the swabs and examined it in the channel of light from the window above her head.

"You shouldn't leave them exposed in this climate." She dumped the contents of the mug into the wastebasket on the wooden floor.

"Have you come to clean me up?"

"Just the opposite," she answered, and grinned like the teenage flirt she once was, taking satisfaction in the ambiguity of her reply.

"Things were a mess, everything got so shitty," she went on, elaborating without any cue from him. She stood on her tiptoes to open the high window that ventilated the room. With a finger she probed the dirt in the pot of philodendron on the sill, its cordate leaves drooping down the wall, green valentines with brown edges.

"What went wrong?"

"A to Z, you name it."

She reached for the water glass on the rim of the basin, filled it with a sputtery gush from the faucet and saturated the roots of the plant. Mitchell read an extreme significance in each move she made. It was not unlike being colonized by an equal or even a greater power, this business of coming back.

"You know how everything can get. You just have to leave."

"You're right," he smirked, "I know," curious at how frail she sometimes seemed to him, as if there were a disease within her she did not yet know about even as it consumed her strength. She dissociated herself from her own events, from the ruin of events, and went on without a fare-thee-well. Johnnie had been an example of a pervasive counterculture phenomenon, a rebellious student but by accident a great educator. She had taught him about evasion, flight, the strategy of escape, those radical cures, about the bitter medicine of goodbye, she, the refugee from her own perpetrations, a woman who practiced self-exile as naturally as other women mastered attachment.

She replaced the glass, enquiring with a sidelong glance. "It's really bugging you that I'm here, isn't it? Should I leave, Mitch?"

He looked at the floor. "Of course not."

"Well," she taunted, and lapsed into a pantomime of pulling her hair out, "all your silence is getting on my nerves. Would you like to bat me around a little bit to warm up? Do you keep a two-by-four in the house?"

"Tell me what's happening. Are you in trouble?"

She sighed, flapped her arms as though she were giving up. "You know me—a sucker for fast moves. A girl who likes a good race, even when there's nothing there at the finish line."

"You're in trouble."

"I was, but not anymore."

"Want to talk about it?"

She made her *no* clear without saying a thing, then averted her eyes. "Not until I'm ready, okay? Until I know you're ready too. It's just one of those things, you know what I mean? I want to get it over with, tell you everything, Mitch, but every time I go to open my mouth I run empty on courage."

Saying this much made her brighten, seemed to make her feel that she had earned a temporary reprieve. An oily forelock kept lolling down into Mitchell's face like a slow tic. It made him realize how filthy he felt, and it made him angry. "You descend out of nowhere," he said, fingers assaulting the buttons of the shirt he had just put on. "I'm unprepared, you understand, so you're going to have to coach me on what it is you want me to pretend—don't look at me like that, I'm not cute when I'm pissed. What do you want to talk about until you're sure we're both ready? Cost-benefit analysis? Start-up capital?"

Her lips concealed a smile, deferring to his irritation. "More or less," she said.

Mitchell hung his shirt over the doorknob and opened the tap, maneuvering his scalp down into the grimy oval of porcelain, water shooting all over, hawking to find out if his nose was still draining blood. He asked for the shampoo in the shower stall and she handed it to him. He lathered up and heard familiar noises that were still one more premonition of the madness his life and its bachelor rituals would have to face in the days ahead. Mitchell opened his eyes to slits and groaned.

"Wait a minute, what do you think you're doing?"

Johnnie had bunched her heavy skirt around her waist, lowered the toilet seat and settled on it, the sheen of navy blue panties binding her knees together, a section of white tissue clutched absently in her fist like a ticket she waited for someone to take. A burst splashed into the bowl. Her behavior made him stiffen, aghast, not that she proceeded with casual disregard, wiping herself, exhibiting no trace of modesty, but because of what she took for granted. (I'm just a girl she once told him. I don't know what else you want me to be.)

"You can't just come in here and hike up your skirt. As if we were some ma and pa show."

She careened forward and laughed privately into the space between her knees. "La la la," she said, cocking her head to look up at him. She stood and her skirt parachuted back into position. Bathroom democracy, domestic peace itself. *La la la.*

He cooked breakfast while she unpacked her belongings, apportioned to the spare bedroom in the shady front of the cottage. The interior walls were built in the style of the colonial period, late Victorian in fashion if not in content, a sensible adaptation to the swelling heat of the latitude, designed to exploit the persistent and welcomed flannel breezes called the Trades that blew across the Atlantic from the northeast and made European contact with the Americas inevitable, an intercontinental highway of wind and current to ride to the west. Under a steep-pitched tetrazoidal roof lathed and sheeted with rusty tin, the board walls went up only so far and then stopped, like tall office partitions, allowing the air to circulate room to room from outside to inside through a bank of louvered windows installed the entire seaward length of the house. The construction favored openness before privacy and Mitchell was acutely aware that Johnnie was breathing down his back from the first moment he went alone into his room to change clothes. Her feet resounded on the old wood floors, her comments about the local batiks tacked to the walls seemed to carry the pressure of her breath right to his ear. The intimacy grated, and he could only take comfort in that the two bedrooms were separated by an entranceway, without a common membrane to amplify the indiscretions that were better left unheard. How priggish, Johnnie would say if she could read his mind. *You're acting as if I never had access to every piece of you, every mortal sloppiness.*

The hallway led straight ahead to a boxcar-sized kitchen which shared its half of the house with an empty dining or living room to its opposite side, and still ahead through a back door was a veranda that ran from one end of the house to the other, its deck ten feet off the ground on stilts, the land underneath sloping off to low cliffs rimming the water with ironrock, and beyond that the fantasy of Howard Bay, its blue ear resting against the land in an act of docility. In the near distance you could see the eastern jaw of Pilo Bight, its brown humps like knuckles worn through a green yarn glove. Beyond that was the haze where the coast turned north to be scoured by the brute waves of the Atlantic. To the south the Los Muertos Channel cut a wide river between St. Catherine and her cays to the east, fragments and atolls known to sailors as The Necklace, and below that the cloud-shadowed slab of Cotton, a dwarf sister island and recently a sandbox for the rich. It was a millionaire's view. Each evening, home from his office at the ministry, Mitchell would come out on the veranda to sit and jab the sunset with a rum and tonic.

The owner's furniture, a few fine cedar and mahogany pieces handed down through the family until they were antiques, remained behind like ghosts, unable to disappear with the bodies to which they belonged. Even so, the guest room was without a bed, and Mitchell borrowed a lumpy object Tillman called a mattress from Rosehill's storeroom and put it on the floor under a gauzy envelope of mosquito netting. No pillow. There was a pillow shortage on the island, and he couldn't hunt one down. And with its double windows shuttered for the night, the room had the bleak look of incarceration, so yesterday he had made the time to get to a dry goods shop where he bought yellow material printed with bright red hibiscus blossoms, then to a seamstress to have her cut and hem the fabric into curtains. There was a wardrobe in the room, and a small primitive chest of drawers, and a Colombian moa nailed on the molasses varnish of the wall planking. Also, Mitchell had dug an elephant's ear on the edge of the lot and potted it in a five-gallon bucket. It brooded in confinement along with a young jacaranda stoically celebrating with a single lavender bloom, a fertility plant dropping its babies in a circle, and a mayonnaise jar crammed with flowering fragrant ginger stalks he had cut fresh prior to waking Isaac for their disastrous ride to the airport. These duties of his hostmanship Mitchell performed without thinking beyond the desire that the sincerity of his hospitality not be held in doubt. Shelter from the storm was a basic rule of humanity and yet not to be misunderstood as an invitation.

And breakfast was being served on a while-it-lasts basis.

Opening the brown skin with his fingernail, Mitchell peeled a plantain and sliced the dry-smelling fruit lengthwise into strips. The oil in the pan on the hotplate heated up, spitting when he crushed a garlic clove and threw it in, followed by the plantain.

"Beautiful smells," Johnnie crowed from across the house. "Coconut oil and garlic."

Mitchell looked up toward the network of roofbeams as though she might materialize there.

A pot of milk bubbled. Into it he crumbled a waxy plug of cocoa, stirred in ground bay leaf, salt, and sugar. The plantain strips turned the color of old teeth. The countertop refrigerator periodically contributed its own scat riffs to the music of the cooking, a three-beat gurgle, a two-four chug. In his better moods Mitchell would drum on it with fork and spoon. From its sweating interior he took a mixing bowl of day-old batter.

"I'm cooking tree-tree fritters," he announced. He speared the plantain to one side of the pan and ladled in four globs of batter. There was a loud sound, the wardrobe being shoved across the floor. Johnnie rearranging her new hideout.

"Were you talking to me?"

"Tree-tree."

"Ye-eah?" A scrape and rumble, and then a bang.

"Tiny little fish that swim from the ocean into the river mouths, the same time every year. Millions of them, no bigger than pins. You didn't know that you timed your visit for tree-tree season, did you?" Hammering vibrated through the house. "What are you doing back there?"

"Just livening up this dark space . . . did you say we're having fish?"

She came to the kitchen singing, a cappella, a capriccio, notes released from her mouth like sonorous bubbles, sort of a parody of a torch song that she sang, it was clear from her face, because she was happy. In her hand she wielded the blunt instrument of a wooden-soled sandal. Mitchell stood by flipping through the *Crier*, St. Catherine's one independent newspaper, printed twice weekly and distributed on Tuesdays and Fridays, Saturdays at the latest, having chartered itself with the imperative of entering a few facts into the national dialogue.

"It says here," he said, reading, "'A man the people of Plaisance call Booty, or some call Sneak, though that is not the fellow's name for he is in truth named Cyril Balcombe, was apprehended Monday last for the crime of praedial larceny, whereupon, in accordance with recent legislation sponsored by the Honorable Joshua Kingsley and the PEAS coalition, the said legislation designed to halt such piratical acts, Mr. Balcombe was taken before the steps of the Town Station the following day by order of the Magistrate, removed of his trousers, and caned on the buttocks by the Corporal there on duty in full view of the public and children, who loudly counted out the entire sentence of strokes, twenty in all. Mr. Balcombe was then required to pay a fine and permitted to return home on probation, where he was later that same day seen at rest in his yard hammock in a position favoring his recent injuries. Mr. Balcombe occupied his recovery by dictating to his son, who loyally recorded the father's words in his grammar school composition book. When asked by a neighbor what it was his son copied for him, Mr. Balcombe stated that the beating he had just received at the hands of the authorities had inspired in him a calypso, which he hoped to sell to an unnamed performer at some future date to advertise his innocence in the affair. Mr. Balcombe added that the name of the calypso that "had been lashed from me" was "I Tek a Whippin, Jack Nasty Tek De Pig."""

"My goodness"—Johnnie rolled her eyes—"did you just make that up?"

Mitchell glibly told her that in St. Catherine all the old thrills were making a comeback. The minister of agriculture had reinstated classical punishment by delivering the first hot stroke of justice to the first guilty arse the government could lay its hands on. The countryfolks loved it. "Teef a cow, tek a bow," the schoolchildren rhymed. Mitchell had been there—it was at an agricultural fair in Kingsley's home parish—and the audience cheered: "Lash him, poppi, strike him straight on, mahn." You could call it Bligh's legacy—breadfruit, the bull pizzle, the cat-o'-nine-tails. Food and discipline as the base ingredients of civilization.

"Hawaii could use a system like that," was all Johnnie said on the subject.

Oil foamed around the islands of fritters, heat escaped through their centers to the pimpled surface. Johnnie took up the spatula in her free hand and poked at them, bending closer to look. "What are these?" she asked.

"I'm doing that." Mitchell folded the newspaper closed and blocked Johnnie out of his way, grabbing the turner.

"Jehovah cooks breakfast. Oh yes," she said, playfully waving at his head with the sandal. "I have not forgotten Mitchell's house rules. Thou shalt not interfere with thy cook. Thou shalt not leave illegal things lying around in plain sight. Thou shalt tidy up thine own mess, wherever it comes from. Thou shalt not covet the rewards of thy lover's ambition. What have I missed?"

He flipped the fritters, thanked by a small ovation of grease. "Stop threatening me with a Dr. Scholl's," he advised. "Are you ready to eat?"

"Almost," she said. "Do you have any tacks? It'll only take a second."

"What is it you're doing?"

"Hanging up a map of South America. *National Geographic*—big."

He gestured toward a column of drawers in the row of cabinets set underneath the counter. "Look around in there," he told her, and kept busy cutting ripe guavas in half. She pulled open several, dug through them, closed all but one back.

"Mitch?"

"Yeah?"

Her tone was incredulous. "What are you doing with so many rubbers?" she asked. "There must be two hundred of them." She scooped a fistful and let them trickle.

"I'm a very popular guy on this island."

"I guess so."

Embarrassed, he went to the cupboard for the enamel plates and silverware. Johnnie found the tacks in the bottom drawer and, whirling on her heels, marched out of the kitchen. Mitchell turned around just in time to see her stick her tongue out at him. Seconds later, a rapping fired through the cottage, a house now inhabited with echoes from another place they would call their own. A house where a woman's words could drift freely from corner to corner and gather in the cobwebs under the roof to form with his, as if their business together would be best conducted, like comic strip characters, in the neutral space above their heads.

In the fullness of the morning, the air on the veranda where Mitchell had carried their breakfast smelled much like baked grass, a lulling scent with an arid sweetness to it that passed across the house from east to west stowed on the Trades, a caravan of fragrance, interrupted at intervals by the effervescence of a thousand buds and oils and essences of the warming land itself, their syrupy heaviness levitating in the heat, thronging the atmosphere like an aromatic muster of souls. He filled his lungs a few times because it was impossible to resist the intense intimacy of the land, not just to smell, but to breathe as if it were an act of drinking, to respire and absorb. A maverick whiff of crotchy odor from the forests would sometimes stray into the stream, from off the inland hills, and eddies of saltiness, like the smell of damp saltine crackers, as the lobe of Howard Bay twitched against the open jaws of the shoreline. He drew hard, but this style of breathing also made him wince, reminding him of the fatness of his clobbered nose.

"Doesn't it hurt?" Johnnie asked, breaking open a tree-tree fritter and with a chary look inspecting its countless white threads, pinpoint beads of black eyeballs attached to each strand. She looked over at him, her brow pinched. "It looks swollen. Maybe you'd better see a doctor."

"No. Don't need to."

He drank from a cup of oily cocoa tea, put it back on the packing crate they were using for a table, opened his mouth but thought better of it and said nothing more. She raised her eyes expectantly but hesitated herself. The flatness that was suddenly upon them appalled Mitchell and he wondered what to do. Johnnie finally took a prim bite of a fritter and chewed experimentally.

"What is this I'm eating?"

"I told you before but you weren't listening. Those are worms. A breakfast special."

She looked, appropriately, nicked by the sarcasm of his tone. It was clear he wasn't trying to get her to laugh. She returned the fritter solemnly to her plate and spooned a purple-pink hemisphere of guava instead, her mouth purse-lipped from its tartness. Mitchell was bored with his seriousness, bewildered and alarmed—even though he had figured it would happen this way—by the chip that rose on his shoulder at the first sight of Johnnie. This weary business of memory, wholly errant. The brain briefing the glands from dog-eared files. Sniffing sniffing sniffing at her passage through the house, an enraged fascination with the intoxicating trail. Goddamn it, he said to himself, enough, enough—this wasn't his life, this wasn't what was important. What he truly needed was an opening in his perception of her, a way to appreciate a new Johnnie, even if he couldn't persuade himself that that was what she was.

It was not a miracle, her return, nor was it a curse. Don't be stupid about this, Mitchell warned himself. Don't make it such a big deal.

Johnnie took a slow deep breath, pressed her knees together to reinforce her composure, and looked at Mitchell with more earnestness than he ever thought possible. Academy Awards, he thought.

"Talk to me, Mitch, okay? Please? Do you want me on my knees?"

Mitchell fidgeted on the crate he sat on. "I don't have any control here," he protested.

"Well, that's not true," she responded immediately. "You can make this into anything you want."

"*Oh?*"

His mouth remained in the sulk that the vowel had sponsored. He could feel his eyebrows declare independence—they saluted, they chopped down, they came together like two fuzzy magnets. He was trying to see into her through a kaleidoscope of minced feelings, the composition altering with each degree of rotation of the Johnnie being revealed, splitting and shifting and merging from one instant to the next. Well, brother, what do you say to a girl not seen or heard from for five years. Who, what, when, why, and how, the reportorial motif? *Oh, it's you,* as though the time apart was of no more consequence than a nap, an errand in town. Oh, it's you, where the hell have you been? Without a working hypothesis, the gulf between them widened and shrank, drained and filled on a confounding schedule. If his mute resistance was getting to her, it was also affecting Mitchell in an even worse way, tipping the rocker.

Whatever Johnnie was thinking, she appeared to surrender to it. She screwed a cigarette into the groove of her lips and sent a beam of smoke down toward the piebald waters where the reef scalloped the bay. The sea was a peacock blue beyond the fields of turtle grass until coral spotted and ridged the bottom, and roved by gasps of wind printing blurred foil tracks on the clean surface. The friction between air and water, these hot patches of light, leaped randomly throughout the harbor on their inevitable course to land to where Johnnie and Mitchell sat in resigned meditation. Everything that had happened between two people, Mitchell saw, could be remembered if you just kept focused on the sea, and everything could be dismissed and forgotten with the future always forcing its pulse, wave after wave rolling out from the great silence. Johnnie seemed mesmerized by a frigate bird set free in endless space. He stole a glance at her profile, saw her eyelids lowering, the lashes knobbed with heavy bits of mascara. She was about to fall asleep. The silence was conspiring with an intolerable sorrow.

"You've got to be tired."

Her eyes slowly reopened. "I'm all right."

"Why don't you go in and go to bed."

"Not yet." Her head started to bob but she made sure it didn't, straightening her spine. The skin of her face had slackened, allowing the promise of future jowls and a loose chin. Her eyes were rimmed with the price of traversing oceans, the jump of time zones. And, too, her constant sniffing made it obvious she had been helping herself along the way to the drug in the diaphragm case. "Mitch, why did you send me all those letters? They made it impossible to forget you." She set her breakfast plate down from her lap. "Okay, I suppose that's why you sent them."

"Well then."

"*Well then!* You have to say more than that."

"There's no more to say than that."

He tried to recall what it was he had written to her over the past years. Second-page news, miniature visions, adolescent restlessness and chitchat, oblique hints of lust, queries about beaus, peculiar events witnessed, the illness of his father (she had liked him for the plodding bureaucratic thoroughness with which he kept up his wooded property, which is just about the only place she ever saw him), incidental juvenile musings on loss and pain, all the funks like Fifties tearjerk tunes, rigidly objective abstracts on the absurdly powerful astonishment of heartbreak. Consistently some wit or clever attempts to pitch at her, keep it fresh in her mind what a smart guy he was, always good for a chuckle, yet why he did this he really couldn't say. Not to play coy with himself, but each time he wrote her he believed had its own isolation and purity, not linked to any greater motive than could be assigned to ham radio operators—which Mitchell knew was no more true than the idea of birds migrating arbitrarily but he would not, certainly not now, confronted with the deed, admit it.

"If there's so much to say," he dared her, "you say it. Nobody twisted your arm and made you write back."

She was pleased that the moment had come, after these dodges and dead-ends, for her to address the apocrypha of their relationship. She smiled eagerly and stubbed her cigarette, which had stayed in her mouth even though it had burned down to the filter. She lit another, craving everything all at once, and told Mitchell what he never knew—what the letters had meant to her.

"At first it was like being tailed by one of those guys who gets a fix on you, you know, takes an interest after seeing you once in a restaurant or pumping gas into your car, and you become his obsession. You begin to notice him everywhere you go, and you realize you're not having any luck in getting rid of him, you can't shake him loose. You feel as if you've been adopted by a pervert, some nimrod, and there doesn't seem to be much you can do about it. I wanted to shriek, every time I went to the mailbox and there was a Charlottesville postmark. I wanted to scream, Why don't you shut up? Why don't you go away? Stop harassing me. But Daddy kept forwarding your letters as I tramped west, and like a dope I kept opening them."

She laughed lightly, holding up a finger when she saw he was going to interrupt. "Let me finish what I was saying about the letters, before you start stewing again. Unlike the way things are going at the moment, you refused to be silent. That was your secret weapon, that's what you were doing, wasn't it? It amazed me, to tell you the truth, that you could be so stubborn. It was so nonchalant, so cavalier, your defiance, so gentlemanly, and I didn't expect it. It dawned on me I really meant something to you, you know. It rattled me that you could still care, considering what I put you through. I mean, that was terrible, Mitch. And I didn't think your caring was very healthy."

"If caring wasn't a form of sickness, your father and every other shrink would be out of a job."

"Look," she went on, becoming more animated. An ash from the cigarette had landed on her breast and she brushed it off, leaving a gray smudge above her left nipple. Mitchell aimed his attention there as if it were a problem to be solved. "Look, I thought your game was to haunt me, to keep reminding me how fucked up I was. But you never tried to nail me into a coffin of guilt—or if you did, honey, you were sure shrewd about it, you know. None of your letters were like you're being now . . . so how could I not respond. I mean, am I supposed to be from another planet or what. Why sack everything, why go for the total wipeout? That's how whores are treated, trash, and as mixed up as I was, that's what I thought I had coming. You know? But there you were offering me something beautiful and I admit it, I was confused by that. Who wouldn't be? It took me a while, but I had to write back, send you a card like on your birthday or Christmas. Most of it was pretty superficial, I know, and I know how crazy it sounds now, but I started to believe that we had never split up, that an accident had separated us but that it was only a question of time . . . do you know what I mean?"

Mitchell rubbed the back of his neck, scowling. He knew what she meant, and it put him in no mood for clearing up their relationship as neatly as she was doing it. A sugar finch landed on the feeder that dangled from the eave, just a calabash shell with sugar water in it, and he watched it, not knowing why it could contribute to his rage.

"Don't make it all sound so goddamn noble," he said. "It's been five years. I've had other girlfriends. I write letters to plenty of women. They write back. They fly in infrequently though." The things he wanted and the things he didn't want—Johnnie had them all in a tangle. Lately Mitchell had been wanting a girlfriend and he kept finding candidates too, when he was drunk, and discarding them when he was sober. Here in front of him was the only woman he had known whom he couldn't evict from his thoughts, an early Christmas for his loneliness, and he was maneuvering to make her cry and do what she said he was too much a gentleman for in his letters, an objective he apparently had no qualms about face to face.

Johnnie blanched. "I didn't think about other women, I guess," she said. "You always left that part out."

"Did you think you had crippled me?" Mitchell was grinding his teeth, fuming, provoked by her dispensation of honest secrets. "Give me a fucking break, okay. Why should it all mean anything now?"

"It doesn't," she moaned, and wrapped her hands in the cloth of her skirt. Her face reddened, on the verge of tears. "Please don't be a son of a bitch, Mitchell. My life has not been easy. You have a right to do what you're doing, but please don't go after me so hard."

"Lord Almighty. How subtle you've become."

"Fuck you," Johnnie said in anguish. "You have to be able to afford to be subtle first. I have to pay my way as I go."

"So go ahead—confess, confess," he shrugged. "Catharsis"— a pop of dyslexia went off behind his eyes—"th-the cathartic ecstasy. Make us both wretched . . . more wretched." He was becoming demented. "So, tell me, how's the you-know-what business these days."

"Aren't you smart?" she said furiously. "Of course it's drugs, you prick. Drugs, sex, rock and roll—all the naughty stuff, all the decadence, I'm behind it all. I'm the queen bee of the generation." Mitchell started to tell her that he knew all along but she stamped her foot so he wouldn't go on. "Man, would you just fucking *listen. Please.*" Her expression was as willful and wild as he had ever seen it. She couldn't moderate her voice. Mitchell listened to its quivering and thought, breakdown time. "When we lived together—it wasn't very long ago but the world was such a different place then. And I didn't know anything. I had nothing to compare you to."

"You once compared me to a jackass."

"Oh, you are a jackass, you. Just *listen* to me, Mitchell." Her rueful laugh frightened him. "The men I've known these past five years, they've been beasts, monsters. I didn't deserve them, I really didn't, but there they were, worshiping themselves and making me feel like shit underfoot. Through it all, you jackass, you were in the motherfucking mailbox—"

"Old jack-in-the-box."

"Damn it, will you please let me finish. There you were, a phenomenon, a precious phantom. Finally, I suppose I romanticized you—how could I not. You persuaded me to have a second try. Wait—" Anticipating him, she stiff-armed the air, then dropped her hand across the crate onto his. A sheaf of hair fell across her eyes and she tossed it back in frustration. "Don't say it. I know you weren't trying to encourage me."

Mitchell couldn't comprehend why she was working so hard to sell her story. The door was open. Here she was. Why press the case? "You can stay as long as you need to," he said wearily. "Okay? No more interrogation. I'll leave you alone."

She withdrew her hand and brought both of them to cover her face, her fingers fanned from cheek to cheek, barring her inchoate eyes, their light now more brown than green, and sad. "You wanted to see me again, didn't you?" she murmured. "Despite all this, you wanted me back, or have I really messed up?"

"That's a very interesting question," Mitchell said.

"*Interesting!*" Her head flew back and she pushed out of her sitting position, maddened to the point of assault, clamping her hands on his ears as if she were about to twist him around until his neck snapped. "You sit there like an Indian and tell me I've raised an interesting supposition. You spook in the mailbox. You cocksucker." She dropped all her weight against him and they tumbled off the crate, Johnnie atop him, squatting on his stomach. "Don't you dare say that, you nasty martyr. You Saint Mitchell."

"Get off."

"No."

"Come on."

"Not until you confess what's in that heart of yours." She cocked her head and pretended to listen carefully.

"That," he said, imperturbable, "is the sound of the little fish of charity, swimming in circles, happy to be of service. They only come once a year and you want to show them a bad time." He moved his hips to budge her off but she strained against him, a counterthrust that shocked with erotic energy. I don't want you to touch me this much, this quick, he thought out of self-preservation, the round dull blades of her pelvis digging into his groin, their bodies poised for a large lapse into sexual fluency, the language of that distant intimate world where they had grown up together, a small alphabet with a boggling capacity for meaning. Maybe we could dance first, something, anything to work up properly to this level of mock copulation about to turn real. It was merciless, this itch, and Mitchell was beginning to see that the largest share of Johnnie he had held on to as his own, his mnemonics of her, his mantra and his movie of this woman, was a spellbinding sequence of carnal images and sweaty vignettes, an index of lovemaking that dominated the archives of his memory of her. The notion crossed his mind that, healthy or aberrant, fair or unjust, in her long absence he had distilled Johnnie into a private stock of pornography. Reduced and reproduced through countless daydreams and night visions, transmuted into a benevolent succubus, she had lived with him twice the time as in the original version, and this newest Johnnie of the batch, mounted above him, was a source of pure upheaval.

She resumed her tricky polemic, her pitch. "Something kept shining on, Mitchell, bright as the north star," she said, an alluring whisper, her voice dropping lower and lower, "and I followed it here."

Mitchell felt too furtive and pathetic and would not respond. The heat from Johnnie's legs and bottom sank like radioactivity into his flesh, cunning isotopes. He squirmed under her. She rocked perfectly in sync with his movement so he stopped.

"Johnnie—" he started to say, but she placed a finger on his lips. Bold, worn out, plumes of hair-thin crosshatchings framed the expression of her eyes where one emotion collided with another and paid the toll of contradiction, like shoals thrown up where two currents opposed each other. Deception, passion, their separate reversals—Mitchell could see exactly where they met, barely visible still but given a few years they would advertise an overt brand of duplicity.

"What we had should never have ended. I invite you to gloat," she said to him, yet she seemed the one to be gloating. "If you want a true confession, there it is."

"What did we have?" The question seemed justified.

She hovered over him, inches away and bending closer by fractions, her smile enlarging from seductiveness to a wide leer, her makeup breaking down into crystallized particles, a granulation meshed by pores swelling in the tropical heat, the relentlessness of travel; layers of her skin dissolving before his harsh scrutiny; the leathery chap of her lips; a yellowness to the teeth farther back in her mouth, scored and packed with amalgamate. Mitchell blinked and the grotesque focus relaxed, softening her features.

"Do you want me back, Mitchell? Just say it, one way or the other."

"Hey, forget that question." He propped himself up on his elbows and Johnnie, gripping his biceps, pushed into him.

"I believe you, Mitchell," she whispered urgently.

Through an injured nose Mitchell inhaled whiffs of her hair, her soap and protein. Nothing registered was recognizable as belonging exclusively to Johnnie, and nothing she had said made sense except as subterfuge, because all she was was a runaway, and she had run away from so many people and things that she had begun to repeat herself, lost in her own momentum, a child resurrecting old toys. Her pubis was like a mallet struck against his own, urging him to acquiesce, and her breath pumped into his ear, a narcotic. Mitchell visualized a hormonal flow chart that resembled a metropolitan subway system, all lines headed for the downtown station. The picture went black and he rolled out from under her.

"You too fahst, gy-url."

Johnnie stayed flat on her back, staggered, her legs and arms

spread-eagled as though she had fallen from the sky, coaxing her breathing back from its galloping pace. She lifted her head, chagrined but still not thoroughly daunted, her look telling him she understood—whether true or not—what had happened. "Shit," she said, and let her skull thump back on the floor.

"I'm sorry, I have to go to work."

"Stay. Take the day off. Celebrate me. I need to be celebrated. I really need it, Mitch."

"I can't. I'll be home in a few hours."

He took the guava skins from the plates and flung them into the trees and vines where the side yard ended—just for the relief of throwing, the response of muscles, the useless power. A path led through the underbrush to the shanty of a woman named Mrs. Fetchalub, his closest neighbor. Her weedy children would scamper up to practice karate in the clearing of his property. The playing inevitably ended when one of the kids whirl-kicked another and the victim would crawl off into the bush, yelping like a puppy.

"Mitchell?"

On the floor of the veranda, Johnnie appeared expired, undone, physically rebuked, her toes and fingers and eyes swollen, her hair spread in limp swirls, the blue skirt wrinkled and misshapen. She wasn't looking at him; in fact, her eyes were closed.

"I'm not a bad person," she said. "I don't want you to think that."

Chapter 7

Too weary to ride his bike the three miles into town, Mitchell walked up to the road and took a jitney, grateful for its rank overload of passengers, as anonymous and without expectation as detainees being delivered to a labor camp. He stayed on the transport all the way to Scuffletown, the endlessly propagating pocket of coastal slum on the far side of Queen's Drop. He could think of nothing else outside of the travesty of Johnnie's preposterous and damningly provocative justification for being there, until the driver got involved in a race with another jitney around the loop of Belmont Park as they entered the capital, and the sudden violence of speed jolted his concern for Isaac, and Isaac's troubles restored some perspective to his own.

Scuffletown was what the world would be—what the world was, actually, in a great many places—without technology, or without a respect for craftsmen and a simple communal standard of caring. It was an overpopulated sprawl of throw-together, condemned by a process greater than any single man's lack of ambition or resource. It smoked and smoldered and festered like the waterfront encampment of a shipwrecked army, without the heart to live in anything but temporary quarters. Latent removal, kinetic transience, those were the essences of Scuffletown. Everyone who lived there believed they would walk away from it tomorrow and never return. Its crowded haphazardness, so offensively threatening to Mitchell's sensibilities, was inherent in this disavowal of permanence, and so the community depended not on the government or populist campaigns or even a modest self-reliance for general housekeeping and renewal but on such catastrophes as hurricanes and fires. Scuffletown, ultimately, was the civil service's pet metaphor for its own ineptness: you'd sooner find a property title in S-town, the hackneyed joke went, than modernize the national hospital, or make sense out of a ministry's book-keeping system.

Mitchell knew he didn't belong here on its sea-damp unpaved lanes, carefully stretching his legs across sewage trenches, deaf to anyone who approached him for any reason. Scuffletown was semiferal, a bit of behavioral wilderness sometimes dangerous because you could never tell what would be found inciting by the short-fused people you encountered there. One time a man powdered head to toe in sulfur-colored dust had demanded Mitchell give him his tennis shoes. He blocked Mitchell's way but then the condition for passage was abruptly dropped and Mitchell walked on. On another trip to Isaac's, when Mitchell stumbled over the point of a rock embedded in the road, a teenage boy came hurtling out of a yard to curse like a psychopath in his face, as if he were a dog asserting its territorial domain, its instinct engaged at the moment Mitchell's gait faltered. But all in all Scuffletown was not as it appeared. Behind the hellishness there were often extraordinary humans going about their daily business, carrying on a struggle for sanity, grasping at middle-class straws. Such was Isaac's mother, who had been raised by her grandparents in the country, where she had learned about the island's wild herbs and bushes. Now, when she wasn't cooking meals for the Jesuits at St. Mark's Secondary, she practiced folk medicine out of the three-room house in Scuffletown where she lived with her four sons, Isaac being the eldest, and for her service she collected a trickle of coins still called shillings by the poor.

That area of tamped and oil-stained sandy dirt in front of the shingled house, previously reserved for *Miss Defy*: its emptiness filled Mitchell with regret as he came past an untrimmed hedge of ixora into the Knowles' family compound. The yard was spared the neighborhood's general desolation by a giant cutlass-scarred hulk of an almond tree and its green chapel of limbs, a bench and a seat from an old schoolbus near its base to accommodate the men and women there to consult with Scuffletown's bush doctress and receive her herbs and tonics. Mitchell had never been to the house without seeing the seating fully occupied, S-town's seniors arthritically husking nuts until Mrs. Knowles walked down the hill from St. Mark's twice a day between breakfast and lunch and again in the afternoon, when the top half of the dutch door would fling open and she would call her patients up to the stoop. For any condition dire and unmanageable they had to drag themselves to the government doctor at Public Health, but for treatment of everyday maladies—the rheumatics and gizzard ache, swamp chill and numerous varieties of rash—Mrs.

Knowles' cures were just the thing, and the price never compounded the ailment.

Mitchell nodded at the almond pickers camped in the shade, a quartet of uniformly skinny turkey-necked old men, outgrown by their trousers and fiercely bleached shirts buttoned to the throat. To escape astronomical tides, the unpainted house was lifted off the ground on short posts, and he climbed a set of uneven steps, stopping at the threshold, to present himself to Isaac's mother. Mrs. Knowles sat just inside out of the sun, her feet on the floor and her bottom resting on the edge of a stool drawn up to a sewing table with the undercarriage stripped of its machine. She was emptying the contents of a stone mortar, a tobacco-colored crush of leaves, onto a scrap of coarse paper. A pestle lay nearby next to a modest pile of assorted coins, a pocketknife, a bottle of rubbing alcohol, a ball of string, a juice glass full of powder-blue berries. She twisted the corners of the paper together into a wick, and, raising her voice but not her head, summoned her customer from the yard.

"Mistah Chubbs," she commanded. *"Come."*

Mitchell stepped aside to make room on the stoop for feeble Mr. Chubbs, who pocketed his remedy in the tent of his pants, counted out his pennies, and left. Mrs. Knowles reached behind her for a ledger on a shelf, opened it, and recorded the transaction with a ball-point pen tied with rubber bands to the belt of her housedress.

"Good day, Mistah Wilson," she said finally, bringing Mitchell to attention with her oblique courtesy. She closed the book and peered up at him over the frame of her reading glasses. There was an unaccountable authority to Isaac's mother, as if she knew very well the habits and manners of a life different than the one she had settled for, in circumstances where dignity was more than just a refusal to be common. She studied Mitchell with her customary expression of controlled distaste, as though she had a privileged knowledge of him, given access to a dossier he himself had never seen, the contents of which were apparently not flattering.

"Good day, Mrs. Knowles," he chimed in response to her own reedy voice. Her presence was like the law. He felt an intractable obligation to be on his best behavior in her vicinity.

"I've come to check on Isaac."

She said he hadn't been home for two days. Mitchell cringed inwardly, dreading the report he must now make. She listened to the bad news without any noticeable reaction.

"Yes, someone come tell me he see Isaac's vehicle in de field cane."

Her steely motherhood enervated him. Of course she would have gotten wind of the mishap through the island's network of eager witnesses. "Well," Mitchell uttered with downcast eyes, chastened by his exposure to Mrs. Knowles, "I only wanted to make sure Isaac was all right. He got bumped around . . . nothing serious though."

"Be it so, Mistah Wilson. I shall tell Isaac you stop in when he reach home." She clasped her hands in a prayerful attitude, the gesture of a headmistress or a nun dismissing a mischief-maker. He started down the steps but turned back. Mrs. Knowles remained immobile.

"I was wondering, do you have anything to make me sleep better?"

Wordlessly, she stood up from the stool, aging and diminutive but by no means frail, and swept to the rear of the room, behind a vinyl-covered sofa to a pressed tin cupboard, a plaster Christ, garishly painted, hammered above on a cross, blessing her secrets. She returned in a minute to hand Mitchell a twine-bound bundle of green sprigs that smelled like musty basil. "Boil de leaf and drink de liquor," she instructed. She gave him something else inside a twist of brown paper. "And dis," she added, "if de nose continue to bleed, nuh?" She looked beyond him out the door. "Hallo, Mistah Atkin," she called. "Come straight up, please. What is it you wish, mahn?"

In all his life Mitchell couldn't recall a day being so queered by what fell unprecedented into it out of the blue, and on his walk back to Queen's Drop and the esplanade he ended up with a dollar haircut, another of fate's small extortions that he hadn't planned on and definitely didn't want, unless it was going to advance his sense of a world brimmed with queer opportunity. Instead, he was being used as an example for the other side of the debate, set out in a pond where chance and coincidence circled like sharks. As Mitchell hiked through Scuffletown on the nameless harbor street that was little more than a widened ditch, clogged with motor scooters and foot traffic and an occasional rogue flatbed truck hauling sand away from the dirty beach, and donkeys with swollen panniers of charcoal or yams or stockgrass, he began to feel pressed and soon enough he was certain that someone inhabited his shadow—in the S-town idiom, a dog-dance, someone keeping cadence with his own determined pace. He was always a push-ahead walker through the stony looks and silent mendication of the streets, past the burlap-shuttered windows of the dismal shanties, the morose self-absorption of rum shop clientele, the vagrant hostility of youth gangs lounging against broken-down walls, clustered in garbage-sown lots. There was much to see but frankly Mitchell didn't care to see it. It was out of character for him to slow up so he changed his line of direction instead of his swift step, hoping the hound would move ahead and be gone, but all this accomplished was to provoke a hissing campaign. Terrific, Mitchell cursed without turning around. He was being dogged by one of the militantly useless.

"Ssssssst . . . *blaireau.*"

A blaireau was not much of a beast, but the anachronistic Creole slur tweaked Mitchell's curiosity. If he was to be identified as a carrier of geopolitical virus and racial infection, he would have chosen to be represented by a varmint with a more noxious reputation than the blond island raccoon. What kind of a world was this anyway where raccoons had to take the blame for rats. For the most part, Mitchell didn't care any longer who fucked who, when, how, or why, because there was no doubt in his mind that he was not the oppressor or his direct descendent or his surrogate, and he knew that guys like the one probably on his heels were revolutionary fantasts, prodded by demons which for lack of a better name Mitchell called the Barbeques, since these particular malefactors were great advocates of arson, enraptured by the vision of persons, institutions, countries, and even systems of thought bursting into fire.

When Mitchell stagger-stepped, his shadow, thrown out of dog-dance rhythm, walked smack into his back. Mitchell pivoted reluctantly to get the confrontation over with. Dressed in surplus camouflage pants and a pale blue tee shirt advertising Disney World, his ridiculously large paratrooper boots worn with no better reason than as weapons, he shifted his weight from leg to leg, a surprisingly puny but lithe youth with brimstone eyes fixed unwaveringly on Mitchell's own. In proper acolyte fashion, the guy's head was shaved right down to his nicked, morocco scalp. His sour lips were encircled by a devilish mustache and goatee, or rather a goatee that would have been truly evil-looking on a less boyish mug. Born to be a fucking nuisance, Mitchell thought, perhaps giving himself too much credit for upstandingness. Mitchell took his cue from the Latter Day Saints, smiling.

"Are you going where I'm going, brother?"

The youth was momentarily stumped, but recovered enough to extract a handgun from the baggy pockets of his fatigues, and although he didn't exactly aim it at Mitchell, the way he enjoyed testing the weight in his palm suggested the aim would follow the splendid thrill of having a gun in his hand, in daylight and on a crowded street. Here we go, Mitchell thought, still smiling with sham crusading fellowship of the heaven-bound yet unable to speak. The

Barbeques were really mixing it up in this rookie's brain. It was no use trying to pacify him, and no good trying to explain, if Mitchell could, that he was more or less on his side, that Mitchell too believed in the folk remedies of change and justice—and Mitchell sure as hell knew they didn't look like this. Here was what happened when the Barbeques got excited and lifted one of St. Catherine's assholes out of the slumber of Pavlovian drool and snarl, promoting them to *assholes with a vital agenda*. Mitchell squinted at the pistol—he had seen so few handguns in his life he couldn't even be positive this one was real.

"Where you belong, eh?" It was an ambiguous challenge, almost a repartee to his own inquiry, and the guy scowled, shocking Mitchell further by slipping the gun back into his pants. He wasn't going to be shot—immediately, anyway—for being smug.

Likewise, he wasn't going to stand still as a bull's-eye for every fucker's manhood on the island. Mitchell pivoted a second time and began to hurry away. The guy's hand dropped on Mitchell's shoulder. *Where you belong?* It was a damn good question but Mitchell wasn't in the mood to open up for it. Without looking around, Mitchell dipped and side-stepped away from under his grasp, its pinch of overgrown fingernails, and ducked briskly onto a footpath that ran between the shanties to the first sanctuary in sight, two outdoor barbers plying their trade on the bottle-littered beach. One of them worked on a drowsing customer who sat on a plank of driftwood stretched between the trunks of two coconut palms undermined by erosion, their crowns phototropically bent, reared like snakes on the defense. The other barber perched nearby on a limestone outcropping and ruminated on the view of Queen's Drop's placid harbor, two freighters off-loading at the wharves. There was an available seat, a metal kitchen chair with its back snapped off. Mitchell plunked down on it as though he were late for an appointment. The barber engaged with his client paused. The one on the rock looked over slowly, highly suspicious. The emissary of the Barbeques had tailed Mitchell as far as the top of the beach and hesitated to come closer. Whatever prevented his approach did not however apply to his tongue.

"You ain belonga we, eh? Which side you from?"

Did he mean Windward or Leeward, Mitchell wondered. Or did he mean right or wrong?

The barber on the rock stood up, quick to understand what was happening. He advanced with his scissors pointed at Mitchell's assailant's chest. Mitchell couldn't make up his mind to warn him about the gun.

"Move on, toughie," the barber commanded in a voice not easily ignored. "You ain trouble today, bwoy." The barber, who had a pugilist's face and muscles that seemed flexed even in their relaxed state, clearly was a local personality of no slight reputation, someone you didn't fool with, even with an armed advantage. More than the potential for violence, the youth's grin, a reptilian disfigurement of an attitude that had already gone too far, got to Mitchell. He decided he was staying put. The barber came back to his rock and sat down.

"Pay him no mind, mahn," he said, staring back out into the harbor. "Daht bwoy juss noise on de road."

The second barber, plump and correspondingly jovial, resumed his leisurely clipping after cutting his eyes in the direction of the militant shadow. "Daht bwoy," he explained while gently stroking the pate of his still-drowsing customer, "him go off on a wuk boat lass year . . . Panama line, eh Jonesy?, and come home wit he head spinnin in shit. Pay him no mind, skip."

"He has a gun in his pocket."

"Oh ho? Maybe so, but him ain got no bullet."

Out of the corner of Mitchell's eye, he could see the youth dawdling not so far down the erratic row of gray shacks, in no rush to disappear, and could hear him cussing and mumbling as his boots bulldozed through the sand.

"Can I get a haircut?" Mitchell asked.

The proposition alarmed the barber on the rock. He thought about it, frowning, his face seamed with doubt. He glanced over at his colleague and then back at Mitchell.

"I ain ahs yet cut a white mahn's locks," he confessed, adding, "I ain so much ahs touch a white mahn's head in me life."

"You pussy, bwoy," the second barber hee-hawed. Mitchell saw him wink his way. "He fraid, skip."

Neither barber, in their tight-fitting tee shirts and faded bathing trunks, appeared lacking in backbone or mettle. Both were as burly as stevedores, which likely was their preferred profession. The one named Jonesy, looking undecided, spread open the scissors in his hand and, in one of the many thin channels of ideograms worn into the limestone, began an irresolute sharpening of the blades. There was a rock like this one, custard limestone, to the rear of the beach in Howard Bay, the site of the first white settlement on the island, where for centuries men had honed their cutlasses, their machetes and butcher knives, the steel filing an inscrutable map of lines sliced deep in the stone. Tillman, when Mitchell stayed at Rosehill Plantation during his first weeks on the island, had been the one to show Mitchell the block. He remembered him saying, Here, look at this . . . this rock is St. Catherine. It's all right here in the limestone.

Jonesy shook out the cloth he had been sitting on, a flour sack with its seams unstitched, and draped it over Mitchell's shoulders, tucking the top edge into the collar of the white man's workshirt. He stood back with his hands on his stout hips, sucking his teeth, sizing up the intricacies of the job before him. His misgivings seemed to cause him indigestion. He burped nervously and took a step toward Mitchell.

"I ain know about dis," he worried. He was on his guard, watching Mitchell as if there were a wildcat poised on his skull. "I ain know but one style."

Mitchell too was beginning to think the haircut was no longer a necessary tactic. The conflict had been effectively preempted, the kid had shoveled himself out of sight, and Jonesy seemed to think he couldn't lay his hands on Mitchell without a degree from beauty college. But the other barber merrily taunted his partner forward until the issue became a point of honor, advising him to just trim around until he got a feel for it. Jonesy bent his knees and walked a circle around Mitchell, scrutinizing the length and thickness of his hair, the wave of incomprehensible curls that swept back from Mitchell's forehead past his eyes, the feathering at the nape of Mitchell's neck. He reached for one of these bunches and rubbed it tentatively between thumb and forefinger. "Oh ho," he said, enlightened, locating by his touch a problem that confirmed what his professional eye had suspected. Taking a primitive turtle shell pick-comb from his waistband, he raked Mitchell's hair with considerate strokes first one way then another, learning who knows what from his experiment. The partner observed this grim procrastination and told Jonesy once again that he was impaired by fundamental pussiness. Eventually Jonesy settled on a starting point—to the front of Mitchell's right ear, where the flaxen current of hair rippled into an abrupt sideburn—and commenced snipping, strand by individual strand. After only a minute of this fastidious work Jonesy's colleague hummed critically, and then he began to scoff and kibitz.

"Nah, daht ain de way you snip a white fella's roof."

Six more hairs fell, one at a time, all cursive els to the precise zeroes and cramped esses the barber customarily manufactured with his scissors. Mitchell watched a bead of sweat slide from the barber's forehead and off the tip of his meaty nose.

"Nah, you too shy, bwoy, peck peck peckin so, like de mahn have a

blahck fella's wool." The rounder barber abandoned his own somno-
lent customer to shamble over and supervise Jonesy.

"Lean into it so." The second man pantomimed hedge shearing.

"There's no hurry." Mitchell flinched.

"Progress slow, bwoy. By de time Jonesy reach de next side, de
bush grow bahck on de fust."

Jonesy jerked his head with exasperation toward the forgotten customer. "Gwan bahck to Alphonse. Him goin wake up soon."

"Here now, look," the second barber said, unable to keep himself
from intervening. There was a slicing bite from the slim metal blades.
A sheaf of sun-lightened hair bounced down Mitchell's arm into the
sand.

"Too deep, nuh?" said Jonesy.

"Fuss, fuss. You ain see ahead to de finish line." Another batch fell
free, scattering in Mitchell's lap. "Look how she smood right up,"
boasted the happy barber. Jonesy was sent away to continue groom-
ing the drowser, who had just come from an eleven-to-eleven shift at
the Ju-C bottling factory, according to Mitchell's new attendant.
Mitchell shut his eyes, resigned to the usurper's brazen self-confidence, his native enthusiasm for defoliation. The scissors drove and
plowed everywhere on Mitchell's scalp, giving the impression that his
hair was being scythed by a mad anarchist, an outcast of the trade.

"'Scuse, skippah, but I does enjoy conversation and psychology
while in operation."

"I think you might be trimming it too short."

"Too shawt? Nah, skip, plenty locks left up here." The barber tou-
sled what remained on Mitchell's scalp to prove his point; Mitchell
felt bristles springing back into place. "So, skip, Abdul give you a
fright, nuh? Daht bwoy low on brainage."

"Who's Abdul?"

"Daht bwoy people does cy-ahll Petey. He name heself Abdul,
heh-heh. Abdul, like ahn Arab mahn. De fella tryin to hawk de gun."

"Wait a minute," Mitchell argued. "He wasn't walking around trying to become salesman of the week."

"Aw," sympathized the barber, "doan pay him no mind. Petey got a
rude technique, eh? Him a dontcarish fella, a simple bwoy wit rough
fancy. But de bwoy's muddah sick, ya know, and I does believe he
lookin to sell daht gun he teef someplace when he ship out."

Mitchell didn't welcome the barber's rationalization, though it
explained the odd way the kid had displayed the gun. Now everything
seemed foolish again and Mitchell felt queasy, a player that can't be

retired off the field no matter how many wrong moves he's made. He tried to look over at the drowser, full of envy for how well he was handling his affairs, but the barber twisted Mitchell's head like a top and Mitchell closed his eyes, willing to let things happen.

"So, skip," the barber talked on as his scissors harvested, "ain many tourists take de Queen's road ahll de way to Scuff Town."

Mitchell had a weakness, one that he was overly conscious of, of describing, popularizing, and, if it came to that, defending his presence on the island.

"I'm not a tourist," he answered glumly, still finding it hard to break the routine. "I live in Howard Bay."

"True?" said the barber. "So how you find life on St. Catherine?"

"Piss-to-windward," Mitchell said, which was the accepted Catherinian response. In the wake of the barber's explosive laughter, which affected Mitchell like a gate swinging open, he pushed right along into a rant, a billingsgate monologue of details about Johnnie.

"Mmm, mmm," the barber grunted happily, a confidante to many tales of woe. "True, true," as if he had known everything all along.

"The contact had worn thin. In another year or less, she would have vanished into oblivion."

"Right, right." The barber wheezed with pleasure.

"And now here she is, staying at my house. Like a robber come back to the bank to open an account."

The barber, who had ceased his clipping at the start of this outpouring, nodded appreciatively. "You see daht a lot in Scuffyville, skippah. We is dy-ahmn funny daht way."

"The thing is," Mitchell lamented, "she knows I know. So why the snowjob?"

"Snowjob?"

"Exactly. Why can't she just play an old friend passing through and leave it at that? Instead, she's going in for this big Hollywood performance."

The barber paused to mull this over. "You must outwit she," he decided. "Employ psychology."

Mitchell realized, beyond the concord of the moment's dialogue, they were both incurable in their separate points of view. He shut his mouth now that the fellow had passed on his wisdom, and resolved to shut it in a more than immediate context, that is, to leave Johnnie alone, to help her in any way she needed to be helped.

The scissors passed over his head in a final strafing. A thunderstruck congregation of bowl-bellied raglings and uniformed schoolchildren, off for lunch, had swarmed out of the dirt yards and shanties to witness this mysterious event, a white man getting scalped on the Scuffletown beach. Only now, surveying the amazement on the children's smooth faces, Mitchell felt utterly estranged from the surroundings, and saw what only a camera would compose: a young man hunkered on the fringe of a foreign slum, a North American with an anemic hard-luck story he has recently divulged to the gathering. His ankles are reddened by sand-flea bites, his head has been shorn to indicate his reduction in status. The expression on his face suggests he has unraveled under cross-examination, that he's been placed on trial before a mob of youngsters and beachkids and defended himself without cleverness, and that momentarily the children will bind him up and stew his unworthy carcass in a man-sized cookpot on the once glorious strand. A wanderer, the camera would show, on the brink of the disastrous.

The barber swept the clippings from Mitchell's neck and shoulders with a palm frond. One preschool ragling, whose tee shirt wouldn't have made it at a carwash, asked a companion with white paste smeared around his mouth if Mitchell were the queen. A girl in a school frock rapped the questioner from behind for this gross mistake. A number of mutts shook themselves out from the throng and discovered each other in the open space between Mitchell and the ring of children. Two scabby males lunged together, fighting at, and then on top of, his feet. The barber who would employ psychology stepped into the fray, kicking the closest dog with such force that, instantly, it pissed blood, squatting like a female. Its former foe did the yipping and crying, however, racing down the windrow of the tideline like a haunted fox.

"Pay dem beast no mind," Jonesy said, still engaged with piecework on the drowser, the most carefree soul in Scuffletown.

The Ministry of Agriculture, emptied for lunch, was a veritable Swiss embassy of escape, a haven from the outlandish conspiracies of the outside world. The greatest loss of the unemployed on St. Catherine was that they were without a workplace to hide in. Mitchell trudged down the hall toward his corner office, detouring into the washroom to assess the damage to his hair. The cut wasn't so bad, actually, only shorter than it had been in many years. He stared at himself in the filmy mirror, accepting the conclusion that short hair made him look older and, unfortunately, mean.

On his desk were two memos, reminders that Mitchell was part of a greater plan and bigger operation than the bagatelles of his private life. One informed him that the team he worked with had gone up the leeward coast for the day—another survey, the third, of the Phibbs Estate. The second memo officially required his attendance at a staff meeting called for Friday, the day after tomorrow, written and placed there on his vintage manual typewriter. The note was signed and dated by the chief agricultural officer, Mr. Samuels. *Work to do,* Mr. Samuels announced. I work, you work, he she and it works, Mitchell muttered, making an effort to focus on what he should be doing, the churning distraction of Johnnie reestablished in his head, a nagging grind, like a cement mixer operating one street over. God works, the devil works, the planet resonates with the dialectic of their labor while the idle luxuriate in desolation. That's right, Mitchell said, responding to his own rhetoric. Slackers beware. Something unexpected had come up, the note told him. Quite right. The unexpected always does.

He didn't have to be at the ministry today, especially now that he knew the Public Lands Development Programme (PLDP) team was out charting the hills and ravines, the disputed pasturelands. Indeed, no one ever said a word to Mitchell on the days he failed to show. When he had moved in last September, he was delegated responsibilities, anointed with a puff of confidence, allowed all the occupational freedoms and available resources he should require, and subsequently ignored. Well, it didn't disturb him. Mitchell liked his work, even as he was beginning to discover it was irrelevant, that its contribution would be negligible, until certain political matters within the coalition were laid to rest. Then perhaps he would be called upon, and he would be ready, sitting on the answers in a lotus position, the ministry's own imported guru from the Church of the Impossible Reform.

There was little reason to be there today, but anywhere was better than Howard Bay, making cocoa tea for Johnnie. Forget that. How much time would it take to recover from the lightning bolt of her reappearance, that smelly sachet of words she unpacked to set up housekeeping. Am I to be loved? Mitchell wondered, but it was not a serious question. There was love and there was leverage, and no mercy to the fools caught between the two.

Using a pencil, he slit open a thick package of current market reports posted from USDA/Washington and spent the rest of the day trekking through a friendly forest of statistics, updating forecasts he had compiled for the island's crops, rewriting sections of the PLDP proposal newly affected by trends he determined in world prices. Keeping the ship in shape, no urgency to it. He could have been daydreaming in a cathedral to the vaulted echoes of an Anglican choir.

Numbers and music shared of course the same patterns of elegance, even when the figures exalted only aubergines.

Or . . . *bananas*, Mitchell stage-whispered, giddy as the afternoon slipped on. The people of London are rioting for bananas. They must have more of these sweet yellow tubes—they demand it. More vanilla for their cakes. More ginger for their beer. The people in London are begging for their goddamn bananas.

Mitchell occupied himself this way until late in the afternoon when his ability to manipulate the ten-fingered chords of calculations faltered, the sheets of statistics fusing together into a jungle of Sanskrit. He admitted he was dead tired and therefore must return home.

The windward coast jitney dropped him off on the road above the cottage at dusk. He thought he would be greeted by an atmosphere he was less accustomed to than the silence he found behind the door. Johnnie? he said, without getting a response. Maybe she was gone already, another of her assaults on this day of inexplicable recesses in reality, but of course the house would feel different, would feel *right*, if that were true.

"Hello," Mitchell said. "Johnnie?"

He went to the kitchen and drank orange juice out of a jar in the refrigerator. Through the bank of louvered windows he checked for her but she wasn't there, even though that's where he had pictured her, in the hammock reading a book, watching the waves strike the reef, writing postcards to her chain of exes, painting her fingernails. Mitchell needed now to see her perform the most ordinary habits. From the primary specifics of her life, perhaps, he would gain a foothold on this slippery business of being near her again.

He returned through the house to her room. The door was half opened, the new curtains drawn but the windows unshuttered, inhaling and exhaling the last hour of light with the breeze cuffing the shore. She was fast asleep under the mosquito netting, stopped in her tracks by sleep, her lower legs off the mattress as though she had collapsed without the strength to make herself comfortable. Her skirt and top lay puddled on the floor where she had taken them off. Her body was twisted, her spine flat but her hips rotated at an angle, one thigh thrown over the other, her hands pressed between the flesh below her crotch. The blue panties narrowed and vanished into the gaunt hemispheres of her buttocks. It brought on an unwanted craving, to see her like this, to be able to study her without any emotion or misunderstanding or ploy raising a barrier. If Mitchell held her right now, without disturbing her, the embrace had the potential for innocence, a contact timeless and sublime. Yet she would wake at his touch and misinterpret what he was feeling, his simple desire for holding her, and he would be unable to articulate his motivation. Even thinking about it ruined the moment of anticipation, made the mood illicit, and then the whole scene was trapped in artifice, as though he had walked in on a setup.

What a strange girl, Mitchell thought, lifting the gauze, bending over her sleeping form, examining her mouth, the lips parted and peaceful yet constrained by a tension that began in a heaviness near the corner of each eye and weighed through the flesh to meet, in parallel swoops, at her chin. Five years ago, losing her was like a practice session with death. Beyond the skin and tissue and blood of that mouth were biochemical imprints, like an abandoned code, of what he had been, and it was just fine with Mitchell that she had taken that other self of his away with her. Whatever else Johnnie intended to bring back to him besides herself, Mitchell wanted no part of it.

He took a final step and crouched down only inches from touching her. Her breasts were much smaller than he remembered them, and there was a reason for that. They were evenly though lightly tanned, capped with nipples like tarnished pennies, and their shape did not flatten out like jellyfish the way the breasts of most women did when they were on their backs. His nearness must have probed into the gravity of her sleep; her mouth twitched and her eyelids crumpled, papery and blue. Mitchell slowly withdrew, again tracing the length of her with his memory. Her abdomen had a slight, robust puff to it because of the way she was folded. Her legs shifted a few inches as he backed up another step and he saw the first of the other girl's secrets, a longish scar on the inside of her right knee, a bubble gum cigar where something had taken a chunk out of her. He winced and looked away, finishing his inspection. Her feet were black-soled and much abused. Maybe she had walked barefoot for five years. One of her big toes had an old sticker of scab on it behind the nail. The toe next to it had obviously healed crooked from a break. The sides and bottoms were padded with hard-looking calluses and spattered with the gloss of little scars. An attempt had been made to resurrect their femininity, red polish dabbed on the nails, but nothing could save them from looking like the feet of a homeless vagrant.

Mitchell let out his breath and stood up, worried about what would happen next. He had never meant to reclaim or re-create her, not in the flesh. That wasn't it at all. That wasn't why he wrote the letters, sent the cards, phoned once a year on her birthday, but now he was drearily confused, divided, and as Johnnie had known, *unready*, a state of being he seemed dumbly fated to keep rediscovering, for what he did next was to step quietly over to the chair next to the wardrobe and do a bit of snooping through one of Johnnie's straw handbags. Dollar bills and ECC bank notes, a packet of airplane peanuts, cigarettes, Tampax, Chapstick, a plane ticket voucher booked one-way: Honolulu, Los Angeles, Denver, Miami, Antigua, Barbados, St. Catherine, with a return leg to Barbados. Johnnie's Atlas of Mundi Novus, her own New World. And her passport, her picture flirting with the camera, issued to Johanna Mae Fernandez. Somewhere out on the trail, Johnnie had taken an alias or gotten married.

He got out of the room, carefully shutting the door behind him. Food and convalescence were as far as Mitchell needed to think. He went back through the dark house to the kitchen, not bothering with lights, and set a pan of water to boil on the hotplate with Isaac's mother's leaves. He fixed a bachelor's dinner, a sandwich made with a stale roll and canned cheese and mustard, ate it while he walked around, restless, making sure the doors and windows were locked for the night. In another hour the southeastern district where he lived would be plunged into blackness as the island's utility company cut the power, shedding electricity for a four-hour span, rotating districts each night to conserve energy and distribute hardship equally. Teef time, the islanders called it.

The tea had a mushroomy flavor to it, woodsy, with an aftertaste of quinine. It seemed to parch his mouth as he gulped it down. Mitchell went to his own room, lay on top of the bedspread, anxious to feel sleepy, praying to be taken out, but his mind started up again like a squirrel on a tree limb somewhere above, nattering rodent invective, and just as he was beginning to despair that Mrs. Knowles' bush tea was worthless, he became concurrently afraid that it was something more than a mere sedative. There was a sensation of a hallucinogenic door being swung open. Mitchell's squirrel brain was chased off by the gathering presence of something owl-like and large, a winged shape which kept expanding, and he felt himself being squeezed so hard that tears came to his eyes. This near-panic was followed by a relaxation of the effect and then an overwhelming sense of well-being, but—and this was entirely lucid—there was a horizon defined by a profound melancholy, and he was traveling toward it at great speed. Before he could get there, Mitchell felt himself being slammed down, getting knocked to his knees in rough shorebreak and sucked along a silky bottom into unconsciousness.

Chapter 8

The minister of agriculture's three-car motorcade ascended a dirt road to an isolated clearing in the humid bush from where Mitchell, his imported American, had spent all morning surveying the possibilities of the land below, a high jungled-up valley in Kingsley's home district, a copra plantation until the end of the second world war. Evidently, Kingsley had ordered the rugged excursion on impulse, interrupting an audience with some visiting delegation of what—investors?—to drag them all out into the countryside. His solemn entourage followed a step behind him, perspiring in their business suits, while the drivers remained with the vehicles. The noise from one of their car radios sounded thin and ineffective and even, Mitchell thought, oddly nostalgic and comforting within the scope of the mountain and all the territory opened up to the view below them.

The minister, it seemed, had an urge to hear Mitchell talk. *Tell me about what you see, Mistah Wilson,* he said with a disarmingly shy grin, this fat old man with power. *Please, go ahead. Say.* He encouraged the air with his hands. Runnels of sweat darkened the front of his white shirt and spread in a line along his waistband. Stickers clung to his trousers from the grasses he had walked through.

Mitchell explained how the valley could best be transformed into a showcase of agrarian production: diversify crops, introduce high-profit exotics, irrigate the lowlands and plant labor-intensive rice, establish a regional base of agri-industries. Arable land was such and such a percent. Grazing land was such and such.

Kingsley stood by and listened, nodding serenely, as if there were a rare pleasure to be gained from hearing an outsider speak of the future of the land the old man had been born to. He radiated peace of spirit, love of home. Then, without a visible change of mood, he became inscrutable.

And Mistah Wilson, you have seen my bad children, nuh?
Sir?
Here. Up in the bush.
I don't understand, Minister.
Jack Nasty? You see him too?
No, sir. Nobody.
You have become very important to me, Mistah Wilson. To our efforts,
he said, his expression darkening, not to be trifled with, and then he
left, followed by his flock of puzzled guests, without saying another
word.

Not without difficulty, the three cars were turned around in the
rough clearing and disappeared in front of a column of yellow dust.
The dust, chasing the invisible cars down the mountain, had its own
dislocated beauty, like sky writing, or a long celebratory streamer
being unfurled on the slope. When silence returned to the mountainside, Mitchell sat down on a flat rock with his notepad and, for a reason he could not fathom, sketched smokestacks and freeways and
skyscrapers into the panorama of the valley, a fantasy of urban defile-
ment that he exed over and threw into the weeds.

Kingsley was one of the Katie-boys, one of the few, who had the
authority to get things done, but what Mitchell had seen for himself
of Kingsley was not sufficient to develop a reliable opinion of the
man. They had met only once before, on Mitchell's first day of work,
directed into the Honorable J. W. Kingsley's unpresuming office
through a door no more auspicious than a broom closet's to have his
hand taken indifferently into the minister's corpulent paw. The new
agricultural economist, the CAO Mr. Samuels said, introducing
Mitchell.

You shall learn something here, Mistah Wilson, Kingsley told him.
His countenance remained impersonal, tutorial, as if it were essential
that Mitchell understand that his education had begun at that very
moment. Mitchell felt an old instinct return, the rebelliousness of the
precocious student, but the chief agricultural officer ushered him
from the office before he could diplomatically remind the minister
that their incipient relationship was not conceived as a one-way
street, that the island's request for assistance was not the equivalent
of creating an opportunity for a white boy to earn postgraduate credit hours. He would have stuck his young foot in it too if Samuels
hadn't whisked him away to a sequence of more affable introduc-
tions, fellows genuinely pleased to have Mitchell aboard.

Like everybody else on St. Catherine, Mitchell tried to remember
to dial in Kingsley's Sunday night radio speeches— monologues

about bizarre phenomena, seasoned with religious metaphor and mysticism, cunningly pierced with one-line directives concerning the most current legislation, and innuendos about unnamed enemies. He had heard Kingsley give a speech on sunglasses and hats, the effects these items produced in their wearers—the minister did not like caps or tinted glasses that obscured the face; he considered them styles of the criminal class. The hour-long analysis ended in an exhortation to plant seven more tons of carrots in the northern co-ops. Mitchell had heard a speech about Savannah, Georgia, which Kingsley had apparently visited in the wintertime as a young cook's mate aboard a freighter. This particular and peculiar soliloquy focused on grilled meats, the inhumanity of racism compounded by cold weather, and finally the efficacy of the Monroe Doctrine, which Kingsley was all for, he vowed, though he lambasted its inconsistent interpretation by American presidents. There were speeches about telekinetic force and herbal cures for cancer, one about how Moses and Joshua divided the land beyond the Jordan River for the men of Israel, one which ended citing a new charter for the Marketing Board but which began with a tribute to Lord Mountbatten, a strange thirdhand account of episodes with the earl in India during the world war. The plagues of communism, Arab control of the planet's oil, muckraking journalism, and insupportable tariffs were noted at random throughout most of Kingsley's presentations. His broadcasts were, in fact, sort of a folk hit, a screwy evening's entertainment in the shops and shanties burning their lanterns throughout the isolated countryside, like boats at sea dependent on the air waves to assure them they were part of the black, larger world beyond the light.

Why had Kingsley sought him out this morning, far out here in the bush? Mitchell couldn't say, but the minister's appearance, so unlikely, disturbed him, providing notice that attention had somehow gathered around him, and Mitchell wasn't a person who appreciated unsolicited attention. Instead of returning to the ministry offices to do the paperwork he had planned, Mitchell stayed on that flat rock throughout the afternoon, staring at the land below like a hawk, like a lone wolf, secure in the knowledge of being far removed from the necessary pursuits of bureaucratic survival.

He sat, perched in the sun, knowing this was the last frontier for the convertive passions. The tropics. Impure and trodden though it may be, the world between Cancer and Capricorn was remote enough to still have its hinterland attraction, that psychic glint and sparkle in the smoky rags of its wilderness for pioneers born belatedly into the Aquarian Age. For what passed in the twentieth century as

frontiersmen: would-be individualists rebelling against the vague bru-
talities of middle-class lives; centurions from the suburbs, the offshore mavericks, the missionaries of industry and guardians of the
endangered thing; the mall culture fugitives, the explorers of psy-
choactivity; the Marco Polos of consumerism and the Magellans of
avarice; the cinema bwanas, the pilgrims of strangeness, the glory
dreamers—all the restless souls who were going to jump right out of
their skin unless they moved out in the direction of the equator, latitude zero, a band of the world that offered opportunities of the absolute—absolute success, absolute failure, absolute depravity. They
came to it not as they would have in the past, as men encountering an
enslaved virgin who would acquiesce to rough treatment, but as
courtiers trying to win the attention of a harridan widow, a mauled-
over bitch who had inherited the broken kingdoms of her ancestors.
Either way, you could hardly call it romance.

When Mitchell was growing up back in the Sixties, it was supposed
that the Western nations had launched a war of money against the
world's weaklings, paving the filthy streets of their cities with gold,
but whoever believed that was conveniently deluded. The cash
boomeranged back home into the accounts of all the players, or fattened the waistlines of baby-faced potentates by another twelve inches. Sometimes the money never existed at all, except as an imaginary
understanding, like Peter Pan, or the tooth fairy. It was a magic act,
the foreign aid biz. One hundred percent overhead. He had never
heard it discussed in terms of changing some poor fellow's hard life
for the better except in classrooms or on television. Almost every
economist he knew at the university behaved like a demagogic oracle
from the Middle Ages. They found more ways to explain things then
there were things to explain. Out in the field, the only programs that
ever got off the ground played as a quick fix for junked-out clients.

Mitchell believed he understood most of the underlying falsehoods
of the business before coming down to St. Catherine but he was
blinded, or chose to be blinded, by the magnificent prospects of
Edison Banks' reform movement. What exactly was the relationship,
he wondered, between the need for reform and the desire for revolution? No one doubted that everything on the island had to change,
and maybe it was time, maybe Mitchell could shoulder some of the
work and learn what he really didn't know—the secret to accomplish-
ing something good and just on this earth, like rescuing a child-
nation that had fallen, and was floundering, in a pigpen of greed.

He added up the odds, though, and wasn't moony about his
chance for enlightenment. He was aware of the scale of the hustle,

the grand imperial benign vastness of it, the unaccountability of its nature. He even knew some of the dirt about Kingsley, the Great Manipulator, whose career could be identified by the reek of burnt cane, and knew that Edison Banks was not much appreciated by the overseers in Washington. And suppose a rebellious nephew like myself sympathized with a leader like Banks, Mitchell wondered, and practiced his own small subversion against the family back home. From Uncle Sam's point of view it didn't much matter, that boy's game. It didn't even warrant a dressing down. The nephews took their paychecks, and they were very plump ones indeed, whether issued by Texas A&M, as was the case with Mitchell, or the USDA, or AID, or a phalanx of other acronyms acting as brokers in these arrangements. It didn't matter because the wealth eventually came back to its origins, even if nephew stayed out there in the jungle to eat shit and bark at the moon. In the meantime the boys were afield guilelessly disseminating the doctrines of rationalism as if they were bread itself, charming the rustics with technocratic voodoo. Eventually all the boys came home to reminisce in old age over their fling with the exotic. And for meaning, nephew, if the spell had not washed off in the Jacuzzis of retirement, had the mystery of his own altruism to ponder, to weigh on the scale of what had not been achieved, and to measure what had failed in his soul against what was never going to change anyway as long as we were men and not gods.

At the end all there was was the knowledge that you took the job to not be cuckolded by opportunity. You let it happen, you let yourself live. You were not afraid to look. You were not afraid to act.

Mitchell put notebooks, topographical maps, camera, and tripod back into the Land Rover and called it a day once the sun entered its fourth quadrant and blasted straight into his line of vision. Back at the ministry, he returned the vehicle to the motor pool and bounded up the wooden steps to the second floor of administrative offices to retrieve his bike. The secretaries in the front bullpen were consistently titillated by the sight of him, their damp mint-eyed white man. Most of them were too shy to talk to Mitchell but not shy enough to be amused among themselves every morning when he appeared. We are black beauties, he imagined they said to him with their eyes. We are lost queens—isn't that amusing? He nodded their way and walked past into the narrow corridor that led to his section.

There was irrefutable proof that words and numbers were the perfect commodities for export. Not money, and not technology, unless it was as fundamental as safety pins. Thus the proliferation of fellows who did what Mitchell did—the statisticians, the language wizards, the analysts, overeducated people born with a passion for ratiocination, who had a feeling for land—any land, all land, the vitality of it, in it, under it—land, the one issue that was eternal. They were the sturdy facade, the ulterior design for a very canny flow of resources. The pearls of research were meticulously logged and stowed until their time of political expedience, which might never come. What is your view on the banana, Mistah Wilson? How best to ensure the policy of our little coconut oil cartel? If not sugar than perhaps you can suggest an intensification of tobacco? Yams? Nutmeg? Cocoa? Lemons? Arrowroot? Pigeon peas? Sorrel blossoms? A cannery for hearts of palm? What are the prospects on the Caricom market for another quadrillion metric tons of sweet potatoes, eh? Our farmers are excellent cultivators of the sweet potato.

Near the end of the hallway, Mitchell opened the door to his office and strapped his briefcase to the carrier on the rear fender of the bicycle. He had left the two windows unshuttered and now latched them, closing out the noise from the schoolyard at St. Mark's Secondary, and a shifting light which penetrated through the banyan tree outside the windows and polished the fine old hardwoods of the room. Johnnie tried to slip back into his thoughts but he shut her out too, and sat down behind his desk, rummaging through the backpack he had left there that morning.

Through no fault of his own, what Mitchell had to offer to the ministry's success was marginal, but he was equally sure that even a little was enough to make a difference, despite perpetual reinvention. Mistah Wilson, the Blackburn study is inactive, we now rely on the Bedford study. No, no, the Bedford study no longer reliable, mahn. The PM has asked us to heed the recommendations of the Vertell Group. Faces turn quizzical—*de what group you say? Vertell?* Look dem Vertell numbahs, mahn. Dey find a nice setta numbahs, true? Look how click-click-click. All of those expensive reports, the reports before the reports, and the reports after the reports, say, said, and would reiterate only one message far into the next century, the one truth that was so true it mocked the legions of lesser truths that flourished in its light—we fuck around while people go hungry. Excellent truth. Everybody loved it. Nothing produced a crop of bullshit like the Green Revolution.

Cassava, Mistah Wilson? But what you think of rice, with proper irrigation, eh? Soil's so rich, mahn, so giving, on St. Kate. Oranges? Dairy production? Carrots? We can grow anything here, you know, just throw seed on the ground and get out of the way, but *dese people, dem lazy. Dese people, dem chupid as frog. Fuckin baboons, nuh?* The second week Mitchell was here he had made the blunder of opening the files kept in the office by his predecessors, a tag-team of foreign experts passing through St. Catherine during the past sixty years. It seemed that every pebble, puddle, and pismire on the island had been evaluated ad infinitum by this distinguished procession of developmental solipsists. They revealed, as a group, an extraordinary penchant for repetition and simultaneous contradiction. One would say, Dig a ditch right here. A second would arrive afterward to say, Clearly this ditch belongs over there, not here. A third pundit would follow and say, Oh Christ, we don't think ditches are the thing anymore; you should fill them in. These absurd, disembodied dialogues had been going on in the present vein for ten, fifteen, twenty years.

So, white bwoy, tell me. You come to mek some big experiments? Mek some studies on dem poor peoples? Dem slavery mentalities?

Mitchell straightened up from binding his pant legs with rubber bands, considering the risky business of going unarmored and unengined into foreign traffic.

Mister Wilson. Up in the bush, you did see my bad children?

He thought about it again, this riddle, and decided it was nothing more than primitive, cagey humor, a joke from a trickster, a politician of trivial intrigues. Again, he lingered in his office longer than he should have, considering the guest alone in the house at Howard Bay. Certainly he stayed longer than was necessary, afraid of Johnnie—Mrs. What's Her Name—yawning, putting in an extra hour for a workaholic's merit badge. He reviewed the maps of the former copra estates, weeded productivity assessments, examined market trends and commodities stats until he hated it all but at least he was forming a comprehensive, lucid picture of change in this no-account nation, changes that were simple and elegant and precise in his notes and made him feel light-headed with a premonition of their impact. Once, the Eisenhower-era phone on his desk gave an abrupt chime and then dribbled a stream of gummy bell-notes. Mitchell picked up the receiver and a woman squawked, "Ministry's on fire, baby," or so he thought. When he went down to the reception area, there were no flames, no smoke, and the secretary nodded to an old man sitting on a folding chair, watch cap in hand. "Dere he is," the woman told Mitchell.

"Who?" Mitchell asked.

"What I juss tell you," she said officiously. "De mahn is here who need to know about de tree you hire him to chop down."

Mitchell didn't have a tree to chop down, and when he spoke to the old man, he couldn't understand his answer, and sent him away.

Finally Mitchell took his Gitane out on the cobbled streets of the old careenage where he became a fluid thread of speed through the early evening traffic, the noisy mix of people queuing up for jitneys, the pods of cattle and goats, the lorries that wanted to skin him. The gears of the bicycle clicked incrementally to adjust to the difficulty of the slope as Mitchell passed out of town into its alternately ramshackle and wealthy outskirts. The southeastern face of the mountain rose off his left shoulder, channeled with darkness, and the sea ahead gathered a soft woolen shadow far out on its rim. He pumped the pedals hard until he was gasping, which made him exuberant, thinking this was what it meant and how it felt when it was good, the breeze in his face carrying the smells and conversations of the open shops, the people and the architecture jolted into impressionistic messages, scrolled ironwork, flowered dresses, a girl toting a calf's head by its bloody ear, a many-gabled boarded-over house, a line of women jogging like Masai warriors, single file on the path flanking the road, shallow baskets of plantains and passionfruit balanced on their erect heads. Mitchell pumped for more speed as he crested Zion Hill, crossed Brandon Vale, labored up Ooah Mountain, and began to coast downward toward Howard Bay, purple land crabs scuttling out of their sandy holes and jigging on the black road in front of him. He was flying, free and unburdened, wishing he had no place to go.

Chapter 9

A cat was in the kitchen sink eating a plucked, half-frozen chicken. Straddled around the carcass, it was stripping the bird to the bone, with all four sets of claws sunk into the meat for leverage, finishing off a drumstick when Mitchell entered the room. The cat's mantis-shaped head held sideways, she emitted a vicious rumble from deep in her mean bush soul, pressing a cheek into the bird so she could go on chewing and growling while she kept a fierce yellow eye locked on Mitchell. As he came closer the cat ate faster, choking down bites.

"What is this?" Mitchell yelled. "That's *my* chicken!" He had roamed Queenstown during his lunch hour at the beginning of the week before he could find a roaster for sale. Mitchell picked up the flyswatter and slapped the cat's face with it but she retaliated, lashing out to strike her own blow, carving three beaded red lines, perfectly parallel, across the top of his wrist.

Mitchell thought all animals understood certain tones in the human voice, especially the one that threatened punishment and death—but not an island cat. He changed tactics and quickly turned on the faucet. The cat moaned, yet her resolve was no less for the drenching she underwent. The drain clogged and the basin began to fill. The chicken bobbed, careened in the rising flood, the cat astride it like a werewolf afloat, its fangs still gnawing away. Mitchell adjusted the spigot so that the stream splashed directly into her mouth, and though she held out as long as she could, he seized her by the scruff of the neck at the moment she abandoned ship. Into the air she went, loose skin and soggy fur bunched in his fist, as Mitchell gripped her in a manner temporarily paralyzing to feline criminals, hind legs and tail folded into her white belly, front paws extended as if she suffered a stroke while playing a piano, eyes stricken with desperation, decerebrated and utterly at Mitchell's mercy, which had run out.

"We'll see about those nine lives."

The prisoner was hauled out to the veranda. To the left the drop was about twenty feet. A cropping of gray boulders turtled the ground, any one of them a substantial target. He suspended the cat over the railing so she could appreciate the severity of her predicament before he launched her. The cat flexed, squirmed ineffectually, and desisted.

Then Johnnie was in the doorway between the kitchen and the veranda, wiping her eyes and calling his name with concern. Her hair was snarled and her face girlishly sleep-ridden. Her uncovered breasts pointed at Mitchell like twin judges, blindly accusatory. "What are you doing?" she asked, coming awake.

"I'm talking to this cat."

"What's wrong?"

"This is private."

The cat cashed in one of her remaining lives to express an appeal for clemency. The body of the animal became resonant, like the soundbox of a viola, an invisible bow of repentance drawn across its strings. The plaint was almost supernatural, a forlorn otherworld yowling. Mitchell was impressed.

"Awww," Johnnie commiserated. She crossed her arms, perhaps realizing how absurd it would seem to scold a man while she stood before him bare-breasted. "What did the poor cat do to deserve this treatment?"

It dawned on Mitchell that the only way the chicken could have traveled from the freezer in the refrigerator to the basin of the sink was if Johnnie had removed it to thaw for dinner, and she wouldn't have known to take precautions, to make the bird catproof. He brought the animal back over the rail and shouted into its face, *BAD CAT!* Her mouth twisted into a little pink gremlin's grin, her cat tongue panting fast as a hummingbird's heart, and Mitchell wished Johnnie wasn't around so he could wallop this hardened feline ruffian on the nose. He released her and she took off across the veranda and down into the bush like a skyrocket.

"Why do you abuse that creature?" Johnnie asked. "Is this a habit of yours?"

"Stop looking at me like I'm a barbarian and instead go look in the sink."

She whooped and put a hand to her mouth, then propped both hands on her hips. "Oh no! She didn't, did she?"

"You can make bone soup."

"That sneaky little bitch."

"That's the spirit," Mitchell said, vindicated.

There were no backup provisions for dinner. Mitchell rarely kept more than a throw-together stock in the house—an onion, a tin of Australian corned beef, a wedge of moldy unidentifiable cheese that came in large round red cans, eggs of varying sizes including a goose egg that he was frightened of, mangoes, guavas, and rotting bananas, a huge hairy dasheen and other popular island roots that he didn't know how to use, a cucumber, a carrot—somehow okay for one but glaringly inadequate for two. Johnnie apologized for the loss of the chicken and volunteered to go get another. "I'm afraid you can't," he told her. "Chickens top the endangered grocery list on this island," alongside beef, pork, fish, and mutton. They were sold to restaurants or exported; in consolation you could get all the necks, backs, wings, heads, and feet, locally known as scratches, that money could buy. To locate an entire bird or its nobler parts for sale you had to see a guy who knew a guy who had a friend, et cetera.

"I've never heard of a place with no chickens," Johnnie said. After all, chickens were so trivial and she wasn't prepared to accept anything that magnified the trivial into a national shortcoming. He assumed she had never been out of the States before so her naïveté, however incomprehensible, wasn't as vulgar as it might have been in another person who might tend to judge a place by what was missing, the cancellation of entitlements. "Something's wrong here."

While she talked she had slipped both index fingers into the waistband of her panties, ran them in sync off the opposite crowns of pelvis and met below her navel, pointing into her pubic hair. Back and forth, back and forth she did it, and Mitchell wanted to tell her to stop doing that, her hands like a gate opening and closing. Johnnie moved over beside Mitchell on the railing and since he wasn't looking at her face, and couldn't look at her hands, he found himself staring, abstractly, at her wonderful breasts, thinking God, tits can really rule a field of vision. Johnnie tapped her foot against his, detouring his attention down the length of her battered dancer's legs.

"So what do people eat around here?" she asked innocently.

"Well . . ." Mitchell glanced up—her hair was on fire, her head bonneted by the sunset. "There's some excellent recipes for shit in this part of the world." The parched way Mitchell said this made Johnnie laugh, and Johnnie's laugh was a cool wetness wrapped gently around his stubbornness.

"I hope you're doing something about that," she half teased.

"Right," he said. "That's the heart of my job— conceptualizing menus."

She nudged against him, enjoying this game of conversation, and Mitchell thought in the unworldliness she had exposed he recognized an element of flirtation more conscious than the fingers in the band of her panties: the lure of vulnerability, the invitation to provide protection against the unknown. Now they had succeeded in doing what lovers do—make the world less serious so romance could have the greater power; catch flashes of substance in nets too fine to hold their weight beyond a moment, but in that moment to know from the feel that something of meaning had been there in the mesh and broken through, returning to the immensity of the distance between them. She bent forward as if to see him better, her arms slowly outstretched, clearly wanting a hug, the kindness that he had not yet expressed, and Mitchell wished she'd put some clothes on.

"Another woman hooked by the glamor of economics," he said sardonically.

"Will you hold me for a second, Mitchell?"

He decided that, as she was, he couldn't be alone with her a minute more and so he stood away, telling Johnnie he was going for a quick twilight swim. When he came back they would go to Rosehill Plantation for dinner.

"Okay," she managed to whisper, visibly hurt by his escape.

At the cliff Mitchell hung a towel on a sea-grape branch and scaled barefoot down the rocks to the colorless water. With a momentary ebb in the tidal surge, he left shore like a crocodile, slipping forward on his stomach, crawling to deeper water where he didn't have to be as mindful of the black urchins that clotted the bottom like military defenseworks. As he breaststroked out from the jagged shoreline without splashing, the ripples rolled ahead of him, tremors through the silvery illusion of ice the crash of sun coated on the bay at this hour. Froglike he kept shooting himself onward until he had passed the red buoy that marked the boat channel. The bottom was thirty feet down here and he submerged, a firm sleek angling outward that twirled him down into the chilled density of blueness, spinning on his head inside a pleasure like no other, a dream pleasure because it required submersion within an altered state, a willful plunge where no earthly metaphor could possibly follow. Mitchell sank until his ears ached with the pressure, then reversed direction by tucking and uncoiling, which made him spring back toward the surface, breaking through the skin of mirror, and then floated on his back, only the darkening sky in sight, his eardrums rubbed by the static that issued from the depths, only the fresh night sky in sight as though he had been tossed out in space like a satellite and suspended in oceanic nothingness.

What a world, Mitchell thought, and whose idea was it anyway? Being in the water, safely lost throughout the time when everything has become bound to darkness, was like being saturated in a divine aphrodisiac. His feet slowly descended on their own once he forgot to keep them afloat, and his head thrust out of the water. The shore blackened solid; the sky and sea merged densities into one thick vapor with no visible definition. Occasionally zephyrs of sound were released from the land: the burr of a motor, the homeward lowing of cattle, a steel band that practiced somewhere in the village of Augustine, spurting brief celestial phrases of melody. The falsetto laugh of a woman suddenly delighted, her voice filling the entire bay for an instant. Rafts of sound out there in the darkness on the water with him.

A star signaled overhead and he saw it. Good evening, Mitchell said. Here's a wish if you're still in the business. Let's not let lust interfere with this bad arrangement, let's listen and wait and see what's what or else Johnnie and I are in trouble again, we'll never really meet a second time, the first in this tattered new world we've been brought to.

He snorted water out of his face and gave a vigorous kick toward shore, racing down the path of a thin wire of light cast from his own kitchen above the cliff, an idle meditation about wishing and stars occupying his swim back in. Were stars still taking orders for wishes or were they boycotting the twentieth century? Did other folks still wish upon stars—mailmen, lawyers, carpenters, politicians, mechanics, academics, IBM executives—or was the tradition reserved for children? What was the going rate, his professional self asked, and was it adjusted to a sliding scale? Was it still considered de rigueur that wishes were meant to be secrets, and did stars ever make book on the odds of a wish coming true, or reveal to other stars what they were up to? Were wishes treated with moral impartiality; that is, did a wish to harm someone have the same chance to come true as a wish to preserve? Was the wish of a bad person given the same attention as the wish of a good person? Were birthday cakes, wishbones, wells and fountains, or churches better than or equal to stars? Animal sacrifices? Did stars take retractions after you wished your enemy would get hit by a truck? Did a person's wishes exist forever, notched on his soul and on display in the afterlife, all those secrets that would never be erased, the wishes of greed, of frivolity, of malice, of prurience side by side with more honorable requests, the only honest record of who you had been in your own eyes?

But then that would mean the end of wishing, Mitchell thought, wouldn't it.

Johanna Woods, veteran of another timeworn paradise, took the walk along Howard Bay for granted. For all her nonchalance the beach they descended to from the house could have been the street she grew up on in the suburbs of northern Virginia instead of a mother-lode source of all those generic logos—the powdery golden shore, the overweight apricot moon, the silhouettes of palm trees—that advertisers used like flybait to entice the northern swarms. She scuffed across the sand next to Mitchell, sandals dangling from her hand. Her loose cotton skirt and peasant blouse, both white and unpressed, softened with friendly wrinkles, were a warm luminescence, like an antishadow, hovering on his left. Every so often she whistled sad, contented notes.

"You know, I haven't slept so long in years," she said. "I feel brand new."

She wanted to know how his job was going but Mitchell was in no mood to attempt a translation of that madness. He felt sulky, a rash of rude ambivalence inside him, and without thinking about what he was saying, he told her that he had been down here by the water on Christmas Eve when the villagers from Augustine brought their cows and pigs to be slaughtered on the beach. Blood puddles, fat flies, and stacks of bowels were everywhere, and the next morning the bay was full of swaying gore. A week later, out on the reef skin diving, he saw what he thought was a large eagle ray patrolling the bottom and dove down to it. It was the flayed hide to a bull, winging on the tide out to sea.

Johnnie interrupted the rhythm of her step. "What an awful thing to tell me on such a pretty night," she said.

Readily exchanged worlds, confused times, spontaneous cynicism and intransigence—those were the benefits of easy travel for you. Her indifference to the surroundings had deprived Mitchell of the opportunity to give, to introduce and present, to dole out the exquisite beauties, to remark upon the specialness of things. And on the other side of that impulse was the relief he felt in not being able to exploit the natural glories as he might with another woman, claiming a right to a reward for details that he could not account for. The bay, the flora, the people, the fragrances were not props, but often it was hard not to think of them in exactly that way.

"I wish you'd just relax, Mitch," she urged, taking his hand and giving it a squeeze. "You're being so moody and nervous, I don't know what to expect. What's wrong with you?"

Stones in his mouth.

She slowed up and spoke crossly. "Look, give it a couple of days, okay? If it still doesn't feel right for you then I'll leave. Deal?"

He made her start walking again.

"Mitchell," Johnnie called out, hurrying to keep up with him. "You're on the march. Slow down."

She stumbled as she returned to his side and he grabbed her to keep her from falling, and she turned in his arms, looking up at him, still about to drop if he let her go, and he couldn't help but pause before he forced her to support herself on her own legs. Her voice turned husky.

"I thought you were getting ready to kiss me."

"No, I wasn't," Mitchell lied. How quickly he was able to lie, how baldly, quick and bald, and it lifted his spirit.

No longer were guests comforted by the approach to Rosehill Plantation, as they might have been, as they surely would have considering where else they might end up on the island, when civilization first landscaped its wild gardens. The ride up the hill from the beach disoriented their sensibilities, and they wondered what in the devil they had gotten themselves into, because the closer they came to the manor house, the more it appeared they had crossed the border of their brochure-fed images into a Botswana of the imagination, which would, soon enough, test their overall fitness with an array of Darwinian challenges. Disciplined royal palms flanked the drive, the lines they produced as solemn as sentries. Their original intention was still oppressively clear, to welcome Rosehill's visitors to a bastion of privilege and moral standard among savages, that a little higher up they might enjoy the rewards of society and culture if only they had the fortitude to mount the hill. But in modern times this sobering effect had been substantially reduced by the untended proliferation of hedges long since ballooned and bubbled out of any geometry they had been set to. Now all the old campaign soldiers hidden within the gray trunks and panache of fronds of the royal palms wore hoop skirts of oleander and hibiscus, ixora, bougainvillea and poinsettia. Impenetrable and unbroken, the species clumped together in bright primary splashes and prospered, like the islanders themselves, as one incestuous mass, two flowering and fragrant seams that opened ahead and closed behind as you moved along the drive.

It was pitch dark there at the cobbled entrance, the sort of darkness with a hallucinatory texture to it, a fizzing flickering nonlight, antilight. Mitchell could hear bats swoop down into the tunnel of vegetation, licking the insects out of the currents of the night.

They walked for several minutes under tall reeds with crisscrossed stalks and tops like mutilated umbrellas. The slope flattened out but did not yet suggest a destination. The vegetation heaped up again, swatches and feathers, thunderheads and inky lace, opaque on the screen of night sky. The drive followed a bend, widened, opened, and presented, not in fragments but at once, fantastically, the hotel, defined in a grottolike aura by hundreds of tiny Christmas tree lights strung along its balustrades, rigged in the frangipani, draped over bushes, sprinkled in an almond tree, dripping down through layers of a Norfolk pine, an immense twinkling spiderweb, the radiance contained, ensnared, an interior glow to every dab of light, like jewels.

Johnnie stopped abruptly. Her face was blue bleeding to red as the strand of bulbs nearest them blinked. The hotel, built by two eighteenth-century decadents run out of New Orleans, looked like a beached riverboat. "Well, it's certainly gay, isn't it," Johnnie said, pinching Mitchell's side, charmed.

Mostly the second sons of British aristocracy had made their residence on the estate, dismissed to the New World to stop their petulance and reform their London habits. Some were gentlemen farmers, or tried to be; others were distraught by the fate of being superfluous progeny and succumbed, at the first opportunity, to the lowest pleasures from which they emerged in coffins, murdered men, or gilded carriages, indomitable bastards with one unquenchable desire—to defecate on this new world and everyone in it.

The old brick walls had endured a cannon volley from a French warship, two gutting fires and countless hurricanes, a volcanic eruption and subsequent earthquake in 1902, vandals and the descendents of vandals, intermittent years of neglect, and unimaginative conversion into a hotel by a corporation of alcoholic realtors from Florida. Once upon a time the house reigned over two thousand acres of sea island cotton, sugarcane, and nutmeg groves, a salt yard down along the bay, pastures of oxen and prize-winning bulls, a stable full of champion horses raced on the beach for handsome purses. Peacocks, guinea hens, even an ostrich (said to have kicked a slave to death for teasing it) had strolled the grounds. String quartets were hired from as far away as Trinidad and Jamaica to perform for ladies' birthdays and Boxing Day festivities. The old masters had triumphed over so much that was against them, man and nation and nature if not God Himself, that the first and last belief they took as divine ordinance was their own superiority. They warehoused great fortunes and when the time came failed quietly and went who knows where, or descended into the rich soil themselves to poison it with their humors. The cycle would spin, the estate would fall into new hands for another generation. The taking-from would proceed. The giving-back—Well, they asked themselves, what in the world was there to give back *to?* Niggers? Jungle? The fireball sun, the treacherous sea?

During the Sugar War in the Fifties, a year when the past was chased the length and breadth of St. Catherine, caught, hammered into a strongbox and pitched into La Soufrière, Rosehill's last secular owner looked into the future and decided he was sickened by its prospect, that it provided too many disappointments and betrayals for nostalgia to survive in peace. The realtors from Boca Raton prescribed to the unusual opinion for the time that in the coming years people would travel in droves to places like St. Catherine, paying through the nose to search for fun and relaxation. The owner thought the realtors were crackpots but sold out to them anyway, even shaving a quarter of his asking price off the deal. They hired a Canadian architect, a genius of insensitivity and budget, and he Balkanized the inside of the manor house with partitions, fractioning rooms that were once airy and naturally lit—qualities that Tillman Hyde was slowly redeeming. Only the ballroom outlasted the architect's reductive frenzy and served now as a restaurant. Tillman, who inherited the establishment after his father died, thought of his job as a private war, an attitude consistent with the stewardship of the plantation throughout the centuries. The difference was that Tillman loved Rosehill, whereas from all accounts his predecessors had not.

The driveway circled a lily pond which Johnnie and Mitchell, deadlocked in the negotiation of their togetherness, padded around in silence toward the haven of Rosehill's restaurant. Rental cars and mini-mokes were parked haphazardly on skinny strips of lawn—those remaining patches of Bermuda grass yet to be consumed by the gardener Abel's—aka Grampa Hell—rejunglefication program. Adrian met them as they entered the restaurant. Their arrival seemed to exasperate her; she guided them to a table in a huff. "Can you believe this?" she said. "I come for a vacation and the guy puts me to work like a Chinaman."

She skated off abruptly, called to service by customers who had caught the virus of her mood and were equally annoyed. A distinguished-looking sunburned gentleman, speaking in a voice with no ability to withhold condescension, asked if it were at all possible to see a menu, since where he was sitting was reported to be a restaurant serving the general public of which he was unwillingly a member, he was here to pay for that service, he and his dear wife were exceedingly hungry, and what did it take to be fed in this goddamn boonie place anyway.

Adrian visibly simmered. "Where do you get off talking to me in that tone, you horse's ass?" she snapped back. She did a first-rate job of sneering at him, returning his airs in force. "The menus no longer apply," she said icily. "We have a beef dish and some kind of fish. Think about it. I'll be back."

She spun away, refusing to notice other diners who sought her attention, and flew intemperately through the swinging door that led to the kitchen. A minute later she battered back through it; at her waist she lugged a round aluminum serving tray crammed with orders, too big and too heavy for an untrained person of Adrian's build to carry successfully. She staggered toward an empty table, landed the tray just as it seemed about to tip and drop, and, after a deep breath, curled her shoulders, hefted the load, staggered forward to another table, crashed it down, picked it up again and in this fashion made her way across the floor to a family of six who became more and more distressed as they realized Adrian was headed for them.

Adrian, the tyrannical waitress in a foreign country, had them all spellbound. Johnnie asked Mitchell what he thought was happening. "Rosehill has been going through an ordeal with its help," he told her as she lit her second cigarette since they had taken their seats. Carelessly she blew smoke in his face and he waved his hand. "Don't blow your smoke my way as if you were some kind of moll."

She apologized. Her eyes crinkled, filled with rueful luster, and she reached across the table to touch his cheek, once, lightly, with the tips of her middle fingers. "So much has happened," she said wistfully. "Forgive me." The golden hair above her jaws was a swirl of lighted fibers.

"Suppose I told you you're too late?"

"Okay, say it."

"Don't think I can't."

"Fine. So tell me."

"I don't think I can."

"Fine. So jolly up."

Put a woman in a manor house and she'd find these Anglo-Saxon phrases to paddle you with, Mitchell thought. He related to her the tragedy of Tillman's mother, who had died on the premises two months ago while on an unexpected and rare visit to her son. For a while, the local police had suspected Tillman of poisoning her. There was no truth to that—every misfortune on St. Catherine was initially explored by authorities sniffing its possibilities for game or profit. Tillman had stored the corpse in the kitchen's walk-in freezer until it could be buried, which gave the cook and her staff the willies, causing them to quit on the spot, and at the same time the bartender down at the beach bar had an unrelated fit of insubordination and came after Tillman. There was an exchange of animosity involving gunfire. Many of the registered guests had not tolerated the resulting decline in service, a decline that proved less temporary than Tillman had foreseen, and he was still campaigning to restore the image of Rosehill as a peaceful and predictable destination.

Johnnie stubbed out her cigarette. "Adrian's terrorizing people with that tray, isn't she?" she said, seeing Adrian shoulder open the kitchen door again. Apparently the new staff Tillman had hired hadn't lasted very long.

Adrian wobbled desperately between tables and stopped. "Can somebody grab this from me?" she demanded. She seemed determined not to budge. No one moved. "Come on," she pleaded shrilly, "it's breaking my back. Can't you see I'm being taken advantage of."

"I better give her a hand," Johnnie said, sliding out of her chair, "before she drives everyone off."

"Terrific," Mitchell called after her. "I want the beef dinner."

Mitchell touched the silverware in front of him, rubbed his thumb in the hollow feminine side of the teaspoon. He regarded his sun-browned hand, the traditional table setting, the rightness of the contact—convex to concave, these shapes that lure fish to a hook, attract signals from outer space—of his finger to the shallow cavity of the spoon. In no time at all Johnnie had achieved a truce among the diners, who really had no easy alternative to their plight for food at this time of night on St. Catherine, nor to their predicament with Adrian, who also seemed without recourse. Johnnie's voice worked the hall, mellifluous, seductive, flattering, repairing the climate. There was always a power of inevitability generated by a self-confidence that made things fit together well. Some of the older customers responded to her as if she reminded them of a favorite daughter, or rather the fair ideal of a daughter they had once hoped to sponsor through the world. And yet if she were that cherished offspring, if they had to claim her as their own flesh and blood, soon enough they would not know how to speak to her, the words would grow thorns of disillusionment and become lodged at the bottom of their throats. Her own father, on the other hand, never conceded the surprises and upheavals his daughter had in store for him, not even when he found out she was jabbing a needle in her arm. Instead, he pumped away on her in a deductive rape, not abusing her body but her mind in the most perversely clinical manner, his intellect as cold as any speculum inserted into her subconsciousness.

Johnnie had showed Mitchell how to use a knife and its accompaniment of forks when they were properly set—an etiquette she rejected with a vengeance before she had the opportunity to take it, independently, anywhere special. That was . . . some time ago, when she was a girl, a clean fresh laundered correct and bright package of girlhood with a craving and exuberance in her, a hot pulse and a heart ready to catch fire. Mitchell once imagined he was the match set against her fuse but it was a bigger flame by far that set her off. She self-combusted with the nation, an immaculate conflagration, an electric guitar searing the "Star-Spangled Banner" like a laser knife. Our brilliant generation, Mitchell thought—we made music and we made war in the jungle, and sometimes it wasn't easy to tell the difference. Kids are better killers than they are lovers. One takes practice, the other doesn't. One looks at the world and believes it is as simple to change as a television channel.

What finally identified the limits of their precocity was that they had no plan for surviving themselves, they were kamikaze pilots cheated out of their best moment, left without a war, without patriotism, without homes, marked indelibly as footloose children, Hansel and Gretel hiking farther and farther into an infatuating darkness of diminishing knowledge, failed faith. Girl entering the world, girl leaving the world, girl trying to circle back. Mitchell did not flatter himself as being that world, only its channel marker, if that; its sideline of involvement. He dropped the magic spoon onto the table, demoralized. It was bad to dwell on the outdated fashions, the skewed mental habits, of those years with Johnnie, tempting himself with a pose of exile and betrayal. He told himself he was less fraudulent than that, more serious, nothing being more insipid than to cry over growing up, though the impulse was real enough. He didn't want to give into it, and for what he knew was a selfish—and therefore, inexplicable—reason, he didn't want Johnnie doing such a good job warming up the tourists, all humanity's hostess.

"You didn't take my advice." She had whisked over to rouse him. "You were supposed to jolly up."

"I'm going to leave. I'm tired. It just hit me."

She snatched her purse from the table and pulled him to his feet. "Oh no you don't," she said. "You're needed here."

"Look, I'm not up to it."

She led him through the tables, whispering in a droll voice. "I go away for five measly years, and you won't stop sulking."

Mitchell dragged his steps, his feet telling him to become an immovable object. In front of them sat an obese woman, her pink bloated arms hanging out of a garish orange and yellow muumuu, observing their progress with beaming optimism. "I know I haven't lost my sense of humor," Mitchell growled in Johnnie's ear, "because I'm not strangling you in front of these people."

At the far end of the ballroom was a bar, unmanned. As they went behind its counter Johnnie squatted down, out of sight to the customers. "Mitch, get down here," she commanded. He hesitated— they'd squabble on their heels like two merchants in a bazaar—but he looked at the restaurant looking at him and sank, kneeling beside her. She unclasped her handbag and fished through it.

"Second wind?" she asked.

Drugs so overtly used in peacemaking were a bubble, a sphere of transparent fellowship that formed around you and lifted you off the ground until pricked by the needle of passing time, dropping you from that high place back to the unforgiving crust of where you began, everything the same—or worse—as you left it. Mitchell wasn't even very fond of cocaine; it made him feel metropolized, under the influence of a crucial desire for fulfillment, a seeker seeking to accomplish something wonderful but of absolutely no importance or merit. Still, he reasoned, the day had been extraordinarily long, especially tagged on to yesterday, the day before, the day before that, the month, the year. Rest or recreation, he had to choose. Johnnie dipped a fingernail into a tiny plastic packet, her eyes sewn shut but tearing open when she had finished. White dots of powder stuck to her lip and Mitchell brushed them off.

"I think," she said, "that we have to pretend." Her forehead nuzzled against the top of his arm.

"Pretend what?"

"That we're meeting each other for the first time, and it's a little awkward, and here we are, after a rocky start, both of us beginning just a little bit to enjoy each other's company, and fantasizing about how nice the rest of the night might be." She raised her head, eyes blazing, to see what Mitchell thought of the idea. "Don't you think it will work?"

"I don't know. I was thinking the same way when I first saw you at the airport."

"Well, come on then," she urged. "Besides, Tillman's going to stand the house to a round of drinks. Somebody's got to mix them." Johnnie scooped with her fingernail, sprinkled sorcerer's dust. Mitchell grimaced at the pain, a freak arctic wind cutting through his busted nose and then the spectacular hush, energy flowing exactly like an electrician had been at work inside him, rewiring the old house, floodlights snapping on inside his skull and a new attitude, one with a top hat and tap shoes and kazoo, retiring the act of infinite propriety. His eyes watered, a diamond-hard numbness drained into his front teeth. Good-bye, social hypochondria. The spirit of performance had made itself known.

"Here's the list," Johnnie said, ripping a sheet from the pad she took from her blouse pocket. Twenty-three rum punches, fourteen piña coladas, thirteen scotch and sodas, four scotch on the rocks, a vodka martini straight up, three lime daiquiris, one Blue Hawaiian, three lime squashes, eight seltzers. Beer.

"What in the fuck is a Blue Hawaiian?"

"Here's your chance to make a real difference on this island, boy," Johnnie said, rolling back off her heels in a laughing spasm. Mitchell thought he should help her sit up so he took hold of her, a lifeguard's hug, her rib cage heaving under his palms. She quieted at his touch and studied his face.

"We're having fun," she finally said.

"Sure, sure. Old times."

"I mean it." Her eyes flashed provocatively but she shifted to her knees. "Ready to stand?" she asked, but there was no opportunity to stay put because they were already surfacing, Johnnie tugging him so that Mitchell had to go too, gnashing his teeth. "Ladies and gentlemen," she addressed the dining hall, all eyes turned on them in anticipation. "This lousy son of a bitch martyr won't kiss me when he's given the chance but at least he's agreed to be our bartender." Several diners clapped. She scooted out from behind the counter back to the kitchen, leaving Mitchell too stunned to react.

As long as Johnnie was in the vicinity, he mused, his life was headed for a state of throwback, retrograde impurity, capricious fluctuation of the emotional gyroscope. What was there to do, though, but to uncap a beer and go to work. When Johnnie and Adrian reemerged through the swinging door they had created a blithe alliance, Adrian pixiating, undoubtedly reformed and stirred to duty by the fast medicine in Johnnie's clutch, bewildering the community of diners with her newfound willingness to serve. In sympathy for their original expectations upon coming to Rosehill, and the damage those expectations had undergone, Mitchell blended a silky punch with twice the overproof rum the recipe varnished into the countertop intended. A good rum punch was the wiliest of cocktails. It was the drink to which teetotalers relented because of its healthy tropical image, all the ingredients of a vitamin-ladened breakfast juice therein, the uncommon flavors of passionfruit and nutmeg, bitters and lime that imbued enough natural ping to disguise the devilish proportion of alcohol in the glass. A superb rum punch had all the characteristics of merciful execution. It assumed no virtue in going slow so that the victim might pause to lament what was being lost, and it valued stealth, the surreptitious wham: the victims of a superb rum punch never knew what hit them. They were swept from one shore of reality to another more liberated coast, a new world where they had temporary license to do absolutely anything that entered their heads, play any scene or voice any pronouncements that suddenly they fancied. This, Mitchell thought, having another slug from the plastic bucket he had utilized, was a very good if not excellent cane punch and should be approached prudently, especially on an empty stomach. He poured twenty-three orders and the bucket was still almost half full, allowing for twenty-one extras, which he also measured out. When the women arrived to collect the drinks, they found him slopping piña into colada, making a frothy mess.

"What are all these?" Johnnie asked.

"Deliver one to everybody in the room except the very young."

"Not everybody wanted a punch."

"Doesn't matter," he retorted. "Not everybody wanted a kiss either."

"Mitchell," Adrian said, "thanks for volunteering to do this."

Mitchell looked down at this tiny kite of a person and told her he didn't volunteer, he was appointed, which was the worst thing that could happen to anybody. "There was so much grumbling out there I decided to go for a first strike," he said, shoving glasses forward two by two. "Get them before they get us. You left no alternative."

Apparently this was a woman who insulted easily. She stiffened, closed her eyes and fluttered her lids, a neurotic habit Mitchell had noticed at the airport. She delivered two glasses of punch to the nearest table but didn't return for more. He emptied a bottle of white rum into a sticky pineapple brew.

Johnnie cruised away with another tray of cocktails. When she looped back, she said, "Adrian's upset, so I don't think you should blame her for the impression she's making."

"Why not?" Mitchell protested, remembering Adrian's critical assessment of him at Brandon Vale, her superior tone in the terminal.

"She's feeling she's been imported to Rosehill as a handmaid. Tillman worked her hard all day, made her change sheets, scour shower stalls. She's mad." Johnnie raised one eyebrow and reversed, sending out faint vibrations of the effect of her own bumpy arrival, his reluctant welcome. "Off again," she chirped, her tray replenished with its cargo of goodwill. Bending down to look for club soda, Mitchell discovered the restaurant's stereo and album collection hidden behind a sliding panel. Reggae was what was called for, some subversive atmosphere in the place. He lowered a record on the turntable and set the volume midway. Conversations in the dining room hall rose gaily, laughter rippled here and there. A man in a yachtsman's blazer stood up to salute Johnnie with his bottle of beer. Johnnie glowed with exercise and camaraderie when she harvested the last of the drinks.

"What are you doing when you get off work?" Mitchell asked, straight-faced.

"Sorry," she said, "my boyfriend's picking me up." She took a step backward but canceled it, resting an elbow on the bar, and spoke confidentially. "He's one of those guys who rushes home to ball five pounds off me. The next day I have to go out and buy all new clothes." She winked and paraded back into the tables, swinging her hips.

"Glad to hear you're being taken care of," Mitchell muttered, never accustomed to women speaking brazenly. At five pounds a session she had better go easy or there'd be nothing left to penetrate. A light rum and tonic in hand, he abandoned his post for the kitchen to forage for food. Hunger made him stare at the diners as he trudged past, envying the plunge and stab of their forks. Little bunnies, Mitchell thought drunkenly, in God's own clover. Watch out for that old bone-crusher, the serpent in the cane. He could be hiding anywhere, flexing his maw, anticipating just such a treat as you.

Chapter 10

Tillman hovered over four blue flowers of flame, deciphering the order chits attached by fishhooks, like laundry, along a string, his spatula and wooden spoon poised above frying pans and caldrons smoking on the stove. He reminded Mitchell of a symphony percussionist reading his score, informed by the sheet of notes and symbols to stay alert for further banging. Bites of hot grease speckled his forearms, flour whitened the front of his jeans, and his tee shirt displayed blotted samples of the evening's fare. He flipped and stirred, measuring lumps of rice onto plates which he then smothered with a brownish stroganoff. Nothing about the manner in which he performed suggested the adverse condition of a man under the stress of an impossible enterprise. Instead, when he eventually noticed Mitchell was standing behind him, Tillman grinned more brilliantly than the old copper tiles banded along the wall. He raised his utensils like scepters, blessing all who entered his kingdom.

"Aha!" Tillman said. "Just the guy I wanted to see."

"I was hoping I was the man you wanted to feed," Mitchell replied. A steamy surf of spice-bearing molecules pumped out from the pots on the stove. Mitchell's mouth watered obscenely. Starvation was turning him into a visionary. He kept seeing a steak with his name written on it in béarnaise.

"Chickens," Tillman disclosed. "And pigs. Cows and ducks. Herb gardens. Vineyards. Tomatoes, potatoes. Crisp leafy lettuce. Shallots and mushrooms. Get this nation on the move, Mitchell."

"Don't talk to me about chickens," he answered morosely.

"People are clamoring for them, buddy. Where can I buy more chickens?"

Mitchell found a dirty fork and speared a piece of Spanish mackerel from one of the frying pans, cramming it into his mouth before it had a chance to cool, rewarded with a burned tongue.

"Hey—don't pick." Tillman scraped the last gummy grains of rice out of a cast-iron kettle, dribbled sauce onto a plate and floated a skinny fillet. "There's not enough to go around as it is." He asked if Adrian had posted the Closed sign on the entrance door. Mitchell didn't know.

"Come on," Mitchell needled, "don't you have a bit of meat I can chew? What about a bouillon cube to suck on?"

"Nope." Tillman was at an impasse; the food had run out and there were two more orders left to fill. He redistributed clumps of parsley, a garnish that for some reason never failed to be available in the markets. The plates still looked barren as a prisoner's dinner so he hacked a solitary pineapple into thick doughnuts and added these beside the niggardly entrées. It didn't matter, Mitchell told him, since his customers were reaching a stage where forks wouldn't stay in their hands.

"What's happening out there? How are the girls doing?" Tillman twisted the stopcock on the bottle of gas that fueled the stove; Mitchell watched the fire sputter and retreat as if he had been deprived of his basic human rights. Adrian had forgone charm, he said, and seemed to think that everyone had gathered in the restaurant for encounter therapy; to ease the mounting aggressions, he had mixed a rum punch so strong it would make monkeys bark.

"Well . . . she's teed off at me." Tillman compressed his lips and, with a butter knife, dug at a smudge of paste stuck to his tee shirt. At that moment Adrian's backside bumped open the door, filling the kitchen with a surge of cackling and bass-heavy music. Muscling a plastic tub of dirty dishes, she wheeled around and glared at the two men as though they were a pair of worthless sloths. The tub crashed down on the sinkboard; straining theatrically, she hoisted the tray Tillman had newly set and was gone without a word, pounding open the door with a thrust of her boyish hips.

"You don't say," Mitchell said.

"Yep, but I don't see what I can do about it," Tillman admitted, going to wash his hands with a lump of soap resembling processed yam.

Mitchell probed the leftover debris on the plates Adrian had bussed. Flecks of gravied rice, morsels of fish attached to gray rubberish skin, french fries with bites taken out, gum wrappers, cigarette butts and cigar ash, dirtied napkins, toothpicks with bloodied points.

He ate whatever appeared digestible. "You're a cruel bastard, I hear," he said with his mouth filled with waste.

"Oh? You've heard reports?"

It was a masticated fray of gristle that finally woke up Mitchell's self-disgust. "Yes," he answered Tillman, straightening up. "You are accused of exploiting affluent white women, luring them to this tropic sweatshop with lies about sunbathing, sailing, and other deceptions."

"I'm afraid what you say is true." He ran hot water into a square aluminum sink. Mitchell handed him grease-smeared tableware. "As long as you don't let them unpack their luggage and settle in, you can get a lot of work out of them. Once they set foot on the beach though, Wilson, that's it, they're not good for anything."

Mitchell had his eye on a dusty can of black olives, high up on a shelf. "I approve of your policy," he said. "In fact, why don't you just take Johnnie and keep her, put her to work."

"Now there's a helpful woman," Tillman noted, his arms submerged under a film of ugly suds.

"Can I have those olives up there?"

"Help yourself. Whatever you can find in the refrigerator too." Tillman explained that they could have handled the evening's crowd but his local girl bailed out right as the restaurant opened. She and Adrian had a disagreement over how the tables should be set and who would waitress which stations. Adrian scolded her; she took a hike.

Mitchell opened the can of olives and inspected them. They looked like small pickled testicles, and tasted rotten. He threw them in with the trash and went over to the ancient Kelvinator, its surface hammered with rusty dents, splashed with grime. He clucked at Adrian's New York temper. She had taken a lesson in what an islander's feet were for—to retreat from shit and into misery.

"Didn't you tell me you had hired an entire new staff?"

"Two sets of them in the past month. They won't stay." The former cook threw in the apron when Tillman's mother died, deciding to go home to her village on the leeward side where she was born. Now she was raising grandchildren while her daughters froze in Boston and Montreal. He had hired several cooks since then, same with the maids. After a day or two they complained of headaches, cramps, shivers. They believed there was a spell cast on Rosehill and claimed to see the duppy of Tillman's mother swimming around the corridors of the manor house, enticing them with a fruit slice on a spoon. With the next group of people he hired, Tillman said he would bring in an exorcist, or fake an exorcism, something to soothe the native imaginations of the labor pool.

In the refrigerator, there was some unlikely aborted thing squashed into a stainless-steel bowl. Mitchell suggested the exorcist start here. "What is this creature," he asked, poking its plastic-white surface. "And is it edible?"

It happened to be an octopus a fisherman had brought Tillman two or three days ago. He had removed its skin and parboiled it and there it sat, chilled and bald and dead, a snack of weird marine life. Mitchell ruminated on the hideous milky flesh, thinking, I am going to eat that octopus. He lifted the animal by a flaccid, slippery tentacle and bit off about four inches, the tasteless meat expanding in his mouth as he chewed, the sucker nodules like hard silicone jujubes, and his jaw soon hurt from grinding on it. He tried to swallow but gagged. Johnnie came out of breath into the kitchen while he stood there choking, holding the octopus like Medusa's head.

"Fucking Christ!" She did a double take. "What in the world are you trying to eat?" She set her tub of dishes down and fanned herself with a saucer, her face flushed. Mitchell slipped the octopus into the slops bucket where it would be delivered as breakfast to an island pig, and tried to recover his dignity.

"You look as if you've been dancing," he said.

"I have. Your rum punch has made people stinko. I've been goosed and hugged I don't know how many times."

"Where's Adrian?" Tillman wondered, drying his hands on the curtain above the sink.

Johnnie rolled her eyes and said Adrian had been captured by an obnoxious German and made to sit in his lap.

"That may be merely justice at work."

"All right," said Tillman as he switched to a clean shirt. "Let's all escape." They had prevailed with great courage in the trenches of tourism, but enough was enough.

On the other side of the door, the restaurant was experiencing a communal release of inhibition. A foursome of silver-haired diners were on their feet interpreting the loud reggae music through geriatric experiments in body language, their dancing a quasi-erotic hybrid of the polka and the twist. A young man and a young woman who had dined separately had discovered they were both from the Midwest and were introducing themselves with vigorous kisses and bottom squeezing. A man Mitchell had last seen sullen, dressed in a polyester suit like a television deacon, sang the chorus of the island's most current hit, "You Sexy Thing," to his pudding-faced wife, who reacted with a fierce broadcast of contempt. A trio of marmish women, red as radishes from the sun, hooked their arms around each other and sought to make a respectable exit but entangled their six feet and crumbled, in slow motion, down. Another pair of women with bleached hair and big red mouths slandered one another, their Long Island accents like dentist drills whining through the general turbulence while their husbands slumped in their chairs, puffing cigars. Other ladies cooled themselves off with napkin fans, tugged their skirts up past midthigh, loosened the top buttons of their blouses. Half the diners seemed to be sharing wanton jokes and coarse anecdotes with the other half who, trying to be receptive, fought to keep their eyes from crossing.

They rescued Adrian from her Aryan kidnapper just as he began to fold with sentimentality. Tillman locked the kitchen and the bar cabinets and put another record on the stereo, a Sinatra album to sedate his guests, nudge them toward the maudlin stage of intoxication that the German had pioneered. In a short speech Tillman bid the customers good evening, told them they were on their own, encouraged them to feel at home—which meant they should not destroy anything on the premises.

"Douse the lights," a celebrant yelled as the Sinatra came over the sound system, and his call was approved by consensus.

Out in the breezeway Tillman confronted Adrian. "Did you make that man cry?"

"No! That ass told me he cried all the time because he had missed the war."

Inside the foyer the night desk clerk, a slim young black woman with a dandelion puff of hair, was asleep on her stool, slumped onto her arms, a pencil planted in one fist, a neat stack of schoolbooks off to the side. Adrian snorted. "Why couldn't she help out in the restaurant when that other bitch quit?"

"That person's doing exactly what I pay her to do," Tillman said, unaffected by Adrian's tone.

"She seems absolutely useless to me," Adrian replied as they walked past the unconscious girl and out the front door. "I don't see how you can run a business this way."

Tillman said he thought getting accepted premed at Harvard hardly struck him as useless, that the girl had no peace at home, and no money, and so on the contrary her presence was useful because it made him feel useful, able to provide her with a small amount of both. Tillman put his arm around Adrian's shoulder.

"I didn't mind that much, really," Adrian cooed. *Oh, brother,* Mitchell thought; Johnnie suppressed a snort. "But my feet are killing me."

"Shhh." Tillman made everyone stop. "Listen . . . hear it?"

Quietly they huddled together on the cobbles of the drive. Artificial embers of colored light were suspended in a fragrant moist hush of darkness pinholed high above by brighter than ever stars. The ubiquitous flora gushed in waves around them, soft, curling, ticklish. They listened with progressive expectations—What do you want the world to be? the night asked, and could this be it? There was a big noise. Invisible insects and frogs transmitted a fuzzy radio hum of startling magnitude. A breeze fluffed the topmost branches of a mass of mango trees so that the leaves reflected scratches of light and looked like a school of bait fish changing direction, turning toward the attraction of a rising half moon.

"Hear it?" Tillman repeated.

Smooth pebbles plunked into different volumes of water— music. Round notes effervesced up the hill from the beach, were lost in eddies and dead pockets and then recovered, fading but heard again as if they rode a tidal flux in the atmosphere. Pan music, the latent harmony in metal, resurrected from debris on the wharves and refineries of Trinidad by illiterate laborers. Those men had taught themselves how to seize what was empty and refill it with desire. For any magic, emptiness was the first criterion—a space, an object, a human soul or a steel petrol drum drained of its former content and then reconstituted to carry the flow of something vital, like these sounds in the night.

The spell of listening was broken by Grampa Hell the gardener materializing out of the darkness, greeting them with a grunt and a flash from the blade of his machete before he disappeared again into a tunnel of his own making. Tillman led them onward to his estate runabout, a battered but rebuilt Mahari Citroën, roofless and windowless with lawn chairs for seats and a body of shellacked plywood. Underdog, Rosehill's mutt, was asleep in it and they chased him out, climbed in themselves.

"Are we ready?" Tillman asked, picking through his ring of keys. Mitchell wasn't but failed to say so. He wanted to remain as they were for eternity, in the dark and ready to go, Rosehill all lit up with pointless celebration and the liquid music from below heard and not heard, spindrift melody so delicate you could believe if you wanted that it came from inside yourself.

"Fire her up," Johnnie said. Adrian bounced in her seat.

"Ready, steady, go."

Inserting the key, Tillman demolished every illusion of peace born by the night air, for the Mahari without a muffler had the vocal chords of heavy machinery. Mitchell, who had lost faith in modern forms of transportation on Ooah Mountain, was nervous in his flimsy seat, expecting the worst, a part of him even welcoming it. "Into the sea," he shouted over the noise. Tillman wiggled the shifter into first gear and they chugged forward down the ravine of the drive, the volume of the puny two-cylinder motor reaching a warlike howl, each cobblestone registered rudely through worn-out shocks, steering around crapauds illuminated like petty thieves in the sweep of headlights. Next to Mitchell Johnnie did something mildly exaggerated and rambunctious—she stood up for the thrill of the wind, though they couldn't have been more exposed to it as they were—and even though at first Mitchell tried to restrain her he stopped himself and simply held on to her knees and watched her above him, anonymous in the rush through the dark, and continued on a train of reasoning he had boarded since seeing her at the airport, hearing her inadequate justification for her return. He was forced to recognize that, for the sake of love itself, every statement of love must be judged harshly, that the planet was inflated with unwarranted statements of love, swollen with the prayers and invocations of love in books, on television, in advertisements as well as on gravestones, a frightful escalation in the volume of love's voice that was slowly scarring his inner ear, rendering unfit his ability to hear what others truly felt, and if it kept on, one day he would likely find himself tone deaf to humanity, which is a way of saying he would mistake every human sound as the plea of men and women he could not possibly help.

Rosehill's beach bar had a personality that made it ideologically separate from the hotel on the hill. If the Plantation was, in a manner of speaking, a tomb or theme park or museum for the march of European sensibilities through the West Indies, then the beach bar was one of the island's stewpots for tomorrow's national picnic, the we-ahll-is-one picnic promised by the calypso singers, the trade unions, the ministers, the churchmen, by men as opposed in their vision as Joshua Kingsley and Edison Banks. So the beach bar complemented the mother operation with a life of its own, the offspring of a parent who found it necessary to draw a line between who could be brought home and who could not. A hotel overrun by local characters whose profession seemed to be overrunning places was not colorful and authentic, merely volatile. The bar therefore existed as a buffer, a free-market zone serving anyone who bellied forward into it with no apparent mischief in mind. The concrete dance patio was available to every kid courageous enough to come out of the bushes, any teenager with enough aplomb and pluck to approach the young women of another country, another class, a different race; any coconut higgler or hand-line fisherman who secretly believed there was a playboy prince inside of him, waiting for an invitation to rule a corner of the world. And for tourists the aura of the beach bar was in fact an exotic authenticity, and though it wasn't as raw as they eagerly perceived, it was a legitimate Third World medium for them to stir themselves into, a genuine *black* experience of the type they feared and avoided at home.

For a time the popularity of the bar had declined along with the hotel's due to the former bartender, the spiteful Jevanee, who favored local thugs and took forever to attend to paying customers. Now Jevanee was gone, jailed for assaulting a police officer who tried to prevent him from hacking Tillman to pieces with a machete. A man of notoriety in the islands, Winston Peabody, once known for his devastating arm as a cricket bowler until disabled in a car accident, replaced Jevanee behind the bar, and was given full authority to manage the establishment as he saw fit. He fired the Mind Invaders, the steel band that had been a fixture at the bar for years, and replaced them with Monkeyjunk, a band of pansmen Winston was promoting for carnival's Road March competition. The combination of Winston's solicitude and the unorthodox tunes of Monkeyjunk—an eclectic repertoire of original compositions they called tropoblues, well-known calypsos, Hollywood show tunes, and baroque concertos—revitalized the failing beach bar. It was hot again with action, busy on week nights, pulsating on weekends.

The palm grove that horseshoed around the bar and opened up to the water of Howard Bay was pegged with onlookers, villagers from Augustine, a line of stoic hucksters, old women or girls with wooden trays of cigarettes, homemade sweets and roasted peanuts, Chiclets, fruits and cakes, roti and small plastic baggies of moonshine rum. Children, some only toddlers, played half dressed in the sand at their feet. A gang of self-conscious boys who hadn't yet found the backbone to step from the trees to the dance patio, to come out in their tattered clothes and uneducated minds and parrot what they had been taught to say—We *ahll is one*—to learn if it were true or not, evaluated and processed every detail of the spectacle before them as if it were a heavenly apparition in their eyes, without precedent in their pubescent lives. As the four of them walked from the parking area along a fieldstone path, Adrian was made uncomfortable by the presence of the boys in the shadows. "What are they looking at?" she said, making a hostile face at the shapes standing among the trees.

Tillman suggested they were looking at a way of life, nothing more ominous than that. But that was ominous enough for Adrian. "My way of life doesn't translate to foreign black boys," she said, raising her voice so it could be heard by the shadows. "I wish they'd look somewhere else and not at me."

Mitchell laughed unkindly. "That's exactly what everybody in the government says."

Tillman, mollifying her, told Adrian not to take the attention personally, and led them into the crowd, past the crush of the dance floor to an empty oceanside café table under a shelter of rustling palm thatch resembling a hairy mushroom cap. Johnnie lit a cigarette and leaned back, a visiting queen of the night. What made her beautiful was the way she responded to all signs of mobilization with a conspiratorial nod, affirming whatever was buoyant and fast and prodigious, as if she had a private arrangement to be welcomed as a member of any group seeking pleasure. She could thrive in a place like this, and more than once Mitchell had looked at her and felt she might do or be anything at all, that she was a woman on the fringe of a glittering potential, moving closer and closer toward its center. It was Mitchell's most generous thought of Johnnie.

Tillman and Mitchell collected round after round of drinks from the bar, and for a while they talked, inhaling deep luxurious breaths of the moist air off Howard Bay—Tillman's attention wandering to the two resident misfits who lurked among the customers, one named Davidius and the other dubbed by the locals The Missing Link, for his apish appearance and retarded intelligence, two defective roosters prospecting the henhouse, operating on the not unheard of theory that white tourist girls would fuck a black man for the asking. Adrian shuddered as Tillman pointed them out, the small and twisted Davidius, broadcasting animal rut and violation; the hulk of the Link, with an idiot's fascination for the female gender, animated baby dolls which he bumbled behind and groped after with the clumsy love of a nursling.

"You shouldn't allow them on the premises."

"Who . . . the tourists?"

"Of course not," Adrian said. "*Those* two. They're not even human."

Mitchell drawled that exclusion was the rule of the past that led to the excesses of the present. Democracy must be an open door, and so on.

"Oh, don't go on with that," Adrian said. Adrian saw Mitchell studying her with soft menace and asked, "What is it you do on this island? What brought you here, if you don't mind my asking?"

"Agricultural adventurism." Mitchell suddenly felt very short-tempered. "And you?" he asked, leaping right into an answer. "You've come to stain yourself a little before going off on a real vacation somewhere where the prices on the wine list exceed the per capita income of a country like this one."

To his great surprise, Adrian burst into laughter. "That's such clichéd thinking, you know. Not to mention sanctimonious."

But clichés get superior mileage in the Third World, Mitchell wanted to say, thinking, Why bother? She was twenty-four years old, pretty, and successful for her age. Europe was her model, her reference, for the world outside of the States. "Look, I don't want to be a bitch," Adrian said, starting to raise her chin and then catching herself. "I've been running nonstop in the city for months. I was ready for a time-out, I wanted to sit on the beach and read and get a tan—and look what I got. I mean, there are just certain things you'll never get me to accept." But she was focused on Tillman now, showing him a pouting smile. And Mitchell wasn't listening. Johnnie, looking away out over the water at the semaphore of a thunderhead signaling from the south, had reached under the table to take his hand.

"Let's dance," Johnnie whispered in his ear.

Mitchell made excuses, but she ignored his inertia, made him get on his feet, walk, hold her. He felt drenched in warm soft pellets of musical rain. What notes were these anyway, banged out on a pan, petrol drums forged into spinets and harpsichords? In their plumage of tie-dyed tee shirts and red drawstring pants, Monkeyjunk was beating its wings upward, their drums yielding breath after sorrowful breath of continental sentiment. He had a weakness for the lament of a keyboard and the pansmen were reinventing something very sad, something that venerated beauty and sadness. The music sifted down upon them, and Mitchell felt astonished by the unreality of the woman he held in his arms, tortured by the substance of her.

Bach? he wondered, amazed.

"Mitch, are you okay?"

Though he knew he looked strangulated, contradicted, he nodded.

"You were just looking so down."

They revolved under the stars. Her forehead was pearled with moisture, her arms glistening and her body so hot he could feel the change of temperature she caused in the air. He saw The Missing Link pass by, shambling like a bear, everybody's partner, craning and witless, his steam-shovel jaw slack on its hinges. The music clattered like a piano left out in the rain. This was their togetherness, she facing the mountains, he facing the sea; when he saw land, she saw water; this chaining, a troublesome irresolution, a troublesome certainty; her, her. Whatever direction they slid and balanced, the world was this timeless cruel harmony of yoked opposition, a pattern difficult to follow gracefully outside the steps of the dancing. The heat and careful pressure at the base of his spine came from Johnnie's hand, and she whispered to him about the fulcrum of his own hand on her, how nice it was—five years of not-knowing reduced by their hands held just this way to one knowing touch. The moment of gliding touch across the contour of a hip, the oiled texture of skin, network of muscles; the discovery that years could be preserved or lost in fingertips, could be inventoried and warehoused in the most delicate conduits of flesh.

To Mitchell's relief, the music faded into cottony vibrations and then stopped. The liquor on an empty stomach, the thick cloying fumes of jasmine, Johnnie—he had become dizzy in spurts. Dropping their hands away from each other, she froze under his scrutiny, averting her eyes.

"Oh, Jesus," she said, daring to look at him again, seeing his confusion, the inertia, the twitches of, what? Revulsion? Self-revulsion? "You really hate me, don't you?"

It was terrible to think she could again be his—more terrible to think he could be hers, that she could swing down the blue arc of the atmosphere with a receipt for five years' payment on this whatever it was between them, held in escrow. What, after all, would their lives have been had she stayed? He felt the immediate futility of thinking that way.

The music ignited again—raving, ferocious, police truncheons playing the skulls of the mob like blacksmithing. Johnnie and Mitchell were jostled by the dancers; tears condensed in her eyes. He tried to lead her off the patio but with sobering force she pulled his hand back to her waist. Her face contorted; she fought against being overwhelmed but her arms hung limp at her sides, tremors jerked her shoulders, black ribbons unfurled from her eyes. He hated the sight of her alone in the world, the agony of her, her homelessness, yet he still could not comfort her.

"I'm so sorry," she said, gasping for air. "Mitchell, I'm so sorry."

"Don't be sorry. Find something else to be. We just met, right?"

Johnnie stepped into him, her fist clenched and unclenched against his shoulder blades, the basket of her ribs so lively, a wetness on his shirt, smeary with mascara, where she pressed her face. He could barely hear her. Something about how she had hurt him, how she didn't understand how much until— He resented this diagnosis and unlocked himself from her arms, walking away, leaving her there in the mayhem of the dancing. There were empty stools at the bar and he sat down, queasy from the whorehouse perfume of the jasmine banking the patio. "I seem to be getting drunk again," he told Winston, and then added petulantly, "I deserve to."

"Who don't?" nodded Winston. "Daht a very Catherinian declaration."

"The fucking pledge of allegiance."

He marked this trespass into the private clubhouse of cynicism and reproached himself for it. There were better ways to disgrace himself than a descent to some sort of glum spiritual unification with a chorus of derelict expatriates slurring dirges to a bottle. The self-exiles, their rotting hearts and negligent remembrance of what they had left behind, this deluded out of the frying pan into the fire reflex, back issues of *Punch* and *The New Yorker* growing musty in their parlors.

"Give me something to finish me off," he said, and Winston brought a coconut mug with the last potent dregs of the night's batch of toxic waste, tasting of green rum and Kool-Aid. Mitchell asked for a regular glass, just put it in something regular, would you?— "Winston, you drink out of a fucking coconut shell at home?" Winston snorted and massaged his metal knee, hovered nearby funneling a half-empty bottle of scotch into one half-full, disregarding the difference in labels. Mitchell brooded, slipping back into the tide, the sexual undertow, the currents that took him nowhere but down, feeling railroaded, in the midst of a grand entrapment. Winston hobbled down the length of the bar, pocketing tips before the urchins could steal the coins.

Then Johnnie stood beside him, glazed, recomposed, refusing to sit down when Mitchell asked her to. Her capacity for new beginnings, for pouring out yesterday's wine, was in effect. She had been in the bathroom stabbing cosmetics across her features with sluttish extravagance. Underneath it all the fragility and fatigue were highlighted like never before. She asked in a controlled voice if he were mad at her. No, he wasn't mad, he wasn't anything, just high, very high, indecently high . . . shouldn't be this high, he muttered. She wanted to go back to the house. Her period had started, spewing with such quantity into her underpants that she had to remove them in the restroom and throw them away. Mitchell had trouble connecting with her urgency.

"I'm leaving," she said.

"Wait, wait. Have another drink with me. You can't walk home by yourself. The boogieman will get you."

"I can take care of myself."

"You don't even know where the fuck you are."

"Look, damn you." Her hand went up under her skirt. Mitchell leered at this indiscretion. "I'm bleeding all over myself."

The hand withdrew, three middle fingers slathered. His vision switched between two or more separate channels as he watched, stupefied, the hand track in segments and stamp his forehead with its pungent brand. She picked up a cocktail napkin to clean her fingers. "Can we go?"

It took Mitchell a second to understand what she had done, this inconceivable act; that she had fouled him. He became infuriated at his humiliation. In a daze he ran for the sea, his rage spottily illuminating areas of his blurred vision like flashbulbs, and splashed into the bay to scour the debasement that was an acid in every cell of his skin. Galactic fields of phosphorus sparks opened and spread just below the surface, green swirling chips of submerged light that seemed to pour out of his fury and diffuse through the ocean. Johnnie stood at the tideline, a virginal apparition begging him to come out. He had not invented her after all, as he had often wished, and so there she was, and time alone could not evict her from his life. He thrashed in the water, the foxfire blooming brighter with each swipe, until he exhausted everything, all the sorrow and condemnation and acrimony, all gone and even forgiven, expelled with the salty-sweet bile, the rum and brine evacuation of all the emotional troops he had marshaled against her. Finally he crawled out onto the sand, emptied but still gagging weakly, and lay down at Johnnie's feet. She knelt down and cradled his head.

"Come out of that dark place, Mitchell. Let it go, let it go."

Didn't the entire world dream this same dream, the reinstatement of love? They could lie about it, they could deceive themselves until all the endings fused like barrier islands around their lives, but he couldn't anymore. He wanted to, fought for it, but couldn't. And in that toppling moment he believed that all hearts had been issued a general amnesty, that the exiled, the banished, the deposed, the deported and the excommunicated, all the expatriates and émigrés of love, could now return to the countries they once inhabited, and even the totalitarianism of families had been at long last overthrown, children and parents reunited in an original state of grace, and old friends who had quarreled divisively were getting back in touch, brothers were mending their civil wars, dogs that ran away were coming home, and everywhere people were excavating the cemeteries of albums and scrapbooks and box cartons of photographs, raising their beloved dead.

She hushed him, saying, *Yes, you were right, Mitchell. You were right to keep believing.*

They broke a window to get back into the house because Mitchell had lost his key in the water. She tugged off his wet clothes and directed him into his bed while he mumbled feeble protests, mistaking her intentions, before he passed out, breathing loudly through his slack mouth, his wounded nose packed with tissue paper because of its tendency to seep into the pillow at night, and then she doctored her own profuse flow in the bathroom, leaving coin-sized magenta drops on the scuffed wooden floorboards, a smear on the toilet seat, on the side of a stack of Kleenex so that the stain was layered deep into the calendar of the box and would be peeled away, day by day. She went to her own room and, after taking off her clothes, lowered herself into bed, but a few minutes later her stomach cramped violently and she got up from the mattress to go out on the veranda and sit in the hammock. Once she heard Mitchell lumber into the bathroom to cough and spit; when she went to check on him his door was open but he was back in bed asleep. For a while she looked in on him, disappointed that he wasn't awake, because it was time to tell him everything, to bring the tyranny of the past to a close and start over again one way or another, pure. She went back outside and rolled into the hammock, staring blankly at the canopy of stars, dipping into a crystalline packet with her fingernail.

Sometime before dawn, Mitchell dreamed about the elderly beggar at the airport, saw him walking around the bush, half starved, wearing the bloody shirt Mitchell had given him—the dream woke him up, and for a moment he thought the man was there in the room. He got up and went out on the veranda for air. Johnnie was rocking back and forth in the hammock, a braid of moonlight twisted on the bay, incandescent. She turned her head without a trace of disturbance or surprise, watching him come near her as if she had anticipated or even conjured his appearance. Her eyes were wide and wild in the thin blue light. Suspended in the almost invisible web of the hammock, she seemed somehow at the center of the night, floating, a lone witness to the secrets of complete desolation. A *visitor*.

"What time is it?"

"I've lost track," she said.

Their voices were feathers, falling leaves, water seeping into its table. He spoke with a gentleness he had been unable to express for a long time.

"What are you doing?"

"I've been singing."

"Oh," he said, still not fully conscious. He told her he didn't know any songs.

"It's easier late at night, when you're alone, to remember them."

She shifted and spread the netting with her feet and arms, unfolding and opening, making room for him in the airy expanse of her solitude. He dipped his upper body over the hem and let himself fall, rolled in alongside her, adjusting themselves until they found the place where they were equally balanced, cocooned, harnessed, twins in utero.

Chapter 11

At daybreak Mitchell was roused by the sounds of steady chopping, as mechanical as the *tock tock tock* of a metronome, the strokes issued with such hypnotic regularity that at first Mitchell thought, Tennis? as if he had been dreaming of two well-matched players engaged in an endless rally. He threw his legs out of the hammock and jerked upright in a clammy sweat of bad sleep and foreboding. He slipped out of the netting, and Johnnie, asleep slanted on her face with her hands above her, stayed put, seemingly undisturbed. She looked like something wild that had died, trying to claw its way out of a trap and it was with this awful sense of respect for the dead that he reached out and stayed the hammock's lullaby. Unwanted discoveries were on his mind.

He went quickly through the house to the front room and drew back the curtains. At the top of the drive a grizzled madman hacked at the trunk of the royal poinciana with a machete so sharp each double set of blows spit a melon-white wedge from the pulp of the tree. Mitchell stepped into a pair of gym shorts and dashed outside, shouting for the fellow to stop what he was doing.

Despite the man's age he appeared unaffected by his labor, it was no trouble to him to work with such hot effort, and he looked too bony and juiceless anyway to make a sweat rise to his ashy skin. His flashing strokes, overhand and then underhand, were clean and accurate and had already done irreparable damage to the girth of the poinciana. He acted as if he hadn't heard the order to cease and Mitchell was compelled to take his shoulder and pull him back out of his cricketeer's stance. With a final swipe he left the long blade of the machete sunk in the wood and turned, removing his straw hat with an obsequious flourish that dumped a padding of folded newspaper at Mitchell's feet.

"Is a fine mornin, mahn!" he said with the heartiness of a lifetime early riser. "God give we anudduh sweet dandy."

Mitchell clenched his teeth and pointed disbelievingly at the damage the man had done. "You're murdering this beautiful tree. What the fuck do you think you're doing?"

"Oh, ho!" Mitchell's anger seemed to take the old man by surprise, but his concern became a polite chuckle and he clapped his hands on the top of his legs, as if he were laughing at a joke Mitchell had not told well.

"Missy Bain say tek de tree out." He gave a blameless look and shrugged. "Missy Bain mek a lettah to Missy Carlisle and say find Mistah Quiddley and tell him tek de tree out. Missy Bain say daht tree she have up by de road fulla bug, mahn, and—"

"What bugs?" Mitchell interrupted, baffled. "Who's Missy Bain? What in the hell are you talking about?"

"Well, sah, I ain seen no bug, ya know, but Missy Bain mek a lettah to Missy Carlisle and say find Mistah Quiddley and tell him tek de tree out daht stand by de road, it fulla bug and de bug gettin into de house and eatin up de place so best tek out de tree 'fah de whole house fall down and de white mahn goes somewhere else and she lose daht money she need to send dem two gy-urls to school up dere where she livin, some place dem callin Toron-to, so Missy Carlisle come by to where I stayin wit me wife and say Missy Bain got a tree she doan want, Mistah Quiddley, and me wife say, Eh, doan boddah wit daht, mahn, St. Catherine fulla trees waitin to drop, but Missy Carlisle reach deep into daht red bag she carry and tek out twenny Uncle Sammys"—the old man fished around in the pocket of his trousers and produced the twenty-dollar bill in question—"and she give me dis same note you see here in me hand and say, Here's fah de trouble of chop-down, Mistah Quiddley, and Missy Bain say is all right to dig de coal pit right in de side by de drive, and—"

"Wait a minute," Mitchell said. "This is inconceivable."

"Eh?"

"Why wasn't I consulted about this? This tree is ruined."

Mr. Quiddley scratched his ear thoughtfully. "I stop by, ya know, sah. I come by de ministry." He maintained the merriest smile possible although his eyes darted, avoiding Mitchell's, as if he feared his explanation would be misconstrued as impudence and any second he'd end up knocked to the ground by the white man.

Mitchell was furious and unable to shake the conviction that he was being victimized by insensible directives from abroad. He stepped forward to the poinciana to give Mr. Quiddley back his cutlass and send him on his way. The shaft had bit so deep that he had to use both hands to unlock the steel from the wood.

"I loved this tree," Mitchell said. "No more cutting on it, please. I'm going to talk to Mrs. Carlisle."

"Tree finish up," Quiddley reminded him, still with his broad, obsequious grin that was making Mitchell feel irrelevant to the situation.

"Just leave it be," he demanded. "There's no virtue in this sort of intervention."

"Now, you lose me on daht, mahn," Mr. Quiddley confessed, and grew sullen.

Mr. Quiddley had exhausted him, he wasn't going to talk to him anymore but went back into the house to prepare for town. He put water on to boil and took a cold shower. While juicing oranges in the kitchen, he heard a vehicle come to a stop in the gravel at the top of the drive, and then a persistent horn, calling him out. There was one of the ministry's olive-green Rovers. Godfred Ballantyne, the forest ranger, had his head out the driver's window, chatting up Mr. Quiddley who had squatted in the side yard using his machete to scoop a crater that was already knee-deep.

"Now what, Mister Quiddley," Mitchell said, advancing. "I thought you went home."

"Wukkin on de pit, mahn."

We're not traveling on the same wavelength, Mitchell thought, surrendering. Not even close.

"Mek a few bagga coals," said Quiddley.

Ballantyne honked the horn again, as if to change the subject. "I come fah you, Wilson," he barked.

Mitchell went back in the house for his briefcase, ignored his tea but gulped his orange juice and wrote a note to Johnnie, asking her to go to the market in Augustine, and *wear a skirt in public, please,* that's the rule if you lived here, *no trashy women in residence!*

All right, Mitchell growled to himself as they drove off, *I see how it is now.* How easy it was for people to disrupt your home and environment, even from distant shores. No one seemed to need permission.

In his haversack, Ballantyne had two fresh loaves of bread, still hot from the bakery oven, and a sixpenny cake of guava cheese wrapped in a sheet of newsprint. Mitchell felt light-headed with hunger the second he smelled them, as shameless as a street urchin inhaling fully, his eyes closed in appreciation. *Eat,* Ballantyne ordered. He loved issuing commands. *Eat. Run,* quelling any thought of disobedience. Where had he been educated? Mitchell wondered. Were there Jesuits on the island? Greedily, Mitchell tore apart a spongy loaf, crumbling the cake of guava cheese and pressing its pieces into the fragrant center of each hunk. Once his mouth was as full as he could get it, he refocused on the world, chewing more and more pensively as he realized something was not quite right, then faster, once he understood, so he could swallow and speak.

"Where are we going?'

"Leeward."

"Take me back," said Mitchell. His neck tightened and he heard an unnecessary urgency in his voice. "I can't go to leeward this morning. There's a staff meeting. I have to be there."

Ballantyne kept his eyes on the road. "No you don't," he said. They were speeding along the flat, goat-gnawed coast of Bambarra. Ballantyne turned on the windshield wipers to smear the film of salt exclaimed into the air by the dangerous waves pounding the emptiness of the beaches. The Rover's engine made an oceanic roar, the rhythmic crash of the sea was like a demolition machine crunching down.

"Ballantyne, what's going on? Why do I feel like this is not a friendly act, you picking me up?"

Ballantyne snorted and looked over, his eyes a mystery yet nevertheless playful. Clearly, it put him in a good humor to make his passenger uncomfortable. "You too nervous, Wilson. Dey postpone it, you know."

"Why?"

"Who am I, mahn? Dem big shots ain goin tell me."

"So why are we headed to leeward?"

"Kingsley."

Mitchell sat back, giving this idea solemn consideration, both flattered and wary that he was being summoned to an audience with the honorable minister—the crackpot, the tyrant, the has-been. Well, okay, good; he had something to say to Kingsley and it was this: Listen, I'm one of the planet's last humanitarians, I'm a ready-made fairy godmother, but I don't know what the fuck I'm doing, I don't know who wants what, why don't you tell me what to do? He put another piece of bread in his mouth and chewed. Ahead of them, not far inland, a bulldozer nuzzled the pale saline-drenched crown of a modest hill, pushing dirt around in a pretense that this stretch of forsaken littoral was somehow livable. There had once been an ancient Arawak village up there, Mitchell had seen the shards during the survey, and now it was being turned like a thin compost, the infertile clay hidden under a sedimentary blanket of volcanic ash and goat droppings and useless minerals now exposed and yellowing under the wet sun. It was a Public Lands Development project: peasants from one of the northwest estates would be resettled here, he had heard. Mitchell didn't have to be a soil expert to know that unless the newcomers were given livestock to graze they would be better off in Scuffletown, since they would not survive here, let alone prosper. Nobody ever had and nobody ever would grow anything on this coastal plain, pressed so hard by the Atlantic. He had recommended the peasants remain where they were until a more forgiving site could be identified and purchased, if need be, and although the chief agricultural officer agreed, there was nothing to be done about it because now the coalition was insisting on the relocation—turning people off good land and marrying them to bad. The last bite of bread in his mouth turned to mud, and he could not swallow.

"What do you know about this," he finally asked the forest ranger, driven by the need to have an ally.

"You get mixed up wit some shit is all I know."

It was not what Mitchell had expected to hear.

The coast changed. The land convulsed upward, the spine of a mountain snapped off into the sea and beyond that another giant opened wide, spreading its spurs like two burly legs, the white cascade of a river dribbling from the crotch into the ecstatic blue of a bay. Still not in view but not far now was the old town of Ferguson, once a thriving sugar port but now barely inhabited. There they would turn off the coastal highway onto the inland track that serpentined down into the valley named after the seedbed of civilization, Sumeria, and then over to the leeward village of Cape Molasses, so christened in 1743 in remembrance of a family of French settlers boiled alive by the Black Caribs in raw cane syrup the previous year, on land that would one day be known as Jack Dawes Estate.

On the road west they passed a seemingly arbitrary sequence of twice-forgotten hamlets, incestuous clusters of families with piercing eyes, where even the chickens wore their feathers like shreds of rags, and larger jungle-crushed villages, vibrating in silence, small lots of humanity impacted in time, unmapped and nameless in the house of their nation, the world itself unnamed beyond the few steps it took to draw water from a spring, to pull a mango from a century-old tree, to pry a stone from the ruin of a mill to use to bank a cookfire.

As they neared the leeward coast and entered Kingsley's home parish the lurching, twisting rhythm of the journey changed.

Ballantyne stopped frequently, here at a shuttered rum shop, here where a bridge spanned a silty, gurgling river, here under a tamarind tree where two men sat on buckets and slapped domino tiles on a plank they supported with their knees. A man put a large green pumpkin into the open bed of the Rover and shimmed it with a rock, to keep it from tumbling around. One woman gave them a potato sack of crayfish her children had collected from the river, and another added a cardboard box full of cashew fruit. The man at the bridge contributed a dasheen root that resembled the testicle of an ox. The man at the end of the footpath produced a stubbly hand of maughfaughbaugh bananas. The bed of the Rover piled up. A girl handed six anthuriums into the cab. Further along they collected a fighting cock in a reed cage, a soup turtle, an oozing lump of honeycomb bundled in ginger leaf, a dead monkey, rank and stiff as a board, a bag of cherry tomatoes, a braid of garlic bulbs, a tray of roasted groundnuts.

No price was named or money exchanged. At first Mitchell was left to imagine that all this booty deposited into the Rover, the fruit of a deceptive abundance, a deception that was also a way of life, a way of life that was only a limited dialect of the language of survival—all this was being gathered as a form of tax or tribute. But Ballantyne clucked at such a theory. These people *knew,* he said, these country people knew who they were, where they were going, when they might pass. They were Maroons—nobody told them but they knew. Nobody asked them to go into the bush or into their scrappy gardens, harvesting what they chose to spare, and then materialize like visions of tormented saints in the niches and cavities of vegetation, dressed like John the Baptist, flagging the minister's Rover to a stop when it appeared, long after they had recognized its sound in the valley, around a bend. Nobody said, *Love Poppi.* Nobody instructed the land or the servants of the land, *Give to your father.* From a speechless people, a world with no tongue, these gifts were the currency of expression. Only Kingsley knew how to interpret them, he was their translator, the interlocutor in the redundant dialogue between silence and power, he was the host, the medium through which their lives might be channeled into a fist of words to shake in the face of something unseeable filled with wild, confusing, ravenous energies. Along the lane to Jack Dawes Estate, Ballantyne was waved over to take on a cargo of waternuts, yams, sapodilla and soursops, a brindled piglet, starved and squealing with worms in its eyes, oranges and lemons, melons and christophenes, and each giver added to an inventory of whispered petitions kept by Ballantyne.

—Speak to Poppi, sah. Water comin foul from de white dust de men put on de hill and me wife and kids all crampy.

—Tell Poppi me cy-ahnt find no rice and no oil in de shop.

—Speak to de ministah, sah. Please fah me. Me husband twist he leg and snap it and now Juney say he lose he job and a next fella come from St. Vincent and tek it.

—Hear now, Ballantyne. De mahn say pull up me croppa onions and bag dem and leave dem by de shed fah de truck. Truck doan come to fetch, eh? Rain wet de bags and de onions tek up a smell. Truck suppose to come on Monday but ain reach till Friday. Dem onions rot up and de mahn say dem onions no good, bwoy, and he ain pay a cent.

—Tell Poppi teef come and eat me next goat, and daht one de nanny.

—Tell Poppi dirt fall down from where de fellas plant arrowroot and break me house.

—Tell Poppi worms get in me new baby and mek she dead.

—Tell Poppi me faddah lose he hand in de machine at Blackstones and de clinic fella won't come to help, him say he busy.

—Speak to Poppi. Tell him *massas day done* ain reach here as yet.

He was seeing too much of this, the prolonged despair throughout the countryside, it made him feel empty and far away, after a point the distinctions began to blur, and you argued with yourself that there was no such thing as the modern world, that it didn't exist, anywhere, but then after a while you went home and there it was, right inside the door, and then you almost stopped believing in the incurable epidemic of misfortune and put all your faith in that boy of Miss Sindra's or Miss Bynum's whom the government made a foreman. Juney, moving up in the world, taking no one with him.

Then, even at a distance, there was a chance you'd begin to think like the Barbeques, that the solution to problems so multitudinous as to form a critical mass of suffering was pyromania. Burn everything down.

The sky had darkened by the time they pulled into the clearing where Kingsley had built his two-story house. Ballantyne parked near the kitchen door to unload the cornucopia but wouldn't accept Mitchell's help, instead sending him around the yard and its neatly tended flower beds to the elevated veranda, where he tapped on the glass pane of the front door and watched through the lace as a woman shuffled across the floor and let him in, telling him Kingsley would soon be there and take a seat, she would bring him something to drink. Mitchell sank down into a cushioned chair, its gingham fabric reeking of mildew, placed at a right angle to a vinyl-covered couch. The room opened at back into a dining area, an oval table made of maple, or maple-colored, six ladderback chairs. Nothing he could see identified the occupants of the house beyond the functional, no art on the walls, no icons or family pictures or degrees or certificates or framed commendations, no trappings of influence, nothing to suggest a personality or boast an achievement, only a round wall clock and unstained wood and a chapel-like hush disrupted at intervals by pots clattering in the kitchen, the entire space cooled by a watery green light diffused through floor-to-ceiling windows that fronted the veranda. I am in a jungle, Mitchell told himself. I am in a small place cast off from the world, the land a hot lake on a blue prairie of ocean. Start there, with Caliban ascending the throne. All this time on St. Catherine he had been thinking there is a beginning and we have left it and we are traveling ahead, but the movement was an illusion, its current proof none other than Johnnie. There was only a beginning and it kept layering outward and then folding back into itself, always re-creating an unresolved zero, as if it were an irresistible force, known and preferred. Why am I so moody, he wondered, I'm not like this, am I? I'm gung-ho. The door had been left open and a crow walked in off the porch, cocked its head at Mitchell and flapped back outside. He wanted a drink, scotch, he wanted to sleep. What he couldn't understand was why he had ever considered something so self-defeating as innocence to be a virtue.

Without realizing why it was happening Mitchell watched the room lose its tranquil submarine radiance, the light becoming so heavy it seemed to collapse, and then it began to rain. The downpour did not intensify by degrees but simply gushed forth with biblical fury, vertical and windless. Outside the row of windows everything blurred into vague gunmetal shapes sagging in the torrent. The rain blasted against the zinc roof, humming and buzzing, rattled cutaneous leaves into an uproar, a cataclysm of swirling particles and splintering forms. A rust-colored spray rebounded as high as the top step of the veranda, kicking a mash into the air that would later dry and stipple, leaving the false border of a floodline. He reevaluated the room he was in and concluded its defining motif was *nothing to steal.* Thus the invention of Switzerland, to hoard it away. A mist entered the house and dragged over him, spreading an even weight against his skin when a minute ago there was nothing. I can't be rescued, he thought, because that's what it felt like to be sitting alone in Joshua

Kingsley's country house, isolated in the turbine roar and thunder of the rain, without a clue, really, why he was here. This land business. Reform. He was biased—money, love, power, memory, blood, food, and finally a grave, that's what land was, everything, actually, and it was no secret though maybe some Zen-like riddle that to reform it all you had to do was reform the reformers, who he believed were committed to the ideal that justice was a matter of ownership, when it was nothing quite so elementary and absolute.

His co-workers at the ministry told him, This is an asshole country, but they couldn't truly tell him why. A Brit who had spent three years on a soil conservation project in Africa had pulled Mitchell aside at a party to confide that he hated to admit it, but blacks could not work together. Sure, Mitchell agreed with a nasty look, You're right, the blacks should model themselves after the Europeans, who had a splendid record relating to each other during the twentieth century—or any other century you'd care to name.

How did he come to be among such men? he asked himself. Couldn't they persist in their glories and failures without him, rocket to the moon and banish plagues back to their source in the underworld, build cities as extravagant as an emperor's birthday cake, trade hearts with corpses, spin a symphony into the ether and retrieve it in Hong Kong, start their wars and finish their wars and rip off each other's balls, *all without him?* But now he had his finger on what he needed to be rescued from most, this screaming desire to give it all away, to say It's all yours, have fun, don't break your neck on it. All yours—*let me be.*

The rain had made him deaf, gave him, gave him vertigo, a sense that he was unmoored and drifting away. Even with the minister in the room, they wouldn't be able to hear what the other had to say. What is this like, what does this remind me of, he asked himself. To be here, to have this happening, the claustrophobia of their fatuous intrigues? He felt as if he were about to be prosecuted, that's how alone he felt. This lush, seething insularity—what am I supposed to be learning, what are the lessons here? The self-reflection, the eclipse of the rain, the constant waiting for answers. If ever he was a being in suspension, dangled in some huge amniotic sac of ambivalence, this was it. Maybe the house shifted, maybe the rain slowed—things began to change. For no good reason besides being broken his nose began to bleed, he could feel it get hot and wet inside, and he put his head back, stared at the beaded ceiling, its paint blisters and its cobwebs and its silent roaming lizards, and drank the flow until it stopped. I can't be rescued, Mitchell thought; rescued from exaggeration, rescued from the malicious inflation of everything I know to be true.

The kitchen door opened a crack and a servant, her head bound tightly in blue cloth, peeked into the room. Her lips moved but it was not clear if she was talking to him or somebody else behind her because he could not hear in the whitewater din of the rain. The door opened wider and Ballantyne passed through as the woman stepped aside with a smirk in Mitchell's direction, apparently in response to something the forest ranger had said. He carried a tray—two water glasses, a bowl of ice, a plastic pitcher of water, a bottle of Pinch— over to the table and then returned to the kitchen. Mitchell marveled that despite the humidity, and the activity of the morning, while Mitchell's own clothes looked like he had slept in them, Ballantyne's khaki shirt-jac looked, with its fastidious creases, as if it had just been ironed. Its square tail flapped over his buttocks, which appeared enormous, twin sacks of cement, in Ballantyne's tan slacks. And those feet. His toes fanned out from the front of his rubber sandals like a cluster of cocoa plugs.

It dawned on Mitchell that the forest ranger had somehow been awarded immunity from bureaucratic process, given an enviable measure of independence in a ministry that was timid about personal responsibility. He rarely saw Ballantyne at the compound, entering or leaving the office of Mr. Samuels, the CAO, and never at a staff meeting. There were infrequent times in the field when Mitchell would cross his path, Ballantyne engrossed in some form of woodsmandry, the planting or felling of trees, orchestrating slash and burn, appearing and disappearing through the smoke along a line of transparent flames searing a hillside. Or they might pass on the road, Ballantyne at the wheel of the Land Rover truck assigned to him by the ministry, the bed crammed with day laborers bounced around and knocked into each other, their faces forever stoic, captives of Ballantyne's driving. And once Ballantyne had come to Wilson's desk seeking information about the mahogany trade. He had purchased some land in the high country behind the volcano, virgin forest, and hoped he might find a better market for the lumber he milled than the regional one provided by Caricom. Mitchell promised to look into it and, at Ballantyne's insistence, they adjourned to Bim's Creole Kitchen for lunch. Bim's occupied the first floor of the Seamen's Union Hall. The air inside was rank with the fishy oils of stewing porpoise. They sat on folding chairs around a plywood table, drinking brown beer until they had achieved a state of alcoholic bonhomie. At some point, Ballantyne's preferred topic became that of the hunt. Working in the mountains, he often carried a rifle strapped to his back to shoot agouti and manicou, tattoo, mongoose, wild pig and goat, blaireaux, bush fowl which he called ginny birds, monkeys that hung in the layers of jungle canopy as passively as fruit. He called them apes. Wilson had asked if the forest ranger was ever worried about bandits. The police checkpoints on the roads entering the northern parishes were at least a cosmetic attempt to stem the recent spread of what was being called Jack Nastyism. The government had reported an increase in violent crime in the north, though no one could point to a parallel increase in arrests. Even the existence of such incidents was in dispute, since murders were recorded without the evidence of bodies, and robberies without the corroboration of victims. The perpetrators were alleged to be hiding out in the mountains, but Wilson hadn't heard about anybody up there, bivouacked in the roadless forests, except doubtful rumors of a handful of Rastafarian clones who grew vegetables and herb and supposedly ran about naked.

Ballantyne had scanned Mitchell's face with a look that, though not hostile, suggested that he didn't like his courage to be questioned. It seemed to be a sore point with him. "Nobody trouble me," he snorted. Don't believe it, he said. There are no bandits.

"Why the reports?" asked Mitchell. "Why all the bad news?"

"Daht is Jack Nasty, mahn. He movin up in de world."

"Who *is* Jack Nasty? Who's he supposed to be?"

"You tell me."

Ballantyne changed the subject back to his infatuation with hunting, firepower. He hoped one day for the opportunity to indulge in his greatest fantasy—firing a machine gun, preferably into something big: a cow, or an automobile. Just once, to see what it looked like and felt like, then he would know and get it out of his mind.

Everybody's got a dream, Mitchell said, and was pleased and relieved he had made Ballantyne smile.

That's right, the forest ranger said, everybody's got a dream. Just watch out for the other guy's.

The table was set and out came food; lunch, or so it appeared—two steaming bowls of ocher-colored callaloo, a communal bowl of rice, from the smell of it, Guyanese and inferior; plates with a strip of dark gravied meat and avocado halves. It was almost midday. He watched the rain ease, and waited. It made him feel very strange—he was going to have lunch with an important man.

He didn't expect to see Kingsley's white Impala drive up, he hadn't noticed its absence from the yard, he had assumed the minister was home, upstairs, on the second floor, but here was the Impala, splashing into the yard, throwing mud. Kingsley's personal secretary, a slight jaundiced man with a Hindu's melancholic features and droopy eyes, got out from the driver's side, opened an umbrella, and sloshed around to open Kingsley's door. They looked like nurse and patient, managing the slippery steps. The minister wore galoshes. He wore a black suit cut twenty years out of style, a shiny green necktie poorly knotted under the dewlaps that hung from his throat. His steps began with a drag of his shoes before he lifted his rheumatic feet off the ground and set them down again, victims of the rainy season that had begun prematurely. He might have been a pathetic, comic figure if not for the raw mystique, the undisciplined charisma, an envelope of sparking frictions, that accompanied his elephantine presence— that, and his power. With a dismissive gesture, he shook his attendant off his elbow and waved him away, toward the kitchen, as if he were aging only as a consequence of his secretary's ineptitude and shallow faith.

As Kingsley padded down the length of the room he kept his head cocked toward Mitchell Wilson, watching himself being watched, disavowing the obvious discomfort of his steps, as though he were challenging Mitchell to feel sympathy for him, or mistake his strength. His labored breathing, faint wet snores and whistles, somehow manufactured a connotation of excitement, a slightly mad pleasure, as if age and obesity and inflammations were small matters solved by the lust of the spirit. As he neared the head of the table and the food set out for him his long face became illuminated with anticipation, and down he settled into his chair, the frame creaking with the strain of his weight, his head rotating on the hills of his shoulders, an amphibious puff to the flesh as though he could survive anywhere, even underwater if he had to, with gills as well as lungs. Watching Kingsley out of the corner of his eye, the gross performance of his body and the shadow of senility behind his movements, Mitchell was alarmed by the contradictory impression that here was a man whose self-possession was absolute, someone who had made a successful career out of tempting fate—a patrician sitting down to his lunch.

"If you wonderin what the protocol is, Mistah Wilson, the protocol is, Come eat. Very simple, here up leeward. Please, join me, mahn."

He came and sat at the second setting, to Kingsley's left. The minister poured himself half a glass of scotch, tilted the bottled toward his guest.

"Yes," Mitchell nodded. "Thank you."

Kingsley toasted him, a sober *Cheers,* and closed his tarpaper eyelids while he drank. The servant woman stepped out of the kitchen to see if everything was all right. She smelled of horse sweat and the greasy shit smell of canned butter heating on a kerosene stove. Kingsley asked for bread, then told Mitchell the callaloo was getting cold, and so they began to eat. Mitchell watched Kingsley stab his spoon between bloated jowls, his throat stretched and swelled. So much like a fat toad, a bad impersonation of Buddha. There were too many strong odors in the room—foremost among them, the decaying breath of Guyanese rice, spoiled in the holds of ships. Incredibly, the minister was redolent with baby powder. His personality was inseparable from the rain's. He was best of friends with his erstwhile counterpart the prime minister of Grenada, Sir Eric Gairy, who had recently warned his enemies, "He who opposes me opposes God."

Kingsley rubbed his jaw neurotically, plucking at the white wisps of his billy-goat beard, wiping away imaginary dribbles of soup. "I believe you follow the picture better than some fellas who been here all their lives, Mistah Wilson," he said. The prime minister had informed him yet again that he was anxious to implement the Public Lands Development Programme.

"Banks worryin that we draggin we ass. Should the prime minister concern himself, Mistah Wilson?"

He shrugged and faced Kingsley, declining any pretext of accountability. "Hell, I don't know," he said. It rankled him to be coerced into this game.

It was Kingsley's former government that had inherited the estates when the owners had had enough, Kingsley who made it impossible for the old gentry to survive. And then—nothing. Squatters and neglect and ruination. But the properties were clustered along the fertile northwestern coastal plains, its foothills and valleys, in the minister's home district, and were a primary source of his power. Fifteen years ago Kingsley had encouraged the peasants to move onto the land; now he had been commissioned to get them off, to plow under their plots and gardens, level their shacks, and oversee their removal to other sites.

For progress. For the good of the nation.

A schedule of operation was painstakingly abstracted and colored in, but was not adhered to, because it was too ambitious, its timing too compressed. The staff meetings had factionalized; Kingsley proselytized about the merits of Christianity, how he was going to do unto others, et cetera. The younger men were cynically attentive, petting their carefully trimmed beards inspired by Edison Banks. The more tenured civil servants doodled on coarse notepads; the senior staff dozed. The meetings had become an abomination of sense and reasoning, a forum for incriminations, they were an embarrassment, people sniggered out loud, they were openly scornful, they were mistrustful, they shouted *Rubbish!* and left the room in protest. They had no other recourse, Mitchell allowed; they were justified, they were men of science being made a mockery. They were the people who knew how to get things done. Things were not getting done— but for the wrong reasons.

"My involvement has been limited to one third of the term of the program," said Wilson, being diplomatic. "That question would be more properly directed at CAO Mr. Samuels, who's more qualified to answer it."

The minister pursed his lips and squinted, wry and half menacing. "I am not askin Samuels, Mistah Wilson, I am askin you. We draggin we ass—yes or no?"

"No, sir. Not the people I'm working with on the team."

"You gettin impatient, Mistah Wilson? Change comin too slow to St. Kate to suit you, mahn?"

"No, not really, Minister," Mitchell said, sick of the thousand tastes of Kingsley's make-believe. It was ridiculous, to have been brought here.

"Who speed things up? You? Who is responsible for this—*you?*"

"No, sir," Mitchell protested. "There's a political nature to the program which I don't fully comprehend at this time, Mr. Minister."

Kingsley laughed, dry asthmatic squeezes of air. He plumbed beneath his collar with a finger, then loosened his necktie with a tug from behind the knot. He leaned forward, cupping his glass of scotch as if it were a votive candle, he the protector of its delicate flame.

"They stealin my people from me, eh? Mistah Wilson?"

"Honestly, Minister, I don't know what's going on."

"They movin them out too quick, movin them too far away, onto worthless land. That is not right, eh?"

"In a larger sense, I think you're right," Mitchell said.

"Yes, yes," agreed Kingsley, contemplating him with amphibian serenity. "I believe you understand." A fly settled on his knuckle and he waved it off. "I see how this goin and I don't like it, Mistah Wilson, but let me tell you something, mahn, this plan goin backfire, this plan goin blow up in they face. I am glad you understand and agree."

"That's not actually what I meant," Mitchell worried.

"Please, Mistah Wilson. Eat."

"I meant . . ." but he wasn't sure what he had meant, *in a larger sense,* and fell silent, cutting into the meat on his plate, not realizing until he had put a forkful into his mouth that it was liver, pork liver, and it sickened him. He swallowed without chewing, trying not to puke, laid his fork and knife down, washed his mouth out with water and sat there, listening to Kingsley's fleshy, licking sounds, staring at his plate. Kingsley baited him, asked if he was a vegetarian. He said he would call for the girl to bring Mitchell something more to his liking. Mitchell explained he had no appetite, the callaloo had been sufficient. Kingsley talked with food in his mouth.

"You workin hard, Mistah Wilson? You lookin fagged out, mahn. White people does work very hard to help us keep the wolf from the door of St. Catherine, not so?"

Thanks for the irony, Mitchell would have answered, on a day he was feeling brave.

"Here," Kingsley said, holding out his empty plate, "slide it off to mine, I will take it, Miss Rebecca get testy if she food sent back to the kitchen."

The minister continued eating. Mitchell's mind wandered. On the ground level of the ministry, where the warehousing rooms were unbearably odorous, stinking of nitrate fertilizers, formaldehyde, sulfates, and fresh manure, was the veterinary section, where you could always find Morrison, the vet's assistant, a guy about Mitchell's age who seemed to spend his time creating boyish scenes of revolutionary executions, swatting off the minister's head with a cricket bat, playing soccer with Kingsley's leering skull on the streets of Queenstown, renamed the city of Jamona. It was sort of fun to go down into the stench and listen to him. Morrison loved an audience.

Kingsley was speaking again. "I ask if you ever been baptized."

"What?" The rain had finished, leaving in its wake a vast, permeating leakage, the river noise of runoff. If the sun came out now it would be murderous. Mitchell met his host's eyes, Kingsley watching him, rummaging through his interior, this idle biopsy, assessing the fancies and ambitions and limits of his imported American. Mitchell looked away, chafing against this infiltration, of being led by Kingsley to recognize himself, the meaninglessness of his position. Follow me into the darkness, Kingsley's look said, and I will show you who you are, who we are. It wasn't ridiculous to be here, it was surreal.

"Sorry, I didn't hear what you asked, sir."

"Why is it taking so long, the prime minister wish to know?"

"Mr. Minister," Wilson calmed himself and reported, "I can't tell you why some of the projects we designed haven't been initiated.

Both funding and material are available, on paper, at least. We're prepared to move ahead, right now, on Jack Dawes Estate."

Kingsley was studying him intently—Kingsley was *always* studying him, observing his white mouse probe the maze of his nation.

"To a degree," he continued, "I feel the hesitation is valid. Some of the proposed relocation sites seem to me to be unsuitable, though that can be worked around."

Apparently his answer was unexpected good news for the minister, the Holy Ghost had descended into his soul, from the expression on his face, and he beamed and pressed on with his interview, Mitchell immediately suspicious, he was making the toad of power too happy and satisfied, telling himself to use his wits but he had lost the capacity, he was without guile, of all the people on the staff he had been shoved out front, alone. Kingsley queried him about the final PLDP report, why it was taking so long. Banks was upset about that too.

"From my point of view, I think it's because we're trying to do a good job. Because what we are trying to accomplish is complex, and not easily attained. It's no more than that."

"Ah, yes." The old man peered over at him, showing his pine-yellow teeth through a disarming smile. His pleasure radiated into the room, he extended his swollen hands, palms up, imploring an invisible witness to appreciate the conversation. "I say so myself to Mistah Banks—'We doin the best we can.'"

"That's my view."

A recurring frustration troubled him, the trapped feeling that he was really nothing more than a formal presence mailed to the ministry to be used like an official stamp on certain pro forma documents, a stamp that guaranteed the money would spill in from the international agencies, all the acronyms like an alphabet soup cooked up to nourish the world's dispossessed. His strongest desire had been to overcome, to transcend the awkward formality of his presence. Now it had happened and somehow the personalization was worse, almost an act of corruption. Why did he have to be manipulated to admit what he genuinely believed, regardless of the political smokescreens. He felt gullible, patronized, bamboozled. It was the system. The disease was in there, metastasizing.

"And how much time you say it take, Mistah Wilson?"

"I'm not sure. Three to six months. Perhaps longer."

"Six months," Kingsley repeated, ignoring the shorter estimate.

"Maybe," Mitchell said. Maybe by then Kingsley would be house-hunting in Brooklyn. This was out of his league, he couldn't make it his business, he wouldn't, he practiced science, its quotidian concerns distinct from its secular sponsor, his messianic vagaries. No matter what, the science would endure long after the childish scheming and elbowing had been forgotten. Such was the age, and even if he didn't know who he was beyond his surveys and analysis and his good intentions, and didn't know who they wanted him to be, it didn't matter, there was a momentum in place, and they were caught in it and carried forward.

"It's probably a good idea to have the CAO verify this time frame. I'm just guessing."

"Samuels been reassigned," said Kingsley, his eyes measuring Wilson's reaction. He became visibly agitated, his chair singing the strain, his gaze scorching from underneath his brow, this manner familiar to Mitchell from the freewheeling insubordination of the staff meetings. "Some fellas too ego-ed up for God's plan. Move ahead, you see. Or move out. Hudson, from the Marketing Board, take his place."

Well, thought Mitchell, taken off guard, I *do* see, at least Kingsley's announcement explained part, if not all, of why he was here. The Marketing Board chairman was one of the minister's trusted few. Kingsley was circling his wagons, under seige by the members of the coalition who wanted him gone.

"Excuse me, Mr. Minister," Mitchell said, feeling bold. "I have no loyalties here on St. Catherine either way. I only care about doing my job."

Kingsley seemed deeply perplexed by this statement, as it if were the pretext of still more elaborate pretexts. "But, what is it you believe, mahn?" he asked softly, with priestly concern. "You believe in doin right, true?"

Indeed, he did. He believed that the old plantations would become, slowly but certainly, showcases of modern production, new boot-straps for a penniless nation, that they could finally coordinate the organic mysteries of demand and supply, that he would leave here after another six months knowing something morally right had been achieved. He opened his mouth to speak but nothing came out so he nodded.

"Good, good," said the minister. "But you aren't a Colonel Hillendale, are you, Mistah Wilson?"

Mitchell had not heard of a Colonel Hillendale.

"No, I see that you aren't," Kingsley answered his own question. "Truth is a process, Mistah Wilson. Do you wish to pursue the process? Santayana was wrong. Too much attention is paid to the past, and it means so little. By rememberin our past we are condemned, nuh? Look straight ahead, not behind, at all that dirty business."

Truth, Mitchell whispered to himself—*troot*, in the minister's raspy dialect—and he recalled something Johnnie had said years ago. What good is truth, she had asked him, if it can't provide at least some small happiness? Then she had lied to him later that same night, making promises about love. Proving perhaps that falsehood could bring its own joy however temporarily into the world. All that dirty business—Kingsley could be alluding to his own reputation as much as anything else. As a young man he had been flogged for using his cutlass to strike off a policeman's ear, and during the Sugar War he had beaten a turncoat into a lifelong state of insensibility, with his own hands, and had masterminded a campaign of terror against the family of a recalcitrant estate owner whom he wanted to make an example of. It was said these were, for men of his generation, forgivable acts, and must not be judged with sentimentality. But Kingsley had thrashed his first wife, busted her teeth and ribs in a rage of jealousy and sent her fleeing for her life to exile in Trinidad. With the butt of a pistol he had knocked out the eye of the captain of the harbor launch for a petty disagreement, and he had once sprained the neck of a typist in his office when he was prime minister, backhanding her for granting a member of the opposition access to his files, and at a nightspot in Queenstown he had slapped a French tourist when she ridiculed his sexual advances. The stories about Kingsley were abundant—Mitchell's favorite was the one that purported that during Kingsley's first campaign for prime minister, he swallowed gold coins and then shit them out in front of cheering crowds of peasant supporters. Some of the tales were the apocrypha of his enemies, others Mitchell never doubted to be true.

The minister was silent, he had paused for reflection, drawing with his water glass in the ring of condensation that had dripped onto the table. He looked bedazed, his eyes filmy with the uninvested, measureless drift of a deteriorating mind. The upper-class citizens of Queenstown, the old merchant and banking families, liked to say that Kingsley was tainted, he had Carib blood in him from his mother's side, manifest in his rounded hook of nose, the pendulous lobes of his ears, the lateral cheekbones like bands of armor below his eyes. Kingsley rolled phlegm in his throat but remained with his head bowed. Mitchell had never met a politician of high rank before coming to St. Catherine so he had no idea what to expect. Anything but this. The Shakespearean illusions, the pose of madness and threat unraveling in chilling circumlocution. He felt the urge to applaud. It was all incredible. The innate scandal of leadership. Mitchell was on the edge of his chair, seduced.

Kingsley began to massage his forehead with his meaty, veal-colored fingers, and when he took his hand away, his eyes were once again clear and alert, absolving, condemning, ordaining. Small lenses of moisture percolated to the surface of his shiny brow. The white floss of hair that circled his pate had uncombed itself. He sighed grimly. "Let us speak of some private situations, Wilson. Isaac Knowles is my godson, you know?"

Mitchell's lips parted silently and Kingsley registered this reaction. He was a bad friend, guilty—with the advent of Johnnie, Isaac had slipped far from the forefront of his thoughts. And now this—Isaac's symbolic guardian was Kingsley.

"I see you don't know that. Isaac never say, eh? Well, he slow to claim me." Kingsley said he needed to know what his economist and his godchild had been up to. Mitchell didn't understand the question; Kingsley repeated it.

Mitchell was utterly puzzled by the minister's implication that he and Isaac were "up to something." They were friends, they ran into each other regularly. Mitchell was stumped and said so, unable to imagine the basis for Kingsley's concern, its ominous, patriarchal overtone.

"Nothin then?"

Mitchell replied with an inquisitive, baffled smile. "Nothing."

Kingsley sat immobilized, only the muscles of his jaw pulsing. He seem bored now, and he blinked at Mitchell with imperious indifference. "Don't you cause me some trouble, Mistah Wilson," he said. "Watch what you do."

"I don't know what you mean. Really."

"You're an American, nuh? Americans cause trouble."

"Not me." Mitchell stumbled in his response, losing his composure. "I wouldn't know where to begin."

It got worse. Kingsley made Mitchell's blood jump and left him speechless by telling him to send away the woman who had come to visit him, that she was a fugitive, though from what he wouldn't say, that she had the wrong friends, people it would be very unwise for him to be associated with. He was put in the awkward position of defending Johnnie, which he did with feeble conviction, his instincts telling him whatever Kingsley knew about her, and however he knew it, was likely to be right. Still, he resented it, this intrusion into his private affairs, he was a free man, not a bootblack, but it made him feel as if he were spiraling down a hole.

"Somebody's telling you lies, Mr. Minister."

"Everybody's tellin me lies, Mistah Wilson. How sweet they sound." He looked at his wristwatch and sat straight. "But suit yourself, mahn. The girl leavin in twelve days regardless, Immigration tell me." His face contorted in loose ripples of effort as he stood up energetically to take his leave. The lower buttons of his shirt had come unfastened and his stomach ripened outward like an enormous eggplant. Their eyes connected for a moment and he looked at his economist as if Mitchell had conducted himself shrewdly, yet he had no glimmer of what manner of infidelity Kingsley imagined of him. He pressed Mitchell to visit him again, anytime, he enjoyed visitors and their views.

"Ballantyne say you run fast," Kingsley said as an afterthought. "Very fast."

Chapter 12

They took the leeward coastal route south, crossing the Waterloo Range and down onto open but haphazardly cultivated land along the placid littoral, driving right through the middle of Plaissance, a former cocoa plantation, the trees now old and unproductive, a spare harvest of beans spread out on mats to dry along the roadside. Mitchell had been here a month before with two PLDP interviewers. They registered farmers hoeing their fields by hand, clearing bush, farmers coming out of the jungle shouldering gunny sacks of cassava, farmers in trees, farmers in mud, farmers in the rivers washing carrots. They talked with farmers stretched out on rough-hewn palettes roofed with banana leaves, sleeping off their midday meal, farmers in their wattle huts, the more industrious in their board or block houses. There were no landlords and many of the tenants couldn't afford the token annual rent exacted by the government. What do you grow? they asked them. How much do you grow? How much do you sell? Do you keep livestock? Do you need help, do you share the harvest, do you do it all by yourself? Can you feed your family? Do you have work elsewhere? Where? they asked, to a man. Hope flickered. With lowered heads and timid voices the farmers would answer the interviewers, Mitchell uncertain if it were possible they were ashamed of themselves, their meager livelihood, or if they were only shy, introverting themselves as a defense, because these men who were asking the questions were the government, and it was the law to answer. But in between questions they directed themselves at Mitchell, imploring him with bleary chestnut eyes.

On the outskirts of the town of Peru, Ballantyne ignored a police checkpoint, downshifting but not stopping, acknowledging the uniformed trio with a cavalier wave of his hand.

"They know you around here," Mitchell remarked, but Ballantyne ignored this, too. Farther down the road, he swung out into the oncoming lane to pass a convoy of three trucks, of the type used to transport livestock, open-topped, the bed enclosed with high slatted walls, only these were filled with people, peasants, about a hundred packed into the back of each truck with their belongings, flour sacks of clothing, kerosene lamps, garden tools, wedding photographs, cook pots. They looked as if they were being detained. They looked like refugees. Mitchell asked Ballantyne who they were. The forest ranger craned his neck to inspect them as they went by.

"Dem from Plaissance, I believe. Bein moved off to Windward."

"They don't seem happy about it, do they?"

"I doan believe so. Dis business gettin out of hand, bwoy."

It disturbed him, it made him discouraged, the land program was meant to be an occasion of opportunity and celebration, but now it seemed increasingly infected by cross-purposes, souring by the day. Where that put him he couldn't yet see but he had a contribution to make here, nobody could refute that.

Ballantyne took a left at the intersection in the center of Peru, then turned again onto a dirt lane that brought them to a concrete house, painted pink and shaded by a grove of avocado pears. They would only be a minute, Ballantyne said, tooting the horn and parking. A man trotted out of the house, in shorts scissored off from a pair of workpants, and a soiled undershirt. The shape of his face was a bit pushed in and he had frantic eyes, but he greeted them with a wave of cheerfulness and embracing hospitality, insisting they come inside, they would talk inside the house, they would have a little drink, Mitchell too, this was an honor.

In the main room—Mitchell could hardly call it a living room—they sat on upturned banana packing crates, low to the floor around a primitive table. The shutters had been thrown open to receive the listless breeze left behind by the rain; a green parrot preened itself on one of the windowsills. It seemed the man had cut down some timber and wanted Ballantyne to purchase it; Ballantyne, on the other hand, was trying to harden his bargaining position by explaining to the man he had cut the wood illegally, since he couldn't produce a permit, and Ballantyne had seen the wood, it was on government land, it wasn't even top quality, it wasn't worth the trouble to him and so on. They negotiated, firing away at each other in patois so deep and quick Mitchell could barely understand it, let alone develop an interest in the topic, and his thoughts wandered off in a direction of their own. He had to track down Isaac for an insight into Kingsley's reprimand, bizarre paranoid nonsense, if that's what it was. And yet the minister's stage managing and duplicity had no peculiar effect on him, now that he thought about it, except for giving him a vaguely imperiled sense that he had been discovered, he was no more an outsider, invisible, untouchable. The situation wasn't bad though, it was just screwy, and there was no compelling reason to walk away.

Johnnie, however, was another story altogether. He was being haunted by Johnnie, and it horrified him that Kingsley and God knows who else had found her worthy of their attentions. Apparently she was a Telex celebrity, had found her way onto lists. The escalating nightmare of the drug business, the old college crowd being withered by more serious players, would be the context for such notoriety. She had tacked a map of South America to her wall. She had the wrong friends, according to Kingsley, which didn't bode well for her independence, but he wasn't going to ask her, she would have to tell him. Or not. He dared himself to turn off the lights, deny her haven. He talked to himself, conjuring up the circumstances under which he had fallen for Johnnie: *Could you run that back in slow motion; I must have overlooked what was there, just plain missed it.* The phrase *in love* needled him. He grounded there as if it were a shoal surrounding a harbor where he planned to anchor. Lean hard enough on those words and they swung open like a trapdoor. You were evicted from one country and fated to dwell in another where everything you once knew would be useless, where all the sensory images a lover collected—the way her fingers lodged in the hair on the back of your head, the smell of her wardrobe, her makeup arrayed on the bathroom counter, the flavor of her mouth, the sounds she made when she cried or when she came, her look when she disagreed with an opinion, the luxurious or scatterbrained way she dressed herself in the morning—where all the echoing intensity of emotions and the arcane catalogue of memory with its obscure dates and locations and fragmented events never aggregated into an answer you could rely on, except in desperation, a last-ditch act of faith. In love perhaps was another way to describe being lost, without the impulse to remember where you came from. He excised the words from his vocabulary until further notice and received in return the scene he wanted, the one that begged review:

Nighttime; a school parking lot; in the near distance, the dome of artificial light over the football field, the off-key halftime sounds of the marching band oompahed into the frosty air. Johnnie's red Volkswagen, the door open, the radio on loud. Johnnie, wearing a Villager blouse, a white sweater tied over her hips, a Scottish tartan wraparound skirt fastened with a large gold safety pin. Black stockings that made a girl's legs transcend flesh and blood and become art, a dangerous incitement. She held a bottle of white wine to her mouth like a crystal trumpet, and she danced by herself, waltzing steps meant for the late September moon, a white eyelash caught on the screen of heaven. That was it, scant evidence for all that followed. A sentimental snapshot of the wholesome past, encoded with painful contests of will and future abdications from reality. He watched her, holding his breath, riveted by her boldness, her unilateral claim on the night, the thrilling aura of confidence that surrounded her which he mistook for self-knowledge, he watched her until she sat back down in her car, singing, and then he backed off into the shadows and retraced his steps back to the much diminished glory of the game, knowing enough not to disturb her, not yet, not until he could match the tenor of her optimism, the autonomy with which she guided herself into the world. One way or the other, he had been watching her ever since, mesmerized. He couldn't stop watching her; it wasn't possible.

The head of the household prodded his guests to join him in a drink. On an enameled tray he brought out a pitty of strong rum and three teacups, the porcelain stained and crackled like the mesh in the skin of a snake. He quartered a lime with his pocketknife and poured out an extreme dose into each of the cups, emptying his own down his gullet to set a manly example of style. Mitchell sipped the homemade rum tasting of jet fuel, looking over the rim of the cup at the man who monitored his progress with unabashed scrutiny. There was a devious air to the farmer's hospitality that made Mitchell uneasy and he frowned back at him, thinking, What is it that *you* want? Ballantyne took a refill, as content as a plant being watered, disregarding Mitchell's restlessness. Without his help, the two black men finished off the pitty and a second one was brought from the kitchen by a chubby hippo-faced teenage girl, her skull bound with a red bandanna, her teeth oversized and square as dice. The backs of her shoes were crushed down by her heels and she did not pick up her feet when she walked. Her dress, a brown polyester shift, was unzipped in the back, her bra visible across the darkness of her flesh like a plaster bandage.

This is my daughter—*Dis me dottah*—the farmer declared, after she had slogged back to the kitchen. His pride in her was distorted by his anxious, lopsided grin. Ballantyne grunted indifferently. Mitchell put his cup to his mouth. The man divvied the second pint of rum.

"Priscilla," he said, naming the girl for them.

"Yes, Poppi," she answered from back within the house, thinking she was being called.

"Blasted gy-url," the farmer said to himself out loud, then shouted back for her to hush. Mitchell was shocked to see the man signaling him with sly winks. He thrust out his lower lip and jerked his chin toward the kitchen doorway. "Want to mek a baby wit she?" he asked in a conspiratorial voice.

Ballantyne sniggered and Mitchell chuckled too. With an awkward smile he gulped what remained of his moonshine and set the cup on the table. It took so little to get fucked up on a hot day, you were already halfway along the second you stepped into it.

"Yes," the father of the girl continued with unyielding enthusiasm. "Mek a baby wit she." Priscilla came to stand on the threshold of the room, her eyes downcast, her hands straight at her sides. Mitchell couldn't believe he was giving her a second look. Thoroughly unable to perceive her sexuality he turned away, mortified. He looked at Ballantyne, hunched over and bug-eyed, ready to die laughing. "No thanks," Mitchell blurted out. "Really." His cheeks felt feverish from the blood rising into them.

"A baby," the farmer persisted. He gestured with his head for Mitchell to turn around to inspect the scene behind him at the end of a short hallway. A door opened to a bed with rumpled white sheeting, a wrought-iron headboard with two graceful arches dovetailing at the center, like a boldline drawing of buttocks. A beam of sharp light cut the mattress in half. Mitchell was struck by the absence of pillows. He looked back at the eager, expectant farmer, his face expanded with a lurid grin, and allowed his repugnance to show, though that was the extent of his failure of etiquette.

"I'm sorry," he said. "I have to get back to the ministry. She seems like a perfectly lovely girl."

Ballantyne smothered his laughter. Mitchell, incredulous, listened to the girl's father's jovial reassurances. "It ain goin tek a full day to give she de medicine, bwoy. You jus mek it. We tek charge of de after-wahds."

The man's sincerity was so outlandish Mitchell panicked. He stood up suddenly and made for the door, getting knifed by sunshine as he hopped down into the dirt yard and marched to the Rover and sprawled across the seat. Jesus! he thought. Unwillingly he pictured himself screwing the girl zombie on the sagging mattress, mommi and poppi standing by, murmuring approval. The notion came to him again that he was some current brand of freak centurion of an over-rated empire, wandering into these out-of-the-way villages to be her-alded as the arbiter of freedom.

"She clean, mahn," he heard the man propose loudly from inside the house, a final attempt to negotiate a profit that was beyond Mitchell's ability to calculate. Was there anyone in the world for whom the girl could offer a soul, a heart, be anything more than meat, subhuman. The images of intercourse with the girl made Mitchell feel blasphemous, then indignant. He toyed with the truth that the man inside the house didn't deserve to live. Ballantyne stuck his head in the window, snorting, and Mitchell sat up to let him in.

"Fuck you," Mitchell snapped. "Go ahead and laugh. You probably get a commission."

Ballantyne was so amused that tears rolled from his eyes and he thumped the steering wheel with his fist.

"Why didn't he ask you to fuck her? Tell me I'm a bigot, I don't give a shit."

Ballantyne finally controlled himself enough to say you wouldn't catch him poking his thing into such a homely cow of a girl. As Ballantyne fit the key into the ignition, Mitchell noticed the man come out on his stoop, holding his jaw, blood running from his mouth through his fingers as he stood watching them drive away.

"What happened to him?"

"He decide to sell."

"You have a daughter, don't you?"

"Two. He give a very good price, you know."

They rode back to Queenstown in a silence made steamy by the aftermath of heavy rains.

Walking from the Rover to the stairs up to the main floor of the min-istry, Mitchell noticed the veterinarian's assistant Morrison lurking in the mouth of the cave that was the supply room which doubled as his office and decided to stop in. Morrison was incapable of concealing his hostility and Mitchell realized he found the vet assistant's displays bracing, cathartic, mildly addictive, and he naturally assumed that his own skeptical attitudes made them comrades in subversion. He had nicknamed Morrison The Prophet.

"What's up, Morrison?" asked Mitchell as they gripped each other's hands.

"Mahn, I ain goin vaccinate no more sheeps. Dey does piss all over me pants and shoes. A fella cy-ahn only tek so much piss before he move on. Wilson, you hear de big news?" He drew his finger across his throat from ear to ear. "Dey unload Samuels dis mornin."

"I heard. What do you think it means?"

"It means Kingsley is next, mahn. Banks goin string him up." Morrison had a gleam in his eyes that Mitchell described to himself as the end of charity.

"I don't know," Mitchell worried. "This crusade might be a little hasty, at least in its method of enforcement." He mentioned the trucks he had seen on the road north of Peru, ferrying off the peasants who had settled on the common lands of Plaissance to a relocation site that as far as Mitchell knew was unspecified, and likely unprepared.

"Banks ain move dem people. Look to Kingsley, Wilson."

"Why would Kingsley do that? He's the one hollering they should stay put." Morrison glared at him and scoffed. "You tell me, mahn. You tell me. What you is doin anyway, lickin Kingsley's arse?"

"Me!" Mitchell protested.

"Puppetshow," said Morrison, and made himself busy.

Mitchell went upstairs, wanting to hide out in his office and ruminate on Kingsley and his latest chicanery. But his office wasn't isolated from the world, everyone from old women hucksters to muddy farmers in from the countryside, town drunks and curious children, once even a black-bellied sheep, had materialized at his door, and as he walked down the hall he knew someone was in there now, waiting for him, telegraphing his presence by slapping out a syncopated rhythm on the surface of his desk. At first he didn't recognize the kid, but then he looked closer and identified him as one of Isaac's younger brothers. Without a word he sprung to his feet and handed Mitchell a note, folded carefully into quarters. Mitchell opened it.

>Dear Mr. Wilson—
>We are missing Isaac. He has not come back.
>Signed, Mrs. Clara Knowles.

"Where does she think he is?" he asked the boy.

"Me no know."

He told the boy to tell his mother not to worry, he'd find Isaac—either in bed with a woman or in a bar with a bottle, taking consolation for his loss of *Miss Defy*—and encourage him to check in at home. "Cool," said the boy, full of high nervous energy, and left.

Mitchell put his briefcase down, closed the door, removed his bookpack from his shoulders, and changed into the fresh oxford shirt he always carried in it for times when he'd return to the ministry, drenched in sweat from being out in the field. On his desk was another note, this one from Johnnie, telling him she had come into town to have lunch with him but no one knew where he was. Next to it was a mimeographed memorandum signed by the deputy minister, announcing Hudson's appointment as CAO. Mitchell crumpled both and pitched them into the wastebasket.

He went to the window and watched the cars, beat-up minis and dusty sedans, entering and leaving the compound. The late afternoon sun faded all the bright tropical colors, emptied streets, made the Friday tailings of commerce and labor ugly. All the myriad annoyances of island life that only yesterday seemed so inclined toward comedy today produced in him a latent rage of incapacitation. Without success Mitchell tried telephoning Tillman at Rosehill, to learn if he knew of Isaac's whereabouts. Twice the phone was picked up at the other end by people who seemed part of a practical joke. His third attempt was even more farcical. Somehow the operator connected him with Radio 805. It was the daily "Bob Marley Hour," call in your dedication. He could hear the music and its pile-driving thump in the background. The deejay asked if Mitchell wanted to request a tune. A cleansing breeze puffed through the window; the papers on his desk vibrated and floated and then landed. To prevent documents from blowing around, there were small round beach stones throughout the ministry, as though they had been issued by General Services.

"No thanks," said Mitchell. "I think I'm getting the Marley thing all mixed up."

He asked the switchboard to try to put him through again, weighing down his papers with the stones as he waited. The phone rang. A lorry hammered along the street below the open windows, its load of cement bags bouncing up a gray dust that wafted through the leaves of a colossal ficus tree. Somewhere in the whitewashed recesses of the building a secretary tapped in indecisive spurts on a manual typewriter. At the other end of the line, Tillman answered the phone.

"Hey, buddy," he said jauntily. "We're bachelors again." Adrian, Johnnie, and Big Sally had talked their way aboard one of the charter planes and were down on Cotton Island. Saconi was having a party.

They discussed Isaac's disappearance and Tillman, speculating on the various possibilities, confirmed Mitchell's own sense of what had happened to their friend, and his mind was eased.

"Did you know that Kingsley is Isaac's godfather?"

"No kidding?" said Tillman, but he wasn't surprised. "These are all one people, one family here. That's the problem. Hurt one and you hurt them all, but you can only help them out one person at a time."

"I'm not ready to believe that."

"Yet."

Chapter 13

Gleaming puddles, clean black windows into nowhere, lay in a sheet of patches across the uneven stones of the floor—if they gave him no water, is that what he must do, lap them up like a dog; now it has come to this: *dogness?*—and it was from within the puddles that the depth and cold smell of silence seemed to emanate. High up on one of the walls, out of reach, was the joke of a bare light bulb, its topside crusted with filth, its socket combed with mud dauber's nests, and higher still a white lance of daylight shot through a hole no larger than a loaf of bread where the rock wall intersected with the mossy bricks of the vaulting. The casement was splattered with bat lime, the wall covered with a long beard of it, almost to the floor. Up there was ground level, where the world began. He knew exactly where he was—in *the hands of the Allambys*, that family of moneylenders and debt collectors who had spread throughout the islands in the nineteenth century and were the source of the popular expression which meant to be in a hole with nobody to throw you a rope, to be in a bad way without the chance for a reprieve. *In the hands of the Allambys*, which meant don't fret yourself with being saved because nobody listening.

The under-the-earth air, its uncirculated sadness, was not unfamiliar to him; was, even, reminiscent of childhood games, crawling into dark spaces and beneath floorboards and under porches, hiding from his brothers, escaping punishment, which ultimately could not be escaped but only deferred, and bwoy he take some good whippings in his day, but here the odors of concealment were institutionally poisoned with carbolic acid and lye, and it was frightening for a space this size, which could sleep a dozen men, all lying on their own pallets, to be without people, to be without enterprise, and to be without noise except for the batbirds and rats and ghost lizards and such.

It was a room unlike any Isaac had ever known or entered, and that fact alone was worthy of fear, opening upon a side of his life he had never bothered to imagine.

Loneliness.

Like himself a plot of rich green thriving guinea grass, and the loneliness a hungry herd of goats grazing him bare, mouthful by mouthful.

He had used a tin bucket before, and worse, but this one was a nastiness, with its dry turd like a moldy egg of shit at the bottom.

Still, it was not terrible to be here, as if he were packed away into the eroded recess of the roots of a mighty tree that sat perched on a channel of silence, and time flattened into a cool riffling peace, eddying into a harbor that would accept only the shallowest draft of thought, by the bargeload. There was no misunderstanding—he was here, forgotten in a rockstone dungeon cell above the careenage in old Fort Gregory because duplicity and swindle were something big men did to little men without thinking too much and perhaps even without malice, as though they were unable to step around it, as though it were how things got done. He had anticipated it, almost, climbing into Archibol's car, and now here he was with a bung-up ear and mashed rib and the dogness that was an empty belly, and it was harsh but not so unpredictable, and no longer ridiculous once the heavy wooden door closed and locked behind him and the fellows on the other side, the one who delivered him here, said, *Here now, that was nobody,* and the fellow already here, the one who received him, said, *Eh-eh, true, true, since him end up no place,* and they receded like duppies, and that was how long ago?

He spit. Niggerbwoys in uniform. Mahn, what is *that* nonsense. And the worst of the lot was Selwyn Walker, he in his khaki shortpants and half-sleeve blouse, the patent leather shoes with their gray film of dust, the drab knee socks with limp tassels, the kneecaps of his skinny legs like chocolate biscuits, his bootoo swaggerstick tapping his calf. That was schoolboy puppetshow in truth. In his office there were no windows so you could say he lock himself up too in a fashion. There was a plastic couch, and a chair with arms and cloth cushions. In one corner, where an umbrella stand might be, was a rock carving so large it must have taken a gang of men to fetch it up. The petroglyph's design was of a headdress, or a rising sun, or a ceremonial axe, a handle leading to a half circle of blade. Isaac had seen that sort of thing plenty out in the bush, along the rivers, and it never failed to spook him. There was a bigshot desk and a bank of radio equipment stacked like crates on a table; a metal supply cabinet and a glass-enclosed bookcase. Shit on the wall, paper certificate and such. A row of perfectly polished hardback shoes on the floor near an empty water cooler, hot plate with an enameled teakettle, clump of soggy bags on a dish like old Kotex. If this how bigshot lookin these days, Isaac had told himself, I ain impressed. Walker wanted them to sit on the couch. They took opposite ends. Walker removed his officer's cap and crossed his tantieman legs and began this same line of bullshittyness about Isaac's father. I knew Crissy well, you know, he said. He was a hero of independence, St. Catherine's own son. All the bigshots knew his father, all said the same thing from the same page of bullshit, he was this and that and would be PM today if he weren't such a jackass fool as to listen to them and finish up the only man killed stonedead in the Sugar War. But there were no songs about Crissy Knowles, even Saconi had missed that boat, no plaques in commemoration, no fucking liberator on horseback statue courtesy of that shitass Archibol, no Crissy Knowles Memorial Park, no scholarship fund, no schools bearing his name. He was the hero whom everybody wanted to go away, stay buried in his poorman's grave.

"He would have made prime minister, you know," Walker said, petting the hat in his lap like a house cat. "He gone too soon fah St. Kate but not so soon he miss seeing how things turnin out, nuh?"

Selwyn on parade to kiss a deadman's arse! Like father like son, that was the point he was steering toward, and Isaac couldn't help himself, he let loose with mouthyness, and said No, sah! I ain dead as yet but you can kiss me ass too if you gettin into the habit, bwoy.

End of talky-talk.

Without stirring, he sat on the edge of the metal webbing that served as a cot, the frame anchored into the stones, sitting long enough for his mind to empty and refill with the pure solace of remembering, vents opening and closing throughout the tunnel of time that was his past. He ached for a taste of scotch whiskey, to be sharing a tall golden bottle of it with his boyhood friends in the villages that formed like carbuncles on Jack Dawes Estate, to be with those simple people again, earth-nurtured people, not lord-it-over-everybody cityfolk, laughing and scuffling and crawling around the bush like berrypaint Indians. His childhood home had smelled of saltfish and gardenias and Limacol, and when they left all they took with them was the white rose his father had planted in front of the old mud-walled house the day he married his mother, and now she kept it in an oil drum filled with Jack Dawes dirt in the rear yard. He resolved then and there to flee the city, go country, back to the land, and be . . . be like what? he wondered, and heard the answer in his head, like Rasta John Baptist wandering the wilderness in animal skin and monkey-free, eating fruit and root. The reality of being cast down into gloomy purgatory returned, the feel like a molten corkscrew being tugged and twisted through his gut, and he thought, I ain care for this shitass country anymore, I ain care if them all die-up. In his bone weariness, he rocked back and forth, in and out of sleep, sideslipping down like a leaf into unconsciousness and then bursting out, seconds later, into a fragmented appreciation of his predicament. Calling up the old men under the *bwa homme* tree—the heroes of the bedtime stories his mother once told him—because only the domino players could help him face this tribulation, for they were—he had made them into—a tribunal of absolution, for even a stop-short-educated country-come-to-town boy such as himself knew that the dead were no more than the dark hidden half of the same journey to which the living were also committed, and these men, the ancestors of his imagination, held no grudges though it was true, yes, it was true that they were fallen men, defeated men, men who never had a cockroach chance against a life-time of rascality and foul play, and when his mother's voice mother-preached tolerance and generosity, he was baffled, he would not claim these things as his, and it was then that the domino players were born into voices of their own, all except justdead Crissy, who hadn't ripened yet to these empathies and was part of no community of for-giveness. All this to occupy Isaac's interpenetrating undercurrents of thought, half asleep, half awake, and increasingly miserable on both sides of the divide. Like-father-like-son was his great temptation. He felt oppressed by the merchants of forgiveness who were powerless to help him, the least able to right a wrong, because more than any-thing else in his life, now that he had to stop to think about it, he needed to be contradicted in the pain that was his alone. If he had less of an imagination he would not have a sober day to his credit, or if he had lost control of it he might have waged a futile, centerless war against any target in striking distance. Who or what would be ineligi-ble, he could not say, not comprehending the nature of the desire to forgive. What act of forgiveness was not diluted by the endless range of cause and effect through which it traveled? Who was to blame for the sediments of misfortune that composed the history of a place like St. Catherine, or a man like Crissy Knowles? God? Was God the one who must be forgiven? Wasn't that itself an unforgivable act, to behold God as an object of forgiveness? No man could afford God's scrutiny by being so brazen. Things bad enough—don't tempt God. But if God is a sinning God, who confess God, eh?

177

Oh ho. God. The outside father, the never-home father. I ain going waste my breath.

He lapsed into an arduous counting that seemed destined never to resolve itself. *Miss Defy* was gone—okay, so it is so. He liked cars but most of all he liked the rituals that were the small private pleasures of possession, so it was these he counted. He counted the favorite tee shirts and jerseys that had become the rags with which he bathed *Miss Defy* over the last three years—the two-stripe one, the baseball one, the play mas one—counted the countless times he had wiggled on his backside in the dirt to lie underneath her and view the filthy beauty of her manifold and pans and hoses, counted the times he had driven up the well-paved east Edison Banks side of the island to jook country girls in the rear seat, counted the spidery wirings he had improvised in *Miss Defy's* electrics. When he finished counting the number of times it was absolutely mandatory to honk the horn on any given day when you drove from Front Street to Cyril Abbott Square, he counted a day's worth of errands and stops and hellos, run-insides and pass-bys and pull-overs and go-arounds and drop-offs—all of which he was being denied like a banker denied his deals, car or no car, and then forlornly he counted the forms of employment he now had little choice but to beg for, mantling himself in subservient manners—Mistah Honeychurch, you does have work fah an honest bwoy?—humping bananas, watching cow, rowing boat, carrying sack, sweeping floor, digging hole, painting board, fixing engine, breaking rock, pounding nail, chopping tree, making road, pulling root, emptying can and such but oh ho, you can't cut Crissy's cane, hear? And now Isaac in a whirlwind dream of hurried counting made an inventory of the things he loved the most but took for granted, these were the everythings that were the songs running through his heart, in and out of the vents through which mortality flowed—eh-eh—picking bush tea with his mum, talking to women on the phone, smell of baby powder on a girl's bubbies, the noise and flood of a river after heavy rains, the ale of his grandmother's breath when she kissed him good night, the streets of Scuffletown first thing in the morning, the music of calypso and all that jump-up craziness; the sight of the old-woman higgler Miss Elizabeth being rowed home at twilight across the harbor in a pirogue, standing straightback in the stern like a proud schoolgirl, buttermilk and sugar finches and the smell of pussy and land-crab stew, old-timers dancing the quadrille dance to the music of jawbone and washtub, the ivory palaces of thunderheads and the glass-blue of the sea, that is a good good thing; and jokes, such as he and Juney Gonsalves sneaking into the funeral parlor where them had laid out Old Fire and Brimstone, the Jack Dawes preacher who had been hell on all we boys and girls, and he held open the lid of Old Fire's coffinbox while Juney taped the center picture of a *Playboy* magazine to the inside so preacher have a naked white gal in his face for all eternity; and a hot hot cup of salty cocoa tea; and this word *camphor,* the way it was said: *cyam-pha,* which is the big soft noise of a ship's engine starting up below deck, and them British and stateside paperbooks with the good news of kookooma science, blood pudding and souse and roti dripping grease, bwoy, and wind-shaped trees high on the cliffs, the ocean scaled of its burning light, and the beauty of a strongback horse wading in pink seawater at sunrise; all the pretty pretty faces of the girls, and the sweet anticipation of seeing their dark eyes overtaken by the pleasuredream (and what is this the papers does say, that if a fella misses sex fah one month, sperm go to his head???), and the Friday night lorries headed out of town with all the happy people going home sweet home, and *m'pé, m'sen,* my father, truth is a process which is infinite, and love is a hole you drop into, it is a grave. And Isaac climbed an echoing ladder of footsteps to an aureole of consciousness, rolling his eyes open like a crocodile's to see that his life had seemed to rush backward within the song, as the lives of those who are dying are said to do, and he stopped, terrified, feeling the presence of truth in his blood, with time so endless we are all lost forever in its chambers, and his eyes rolled open like a crocodile's only a second before he was brought roughly to his feet, and he was taken in escort across the courtyard and dragged down a flight of slippery wet steps, which he counted one by one and then began again, counting one by one while his body was stripped bare and his head crudely shaven and then in a circle of yellow light he learned that he was incapable of answering questions in such a way as to save himself from dogness—but tell me what is all this royal pop-pycock ratshit fuss they making about the guy Wilson?—and when the two men who held him and the two men who beat him had finished, his testicles were like churchbell clappers, and the men under the *bwa homme* tree had converged on the pitiable novelty of Isaac's doghood, commenting on how well it suited him, his friend-of-man attitude toward the world, trying to lift his spirits by baying in solidarity while Isaac bayed the lead, marveling at the ease of canine speech in his throat, how well it expressed the vital particulars, a language of liver and lungs and glands, until finally he lay down on the floor, urinated blood with great relief, and pulled an invisible blanket over his head.

Part II

In a poor isle and all of us ourselves
When no man was his own.

WILLIAM SHAKESPEARE, *THE TEMPEST*

The St. Catherine Crier

April 7, 1977

Low & Behold
by Epictetus

Eppy: Well, gents, the grandkids had a puzzler for me since last we met in our seminar of the streets. It seems the schoolmarm entered some confusion into their heads.

Sir Cease-All: I understand that's the modern method, imported in the barrel of independence from the world's great centers of learning.

Beau of the Bawl: What, we still import stupidness to St. Catherine?! But we oversupplied as is with the home-grown variety, man.

Joe Pittance: Not being as educated as you fellers, I can still say Old Rod and Master Cane never failed to explain a lesson clearly.

Eppy: Here's the nut, now see if you can crack it. The innocents went off to form believing they were sound Catherinians, and after a day at their desks, returned in doubt of their common identity. One child was Spanish, one French, one African, one English, one Portugee, one savage Indian and the like. What shall you make of that?

Beau: What history herself has made of it: a d—m scramble. Since we have proved unable to make history, history tried to make us—but couldn't even make up she own mind, eh?

Sir C: Such a hee-haw this man makes. We share a Queen with the great Commonwealth and have been lucky in that regard for as long as anyone here can recall. We're as English as Aunt Nellie's knickers—that's the end of it, sirs.

Joe: With all due respect, Your Honor, God issues souls and nations issue passports. The skin you're dressed in was not issued by Her Majesty's Government. We are Africans first, all else second.

Beau: Heh-heh, that's a good one, boy. All these fellers screaming black power yet when was the last time one of them purchased airfare to the dark continent. You couldn't pay a feller from around here to go back across the water, yet he will teef to make passage to London, Toronto, or Brooklyn.

Joe: What is sweet in our natures carries over from Guinee. What is sour comes from pretending to be what we are not.

Eppy: Rein you horses, gents. You've done a fine job of enacting the puzzle, and I thank you. But is there no one answer we can agree to on the question: Who are we people of St. Catherine's? Can history tell us? As you well know, the Admiral of Castille discovered our fair island upon his third voyage in the year 1498 and named it Conception, to honor the Immaculate birth.

Beau: Family Planning looking to rechristen her Contraception, eh-eh, to chastise our national pastime, immaculate or otherwise.

Sir C: I protest your play with morals not with words. Blasphemous play to boot.

Beau: I mistook you for English, not Roman.

Sir C: As my parents believed so do I, and the better for it.

Joe: And so do I though I suspect none of you will hear of my old folks' country ways. But "discover" is not a fair word, for the island had a name before Columbus saw it—Haroon—and a population that we could say "discovered" Spaniards.

Eppy: I see we cannot quickly direct history to our goal, so back we go to our question. Think, now, so that I may straighten out the kids. Who are we Catherinians? Beau?

Beau: We are perpetual knockers on the doors of houses other than our own.

Sir C: Each to his own opinion even if it serves no one. We are a modern nation, sirs, newly born but nevertheless free and on the road to maturity, aligned with a greater power for greater benefit and security. We are, as they say up north, a melting pot.

Beau: Melted pot is what you mean.

Joe: In my simple judgment, until we are at peace with ourselves we are only abandoned oxen, some mooing at coattails of those who have left us to our own devices, some bulling around as if they would replace their former keepers in the drawing room, but most only lost and unable to reconcile the injustice of their position.

Sir C: Negative, negative. You have practiced a speech, Joe.

Beau: The barnyard ain't need a keeper for a cock to rightfully rule.

Eppy: I suppose the rightful question is not who we are but who we are becoming. By the way, why is it that the streets have been turned into dance halls, playgrounds, sports arenas, and the like by young idlers and their corner gangs? Now the latest fad is flying kites in the middle of the road, joining in with the karate practice and stooping and gambling. The Police are seemingly unable to do anything about it, especially against the use of the foulest language accompanying such vice. Let's be positive about our image and clean up the streets. And speaking of sport, congrats to our boys for taking the third Test against India on Sunday past, winning convincingly by six wickets. Until next week then, *Clarior E Tenebris.*

Chapter 14

Start on Cotton Island, where nothing of consequence to the world ever started, where even by the primitive standards of the sleepy island, twenty-two years ago, before the airstrip was built and the atoll became a fashionable place for wealthy Europeans, the birth of Cassius Collymore came to be known for its unwarranted crudeness, the baby expelled into a windrow of sea trash on the beach sand down from the old wooden dock near the anchorage, a place where the air is never fresh but a pungency of creosote and tar, iodine and rotting marine life. Born collectively, as it were, to an island sect of the Pentecostal church—The Church of Christ of the Crossroads— at the pitch of the moment most sought by the celebrants, in Creole known as the *crisis de loa*, when Jesus and his court of lesser gods mount their human horses and express themselves.

Only, the night of the birth of Cassius Collymore, they chose to express themselves in the language of impossible love, manifested in blood, pain, and excrement—the brawny, lust-ridden Erzulie Mary, Lady of Sorrows, the Black Venus, demanding that the child forfeit the flesh and spirit of the mother, so that the goddess might inhabit them herself. Into the fetal ear, Erzulie Mary is said to have ordered, "Go down into the world and leave these waters." A mother has the right to intervene on behalf of her child, to prevent the unhealable wound of being supplanted, but Miss Diedra was fourteen years old, a simple god-struck girl, favored by Erzulie Mary for her promiscuity, the abandon with which she had given herself to the fisherman Collymore, and could make no other choice than to seek the unattainable perfection of all her passion.

Foolish girl, her stepmother clucked, seeing Miss Diedra dress in her smock and turban, wash her face with holy water: stay home in bed with your jerking belly. Her smock was a white whale, its immensity foreshadowing the labor that seemed to begin with a deep puckering contraction that faded seconds later, leaving behind a sense that the folded, circling emptiness between her legs was loosening, just as her bowels would slacken involuntarily when she was ill. Those hard lips, so loyal to their secrets, were swelling and opening and losing their ability to harness whatever ecstasy was farther up inside her, shoving out. Still, she wrapped her small head in white binding and sat in the kitchen of her stepmother's house, her skinny legs open like a compass, her adolescent body crushed by the boulder of the pregnancy Collymore had thrown on her, and waited to be collected for Sunday evening service, always held on the beach under the stars. In a mirror, Miss Diedra had practiced being a lover, making her eyes try to be Erzulie Mary's eyes, eyes that could cry red tears; making her mouth try to be Erzulie Mary's mouth, a mouth that could jealously accept a penis half a yard long, a mouth that could eat dreams and express pleasure beyond human capacity. Now she made her lover's face unknowingly, and sang: *Where are you, beautiful woman? Oh, come to me. Here you are in the water. If you need me, come to me. Come—*

Before she could even say why she was up out of her chair and waddling like a frightened goose, down the back stoop to the outhouse, the water pooling for a moment inside her heavy panties before it bathed her legs. With shaking hands, she took a match from a can on the wall and lit a candle, illuminating the shed of foul darkness, its palm crucifix and faded chromolithograph of the Madonna and child nailed to the door. She sat over the rough hole and removed her underwear, left them on the floor, sponged her aching thighs with paper as she dripped into the latrine, terrified but blessed with an affirming ignorance which made her as thoughtless and accepting as an animal. She closed her eyes and experienced the impulse to lie down on her back on the floor of the outhouse. *Erzulie Mary,* she sang in her mind, *you bring me joy.* Then she gasped as the baby stabbed her, and she thought of it rapturously, its weight and restless movement undammed, on the verge of cascading down the sluice of her cunt, as the god of the sea launching his boat. *Where are you, beautiful woman? Here you are in the water.*

Voices called to her from the shell-white road that ran past her stepmother's house to town and the beach. She stood, tottering so that it seemed she was thrown at the moldy image of the Madonna, which she gave a feverish kiss, already half given to the spirit herself.

The hem of the long smock descended like a bell of light around her legs. She blew out the candle and let herself be carried in Erzulie Mary's arms up to the road.

The congregation moved forward like a tribe of ghosts, the women floating and faceless, white clouds blowing seaward, the men chopped in half, wearing dark pants but white long-sleeved shirts, their heads invisible except for the bobbing crowns of their felt hats. At the beach the priest took his walking stick and drew the *vévés* of all the gods in the sand, beginning with the cross and the fish, the symbols of the Christian lords. He sacrificed a chicken, singing *Our fathers who art in heaven,* so that the gods would find nourishment when they arrived. He sprinkled the sand where they would dance with the chicken's blood, and then wet the sand again with an offering of bush rum, dribbled from a bottle labeled Château de St. Amour. His assistants began to beat their crude goatskin drums, softly, since those not of their religion considered drumming a backward form of worship. In the rhythmic surf of handclapping, the priest sang the names of the twenty-four apostles of Christ of the Crossroads, twelve white and twelve black, sang the names of the forefathers and wives and divine children, invoked the gods of the hearth, of the forest and of the wind, until the words of his song were far away in the minds of the dancers, muffled and incomprehensible, as the prayer jumped like electricity from one pole of reality to the next, becoming a prayer of flesh, without which the mysteries would not present themselves. In the starlight, an old woman had been watching the girl, her moans and shudders others mistook for piety, and had realized what was happening. "Child, is your time, you muss go home," she said, taking Miss Diedra by the arm as the dancers weaved and interweaved around them. Peering closer at the girl's face, she saw her eyes rolled back, leaking the red tears of Erzulie Mary, her dark lips flecked with foam. Suddenly the girl convulsed. The old woman struggled to hold her up, but she wheeled away, mounted by the goddess, into the dance. There was a great agony in Miss Diedra's dance, not unfamiliar to the others, and they swirled together like white storks in the darkness, the black water of the harbor lapping their bare feet. Down to the earth the girl—though she was no longer merely a girl, but a servitor of the angel that was dancing in her head—summoned a surplus of grace and, one by one, the other women became flames of the Holy Spirit, flames and doves, tongues of flame and wings of doves. Amid the ululation of their praise, her cry was most piercing, her gift most convincing, but she did not know how to respond to the extravagant demands of Erzulie Mary, and as the child battled with the angel for its sanctuary, Miss Diedra realized she wasn't prepared to offer such absolute fidelity to such an insatiable spirit. The celebrants flew around her, a whirlwind of shining, flaming birds, while she heaved and screamed, unnoticed except for her exquisite fervor.

"She serves the Virgin Mary," a man sobbed in a guttural voice. And from another, "She dances with the hand of God!"

Startled by the brutality of her dance, the priest rushed to catch her as she seemed to collapse; he was afraid, because now he too, like the old woman, knew the nature of the girl's dance, which was unprecedented in his experience, and he feared for the safety of that part of her that he called, in the old language, *petit bon ange,* and because he understood that you could not always know where the powers of evil reside. In his arms, the girl shrank back upon her heels, squatting and shitting, and with a wail as high and unbroken as a steaming teakettle, released one spirit from her womb, and went limp at the entrance of a dominating, intractable other. As tiny as Miss Diedra was, the priest could not support the massive bulk of Erzulie Mary, and let the girl fall back in the sand. At her feet squirmed a glistening shape, in a sandy puddle of blood and feces and seaweed, a baby swaddled in cord and placenta, steam rising from its heat. The celebrants fluttered between the higher and lower worlds and were slow to stop their dance, being more inclined to elevate the girl and her miracle back into it. *Madonna Madonna,* some of the women chanted, among them Emma Quashie, who believed that Miss Diedra had indeed been transformed into a vision of the Holy Mother, and when she stooped to the child and picked him up, and bathed him in seawater until he screamed from the salt on his new flesh, she acted in response to this vision, to the ancient savage glory of the epiphany, the gods' signature on hapless human creation, and not because her heart went out to the infant though she was a mother herself, with a nursling at home. She found a bird's nest of nylon fishing line in the windrow of soggy turtle grass, plucked its ends from the ball and tied off the child's umbilicus, pulling the second knot tight enough to sever the cord. The celebrants formed a white wall of faith around Miss Diedra, who lay dazed in the sand, exhausted by the unimaginable violence of the spirit named for love. Below her waist, the fabric of her smock filled with the black clots of her hemorrhage. Without a word to the others, Emma Quashie slipped the blouse of her dress over her meaty shoulders, put the baby to her nipple and took him home. Miss Diedra was now nothing more than a dead person who seemed, incidentally, to be alive.

The men carried the unconscious girl back to her stepmother's, and eased her into her narrow bed. The women undressed and washed her, thickening the shadows with prayer. As if she were an icon or the prostrate statue of a martyr, they stole kisses from the girl's waxen forehead. The oldest midwife on the island was summoned, a hag like a burnt, elfin wraith who had delivered hundreds of babies without ever losing a mother. She placed a poultice between the girl's legs, wedging it into her torn vagina, then crossed the legs tightly shut, right over left, and bound them together at the knees and ankles with strips of bedsheet. Finally, the priest came from the front room, where he had been swilling bush rum while the girl's stepmother argued out loud with herself for the benefit of all in earshot, that the girl was no good, that she had warned the girl to have nothing to do with men, that her dead husband would have beaten his daughter and locked her in her room if he were alive, to save her from turning into the green whore she had become; that this was a good house, until the girl had corrupted it with sin. The preacher knelt at Miss Diedra's bedside, tormented by his own devotion to the Black Venus, and begged Erzulie Mary to dismount the girl, but the saint mocked the priest by exchanging the suffering in the girl's face for a look of sensual beauty, moving the girl's right hand so that it clutched the nut of her left breast, and pulling the other hand down to plant its fingers in the wool of her pubic hair. The next day, a doctor arrived from St. Catherine on the afternoon ferry, carrying his soupy bags of plasma in an ice chest, but the transfusions only funneled life back into the girl's veins, not health or liberty, and she remained an angel trapped on earth, the living temple of the Lady of Sorrows, Erzulie Mary, bedridden in the house of her stepmother for five years, speaking infrequently and then only in the language of unutterable obscenity that composed the benedictions of her mistress. In due time, the priest of the Church of Christ of the Crossroads built a shrine in the girl's room, and fornicated with the goddess on Tuesdays and Thursdays, her chosen days, and with the stepmother, when she would have him. The baby, being nothing, was neither remembered nor forgotten, as if it had come no closer to the lives within the house than a shooting star.

Ten days after the birth of his son, Collymore returned to Cotton Island, his pockets full of money from a week-long expedition aboard a freezer ship, fishing grouper on the Leeward Banks, along the bluewater edge of the shoals. For two days and nights he feted himself in Mama Smallhorne's rum shop and, after sleeping straight through the third, visited the girl Diedra on the fourth to verify the jokes and rumors that he had given the world another mouth to feed, again. One visit was enough, and more. The unwelcoming stepmother wanted to know who he was, and what business brought him to her door. "Mahn's business, eh?" he answered, and stepped around her. The girl herself revolted him, with her deflated body and swimming eyes, her odor of embalmment. She spoke in a rasping, throaty voice but made no sense, though there was not much sense to her to begin with, only a hunger he could clearly see had itself been devoured. Relieved she had no claim on him, he backed out the door, nodding all the while, as if she were telling him not to come back, and he was bravely agreeing to obey her wish. Then, with no regrets, he walked a mile down the road and another ten minutes down a gully path to the Quashie house, to get a look at the baby and get a feel for the extent to which he might be held responsible for its welfare. He filled the doorway of the small frame house on Hammon's Bight where the child had been carried the night of its birth, declining Emma Quashie's chilly invitation to step inside.

"You know I does fish fah me bread and buttah, Emma Quashie."

The baby was wrapped in a clean yellow crib blanket. His open eyes were almost slanted, like Collymore's. Emma held the baby propped in her arms, displaying it like a vendor at the market. "Collymore, what you sayin, mahn? You ain tek you own baby?" The infant had colic; his raw umbilicus, infected, protruded from his gas-inflated stomach like a sausage; he cried throughout the night, throughout the day, and as if on cue, he began crying now, mucus streaming out of his eyes and miniature nostrils. Emma was accustomed to these tribulations of child-rearing, but never had she seen her husband Rupert so short-tempered and disapproving. He didn't like the time she gave to the church—he thought of the group as a cult of religious fanatics, backward-thinking, and told her so, told her to join a proper Baptist church. Told her, the night she came with the baby, "Here now, how you reach home wit pickaninny of a crazy gy-url! Womahn, you would let dog suck you titty." For his benefit, Emma quickly discredited the vision of the epiphany that for a moment had bathed the beach in celestial light, but her superstitions were not easily dismissed. The child had survived a divine confrontation. If power were a Barbados lily, its pollen would have dusted the baby's eternal soul, from his brush against it. If this meant good fortune, she wanted to keep the child at whatever cost, but surely the infant could be cursed with bad luck too. Time would tell her so. Her maternal instinct, however confused and complicitous, made her righteous and bullish. She squared her shoulders, cocked her head at a fierce angle, and raked Collymore with scorn, almost shrieking what she had to say. "Muddah won't come. Stepmuddah won't come. I try to help in crisis but who appreciate it! Now de faddah come and him useless, him shiftless, him assified, him a mahn who pay you back on Nebruary mornin, him a contriver and him just one more chupid nigger-buck wit roostah fah brains!"

Collymore had heard too much of this in his life and had learned to be amused by it, though on the sea each day, he rehearsed his revenge against all who had no time for him, a hardworking fisherman, he obliterated their images and their judgments and their lack of respect. With superior mind power and superior muscle power, he conquered their shadows. This Emma Quashie, he knew her from way-back, another hungry, grab-a-bwoy island girl, before she married the Guyanese cop, and take airs. He knew her when she but a girl hung with rags, her new bubbies sore like bee sting, poking carrot up her pee-pee to joke the boys. She saw how he smiled at her, and smirked back at his arrogance, but now that they recognized themselves in each other again, top to bottom, now that that was clear, Collymore set his mouth and became serious.

"When he pull a line, he cy-ahn come by me, eh?"

"Bwoy, you sit in de hot sun too long. Me ain feedin no pickaninny to send by you when he raise up. Step down from my stoop, Collymore."

"Here now," he bargained, "you ain tek fish fah you pot?"

Emma Quashie wouldn't soften her manner, for fear of seeming pleased with this arrangement. "Send a piece *each time you reach,* nuh?" she said with strict precision. *"Each time."* As if she wanted the buyer to verify the quality of his purchase, she held the baby out in front of her, indifferent to the infant's pathetic bleats, the void of comfort in which he writhed and squirmed. "You wish to hold de child?"

Collymore snorted. "Soon enough," he said, and so the deal was struck.

In those days, the colonial administration still rotated the members of its police force throughout the West Indies, and Rupert Quashie, from British Guiana, had been assigned a year's duty to out-of-the-way Cotton on the principle that outsiders, by nature, would never get in too thick with the locals, who were gaining a reputation as interisland smugglers. But Quashie married a Cotton Islander, and gave her two children, both girls. He savored the tranquility of the breezy island, the illusion of its expanse and the snugness of its insularity, after having known only the slums of Georgetown. So much so that when he was scheduled for promotion and transfer to Antigua, and his hard-headed wife announced she wouldn't live in a country that operated gambling houses—an objection he knew masked her inability to forfeit control over her life—Rupert decided not to argue with her about getting ahead in the world, because now it seemed that getting ahead actually meant going past a good thing. In this small place, his aspirations were not being denied him—he had a family, a house, respect from the community, extra money from being on the take with the contraband runners—and because he had married Emma, and was an outwardly honest and obedient policeman, he was allowed to stay where he was, though his promotion was indefinitely deferred.

Once his anger at his wife's impulsiveness subsided, and the mad fires lit by obeah flickered out within her eyes, he saw the hopelessness of the baby's situation, how grim and unwelcoming his deliverance, and granted the child a home under his roof, and then within his own healthy heart. It was Emma who named the child Cassius, after the priest in her church; it was Emma who nursed and changed him, washed him, then later took him to the markets and every Sunday noon to the one-room church on the hill above town, but it was also Emma who filled his head with a chaotic pantheon of white gods and black ones, of saints that could at any moment turn tyrant, and of an almost-visible underworld about to burst though the doors and windows of the house and fill it with galloping, darting, merciless devils. The river of her fantastic whisperings eroded into the child's consciousness, as it did with his two sisters, and made the Quashie children famous among their playmates for being easily spooked, with imaginations as fertile as volcanic soil. As for his sisters, they treated Cassius no differently than they did one another, with no more meanness, and no less affection, and he loved them without ever thinking about it, and with no notion of what any mirror would try to tell him, that he was not their brother.

As for Rupert, he was all the god that Cassius wanted, there and not there, occupied by the most vital events in Cotton's universe. His unpredictable appearances were profound and joyous, to look up from the yard, or from the kitchen table, or from the bed where he slept with his sisters to see the giant that was his father, to be successfully appraised by this power, the nighttime of his stern face dissolved by the waves of radiance that were his smiles, to see how handsomely he wore his fine uniform, how well he suited the justice of its red, the authority of its navy blues, to touch the high black polish of its leather, the glory of its gold buttons and fastenings; and the most unnerving pleasure, to slide near enough to inhale the oiled metal of an absolute and forbidden marvel, the stone-heavy pistol strapped to its triangle of holster. It was the sight of the gun, and the sight of his father with it hung on his hip, that made the boy Cassius believe that the world had a place for its heroes, which was a conclusion he came to in full innocence, without a child's violent make-believe of the gun shooting or destroying, because Rupert Quashie wished to be a good father and a kind though wide-awake man, and he was. Meanwhile, day after day, Emma matter of factly described a parade of invisible horrors lurking about, indoctrinating the young Cassius to the philosophy of a volatile world, its dangers requiring years to enumerate, wholly vulnerable to catastrophe. It was in this way that she programmed a happy child for the future. And it was only a few months before his fifth birthday that the future showed itself, if only for an afternoon.

Miss Emma was sent word from Cassius' namesake—servant of God, minister of Jesus, priest of Legba and Erzulie—to come bring the boy to Miss Diedra's house, for she was fighting against death and needed their support. Emma was not eager to go, and sent a note in care of the driver of the island transport: *Tell me,* she scrawled, *how we can help keep dead from dying,* and within an hour, received a message she dreaded in reply: *the boy, son of Erzulie M.* She called the child in from the yard where he was batting rocks with a stick and dressed him in the Sunday suit handed down to him from a Quashie cousin. Cassius was runty and the suit baggy, the tip of the necktie tucked into the bunched waist of his pants, the socks hot and the hard shoes like buckets on his feet, but still it thrilled him to be made to look special, the knots combed out of his hair and his cheeks patted with his father's bay rum, his mother fretting over him like she did his sisters.

His mother cussed at his fidgeting, the parakeet-like energy of his excitement, his unanswerable questions. When she took him by the hand, he made sure their fingers interlocked, and together they walked around the harbor road, Emma tugging him onward when he slowed down to inspect a bug, a flower, a lizard, a grazing horse, an interesting piece of garbage, another child of this flake of paradise, until they came to a sandy yard and a path lined with conch shells that led to the place called Miss Diedra's, where sunlight faltered at the threshold as they stepped inside.

Emma's anxiety reared up and the boy sensed it, his grip tightening, sweeping the shuttered dusk of the room with his worried looks. She had only come to this house twice since the night the boy was born, the first soon after to say the baby was well and come fetch it when Miss Diedra was feeling able, the second to pay her respects to the stepmother, dead two years past from a cancer. The hush that surrounded them was the same a sleeper awoke to in the middle of the night, having dreamt of an intruder. *Mommi?* the boy said, and Emma shook his arm to silence him.

"*M'pé,*" she called into the shadowy depths of the house, shamed by the tremolo she heard weaken her voice. Foolish girl to come here, she thought, but twice as foolish to be afraid. "Faddah?" She listened but heard nothing. "Is we who you have summoned."

From the back of the house they heard a man's baritone voice, hoarse and lilting, choked off by coughing before they could understand what he said. The coughing was like strangulation, then it lessened, punctuated by an ellipsis of wet growls, a rolling of phlegm that became an eerie creak of footsteps passing through the floorboards like the noise of rats. The colorless plastic ribbons dividing the front room from the hallway danced apart to frame the priest of the Church of Christ of the Crossroads, a short and once stout man now bloated by the countless bottles of rum of his grief, the sack of his stomach bouncing nakedly between his sleeveless undershirt and the dungaree trousers that sagged from his hips, meant to be buttoned around the waist of the man he once was, not the man he had become in his years of deceitful marriage to a girl—a child—who had lost her mind; not the man who had inherited a wife by divine plan, the way Satan inherited a doomed soul, and not the man who now worshiped far beyond salvation the most profane treasure, the unchallenged ownership of another's flesh.

Driven into the priest's mouth like a wooden peg was the butt of a hand-rolled cigar. It twitched as he chewed and sucked the black juice from it, scrutinizing the woman and the boy with bloodshot eyes sunk into the alcoholic bloat of his face. "It is not I who mek summons," he wheezed. "Not I. I mek no summons." He fixed a menacing stare upon Emma until she bowed her head, nodding agreement, and when he turned and receded back down the darkness of the hallway, she pushed the boy ahead of her, through the strips of plastic that licked across his face like a nightmare of tongues, and they followed the verminous sound of the priest's steps, into the temple of Erzulie Mary. Arrows of feelings were flying at the boy—was this the wolf thing his mother had warned him about? was this the *zobop* thing? the *baka* thing? the hairless thing? the serpent thing? the thing that caught you from behind?—*it seize you unawares*, Emma had threatened—the thing that killed and ate everything? So close now was panic he could hear its lion's roar, and he began to discover ways to hide within himself. But then the door eased open upon magic, and it was beautiful.

A white forest of tapered candles sputtered on the floor, on the dressing table, along the sills of the shuttered windows, lakes of pearly wax overflowed the upturned jar lids in a glacial flood that layered the floor, the furniture, the walls beneath the windows, which elsewhere were painted sky blue, and moved like water in the golden nervous light, tossing a gallery of pictures on its liquid surface—paintings, postcards, bold drawings made with a stick of charcoal, pages torn from magazines—each one of a lady, some in robes and jewels, some without clothes and others with haloes, some on thrones and some with a breast fed into a baby's mouth and some with wings like a pelican. There was a wooden pallet on the floor against one wall where the priest sat on a crumpled blanket, gesturing for the woman and boy to sit in the two rickety chairs at the foot of the bed. The boy covered his mouth and nose with his hand, because the room stank, smelling of sour tobacco and a stomach-turning perfume of rotting gardenias; something worse too—a pungent, fishy stench, not quite as bad as shit, not as searing as a dead animal, but nevertheless a sweetly noxious essence that made his head spin while his eyes dilated in wonder, feasting on the dazzling mysteries of the room.

Roots of tree daht shade de crossroads, deep and numerous, the priest commenced the invocation, bending toward the fruit-crate altar to the side of the pallet. *En bas de l'eau,* in the Creole of the French who had ruled the islands for one hundred years, centuries ago. Two pickle jars were set at opposite ends of the altar, one filled with holy water, the other with crimson flowers. Carefully arranged between the jars was an arc of liquor and wine bottles, each filled to a different volume with a clear or amber liquid, and at the center of these glass pillars stood a foot-high plaster statue of the Virgin Mary, tiny bead necklaces draped around her neck, a small baked-clay lamp of palm oil burning at her feet. To her left, a mound of basil leaves and cinnamon sticks, to her right miniature perfume bottles and pieces of costume jewelry. The priest's chanting grew lower and lower until he only muttered with closed eyes, and then that stopped too. He uncorked one of the bottles on the altar and swigged from it. The odor of strong rum made a greasy pass through the room. He leaned his head over the oil lamp and through tight lips sprayed a mist of alcohol into its flame, creating a small ball of blue fire between his mouth and the altar. Then, with hands that were supernaturally steady, he lifted the crate of the altar straight into the air, not one of its bottles rocking, to reveal a live rooster, its legs bound with twine, lying on its side. Exposed, the bird percolated calmly, as if it had every intention of being reasonable.

"Bwoy, come. Move dis cock aside."

Without a change of tone, the priest repeated himself before the boy, glancing at Emma Quashie for approval, went and dragged the fowl out from under the crate, and remained watching, mesmerized, as the priest set the altar back in place, as cleanly as if the crate and its array of objects were a solid piece, only the liquid in each bottle canting gently. The priest Cassius then took a cloth pouch of cornmeal, and on the floor between his gnarled feet and the boy's shoes, tapped out the yellow powder in the design of a valentine heart, then a second sifting of lines that pierced the heart with a gold-dust sword.

"Stahnd in it," the priest barked, nodding at the paralyzed boy to step within the pinched and pointed shape of the heart. "Stahnd in it," he said, his gruff voice echoing in the room, "Stahnd in it and meet Erzulie," he said a final time, then took the boy by the belt of his pants and dragged him forward. "Sistah, come," he commanded Emma, and as the boy heard the scrape of her chair, her lips spilling a torrent of prayer, heard the man tell her to remove his coat and tie and shirt, felt her fingers picking and tugging at him, felt the fetid heat of the air on his upper body—*Hold him now*—felt his mother's fingernails press painfully into his shoulders, saw the silver serpent of the machete strike and the bird flutter headless in the priest's right hand, disgorging its blood from the hose of its neck, saw the priest sprinkle red drops into the flame of the oil lamp and then felt the sweaty fatness of the priest's hand lock over the insignificance of his own tiny wrist and turn his right palm upward, felt how he was made to cup the sticky life of the chicken in his hand, felt how the priest swabbed the ever-lessening flow up and down his small arm, making its length slick with blood, as he heard and felt these inexplicable acts, it was then the boy became aware of the sinister presence in the bed behind him, heard what he had been too enchanted to notice before now, the faint labor of weary lungs, as if the air was being nibbled and not breathed; a rustling of fabric no more distinct than the velvety flight of a bat, and now—but he wasn't sure if this was a noise he made himself or not—a whimpering, a rhythmic trickle of fear. Then the trickle turned into a cold rain and he began to quiver, telling himself, Don't look! Don't look! as he felt the tears of his mother, hotter than blood, carving down the back of his neck.

"Face me, look aht me!" The priest took the boy's chin and wrenched the tiny head up straight, the child's eyes wide open like a doll's, round and inanimate. "You must reach in and pull Erzulie Mary from you muddah. You must reach in and remove de *loa* from you muddah, or she will die!"

Don't look! he pleaded with himself. The thing that caught you from behind! the red-eyed *baka* thing! the big dog thing!

Emma Quashie was a tree in the wind, swaying above him in a storm. "Oh Gaawd," the wind moaned, "No . . . no. No . . . no."

Lumbering to his feet, the priest crossed to the bed, throwing back the sheets, and prepared the inert body of the girl for the ritual, the purifying rite that had been delivered to him in his cane-sodden dreams. He made Emma Quashie turn the little boy toward his true mother and escort him to the side of the bed, and Emma hummed in a gale force of misery, turning her eyes away from the blasphemous sight of the naked skeletal creature she had known as the girl Miss Diedra, the stick legs banked open and emanating rancidness, but she obeyed the priest in the powerlessness that was ancient and human, to ease the tremors of her own mortality, and held firmly to the shoulders of the unseeing boy while the priest grasped the child's hand, lubricated with the blood of sacrifice, rounding the fingers into a snake's blunt head which he guided up through the narrowing channel of Miss Diedra's thighs until the tips felt the scratch of a strange fluted kiss, and he made the boy lean forward onto the mattress and press, his hand nuzzling deeper and deeper into the yielding lips. The room was a squall of light, teardrops of fire raining upward from the candlespouts, the undersea women of the walls immaculate and secure amid this stormy luminescence; they allowed the boy to run to them, and shielded his face from harm. He pushed into the dry toothless mouth that constricted like the elastic cuff of a pajama sleeve. His hand burst through the ring of throat into the silk center of a warm cloud, not an unpleasant sensation, while the rubber mouth of the cuff inched up his forearm to suck at his elbow. A cat climbed onto the bed to sing with his mother Emma. The child felt sleepy from the bath of clouds where his arm rested, and felt the desire to immerse himself.

"Find Erzulie Mary, bwoy. Pluck she out."

It was when the priest pushed his arm impossibly forward that the boy realized he was being swallowed, and when his fingers brushed against the hard skin of the fetish that had been implanted inside his mother by her wretched lover, he shouted out, and jumped to withdraw his arm but couldn't budge against the weight that held him. The clouds roiled and bucked around the limb of his right arm; Emma Quashie heard the goddess within them speak in a thunderclap—*Cock of Almighty Christ*—and struggled with the priest to make him release the child. *Don't look,* begged the women of the walls, where he had been hiding with them, below the water. But now he was too afraid to stay with them. He ran squealing from this safe place, opened his eyes, and looked upon the first heartstopping assault of the demons that had launched an invasion into his life and there in his hand, when he finally twisted away and his devoured arm was spit back onto his body, the claw thing, black and scaly, its talons wrapped around the blue eye of a marble. The women called him back and he went toward them haltingly, having lost trust in their protection, and he barely noticed the priest douse and wash his arm in white rum, was less and less aware of his mother dressing him, and then he was being lifted up into the embrace of the undersea women and carried home to bed.

"Where is Cassy?" Rupert Quashie asked at supper that night, and his wife told him the boy seemed to have a touch of the influenza. Less than a month had passed when his father stopped home to tell Emma that a house had caught fire early that morning, the house where Miss Diedra and the priest lived, and them burn up.

"I ain surprise," clucked Emma. "I ain surprise." The man so careless with rum and candles.

Chapter 15

At ages five, six, and seven, Cassius went to school with his sisters, and though he wasn't smart, he wasn't dim-witted either. Dutifully, he learned his letters and numbers and was taught to read his primers. With the other boys, he began to reverse the course of the mothering that had circumscribed their lives. He learned to play marbles and kick a soccer ball, lash the air with a cricket bat; learned to push back when he, smaller than the other boys his age, was pushed; to hold his tears inside and to show no public respect for girls, but to obey teachers, parents, and the old people. Roaming with schoolmates in the afternoons and weekends and holidays, he found out how to capture land crabs for his mother's cookpot, and catch iguana, though he hated them, with a stick and wire; how to hit birds and bush cats with a slingshot; how to take a cow to pasture, and bring it back when it wouldn't come, and how, with the other boys, to hold a she-goat by the head and slurp milk from her titties, and how to beg a shilling from the tourists who came on the ferry, and in sailboats, and to crawl and paddle in the shallows of the harbor without stepping on the spines of an urchin; how to steal fruit, how to climb mango trees and shinny up coconut palms; how to race down a hill alongside an old tire, keeping it upright with a flat stick, and how to use a machete properly so you didn't hack off your own fingers. How to jump from rock to rock atop the windward cliffs, how to tell jokes and how to lie, and how to run fast enough past graveyards before the duppies saw you, because he, of all the boys, knew what would happen then. In the midst of the other children, he was an able student of all these things, helping to construct their happiness, and his, and the wonder of that pretty sunswept world, where nothing seemed too much out of place, or wrong. As for the priest and Miss Diedra, they had dissolved into smoke even before they had burned themselves up, so that when he heard his parents speak of the fire that had consumed them, he, the boy Cassius, didn't know who they were talking about, though sometimes late at night would come a whiff of their char, and he would know without knowing, and remember the undersea women.

But for one responsibility that had been given him by his mother, these years of his boyhood would have remained spellbound by precious normality, especially since his mother had given up on the church. Instead, Cassius had cause to learn the meaning of rage, and what it felt like to have an enemy so strong as to be immune from defeat. Rage meant you couldn't stop somebody from making you do what you didn't want, and having an enemy felt like you never knew what bad thing was going to happen next.

While the boy was still small, Collymore sent Emma Quashie's fish up the road with one of her neighbors who had come down to Norman's Cove in the afternoons to buy from the boats. He was an unreliable supplier, though, skipping days, sending trash fish or the first caught, uncleaned, gone dry and soft in the sun or flattened under the bigger, fresher fish. Exasperated, Emma went herself one evening to the spot where Collymore rigged his scales on the limb of a sea grape. He was stooped at the water, yanking the skin from a jumbo-size oldwife.

"Collymore, how you get so clevah to cheat me, eh?" she said, hawking at her feet. "Come, give me daht nice oldwife, or is baby you muss mek room fah, in de boat."

There was no escaping it: fish must pay for the boy, either with Emma Quashie or the next house. And his own mother already keeping two pickaninnies he make, and put she foot down, won't take three. And them babies but fancy-pants girls, sad to say, and each one due a piece of fish. And Quashie have the only boy, and the mother dead. Resigned, he held the oldwife out to her, because he *wanted* that boy.

"When he cy-ahn row a boat," he reminded Emma Quashie, "send him down by me."

This was their agreement but as time passed, Emma thought little of it, considering only that the fish was rightfully hers.

The day she decided that Cassius was old enough to walk the road by himself, she gave him an errand that from then on would be his alone—to go to Norman's Cove when the fishermen came back ashore and collect a piece of fish from the man named Collymore. His instructions were to take nothing less from the fisherman than a *nice piece*, and so he set off over Paley's Hill, wearing a frond basket like a chinaman's hat, eager to serve his mother. In front of the one pointed out to him as Collymore, he stood happily and repeated what he had been told to say: *Me muddah wish fah a nice piece.* No one had to tell Collymore who the boy was—he had Miss Diedra's puniness, her turned-up squash of nose and cocoa coloring, and Collymore's own slanty eyes. The fisherman ignored him, looking over the boy's head to the knot of customers higgling with the catch, and served them all, tucking their money into the pocket of his frayed bathing trunks, until only the boy remained, timid now and puzzled, his basket held out in front of him like a beggar's bowl. Cassius had not been given money; he worried that his mother had made a mistake, that the man knew about it and would be angry. He came and towered straight over the boy. All Cassius could see was the thick rope of the man's penis, tented within the fisherman's damp suit, and he quickly took a step back in the sand.

"Who you, bwoy?" Collymore demanded.

"Cassius Quashie." By now he was sorry he had come to Norman's Cove.

"Lehwe see you money."

The boy wasn't going to talk about money, since he didn't know about it, and he stood his ground, only hoping his mother had not been wrong. Collymore asked him how old he was, but Cassius wasn't going to speak again.

"You is a fuckin peewee, nuh?"

The leering disgust in the man's tone caused the boy to flinch, his face contorted as if he were trying to hold back tears. Collymore strutted over to his boat, raised a sleek machete, and gutted an unusually large parrot fish that he had set aside to sell to Mama Smallhorne for her two-table restaurant. It was a giant fish—a fish as big as the boy himself—and with a mordant grin, he held it horizontal, an extravagant offering, above the boy's basket and let it drop. The sudden weight was a stroke of sleep, deadening Cassius' grip, flicking in and out once through his head. There was the basket in the sand, the fish's big square clown's head and rigid fan of tail overgrowing and crushing the rim, something funny in that but he wasn't about to laugh, and only because he hated the fisherman so much for persecuting him was he able to make himself not cry.

"Tell Miss Quashie here is a nice piece and to hell wit she. Tek it up, peewee. Go, I tell you!"

The boy was being stupid now, staring at the bright turquoise-armored fish as though he were waiting to hear it confirm its own impossible heaviness. He had to leave, to get away from the man

Collymore, who was still there to bully him, yet each time he tried to lift the basket he couldn't find its balance, and the fish plopped out until its slime had a crust of sand stuck to it.

"We is on de tough-up program now, peewee, you and me. Pick it up so, eh?" Before the boy could jump back, Collymore had him by the right hand, forcing it into the slit belly of the fish, sliding it upward across the wet surface of flesh to where the line ended at the finned peak of its throat. The boy's heart pounded madly and he didn't know why, just that his eyes hurt, and he could be made sick touching the fish this way. He tried to run but the fisherman held him fast, helped him raise the fish by the bones below the gills, then took his own hand away, and the fish fell back to the sand. "Pick it up so," said Collymore and then, losing all interest in the boy's dilemma, walked away back to his boat.

It was the first time the boy was seized, complete and head-on, by hatred, and he knew instinctively that you do not provide satisfaction for someone you hate, but do all you can to deny them. Somehow he managed to scoop the fish back into the crumpled basket and drag it like a sled down the beach to where the bush began, and the path went up into it to traverse Paley's Hill, taking him out to the road and then the hamlet out on Hammon's Bight. The sun had just stepped down from the last bank of clouds on the horizon into its perfect form, became a living, tangible object, prepared to die in the water, and the sight of it goaded the boy, because he was terrified of being outside of his own house after dark. It was not fear, however, but his newborn brawny hatred that hauled the parrot fish up Paley's Hill. Encircling the sand-pasted body of the fish with his short arms, he hoisted it against his chest, its bone head gluey, pressing into his face, its leak of pink syrupy fluids soiling his clothes. As he walked and stumbled up the path toward the summit, he could feel the gritty scales shaving his bare arms, the tail fin slapping his knees. Near the top, his foot banged into a rock and he toppled over, his fall cushioned by the fish, although the dorsal fin punctured a line of stigmata through the flesh of his arm. He was used to being a mess, and even liked it, but this was not the kind of dirtiness he could be friends with—the smeared snotty slime on his clothes, the foul stickiness drying on his face, the stinging blood on his hand. He felt unclean as he never had before, out romping in the yards and mud and scrub. He ran back down the path for the basket, smashing it in frustration into the branches of thorn acacia and pigeon pea through which the foot-path tunneled. He lifted the fish again, made the crest of Paley's Hill and started down but now his arms ached so thoroughly he knew he could no longer carry the fish this way, and after the drama of several lunging steps, he threw it down again. Almost in a panic—the shadows looked like closing teeth as the sun went down, below him, out at sea—he hurried back for the basket, then back to the fish, its position marked by hovering gulls. This time, when he tried to raise it, he felt the sear of hot needles along his arms, sprinkling down his legs and the tops of his feet, and saw too late that the fish swarmed with fire ants. The birds told him to leave the fish where it was, for them, and go home. In a fury, he tore a leafy branch from a bush and swept the ants away, then remembering about the gills, threaded the broken end through them and out the fish's beaked mouth so that the branch became a handle and in this way, walking backward in a crouch, he dragged the fish down the harborside slope to the edge of the road, scurried back up the hill for the useless basket, and each step back he found himself deeper in the spreading black fog of night that was his poisoned imagination. A raven had landed on the fish and was pecking out its eye. Before he could chase it off, a cat pounced out of the dark weeds, and then two more, wild, screeching duppy noise. He felt more helpless than ever as he watched them fight among themselves over the mound of the fish, ripping at the cut in its belly, and when he kicked at them they slashed his ankle with their claws. He found a big stick and beat at them mercilessly, blow after blow, for how long he didn't know, until out of the darkness a hand grabbed his arm and he swung the stick to beat at it too but the stick was taken away from him. He was lifted into the air and put on a donkey, and given his basket to hold. The fish was loaded into a pannier, and he was taken home, a man he couldn't see leading the donkey by a rope. "Miss Quashie," the man called out when they were in Cassius' yard, "I find de child along de road, tekkin a dislike to parrot fish. Him flog it so, I say to meself, what bahd baka ting is dis." Cassius was a small boy, six years old, his size held back a year by Miss Diedra. The dead fish had felt as heavy to him as the cross they made Jesus carry, but he carried it anyway, until the baka things came, and fireflies boiled in his vision. When he saw his mother open the door he cried.

Emma Quashie said nothing to soothe the child, other than to go wash himself and hush, because even bunged up and filthy, the parrot fish was a great windfall for her kitchen, a private's wage in the colonial police being nothing to brag about. But, *eh!* what a damn dirty trick Collymore play on the boy, she thought, and at dinner made a point of praising him for his strength, to carry such a cow of a fish over the hill. The boy's face brightened momentarily, but it would take more flattery than she had to give to dispel the stubbornness that had come into him, a companion to the hatred. He had been strong, that was true, but the way it came to him was an unwanted discovery, exhausting and frightening. He ate only the rice and peas on his plate, avoiding the chunks of fish his mother had stewed, though only yesterday they were his favorite. Later that evening, when his father came off duty and entered the children's bedroom to kiss them goodnight, Cassius reached out uncertainly to touch the spot on his father's belt where he wore his holster. He had seen men carry rifles to hunt birds or wild goats, but he wasn't sure for what purpose his father wore a gun, only that it was something of indescribable power, like a bolt of lightning.

"Where de gun, Poppi?" he asked sleepily as his father brushed his lips on his forehead.

"Put away, like you, in its bed."

"What it fah?"

Rupert Quashie chuckled softly. "To save me arse from bahd men."

"Huh?"

One of his sisters poked him to be quiet.

"A fella give me de devil, I muss fire it, ya know."

"Wha happen?"

"Him fall dead, and ain trouble nobody again."

"Poppi," his oldest sister tattled, sitting up in bed, "Cassy want you to fire de gun upon de mahn Collymore." The boy nodded his head shyly, hoping this was not too much to ask.

"What you say, bwoy?" his father said, merry with feigned alarm. "What Collymore do to you?"

Cassius described his ordeal. When he held up his hand to show his father the puncture wounds he had received, his father kissed them, sweetly laughing, pulled the sheet up on the boy and his sisters and petted the tops of their heads, like melons in a market.

"Yes," Rupert comforted the boy. "But you bring de fish anyway, eh?" He loved children but knew Emma was tired out from making her two, and now swallowed clinic pills to thwart his seed. He knew that Collymore sent fish to help feed the boy, but did not think of him as a son, as Rupert did. "You triumph. Collymore muss believe you is special, to give such a faht fish."

Cassius remembered the spite in the fisherman's eyes, how he held the parrot fish above the basket and released it like a brilliant blue bomb, and was not swayed by his father's words. Collymore tried to defeat him, Collymore desired to see him cry. The boy couldn't accept this behavior, except as he knew it in the schoolyard, where boys pushed each other down on the soccer field. But grown-ups ain push you down, he rationalized, but does give you a spank if you misbehave or talk rude. Collymore use the fish to push me down, the child thought, arriving at a startling but logical conclusion. And now he wanted his father to go push Collymore down in return, but his father wouldn't do it. He fell asleep dreaming though that Rupert Quashie went to the beach and pushed Collymore down with his gun. Thus would a boy's dignity be restored, but it did not happen.

He put the grave injustice Collymore had committed out of his thoughts until the following week when, arriving home from school, his mother met him with a new basket and told him, Go fetch a second nice piece when Collymore's boat reach. He dawdled, afraid to say no or resist her or speak his mind. She took notice of his rare procrastination and broke a switch from the croton bush in front of the house.

"No, Momma, no!" He skipped away from her, feeling the quick hot lines of her impatience on his backside, and ran to the edge of the yard. "Momma, lehwe buy a piece from a next boat," he mumbled. His hatred for Collymore swelled and flooded through him, not letting him forget that it was now part of him, and it seemed filled with the presence of creatures larger than the parrot fish, hideous things he refused to look at, and even harder to carry. Worse, this second surge brought a treacherous discovery, since it had the power to make him feel ashamed.

"You ain fret about de mahn Collymore," Emma Quashie reproached him from back in the doorway where she had gone, too lazy to chase the boy. She had spent the past year godless and melancholic, and she felt as if she were waiting to receive a new set of directions—from where, or whom, or what they might say, wasn't the least bit clear to her. Then, she knew, she would have to reevaluate her changeless life. Naively, she thought perhaps God Himself would call her back into the church. She surprised herself by saying something that would prepare the boy for the time that would come, though there was no shape to that time in her mind, and no clock, and she felt bad as soon as she opened her mouth.

"Collymore is relation to you, ya know. Now, shoo, go on."

To his hatred then was grafted the enigma of relation, which he would not stand for, and that same afternoon tried to disprove. At Norman's Cove, waiting forlornly in the queue around Collymore's boat for his fish, the boy looked hard to see an uncle, but there was no motherside or fatherside to the fisherman's ugliness, and he did not recognize the sharp malice and furrowed insecurity of the man's features as a model for his own. As if attracted by the boy's examination, Collymore scowled, his eyes locking with the child's, and he asked what Cassius was doing back so soon, what business did he have in Norman's Cove.

"You is no relation to Quashies!" Cassius blurted out.

"Me? Ha!" Curling his lips to smile, Collymore repeated an old island saying, "Peewee, I is related to you de way Satan related to sin." He lobbed a yellowtail snapper into the boy's basket, and everyone except Cassius, who didn't understand what the fisherman had meant, had a laugh. He felt the truth of it then, hearing the laughter, and understood to the extent that he could tell something hidden lay between the two of them, a bridge in the darkness, felt its connection inside him but could not imagine what it was and did not want it identified. Throughout the year he went to the beach for Emma Quashie's fish, he brooded over the possibility that Collymore had the right to claim some greater authority over him than any other strange adult, and it was this brooding, translated into a child's somber defiance, that Collymore took pleasure in trying to break.

No matter how he ridiculed or taunted Cassius during that year, pinched his bicep hard trying to find the muscle, no matter how he made the boy so mad he wouldn't step out of the rain to stand with Collymore and the other fishermen under the thatched lean-to where they hauled up their boats, still Collymore wanted the boy, and had no intention of letting Emma Quashie keep him, when the time came. Though he would not admit it, Collymore had become lonely on the water and felt the unlocatable itch of solitude. His succession of partners in the past he had not treated fairly, and everyone now knew better than to fish with Collymore. From his first sight of the boy, Collymore determined he was not a born seafarer; he could see it—there was too much churchy, go-dizzy woman in the child; there was no swagger, no love for the makings of a boat, no eye for the handsomeness of fishes. The boy was only stubborn, and oddly sensitive, and to make him a fisherman Collymore would have to make him rough. To get any work out of him he would have to eclipse his attention from the easy, land-people world of the Quashie house, Collymore figured. Too much a made-for-school boy and pray-to-God boy and cling-to-skirt boy, eh? with his mind overworking needless, no-profit things. But until the boy came of age, had grown into the oars, he would be a nuisance, and Collymore didn't want him, had no more use for him than a pet rabbit.

Yet he got the boy anyway, want or not, when disaster struck the Quashie household, two weeks before Christmas, four months before Cassius' eighth birthday. Emma had fed a pork and bean dinner to the children, gathered them in the parlor for a half hour's Bible reading—having swallowed her pride and joined the staid group of Baptists her husband favored—and then sent them to bed, Cassius still in the same room with his sisters but now with a narrow cot of his own. When the house was quiet again, she went to sit in the kitchen, waiting for Rupert to come home, hungry and full of gossip news. Lately he had been assigned to night duty, sleeping in, leaving in the afternoon, returning at eleven—an hour before he was official-ly free, but no one bothered about that. Night shift mostly entailed monitoring the short-wave radio link with St. Catherine, napping, playing cards with whomever came to sit in the free light, drinking a cold beer.

That evening though, around ten o'clock, there was a rare sort of emergency, and Rupert was called upon to respond. The station tele-phone rang, a rarity in itself, since phone service on the island was virtually nonexistent. On the line was Van Jones, a white man, a licensed ship's captain and a well-known smuggler, the descendent of Cotton Island planters who had supplemented police-force wages for generations. Jones was furious, and Rupert Quashie had to hold the receiver in front of him to listen to the tirade, or else have his eardrum damaged. One of Jones' workmen had come breathless to his house on windward, telling of a Carriacou boat, emboldened by the opportunities of the holiday season, unloading cases of contra-band liquor, cigarettes, and transistor radios on the beach at Scuttler Bay. For obvious reasons, Jones demanded that Private Rupert Quashie take action against these trespassers, and Quashie said he would see to it. His plan was to go to Scuttler Bay, fire shots into the air, and go home. That would be the end of the affair, since contra-banding was a stable, well-defined, and coded enterprise, and nobody would do it if they thought they would be shot for their trouble.

But scaring off maverick smugglers from Carriacou was not the simple business Rupert Quashie imagined it would be. Later that night, he was pushed out of his government-owned Land Rover in front of Van Jones' gate, sending the two Alsatian guard dogs into a frenzy. He was alive but beaten unconscious, bleeding from the mouth, nose, and ears, and had been shot at close range in the knee. Emma, who had fallen asleep at the kitchen table, awoke at dawn to a pounding at the door and a man who brought her the inadequate explanation that her husband had been mashed up and taken by speedboat across the channel to the hospital in Queenstown. They brought him back to her six days later, ending one vigil of sleepless prayers and beginning another. His head was wrapped with tape and bandage because his skull had been fractured. What she could see of his face remained puffy from the blows, and his right leg was in a cast, the knee ruined. She fed him from a carton of sedatives and painkillers that arrived with him, not being able to bear the sounds of his misery. There he stayed, alone in the bed of his marriage, enfeebled and listless, neither incoherent nor lucid, neither suffering greatly nor healing quickly, but in any case dormant, lost in the backwater of the violence that had washed over him, day after day. There Emma stayed too, round the clock, in a chair pulled next to the bed, holding the galvanized pan into which he emptied himself, cleaning his withering body with a wet dish towel, even—once—relieving the pressure of his seed with her hand, and all the while petitioning the Lord Jesus with nonstop prayer until, inevitably, she brought Legba and Erzulie Mary and the rest of the ancient spirits back into the house, and with them came the forgotten image of Miss Diedra in ecstatic repose, and Emma's jealousy for the god-favored girl got twisted up with her anger over her husband's tailspin of misfortune. Lack of sleep and lack of hope were making her lose her mind, but out of the stray of her thoughts, a truth formed, bright and bitter and redeeming—she had forsaken the old ways, the oldest the island knew, and Erzulie Mary had placed a curse upon her in revenge. Now, without the priest to advise her, Emma Quashie would have to concentrate on a solution.

Only the children fully witnessed the bewildering progression of her madness. Always temperamental, she now terrorized them with a campaign of scoldings and shrieks and unwarranted spankings whenever she stepped out of the bedroom. Then, it was as if the children no longer existed. She stopped cooking, and for days the boy and his sisters ate stale bread and tamarind jam by the spoonful. The fish Cassius returned home with lay in a plastic basin in the kitchen, spoiled and stinking. She forgot washing too, and simply threw her own underthings out in the yard, where dogs would come and eat them. Often the children would snap awake in the middle of the night to hear her singing hymns in a voice that wavered eerily, and then one Sunday after sundown, they watched her dress in white, tie a white bandanna around her head, and leave the house. Hours later, she was carried back through the door in a faint, and dripping wet, because, guided by the new priest that had finally emerged from within the ranks of the Church of Christ of the Crossroads congregation, she had been mounted by Erzulie Mary, and the goddess had ridden her into the sea, looking for Agwe, god of the water. The men who brought her into the house were sent outside; the women came in to dry her and slip a nightgown over her head. By then Emma was conscious but unspeaking, her eyes still looked ready to pop out, and they took her arms and helped her walk to the children's room, laid her down on Cassius' narrow cot so that the boy found himself sleeping with his sisters one last time, and they hugged each other with desperate affection, counting their mother's snores which seemed to them full of pain and torment. Here in the room with the children was the first Emma had slept straight through the night, other than her noddings and driftings in the chair next to Rupert's bed, since they had returned his wickedly injured body to her. In the morning she awoke to the children standing over her, but she did not move or talk to them or calm their apprehension, until finally they took themselves off to school. The rest did not cure Emma Quashie, but it focused her, and she stayed where she was throughout most of the day, hearing her husband's weak voice call to her for his bedpan and tea. Her mind returned to the beach, the possession which had begun in the usual way with an emptying of herself through the hymns and the rum, the drumming and the dance, the seizing of her thoughts by a purple fire, but then the transformation had assumed an unimaginably violent character. Her spirit self had understood—had collaborated—with what was going on—she was taking the beating and torment her husband had suffered, taking it away from him, taking it upon herself so that he might be free of it. This was the commerce of the gods, the only trade they valued. When she could no longer bear up to the savagery of it—her mouth and eyes shut from the iron-hard blows, her head split open and one leg like a twisted scream—she collapsed—but this was the worst of all—into the bone arms of the dead Miss Diedra, who couldn't support her, and together they were thrashed and tossed into the sea as if by an earthquake. Miss Diedra had a mouth like a dead horse's, with its fire-scarred vise of long teeth, seeking Emma Quashie's ear. Her voice flowed into Emma like a molten cloud: "We is blameless, when we do she mischief." Now that Emma had spent the day staring through an aperture in the world at the vivid image of this revelation, she knew exactly how she must interpret it. Miss Diedra's blood—the blood of her spirit manifested in the blood of her flesh—was a carrier of hardship and woe and damnation, and walked the earth to this day in the vessel of the boy, a new generation of calamity. Miss Diedra had been his first victim; Rupert Quashie his second. This is what she now saw clearly, that the boy was marked by evil, and gathered it as innocently as the flowers he often placed on her pillow in the mornings, and he must leave her house, forever. The children returned from school, cautious and hopeful, and stood quietly at the foot of the bed. Emma had no strength yet, or will, to raise herself and do what must be done. She let them kiss her, made them promise not to be spranksious—*Never trouble trouble till trouble trouble you!*—to go help their father alone in the bed, and to feed themselves, and wash, eh? and pray. When night fell they slipped back into their room, curling like cats on the second bed, careful not to disturb their unconscious mother. Cassius fell asleep dreaming of the *flims*—films, the movies Rupert would parade them to the last Saturday of every month, when the flim man arrived from St. Catherine and set up his sixteen-millimeter projector in the old cotton warehouse, and hung sheets from the rafters, and the white man from windward came with his generator and made electricity—spent a last, foreshortened night in the Quashie house dreaming of the glorious charioteers he had seen in *Ben Hur,* the horses racing and pawing behind his fluttering eyes, and awoke suddenly and in confusion to the dark middle passage of his journey into manhood.

Because it was a school day, when his mother shook him before sunrise and told him to get dressed and come with her, he put on his blue shorts, white shirt, and hard shoes while his sisters observed him with sleepy detachment, not yet awake enough to comment on their mother's inexplicable behavior. Then, without food or tea or extra clothes to prepare him for the life ahead, she pulled him by the hand, out the door and down the road, the boy embarrassed that she was outside in only her thin nightshirt, like a sleepwalker. When she turned off onto the path up Paley's Hill, Cassius knew where she was taking him, but could not begin to imagine why. When he asked— twice; and minutes later a third time—she ignored him. From the top of the hill he could see dawn break its seam far beyond the ghostly silent churn of the waves on the windward reefs, the phantom white walls building and toppling like a movie without sound. The sight somehow made him remember his wonderful dream of Roman heroes, but with this memory came a longing for his father that was so forceful, like a punch, that it took the wind from him—Rupert had gone, he had lost Rupert, his father, the proud and happy man who took his three children to the cluster of houses and stalls that served Cotton Island as a town, every Saturday morning, to buy them ice cream, when it was to be had, or candies when it wasn't. The only disappointment Cassius had felt on these excursions was because his father would not wear his uniform. In fact, only at home, coming and going, had he ever seen his father in uniform, which led all the

Quashie children into the bad habit of bragging to their playmates that their father was a soldier or a general or an officer for the Queen—it was all the same to them. And now the man Cassius had revered, the man who sat with him and his sisters on the benches of the dark warehouse with the crowd of bawling and spellbound children, had been thrown down, and his mother had gone crazy and was taking him to Collymore.

Below in the cove, the lanterns of the fishermen bobbed as they readied their boats for sea. Emma Quashie tugged Cassius down the path to the gloomy sand of the beach. Collymore's boat was half in and half out of the water. The fisherman himself was a black shape just now stepping out of the sea grapes that concealed the decrepit shanty where he lived. On his shoulder, like a gladiator's lance, he toted his boat's mast with its wrap of lines and sail. He couldn't help but see the woman and boy off to the side of his boat, waiting, but he behaved otherwise, stepped the mast in the bow of his catboat without acknowledging them, stowed his fishing gear and began to push off into the shallows.

Before the boy knew what terrible thing was happening, his mother had swept him up and charged knee-deep into the water. He began kicking when she tried to put him in the boat, but she did it, letting him fall onto the middle seat, and there he was, insensible, stupefied.

"Go wit you faddah," she said to him, nearly bellowing, and to Collymore, "Reap what you sow, mahn. He stayin by you now." And then she was gone, whirling away in the lavender shadows of dawn. For the boy, all was movement, unfamiliar and already sickening, and himself locked into the center of it.

Collymore unfurled the sail and let the boat be nudged seaward with the light breeze running off the land. Cassius, facing Paley's Hill, began to shiver, squinting hard to see—but not seeing—his mother mount its slope toward home. The hill itself flattened, revealing the shape of taller hills behind it. Even then he stared miserably at the spot where he hoped to see her, so that he would not look at the fisherman Collymore. But he could see the black petals of scars on his legs, the brute hands clutching the ropes, and that was enough to terrify him. As they passed the headlands of the cove into open water, Collymore spoke to him, gently.

"Peewee, duck you head—we's tackin, nuh?"

Cassius remained immobile, his eyes on the near distance where the land shrank away in the feathers of their wake, as if he had not heard or understood. Collymore brought the boat slowly around, until the patchcloth sail luffed, and the boom tapped, lightly and unheeded, against the boy's shoulder."Drop you head, bwoy. Drop it." Eh, but the damn boy plug up his ears! "Suit youself, toonkins," he said, surprising even himself with this term of endearment, "but ahead lie plenty to-do-ment, so on we go."

Collymore showed no anger, only determination that the boy learn. The boat swung around to its new heading. He had changed course delicately, but a gust whipped the boom smartly across to the opposite beam, slapping the boy hard enough on the side of his head to drop him where he sat, dazed, a welt rising near his temple, his face contorted with betrayal. Why had he been abandoned? He could not understand this—could not! Why was he being taken out on the treacherous ocean—yes, yes, the *Sinbad* thing—by the one person he hated? He could not understand. Why had his mother said this man who caused him so much dread was his father? He could not understand, and he was powerless, no one could help him, and he wished he were dead.

Collymore got no answer when he asked the boy if he were all right. This business going take time, he thought to himself, but here he was in his element, a fisherman, and had no problem with time as such. He unraveled a troll line, put a lure off the stern. They sailed on over the friendly shallows toward the sun, levitating behind the waves on the reef. Cassius felt the warmth of the first ray play on his back but he still shivered uncontrollably, in the position he had been knocked into, head cradled in his arms, his legs dangling awkwardly over the boards of the seat. The tips of his school shoes dipped in and out of the water that collected imperceptibly in the bottom of the boat.

"Breeze sweet dis mornin, peewee. You will come to love a breeze dis sweet." Collymore laughed—he was happy. The boy was small, too young, without experience and afraid—Quashie bring him down unripe, eh?—but Collymore looked forward to teaching him, being the expert, the authority—and sure the boy have capacity, nuh? since them already take him to the schoolhouse. But—*tch!*—him mule-headed.

Halfway across the flats, the troll line sprang so taut the peg in the gunwale it was tied to creaked and hummed with tension. Collymore yoked the steering harness around his legs, clasped the sheetline in the gap between his big toe and the others. Bending over the side, he began to haul in the fish, stiff dripping loops of heavy nylon balling haywire at his feet.

"Flats always bring a nice barra at sunrise, ya know."

The boy heard angry, powerful splashes. Heard the fisherman grunt and curse admiringly.

"Watch youself, peewee. Mistah Barra is a mahd, mahd fellow."

Cassius didn't care. He lived on a small island, ate fish regularly, but never had to bother with a live one. He didn't care about the barra—*why should he!*—or Collymore, or the boat, or his wet shoes. Even the pain in his head and the dizziness in his stomach were things not to care about. *Go* to hell, *go to* hell, *go to hell,* he prayed to himself. *Mahn,* you go to hell.

Then the barracuda, huge and enraged, was in the boat between them, flashing like the blade of a cutlass in the heat of battle. Almost immediately, both the boy's legs were slashed and bleeding and he was somehow up in the bow, holding on to the mast for his life, watching in horror as Collymore crushed the murderous head of the fish with a lead-weighted pipe, and blood sprayed.

"Oh ho, what I say, bwoy? Cy-ahnt be dreamin when barra reach de boat."

Cassius hyperventilated, his nostrils dilated and his eyes bulging. Bright blood was splattered across the chest of his starched white shirt as though it had been shaken out of a mop. His fear made him wild inside, made tongues of flame spin behind his eyes, he felt an incomprehensible impulse to jump out of the boat, dive underwater to find—*what?*—at least to get away from what was now perfectly clear to him, because his father Rupert Quashie had taken him to see *The Adventures of Sinbad the Sailor,* so his nightmares were no different than this moment, and his life was now no different than the film, out here so far from land with Collymore, and the sea ruled by monsters who lived within the night below the surface. He bawled inconsolably. He chattered nonsense. He trembled and clawed the mast as if he meant to scale it.

Collymore pointed the catboat into the wind. After tearing the spoon from the ferocious jaws of the barracuda, shoving the fish under the center seat to protect it from the sun, he stood up and walked the length of the boat, a master of balance. The boy panicked and tried more desperately to shinny up the mast. The delirious noise of a small animal came from his throat.

"You ain no pussy cyaht, peewee," Collymore said with firmness in his voice. He peeled the boy's fingers from the wood and swung him over and down, replacing him on the seat. "You ain no monkey, mast ain monkey tree. Here now, hold steady so I cy-ahn speck how Mistah Barra nasty up dese legs!"

With the calabash bailer, he scooped seawater and washed the boy's cuts. They were many, as if a comb of needles had been dragged across both shins, but only superficially, and there was no cause for concern, at least no cause that Collymore could recognize. The salt-water stung and the boy winced through his tears, not knowing it was saltwater that had woken him up to the world. Although he felt the barracuda inside of him, alive, shredding him to pieces, each minute he drifted farther down into a strange calm, as though he'd been drugged, and a blankness settled across his face, masking his anguish.

Collymore returned aft, trimmed the sail, and the boat speeded ahead. "So now you introduce to Mistah Barra," he chuckled, feeling for the first time a great bond of intimacy with the boy, now that he'd been bloodied. "Dey ain teach you about Mistah Barra in school? What! True negligence! Me Gawd, daht was de ABC of barra, peewee. A-B-C!"

The fisherman brayed laughter, pleased with his joke, and delighted to see the boy had composed himself. A tenderness passed through Collymore like a bird, and he wanted the boy to come to love the sea as he did, because it was beautiful and honest in its indifference, it gave a man the only freedom that tasted pure, and because there was nothing else in life to love. But Cassius—whatever he would have been otherwise without this fate, his soul—was an uprooted seedling.

The sea grew agitated as they approached the lee of the barrier reefs that sheltered Cotton Island from the unchecked force of the Atlantic, the eternal sweep of currents from an Africa submerged far off in their lives. The concussion of surf began to thicken the air; an arcade of fragmented rainbows shifted brilliantly along the spine of collapsed breakers. Coming so near, like this, it was a great spectacle, both exhilarating and of a consummate threat, like stepping aside as a herd of wild horses galloped past, and it left all men speechless—the immeasurable upswelling of the universe of ocean against the fragile coral defense of an island so small that even now, this close, it was no more than a mere smudge on the horizon. Collymore bid the boy to look, for it was a sight as irresistible to the eyes as a city ablaze with flames in the night, but Cassius remained hunched and dull-eyed and removed, far back into himself. Yet when the fisherman piloted the boat through the turbulent cut in the reef and into the high swells beyond, which surrounded them, tossed them high and low like a door perpetually opening and closing upon a boundless field of tow-ering indigo cusps, the change of movement commanded the boy to awareness. He lifted his head and looked fully around, stricken, final-ly looking at Collymore in frozen, silent appeal until, with a roll of

BOB SHACOCHIS

his eyes and a resignation that overcame even horror, he vomited the thin contents of his stomach into his lap. Like an invisible boxer, the jar and rock of the boat pummeled him, even as the puking spasms made it impossible to support himself upright. He tumbled backward, throwing himself yet being thrown, to crawl along the bottom of the boat like a beaten dog and lay propped against the ribs of the bow when he could go no further, moaning and heaving, foamy bile hanging off his chin, then pissing too into his blue schoolboy shorts, knowing that this was the worst—that he was nothing; that nothing could be altered; that nothing could be forgiven.

For a good ways more, Collymore sailed onward to the offshore banks and then anchored. He fished into the middle of the day for red snapper and was lucky. Occasionally he spoke to the boy, but only to hear his own voice; he pitied the child, understanding there was no comfort for him on earth but land itself. Beyond this, he had no other insight into the boy's misery; nor, on his terms, required one. By the time Collymore restepped the mast and hauled his lump of heavy scrap iron from the deep, the boat was carpeted with gold-orange fish, and six inches of bilge water lapped against the boy, soaking him with blood and slime. As they sailed, Collymore bailed with the calabash shell, his arm dipping mechanically and his face serene, and he sang a Jim Reeves ballad popular among the fisherman—

Put your sweet lips a little closer to the phone,
And let's pretend we're together, all alone.

Collymore had never spoken into a telephone, but he knew plenty of women with sweet lips, and the goal of his life was to be alone with them all.

Inside the reef, on calmer waters, the boy gratefully nodded off to sleep, exhausted by his ordeal. He lay mostly on his stomach, hugging the angle of the hull, his underside drenched with filth, a reddish hue to his exposed skin where the sun had cooked him. Collymore steered off his heading to the islet called Palm Cay and sailed the boat aground on the sands of its isolation. He lifted the groggy Cassius in his arms and perched him on the bow and removed his shoes, pouring a pink syrupy bilge out of their interior, stripped the listless boy and lay him mercifully on his back in the clear, tame water where the child bobbed, half submerged, eyes closed like a shipwreck victim. Collymore rinsed out the soiled clothes and spread them on basalt rocks, farther up the tidal slope of the beach, to dry.

"You will find it come easier, peewee," he said as he slapped the first of the fish down on planks of the bow, and opened it with his machete. "Tomorrow and de next time and de next, it will come easy, come nice, and you will say, 'Mahn, here is a life I does like.'" The boy gave no response but only floated, still listless, feeling as hollow and light as a balloon while his clothes dried and Collymore cleaned the catch, throwing guts to the pelicans that suddenly appeared, and he listened, whenever his ears broke out of the water, to the wild, Sinbad wind of their wings.

That night, put to bed on an old car seat in the front room of his father's shanty, Cassius rose with the late moon and ran away, back to the only place his running could take him, home to the Quashies. He was dressed in an oversized white tee shirt, yellowed from wear and containing the sulfuric smell of its owner, that Collymore had given him, so that passing through the bush on Paley's Hill Cassius reproduced the image of his own mother in years past, immaculate in her white smock, leaving her stepmother's house to join the Holy Rollers on the beach. He moved fast along the path, as much in dread of having his liberty aborted by Collymore as of the baka things that were out there too, roaming the darkness with him, and he was out of breath by the time he reached the Quashies' stoop; tears had painted two silvery lunar channels of reflected light down the length of his cheeks.

He threw himself hard against the dutch door, beat it with the heels of his hands and kicked, crying for his mother and father to take him in. The hamlet dogs erupted, formed a pack and dashed into the yard, barking madly, and the boy's own wails were absorbed by this invasion of noise. Only he could hear himself, and what he heard was only another voice in the general blow-up—the weakest, the one that no one heeded—and yet his place in the dogs' chorus made him stronger, as if they had come to be his allies, as if they understood what he wanted, and how to make it happen. From inside, he heard Rupert's weak voice interrupt the darkness: *Emma, wha happen? Cashy outside. Let him in. Emma? Emma?* Footsteps from within, identical to his own heart in sound and rhythm, but they remained clear of the door. Then he could hear the susurration of his mother's whispers, explaining to his father, but he didn't know what she was saying. Emma had in fact experienced misgivings about handing the boy over to his true father, and had not found the courage to mention the act to her husband. Kneeling now at his bedside, in her guilt, she lied and found relief, seeing her husband believe her tale, that Collymore himself had come unexpectedly that morning to reclaim the boy, and she dared not deny the fisherman's right to his own flesh. In the darkness, she sensed her husband's sad acceptance of the act, and when his hand searched out hers in comfort for this loss of their adopted son, she herself was half convinced that her story was true, and nothing could be done to change its consequence; nothing would ever make it different. She resolved, patting Rupert's hand and replacing it on his chest, to let the child bawl himself out and then, with no attention paid him, he would readily find his way back to where he belonged. But, eh! what a scene he make, screaming so, walloping the door, and them dogs like baka brothers to him, joining in.

Meanwhile, the side shutters had burst open, and Cassius raced to them, roaring with hope, his sobbing intensified by the flare of hope through his body. There he stood below the sill, transfixed in anticipation, tongues of flame darting at the edge of his vision as he stared up at the pigtailed heads of his sisters, gazing down at him with interest. "Cashy," the oldest whispered conspiratorially, "*bwoy*, you mek a row! Is you ahll right? What is fishenin like? Did you reach St. Kateside? Mommi does say—" They were sucked back into the darkness, vanished, replaced by his mother's plump forearms, drawing the shutters closed and, with them, his heart. He had not seen her face, and never would again. The dogs seemed to find significance in the latching of the shutters; they grew bold and chased the boy down the road, where the baka things waited, to harry him up Paley's Hill and—but he would not say or think it—home.

Chapter 16

By summer, Rupert Quashie's injuries had healed as well as they would. He asked to be returned to duty; was offered—and accepted—a promotion and minor administrative posting on the island of Montserrat. Two months had passed since Emma had exiled Cassius with only the clothes on his back. Even now, she refused to think of him, and as she packed what she could of her house into cardboard boxes and baskets and a rusty footlocker, when she came across the boy's few things she began to throw them out, and would have, if Rupert had not noticed what she was doing. How the boy get by with no clothes? he wondered, but restrained himself from asking why she hadn't sent them. Since his recovery, she had been high-strung and testy; his transfer seemed to rejuvenate her, and so he was more inclined to let her be, and simply picked the clothes out of the trash pile himself, while she was at a neighbor's, folded them, inserted an envelope and a gift into the center of the stack, and tied the bundle with cord. He knew the boy had been schooled long enough to read and write, so he had written a short note: *Cassius: Here is clothes you leave behind. Miss Emma and I and girls going to Montserrat—2 days. You was a good boy and we miss your many smiles. Love, Rupt. Quashie P.S. Why Collymore not come to collect the clothes? Tell him I say he must treat you right.*

The gift he sent along was his brass-plated police badge. In Montserrat he would say it was lost, and be issued another.

He enlisted one of the girls to deliver the bundle to Norman's Cove where she set it down in the sand in front of Collymore's door and left in a hurry, ravaged by the clouds of mosquitoes that hung in the stifling air. When he returned that evening from the sea, as mindless and unseeing as a zombie, his knuckles scraped and his hands cut and swollen from a day of line-fishing that would have exhausted most grown men, Cassius walked straight past the package and into the shack, to his car seat, and lay down, his flesh throbbing and vibrating, the hallucinatory nature of his fatigue already shifting beyond consciousness, into rapid-fire dreams. By now his school clothes were as odious and torn as slaughterhouse rags, with fish scales permanently affixed to their threads, never completely dry, and starchy with an accumulation of salt and crud. Gone-to-the-devil, Collymore had remarked, not with concern, for he himself was proud to fly the stained flags of a fisherman's rugged life. Still, returning home from his rum shop meal, it satisfied him to find the bundle of clothes at the door. He picked it up and set it inside the front room, and left a bag of blood sausage and bread for the boy's breakfast on the small table, the room's only other furnishing, against the wall.

Not until the weekend did Collymore remember the bundle and tell the boy—he had to be told—to untie it. There were three pairs of pants, three long-sleeved shirts, three undershirts and underpants, and a handkerchief—his rightful inheritance, and no more. He read the letter from Rupert without expression; its message came like a stale breath that had somehow been exhaled from a corpse. The page was undated, but the boy had lost track of the days anyway. As far as he knew, the Quashies had not yet departed Cotton Island, but the implied invitation to come say his good-bye was unintelligible to him: it rang once against the shield of his heart and echoed away into a fog. There was a constant gravity to the boy now that did not allow for human affairs that existed outside the sphere of Collymore.

The badge, however, attracted him, with the same ravenous and inexorable appetite of a fish committed to a lure. Immediately, the badge became an emotional horizon for the boy, reduced to seductive flashes but in proximity, bearing the illusion of attainment. He pinned it to his fresh shirt, the fabric retaining a trace of the garlic smells of his childhood, and wore it continuously, despite the teasing it earned him from the fishermen, and the apt nickname, Private. The weight of the badge became a timepiece, measuring a basic cycle. Only when a shirt became so threadbare it would no longer hold the formidable brass pin would Cassius throw the garment away, and wear another from his scanty wardrobe. As if his own needs were at best equal to the requirements of a piece of metal. It was a primitive's love, a sensation, and nothing more, so completely had he been severed from his past and its symbols, and as a pretty thing that suggested unidentified powers he wore it daily for two years, until he lost it, capsized in the water, on a day when Collymore was reckless enough to flaunt a squall, attempting to outrun it in a catboat overloaded with a bounty of conch. The wind filled the sail like uncontrollable anger. With no freeboard to counterbalance, the leeward rail pressed down, admitting the flood, and the boy bailed furiously. Collymore, exalted by their speed, the bravado of their furrowing wake, refused to release the sheetline until it was too late. A severe gust blasted into them, standing the boat on its beam so that it swallowed enough water to plunge to the bottom, thirty feet below. For hours, Collymore and the boy swam toward shore through a tempest of gale-driven rain, the surface a gyrating hive of transparent liquid bees. The boy dog-paddled with closed eyes and followed the sound of Collymore, not having learned how to swim properly, and since his mouth stayed mostly in the water, he whimpered through his nose, expecting any second to be pulled under and drowned by an inhuman hand wrapping like a thick noose around his ankle. When they finally made the coast, Cassius discovered the badge was gone, and no search would bring it back.

The catboat though was another matter. Cassius spent what was for him a pleasure-filled night of restlessness, imagining the storm had saved him from this slavery he had been cast into. He squirmed on his car seat until morning, trying to see the outline of freedom that had been restored to his life, and was never more dejected than when Collymore marched him to the beach and they set out with two other fishing crews and resurfaced the boat. The salvagers even dove up the sluggish conch. Collymore and the boy returned to shore with it; they cleaned the meat from the shells until midday, and Cassius was given the rare reward of a fair-weather afternoon to himself, to squander as he pleased.

As he pleased!—but this was the anxious, haunted liberty of an amnesiac, a cheerless interlude from the drudgery and torpor of the boat; its eternal Present, expanding without change. He felt embalmed in salt and foreignness, walking the road to town, and soon turned back, preferring to stay near Collymore's shanty, craving nothing as much as his bed. He stared at goats and cattle as if trying to determine the secret of superiority. There had been other days too when Collymore had set him loose, but he spent them no differently, without joy or purpose. Because he had no money, he had no business in town, with its memories of Saturday morning sweets, or the cool magical darkness of the flim shows. Nostalgia was the same for him as starvation, and he could not endure its deep, inner pressures. And he avoided what was, in his mind, the great human commerce and communion of the public dock, because even on an impoverished island where rags and clothes were too often synonymous, his were the most offensive, his body itself was an obscenity of neglect, and he was rebuffed for his crudity and for being the simpleton that the brilliance of the sun out on the water had made of him, framing his thoughts and feelings in a perpetual stupor. Truly, he became accustomed to this state, recognized it as his nature, inescapable, and so was able to provide himself with life's most austere comfort and permitted himself to believe that he deserved his downfall. Most of all, on these miscarried excursions beyond the wilderness of his new world, he could not stand the sight or company of his former schoolmates and their tenacious silence, looking him over, he thought, as if he had become disfigured or deformed. As if they were frightened of him. It was left to him then to bank away his penny allowances of freedom, as if they were given to him in a currency that was not exchangeable, and this is what he did, lingering in the shade of the sea grapes, sitting on a wooden fish box and snapping twigs between his growing fists, smoking cigarette butts he had scavenged off the road, killing mosquitoes and lizards and listening to birds, sitting and waiting beneath the monolithic shadow of his father, a gray soul in a limitless purgatory, waiting for the shadow to be thrown aside, or down.

In the third year of Cassius' servitude, a princess, he heard, came and restored an old plantation house on Cotton Island, a place where she could hide away from the world, and enjoy her holidays. The following year, on the perimeter of her compound, a small but exclusive hotel had opened, inaugurating the island's entry into the age of tourism, and the hotel prided itself on serving its guests enormous lobsters, brought fresh from the sea. To help fill this new and lucrative demand, Collymore had purchased a speargun and skin-diving gear. Though he was in poor shape for diving, and his debaucheries frequently modified his greed, even being bad at spearing crawfish, as he called them, was, for a time, profitable, especially after the ferry service improved, and the restaurant owners from St. Catherine came down to make deals with the fishermen.

One day, before the shallows had been hunted bare, the boy sat in the boat, manning its homemade oars, trailing after Collymore, who was up and down in the water like a seal. On one of his dives, the fisherman poked his head under a ledge of coral, sighting down into a narrow canyon of blue light flurried with motes of plankton, and saw two things that caused him excitement. The first, and first to be dealt with before he could slide deeper under the canopy of the ledge where it cracked and chambered, was an olive-hued conger eel, surely as long as his own leg but with ten times the power in its sleek, flat muscle; and beyond, just the wavering tips visible past the serpentine roll of the eel's body, the antennae of a lobster that he guessed to be as long and round as his thigh. Though he couldn't see the crawfish, back in its hole, Collymore took several blind shots at it, firing beneath the eel, without success. He tried jabbing at the eel with the gun to prompt it out of its sanctuary, but the creature only made threatening feints, brainless and territorial, and Collymore made the unhappy decision that he would have to shoot it. Given such a large and unmoving target, though, he aimed too casually—the shot was poor, not a kill shot—and the eel vanished before his eyes, wedging itself within the rocks, the shaft of the steel spear clanking like the bell of a sunken ship.

Dozens of times, Collymore dove, struggled and ascended, back and forth between the fluid mirror of the surface and the twilight of the coral crevice, without retrieving his gun. Finally, he had the boy hand him the iron-tipped pole he carried in the boat, designed for such occasions as this. Its weight raced him to the ocean floor where he set about splitting and prying apart the coralheads where the eel had receded, fleeing to the surface as his air ran out, then back down again, as Cassius hovered the boat in the current. This was exhausting work—when the eel eventually materialized out of a cloud of pulverized coral, impaled and writhing, a tendon ripped from the flank of a giant, Collymore barely had time to grab the gun; barely the energy to haul this monstrous nuisance to the surface, a greenish smoke of blood trailing from its wound.

Cassius heard the fisherman blow the water from his snorkel. Nothing seemed amiss—Collymore had not even bothered to describe the problem to him, saying only that the spear had gotten jammed in the rocks. The boy hadn't volunteered to anchor off and help. As much as Cassius hated being in the boat, it was nothing compared to the panic he felt being in the water itself, far from shore. He pictured himself drowning, or being eaten—the two most inconceivably desolate and hellish fates that were the flirtations of every sailor and fisherman who ever left land. From this obsession he had only one remedy, a release, one rite of exorcism, however temporary and futile, and he found it in the customary violence of his occupation—the gratification he received from hammering to death a big, bloated fish was immense—and he became his most articulate in the expression of this violence. Each fish became an emissary from the chimeric wilds of his imagination; each blow he delivered to its bony plate of skull was accompanied by a monologue of childish condemnation.

It seemed to him right now that Collymore was resting, catching his breath. If Cassius had suspected otherwise, he would have been prepared and braced, the lead-weighted bludgeon in his hand, for the battle ahead of him. Instead, he was half lost in lassitude, managing a slow-motion tug of the oars to keep the boat near Collymore, who was somewhere close in front of him, off the bow.

"Come! Come! Come!"

Collymore had something for him. The urgency in his voice was not unfamiliar. The boy pulled ahead.

"Kill it! Kill it!"

Without further warning, into the stern of the boat dropped a monster of Sinbad proportions, whirling itself into multiple forms. In the eel's fury, it bent the shaft of the spear shot through its flesh into a right angle against the hull. The boy immediately let go of the oars and stood up in his seat, mortified, breathless, watching the beast smash and toss, strain, all neck, the Sinbad thing, an incarnation of utter virulence, wanting him, wanting at the boy, popping into the air as if it danced on a red-hot griddle. Motion that was pure wickedness, thoughtless and crazy—just to look at it made Cassius feel he was floating. He knew it was going to get him and it did. He knew, because, *"Look—It got me!"* he screamed. Astonishing, how he screamed. *"It got me! It eat me!"*—there it was, a lightning bolt clapped onto his leg. He wasn't even sure what it was, had never seen such a thing, and here it was stuck on his leg, its terrible beaked jaws snapped shut around his shin bone, sinking down into the meat of his calf. He was still a small boy, his youth blistered and festering, but he knew what to say as he grabbed for the pipe and battered it and battered it and battered it, all movement a target, anything a target, holding the pipe in both hands and chopping it down with surprising force, pulping the beast's flesh, his eyes held in shuddering enchantment by the aqueous snake eyes of the eel, and each blow no different than if it had struck himself simultaneously, so said his pain, beating and beating and blood spurting everywhere—*Cunt! You cunt! You muddah cunt! Clot cunt! Cunt hole! Cunt!*

Nothing alive in the world closes with such finality as the jaws of a conger eel. Even after he had clubbed it to death it was part of him, his ball and chain.

Collymore heaved himself into the boat and slapped the boy until his senses returned, prying the club from his mortal grip. He severed the eel from its head, but wasn't strong enough—or cruel enough, *even him*—to unlock the jaws and set the child free.

❖   ❖   ❖

Collymore had long since been fed up with the boy, his weakness and fears, the exaggerated gestures of persecution; the numb, averted eyes, stagnant pools of hostility; his ears that heard nothing—*nothing*—but the distant amorous sighs of land; least of all the ulcerous hate, which wouldn't have been so bad if it provoked the boy, lit a fire beneath his scrawny arse, challenged him, as it had long ago with the parrot fish, made him rise up erect with the vital energies of vengeance—but it didn't: the boy was too slow, buried within himself in an envelope of malaise, to employ even one of the many chastening advantages of hatred. He had no pride in a good day's work, no blood that natural wonder could put a fever into, no home in his heart for stories, not a part in him that Collymore could see that ever warmed up to the world, and this was not what the fisherman had bargained for when he bargained for a son. Collymore's love for the boy blew in and blew out, in their first months together, like a rogue south wind; now he only expected to get whatever labor he could wring out of the boy's body, harden him up for the day when he would not be there in the morning, tucked on the car seat, when he would just wander off and disappear like a wary dog, to fend for himself.

Sometimes when Cassius shut his eyes the sun was brighter than ever; the spell-binding labor of the boat and its intervals of boredom as unrestful as illness. There was no remedy for it, and time slid off its shell unnoticed; no parole except for the unforgettable ache of Sundays with their strange church-echo, mother-echo—the psalm-singing of feral lovemaking from the back room, the radio's melodies a sour harmony, as Collymore jooked the island girls on his mattress pad.

On stormy days Collymore took refuge in Mamma Smallhorne's rumshop and the boy submerged as far as he could take himself into the badness of the weather. At their worst, these days were his only ally, preventing the boat from being launched, sometimes days in a row. On most nights he slept consumed by dreams of fright, something scaring the breath out of him, he didn't know what, dreams as bottomless as the blue water.

Despite his own sense of doom, and the more visceral feeling that Collymore would work him until he was dead, the boy survived, growing into a wiry adolescence. Though he was still and always would be short, with bandy legs (the right one ornamented with a spectacular braid of scar tissue from the eel, like the stitching on a baseball), his leanness concealed the true capacity of his young strength. He had become a tireless spartan worker who never seemed to register ordinary pain or fatigue. He could haul fish twice his weight into the boat with ease, row cheerlessly from dawn to dusk without faltering rhythm. He was morose, and because Collymore both cursed and bragged about him to the other fishermen, he had a contradictory reputation for courage—some swore he had it, some said the boy was the most gutless runt that ever put off from shore in a catboat. No one in the community of Norman's Cove knew him well, no one wanted to, no one saw any benefit to it, and so he remained a constant to all whose lives he drifted past, and especially to Collymore—a vacant, impassive, stony, difficult youth, notable only for his spinelessness. Only a few looked close enough to see in him a silence as fatal as a viper's.

He premeditated nothing. No dreams, no fantasies, visions or revelations showed him a course of action. He was living the Sinbad thing. He just knew. There was nothing he could do to make himself ready for trouble, except to know it was coming.

Came his last summering with Collymore, a day they sailed outside the reef to turtle during the time when the hawksbills and loggerheads and greens completed their solitary migrations to mate in island waters. The breeze was mild, the swells lulling. They appeared to sail forward into an olympian theater or coliseum of sluggish cumuli—to Cassius a basket of smoke; to Collymore, only lazy clouds—spread with an awning of colorless overcast. With the surface so obliquely illuminated, the water was at its richest sapphire, the intimacy of its depths opening upward, magnified, shifting and smeared, then transparent and miragelike. Often they saw birds resting on the slicks, and the seascape itself was a stage-set drama that lacked the energy to gather its elements together and begin.

The first turtle had sounded and Collymore had furled the sail, lowered the mast across the boat's three seats, and ordered the boy to the oars. When his father had first made him do it, years before, Cassius had suffered as an oarsman, fighting the clumsy sticks in their rope locks, but by now he preferred it, the fully occupied mindlessness of the synchronized strokes, the backward-facing position of the rower, the moving ahead without looking ahead, proceeding into a future that required nothing more than infrequent, over-the-shoulder glances. There were calluses on his hands hard enough to stop a thorn. Sometimes he rowed naked, took off his rags and stowed them in a piece of oilcloth until they were coming ashore, but today he wore a pair of tattered swim trunks and a gray-colored shirt, buttonless and with the sleeves removed, like a vest. He stretched, dipped, pulled, released; stretched, dipped, pulled, released and thought about the mongrel bitch that had bellied under Collymore's shanty a month back and given birth to a litter of worms that had now turned into puppies. Yesterday was Sunday, and he had decided to take one of the puppies for a walk. He tied a piece of twine around its neck for a leash. Its legs weren't used to walking. He dragged the puppy around Norman's Cove for an hour and then threw it away, because it was dead, choked by the twine. He rowed on, thinking to himself, *There are one two three four five more puppies. No, six. No, seven. No, five.*

Collymore was on his stomach in the bow, peering into a water-glass, a window into the ocean, trying to spot the turtle which he knew would be suspended below them like a hummingbird as it fed on the reef. *Come in!* he would call to the boy, or *Go out! Slow it! Wait up! Pull!—de boat, de boat, eh? me no say pull you peeny sparrow cock—me say de boat! Pull!*

He located the turtle—turtles! a pair of greens. A slyness tempered his voice at such moments of discovery; Cassius heard it and smirked to himself as he was ordered to rest the oars. It used to be that Collymore hunted turtles with a ring net, as some of the old-timers still did, but Cotton Island had changed over the past five years, and all the able fishermen had grown addicted to the excitement of the gun. Collymore removed his tee shirt, strapped on mask and fins, and eased himself noiselessly over the side so as not to alarm the prey. Cassius handed out the long gun to him; Collymore armed it, stretching its rubber sling to where its metal clasp fit into its notch in the spear shaft. He filled his lungs and dove.

A minute passed. The boy, hearing water clear from Collymore's snorkel, sculled the boat ahead. Glancing sideways, he saw Collymore veer off, roll and gracefully arch like a porpoise, and go down again. Cassius idly repositioned the boat and daydreamed of riding the ferry to St. Catherine, where he imagined it was possible to attend something much like the chariot races in *Ben Hur*; then he dreamed of asking the man he still believed was his real father, Rupert Quashie, if he could have a bicycle. He recited the rote exercises he had learned in school. Naught and one is one. Britain—b-r-i-t-a-i-n. Majesty—m-a-g- *no,* m-a-j— Collymore was back on the surface, his face in the water, a sound like muffled whoops piping from his snorkel, alerting the boy. Cassius rowed, knowing there would be a turtle to load. When the boat was alongside the diver, Collymore handed him the gun; the boy stood up and retrieved its tether until it brought him the butt of the spear. He prepared for resistance, but felt only cold weight, and then he could see that Collymore had done something oafish and ignoble, had shot two turtles at once, and had shot them through the shell, which was considered an amateurish method, and problematic, since the idea was to hit the turtle in one of its fins. Such a shot demanded expert marksmanship but meant the boat took a live turtle. No one would pay money for dead turtles that had ridden in the sun all day, so these were turtles they would have to eat themselves, or give away. Worse, they were small greens, their shells of no value—the male no more than fifteen pounds, the female less. The boy jerked them in over the gunwale, his father giving an unnecessary push from underneath. Collymore slid the mask up to his forehead. He spit out the mouthpiece of the snorkel, his eyes cunning and merry.

"Two fah one," he boasted. "I strike dem while dey was jookin, bwoy." For a moment, he wanted the boy to share his amusement, to applaud his marksmanship. Then he remembered it was an empty cause. The boy had never laughed, smiled, never *appreciated*. If you wanted so little as to hear his mumbly voice, you had to make him speak, prod him to open his mouth. "Who you see as yet get two fah one?" he continued with diminished enthusiasm. "Trevor? Robertson?" He named his two closest rivals in the fishing fleet from Cotton Island, men married to the sea as he was. Uncharacteristically, the boy answered.

"Dem dead up."

Neither in tone nor expression had the boy altered his basic remoteness with this observation, but to Collymore, having starved on the youth's scant responses for six years, having just made what he knew himself to be an infelicitous, shameful kill shot, these three words burned in his ears. The boy would never respect him, never have confidence, never be a worthy companion, never be but an anchor on the few simple glories Collymore labored to raise from the world. He heard *dem dead up* as the first note on a scale of challenges, tantamount to a declaration of forthcoming independence. This meant Cassius had entered into his age of rebellion; the time when they would war against each other for dominance had arrived, sooner than he had reckoned, and this knowledge infuriated Collymore. He reared straight up out of the water to his waist, grabbing the nap of the boy's hair, uncut for more than a year, frizzed and orangish from its bleach of salt, and yanked him flapping into the water.

"Eh, eh," Collymore snarled, replacing Cassius at the oars. "Lehwe see you put two turtle in dis boat, Geronimo."

With the advent of lobstering on the island, Collymore had told the boy he must rotate with him in the water, share the load with his virgin lungs—Here, you ain no garden boy, peewee—but on hearing this news, Cassius had lowered his head, wouldn't go so far as to shake it, and held tight to his seat. Collymore said he would count to five. Cassius closed his eyes and waited, then Collymore had him, was stripping him down to his sad underpants. He fought and twisted and bit like a mongoose, to no avail. Collymore picked him up and flung him overboard and rowed off a hundred feet, watching with spiteful satisfaction, the boy sputtering and treading water and trying not to panic. Cassius had no experience with the mask and snorkel, other than for hurried moments bottom fishing out in blue water when nature itself hurled him overboard, since no matter how much he desired to, he found it impossible to lean backside out over the bucking boat and evacuate his bowels the way his father could. He couldn't do it, ended up shitting on himself and then had to get in anyway. Collymore enjoyed telling him that those deep and wilder waters were dangerous *in truth*, just the place where a mako shark the size of a politician's car might mistake the boy for a duck, swallow him whole, eh? and so the boy donned the mask willingly to keep guard on himself, slide quietly in, spinning in terror, his underpants around his knees, the turds torpedoing out behind him into the blue atmosphere while he stared and stared into the dense infinity of the underworld until his vision blurred with the strain of never sighting anything but the waste of his own solitude.

Throughout the weeks he rotated with Collymore, Cassius brought little to the boat, most of his shots hurried and desperate, thunking into rock, puffing sand into the lobster's insect eyes, and Collymore, disgusted, had rescinded the order and allowed the boy his oars.

He knew how much the boy wanted the mask. He had rowed up current and let the boat drift slowly back to where the boy could hang off. Collymore couldn't see his head, only his fingers curled over the gunwale, the split, chewed nails, and he could hear the boy's teeth chattering. Piece by piece, Collymore dropped the gear over the side, making the boy swim to catch it before it sank.

Reluctantly, Cassius kicked into the current; his shaking arms cradled the gun. His skin constricted from the chill of the water, heightening his awareness of the tension of his own muscles, their taut power. He had never hunted where it was so deep; instinctively, he angled toward the waves on the barrier reef in the distance. Below, a canyon wall dropped off abruptly into blue space, its crown ridged by mushroom clusters of brain coral that in their shape and stillness resembled the weather above the surface. Along the edge of the deepness, Cassius was sure he saw something leviathan; it hovered on the periphery of visibility, threatening to manifest itself, collecting itself particle by particle, but then evaporating with the same dreamlike uncertainty. What was there, what was not there—you never knew until too late. On the ghost-white sand between two stands of staghorn, a school of small sharks swirled like a cloud of gnats. In forty feet of water, out of a thousand shapes of fear, Cassius watched a hawksbill emerge with utmost innocence from a pink sway of soft coral. He had no choice but to inflate his lungs and dive into the clear hissing shadows.

What's there? Cassius chanted to himself, his inner voice as mechanical as the movements of his body. The deepening ticked pain, sharper and sharper, into his ears. What's there? *What's there?* He frog-kicked desperately, down toward a thicket of gleaming antlers, but then his lungs gave out, and he had to return. He clawed through the resistance of the atmosphere, the perilous living blueness that would just as soon keep him, racing his silver bubbles to the surface. Refilling his lungs, he dove a second time.

He was a being who had learned to live with the furtive noiseless stealth of a reef creature, and he felt a strange and inexplicable comfort—something euphoric was happening—this time as he descended, the pressure like a frozen explosion in his skull, and he turned and looked in wonder back at the boat, which had become an insignificant beetle scratching at the surface of a mirror. A nurse shark passed over him like an unmoored blimp. The boy had the distinct impression he was about to meet someone who would welcome his arrival. He coughed giddy laughter into his snorkel, hollow balls of glass. He began to suffocate and then burst through a plane of white anger to the surface. Wherever the turtle was, he had lost sight of it, but he gulped as much air as he could fit into himself and dove again, almost nimble now that his fear had been smothered and extinguished. He felt the spirit of the person or thing pass through him with a pleasure as crushing as if he had ejaculated. Cassius thought, *Sweet!* and was overwhelmed. There was the turtle, directly underneath him.

He ceased kicking and sank. Like a small black angel, he floated downward through the evening-blue realm that had before always been a desolation to him. Now, everything was different. He knew the answer to What's there? *He, Cassius, was there!* He floated alongside the feeding turtle, amazed by its beauty and delicacy, like a breed of angel itself. He thought, *Angel.*

He thought, You're there! *You dere!*

The turtle flared its fins, making itself vertical to face Cassius, its scaled gold neck outstretched in curiosity. The two of them hung in suspended animation as Cassius stared into the turtle's beatific eyes and recognized, there in their lambent gaze, the sheltering acceptance that had at some lost time been a secret source of mercy in the world, his last chance for refuge. They were the eyes of a woman—he almost said her name, but didn't quite know it soundly enough to speak it— and they beckoned to him, filled with the tender honey-glow of amber, as he extended the gun.

They hung in the liquid turquoise air as if they had been painted into its center. Then, from behind the boy, simultaneously surrounding the two of them, a violence splintered the atmosphere of gently refracted light into a whirling current of hundreds, and then thousands, of luminescent pieces, a radiant blizzard that pulsed and swelled like an undersea storm of electricity, light of creation and light of the soul, as the boy and turtle were suddenly absorbed into a large school of bait fish passing over and above and between them at high, convulsive speed. The water seemed to effervesce from their agitation; the boy's own skin tingled with their charge. He leaned forward, straining to see, into this rushing river of light fragments, the cascade of sparks and blades, the intelligence of the whole like a single blast of fire, leaned forward and thus shaped a void in the flow, a perfect seamed resistance, and there, once more, was the turtle, waiting for him, a lover in a grotto.

The pattern of the lights shredded and dispersed. His vision was spotting as he came closer to blacking out. He hurt. Everything hurt. Everything had always hurt like this, when he wasn't careful. He no longer needed to breathe if he didn't want to. That's what the turtle was waiting for, the choice he would make. There was no time left. There was time to speak her name—the name of the woman within the eyes of the beast—but then he got mixed up, and didn't want to. There was one woman, there were many women—???

None of them was his friend.

The spear was aimed at the turtle's fluorescent throat. He pulled the trigger. He saw a bouquet of crystal flowers, blooming upward, up and up, chased and smashed by the ice cobblestones which were his own expiring breath.

Cassius thought: Collymore cy-ahnt grip me hair so. Him have no right.

Collymore took the turtle from the boy and speeded him into the boat. Luck had chosen to run with him today, bwoy—he had sighted a large loggerhead, riding the surface current to the southwest, and had already stepped the mast in order to head off in pursuit. Cassius took his seat, bent over, gasping. Two years ago, Collymore had been jubilant about the boy's unsteady achievements, squandering his praise on ingratitude, like talking to a dy-amn stone bobo; then he began telling what he cared to tell to the seabirds—and then, nothing at all, nothing, never, he had no more to say to encourage the boy. Cassius unscrewed the spear point and withdrew the shaft from the bloody turtle at his feet. The boat sliced into its tack. The boy felt exalted, and spoke unconsciously, his eyes still burned by the incandescence of this, his first kill, the death of an intelligence he had recognized.

"She sit dere and . . . and . . . and let me shoot. I aim like so—*pow!*"

Collymore's eyes were fixed on an invisible point in the distance. He answered out of the side of his mouth, "Eh, so why you not stick him in de fin, nuh?" and the deserved chastisement, so familiar, awoke the boy from his hallucination of happiness and power. But the immobility that had lasted half his life, the glaciation of his spirit, had been ruptured and he could not return to it.

Collymore sprang from his helmsman's seat and, without bothering to furl the sail, deftly lowered the mast, no noise, no effort to his movement. They were in the spot where the loggerhead had last sounded, and now they waited for it to sound again. A dull glare had appeared on the water. Goose bumps rose on the boy's flesh, his arms and legs jittered, but he sat erect and alert, focused on Collymore, and studied his father as if he had never seen him before. The turtle sounded, making its manlike suck for air, thirty feet from the boat; its blunt wedge of head probed nightmarishly through the silvered shine. Cassius thought: *I know dem creature.* Collymore edged over the side and was gone, his shadow fragmenting and then absorbed by the underworld. The bilge was soupy with gore and Cassius bailed with the calabash, letting it trickle out into the sea, which for some reason gave him satisfaction, as though he had discovered a ritual that had been available to him all along. The carnage stained the water, spreading like a cloud of smoke, the blood greenish, the particles of flesh whitening like flakes of ash. He became so preoccupied that Collymore slipped from his mind, so that now he believed he was only imagining his own name being called out in the ocean air, at the brink of the world. Finally, he looked up and acknowledged it, and out on the smoothly rolled aluminum of the swells he saw a violence—frantic convulsive splashing—and though he said to himself, *Cassius is ready, he ready,* he didn't move but stared at the filth swirling around his ankles until his name became the ocean's curse, and then he remembered Collymore, and took his station at the oars.

He pulled obediently in the direction of his father, his muscles not registering the effort, saying to himself, over and over, as if to count the strokes, *Dem magic, I know dem, dem magic. Magic creature. Sinbad creature. Angel. Devil-dog.*

And if saying so made it true, he made it true. There was a harrowing urgency to Collymore's shouting; the watery cries made an electric current flutter up the boy's spine, telegraphing resentment and fear. A weariness too was in Collymore's voice, an unprecedented heavy tone of doubt, as if he were not equal to the struggle. *Good*, Cassius heard himself mutter, but knew he had meant *Bad*. Along the seam of this contradiction, reality divided: he would have to fight, the fight would be terrible, the fight would be heroic. The boat was no more than a few pulls away from the diver. He stowed the oars and let it glide forward, turning himself sideways to look at the Sinbad thing, his eyes glazed. With failing effort, Collymore held the huge sled of shell upright, its top out of the water, the loggerhead's powerful front flippers useless in the air, as long as an osprey's wings but slapping ineffectually, like a drunken man swinging his arms at duppies, unable to run to safety. It looked to Cassius as though Collymore were offering him the turtle, making a gift of this horror trying to swim away into the sky. The head of the animal was the size of a year-old cow's; the boy watched it crane and dip like an imbecile's, its yellowish lizard throat gulping. Now the pair writhed together in a slow, circling dance, Collymore pulled down with it, then bobbing back up, his strength sapped. Cassius could only see his father in pieces, lost behind the barnacled shell, and hear his hoarse, threatening voice.

"Tek up de fin! Now, bwoy! Tek it up, tek it up! If he break away, is you ass to pay!"

He had killed an angel, and its spirit had sent this darkness to swallow him.

"You devil beast," he whispered, and reached out to take hold of its scaly flipper.

Collymore was getting dunked repeatedly, but once the boy had an advantage on the fin, he released the loggerhead and submerged under his own will, grabbing the gun that dangled beneath his feet, attached by a line to the spear that impaled the turtle's backfin. He was safe, now that the turtle couldn't dive. For a moment Collymore was underneath it, could measure its size against the boat—a fourth the length of the hull, at least—the sky blocked out, the uninjured fin raking his shoulder and back. The sudden weight in the boy's hands almost somersaulted him into the water, but he braced his knees against the planks, and hooked his feet onto the ribbing. Then the turtle was going to tear his arms off, and he let go. His father was back aboard, screaming at him, and the turtle was towing the boat through the water like a plodding ox. The gun was braced against the thwart, held in place by Collymore, but he made the boy come put his feet against it, then hung his forearms over the gunwale, vomiting seawater as he tried to catch his breath. Lured by the drama, sharks flew up from below in the deep—Cassius watched their vague streaking shapes forming and unforming beneath the surface, thoughts in a disturbed mind. His father noticed them too but regarded them with disdain. He wanted the turtle boated, now, before the sharks took a greater interest in it—a turtle so big it would be a victory, a legend, back on shore. He began hauling the spearline hand over hand, bringing the loggerhead and its retinue of shadows ever closer to the hull. The harpooned fin emerged. Collymore hollered instructions at the boy, who grabbed the shaft on each side of the fin and pulled. Collymore returned to the water and pushed from below, and they managed to lift the carapace half up on the gunwale, tottering, about to come in, when Cassius lost his strength, the turtle too immense, like a plucked dinosaur bird, and splashed back into the sea. His father swore at him, uncoiled up out of the water to swat at him but missed and plunged away. They tried again but failed, and now the sharks were growing bolder, bumping against Collymore's legs and the boat, so he climbed back in, took the shaft of the spear himself, the bones inside the limb broken now and angled cruelly, and made the boy dip over and grab the forefin, madly kicking, but he could not bring it more than a few inches out of the water before he was stopped by the full stone weight of the colossus. Collymore drove his foot into the boy's hip, to spur him, but the weight was too much for Cassius. He sent the boy to the bow, then, to take the machete and cut two lengths from the anchor line, to use as slings, and two short pieces to lash the left-side fins of the turtle to the boat. Cassius obeyed, but in a wild tantrum, nonsense spilling out of his mouth in a rage. Collymore took the rope from the boy and cleated off the destroyed flipper, made the boy noose the second short piece on its counterpart, dunking into the water past his rib cage, the catboat heeling radically to starboard from the imbalance of weight. Cassius clutched for the fin but it eluded him. Sharks flicked past, everywhere, swooping and turning like buzzards, banging against the turtle to identify it. He was past endurance and blind, but his fingers found the elbow of the fin and sunk into the plastic flesh, the rope somehow cinching itself, then all existence quickened, and to see what was happening, Cassius opened his eyes in time to see a dove fly out of the pale, open beak of the turtle, then came a tug and he was in the water upside down to his hips, and his father had the rope and was raising him up, the turtle's head reared backward on its elastic palm trunk of a neck, the steel-hard mandibles of its jaws clamped on his forearm. His scream exploded like a shattered window into his face. Collymore hauled with all his might and the boy tore his arm away, pouring blood, and flipped back into the boat. Collymore strained and hauled, the mountain of shell rising up over the gunwale, the head stretching outward and away, as if it might disembody itself, the neck extending impossibly far toward an impossible freedom, but even as Collymore saw it and marveled at its resistance, the boy struck with the machete, and the head canted crazily and then collapsed, the neck broken by its own weight, once the muscles had been severed. Astounded, Collymore let loose of the rope with one hand and swatted the boy. The boy swatted back without hesitation, still brandishing the machete, the blade taking Collymore's hand off, right above the wrist that still held the rope. Collymore had sharpened the edge himself so that it would no more than stutter as it passed through green bone, given the proper amount of determination. From his throat came a gobbling sound, which amazed him as much as the loss of his hand. Gushing blood, the turtle swung back down and disappeared underneath the leaden glass of the water, except for the tortured limb still pinned to the rail. The sharks came in like a pack of dogs, ripping apart a rabbit, and the boat bucked and tipped in the storm of their feeding. Collymore lurched to take the machete from the boy's hand, but Cassius chopped him again on the cheek. There were sparkling rainbows of blood. After several lost minutes, not timelessness at all but an exact reckoning of time—*his* time, that had been taken from him—the boy was suddenly aware that Collymore was no longer in the boat, that he was alone, and with inscrutable calm he sat down on the thwart, crossing his arms over his chest, his own blood a silken scarf running into his shorts, his head held high and his wild eyes taking possession of the glorious coliseum of emptiness, the boat jerking and twitching from its center like an exposed nerve. Before sliding the oars into their locks, he held the waterglass over the side and scanned the blue caldron of infinity until he saw the ribboned ball of his father, tossed back and forth between the mad huddle.

"Him have no right," the boy said, and went about rigging the sail of the boat bequeathed him by the victorious shapes of fear.

❖   ❖   ❖

A few scattered lights burned on the ridge of low hills as he arrived in the cove, long after nightfall. It was magic that brought him back, since he hadn't really known the way, knew nothing about navigation that he could say to himself. The boat was impossible to beach without help; he threw out its scrap-iron anchor, took nothing but the Clorox bottle of tepid drinking water, and waded ashore, stepping over the middens of shells in his bare feet without feeling their broken edges. There were no people about, but cattle nuzzled on the spindrift, and they made him nervous, made him hurry along.

There was fire under the gummy icing that blood had formed on his forearm. Inside Collymore's shanty, the darkness pulsed in such a way that he felt an identity within it that was his own. He opened his father's wardrobe and felt around until he found the half-empty jar of bush rum and drank it as he stood, greedily, until it was finished, his first and last taste of the cheap escape that was liquor. Then he swigged the remaining water from the Clorox bottle too, and he would have drunk more, anything that was liquid, but there was nothing left in the house. He wrapped his arm in a filthy towel, stiff with mildew, because he had bumped it, rummaging in the dark in the wardrobe, and he could feel it bleed anew. His head filled with bursting light, splintering, swirling pain. He staggered to the front room and sprawled on his back on the car seat, his feet planted on the floor to fix himself, tormented by the jack spanier sting of a lifetime of curses, the cringing shame of his father's blows, the mongrel's life of debasement in which each day was like their first encounter, and until he lost consciousness, the child that he had been stumbled up the thorny slope of Paley's Hill, hugging the elephantine parrot fish, all the creatures of the sea sinking the bright needles of their teeth into his ankles, and Collymore their master, driving Cassius forward with a staff made from the dried pizzle of a bull. Then, as the drunkenness and fatigue guided him toward oblivion, he was suspended again in the pool of ocean, chalk-blue, the color of the robe of the Lady, maneuvering himself toward the sorrowful eyes to kiss the hawksbill turtle that was transformed—like in the stories of mothers and teachers, like in the church in his days of innocence—to a welcoming angel.

In the lavender silence of dawn, the fishermen came down to the water to discover the oddity of Collymore's boat standing off from the beach, its sail unfurled like a laziness, the hindfin of the loggerhead still lashed to the gunwale, waving toward the men on shore. They hauled in the boat and a boy was sent running to fetch a hook scale from a cattleman up behind the beach. Then they hung the shredded ham of the turtle's leg up and it weighed at 103 pounds, so that they figured the whole animal, before the sharks tore it up, would likely have been over eight hundred. In a group they went to Collymore's shack, impatient for his account of yesterday's adventure, but there the mystery only multiplied. They examined the boy's mangled arm with foreboding, and tried to question him, but he wasn't interested in waking up, and hid his face from them. Someone took mercy on him and walked up the road to flag down the first vehicle to pass, a dump truck carrying rock for the construction of the airstrip, and Cassius was taken to the clinic in town. The doctor came once a week, from St. Catherine's, but this was not his day. There was no novocaine to give the boy either, so while the watchman held him down, a nurse sewed his arm as serenely as a seamstress, ignoring his tears and howls. With no other patients to administer, they let the boy lie on the examining table to recover himself, and in a few minutes his groans had softened into tormented sleep. He was emaciated and filthy, but the nurse did not regard the boy's condition as so unusual for a working boy on Cotton Island. Later in the morning, at the direction of the constable—a Sergeant Marcus—she shook the boy awake. He immediately cried for water, to feed the inhuman thirst that sleeping for seven years had given him, drinking glass after glass and then, with a wave of agony and poison rushing through him, vomited onto the floor. While his poor mess was being mopped up, he broke the abstinence of his emotions and smiled at the policeman, reaching senselessly to pet the starched cloth of the man's uniform. The sergeant indulged this simpleness from the boy, smiling back, and asked what had happened to Collymore, his father.

"Angel tek him," the boy said, which was a proper island euphemism for death, and the boy uttered it without guile. Corporal Marcus had already heard from the fishermen at Norman's Cove, had the details of the grisly shark-eaten carcass of the loggerhead memorized for this three-line report. That was the end of the inquest. The angels had taken another fisherman, which was a prosaic matter, of minor importance, and Collymore's death, as well as the boy himself, were forgotten, except as common mysteries.

As for Cassius, he remembered the last day with his father only for its stillness, its extravagant textured expanse of silence that was the sky, the unending field of slickness that was the water, and he would love this memory of peace.

Before the week was out, he had sold his father's boat and gear for half their value, paid off the debtors that appeared, and arranged to take his supper at Mama Smallhorne's rumshop. Freedom was an enigma to him though, his escape from hell had not led him to any clearly defined place, and once he had taken care of his basic needs, he was at a loss, and for two more weeks he sat in his shanty, stupefied by the pleasures of idleness, until the day Sergeant Marcus came to check on him, and took the boy's welfare into his own hands, bringing him clothes—not new but respectable—and comic books, slices of ginger cake and a wind-up clock, and told Cassius he was a pretty boy, a pretty boy, a pretty boy, until the day, six years later, Selwyn Walker came to the island and rescued him.

Chapter 17

In her kitchen on Ballycieux Lane, Sally stood with the front of her sheer nightgown hiked up and pinned under the pendulous weight of her breasts, spooning yogurt between her legs from a pint container. The sun ascended the fist of mountains to the east. Roosters answered one another throughout the hills of upper Queenstown. A lorry rattled down the road, collecting laborers for the public works division. With babies and radios and idiot cocks and the eversweet arcadian breeze of the morning, there were no late sleepers on Ballycieux Lane. In through the window streamed the meaty aroma of pork cracklings frying in coconut oil, sachets of jasmine and of sewage, the shellfish scent of the city that built its original dwellings at the edge of the tide and then flexed backward, the muscle of civilization, into the higher and wilder land, away from the sea and its whispers of return.

Blended with these smells and what was most apparent to Sally was the strong doughy odor of her fingers. Throughout the night they had clawed unconsciously into the damp folds of her crotch, wanting to rake off the flaming itch that chewed with a hundred hot microscopic teeth. To be a woman in the tropics was to feel you were a most inviting if not cooperative part of the food chain. The bacteria came and went as they pleased, thriving inhabitants nourished in the reef of her sex, resisting the best efforts of the pharmacist and the worst efforts of the medic attending to the biological needs of the multinational cadre of volunteers on the island—a runty, soft-looking but shockingly handsome-faced doctor from Ceylon, a Muslim who lingered boldly during the course of his pelvic examination of Sally, his hand inserted into her, to query in birdsong English about where she was from, did she have plenty boyfriends? how the local fellas size up? did her bladder infection make it painful to do it? could he take her to dinner and dance and so on? Inexplicably, the fool diagnosed crab lice and prescribed Gentian Violet and Sally filed a complaint with the regional office, to no effect. For the yeast infection though, what worked soothing wonders was the female-friendly culture of yogurt, a remedy she learned from the mother of one of her students, one day when the woman noticed Sally absently rubbing the binding of a first-grade primer along the center seam of her jeans.

The yogurt was like the cool tongue of some large arctic animal—a seal, perhaps, or a polar bear, licking the swampy fires. She put the teaspoon and container down on the kitchen counter, humming with relief, and leaned back against the refrigerator, massaging the culture lovingly into her labia, alleviating the stab and ruttish throb. The yogurt drooled down her thighs, splattered on the floor in a pair of thick drops. This squirming, so much like teenage desperation, made her roll her eyes—who was she to complain, with her claim on Saconi and his penis like a great black bassoon. She had never really envied anything about a male's body until she came to this place, and then she yearned for the male's dry exposed outwardness that couldn't be so readily invaded. In contrast, she was an oven, a hothouse for all manner of cultivations. When she danced, when she walked home up the hills in the afternoons, when she made love, when her pants rode up into her, there it was, so much a part of her now, the itch. Or else cystitis swelled her bladder with false pressure, or the flesh under the curve of her breasts chafed with an irritation akin to athlete's foot, when the weather turned humid during the rainy season. Her body paid a daily price for its presence on St. Catherine, if not one way then another, yet something almost magical happened to it too, in the languorous heat, in the ubiquitous fecundity, something extravagant, as if it might be true a woman could be transformed into a luscious, glistening flower in certain latitudes, under the right tendering care. Understandably she wouldn't talk about it, big-boned and broadfaced as she was, but she had never felt more voluptuous in her life.

There evolved a second order of heat, deeper and wider sensations, glowing rings warming by degrees toward another level of therapy altogether, and she hesitated, eyeing the wind-up clock on the kitchen table, then turned her head for an out-of-focus look through the back window, below to the sunny green lushness of a stand of bananas dancing with the wisps from cookfires. The land, its images, were so shockingly licentious—it seemed of a piece, even correct in some vaguely mystical way, to be gazing into it as if it were her lover, as if she were broadcasting her orgasm out into its depth. As if the land had found a home in her, though the real question was, had she found a home in it? She would have gone on, released the tension she had stirred, but someone began to knock at the door on the street side of the house and call—*Miss Sally, Miss Sally . . . Miss Sally*—and she grabbed a sheaf of paper napkins from their grass basket and wiped herself—*Miss Big Sally*—and let the hem of her pink gown fall back below her knees. *Miss Sally.* She washed her hands in the sink, annoyed to be taken away from such dreamy, cozy minutes—*Big Sally*—and God, there was no escape from the world because people in the neighborhood would root on her doorstep calling loudly or just whispering in bashful voices until she responded.

The doors of her bungalow were cut in half, Dutch style, so dogs and children were kept out but the air could come ahead. She unlatched the upper panel and swung it back to its hook on the wall. In the brilliant square of sunlight she recognized Joseph, one of the boys who worked aboard the interisland ferry. The sleeves were torn off the shoulders of his yellow workshirt, the front buttonless and the two tails knotted over the iron pan of muscles of his abdomen. Sun and saltwater had tinted his hair orange; a lopsided ridge of it foamed out from under his baseball cap. The boy never showed up at her door unless Saconi was away, performing on one of the nearby islands. He never smiled and he never communicated more to her than what Saconi had told him to say. Beyond this service he seemed to Sally to have been created by God to disappear into the harsh rhythm of whatever menial task was required of him. It was no use inviting him inside for coffee, juice, a glass of cold water. He would refuse—he always did; shy or afraid, she couldn't tell.

"Good morning," Sally said, folding her arms atop the bottom half of the door. "What's the news?"

Joseph reported his message. He had a sober mouth full of strong teeth, and looked, it seemed, at her ear when he spoke as though he were counting the words as they flew in. He was polite and careful but painfully formal, an uneducated gentleman, and she often wondered where someone like Joseph placed her in his view of the world. Don't touch? If that were the case, he was one of the few exceptions on the island. It made her skin crawl, the deference. That he might elevate her into the imaginary ranks of some royal court of whiteness. And yet, better that, perhaps, than being a target, a punching bag, a she-goat.

"Saconi say come down, Miss Sally." For Friday night—tonight. A goat roast and fete. She could bring whomever she wanted.

"Saconi tell me please to ask Big Sally bring a next set of guitar string. Bring him white shirt, eh?" Joseph shifted his weight and stared hawk-eyed down the lane. "Okay den, Miss Sally, I gone now," he told her but she knew he would not move until he was released. It was a long steep walk up the hill from the ferry landing. She went back to the kitchen and returned with a chilled bottle of beer. If she had asked if he wanted it he'd say no but Joseph would never decline what was simply given.

"Okay then, Joseph," she said, fitting the sweaty bottle into his callused hand. She remained in the opened and closed door—her idea of a perfect door—and followed him down the street with her curiosity. What she once considered oppressive about Joseph, his cold style and impenetrable attitude, now earned her respect. Too many men here were shameless, grabbers and rubbers and worse, the motto of their manhood *Screw them all, bwoy, you might miss a good one.* Even the little boys polished their groins when she clipped by on the sidewalk. Where did the ones like Joseph, like Saconi, loyal and trustworthy, considerate, come from? But the thought had a bad spot of confusion in it and made her uneasy—what exactly was she admiring about Joseph other than the formidable impassivity, his impersonality, which was that of a servant's? *You men,* she sighed, unable to either acquit or condemn them, and went to the bedroom to dress for work. Men were other planets, regardless of detail, wherever you found them. Why fuss about the island variety? Some dangerous, most intellectually barren and tiresome—there was enough to hate, *enough!* A few were magnificent, life-supporting, and you could look around and visit but still you couldn't live there. Like Saconi, who made her wash off her American perfumes before he would sleep with her. Smell honest, is what he said, not unkindly.

With the help of a few desperate mothers, and after months of lip service from the Ministry of Health and Public Welfare, she had created a school—a breakthrough that left a lasting impression on her apprehension of power. At the ministry she smiled until the muscles in her face seemed carved out of wax, and then in frustration she changed tack and began to yell and vilify, unsuccessfully, the civil service staffers until tales of her brash conduct overflowed out onto the grapevine and she became a *topic.* Her supervisor called her in and sat her down.

"Didn't you ever think it might be a cultural thing?" he suggested, irritating her still further with his fatherly tone. "That you might not know how to communicate with these people."

"Did you ever think these shits at the ministry might not know how to communicate with a woman from Kansas?" she replied, gritting her teeth.

She had come to wage peace, only to discover she was equally willing to engage in warfare. The ensuing ideological crisis she experienced kept her in bed for two days, the door locked and the curtains drawn. She gorged herself with starches, those ubiquitous island roots, boiled down to a tasteless but comforting mush, and could feel herself gaining weight by the hour. Sometimes she wept because she knew she didn't belong there and there was a conspiracy to drive her out. She couldn't say how long she would have kept prostrate in her room if the mothers hadn't come, six or seven of them standing outside her window, their round faces like gloomy chocolate moons pressed one by one against the screen, like a confessional, to petition her help in doing something for the children. On her knees, leaning against the sill, she whimpered, ashamed of her weakness. "I'm trying to help," she said, her voice catching, "but they're not letting me."

It was one of those serendipitous accidents: her supervisor at a cocktail party of coalition notables, joking with a Banks appointee, the brilliant and never-tiring minister of education, a mere twenty-five years old, still schoolboyish enough to be convinced that everything was possible if a person showed enthusiasm and obedience. The supervisor related, in an amusing way, the anecdote of his Special Ed. volunteer stonewalled by the minister of health, one of the elite power-hoarders who had been retained in office thanks to Joshua Kingsley, and the volunteer's rather testy and insistent response to the situation. The young minister took an immediate interest in her plight, pretending the supervisor had slighted him. "But why you give her to the Ministry of Status Quo?" he protested good-naturedly. "Education is where she belong. Send her to me, mahn."

"It seems like only one half of the government can get things done around here," sympathized the American.

"Change is comin, my friend."

Sally's elevation was complete before the week was out and left her shaking her head, amazed; for once, she felt *all there*, eligible, illustrious, a part of the enlivening force that had seized the island. The minister of education found her an old building on the waterfront for her school and, more than that, he seemed to want to be her friend. He invited her to his office to hear her progress reports and even introduced her to one of the island's new generation of folk heroes, the musician Saconi, one of his boyhood chums, who raised her slumbering political consciousness into the light of day, though she still argued that if the United States was an empire, at least it was an empire of hope and reason and principle—Saconi of course would snicker.

The months of futility ended without looking back. Her dread of her own worthlessness vanished; she started eating right again, started a social life that seemed richly ored with meaning and, on its own terms, glamor (though she would *never* say as much), and she went to work in the mornings telling herself she had arrived, finally, at home.

It was in her waterfront school where the defective, shadow-filled children of St. Catherine found sanctuary. She harbored the babies afflicted by God—a blame she was willing to assign—the babies carelessly disabled in the womb, the blind lost children who were unbearable bad luck to a family already crushed by poverty, the deaf children timid as finches with no greater faculty of expression than a bird's. All the conventionally impaired were, in their deformity and hopelessness, bitter fruit fallen from the same tree as the mongoloids and autistics—untrainable, unmanageable, otherworldly beings. Occasionally in her canvassing of the villages, she would even find a child collared and leashed to a tree shading the shanty of the resigned parents, utterly frazzled or numbed by their misfortune. Struggling in the middle of the flock were the gently retarded children, submerged in their own strange joys, painful mirrors of love and horror. And even such a gathering of outcasts had its own, orphaned not by death but by virtue of their own lives; empty, nocturnal, estranged—a five-year-old with no arms, no intelligence, and a perpetually scabbed face. A boy born with flippers, which never ceased twitching. A hydrocephalic who apparently survived on insects and weeds when his distraught mother reached the point where she was too appalled by this *thing* she had made to keep feeding it.

The first week of school, one of the autistics, a small girl so feral she might have been the incarnation of an alley cat, had bitten an actual mouthful of flesh from above Sally's knee during a tantrum. With diabolically bright eyes she swallowed the bite and began to *hophophop*, still hopping when Sally returned from the hospital, the wound closed with a black web of stitches, her rear end throbbing because the RPN had broken a needle in it.

Those she couldn't educate, she struggled to pacify and soothe, and the ones who resisted domestication, she battled, for her own survival as well, telling herself it was for their souls.

*　　　*　　　*

The day had been uncustomarily trying, credit that to a new boy brought in from the countryside with scummy eyes, an eleven-year-old named Trevor about whom nobody could say what was wrong, though Sally suspected his was a hyperactivity that could be medicated down to some metabolic level of normalcy. His psychology though was another story. From the time he walked in, Trevor had persisted in a relentless, sexually precise assault on all the girls in the school, going so far as to pinch one of Sally's breasts, *hard*; she had lost control and kicked him, also hard, in the shin, hard enough for obsidian tears to pour down his cheeks. Then she wanted to run away but could only count the hours, tending to one crisis after another, before the day was through and she could bail out to Cotton Island for a weekend's r-and-r.

Keeping the school open past midafternoon was impossible anyway, a matter of passing the threshold of endurance for Sally and her two trainees, for the parents who walked from throughout the southern quarter of the island to deliver and retrieve the students, as they were euphemistically called, since education was really not the point of the school, not yet; and for the children themselves, relief from the exhausting ordeal of unscrambling the humanity that was placed so differently and behind so many obstacles in each of them. The ministry van arrived to collect the abandoned children and the eight boys and girls sent from up the northward coasts. Sally assisted the driver, loading kids, strapping the ones who required restraint into their seats, bestowing kisses, and off they went back to the convent of the Sisters of Mercy where they were monitored like clinic patients and allowed the charity of room and board. She lingered outside, mothering the rest of the group, releasing them one by one to a parent or aunt or older sibling, and then returned to the decrepit building, once a small warehouse for a cooperative of onion growers, smelling still of their harvest, its cavernous concrete walls blackened and streaked by mold. She had been promised paint, cheery colors, but wasn't going to hold her breath waiting around for it. The two aides were straightening up and she joined in to turn the tiny chairs upright, empty the chamber pots, mop urine from the floor, wash the spoons from the daily lunch sponsored by the Rotarians, gather all the toys, donated broken like her children. Sighing in unison, the three women locked the door behind them and exchanged hugs in the sunlight, laughing at the lingering smell of onions they inhaled off each other's clothes.

"Vincent stick a palmetto bug way he nose. I does have to dig it out wit me house key."

"What's Hyacinth's mother like?" Sally wondered. "That little girl has bruises on her back. Her mother wants me to believe she fell down."

"Watch she doan knock you too, Miss Sally. Daht womahn have a mean streak."

"I'm going to say something to her."

"Robert laugh today, you know, Miss Sally. Oh, what a pretty sound he mek to test a heart."

Their throats constricted and they embraced again, wiping tears from their eyes, and said good-bye for the weekend, Sally buoyant, walking away through the crowd on the street, the emptiness that she had once felt back in her other life long gone, the island had filled it in, and why *this* place, so radically different than all she had known, she couldn't say. She could not grasp the meaning of the change, and didn't dare search for it.

She was a farm girl from the western edge of the Flint Hills of Kansas, corn-fed in the heartlands of the continent on an ocean-lonely prairie. Her body, she had told herself in college, watching slides in art history class, was classically robust, yet undernourished by a sequence of fair-skinned square-chested young men who quickly spent their brief uprisings and then settled in to make the most conservative investments in passion and joy—not quite grown-up men with plenty of convictions harvested direct from the soil, but little in their chemistry that could live beyond the county line, past Wichita, past Emporia, past Topeka. Not interested in Kansas City, some would say. Too many niggers.

She taught special children—retarded kids—in a temporary building—a trailer, really—on the grounds of the regional elementary school, after graduating from the state university in Wichita, but within two years, lethargy wrapped around her life like a blanket during a fever, empty minutes building hollow hours, fragile days, an existence that lost its grip on time and began to spoil in its protective shell. She believed herself unborn. I want more experience than seems to be available, she confided to whoever wanted to listen—Sally's problem, whatever it was, something without a true shape. She cursed the professors in Wichita for teaching her to read and appreciate and distinguish, to dream and to believe, as an act of intelligence rather than faith. She cursed them for the window of life's promises they dared to showcase, and she cursed herself for paying attention, when clearly not many did. Why get yourself educated if it only made you unhappy? She struggled to analyze whether this was a naive point of view, or worthless cynicism. Her parents casually suggested that what she was feeling was an unadmitted desire to marry and be a mother, a path to fulfillment they would permit no one, especially their own daughter, to challenge or diminish. *That's not it,* she would snap back, though she knew she was a type, somewhere in the back of her mind—one of those females who could populate the world.

She began dating a guy she had known in high school. Nothing remarkable about him, but he had been sent to Vietnam and there had lost his boyish swagger. Now he was responsible and thoughtful but also a degree withdrawn, robbed of the spark of trouble-making she had girlishly loved to hate, and seemed more than ever of her kind—normal, a good and steady man. Liked to drink, but wasn't crazy. Before long she knew he wanted to marry her but wouldn't propose until she made it clear the answer would be yes. Yes, *darling.* Yes.

She remembered with numbing clarity the day one life ended and another stubbornly pushed out into the middle of an antiseptic wasteland, the day of a spring blizzard that frothed out of the Rockies and raced across the plains with no advance warning, burying the state in cementlike snow that froze overnight after the wind had ridged it into high dunes. She joined her boyfriend in his four-wheel drive truck, reconnoitering the vast pastures of his father's ranch on the lookout for livestock trapped by the weather. It was a profound disheartenment, to crawl across the ranch in the great primitive silence of the aftermath, her boyfriend—Jerry was his name—seeing the future, his future, theirs, knocked back away from him by just that much, what a bad spring storm could do to a herd. Then the truck went off the ledge of an old creek bed tapered by a drift and they were stuck until well after dark, when his father brought a tractor out to look for them.

They waited to be rescued and Jerry drank—not nips but deadening mouthfuls—from the fifth of peppermint schnapps he carried in the glove box. He was, in his unassuming way, a comfortable man to be with though a cautious speaker, convinced that most of what people said between themselves was more than obvious anyway. That was pride. Pride that all he did, every deliberate movement, gesture, and nuance, was rendered perfectly clear by his fundamental decency. He wished to be kind and good, and he was. And yet even that caused a bend of despair in her hope, made her see herself as a prisoner to a methodical man inspired solely by decency. She would be willing to gamble if she knew it would be enough, but she didn't know. When she felt the truck slide and whip off solid ground and sink on its frame it seemed not inevitable but a lucky breach of routine, that what was happening was happening because they were both too weak and proud to talk about what was below the surface of their lives, air out their dreams. Shipwrecked in that frozen sea she craved that conversation then, she wanted the resolutions that would help her navigate the years she would board and ride to her prime, age thirty and beyond.

The tailpipe was beneath the snow and rather than dig it out he cut the engine, inviting the emptiness to join them. They sat and listened to the ticking of the engine fading as it cooled. Within minutes, the windows were blocked out by an opaque film of ice, forcing them to reel in their thoughts to accommodate the sudden reduced scope.

"Well, here we are," she said, much more solemn than she intended. Finally, they were bound together, as they might always be.

There's all this space, she had said, spreading her hands and extending them into the distance they could no longer see, *and all of it pressing in.*

"Do you know what I mean, or at least do you know what I feel?"

She had felt her blood heating up with something other than springtime, as if she were being prodded by an unseen force toward inexplicable acts, obscure desires, but the real point was that more and more she felt unafraid, almost reckless, prepared to take a chance, and that could mean marrying him, or maybe she was understanding that she wasn't settler stock after all. To be born into it was not to be given a choice.

"I wouldn't have stopped here, a hundred years ago," she said, perhaps too fiercely, with an implicit contempt that she didn't feel. She could see she had hurt him.

"I can't see how it matters where you stop," he said, a reproach for denying him the rightness of his own choices, "just so you do. Some day, before you burn yourself out."

I hope it wasn't girls like me you were fighting for, she apologized to him, far inside herself.

"This is a morale problem," he said, combing her hair back from her face with his red hand. "Trust me. I understand."

She exposed more and more of her thoughts, stripping herself, surprised by her brazenness because she had never said these things before, not even in her own head, because they were until now only sensations of hunger and need, bereft of voice, and no telling how trustworthy. I feel isolated, she confessed, almost pleading. I feel forced into place. I feel passed by and forgotten. He grunted and drank his schnapps and let her reveal herself. She asked him, leaning toward him in earnest concentration to receive his response, what he thought he would be doing anyway, fifteen years down the road.

"What you see," he answered, and tucked a pinch of snuff under his lip, and he tipped his head at the coming darkness.

With his bare hand he cleared a circle through the frost on the windshield and squinted out at the colorless twilight spreading through space, even the fence line gone, and no lights on shore. For him it was only a visitation of unexpected weather, and just as it sifted down on them it would lift away. Nothing could prevent its passing and the idea was to hold on. But for Sally the quiet life she had been enduring, what was yesterday only a persistent nagging mood, had bumped against something deeper, something immovable that was not temporary, and she wondered, How did I arrive at this boldness, where did juvenile fantasies end, and an imagination you could work with begin? Was it as simple as loving life *too* much? If that was so, loving life this way was madness, it swept you out on the edge of propriety, it drove you wild. And if you resisted, it poisoned you.

She felt a tremor of real fear—was she wise and strong enough for this, her own imagination—her own *illusions?*—parenting her into another life? But how could anyone possibly know? What she knew was that for the first time she was wide awake to what she would become if she stayed, and the first casualty would be her momentum, that motion or energy that was hers because she was young and unimpeded. Out here—with Jerry or without him—it would unravel into complacency, and there she would sit, a Mother Goose in Kansas, and never knowing otherwise. She wanted to give this expanded idea of freedom a run for its money. It was her birthright, she saw that now. It explained everything.

The window within the window Jerry had made had iced over again, and he pawed at it, smearing out an opening. Outside, with nightfall, a luminous hush had transformed the snow into something peaceful and welcoming, Christmasy. But the feeling only lasted for an instant, receding into the distant lowing of cattle, which sounded like the misery of ghosts being blown across the plains.

"I think I'm going to have to leave," she said and, looking at his reaction, pushed her back against the door, recoiling from his misshapen expression, the way he peered at her, as if she were a serious problem he better find a solution to, *now*. He was drunk enough by then and misunderstood her, imagining she had determined to get out of the truck, defy both his decency and the deadly weather and hike back to the farmhouse. He seemed to fall across the seat onto her, grabbing her roughly to stop her from opening the door, inadvertently tugged her hair and hurt her neck, and she was almost grateful for this, the physical dimension of his anger.

"You're insane, fucking insane," he spit, the words thick and minty. "You'll kill yourself." He looked away to say in disgust, *stupid fucking bitch,* and then snorted, relaxing his hold on her, and then turned back, shoving his red face into hers. "You won't make it. You'll die. You're not getting out of here, understand?"

Instinctively, she brushed his cheek with a kiss. "I love you," she answered apologetically, but she didn't, she said it only to console him, as she imagined she would have to say to him or somebody else, and for the same reason, if she remained out here on the prairies.

She had no money saved, no friends in places distinct from where she was now. Any ticket out was the right ticket. The news made her mother sit by herself in the living room and cry, somehow hurt and then exasperated; it made her father take a second, probing and unfriendly look at her. "For God's sake, where in the world is St. Catherine?" her mother asked in distress. "It doesn't matter, Mom," Sally told her with a smile she regretted. "I don't really care where it is." Her father went to the bookcase and pulled out a volume of the *Encyclopaedia Britannica,* one of the few times she ever saw him with a book in his hand that was not a manual. He scanned the entry for the island and shook his head. "You might as well be in Africa," he said.

"Thank God it *isn't* Africa," her mother responded, thinking only of her daughter's welfare.

After school Sally's time was her own, on those days free of administrative loose ends, and she spent it with a sense of unrestricted wealth, heading for the scarcely populated beaches or the fragrant carnival-like crush of the market. Or she would walk back to the house to write ebullient, almost boastful letters to Kansas, or read her weekly novel snatched from the shelves of the expats; wash laundry by hand and foot in the shower, which turned out to be quite good exercise, or practice the harmonica she had promised to teach herself to play (the irony of "Home on the Range" didn't faze her), or trek to the Botanic Gardens and sketch flowers. On Tuesday afternoons she would brief sponsors at the Ministry of Education, lest they disremember her crusade, and on Wednesday evenings she would go to the club where Saconi rehearsed with his band. And though she wasn't immune to the camaraderie to be enjoyed in the volunteer community, she found that her old reasons for seeking them out—to compare strategies and tell interminable war stories—were moot, once the school was operative, and she felt less and less compelled to spend time among people whose experiences seemed so suffocatingly close to her own. She knew too that some of them, despite their talk about compassion and justice and the other pet ideals that flew like banners in their rhetoric, disapproved of her relationship with Saconi, a few accused her of being a camp follower, groupie, whatever, a plain Jane promenading with her handsome black stud, something naughty to write in her journal, she was exploiting him, he was exploiting her, *blah blah blah,* endlessly and unkindly, until she made a point of keeping separate these two facets of her life in St. Catherine, as much as that was possible in such a dab of a country.

Today, however, she walked along the length of the busy quay toward the center of Queenstown and Government House, past glistening stevedores stripped to the waist, their heads cooled with wet rags, the impoverished fleet of workboats hugging the wharf, their eczemic hulls flaking chips of blue and white paint into the harbor, solitary sails patched and soiled with age; past the herb-heads squatting on the edge of the dock, perched on the huge capstans, lined up like pelicans facing the sea as they brazenly shared a cone of ganja; through a mob of older schoolgirls, forms five and six, in white knee socks and bursting white blouses, their style to leave the blouse untucked over the pleats of their blue skirts, the younger girls from the middle schools in plain jumpers, hair braided with ribbons; past the makeshift stalls of the weary hucksters unable to afford the fee at the government's new covered market, the women with their egglike skulls wrapped in bright-colored cloth, hovering over pyramids of avocado pears, oranges and limes and hideous soursop, papayas, and just-ripe mangoes, first of the season, garlic bulbs and pigeon peas and bundles of coriander and basil and thyme tied with thread, the more competitive of the women barking for Sally's attention but only receiving the briefest fragment of smile. But she returned the long incredulous look of a girl in flowered cotton underpants, her mother beside her in a sack shift, the muscles veined and lumped in the wood of the woman's legs, their feet powdered with white dust, each carrying a rank basket of ballyhoo on her head with the most erect posture imaginable. As if they had not yet been permitted to play in the twentieth century, children too young for school rolled hoops salvaged from old bicycle wheels, guiding the rims with flat sticks, or sat in the packed dirt and shot marbles. A man roasted a breadfruit on a brazier of coals until its skin was as black as a bowling ball. A knot of scampy, tattered boys surrounded the movie advertisements pasted to a cinderblock wall, goggling at the posters: *Hell Up in Harlem* and *Bogard: Beat Him to Win*, plus the latest kung fu neck-busters from Taiwan. The proprietors of the rum sheds nodded amiably as she passed, their sideburns like scimitars, and Sally saw the policeman with the close-cropped mustache who had once humiliated Saconi in front of her by asking him to produce identification, the rotten shit, and up ahead was the crazy man called Long Time who had helped dig the Panama Canal, sailors in straw cowboy hats, fishermen down on the water cleaning a mossy mound of conch, ugly-footed beggars with rheumy eyes, ships' pursers with clipboards and gold-framed sunglasses, a group of idle taxi drivers having a smoke-and-joke, basket weavers, fishmongers, bloody butchers in their filthy stalls, boys pushing wheelbarrows of ice, vendors of hawksbill combs and black coral jewelry, waternut men like artillery captains standing by their mound of shells, curry-makers and roti-rollers, sidewalk preachers, staggering drunks and hefty, handsome women and mutant dogs lapping at jade green puddles and a leper with no nose and a crusty, suppurating mouth-hole, riding a donkey; an osprey ascending into the sky with a dead rat in its talons. And who could say she was not entitled to all she saw, that this world too was hers, a part of the human dowry, that the big-shouldered woman with the hockey player's legs, the white lady dressed in the pink sunshift batiked with frangipani blossoms, the girl bare to the golden upper rise of her breasts and sweating like a man, her inner hair plastered along her neck, a few slick brown tendrils curling across her throat, who could say she wasn't herself part of the life of the city? No one could tell her she didn't belong there because she could no longer say it to herself, not since she had become married to the island's sorrows and frustrations, its threats and wonders, so that what was normal in a normal life had been redefined, transformed, its seams loosened to accommodate her, and not since she had resolved during the days in bed spent grieving for her shattered purity, frightened by her own bullheadedness, that St. Catherine could defeat her if it chose but she was staying, she was willing to assume the costs, whatever the asking price was for this dazzling enthrallment of human energy.

And here, she even frowned at the cruise ship anchored in the harbor for a half-day stopover—God, was there anything worse than a tourist? At least she had found her own way around that problem. *My, my, Miss Sally,* she chided herself, *what's gotten into you?*

She turned landward up Drake Street with its lemon-washed, cream-trimmed colonial facades. The block she was on thundered with music, a calypso from Saconi's new album, *Free Costs Dear,* pumped out for public consumption by the stereo system at Calvin Da Silva's Disc Den. Calvin, in a tiger-striped dashiki and stocking cap, saluted with his raised fist from behind the shop's counter as she passed his open door. Sally waved back. *Are you deaf yet?* she mouthed. She pointed at her ears and shook her head, watching Calvin's lips move, a sentence destroyed by the hurricane of sound. He stood serenely in the calm eye of fanaticism while walls fissured and foundations cracked in the buildings on the street.

She couldn't fathom the point of such loudness, less a gift than a nuisance. In Sally's opinion, Calvin was too shrewd for his own good in his appreciation of Saconi and his music. He emceed the local concerts and was more than a little responsible for the management and promotion that had popularized the musician throughout the Antilles. In return Saconi proudly—and foolishly, she would say—displayed the lack of business sense attributed to artists. The record merchant controlled the books—to his own advantage, Sally suspected, but Saconi refused to discuss such a bourgeois matter. Less than a year ago Calvin, proselytizing brotherhood, persuaded Saconi to break with the distributorship that handled his label because it was run by light-skinned East Indians—*coolies*—in Trinidad. What about double standards? she had protested privately to Saconi, but he assured her his only motive was to assert control over his own future. They screw you for pennies same as dollars, Calvin told Saconi—virile black boys were too ignorant to be anything but what history and nature and foreign entrepreneurs said they were: slaves. Next Da Silva formed his own recording company to shape the range of Saconi's creative and financial affairs, but Saconi seemed no better off than before. Watch out for Calvin, Sally had warned. Try to understand brotherhood, he had told her. But he's not black, Sally had argued, he's rich—there's a difference. Afterward, Saconi composed "Rise to White" in response to the conversation, the number-one single in the Caribbean for three consecutive weeks last fall. Calvin had no inkling he was the subject of the hit.

But Sally had learned, or thought she had, anyway, that Saconi, with sly complicity, encouraged Calvin's ambition because he recognized himself in it, and he could not disapprove of what he himself was guilty. It was a game the two men played with each other, she realized, and throughout her year on the island Saconi's friends had become her friends, both their faults and their virtues acceptable to her. Or at least familiar. They were rude with women but they treated her implicitly with respect. They loved children but they were mystified by the attention she lavished on the ones whom they thought, trapped in genetic cocoons, were better off dead. Individually, the men were solicitous and cheerful but when they congregated she receded from their grace. Though their racial and sexual innuendos never targeted her, no one thought anything of asking her to fix and serve drinks, cook a meal, wipe a spill from the floor, fetch cigarettes from the shop. The women, however, were like any other in her presence, some jealous, some morose and empty, some cyclones of self-infatuation, always a few as easygoing as loving sisters. Despite their differences, there was an abundance of joyous times—the beach cookouts, the backstage parties, the card games at her kitchen table, the exhilaration in the cramped studio when a song coalesced for the first time, the family reunions and boat excursions, the dinners cooked by adoring mothers, women as solid as oak trees who gave her oily kisses and squeezed her hand, regarding her, it sometimes seemed, as a living symbol of their sons' success.

She thought of going back to the Disc Den and inviting Calvin and the others down to the fete on Cotton Island but then she decided no, Saconi would have already seen to it if he wanted them down there and besides, the parties on Cotton Island were almost exclusively European—white, wealthy, and decadent—and for reasons best known to Saconi, he indulged the Princess and agreed to play her private troubadour. Unlike the others, he had transcended whatever insecurities came with being born on island soil, and he would never react to Sally—she believed this deeply—as if she were declaring, by her pleasure, one world inferior to another.

In the road ahead was a man asleep, being licked and nuzzled by a pack of dogs. Traffic detoured around him, honking. She stepped off the sidewalk to try to wake him only to see that he wasn't asleep at all, just lying there with his eyes closed, his mouth curved in a heavenly smile, murmuring endearments to the dogs. She walked on, ever amazed by life in St. Catherine.

Chapter 18

What she planned to do was invite Mitchell and Tillman; Isaac too if he were around, since he and Mitchell, though not inseparable, had a friendship that she could easily envy. With them she would be most relaxed in a place like Cotton, and they would value the break from routine. Too many of the American or European men she had met on St. Catherine were encyclopedias of arrogance and conceit, businessmen and sportsmen and financiers and functionaries who suggested they represented, in some vague but consequential capacity, this country or that multinational, and then launched monologues detailing the most outlandish schemes: a toy factory that would employ thousands; the importation of camels as a source of supplementary protein; a program to train fishermen to navigate with the use of sophisticated equipment that they would never in their lives be able to afford and didn't need anyway. At first she thought these men were innocuous, but after hearing their litany of illusions and false promises again and again, she came to believe that such men, serving themselves with their bedeviled imaginations and lopsided pragmatism, were somehow the enemies of the world. As far as she was concerned, fellows like Tillman and Mitchell, with their ironic professionalism and understated dedication to improving the lot of the island, helped restore the balance upset by the flow of haughty clowns through St. Catherine. They weren't missionaries or closet emperors or ne'er-do-wells hidden in the ranks of the terminally sincere; they didn't pretend to have the answers, they weren't fools but fighters, and they made her laugh. That was enough.

Then too there was the fact that both men had received lady friends out of the sky this week, as if they had heated up with romance according to the same emotional clock, and Sally was attracted by the possibilities the women's arrival offered for uninfluenced female companionship, objective female minds that would not take her independence as a personal affront. She had noticed the four of them coming into the beach bar last night, but her ride back to town was leaving and she had no opportunity to say hello. She looked forward to meeting them because she had an intimation, inexplicably, that one or both of the women had something to give her, if only their confidence, the sense of being a fellow traveler—but how strange, she thought, that coming so far on her own, surviving and even prospering for a year and a half in a foreign land, she felt a hunger for this sort of, what . . . certification? Just don't let them be that certain type of female who will be your best friend *ever* for about twenty minutes, she prayed.

Switching her overnight bag to her other shoulder, Sally mounted the steps to the Ministry of Agriculture. Mitchell was not in his office and none of the secretaries was certain if he had come in that day or not. Sally groaned, asked to use the phone and dialed Rosehill. The line was busy the first time she tried to get through, and seemed utterly dead on the second. She tried the phone on another desk with similar results. She went down the dusty hall to Mitchell's office and explored it for clues but found nothing that could suggest his presence except for a tin cup of cold black coffee. She tried once more to get through to Rosehill, using the phone on Mitchell's paper-scattered desk, and was grateful to hear her call ring and answered.

"Is Tillman there?" she asked.

"Him outside," a male voice said, and hung up.

She left the ministry and went across the road to stand under a colossal pink trumpet tree, waiting for an eastbound passenger lorry to take her to Howard Bay. The shade of a every big tree in the city served as a stop for public transport and as she joined the others gathered there, a gust ruffled through the overhead branches and the queue was showered with hundreds of plump, leafy flowers, stuck in people's hair, burying their feet. Since noon the skies had been patrolled by lone clouds full as watering cans that tipped their content in a vertical deluge as they passed languidly over the island. It would soon rain again, she knew, and she urged the lorry along as she saw it turn up from the harbor, as ceremoniously painted as an elephant in the King of Siam's court, and stutter toward their stop. Its brakes sang in different keys; a boy vaulted down from its flat bed with a two-tiered box of steps. Gunnysacks and parcels were handed up. A grandmother with an Easter hat was half lifted aboard by her elbows. Sally waited to climb on last but an old man lingered behind, exhorting her to go ahead.

"He holdin back fah a look up ladies' dresses," someone on the truck, a woman in white gloves who sat on her bench with her forearms atop her knees, hunched, as if she were on the toilet, observed. She focused on the old man as he hauled himself in and looked for a seat. "Ain what you want get you fat, Mistah Johnson," the woman harumphed. Sally, embarrassed, sat as far away from the dowager as she could. The boy reloaded the staircase and the lorry jerked forward; he pinballed from one passenger to another collecting fares. Mister Johnson had been forced to sit almost opposite his adversary; she glowered at him, tugged the hem of her dress toward the moons of her knees and, farther down the road, began to harangue the dickens out of him, cataloguing every trespass and shortcoming she could name. Obviously the two had known each other all their lives. Suddenly she was on her feet, swinging her big plastic purse by its strap into the side of his head.

"Stop!" she screeched. No one but Sally appeared dismayed by the spectacle. "Stop dis truck! I ain ridin wit dis mahn!" But the driver continued on to the next roadside queue. Only then was the woman able to satisfy herself. She threw the man named Mister Johnson off the truck, sat back down, and said not another word.

"She his wife, you know," the girl sitting next to Sally told her. The girl, in her early twenties, Sally guessed, wore cheap baggy jeans and a man's long-sleeved shirt with the cuffs buttoned, her feet in chewed-up ballet slippers. She had overapplied makeup to sculpt her eyes like Nefertiti's, and whatever she put on her lips made them appear enameled, stiff as cartilage. Leaning into Sally, she giggled.

"He marry six times in seventy years and keep disrememberin dis lady de current wife. She ride de transport huntin fah de old mahn." Sally inhaled the spearmint of the girl's breath and snickered too, opening the envelope of space she assigned herself on the lorries. Their bodies pressed together with the lurch and bounce of the road. The inborn warmth of the black girl's manner appealed to her.

"You de gal dey call Big, true?"

Sally nodded and the girl glanced away, a stranger again. They rode without speaking until the next stop, when the woman changed her seat, making Sally wonder what lies she had heard. Then at the Charing Cross stop she came back, wedging herself between Sally and the man who had taken her place. Tears threatened to spill from the corners of her extravagant eyes.

"I wish you'd tell me what's wrong," Sally coaxed. The girl bent her head in mysterious anguish and her hand sought out Sally's like a lost child. She had heard stories, she said—Sally cringed but she needn't have—stories that said she came to help the children born *mahd.* Sally did not yet know what to answer so she told the girl her actual name.

"Jolene," the girl reciprocated, and wiped her eyes with the back of her free hand. She worked in Scuffletown, at her uncle's upholstery shop. Her own family lived in Retreat, the northernmost village on the windward side, and she was on her way home for her monthly visit. There was a baby in the family—her sister's baby, she hastened to explain. A little boy, four years old, and there was something very, very wrong with him. *Him juss make a moo sound, Miss Sally. Not a word in de bwoy's head. Him goony. And he shake like so*—she held out her hand to demonstrate. Nobody had the slightest idea what to do with him except let him be, but Jolene often wondered if there was a medicine Sally kept at her school to treat such a case.

"There's no medicine, Jolene, but I can help him. Tell your sister to bring the boy down from the country."

But Jolene seemed to resist this solution—the family was too poor, the sister was overprotective, the father was ashamed to have the child in public. Sally tried to no avail to coach Jolene on the arguments she could use to convince her sister.

"No, no," Jolene sniffed, a distant, detached look coming over her. "She doan listen. She ain goin do it."

The road curved down toward Howard Bay and into the path of an isolated squall advancing along the shoreline. The interior of the cloud flickered with diffused bursts of light, and a wavering curtain of rain, dun-colored, cut a line across the ground, obliterating all that lay behind it. The inevitability of being drenched made the passengers glum as convicts. In the popular imagination of Catherinians, a good soaking by the weather was tantamount to falling through ice into a pond. Sally once considered the local attitude about rain an example of mass hypochondria until she larked home one day to Ballycieux Lane in a drizzle, a pleasant climatic change after two months of error-free skies, and spent the next fortnight miserable with walking pneumonia.

A handful of passengers banged on the roof of the lorry's cab demanding to be let off. They sprinted into the underbrush on the roadside and crouched under wild tannia leaves, pulling the plants over them like green slickers. The passengers who remained on board sheltered their heads with schoolbooks, newspaper, purses, nylon shopping bags as the drops began to sizzle around them with a roar like burning cane. The two women hugged each other, Jolene's sparkling head tucked under the white woman's chin, her vinyl suitcase, held together with cord, laid across her thighs. Mother and child in flood, Sally thought, seeing an image of herself from a distance. The lorry splashed along the scoop of coast past the ghost figures of pedestrians, banana leaves like umbrellas raised above their skulls.

"Jolene," Sally urged, hunched into the other woman's heat. "Bring the boy back down from the country with you. I'll take him in, I promise." Licks of steam rose from along the black girl's spine as though her spirit escaped, wisp after wisp, and she shivered, not answering. Sally craned her neck and peered into the silvery heart of the rainfall, trying to locate herself but all she saw were the anonymous outlines of palm trees, darts thrown into the spray. Jolene kept her face hidden, the rain settled throughout the coils of her hair like beads of glycerine.

"When are you coming back to Queenstown?" Sally persisted.

"Monday," the girl answered weakly.

"I'll come find you, Jolene. Where is your uncle's shop?"

Jolene told her, and Sally adjusted her hips to face the back of the lorry, squinting against the heavy drops that sailed into her eyes. She yelped and sprang up from the bench, hammering the back of the cab with her fist. "Shit, we passed it," she yelled above the downpour. "Stop! Stop!"

The lorry fishtailed to a halt. Sally dropped down next to Jolene, whose eyes had become blind, water-filled, her age washed off so that Sally drew back in wonder, seeing not the self-possessed adult who had been there but a teenage girl, *young*, alone and drowning. She petted the rain from the girl's sad face, wanting to bring her comfort.

"When the rain ends make the driver stop and wait for you and go into the bushes and put on some dry clothes. You have too far to go wet like this. When you come back down Monday bring the boy with you. Bring him to my school in the morning. Has a doctor ever seen him?"

Jolene shook her head no. Sally looked at her, feeling strange; something in the girl's sadness, its absoluteness, made her shudder. On an impulse, she asked, "He's not your little boy, is he, Jolene?" but Jolene's eyes stayed averted and she said nothing. "Bring him and your sister to me Monday morning. Okay? Promise?"

"All right, Miss Sally," the girl whispered. The driver honked for Sally to disembark. She kissed Jolene on her slick cheek, sloshed to the rear of the truck and off. The boy who worked for the driver slapped the roof of the cab and away they went, fading ahead into the storm.

        *   *   *

Sally took off her sandals and forged the roiling ditches built by the crown agents, her dress heavy and pasted into her body, sagging between her legs like pink webbing. In the minute it took her to walk back to Mitchell's drive, the rain ceased with mocking abruptness, turning the air fresh and heavy-sweet as a bite of pineapple. Succulents swelled with juice, broadsword leaves looked polished with furniture wax, flowers drooped and bobbed on their stems like bells of velvet flesh, weighted with promiscuity. Johnnie opened the door dressed only in the red-and-black-striped bottom of a bathing suit, her smile plunging but then recovering to a tentative hello. The sight of her breasts unnerved Sally; she glanced over her shoulder for passersby and pushed herself and Johnnie inside.

"You just can't answer the door like that," she said by way of greeting. "Not around here. There'll be no end to the presumptions and the men will drive you crazy."

"I thought you were Mitchell," Johnnie explained, demure but proud, toeing the door closed. She raised her eyebrows at the water that trickled off Sally, darkening the wood floor. "Who are you?"

Sally introduced herself as a friend of Mitchell and Tillman.

"Well, Sally," Johnnie said, "why don't you take off your clothes?"

In the shower stall, Sally stripped off her dress and underwear and toweled her hair. From the opposite corner of the house static alternated with abbreviated gulps of sound as Johnnie scouted a clear signal on the radio. As Sally opened her mouth to call out a number, the tuner settled on a station and the house inflated with reggae. When she dried between her legs the prickly itch flared up to harass her. She sniffed at a brand of perfume she was unfamiliar with and unscrewed the lid off a jar of expensive skin cream to rub a dot on her forehead and nose, as though she was experimenting with luxury. As much as she had tried to protect her overnight bag from the deluge, kicking it under one of the lorry's benches, up against the cab, unzipping it she saw that her change of clothes was soaked as well, and she had nothing on hand to wear except her own wet bathing suit, which was not enough. She called out to Johnnie, hoping to borrow something, a skirt and tee shirt—she could do without bra and panties until her own had a chance to dry—but realized the radio was too loud, she couldn't be heard. Inadequately wrapped in the towel, she padded toward the kitchen, tossing her head to shake out the wet loops in her hair, carry her hand-wrung clothes to spread out in the sun on the veranda where they'd steam and dry in fifteen minutes.

"—where Mitchell keeps the cups?" Johnnie was mumbling to herself, flinging open cupboard doors, when Sally entered the room, wondering why this woman hadn't had the sense, in the interval, to put on her top. Johnnie's lack of self-consciousness made Sally feel rushed into a state of intimacy, and that was not a comfortable feeling. Still, it was her house, more or less, her privacy that Sally had interrupted, arriving unannounced, inviting herself. Johnnie found two mugs and set them on the counter next to a pot of water heating on the hot plate. She took belated notice of her visitor and smiled in a way that made Sally begin to trust her. She dangled a bag of Red Rose tea.

"I may be slow with dress codes but I know something about these hot places and *haole* girls getting caught in the rain."

"*Haole?*"

"Hawaiian for white girls."

Sally felt uncustomarily coy, wondering why it seemed they had reversed roles, she the newcomer, Johnnie the old hand, that awkward sensation of being instructed, and although she had a healthy attraction for nakedness—women's bodies too, well-figured ones like Johnnie's, were always a fascination to her—her midwestern upbringing certainly contributed to her priggishness about inappropriate exposure. There's an audacity to perfect breasts, she thought, looking at Johnnie's surreptitiously, that she couldn't ascribe to her own, their meaty surprise. While Johnnie steeped the tea Sally exited to the veranda to spread her things over the rail in a rectangle of sunlight. The storm was inland now, nowhere to be seen from where she stood, tucking the loosening edge of the towel more securely under the pit of her arm.

Johnnie fortified the tea with rum and brought it out to her. The first sip scalded the roof of Sally's mouth and she set the mug down. "I'm sorry to have to ask," she apologized, "but my stuff won't dry for a while. Do you think you have something I can wear?"

"Oh sure." Johnnie smiled again, creating dimples, wholesome cheeks, an aura of reliability, but she measured Sally's length and breadth with a blunt look. "We're not the same size but something will fit. I like loose clothes. Nothing sticky."

It was the sort of offhand comment that usually annoyed her, other women's silky remarks, calculated or unthinking, about her strength, her bones, the fullness of her athletic figure, sabotaging her to elevate themselves, but she was inclined to believe that Johnnie, who had the ease and distracted confidence of a house cat, had meant nothing by her observation.

"Here," Johnnie said, reaching toward her. "We might as well put this in the sun too," and before Sally could protest, Johnnie's hand had curved in on her to unhitch the towel, and though Sally pulled away instinctively, alarmed but also confused and bashful and then, finally, feeling silly, she stopped and let her do it, relenting to this loss of inhibition, already in a large part forfeited to the rain and Johnnie's own conduct, unbecoming to a stranger but seductive in its indifference, which was not smug but oddly happy. Carefree, Sally supposed, was the word.

"You have a sexy body," Johnnie said, matter of factly, but touched the roundness of Sally's shoulder, a quick and meaningless caress that caused Sally to make a good-natured smirk—only a man could flatter her this way—and retreat into the house, determined to get back on at least an equal footing with this woman and her powers, which she couldn't put a name to.

In the bedroom Johnnie inventoried her modest wardrobe while Sally sat in the only chair, something salvaged out of an old schoolhouse, sticking her ass to the tacky varnish of the seat. It occurred to her that Johnnie had not bothered to introduce herself.

"That's perfect," she said as Johnnie plucked a lemon-yellow wraparound skirt from a hanger and held it out to her. Sally stood up, fastening it around her waist, and with her hands spread the front of the fabric tight across her groin. "You can't see through it, can you? Is there a shadow?"

"It's fine. Now let me find you a top."

"Your name's Johnnie, isn't it?"

"Johanna," she answered, not annoyed but not explaining the discrepancy either. "Has Mitchell told you about me?"

"Not really," Sally said, edging back onto the chair, her arms hiding her breasts. "Just that you were coming for a visit, when we had lunch together, early in the week. Well, lunch isn't right. A snack is more accurate—I eat lunch with my kids."

Johnnie didn't seem to need this explained. "Oh, more than a visit," she said. She handed over a short-sleeved jersey and Sally fitted it over her head, squirming into it.

"Do you mind my asking—are you Mitchell's girlfriend?"

"Used to be," Johnnie answered slowly, as if she wasn't sure how she should reply. Sally couldn't tell if she were being evasive, or deciding how to phrase something too complicated for simple assertion. But then, whatever the dilemma was, she resolved it. "And, yes. Now. I am." There was a quick, subtle sharpening to her expression. "And how about you?" she asked. "Have you and Mitchell been dating? Or whatever?"

"Heavens no!" Her candor made Sally laugh nervously, though she appreciated getting such a delicate matter straight from the beginning. "You don't have to worry about that. I mean, I'm deep into it with a local, Saconi, he's a musician—in fact, that's why I'm here."

The invitation transformed Johnnie, seemed to throw her into a mini-crisis of anxious excitement. Jagger vacations down there, Elton John goes there to fuck boys, Sally told her. Who knows, they might be there too; somebody famous or soon-to-be usually was. Johnnie jumped around the room, searching for something—her cigarettes— and lit one with a shaky hand. Like a child blissfully windmilling, she spun on her heels with her arms outstretched, her breasts swaying.

"It's just a party," Sally said, seeing what she felt was a display of bogus girlishness, though her own sense of adventure was surfacing. It *was* exhilarating to be here, in this place.

Johnnie stopped her sophomoric turning, smiling with mysterious privilege. "I was in a rut but I got out of it," she said, wound up in marveling. "That's why I'm happy. My luck has changed. You don't know what it means to just go to a party and have fun."

Out of effusive gratitude she bent over to where Sally was sitting and kissed her on the mouth, and this time Sally didn't know how to take it, this second act of touching, spontaneous and yet not clearly innocent, and the pleasant sensation of reward. The back of Johnnie's hand brushed lightly—and accidentally, perhaps—across one of Sally's breasts as she stepped back and Sally stiffened, aroused by a crosscurrent of emotion, wondering *what next?*, but Johnnie was unaware of her effect, already moving back across the room to the wardrobe to throw on a pullover, and Sally was embarrassed by her receptivity, her naive willingness to imagine messages.

"When do you expect Mitchell?" she asked, feeling foolish.

"I'm not sure," Johnnie said, sighing, the wind of her mood shifting, her energy drained by just that much. She looked concerned. "He seems to be under a lot of pressure at his job." It seemed important to her that Sally understand this. "When is it we have to leave?"

Sally checked her wristwatch. The last scheduled flight, a twin-engine De Havilland, left in an hour, but if they missed it, there was a chance they could talk one of the charter pilots into a deal. There was also the ferry in the morning, though that meant missing tonight's fete, although they'd still get there in plenty of time for Saturday afternoon's goat roast and whatever was going on that night.

"What should I do?" Johnnie murmured, in a tone that implied no real solution existed, but she would do what she was told.

While her clothes dried, Sally said, she was going to take a quick walk up to Rosehill to invite Tillman and his visitor, what was her name? to come along.

"Adrian," Johnnie said, lowering her eyes, visibly upset. "But what should I do? I know Mitchell wouldn't want to miss this no matter what. And I really think he needs a break, don't you?"

Sally couldn't say, she didn't want to put words in anybody's mouth, but knowing Mitchell, he'd likely want to take part in the excursion, not so much to raise hell—he didn't seem to require that kind of release—but he loved Cotton's reefs, its laidback pace, enjoyed the traveling show of Eurotrash in the little island's one bar. Like any man living in the islands—she didn't tell Johnnie this—he liked to cull tourist girls out of any day's available assortment—the tuna pool, they called it—for one-night stands.

"What you *can* do," Sally said, emphasizing her unwillingness to make up Johnnie's mind for her, "is think about it until I get back. You can either come to the airport with me then, or wait for Mitchell and take your chances on getting a flight out today, or just go on the ferry in the morning. Whatever you decide, it's no problem." Sally got to her feet, checking a last time to see if her pubic hair showed through the light fabric of the skirt. "I should go now."

Johnnie actually seemed desperate. "Are you sure you have to run off so soon?" she said with a troubled look. "Why don't you stay a bit longer?"

They were running out of time. She asked if Johnnie would like to accompany her up the beach to Rosehill but Johnnie, suddenly remote, said no, she'd better stay behind and start dinner, she had promised Mitchell spaghetti and it was probably time to make the sauce. Her eyes seemed to deaden as she followed Sally out into the front room. Well, thought Sally, that seems to settle it. Before she opened the door to leave, she returned Johnnie's earlier kiss with a dry peck on the cheek, from which Johnnie withdrew, agitated, as if such gestures were to be hers alone.

"You're coming back, aren't you?" Johnnie said in a flat voice. "You're serious about going to Cotton Island?"

"Of course," Sally said, feeling again as if she had made a fool of herself.

She left Mitchell's house puzzled and frustrated by the rise and fall and unpredictable turnings of Johnnie's spirit, the opaqueness of her intentions, the strange sensation that here was someone who could keep her off-balance, make her do things that nobody else on earth might. Meeting Johnnie was like a blue-water dive without proper training, going too deep too fast into a place that was as risky as it was dreamlike and captivating. Probably she was making a mistake. Probably she should just go, by herself, rather than attempt to play hostess, fabricate a community of skewed sameness for which she had no use or need. But, but, but. She was already into it, descending.

The woman named Adrian was installed in an orange Yucatán hammock, a Cheshire grin floating between the stanchions of two spindly palms. Tillman sat before her in a rattan chair, a tea service and tray between them on the Bermuda grass; he read to her from a book opened in his lap, cup in one hand, saucer in the other. Behind white-framed sunglasses, Adrian listened with a look of fierce distaste on her mouth, which she aimed at Sally when she noticed her approach. To forewarn Tillman, she said something which Sally couldn't hear and in response he rotated his upper body in the chair and, when he saw who it was, raised his teacup in a facetious salute.

"Hold it, lady," he said, for Adrian's sake, to tease her, because she had supposed Sally was a registered guest. "It's not my fault if your luggage is in Caracas, your husband's in a brothel, your mind is in Kansas City, and your love life is insufficient."

"Everything is your fault," Sally said, feeling fondness for Tillman, his at-your-service sense of humor. "You're the perfect person to blame."

"Whoever this is, I like her," said Adrian. Tea apparently was not one of her rituals. She puckered her mouth over a straw dipped in a Tom Collins glass. The ice in her drink chimed.

"Listen to this, Sally," Tillman went on, refocusing on his book, *The Historie of the Black Caribes.* He read from a dog-eared page, a gruesome anecdote about the mutilation of a pregnant colonialist by eighteenth-century slave-Indian crossbreeds. The woman's womb had been opened with a captured saber, the fetus extracted and replaced with the head of her recently decapitated husband.

Sally sucked her teeth loudly, a habit she had picked up from the islanders. "Tillman! What are you doing reading her such awful things."

"She likes it." Tillman relished defending himself. "She wants to know all the horror stories about our poor St. Catherine."

But Sally stopped him from making a joke out of it. "*Tillman,* I'm not going to let you ruin this island for her. Listen, you like to eat goat, don't you?"

265

"I like to eat anything I don't have to cook myself." He winked at her over his cup, finishing off his tea, and spit a lemon rind over his shoulder.

"I'm sure what she means is, crow is too meager for a mouth like yours," Adrian quipped, a bit too acerbic, Sally thought.

Tillman slumped in his chair. "Now what could that mean?" he said.

Sally, elaborating, was not happy to note that her invitation had ignited a dormant tension between the couple. Adrian looked at Tillman with expectation that didn't couch its challenge and Tillman looked off across the lawns, disassociating himself with a grimace.

"I can't get away, Sally," he said, "but take Adrian with you. If she wants."

Adrian dropped a willowy leg out of the hammock, scuffing the ground to make herself rock impatiently. Sally studied her and concluded, prima donna.

"I don't understand," Adrian said. "You've got yourself a new cook now. Why can't you take time off? If not now, Tillman, then when?"

"Well, soon," Tillman answered, but he sounded noncommittal. "I'll see if I can arrange something."

Sally forced herself to smile; she was too conscious of the crescent shape her lips made, mimicked by the hammock. "His idea of a good time is to work himself to death."

"That would be one thing, if it was just himself," crabbed Adrian.

"It's not that simple. Rosehill hangs on by the thinnest of threads." His tone changed, tried to be magnanimous, but resentment sat heavy in the words nonetheless. "But that shouldn't concern you. You came here to enjoy yourself and you should. Go to Cotton. Sally will take you."

"Sure," Sally chirped, concealing her disappointment. What was she getting herself into, with these spoiled women, their slippery moods? It was the bonhomie of the males she had sought, primarily, as though they could guarantee the quality of the weekend, keep her engaged and protected when Saconi was otherwise occupied, then recede like wise brothers at the proper moment. It was something that a woman had to think about beforehand, but even in this respect her common sense had not prevailed, since here she was, about to be saddled with two strangers, one beyond pleasing, the other one in need of a minder. Well, okay, this is all my doing, she told herself, and I'm not feeble, I have the capacity to deal with it and besides, it's only a party, a weekend, a jaunt across the channel. For the first time since she had walked up, she felt Adrian paying her real attention, forming an appraisal of her personality, now that she might wish to invest in it.

"Come on along. We'll have more fun without this spoiler anyway. Just us girls. Maybe Johnnie and Mitchell too."

"Johnnie's going?" Adrian said, perking up; she seemed to want no further inducement than this.

"Wait, wait." Tillman jumped to his feet, as though he had heard something of great significance. "You've talked to Mitchell? Why didn't you say so? What's the news on Isaac? He's all right, isn't he?"

Sally registered a chill spreading across her shoulder blades. You learned to live with the lack of telephone and reliable media but when the grapevine failed or excluded you, you might as well be living in a cave on the moon. "What are you talking about? What's wrong with Isaac?" she said, firing off the questions. "Mitchell wasn't home and Johanna never mentioned Isaac's name. *What's happened?*"

"He smashed up his old Comet."

Yes, she said, relaxing, she *had* heard that, had seen a crumpled *Miss Defy* too, out in the greening fields of Brandon Vale, and she had heard that Mitchell was with him when the brakes failed at the top of Mount Windsor, and that they were both fine except for a few bangs and bruises.

"But that's not all of it," Tillman added. "No one's seen Isaac since. He's been swallowed up. Hasn't been home, and he's not in the bars, and his girlfriends don't seem to know anything about it." He paused to consider. "There's something eerie about it, don't you think."

"Damn, I don't know," she said, inclined to believe there was some better explanation for Isaac's disappearance than whatever vague disaster Tillman was suggesting. Knowing Saconi as well as she did, she doubted it were possible to canvass *all* of any man's lovers, to have access to his complete list of sanctuaries, or to expect that whatever loss he incurred, he would react rationally. "I'm sure he's depressed, *bad. Miss Defy* was his baby."

"The guy's probably holed up somewhere with a bottle," said Adrian, emanating competence of opinion. "I know I would be."

"No you wouldn't," replied Tillman. He tried to make it sound like a compliment but instead seemed to accuse her of dishonesty. "You'd deal with it. You'd stampede. You'd overcome."

"Maybe she's right, Tillman," said Sally, simply agreeing with Adrian. Making peace between the couple seemed out of the question. "There's another possibility too. Did Isaac know Saconi was going to Cotton?" Tillman thought that was likely. "Well, maybe he took the ferry down yesterday morning. To make it easier to forget."

Tillman seemed to find this notion perfectly acceptable. He faced Adrian and solicited the answer she had yet to give. "Would you like to go?"

"Yes," she said, the spite removed from her voice. "I would. If you don't mind. Then next week, we can do something together, a picnic or a hike." She shoved her sunglasses up into her ginger hair as if this were the only gesture that would validate her sincerity. "I didn't mean to upset you. I'm sorry."

"Nothing to apologize for. Sometimes something bad happens and I think it's me that's the victim, not the other person."

"I know what you mean," said Adrian. "Any woman would." She turned to Sally. "Tillman's hell-bent on reeducating me," she reached up to tousle his hair, "and as I'm sure you've noticed, I'm failing the class so far."

It was impossible to court her with one crisis after another breaking into the flow, but if she would just step away for a day or two, he promised, she would arrive back in a newly ordered universe where she would ascend to the throne of his attention.. Then, starting fresh on Monday, there'd be plenty of time for love.

"It's plain to see," Adrian said with playful affection, "that I am being evacuated."

Sally breathed a sigh of temporary relief—at least there was something more to Adrian than poutiness and vanity. After she had packed an overnight bag, Tillman, who had to go supervise the new cook who didn't yet know her way around the kitchen, offered to have one of Grampa Hell's helpers, Junior, drive them across to Mitchell's and then over Mount Windsor to the airport. Junior, all fantasy life or ego or just plain recklessness, revved the engine of Rosehill's station wagon and set down a patch of rubber exiting the circle turnaround, disinterested in impressing either his employer or his passengers with moderation.

Johnnie met them at the door wearing white jeans and a blouse, a straw bag strapped over her shoulder; she looked alarmingly restive and feverish, clear-eyed to a fault. "You're back," she said with exaggerated relief, as though she had waited and waited and worried and doubted. She embraced one and then the other of her new friends, incongruently skittish, almost brittle with gratitude. With her face ducked briefly over Johnnie's shoulder—Johanna, whatever—Sally sniffed for signs of Mitchell's dinner but smelled nothing more appetizing than the woman's neck-splash of musky perfume. In horizontal shafts, the sun beamed directly through the veranda windows at the rear of the house.

"And you're mad at me."

Sally couldn't keep herself from scoffing; then she understood that this was still another form of Johnnie's random flirtation.

"Girl, snap out of it," Adrian said, light with mirth. "What have you been taking? We have a plane to catch."

Sally had to ask, "Why would I be mad at you?" although any more of the vacillations between coherence and riddling nonsense and she would gladly entertain the thought.

Johnnie tried to explain. "I don't know. I feel like such a mess sometimes. Mad, because I decided not to wait for Mitchell. Because I have no idea where he is or when he's coming home. I went to his office at noon but nobody had seen him. Because I don't know if I should be here. Because this might be an unforgivable mistake. What if he doesn't want to go? He'll be mad at me, won't he? Or maybe he'll be thrilled. I left him a note. Do you think I shouldn't go?" Both Sally and Adrian looked at her strangely, with traces of alarm and sympathy, as if she were a bird flapping hopelessly against a windowpane, and she caught herself, backed up, squeezed Sally's arm to allay her judgment. "Okay, Jesus, you must think I'm a total wreck." They laughed nervously, all three of them.

"Sometimes my paranoia overwhelms me." She bowed her head, shaking it self-deprecatingly and laughing.

Adrian looped her arm around Johnnie's waist and walked her inside. "We spell that cocaine," she stage-whispered, mischievous, and they all giggled again to relieve the tension.

"Mitchell will come meet us, won't he, if that's what he really wants. What he probably wants is for me to leave."

"He'll come meet us," Sally assured her. She didn't know if that was true, but it didn't feel like a lie. "I'm sure there's nothing he'd rather do, if he can get away."

"Let's not squander our opportunities, darling," Adrian encouraged.

"Oh you're right," Johnnie sang blithely, and suddenly it was like she had never panicked. Suddenly she was all resource and resilience. "Everything will work out. It always does."

On the veranda, Sally gathered her clothes, still a little damp and likely they would probably remain that way. How can I trust her? Sally wondered, finding Johnnie's behavior too perplexing for words. She was beguiling, even as a woman in the process of coming apart— if that's indeed what was happening. Even the contradictions from which she so artfully managed to twist free, like some emotional Houdini, seemed part of a conspiracy of inchoate passions, as if Johnnie were in a rush to invent herself, once and for all.

Sally heard the engines before she saw the plane—the STOL De Havilland gaining altitude over the channel. She scanned the glaring skies and there it was, a slip of light, spermatoid, arrowing toward the violent egg of afternoon sun.

"Fuck! There goes our flight. We've got to hurry before all the charter pilots head for the bars."

Forty-five minutes later they were in the air themselves, breathless and trouble-free, the altitude affecting them like a stimulant. The pilot had a cooler of beer on ice, which he encouraged them to start in on.

"I told you," Johnnie reminded them. It would all work out.

Chapter 19

Cassius Collymore had a uniform. It was precious to him, he had paid dearly for it in ways no one could imagine, but even still he wasn't supposed to be seen in the uniform except on special occasions, in the presence of special people, and never out on the streets.

He had a new name too—Corporal Iman Ibrahim—but he didn't have a desk. Not everyone did, although Selwyn had let him sit at one, off in the corner of the small bullpen adjacent to the inner offices of the headquarters of the National Police, five days straight throughout the course of his first week in Queenstown. During the entire week the desk was home, the center of a homeless universe.

Whoever had lived there at the desk before him had carved into its top, gouging through the layers of ancient varnish into the yellow wood—*Me Fuck Owena*—which upset Cassius Collymore. He worried that others might suspect he was responsible for things that happened to this Owena, and he didn't even know a woman with that name, not that he could recall, but who could say for sure, because there were things he *was* responsible for, bad things, and maybe somehow Owena was on that list so you had to be careful. He was learning about lists, they were very important, and that was a very important plan—*being careful*—and he erased the words one by one during the five days that he sat there, near the door to Lieutenant Commander Selwyn Walker's office, methodically plowing the letters with the unclipped nail of his index finger, rolling the scraped-up words into tiny gumballs and flicking them across the bullpen at the clock on the wall, but taking his time at this task because there was no hurry.

He was made to wait four days for Selwyn Walker to come tell him why he had brought him there from Cotton Island and what it was he was supposed to be doing—sell marijuana? collect money? keep an

271

eye out? All those things he did for Sergeant Marcus on Cotton Island, until he couldn't do them anymore. By Friday of that first week he was still at his desk, immobile, until Walker came again, and explained it all again, and calmed him down, explaining that his would be one of the easiest jobs on the Force, since all it required was to act natural and be ordinary.

"You cyahn do daht, eh?" Walker had said with a big, phony smile. He hadn't answered, but Walker took it the right way. The other cops thought he had come to spy on them. He used to but he didn't do that anymore, that wasn't his job; that was someone else's job.

He sat at the same desk now, notified by one of Walker's men to come in for special assignment, so here he was, looking natural and ordinary as he had been instructed almost one year ago: pullover shirt, pants and belt, good shoes, aviator sunglasses, haircut, after-shave water, the holes in his teeth fixed. He sat erect in his chair, arms folded on the desk top, making an examination of the office stapler. He wanted the quartermaster to issue his section—Special Action— its own stapler, but the quartermaster said no—*they was like that*. Every time Ibrahim punched down on the stapler's arm, the staple fell out on the paper already closed, dead. He chopped it again and again, making a school of pinched staples, trying to see the problem. But it's broken, man, the secretary had told him. Yeah, Ibrahim had responded, but *why*? You ever think of that? She was a bitch he would get rid of, if he could, *but dey ain as yet give him real power around de place*.

Ibrahim was hungry. He looked at the clock on the wall, then checked the time against his Jamaican wristwatch. He had liberated the watch from a guy who didn't know how to behave—Jamaican ras-clot. The look on his face, bwoy! The Force had shipped him to Jamaica last year for what was called surveillance training, this play-game action. He went to an office building in Kingstown for school, then a camp in the mountains, then some make-believe business in Negril. There were five instructors—three Jamaicans; two Americans, one white, one black: it didn't seem to matter because they both acted smart. One day they dressed him up like a busy girl, even though he told them not to do it, and then they made him walk down the street. He went blank and there was some trouble he couldn't remember. Later on they showed him a telephone with a bug in it. They had binoculars, cameras, very strange weapons. They took his urine and made a study of it. He heard there was a potion they drank to make themselves invisible, but he had never tasted it. They wanted to teach him what waiting was, and being quiet, and hiding, but he already had that information. Their secrets were not always to be believed. For instance, mind reading—they said they had a machine that could do it, but they didn't prove it to him. They hooked him up to it but they couldn't read his mind. They had some drugs but he heard a voice saying he shouldn't take them. They said his rating was *Good* and awarded him a certificate, very important. Next thing he knew, Selwyn Walker promoted him, Corporal Cassius "Iman Ibrahim" Collymore. He was sent to Panama for another certificate. He went to the States, to Georgia, where they called it that, they could call it whatever they wanted, but that didn't work out, they said he wasn't right. The certificates were in Selwyn's desk where they belonged. He was going to Cuba next, for more training. Classified. Cuba was a very important place, according to Selwyn. Very organized. Selwyn always talked about Cuba.

The important thing about Jamaica, there were holymen there. He met with them, because he had a religious feeling, and they gave him his true name. There were other holymen, but they were like wild dogs, and he didn't trust them. The instructors in the school said, "Well, Collymore, you are one step ahead of us, eh?" and thought he was on to something when they found out about his name. The holymen had cleared Ibrahim's mind about enemies, which he had information on, but not enough. They gave him Muslim words to use, if he needed them. The Muslim said, Protect yourself from men with *ideas.* Right-thinking men were your brothers, your sisters. He was beginning to understand. *Ideas* were such things as imperialism, capitalism, fascism, oppressionism, Zionism. Alcohol and drugs. Maybe sex, but he was confused about that. He had heard Selwyn Walker reject these ideas first, though Walker wasn't a convert to Islam. Or maybe he was, but had to keep it to himself. *White* was an idea Ibrahim had no experience with, but he was learning every day. *Black* wasn't an idea, it was a way. A way through hell.

His stomach growled. He liked to eat, as much as he could fit, and maybe get a little bigger. His arms and legs were strong. In seventeen minutes, his lunch would be set out for him at the house where he rented a room in Scuffletown. Mrs. Pierce gave him a plate, Monday through Friday, for a Biwi a day—goat stew, bean and rice, sardine, jam sandwich, pilau, hash and boiled cassava, callaloo, pumpkin fritter, biscuit, stick of candy, glass of water with ice, sorrel tea, bottle of Ju-C. He refused fish. He told her not to cook pig anymore, not even for herself since it would foul the pots. Saturday he must find his own food—Mrs. Pierce gone country to visit she old people. Sunday he must find his own food—Mrs. Pierce gone church. So, his plan for that was, to buy rotis from a street vendor and eat them in his room. Or pray—St. Catherine had no right-thinking church, so he had to pray by himself. Mama Smallhorne had been the superior cook and cheaper, but she was sour in personality, like she was doing him a favor, and Mrs. Pierce was lively! She with her housecoats and big ass and five pickaninnies and a faraway husband who sent her a big new refrigerator to stand in the kitchen like America or France or such place. On an ordinary day, Ibrahim would eat, then wash his hands and go to the front room that was his, open the closet and inspect the uniform that hung there—he had Mrs. Pierce wash and iron it every week, regardless of whether he wore it or not—and then sit on his bed and read a Trinidadian comic book. He was a good reader; he had read the Koran too, and Eric Williams, and Louis L'Amour. There was a darkroom at the back of the house—he had built it himself to make pictures. They had trained him how to do it, so in the afternoons he would go there, or walk back to the motorpool at headquarters for a car and take a ride, keeping a lookout for the ones who might be getting ideas, snapping pictures with his Japanese camera. Two months ago, Walker had told him to make a collection of pictures of foreign people who worked on St. Catherine, but he didn't know who they were so he just took photographs of whites. It was easy.

The stapler seemed to have ideas too. He gave it one more chance and then threw it out the open window behind his desk, sailing it into a clump of oleander. He saw a black and white cat run away and thought, *Fuck me, I miss a shot.* He hated animals—there was more to them than met the eye. When he swiveled back around, Selwyn Walker was there in the bullpen, aiming his concentration at Ibrahim, but Walker knew he was not a fellow with a flimsy heart. The corporal shrugged and smirked, acting impertinent about the whole thing—*Selwyn doan care fah staple, nuh? Selwyn care fah report. Report, report. Pictures and who-see-who.* That was all that was required of Ibrahim most mornings like this Friday morning when he was summoned in: wait for the lieutenant commander to appear, then follow him into his office and make an oral report, show him some pictures, name some names. *This mahn fix motor, this mahn wuk in hospital, this one wuk fah Kingsley, this one wuk fah Banks.*

Selwyn had recruited Ibrahim himself because he was impressed by the zodiac of scar tissue on the boy, that's what he had said—where you get dem nastiness, bwoy—the two crescent moons on the youth's right arm, the stars on his right leg, the diamond above one eye where Sergeant Marcus had kissed him with a piece of coral stone. Selwyn had saved Ibrahim from limbo and brought him to

Queenstown to serve in the Special Action section with another guy who hadn't been around lately. He was sick, Ibrahim speculated. Or he was on secret duty; maybe he went to the country to visit his mother. Maybe he was dead—Ibrahim wasn't going to stick his nose in it.

Walker came over to where the corporal sat at the desk. Ibrahim gauged the intensity in the lieutenant commander's eyes and made himself ready for it head-on. Selwyn had that look that meant an operation was coming. His uniform smelled like flags. Ibrahim always felt in the presence of strong forces when they were together. There was heat simmering out of Selwyn Walker, deep inside. That was a thing they had in common. Another thing was, they were both clean, which was important. Ibrahim held a powerful aversion to uncleanliness—he had been made to spend the greater portion of his existence bathed in filth, and it made his skin crawl, and fireflies blink in and out of his vision, to remember those times.

He sprang to his feet. A silver rain of staples fell to the floor. The salute, the end of nonsense. Walker let him remain at attention, but that was correct, he had been born and raised with a curriculum of discipline. He could *contain* himself, if you showed him a good system, like Walker's. He wanted Ibrahim to be *an immaterial being.* Tell lies about wrong-thinkers, stay in the shadows, create the fear.

You can do that?

But shit, Selwyn Walker knew he could do that, or else why else recruit him when Walker found him there like a pet monkey, invisibly chained to the stoop of the police station on Cotton Island, during those first days when the coalition took control from Pepper. He understood perfectly how to lime and lie low and don't talk. Walker had gazed down at him, curled in the shade but alert, and he saw that the youth fit his operation.

"What wildness you been up to, bwoy?" That was what Selwyn Walker had said, the first words. "Where you get dem nasty scar?"

He didn't tell Selwyn Walker anything, but the lieutenant commander got the picture, he comprehended everything about him, straight off. He had to say nothing—*it just happen.* Selwyn Walker had made him stand up and turn a circle. Then he went into the station and spoke with Sergeant Marcus; when he came back out, he looked at Collymore as if he had done something wrong, and he said that he should come with him, back to St. Catherine.

He had looked down at his bare feet, self-mortified, and had begun to tremble. *You carryin me to prison, sah?*

Selwyn Walker looked inquisitive and wanted to know why he

would ask such a thing, if Cassius felt that prison was where he rightfully belonged. Cassius had no idea what Sergeant Marcus might have told Selwyn Walker—the man knew some things, after six years of jooking his backside, and playing cover-up, stashing money—but he saw that the lieutenant commander was not a fellow he could hope to deceive, not for long, and there'd be hell to pay for trying. He bowed his head, not in shame but to prevent himself from telling all.

"Yes . . . sah."

"*Yes?*" Selwyn Walker repeated, amazed. "You say, *yes!*" He relaxed himself with laughter, shaking his head in disbelief. "You sometin, bwoy."

Yes. Because there was a restlessness inside of him that no one could see, and was without cure. Yes, because he had mean thoughts. After his father had disappeared at sea, between the time Sergeant Marcus had come to claim him and the situation with the Albritton girl, he would walk all day the way across the island to the villages on the windward side, exploring Cotton as he hadn't since he was a child in another home, with another identity. He would walk all the way across just to drink a grape Ju-C in a shop and then turn around for the walk back, reaching Collymore's shanty at dusk, tired and wanting sleep, so that he would not care so much when Sergeant stopped by. There were months he had spent on the periphery of the construction site for the new airport, staring dully at the machinery and the clouds of dust, and endless hours that would find him on the town wharf, getting in the way of the stevedores, staring cat-faced at the sailing yachts, thinking, *This is my boat. That white woman is my woman. Them men does work for me.* Then he would drag the heavy mindless restlessness of his adolescence back to Collymore's shanty, and Sergeant Marcus would come with his lesson books, and his sport magazines, maybe a piece of sweet cake or can of soup, and a jar of Vaseline to rub on his bum. He became a thief, because Sergeant never gave him enough money. Sergeant had a business with ganja, and Cassius became part of that too—a delivery boy, although he didn't smoke it himself because it brought on hallucinations and panic. There were other things, deals and messages and threats that took him from one end of the island to the other, always walking, walking out the sick energy and the rage, the terrible desires, feelings so ugly and burning that he found them intolerable, until one day, crossing through the bush, the sun so hot it cooked the silence into a boil, and the ravens overhead hissed at the infertile land where even the insects were drunk with heat, he met the Albritton girl, a stupid ugly girl in a torn and dirty dress that was too large for her and wouldn't stay on her shoulders but kept dropping below the swollen pointy nipples that were her new bubbies. She sat on a rock, her feet in the dirt and her legs wide apart, scratching her name in the hard white dirt with a stick. He heard bells in the bush and noticed the scrawny goats she was there to tend. Behind her was a higher rock, and he climbed up on it to look around at all the thorny, rock-strewn, waterless and inhuman solitude of the interior of the atoll.

What you see, bwoy? the girl had asked.

You.

Even in the emptiness and cruel quiet you could always count on people being around nearby, somewhere, even if you couldn't see or hear them. When the girl made too much fuss, he stuffed her mouth with her own grimy, stink-pot pair of panties, and when she kept acting up, even though he told her over and over, *No, no, listen, me like you, hush,* he took the stick that she had used to draw in the dirt and, prying it between her teeth, pushed the panties far back in her mouth to quiet her down, and she quieted down. He remembered that, he would always remember that—the calmness that passed into her, like sweetness. Then he went and stayed by the police station, because he was afraid, and that was the end of the part of the restlessness that walked him all over the island, like a duppy who can't seem to locate his own grave. After that, he behaved better; he knew not to stray too far from his own yard and master.

Then Selwyn Walker came and said he had a proposition for him, and took him on the boat where he was sick, and Walker thought it was his first time at sea, but when they reached St. Catherine and stepped ashore on the quay he felt like he had been set free from a movie he had somehow gotten trapped in, a captivity that was infinitely more mysterious than it was unjust. And Selwyn Walker never asked him to confess.

"In my office," Selwyn Walker said, and Ibrahim followed him in. "Close the door," said Walker, and he did. "Sit down," and Ibrahim did as he was told, and Walker informed him that this was a situation of the highest gravity. Ibrahim knew exactly what the lieutenant commander meant when he said *gravity*: objects, people, dreams, everything, falling into place. Gravity was like the law—it wouldn't let you escape, not for long, unless it wanted you to escape, like going underwater.

Selwyn Walker hesitated, seemingly distracted, and Ibrahim knew that look from the years on the reef spent with Collymore, when Collymore was trying to get his bearings, looking for a hole or a cut or a passage. Walker studied the wall behind Ibrahim's head, full of more certificates, commendations, such things as big shots collect— *On Her Majesty's Service*: We thank you for your years of sub-servience, et cetera. Walker's joke. Then his attention returned to his desk and he fingered through a pile of papers, pulling one out from near the top. Ibrahim recognized the format, glossy and smeared: *dem cable business,* meaning, important message, pay attention. Selwyn extracted a second sheet from the pile and pushed it across the desk for Ibrahim to see. A copy of a picture of a woman was printed on it, hard to make out—just a woman, white; or maybe a man with long hair—and then typing below that: name, age, date of birth, place of birth, 110 pounds, brown hair, hazel eyes and such, scar on knee. Then the story: *drugs . . . in connection with . . .* His eyes slid off the page.

"You recognize she?"

"No."

Walker pushed the other sheet forward. "Him?"

Roberto Antonio Fernandez. Age, date of birth, place of birth: *Cienfuegos, Cuba . . . U.S. Marine Corps, 1968-70. Discharged honor-ably: 9/1/70. Wanted for importation of narcotics into the United States of America; wanted for questioning in the death of Katherine Byrd Mason, 3/3/77, in Honolulu, Hawaii. Indicted 3/13/77; warrant for arrest issued, Pacific District Federal Court. Whereabouts unknown, believed to be in Thailand, Mexico, Latin America.*

"No."

Walker rapped the first cable with his knuckles and sat back. "People in Miami very curious about this girl, eh?"

Ibrahim scanned the cable concerning the woman again: *Whereabouts unknown, believed to be in Thailand, Mexico, Latin America.* But at the bottom of the page he read an update: *Attn: St. Catherine National Police: Please confirm arrival of suspect at Brandon Vale International Airport, 3/30/77. Notify—* "If them boojies want she," Selwyn said, "why they drag feet and let she pass through? Them always have *reasons,* you know."

"Something goin on?" ventured Ibrahim.

"Something goin on *always,* is what I know."

"True, true. Me see it."

"Funny business starting up on this island, bwoy. Airport catch afire, Kingsley stirrin up the coalition, disrespect, nuh? interference, all manner of nastyism up north, opportunism, reactionary thought, hostile moves against the masses, and uneasiness." To punctuate his message, Selwyn sucked his teeth, looking disgusted. "If we have something them Miami big shots want, I must know, eh? And if the woman come this way, I want to know why. What we got here that interest she, nuh? She have negative reasons, eh?"

Ibrahim automatically agreed. Walker picked up the phone and began to dial, his way of dismissing a subordinate he had called into his office. Selwyn Walker was very cheap with instructions to the corporal. He depended on him to use his imagination. Iman Ibrahim stood and backed out the door, saluting. He knew without being told what information the lieutenant commander wanted him to provide. The *who-see-who.* Connections. In a place like St. Catherine, it was a simple job, because everybody was connected to everybody else, either by blood, money, or misfortune. Except someone like him, Iman, who was a fellow born motherless in hell and brought to earth by burning angels to occupy a place where connections broke, and then began again on the other side of him, transformed.

He went for his lunch.

Selwyn Walker spoke to his secretary, requesting his car and driver to be stationed out front, to take him to his own lunch with the foreign minister and the minister of information—a last briefing of Archibol before the man put himself back where he was most useful, in New York, fund-raising and hell-raising. The United Nations was a place you could get things done, these days. President Carter had appointed a black man from Atlanta to the U.N. seat; also, these men were conducting formal negotiations with Havana for the first time since 1961. People were listening, you could assert yourself, your cause. Human rights were on the agenda; whatever that meant, it raised possibilities. Lists were made, lists were unmade.

He would supply Archibol with plenty of evidence: evidence was a foregone conclusion, a wild crop that only need be selectively harvested, then pruned and shaped. Really it was only a matter of using the talent at hand, like a school play. Students would rise to the occasion, given the necessary direction. The boy Cassius Collymore, for instance. He had simply brought him to St. Catherine to be a shadow, to menace and prowl, to be a haunting reminder of Walker's own power, and now his Cotton Island foundling had remade himself into the spirit of the times, a mascot for all the change that was coming— Iman Ibrahim, revolution's smoke. And now Selwyn Walker had accidentally acquired another, though less gifted actor, being readied for service.

This was a very interesting game of dominoes—that was another way to see it. He had been curious about Crissy Knowles' son, had

meant him no harm, but had been forced to throw him into jail for
being rude, for being a smartmouth, to teach him manners. This was
the correct way to proceed. Then he began to think, Why was the
boy so quick to be rude, unless he had an axe to grind? He asked one
of his men to provide a memo on the Knowles boy, his family and
friends, his activities. The results were very interesting. Kingsley's
name came up in an unexpected way. Also, the name of an American
attached to Kingsley's ministry. And now this girl, Johanna
Fernandez, whom Walker already had learned was somehow associated with Kingsley's American.

It boiled down to scurrility, one way or the next. It was a process,
this business, not a policy. Two plus two plus two plus two. What it
all meant, he didn't know, but they trusted him to figure it out—all
the more because the process was mental, an exchange of intuition
and vibrations, and he had to puzzle it out himself from the evidence.

They lunched on steak and chips, upstairs in the old Seaman's
Union Hall on the waterfront down toward Scuffletown. Selwyn
Walker probed Archibol about Crissy Knowles' boy.

Crissy was a patriot, said Archibol, but his friends betray him—
just like his friends betrayin us. Crissy's boys were good boys, he
believed. His wife had been involved recently in a minor traffic accident with the eldest. Archibol had spoken to him, discussed the way
things were with the boy, and had the impression that the boy was a
sympathizer and might be willing to help. Crissy Knowles' boy could
be an advantage, a reminder of how Kingsley had played coward and
fucked up the country, put all them peasants out of work. Someone
from the party should contact the boy.

Were Kingsley and his clique still supporting the family, Walker
asked? Archibol said he didn't know. Lloyd Peters listened intently,
wondering where all this talk about a damn boy was leading.

They talked about the businessmen on the island, most of whom
favored Kingsley. They talked about tourist revenues, money that did
not spread through society, but funneled back into the same old
pockets. They talked about the difficulty in reforming an agricultural
economy based on exports, and they talked about the indifference of
the United States of America, and then, without feeling they were
contradicting themselves, they talked about sabotage. Just because an
enemy was aloof made him no less your enemy.

"Here now, Selwyn, just what is it you surmise taking place up
north?" Archibol asked, looking less troubled than imperious.

"Counterrevolutionaries."

"You jump ahead of yourself on that one, Selwyn," remarked Lloyd Peters, amused. "We ain't as yet have a revo for anyone to counter."

"No?" said Selwyn, mockingly. "No?" he taunted, and, smiling at their laughter, told them he was preparing a case. He was gathering evidence. The evidence would show that the Americans were conducting a covert operation on the island, financing pro-Kingsley reactionaries with illegal funds laundered from drug sales.

"Fuck me in the ass, bwoy!" said Lloyd Peters. He was duly impressed. Selwyn had a busy imagination. He was a pioneer, a fucking pioneer.

As the working day ended, Ibrahim returned to headquarters to make his report. He had been to Immigration: the woman had arrived on St. Catherine two days ago. On her immigration form she had written Mitchell Wilson, c/o Min. of Agriculture, as her place of residence. Selwyn Walker listened stony-faced for details that he didn't already have from his tiring discussions with Crissy Knowles' boy.

Still, this was how a hunter trained his dogs to hunt, introduce them to the scent of the quarry, wipe their muzzles with it, and then unleash them, but not until you'd pictured in your mind the chase and its possible routes, foreseen the outcome and the alternatives to the outcome, so that at the end you'd be there, waiting, to know if your instincts were correct, your art impeachable, and you could step forward, finally, in control.

He was working it out, trying to fathom the design: Here was a truth that proved itself daily—when you were right-thinking and positive and poised for change, then history grew translucent, you could see your face in its reflection, the design spiraled with a life of its own toward convergence, and every passing moment favored you with something new. Corporal Ibrahim had nothing for him, but he had something for Corporal Ibrahim. Minutes ago he had taken a phone call from one of his recruits at the airport, someone in Customs, the same recruit whom he had called for investigation regarding the overseas cable yesterday, when it had been received by Communications. The message this afternoon was that the woman and two others had just taken a charter down to Cotton. Very interesting: why was she not with her man?

Selwyn Walker had not satisfied himself as to Iman Ibrahim's potential, and there was no better time to do it. He had not yet tapped the corporal's sanguine moods, not truly encouraged whatever dark knowledge lay beneath the youth's scars, behind the chilling, roaming psychopathy of the eyes, had not quite utilized the coiled tension of his posture, so that he might better understand how to manage and enjoy Ibrahim's special gift, to find for it a role that was not yet fully apparent, for he would not have it wasted, as the boy's guardian on Cotton Island had wasted it, spent on frivolous craving.

He believed he knew Iman Ibrahim, but he did not yet understand Cassius Collymore. Which was exactly his motive for sending him—*them*—to Cotton Island.

Mek some new friend, eh? Some gy-url friend. You see?

Sah.

Also. Marcus still movin ganj, eh?

Ibrahim shrugged, not knowing.

Mek him stop, nuh?

Cool.

Daht fella exploit de masses, nuh?

Sah.

I am authorizin you to mek him stop as you see fit, nuh?

Sah.

He explained further about how the corporal should approach the woman, then dismissed him, and, remembering another angle of pursuit, wrote something on a piece of paper, a reminder to himself to send his own cable, not to Miami, where the first one had originated, but to the Cuban embassy in Mexico City.

He sat meditating upon his pursuit of Kingsley, and through Kingsley, the colossus to the North, from which he could not be deterred, until the phone rang. It was Eddy's secretary, informing him the prime minister wished for five minutes of his time, within the hour. Government House was only three blocks west but not since he had been promoted to this office had he taken that walk, like a street patrolman. He called in his own secretary and told her to order ready his car and driver.

In the prime minister's office, Edison Banks greeted Walker with courtesy. He stood up from his paperwork to shake the lieutenant commander's hand, then came out from behind his ornate desk and invited Walker to sit with him on the sofa. Before he spoke again, he poured them both glasses of ice water, his brow furrowed as he concentrated on what he was doing. The meeting was brief. The glasses stayed where the prime minister had poured them, on the coffee table, untouched.

"Lloyd stop by," said Banks. "He told me Archie get off okay."

Selwyn Walker nodded. "Good, good," he said.

"You movin too fast, Selwyn."

He kept his resolve, though he had not expected to be confronted about this. "Prime Minister Banks, I ask permission to request military advisors."

"What! You jokin, mahn," the prime minister scoffed. "From who?"

"Cuba. Sah."

"You fellas worryin me, you know, Selwyn." Edison Banks sighed, and absently rubbed an ear, looking out the window. Ever since pre-coalition days, he had authorized low-level contacts between the PEP and the Cuban government, but he didn't want to make a lot of noise about it. Since then, he had let Walker discreetly pursue an advanced training program for some of his police units on Cuban soil, but he was leery of allowing the relationship with the Cubans to warm up beyond that, not until it was clear if this policy shift toward Havana in Washington would prove productive. It would be unwise, it wouldn't make sense, to antagonize these people at such a portentous moment, and besides, he had never been keen on the idea of *anybody's* military to come advise them. Getting them to come was always easy; getting them to go home was like trying to separate two dogs jooking. He had accepted an invitation from Fidel Castro to attend a national celebration in Havana in July. At that time, he told Selwyn Walker, he would raise this issue with the Cuban head of state. The lieutenant commander was not in agreement with the prime minister, and said so.

"You moving too fast, Selwyn. Is it so bad?"

"It will be, Eddy."

"No," said Edison Banks, "I don't believe so, Selwyn. We should save this for the next executive meeting of the party, eh?"

The prime minister checked his watch and regarded Walker with powerful—sudden and startling—aggravation. Selwyn stood, saluted, and walked himself to the door, leaving Edison Banks on the sofa, staring out the window.

Back in his own office, Selwyn Walker waited impatiently while the operator tried to connect him with Mexico.

Government Information Service, St. Catherine, W.I.

PRESS RELEASE: For immediate use.

RADIO: Radio 805 (Please announce three days consecutively)

****

Authorities at National Police Headquarters in Queenstown reported that during the week past, two NPF rural stations in the North Leeward districts of Balmont and Cri de Coeur were the target of attacks by a band or bands of unidentified men. Private Albion Lewis, of the Mansard Station, suffered a cutlass slash to his right forearm. The brigands are reported to have made off with rifles and ammunition. It is unknown at this time whether the attacks are related. A sergeant on the scene however said that the suspects appeared to him to have conducted themselves in a disciplined fashion. The sergeant declined to speculate as to whether the men had received military training, or whom they might represent. Authorities at NPFHQ consider the incidents serious and promise a proper and thorough investigation of the matter.

****

Ministry of Information Bulletin D24-77. Initialed and available for distribution: Hon. Min. LP Fri. p.m. 1 Apr.

Chapter 20

By the time Mitchell arrived back in Howard Bay it was dark, much too dark—a darkness dredged up from another epoch; a thick, nerve-wracking, unyielding blackness. All the way along the coast, from the hill lowering into Augustine out to Pilo Bight, the electricity was off, though inland, up through the steep valleys, occasionally he saw a mountainside sparkled with power. Along the highway, houses were shuttered, lifeless. Sometimes back in the bush a rag-soaked torch slapped a greasy light high up into the branches of trees. In the taxi's sweep of headlights, people walking the road looked angry or dumfounded, like startled animals, ready to defend themselves or run.

His mouth tingled with curry from the dinner he had eaten alone in town. He read Johnnie's note by candlelight. Her absence purified the house again, he thought at first, but then gradually another presence, like an aura or after-image, pressed against his sense of well-being, as if within these walls something fateful had occurred—an accident, a death—and had been cleaned up but not erased. His head began to pound and he patted his way blindly through the house to the bathroom, swallowing what he hoped were four aspirin. Then—he was certain he could hear its hum, entering the silence—the electricity came back and he went into every room, turning on the lights.

He picked away at Johnnie like a scab, vacillating between relief and disbelief. Her very arbitrariness made it impossible to discern what use she might have for him and, frankly, he was getting sick and tired of reflecting upon Johnnie's motives. Like the simplest of fools, he forgave her, too, but being happy about it was like asking him to draw on some inner resources that he did not have. He doubted himself profoundly, that despite all his wounded rhetoric and posturing, he hadn't the stomach to say, That's enough, I'm cutting losses on you, you're beyond redemption, I'm beyond tolerance, and nothing's more inexcusable at this point than hope, not even love. Love didn't require it, love could prosper just as it was, without a future, could be mad, irresponsible and self-generating or self-destructive, as it wanted, a mad molecule that could not be contained, or held accountable, but a relationship was a different matter and had no business existing, an economist might say, without a sense or vision of profit.

She was some sort of international outlaw, for the love of Christ. How fatuous, utterly ridiculous, and unthinkable. How did she let this happen? Selling dime bags of grass to her friends!? *I mean, really,* Mitchell cursed to himself, livid, throwing open kitchen windows, banging ice from the tray in the refrigerator to fix himself a rum and tonic. *Stupid, stupid,* she was completely worthless, this bitch. He took his drink out onto the veranda to stare savagely over the black, soothing water, until it found a place for his outrage.

This time, it had taken Johnnie only three days to cast his life in murk and shit, and here was a government minister, a man he answered to—and who knows what other interested parties, certainly—right in the middle, telling him to measure his distance from this woman in miles, oceans, continents. And that rankled him; he recoiled from that too. A pronouncement. What concern of it was Kingsley's—Kingsley was a crook himself! Fuck Kingsley. Fuck all. The principle of sanctuary still held, could not be revoked by pronouncements.

In its phrasing and scrawl, her note communicated breathless speed, a frantic slippage of control: *Mitch! Mitch! Please come down, join us, be with me, in our own world, I love you, Believe! I want, believe how much I want, you. Now, then, always. I'm going because you want me to go. I'm giving you time to think. Sally says you'll come tomorrow. I'm doing this for you.*

She's doing this for me, he mocked; what was he, the no-longer-elusive project of her life, the subject of her aimless energy, her anxious smoking, her Tinkerbell blasts of cocaine? She was a selfish, corrosive woman—what had she ever done that connected her to forces greater than herself? What actually was the point of her life, he'd like to know. What actually did she identify with, besides pleasure?

The canvas of a sail snapped, luffing, somewhere out in the bay; Mitchell peered into the shimmering darkness as if it had called his name. The pinprick red and green running lights of an invisible boat maneuvered toward the cut into the harbor, difficult enough to navigate in daylight. Uncharacteristically, he felt excluded from the lives that surrounded him, lives that perhaps offered more, and then the irrational fear came over him—*She's abandoned me, again.*

It was driving him mad, thinking about sex with Johnnie. He stood away from the rail, detaching himself from the madness, and went into the kitchen to make himself another drink, more rum this time, less tonic, and came back outside.

If he went down to Cotton, what would it mean? or rather, he corrected himself, what *wouldn't* it mean?

He could go down too—what prevented him? The reefs and beaches were paradisiacal, the pace stuporous, the people happy and unbothered by the aristo invasion that threatened to unhouse them within the span of a generation. Saconi was there, and Isaac, in all probability. An impromptu tribe of celebrities would be lying about in the sugary sand, basking in heroic self-regard, ducking in and out of their hideaways. (What did Mick Jagger have in mind for us at the London School of Economics anyway? Mitchell wondered.) He would take Johnnie diving into the celestial waters and they would emerge from the ocean cleansed, their minds clear and their bodies young and perfect.

Sleep atop the sheets, he thought. Her skin. She did owe him this—a moment, a time and place to reconsider. You never knew if it would be meaningless until you got there.

The decision wasn't so terrible to make, after all. He would take the morning ferry.

Maybe, he thought after a while, it would be realistic to accept that Johnnie has to go, under the circumstances. Yet, under the circumstances, if he had any sense, *he* would be the one to leave, leave the islands altogether, and she could stay or go as she pleased, depending on her ability to manipulate Immigration. He was beginning to loathe the farce of his employment, the wasted breath, the waste, the ephemeral designs of progress, the riddles and convoluting duplicities, the conflicting voices, the oil and water of ideologies, the disguises that peel away upon still more disguises. Toward the plight of St. Catherine he had grown a shade unsympathetic, wary of his best colleagues and hateful toward the power brokers, the ministers and sub-ministers, who conspired in an increasingly bad and tasteless lampoon called Leadership. And it was painful to watch men he admired, men like Edison Banks, thwarted every step of the way on the road to change and reform. Banks was a moralist, he had waged a bloodless campaign against despotism and corruption, he was committed to decency and in that respect, he, Mitchell Wilson, was the same. All he had ever intended was to act decently, in his profession, in his private life, and now look at him. If at first he had felt sorry for himself—and of course he had—now he was simply fed up, enraged, and simultaneously on the edge of despair.

After a third drink, he felt uncommonly sober and lucid, the aim of his thoughts at last properly sighted. The answers he sought about both Johnnie Woods and St. Catherine were of only passing significance, since he could see beyond caring about the exact outcome each answer suggested. What it all reduced down to was this: he wanted their stories; however things turned out, he was their perfect model of an audience, one of the very few who had managed to come up with the price of admission. A high price it was too, but it wasn't as if he sold his soul. His curiosity seemed promiscuous, but it did not seem puerile. Rather the opposite. He had stopped mining events for their comic opportunities, the absurd charms. He was taking it all very seriously. He was profoundly moved by the performance. It was no longer impossible to be serious. Look, he wanted to shout off the veranda, I am serious.

Somewhere up there now was a luscious moon—cantaloupe moon, tangerine moon, mango moon, guava moon—and the night had become porous; a bubble of noise rose to its surface and broke, off down the beach. Mitchell checked his wristwatch—it was too early yet to be tempted by Rosehill's bar. He went to his room, stretched out on the bed to read—a novel about Gettysburg, *The Killer Angels*; it had won a Pulitzer last year—but his mind wandered. What it really seemed to want to do was skip along through pre-independence per capita production figures for the old estates, a little scientific romp through certainty. Most other nights he would have fallen deliberately into the numbers, and the numbers would have scattered into a colorless landscape of sleep, but he was too restless for that. He set the book aside, thinking it would be a good idea to pack, to save time in the morning. First, books. He couldn't help it, he always traveled with books, too many, even when it was clear beforehand there'd be scant opportunity to punch through them. He dug his daypack out of the closet and slipped in the *Speeches of Che Guevara* and a fat treatise by Gramsci. Part homework, part fascination. Agrarian reform was not a new idea, but its newness never seemed to wear off for capitalists, though Mitchell was reluctant to think of himself as such. Successful reform meant building bridges between the shores of two extremes, bridges between ancient habits of greed and insane self-defeating gestures of defiance. He was going to try to read on the beach—that's what beaches were really for, contemplation—and he was going to swim—his suit and skin-diving gear went into the pack—and eat, somebody would be barbecuing something—his toothpaste and brush—and he was going to sleep with Johnnie—one of Sister Vera's party-favor condoms was requisitioned for the deed. A fresh tee shirt, a comb—he could take off for the Congo tomorrow, if he wanted. His camera, with half its roll of Tri-X shot last week in the field. Living in a place infiltrated by tourists had dampened whatever amateurish impulses for photography he had once claimed. It was a discreet form of imperialism, picture-taking, but this would be different, he'd be documenting the migratory pattern of friendship. Images that were innately personal.

The daypack filled, he left it on the counter in the kitchen and, scouting around, as if he had forgotten something, he investigated Johnnie's market purchases. At least she had gone shopping, as he asked. She had replaced the chicken—he marveled that she had found one to buy—but she had stupidly bought cat kibble too, as if the bush cat that hung around had declared itself ready to settle down into a suburban life. There was a plastic package of hamburger that looked like ground fat with sticky brown blood poured over it. Didn't Johnnie once write him that she had become a vegetarian, sworn off blood? Garlic bulbs, rice, noodles, bread, lettuce, a can of sardines, eggs—it all struck him as deceptively normal, her day of grocery shopping.

He wasn't hungry; there were no dishes in the sink or he would have washed them. She kept house apparently; she wasn't disinterested in domestic routine and ritual. He went to the bedroom he had given her and, without second thoughts, poked through her things, not hunting for anything specific, but with a sense of getting to know her, this strangely familiar woman, better. He held a pink pair of her underwear and meditated on its crotch, its washed-out stain, faint but absolutely unreadable, nothing but a poor trace of mundane humanity to stare upon. He decided he liked her clothes, their subdued colors, their implicit rejection of flamboyance. Straight lines, comfort, no use for pretense. No socks or sweaters—she had made herself into an authentic fair-weather girl. No photographs either, no outdated credit cards, no cute mementos, no package of letters fastened with a rubber band, no sentimental trinkets, a teenager's modest hoard of jewelry and not much more, no nostalgic detritus from a life walked away from, admittedly in haste; nothing to circumvent or deny a message of ordinariness. Variety of girl: ordinary. Well, that was bullshit. She deserved nothing, he argued, that she failed to earn, day by day.

In one of the pockets of her knapsack, he discovered a small black chamois pouch, which he unzipped; inside was a rosary, its crucifix silver—it mystified him as much as anything about Johnnie ever had. Had she, a lapsed Episcopalian, a woman as theologically oriented as the commodities exchange, converted to Catholicism? Found God? Found a use for God? Bewildered, he replaced the rosary and left the room, as if rebuked: Say what you like but remember she has a soul.

He shaved haphazardly, nicking himself, eyeing his crooked nose in the bathroom mirror, dabbing the blood with toilet paper. Along the windowsill, a row of Johnnie's creams and cosmetics and shampoos seemed unnatural, like props. Through the opened window, music whispered to him, emanations of happiness, tugging and prodding. He was wound too tight to stay at home on a Friday night, in a house that had never before felt empty.

Instead of shortcutting down to the beach, he stayed on the road where it was easier to walk. Up ahead in the darkness, the music came to a stop and he could hear loud drunken voices and laughter. The roadside flowed with pedestrians, many of them singing—their own songs, church hymns, radio tunes, TV jingles, greetings. Good evening, good night, taking a walk, eh? St. Catherine island was a friendly place, he was willing to say, safe as childhood in Nebraska; provincial, ornamented with crimes of passion and crimes of finance but not made ugly and unbearable with malice. Sometimes he even forgot to lock the door to his house; it didn't strike him as necessary, and the common people were more trustworthy than their leaders.

The bar had its end-of-the-week mob; he had to stand and wait for a gap in the wall of bodies before he could belly up. Winston had two assistants now on weekends, and two more, a waiter and waitress, both wearing white duckbill caps with *Rosehill* stenciled on their crowns, freighted drinks to the café tables. Maybe Tillman would be better off, Mitchell thought, if he unloaded the hotel and rode the faster horse. But he wouldn't; the romance was rooted deep in him. Still, there was always reason to believe that things would get better or, failing that, that the worst wasn't as bad as you had imagined it would be.

With a green bottle of beer finally in hand, he shouldered a path out of the barside crush and looked around, optimistically. He chatted with a huddle of Sally's Peace Corps cronies; some acknowledged him with thin, appraising smiles—they came equipped with a proprietorial air, as if he had trespassed on their turf. The self-righteous ones made a habit of spurning foreign service professionals, contemptuous of their servants and fat salaries, private cars and swimming pools and luxurious houses. And the specialists, many of them, Mitchell knew, stared right through the volunteers, as though they didn't exist. Pretension and snobbery were their common denominators. He flirted with a woman he had been flirting with for months, with no more success than in the past. She had a boyfriend on another island, she was engaged to someone back home, she was not dating at the moment, she was trying to get over a divorce—she was everything but available. Then you shouldn't look at me, Mitchell thought he must say to her, the next time he had to listen to one of her excuses, with that merry flash of wildness in your eyes.

He maneuvered onward, nodding and patting arms; he was an old-timer by now; it seemed he knew or recognized everyone there, the bureaucrats, merchants and teachers, the shopgirls from the more elite boutiques, the students from the technical college and upper forms, acolytes of the ruling class. He couldn't help but notice the towering, leonine presence of the minister of justice and his court of sycophants—a man as famous for his wholehearted participation in the island's nightlife as for his idiosyncratic style of jurisprudence. In close orbit to this star were tight knots of barristers, animated with privilege, ringed by fearsomely glamorous women with Valium and dainty pistols in their handbags, as a matter of style. The European tribes were camped at their customary tables: the hermetic French, the innocuous Canadians, the annoying British, their sonorous pomposity in fine pitch with the gentleness of the evening air. Run-of-the-mill Latin types and loud generic Americans. He consciously avoided a visiting group of World Bank economists, here for consultations with the Ministry of Trade and Finance, restructuring the island's debt. Earlier in the week they had not understood him when he attempted to explain there was no such thing as an American agenda here, unless they had brought it themselves, no contracts issued to stamp out the brushfires of socialism. Not yet, at any rate. There was only himself, endeavoring to help. He was no one's emissary; he hoped he had made that clear.

He stepped off the concrete patio onto the beach itself, removed his sandals and walked to the water's edge, letting the foamy bay cool his feet. The mineral-flavored sea breeze refreshed him. Out there across the dark heaving swells, Johnnie devised her own good time, advancing her role as voluptuary. Being there, he'd want her time, her drifting attention—had he changed that much in three days?—he'd want to sift through what was hidden in her heart, minute by minute, like a buyer at a rummage sale. He could make allowances for her needs, her hungry self. He would.

He listened to the water lapping against the hulls of the sailboats in the anchorage, a chilly, dense sound, the harbor like a vast, unlit, marbled ballroom, echoing with aqueous rhythms. "This is our last bottle of catsup," a male voice said, carried across the water. Someone tuned in the BBC. He watched two people on the stern of a ketch lower themselves over the side into an inflatable launch. An outboard motor came to life with a mechanical tongue-roll of Rs. The launch swung in toward shore, an enormous pale turtle, and beached itself nearly on top of him; he, a beacon for arrivals, not the sort of thing that enhanced a résumé. A woman and a man—archetypically blond, and sinewy; Madison Avenue Vikings in crusty shorts and tee shirts—waded through the shin-deep water to stand, shaky and disoriented, on the miracle of dry land. They had timed themselves to be heralded; the band, Monkeyjunk, resumed its vibrant music.

"Any problem with leaving the boat here?" Mitchell watched them intently, almost in awe—Were sailors the freest people on earth, or the most perversely ritualized and regimented elopers?—before his reverie broke, and he responded automatically, hearing his own voice say, Sure, before he had thought about it.

The woman marched on ahead while the man hung back, convivial, a new face in a new port, a hero come in from the black and hazardous sea. His was the boat Mitchell had spotted from the veranda, ad-libbing through the cut. Rhode Island was its home; he was delivering from Lauderdale to the Grenadines for the owner. The girl was mate and cook, or cook and mate—depending on your point of view—this was the first they had shipped out together. The weather had been good, then bad, then good again, and finally terrible. Any place nearby, he inquired with a wan grin, to get a shower and a bite to eat, something fried and greasy?

"Not likely," Mitchell had to tell him. "Not until morning." Rosehill was not an option this late in the evening. The fellow had a sunken stomach and scorched forehead; he rubbed the golden bristles over his jaw, clearly not ready to take no for an answer. Mitchell saw in him a more streamlined version of a fellow spirit, someone who didn't shrink away from unpredictability for the paradoxical reason that it force-fed their journeyman's faith in logic, the religion of alternatives. Mitchell decided to help him out. "There's my house, up the road," he added, "but the shower's cold."

The sailor introduced himself—Captain Pat—and they strolled

over to the bar for beers, wedging in alongside the woman, who was drinking a can of Coke, her arms folded across her chest, dour-faced, observing the dancers. Mitchell complimented her on their expertise, bringing the ketch through the badly marked cut at night; she would have been up in the bow, hawk-eyed, spooked, vigilant, superhumanly alert, no different than a warrior, really, all the instincts inflamed. But she frosted him with a look of infinite condescension and, without a word, angled her head away from him so she could continue to scrutinize the dancers. Fucking Christ, Mitchell rasped. He didn't drop his voice; if she heard him, fine, this Artemis of the Indies. She was just a cook, a pretty can opener, floating around in a sailboat. Big fucking deal.

"Lucky in love," Captain Pat spoke under his breath.

"Why anybody thinks they can act that way is beyond me. I don't see how it matters who she is or what she's done."

"Don't blame me," muttered the captain. "I didn't hire her and I can't fire her. Take it from me, you're not missing anything."

"Life on boats," Mitchell said, his mouth souring, wanting to change the subject. He wasn't trying to collect women with attitudes, women with pathologies, women who conspired with men in their hatred of females. He didn't want enemies, especially desirable ones.

"She's a sex crime waiting to happen, man," said Captain Pat.

They talked of other islands, adventures at sea, anecdotal evidence calculated to gild the vagabond life. Several minutes later, as if on cue, Davidius, troll-like, dressed like a busboy, materialized on the periphery of the jump-up and stalked bow-legged down the line of customers at the bar, informing the ladies he was available. Captain Pat's shipmate responded inexpressively, simply following after him like a zombie, though her face gradually brightened as she entered the music, moving her body to the raining fusillades of the drums like a shot gazelle. He didn't get it, he would never get it. She's adopted a creature, Mitchell thought; Davidius is as deformed as sin. They would have to spray Davidius with DDT to pry him off her, later on.

"You might want to keep an eye on them."

"She's a big girl, right?" The sailor scowled at his empty bottle and ordered something stronger. "You would think she'd know better. She's been around. You would think she'd have an instinct, a warning light. She's just like any other able-bodied I've ever known. She belongs in the fucking navy, man."

Captain Pat had said enough, in just the right languishing rueful tone, for Mitchell to understand the sailor was in love with the woman. He made a point of losing interest in the conversation and

the scene that had stirred it up. It was all too disturbing and insensible and worse: his own problems seemed to be the message, the
theme, where the emphasis lay, as though his particular deficiencies—
whatever they were, he could not grasp them—were the source of the
enigmatic behavior of women. Out of the corner of his eye, he
noticed George James across the oval of the bar, seated with a pair of
Catherinian women at one of the tables in a row fronting the bar's
spatial perimeter, along a tall hedge of flowering jasmine. The editor
and publisher of the *Crier* habitually commenced his marathon weekend binges at Rosehill's beach bar, before campaigning onward to the
more private and elite clubs, the plebeian dance halls, the neighborhood holes-in-the-wall. James looked up and around, caught his eye,
it seemed, on Mitchell, and seemed to wave him over.

The sail down from St. Barts had been taxing, said Captain Pat,
four nights and three days walloped by heavy cross seas. To wash the
salt off his skin and bite into a hamburger, that was all he could think
of at the moment. Mitchell almost blurted out, I don't want that cunt
you're with in my house, but it wasn't like him to retract his own
largesse, he invested too much of his own virtue in the virtue of trust,
he believed he was a better man than that. He couldn't recall whether
or not he had locked the front door, so he explained where the house
was and handed over the key—the captain could return it to him back
at the bar, or Mitchell would see him up at the house later on. Either
way, Mitchell said, there was nothing to worry about, the captain was
free to go up when he liked, take his crew if he wanted. Mitchell
excused himself then and ambled over to George James' table, bumping through the crowd as he licked the suds from the mouth of
another bottle of beer.

James had lost one of his companions, but was embroiled in an
unpleasant conversation with the woman who remained. Neither one
of them appeared to be aware that Mitchell had approached the table.
James continued chastising the woman for being a nuisance; she
seemed not the least ruffled by the attack. He was married, with several form-age children, but apparently this was not his wife. James
had a reputation for being an incorruptible man, and, as a consequence, his journalist's vanity was immense. He was a caramel-col-
ored mulatto with thin Caucasian features who cheerfully boasted
that his mixed blood was not a mixed blessing but in fact a political
gift, granting him special license to represent everybody and nobody,
as it suited his purpose, and it mostly suited him to be everybody,
reflecting whiteness to whites and blackness to blacks; an American
to Americans, Brit to the Brits, African to the Africans. What he

failed most at, at least by local standards, was being a black Catherinian, but he laughed at this category of criticism. He was well monied and proud—always with an ironic smirk—of his blood ties to the old planter families, was politically astute enough to understand he would always be the beneficiary of change, as long as it reared back from chaos at the last moment, yet he lacked neither courage nor decisiveness, and would not forfeit his principles for the milksoppy, vulgar satisfaction of merely being on the winning side. The *Crier* was mediocre by default, since it could not leave its audience in the dust. James was contemptuous of the uneducable but not of the uneducated. "Opinionated ignorance," he was fond of saying at cocktail parties, "is the chief discourse of the world's undeveloped communities"—pause—"and most of the developed ones as well." When the coalition had dislodged Pepper (with the *Crier*'s wheedling support), James had rallied a group of Queenstown businessmen to finance literacy squads, seeding them throughout the rural parishes until funds dried up. Increasingly though, the coalition disappointed him, regardless of his well-known preference for the Banks faction, and his editorials were now being penned with a tearing bite that caused even his closest allies to wince.

James canted his head two or three times, looking at Mitchell sideways, smiling helplessly, as his companion logged her side of the story in their mutual exchange of faultfinding. *Oh, the hell with this,* George James mouthed clearly and popped up, effusively courteous, to greet Mitchell and shake his hand. Mitchell noticed that James' blue jeans had an ironed crease down the length of each leg, which he associated with impostors. The President of the United States. The woman tilted her head only enough to acknowledge him and said nothing.

"Mitchell," George James declared cheerily, "you are my Tuesday headline, bwoy."

"*Shit,*" Mitchell sighed. "Why?" He sat down at the table, his quizzical look hardening into consternation.

"I will recite it for you, eh?" The editor's hands made chopping gestures to frame the words on the table. "PLDP SLOWDOWN ADVISED."

"Come on, don't get me mixed up in that," groaned Mitchell.

"The lead go like this," George James continued: "*'After consultations the week past with his chief economic advisors, the Honorable Joshua Kingsley, minister of agriculture, announced a course of prudence* ...' You like it?"

"Keep my name out of it, George, could you?"

"Mahn, I lookin to you fah quote, Mitch. A piercin insight, nuh?" he said lightheartedly, but challenged Mitchell with an aggressive smile.

"No," said Mitchell. "I'm not involved in this." He felt nauseated by the thick cloying stink of jasmine and gardenias, evil flowers, which he associated with church and wintertime, riding in the family station wagon with his mother, asphyxiated by her perfume.

"Right, right," James said, studying Mitchell with a look of mild irritation. "But you are the *expert* . . ." He stressed the word, not outright mockingly, but weighing its accuracy.

"You have to understand," Mitchell said, barely able to keep himself from gagging. "Something's happening. Almost overnight, the land reform program seems to have compressed into a flashpoint." He hated the imploring tone that seemed to rise out of his lungs, but there it was. He wanted to tell George James—he wanted to tell anybody, but couldn't—he wasn't on a crusade: I don't come wrapped in a flag, I am not a torchbearer for capitalism, my whiteness is incidental, but the responses would be reflexive—Yes you do, Yes you are, No it isn't—and worse, echoes of his own interior dialogue with himself, and he just didn't need to hear them again, feel their dead immovable weight.

"Yes, I agree about the program—how could it be otherwise?" said James, but before he could elaborate further the course and tenor of the evening changed entirely.

James' sullen companion suddenly perked up, looking above Mitchell at someone behind him and rolling her eyes, signaling she'd had enough. The journalist's eyes, too, shifted up. A waft of scent—rosemary or eucalyptus, something with a tang—preceded whoever had approached, then a pair of hands clamped on Mitchell's shoulders, as if to hold him down. The husky, honeyed, youth-hot voice of a woman whispered into his ear, sealing him into an envelope of audacious sexuality. A mop of skinny braids, interweaved with ribbons and trade beads, swept across his neck and cheek.

"You de white knight come to my rescue, bwoy? Here now, dese bloody people borin me to fits."

He could see her elegantly boned hands, the long whorish nails, their fuchsia-colored polish chipped, the ostentatious hardware of her rings, one a silver ankh, but not her face, though he expected her to be beautiful—the first expectation of any man—because of her voice.

"Dis mahn cyanht leave, ya know," she said out loud to the table, and glided into a river of sassy, exuberant patois while her fingers kneaded into his shoulders, making him speechless but at the same time oddly balanced—rescued himself. Her facetiousness seemed to tranquilize all three of them, bring them up to speed on their moods.

"Dis mahd bickerage you two mek—I ain step out to referee lovers' spat, ya know."

Her fingers fluttered up, one hand warm and open, the palm resting against his temple, the other cupping his chin, and then she turned him with a coaxing pressure to see his face.

"Oh me God," she said theatrically. "He ain so plain-lookin, true?" She gazed down at him, vamping, then overacting a pout, as if her attempt at seduction had already ended in disappointment, and then she bent herself into him, laughing, her scarlet tongue hopping in her mouth. Her face was longish, narrow—flat and stylized as an African statue's—lacked the perfection of beauty, at least in Mitchell's own conception of it, but she was spectacular, a spectacle, an incendiary device. He felt a dangerous surge of attraction. She made him feel expropriated, which seemed to fit a recent pattern of expropriation. Her name, George James said, introducing them, was Josephine. Empress, dancer, and now, he wondered, whore? He must be Gemini, she said. No? *Sahgi?* Oh ho, she knew it, she said victoriously and kept herself delighted by creating these little coups.

Mitchell stood to pull out the empty chair next to him. She sat down, but not before she had done something akin to presenting herself, the deliberate physical fantasy of herself, making sure he had taken her in, head to toe, side and front, her girlfriend snickering at her shamelessness. Josephine's shoulder-length hair had been oiled, painstakingly cornrowed and braided pencil-thin and studded with ornaments—Medusa on her wedding day. It must have taken hours to do, suggesting to Mitchell a rather queenly existence for Josephine. Her dress was an emerald green sheath with a high neckline and a crenulated hem; tinsel had been woven into the fabric, random vertical lines, which caused her movements to gather in ribbed puckers of light, silvery cascades and shimmers accompanied by the clatter of her braids, like a certain type of wind chime made from bamboo. For a Catherinian woman, who tended toward brawniness, she was abnormally svelte and flat-chested, and her stork legs were planted into a pair of spike heels which by themselves were enough to set her apart, for lack of common sense, in a place of broken walks and dark unpaved lanes. It wasn't her blackness that made her a novelty to Mitchell as much as the particular branch of femininity where she seemed to have established herself. Some women were there to marvel over but not touch without special training, packaging themselves to command the strict attention of men, women opulent and robust, taloned with sensuality, assigned to exclusive venues and readily assumed to be playthings and prizes, ultimate expressions of submissiveness feathered over with artifice and coquetry. Josephine was that, or a close call—what else *could* she be? By contrast, the other woman, James' consort, by far the lovelier of the two women, remained opaque in generic beauty, nameless, with a face that translated through culture and race. Josephine's eyes searched his momentarily, a magnetic fix, no longer teasing but radiant with curiosity.

"So who you is?"

Mitchell began to tell her, which brought George James back to life, who interrupted to say he was under the impression that Mitchell was an employee of the United States government. Follow the money trail, Mitchell hastened to explain, and that was where you ended up, but in fact his connection with Washington was tenuous, at best. Private consultant was the more apt description, if anyone cared. No one outside of St. Catherine really knew what he was doing until he filed his quarterly reports. A regional director posted in Jamaica exerted only cursory oversight. He was on his own, which was how he preferred it, since he still had a Sixties hangover from his bash with the Establishment. Josephine asked if he had been a hippie, and she wasn't kidding. He laughed self-deprecatingly, trying to imagine just what it was he had been back then, not long ago. Apathetic anarchist, moderate extremist, sentimental surrealist—all descriptions he had attached to himself in an essay he had written for some shapeless, earnest undergraduate class—Introduction to the Self, or something like that. Johnnie was living with him then, had proofread the paper, pronounced it *Far out*. So much for Whitmanesque self-knowledge circa 1969.

"I was a student," he told Josephine. "Hippies didn't grow up to be economists."

Explain that to me, she said, but he wasn't about to elaborate upon the instant anachronisms of his own life, although he wondered if she saw herself as a beneficiary of the counterculture, and if she did, was it because America had been bloodied, or blacks nominally empowered, or simply because from this distance it all looked like great fun? But he was more interested in the game she had initiated, and where it might lead. George James caught the attention of a waitress and they were brought another round of drinks. Mitchell made the transition that signaled to himself he was there for the evening by ordering rum, like everybody else. James plunged back into their earlier discussion and for several minutes Mitchell allowed himself the dignity of his own expertise, framing the sugar issue, why market forces made its reintroduction on the island pure folly, and proposed that each estate be devoted to the production of a specialty crop, exotics like saffron, nutmeg, arrowroot, sorrel, christophene, tobacco, each crop spawning its own small agri-industry manufacturing a line of slickly packaged products to be exported to metropolitan centers in the States, Canada, Europe, et cetera. Josephine surprised and pleased him when she showed an insightful interest in the marketing aspects of the scheme, but her attention wandered when the two men returned to the conflicts now rising to the surface out of the stasis of the coalition. James alarmed Mitchell by taking a small notepad from his shirt pocket and jotting on it when Mitchell confided that a Kingsley minion had been spreading a rumor that same afternoon, stirring things up at the ministry: Kingsley was planning to issue certificates for land to the peasants who would soon be rounded up and removed from Jack Dawes Estate without his authorization, the intent being that one day they might reclaim their original plots, under what circumstances Mitchell didn't dare imagine. The rumor was not credible, he stressed, willing James to put his pen away; the land certificate idea was absolutely antithetical to the reform program, which Kingsley was committed to seeing properly installed, as the *Crier* itself had consistently reported. James put the pad away, laughing good-naturedly, and told him not to believe everything he read.

"Why doesn't the PEP stop bawling and call a new election?"

"Kingsley would walk back in, mahn. Maybe better off than before. *Elections too chancy fah Banks and dem, eh?*"

The ladies are bored, said Josephine. Mitchell asked her to dance, not wanting her to lose the spirit she had brought to the table. She crossed her legs so she could shift her body closer to his, as if now she were the only subject he need occupy himself with. Her eyes glittered and her face was shining. George James and the other woman dropped away into their own world. Josephine said no, this wasn't her song, it didn't do anything for her. Her father was PS— Permanent Secretary, career bureaucrat—at the Ministry of Culture, a new portfolio born with the coalition, a campaign promise of Edison Banks. He had been reshuffled into the job from Public Works because he played the saxophone. The ministry still searched for an identity, unsure of its role beyond sponsorship of a few concerts and a disorganized, understocked crafts co-op. Josephine's mother, appropriately enough, was from the French Antilles—Guadeloupe— where she had returned years ago, unable to adapt to St. Catherine's backwardness, and since remarried, not once, said Josephine, but four times because no man was ever satisfactory. Her father had remarried too; Josephine didn't live with him anymore, she was independent, she did what she wanted, men couldn't handle that. She bridled when Mitchell said something offhandedly, insinuating she didn't have to work for a living.

"Kiss me black and beautiful ass, bwoy," she said. "I am a dressmaker," and he looked pointedly at her long fingernails to say then she must be a woman good with her hands, and she slapped him in slow motion, playing, so that the gesture was more like an overt caress. "*Now,* bwoy," she said, and since he didn't understand, she feigned exasperation and commanded, *Dance!* her heels already clicking across the cement by the time he got on his feet. Dancing was important in St. Catherine, a mother language; he had been drinking now for a solid four hours, starting at dinner, and it took him a while to find the beat, standing there absorbing the rays of carnality Josephine generated with so little effort, her body like some loose volume of juice poured lithely from hip to hip, the last word in nubility, every move she made adding up to lovemaking. She made him mindless, and he rejoiced in it, yet his body hadn't taken up the slack, jumped into the fire of flesh. There he stood, rhythmless, out to lunch, rocking from foot to foot like an elephant when something much more apish was needed, mesmerized by Josephine and her lewd counterthrusts to an imaginary phallus, her pelvis bouncing in the saddle: *Is dis you cock? Is this your cock?*

Chapter 21

A local named Coddy met them at the airstrip with a doorless, rust-consumed pickup truck, its tires without a hint of tread to their name, and took them direct to the Green Turtle, the island's one bar and gathering hole, down by the ferry dock, for posttransit refreshment. The enterprise was textbook rustic, neo-primitive; the shade of cobalt in the lagoon seemed otherwise unavailable in the world. Across the channel the peaks of St. Catherine formed a diadem on the horizon, and twilight on a tropic atoll had to be the original inspiration for the pastorale, not mountain valleys but this unearthly tranquility of Trade-cooled sheltered water, what greater enchantment could realism aspire to, and it was all undeniably soothing and marvelous, Adrian acknowledged, except for the *stars*, offstage, and they were a bit much, outside their heaven. Anything could fall. Anyone. Here was a refuge for the type.

Saconi was up the hill, resting at the Lord Norton compound. Coddy promised to take them there in a while and Sally, content, didn't object. They were handed rum punches and geared into circulation, she and Sally trailing Johanna, who seemed to be the catalyst for a more ebullient pace. Adrian noticed she deferred to Johanna's ease in the world—not to be mistaken for worldliness. Not the world, but groups, clusters of animation. She had a charming, effortless superficiality that many people would want to call charismatic. The surface of her life was seduction, its midrange scales, its pastels, its easy wins. Go on to the next oasis of faces, opinions, anecdotes, stay in the loop or perish.

It was not necessarily objectionable. Adrian had lived it all before; she had virtually existed at Studio 54 last year, orbiting Warhol and his stunning constellation, the decadence benign and waxed and winking, self-parody as a collective effort, and off to the side, always, permanently emplaced, the arrogance of overprivileged boys, the swollen curling lips of snobbery, the candied snarls and stylized scorn, the drug and sex and studio palaver of the globe's ascendent culture. It titillated her but brought forth her worst side too, tautened her voice with a jaded nasality, made her more ironic than thou, a snoot among snoots, because rudeness was a form of social efficiency, sort of, and a natural defense, sort of, and everybody was that way, out and out rude, free to do what they wanted, free to get away with it, but clearly this was a different sect of rudeness and its practice here among the sociopaths at the Green Turtle. The difference was their blighted eyes, the impudence drained of youth. Their drawstring pants, flowery silk blouses, famished physiques, and thick sea-breezed hair that any woman would kill for all looked cartoonish, more faggotty than faggots, fops of the bankrupt manor. Evelyn Waugh gone to pot. They were her wicked older brothers, they had ridden a crest of boyish rebellion and they were lodged there, yesterday's cutting edge, growing old. They weren't naive, not like the youth of her own city; instead they reeked of the incorporation of innocence and its devaluation. One of them took her hand in his androgynous grip and asked, "When shall we fuck, then?" and then tapped the glass of his Rolex. They were assholes, kinks in the beauty of the nightfall, and yet still they managed some fading puissance, a not-yet-dissipated power to lure her reluctantly forward with a nerve-stretching sense of expectation. They were probably evil. She would probably want to know. *The stars.*

There seemed to be a consensus that they mobilize and move out, everybody, up the beach to Coddy's place. He conferred with Sally— Adrian and Johanna were being given his digs for the weekend, he wanted to take them there now, get them established, rally onward to the mighty Saconi. Coddy, it seemed, because of his light skin and generosity of attitude, had been plucked from the sunny daydream of his life and anointed king gofer for Cotton Island's glittery invasion of rogues and royal understudies. His place, at the dead-end of a crushed coral track that paralleled the beach, set a high premium on castaway charm, more like a meeting house for beachcombers than a space where a person might actually reside, its single room set on knee-high stilts, a large and open rectangle, the lower half of its walls constructed from bamboo, the upper half green nylon screening, the panels sutured together over structural posts supporting its roof, the roofline tacked with gingerbready trim painted brothel red. It sat in humble privacy a dozen steps back off the empty beach, shaded by a grove of palms, tamarind, and gnarled sea grape trees, its yard pocked by land crab holes. Adrian had never come closer to camping out than this; she was going to think of it as an experiment in dirtiness, testing the unwashed appeal of letting her body go, letting her mind chase after it. It was a right she had never asserted wholeheartedly.

A stereo played "You Sexy Thing" through homemade speakers. Coddy told them get used to it, it was the only record he owned at the moment. They got their bags out of the back of the truck; a caravan of mini-mokes rattled into the yard, toy cars ferrying an elite corps of freaks, the vulturish Peter Pans of legendary bands. Johanna wasn't overawed either, but for other reasons; she was already claiming the boyos for her own court. There were people inside, long-termers, smoking ganj, displaying themselves in languid repose, as if they had been there all day, *en soirée*, slothing through paradise. The interior was a museum of the washed-up and overtraveled, all tropotawdry, seedy and fabulous, conch shells spray-painted Day-Glo colors, starfish mobiles, whalebone ottomans, fishing-lure chandeliers, suggestive contortions of bleached gray driftwood, weird seedpods, a dining table made from hatchcovers, pillow cushions thrown into a rotted-out island rowboat to make a cradlelike couch, the summery pennants of drying swimsuits and damp towels, nautical charts and concert posters, a blowup of Haile Selassie in the year of his downfall, and a refrigerator pasted with centerfolds from *Playboy* magazine. Coddy took Adrian aside to tell her apologetically that the head was *out there*. She didn't understand until he pointed out the screen into the scrub to a pit latrine, roofless, its privacy afforded by half walls of corrugated sheeting, its door impossibly warped. *Oh*, she said, *thanks*, but there was no way she was going to enter that thing, let alone shit in it. She looked around the room thinking Here I am in a beautiful nowhere with the idols of no tomorrow. Someone handed her a can of beer, Lord Norton's private label, picture of a playing card whore stamped on front. *Betty at Bedtime*. There was a blond assortment of ghoulish bimbos variously attached to the males of note, sweating through their pancake makeup. Johanna seemed delighted, words spilled out of her mouth. It was like Gilligan's Island, scripted by Shakespeare on PCP. Adrian looked at the one bed, a double at least, inhabiting a corner of the room and wondered how clean its rumpled purple sheets could be. A once-famous bass player began to talk to her as if he were still cock of the rock. He had made a difference, she told him wryly. The world had noticed. We can be in Monte Carlo by Monday, he said, Ischia by Tuesday, then on to the Seychelles.

Sally rounded them up to ask if they wanted to come along on the

Saconi huntdown. The option was to stay where they were and join up later; they could walk to Lord Norton's, she gave them directions. Coddy opened a cabinet to show Adrian where to find flashlights. The place was theirs, he reaffirmed; kick everybody out when they became a nuisance—implying they would. Adrian and Johanna looked at each other, tacitly agreeing. Go on, Adrian told Sally; go find your man. They'd be up in an hour or two, get a lift or whatever. One of the mini-mokes filled with revelers and followed the truck out.

What happened next Adrian never regretted, but never wanted to explain or fully rationalize, especially to herself, except that everybody had a stock repertoire of fantasies they play-acted through in the dark theater of their imagination, improbable but not impossible acts that seemed nevertheless beyond one's scope or courage or sanity, requiring like-minded co-conspirators (sleeping with your father) and a sequence of willed coincidence you weren't likely to pursue. Still, given the moment, you could never be certain how you might respond, the fantasy suddenly and serendipitously there, clichéd by secret repetition and rehearsal or simply by popular desire, Eve's apple at your fingertips. Getting comfortable with the pattern, you could get yourself in a lot of trouble, but the opposing attitude, restricting yourself to know only *this* much about life and no more, was too boring for words. And so was workaholic Tillman, the Quixote of postmodern tourism, married till death do him part to a hotel collapsing flake by paint flake down around him. There was a popsicle's chance in hell she was going to play chambermaid and bus-girl for overweight suburbanites from Jersey. Or worse, Bavaria—forget it. But she wasn't the baby everybody assumed at first glance, she wasn't the hard-to-please little spoiled bitch (though she reserved the right). Tillman was totally occupied, burdened by incipient failure. Or exhilarated by it, she couldn't tell which. She understood that, she could take care of herself for nine days, then flee back to civilization and culture that wasn't so damn authentic, as in *not mine*, didn't make you choose sides, wasn't such a latent threat. Had she come all this way to see a man? Guess not, she'd have to say, realistically. It was not a great shock.

Someone lit a kerosene lamp then switched off the glaring overhead bulb. Weak light jumped restlessly around the room, spreading along its low gold walls, and then relaxed, diffused into buttery haze. The beachy outdoors chirred with insects, the noise combining with the sandy flow of what used to be music and was now a dull, flattened heartbeat, the mechanical pumping of the environment. Another mini-moke loaded up and blasted away into darkness. Adrian went to the refrigerator for a second can of beer, recognizing one of her classmates from Barnard, stuck to the door. This girl, if you were a boy, any boy, you could stand outside the dorm and blow a lifeguard's whistle and she'd come down. Boobs that size probably convinced her even nature saw her as an object.

She sat down on a bench at the hatchcover table, thinking somebody should empty the ashtrays. She said hello with her eyebrows to the men sitting there, these two that the whole world knew on sight, the two others, attachés or valets or olés, whatever. Dealers, she figured out. They were engaged in disjointed rapport, unfamiliar slang that seemed to be about drugs, reliability of sources and levels of quality, like wired housewives discussing where they found their baby-sitters. They seemed fairly worthless away from their guitars, disconnected from the amps. Were any of them collectors? she asked. Mumble, mumble, over and out. One collected guns. One collected old lithographs of horses, birds, dogs. One only cared about grossing her out—he collected pubic hair he had shaved off all his conquests. All the cunts I've banged, he said in a mock-sensitive voice. Goonish hilarity. They were boors, philistines who had stumbled upon an abdicated throne and sat down. She looked across the room where everyone else was, flopped on cushions opposite the bed, loosely circled around a burning candle, oddly quiet and soft-voiced, doing something—drugs, what else—with a fastidiousness that amounted to reverence, but their energy was definitely lowering, like a paralyzing fog wafting through the room. She heard Johanna chuckle, deep back in her throat, with such rich sensuality that the sound rang with attraction, motivating her. If it was coke they were doing she wanted some, she had somehow gotten herself on a plateau and wanted off, wanted a foot up to the next level, wherever it was, whatever levity or sensation, and then they should get out of here, find Sally and her musician, a fresh mix of people, reinforcements with some intelligence or originality or at least *brio*, my God.

The sound of Johnnie's laughter seemed to pull one of the dealers out of his self-absorption. He looked over at her, then back to Adrian.

"Don't I know your friend there, luv?"

"I doubt it."

"Isn't that Roberto's bitch I'm looking at. How'd she end up here?"

"Wrong girl," said Adrian, standing.

"It's a small, small, wee, wee world now, isn't it luv, and that

Roberto is absolutely a crazy fuck, now isn't he? A big, bad bear," the guy said, cackling.

"Fuck off," Adrian said, and crossed the room.

She pulled up short when she saw the man sitting one over from Johanna, his sleeve rolled back, strapping his bicep with a length of surgical cord. Was this what they were doing! Centered on the floor between them on a breakfast tray were the needles, the candle, a blackened tablespoon, a snuff can holding a cache of bone-colored powder. Of all that she had seen in the city she had never seen this before; people she knew bragged they shot up, but not once had someone done it in front of her. She could only stare, fascinated and appalled—needles were nightmare instruments—nothing was more viscerally terrifying than having a dentist lean into your mouth with that gleaming filament of pain-tipped steel, its penetrating icy sting— but no one was dying, no one was winging out of control, no one was freaking. Just the opposite, like, *zuck,* peace, love, drool, googoo, an all-saints rodeo being held in the clouds. It caught her off guard, made her light-headed, her arms tingled, pushed a shard of anxiety from her lungs down toward her stomach. She crouched down behind Johanna, needing to know what her intentions were, did she intend to do this, *abandon her,* didn't it matter that they were togeth-er, wasn't there some small but necessary vow of loyalty between them? Whoa, girl, she prayed, more caution than plea because she was intrigued too, vice had its own piquant style, underworlds their sly dramaturgy, their covert plots. She wanted to watch, sit among the fiends and see what it was all about. People hunched forward like refugees, their heads lolling. The groans they made were like hums of sexual pleasure. She made herself believe she was being nonchalant and not intrusive. As she edged up closer to Johanna her skirt bunched in her lap and she felt a coolness ride up her thighs, the bald-ing wretch across the circle from her had a generous view of her crotch but big deal, she could have been a nun on fire for all he noticed or cared. Johanna tilted her head back at a worshipful angle, as if she sensed Adrian's nearness and expected her to whisper in her ear. She did: You're not going to do this, are you? Shit. Johanna? But the needle was already home, jabbed in the crook of her elbow, the plunger nearly depressed to its limit, and Johanna, her face luminous, beatific, faultless and chaste, that trick of the demigoddess, put the emptied syringe back on the tray as if it were no more than a pencil she had borrowed, something to write her name in the air.

"God, you do this."

Johanna scooted back away from the circle and slumped against the closest wall, Adrian crawling after her, demoralized and equally infuriated, wanting to excoriate this woman, flay her, for not abiding by their interdependence, a sisterhood of convenience if nothing more, wondering just what it was she was supposed to do now, to whom and what did she owe allegiance. The countenance of Johanna's face was a cameo of expanding ecstasy. Her eyes rolled and then snagged into focus, rolled, snagged, trying to meet Adrian's.

"Don't be mad," Johanna slurred. "You knew."

"No, I didn't," Adrian whispered back primly.

"We knew where Sally was bringing us."

"I don't know what you mean."

There wasn't going to be any more talk, and Adrian was loathe to hear herself anyway, prim and predictable. What a bad idea this was. Drugs were in competition with the other universal languages, the new Esperanto of experience. She refused to let anyone see how horrified she was by acting aggressively bored. She hated it that she felt left out, exclusion was the one feeling she couldn't finesse, and so of course she became more and more resentful as she sat there, until her irritation began to suggest itself as a subterfuge, a way to delay the issue. She wanted to unstick herself from the modern gods, maybe, but she needed a hint, a telltale. Johanna gurgled in her perambulator and Adrian looked at her, the serene mush of her expression, and felt cheated; denied, at least. No one had even offered, as if she were labeled off limits or something. Like, she would have appreciated a little peer pressure.

"What's it like?"

Johanna smiled behind closed eyes, opened her mouth to speak but didn't say anything. "You Sexy Thing" played on obnoxiously for the twentieth or twenty-first or thirtieth time. She felt scared and absurdly unwanted, and to feel unwanted was a reckless form of instigation. She couldn't stand listening to the human hush, Coddy's place transformed into a chapel of self-initiation into blessed nullity. She caught herself examining her split ends and dropped her hands.

"I want to try it. What do I do?"

Johanna's smile was incapable of change. She made gestures that were fragments of collusion. Sorry, she managed to say; she couldn't move. Adrian tsked with intense frustration and scooted back over to the center of the circle, her mind made up. This was something you did once, like skydiving. Survival of the highest, Dionysian Darwinism. Who were the fittest for the pleasures of the nuclear age? Not just because it was outrageous but also so she would never have to listen to anybody's shit about what it was and what it wasn't.

Knowledge that preempted fraudulence was always worth a risk, so you were never placed at a disadvantage, but it wasn't like she was putting her soul up for auction. On the contrary, she had one self that was infallible, a wild, volatile core. She was a bit drunk and stoned already, not that she didn't know what she was doing when she picked up one of the plastic-wrapped syringes and crossed the room to negotiate with one of the rock vipers, set her own rules.

"Hey," she said to the one who had been a cover on *Rolling Stone*, how many years ago, "I have some of your albums."

Last year like everybody else she liked disco, this year punk and reggae.

"Ah."

"I used to listen to them when I was growing up."

"Gar, what a contemptuous and brash child we are."

"Not that I've listened to them in years, actually."

"We don't blame you, darling. Paleolithic."

"Can you help me with this?"

He looked at her with his cadaverous eyes, considering. She noticed the phlebitis on the inside flesh of his arms and felt disgusted.

"As a gentleman," he leered. "A gentleman's duty and pleasure."

"Yeah," she leered back. He got up from the table and went with her, kneeling by her side over the tray on the floor. She watched him cook the powder, draw the liquid into its calibrated chamber.

"I hate needles."

"You'll love this one, luvie." He took one of her arms and extended it, a connoisseur of veins, inspecting the dark channels that fed her body, caressing the skin with his callused fingertips. "Oh look what sweet and tender meat obeys," he cooed mockingly. "We're virgin, are we?"

"Absolutely vestal," she said, trying to be flip but she had begun to tremble.

"Right. Let's have a lovebirds' stroll to the sink."

"Why?"

"Why, to get to know one another, darling."

"Why?" she persisted, getting up to follow after him.

"Foresight, luv. Some of us naughty children tend to feel a bit queasy for a second or two. We wouldn't want to make messes for old Coddy, would we?"

"You mean I'm going to vomit? Nobody else did." Her legs shook as he took her forearm in hand.

"Or not," he said. " 'Tis nothing at all. But here's Mr. Sink to receive whatever you can spare. I'll bet many a poor bloke has cut off his bollocks for a nip of this heavenly body, what?" His grip on her arm turned cruel and intractable; she focused on the light of his wedding band.

"Skin or in? Pop or sop?"

"What?" She kept her head down, through looking at him, his studied vileness.

"Mainline or sidetrack? Skin is Sunday service and main is storm troops."

"Just take it easy," she whispered, her courage wavering.

She swallowed hard and winced, watching the tip of the needle tented under her skin, the flower of blood drawn back into the chamber as the bastard hit the vein straight on, his version of the game. His thumb exerted slow and steady pressure on the plunger, letting it take forever. He stuck his face in hers so she could see his manic, menacing grin and he could see her register the velvet violation, the chemical phallus crushing into her.

"You know, luv," he said, whispering himself, taking her into his confidence, "if you ever fucking well want this again from me, before you come begging you might show more respect for your elders who are also perhaps your betters, you can do this by dropping your pants to welcome a visit from old John Wank, who will fly up that dainty perfumed arsehole of yours till you howl awful bloody murder."

Her quivering stopped, dissolved in a warm flood, an ineffable rushing current of power. "Probably not," she answered him, barely able to speak. Her mouth watered instantaneously from the rising spin of nausea.

"Or not," he agreed, withdrawing the needle and tossing it into the sink. "But do you know how to bloody fucking howl?" Stepping behind her, he aimed her over the basin and held her waist. "Give us a good one now. Steady."

She felt the meltdown commence, the divine immanence that was also her stomach sliding up effortlessly as she retched onto beer cans—*Susie at Sundown, Melanie in the Morning*—and dirty plates.

"Atsa girl, the howl needs practice. What say, mates?" He turned her like a storefront dummy, modeling her for the tableside audience. A string of spittle dangled from her jaw. "Let's put you back on the floor with the other angel and let you angels be. Would you say to be a bloody cunt is its own reward?"

She was insensate yet as he guided her across the room she knew his hand was beneath her skirt, clawing under her panties. Through the swaddling steam and imploding illumination of the drug she tried to bat it away but her equilibrium failed her and her arm was boneless when she swung, she might have fallen but then—she gasped at how brutish and sick he really was—he was supporting her weight with a finger driven into her ass, the nasty pressure was there and it should have hurt but it didn't, even her shame was abstract and incidental, he was a lecherous swine and she didn't care, he was nothing, the most profligate of satyrs, a ridiculous filthy worm, laughable—she laughed despite herself, *girlishly*, she was alarmed to hear—and she had ridiculed him, made him out to be the pathetic fool he was before she in effect gave herself over to him, choosing to be powerless like this, her life square in his demonic hands, but as long as she knew who she was it didn't matter—*really*—and he was caged in the impotence of his own irrelevance. The finger was removed with a tearing suck of friction, she felt herself being lowered down like an invalid next to Johanna. With a final smutty smirk he dragged the guilty finger in front of her nose, forcing her to inhale the essence of her humiliation—*Now you know what you are, luv;* he was smut incarnate, barbarian manqué, a repository for recessive genes—but it was no longer conceivable to pay him any attention and then the putrid little sport was finished, he had exacted his revenge and left her alone, aloft in the syrupy amniotic sac of the heroin, a swirling like incipient convulsion swirling but never bursting and out of it leaked an ooze, rubbery and celestial, of orgasmic sap. Coins of pleasure lidding her eyes.

"You Sexy Thing" played for the hundredth or thousandth time. Adrian was half conscious of the fact that Johanna was speaking to her but the golden fatal abyss between them was too great to leap. She had to wait a little more. She wasn't finished here in paradise reduced. She was still a gelatinous, absorbent being, dunked into a radioactive pool of rapturous felicity, it wasn't easy to let it go, the most gorgeous feeling she had ever experienced. Nothing else came near, nothing approached its unlimited escalation of pleasure; even sex, by its brevity alone, and its clumsiness, physical and emotional, was a vastly inferior process. Finally someone had enough sense to enforce a ban on "You Sexy Thing"—it must have been Johanna, there was no one else she could see. The recovery of silence was important, its freshness was a reasonable transition, alerting her to the drug's staleness, its lackluster wake as it passed onward toward extinction without her. She smiled weakly, watching Johanna loom before her, squatting back down.

"Did I wet my pants?"

"Say it again, I didn't understand you."

She did, concentrating on pushing the words forward with the tip of her heavy tongue, biting down with her loose jaw— everything that held her together now seemed dismayingly flaccid.

"I feel like I came so hard I peed on myself," she said, weighed down by torpidity, a vaguely postcoital disorientation. "Like, there goes the dam." She blinked slowly, straightened her legs and smoothed her skirt, feeling dull-edged, tired, and contrite. Did she need help standing? Johanna asked.

"No," Adrian said, yawning, cotton-mouthed. "I don't think so. Where is everybody?"

"Sally was here a while ago, checking on us. She's very loving." She had taken the auxiliary partiers with her when she left, more fuel for the central fete up at Lord Norton's. Johanna went to the refrigerator and opened it, stood there gazing into its coffin of light. "You were still out of it, I guess."

"The bad boys meet the bad girls. Are we in trouble? Are we damned?"

"Of course not. When in Rome. There's nothing but beer. . . would you like one?"

Adrian shuddered. "Jesus."

"What?"

"You know what."

Johanna's spirit seemed to wane before Adrian's eyes, she shut the fridge door and went right to the bed, crashing down, responding with weary, forlorn detachment. "Here I go again, setting a bad example." Her cadence sounded spectral and overdone, as if she were speaking from beyond the pale. She swore she didn't want to be on junk again, it was too much, too retrograde. "I need to be restrained, maybe." She paused. Adrian felt her own nerve-endings cool down to normalcy. "You liked it?"

"I liked it so much I think I'll never go anywhere near it again. Does that make sense?"

"Perfect sense," said Johanna. "I was headed for this. I felt it all day, just out there, knowing it was going to happen. Don't ask me why I don't know better. I should. God, I should."

Johanna seemed in no hurry to unpack her story from its psychic baggage and Adrian, suddenly desperate for a drink of water, wasn't going to tease it out. She wasn't so curious anyway, drugs made for lousy narrative. Standing up was like lifting a sack of sand. She wobbled toward the sink, latching on to furniture for balance. Is this an inner ear problem, she wondered, and then stifled a shriek, her blood running cold until she realized the face at the back screen was nothing more than the outline of a huge nocturnal moth, eye-shaped markings on its wings, but it served as a reminder, a note you stuck on a bulletin board near your phone: Don't think you're not vulnerable. The sink revolted her and made her recall the hostile anti-Svengali routine she had performed with what's his name the wallowing star. Opening the faucet she was determined to wash it all away, poked unspeakable things down the drain with her finger and scrubbed herself up to the elbows with dish soap, ignoring the pinhead of sore redness where the needle had pricked her. She held her hair out of her face to duck her head to the stream of water, its tepid briny flavor only compounding the sourness in her mouth, the awful taste a barrier to the obvious head-clearing virtue of forgetting about what she had just done to herself. She found where she had put her overnight bag and brushed her teeth. Johanna stared at the roof, humming oblique snatches of something heartsick.

"Do you want to go over to the fete now?" Johanna asked.

"I don't know," Adrian replied, but the truth was she felt sated, needing to nest for a while, recoup, decide if anything had changed thanks to her discovery of a place where there resided not the slightest vestige of pain, its possibility, or even its foreshadowing, a stoptime place of all-embracing and continuous pleasure in terrifying proximity—God, it sounded so histrionic but she couldn't help that—to death. The solitary emptiness of everything was tranquilizing and seemed to call for undisturbed introspection, everything handled with care, or else they'd end up lost. The moth was still there on the screen, as if it meant to heighten her sensitivity to the watchfulness inherent in a world gone suddenly quiet.

"What about you? What time is it?"

"Past two."

"I think I'd rather not."

Johanna didn't answer but made an ambiguous gesture, spreading her hands out toward the sides of the bed—was she offering benediction or practicing being crucified?—and Adrian told her she had to pee and was going outside.

Something had happened to the planet while she had been inside, it had come closer to a magnificent threshold that she only now saw and only now acknowledged, rather than slip past with the pretense of acknowledgment as she had done so many times in the past, being a person overdefined by the city, a woman who thrived on citylife and resonated to cityscape, someone trained to believe the true home of myths were media—paint, words, plastic, image—that progress was the only natural dynamic worth one's undivided attention, that only art was without boundaries and therefore the only entity capable of mythic dimension, and she was not at all prepared for the elevated, olympian world she found on the other side of the door, startling in its precious stillness, newborn to her consciousness, undebauched and marvelous. Its expanse shimmered under a dome of honest stars, the harvest doubled or tripled beyond any sky's she had known in the past, and outward, sharing her plane, the placid ocean like endless freedom, the most precarious of bounties, Lord deliver us from freedom, amen. She could hear fish come to the surface, tails slapping the interface. Tonight, *here*, she felt she was encountering the apotheosis of the physical world, passion purged of exotic relativity, its magic foundational, its purity undefiled, so that it made her wonder if another kind of life was possible, or perhaps even preferable. It was hers, all hers, she was alone in it, this exalted kingdom, Gaia, this miraculous earth. The hyperbolic sense of solitude was what crazy, desperate, psychically injured people felt in the city but here, no, here it was—Was this all the drug? she countered in a flash of cynicism. Chemically induced transcendence?—but it wasn't, she knew that, the drug she took loved itself only and had no use for insights. She could attribute it to luck, being in the right place, your gates opened, the wild horses set free.

She removed her clothes and waded out into the water, stopping to urinate when she was waist-deep, unable to distinguish a difference in temperature between her fluid and the ocean. The water danced with sparks when she moved, delighting her, as if the sea carried within itself a dust of latent, beautiful fire. The air was resined with salty aridness, and wherever she looked the world was only itself, no other buildings in sight but Coddy's place, not a telephone pole or highway or electric splash of light to be seen although up north, across the moon-scraped channel, a blue-white mass of storm turtled toward the jagged silhouette of St. Catherine, its gorgon thunderheads blushed with roses of lightning. Aegean was the word she wanted to say, ancient and pagan, but she had never been there, never been anywhere like this, and the pantheon of gods was wrong. A place deserved its proper gods. Who could tell about the gods here?—she wouldn't presume to know them. Some variation of Neptune certainly. She had forgotten whether Caliban was deity or devil. This night changed nothing but it added volumes, Adrian thought, genuflecting until the water reached her chin, afraid to go deeper. Tiny fish groomed her legs; the bottom felt like granulated silk, plush against her feet. The screen door banged and she pulled her knees into her stomach, floating, and rotated shoreward to observe Johanna, ghostly in her nakedness, at the water's edge. Venus, as in The Birth of—the updated version, resubmerging, wearied by the mortal price of love.

"Come on in," Adrian coaxed. "It's divine." She let herself sink down into a sightless antinomous space opposite infinity, hearing her own blood, its delicious throb, and in the background just that, the rasping scrape of infinity the ocean produced in her ears, its clicks and creaks, the static of its own weight and the pulsing comfort of her own weightlessness, and then back up to the air again, and again infinity, so close at hand, the whole boggling theater of the universe opened wide, the black expanding expanse and its spill of stars. "We want Big God," she joked to herself, happy for this moment to celebrate this life. "Where's Big God?" Without making any noise, Johanna had breaststroked out to her, coming to rest by her side.

Neither of them spoke, as if they knew their words would disappoint. After a while Johanna said, "There's something going on here with nature."

"It's Big God," said Adrian, giddily. She put her face into the water, giggling bubbles, but then grew serious. "What do you mean?"

"Something mystical. Something spiritual."

"Something reconciling," Adrian added, though she wasn't sure what she meant. "I feel it too. I adore this place."

Only their heads were above water, their bodies outlined in the shallows by aqueous, smearing flecks of light, like fireflies. Johanna looked so lovely and in her element out here, Adrian thought, her hair poured straight into the water like something metallic, her face shadowed and tender, her teeth so white, her lips and eyes glistening. She wore a puka-shell choker around her throat; it looked ritualistic and it also seemed to cut her off, with the water's help, below her neck, making of her head a bust, disembodied, a marble face trapped in time, something Adrian might have seen on a pedestal in the Uffizi.

"What I feel," Johanna said, "is more like anger everywhere, something spiritual but angry. It's okay though, it's not scary. The anger keeps the lid on chaos."

What she was really talking about, Adrian soon realized, was Hawaii, up in the mountains on Oahu, clandestine trails burrowing through the undergrowth to hidden valleys and canyons where she and her friends had cultivated cannabis. It was there she learned about the anger, she said. You had to educate yourself about taboos, leave offerings in front of secret pools and carvings, never tell the wrong people about these places, because those places were sacred, those places would harm you if your heart was bad. Usually such talk made Adrian chary, she wasn't the right type for the cosmic cheer-leading squad, the steam coming out of the subway grates was suffi-ciently fabulous for her, but Johanna was being earnest, and this was not the setting for being unreceptive. On forbidden ground she had done forbidden work, Johanna said. Her nostalgia for whatever meaning she found in that was so evident that Adrian wondered out loud why she had ever left the Pacific.

The dark sea lapped against their lips. Johanna seemed lost in thought or just gone but she said, finally, that the scene back there had gotten out of control.

"Scenes come apart, don't they," said Adrian. "I think it's a com-mandment."

They bobbed in the water, like children imagining they were dreaming. This was heroin's platonic cousin. Adrian pretended she was waiting for a signal from Big God. Jung came to mind, because the northern perception of the tropics was feminine, and that struck her now as fallacy. The visual softness, the aesthetics of sensuality, these were illusion; behind the illusion, animus, a devastating virility. My God, she thought, I've just argued the psychology of Johanna's anger principle.

"What I meant was, I wanted to use drugs as a positive thing," said Johanna, reviving the conversation. "They have a role to play, in soci-ety I mean. I think they're like an evolutionary agent. I think the future will bear that out. I don't mean heroin. I don't mean heroin at all."

"They're everywhere," Adrian sighed, "but I don't know."

"But my husband," Johanna continued, "had a different idea about what drugs were for. A very different idea. I don't even understand it."

"Wait, you have a husband?"

"He's got this attitude. He hates America."

Only a body's length away, a school of baitfish sprayed through the surface, arcing through the air like a rain of cartoon bullets. Adrian flinched and put her feet gently on the sand. The fish jumped again, twice, each time farther out into the darkness, and then a larger shape came skipping behind them with murderous speed. A chill rip-pled down the sides of Adrian's backbone.

"Something's chasing them," she said. "Let's go in."

"Ex-husband," said Johanna. "I left him." Adrian bounced with featherweight lightness on her toes, edging toward shore, stopped by the incredulity of Johanna's accusation that this guy was responsible for the death of her best friend. "Her name was Katherine, like where

315

we are, like where they've made her a saint, except with a K. Isn't that weird?"

"You mean, accidentally?"

"That's not what I mean. No. It's all very very sick. I'm sleepy. Do you want to go back in?"

There was an emerging bathos, a sense of having dropped too far away from the magic, and Adrian didn't want Johanna to say anything more, she didn't trust herself to be sympathetic. *Is this for real?* she wanted to ask yet she couldn't dare gamble with Johanna's suffering, if that's what it was. But if that's what it was, where was grief? Her revelation was alien and troubling but not poignant, her tone something less than stricken. Tomorrow, Adrian vowed to herself, let's keep our senses.

From the vantage of the water, Coddy's place was the epitome of welcome, insular and secure. They gathered their clothes and hurried across the slope of the beach, slapping at no-see-ums that had discovered here were the only two people that had survived the night. On the steps they tried to brush the sand from their feet, quickly, their breasts hopping in the air, leaning on one another for balance, then dashed inside to towel off. The lamplight puddled in the troughs of the bamboo. *Gorgeous,* thought Adrian, but she was grateful when Johanna extinguished the flame. No matter how many towels she used, she couldn't get to the point where she felt dry. After the water, being inside the house was unpleasant, the air sticky as glue, and her skin prickled with salt itch, even more so when she slipped on the tee shirt she liked sleeping in. And maybe they had always been there and she hadn't noticed, but the room was filled with the whine of mosquitoes and they were torturing her.

She groped her way across the room to the bed, her eyes adjusting to the darkness. Johanna lay atop the sheets, nude, her arms wrapped graceless over her face, her wet hair scattered, her breasts stretched and dispersed, boyish except for the nipples, the string of a tampon hanging out of her like a fuse. Even obscured, her nakedness made an imperishable vision, graphically framed and emphasized by the bed, but this was a night when everything was dissembling, and she didn't trust Johanna's body to cling to its identity. It had the power, she knew, to become anonymous, and then what she didn't want to think about.

Adrian slid in between the scratchy sheets on her side of the mattress, sagging down into a furnace, the sheets like woolen membranes, the mosquitoes shrill in her ears with their shrunken voices. The air refused to move. She pulled the outer sheet up over her, sprinkling sand, buried her head in the foam pillow but the pillow was rank, the sheet suffocating, every evil grain of sand intolerable. While Johanna lay perfectly still, virtually catatonic, she fidgeted and tossed in misery, finally rolling out to peel off her shirt and then she lay back down on the top sheet, gasping, but that was no good either and after a moment she sprang up again to rub aloe lotion on her body and then climbed back into bed, turned away from Johanna, lying on her side, her mind nattering ad nauseam about her penance of discomfort, the bed a crucible slowly devitalizing her, cooking her down with its steam-slick heat into a languorous soup. She was cognizant only of the fact that dawn would soon come and wreck her. Johanna said her name.

"Let me kiss you. Please."

Adrian's eyes were open, watching the false, lifeless eyes of the moth, still where it was on the screen, watching her through the phantom mask of its wings. When she didn't respond, Johanna rolled over next to her, and Adrian felt the broiling heat of her skin near hers, the candescent touch of Johanna's hand on her shoulder, the sultry imprint of her lips at the base of her neck, chaining her with kisses. Adrian strained to rouse herself out of her sudden immobility and rebuke her, but Johanna's arm angled over her ribs to cup a breast—Don't, she whispered feebly—and the kissing continued, passionless but needy, until she felt Johanna's tears lacerating her spine, the mattress jerked by her mute sobs.

"What's wrong?"

"I love Mitchell."

"You love everybody," Adrian mumbled, in spite of herself, now aware that this was Johanna's curse, because Johanna was unpossessable. She turned on her back, conflicted by greed for distraction, anything to get her mind off the heat. Everything was simplified by the sexual flux, the only infinity humans might claim being the infinite ambition of desire, and she submitted to a dream that in the morning would be nothing more than a memory of forgetting; private, incorporeal yearning, a dream that would perhaps be stored as the memory of a painting, astral or animal spirits in a flame-tossed void, the enduring images of the magnificence of everything that burns. Her forehead creased as she felt the pressure of Johanna's hands, easing open her legs. She couldn't even name a man she wanted there, really, any man would do, anyone, any mouth was every mouth when it was between your legs and your eyes were closed and it was this hot and, you were this restless and your body lay swollen and battered by the sea and moon.

It's myself, she thought, beginning to writhe, her hands twisted in Johanna's hair. *It's me,* and she opened her eyes, sensing the presence of another being nearby, and looked again at the moth, staring back at her, but it wasn't the moth, and it wasn't Big God, and she screamed.

Johanna had to calm her down. She got up, looked through the screens, got back in bed. "There's nothing there," she said. "There's nothing there," but now they were both trembling.

Chapter 22

Here is Shoovie, Josephine said.

Mitchell had veered in the direction of the taxis up along the road but she nudged him toward the carpark to a crumpled Deux Chevaux, Cinderella's pumpkin. She took note of his amusement and told him in no uncertain terms not to bore her with commiseration or jokes—Shoovie was her transport, purchased with her own hard-earned money. She didn't have to defend herself to him, and he told her so. "Ain no limit to me a-tall, darlin," she said, feisty, snapping open her clutch for the keys. All right then, he said appeasingly. So she was an ambitious girl, she was going places, even if she arrived there in a battered old workboot of a car. Wrong on that, she retorted, challenging him with a face. She *had* gone places. She was back.

Who would drive wasn't an issue—he'd rather pay attention to her than the road anyway. They edged up the sandy lane, onto the paved road toward Augustine, then at the crossroads turned inland on a serpentine route that led up into the hills, the road swinging under dark canopies of vegetation. Josephine lobbied him to tell her what George James had said when she had gone off to the ladies' room with her friend. She suspected something, said her tone. They had discussed this land reform business and the newspaper; she interrupted him to say, *No, about me.* She cajoled him, going so far as to take one hand off the wheel and put it on his knee, and Mitchell acquiesced, at least to euphemism, telling her that James had said something to the effect that she was all talk and no action. Cockteaser, is what James really said. Mitchell was glad he told her, since it seemed a way to make clear his own honorable intentions, that he had signed on with no particular goal in mind, other than having a type of adventure, an escapade, an interlude, but then he had to wonder how dishonest that sounded, if not to her, to himself. Josephine became subdued, and Mitchell thought she was hurt by James' accusation, though he couldn't make sense of it himself, given the image she projected, and regretted being so disingenuous as to actually tell her the truth. Punished by her silence, he fixated on the air freshener card shaped like a Christmas tree that tossed like a hanged man from the stem of the rearview mirror. The card flung out a noxious smell of disinfectant, and he ruminated about just what it was in the black world view that was symbolized by these things.

Gaining altitude, they drove out along a treeless ridge, meandering south to cross over the coastal range that shielded Oueenstown from view. When he felt ample time had passed for her to lay aside her brooding, he asked where they were headed. Once more she told him, *a spot,* shyly, as though she had embarrassed herself, but she took her eyes off the road, her braids rattling, to beam at him as her enthusiasm for her lark returned.

"You will like it, bwoy, because it is a beautiful spot, a people's spot."

Spot, he had to assume, meant trysting ground, and people meant country, rural, basic. I thought you were an uptown girl, he said, and she answered No, what he saw in her was business, she had business to see after, but she was behind it all a simple girl. *Hardly,* thought Mitchell, cynical about the business she claimed without identifying. Still, she was not remote, only elusive. He wanted to know where she had been and she recited cities in the States, Canada, Europe, semesters at McGill and CCNY, she had been everywhere in the Western world, it seemed, until her father cut the purse strings at the insistence of his second wife, and even then she trouped on as a member of a small repertory group—costume design—until that too became unfunded. Now, no complaints—she was on her own. Dressmaker, costumes—Mitchell was getting part of a picture. The Deux Chevaux farted down a ravine and back up a steep incline, the night air less and less muggy.

"Why did you come back, Josephine?" he asked. How could she endure St. Catherine after she'd been to Rome? It wasn't the pattern. You rented a tenement in Brooklyn, worked yourself to the bone, didn't know the names of the few trees dying on the street, froze in the winter, suffocated in the summer, spending the rest of your life in a nostalgic coma, but you didn't come back. Maybe he didn't wish to hear why, she suggested, but he encouraged her to speak her mind and she did, focused on the dim illumination of the headlights, her voice lilting with bright high-spirited irony.

"Well, so listen den, Wilson, I come back because it wear me down,

320

nuh? It is bein a nigger I am talkin about, nuh? I was never nigger until I go away, I born too late fah daht in St. Catherine. Here I was womahn, true, but de shit womahn eat taste much de same dis place or daht place. But nigger—no, I was not daht. Catherinians are proud and it shamed me and I will not speak of it with my own people but I will speak of it with you. You muss not believe I only givin white people hell, Wilson, it's not so, because even black people in de States treat me third-class. Here is where I think de name Third World come from—we people everyone else in dem better-off places decide to treat third-class." She shot a glance at him to see how he might be reacting to all this. "You asked, you know, you poke you nose in. Doan be vexed wit me, darlin."

It was a down-the-road topic, it was in the way, he definitely wanted no exploration of Pandora issues tonight, this was the last conversation on earth he expected to be having with Josephine at this juncture. He had not only misjudged her, he was in fact in, as George James would surely take satisfaction in reminding him, over his head. It was feeble to entertain for a second the proposition that he had gained insight into her travails merely by being where he was, it being marginally problematic to be a white man in a black nation, but by no means a cross to bear. But he was flexible on the subject, he could be manipulated to concede things he wasn't sure were true. Sighing, she accepted his lack of response and they drove on.

Finally he managed to say, "Josephine, I am an unwilling part of this disease," hoping she'd understand.

There are white boys and there are white boys, just don't play the fool by trying to apologize to me, she said. Abruptly, she stopped the car in the middle of the abandoned road and gave him a biting kiss, sharp enough to make him wince, the surf of insects roaring in his ears, and then, again, they drove on. Mitchell wasn't thinking, he didn't want to think, there was no place happy where thinking would take him.

The spot Josephine had in mind was on the crest of the highest peak that backdropped Queenstown. Its cartographical designation was Mount Archer, but it was called by its folkloric name, Soldier Mountain, indebted for this sobriquet to the British forces withdrawn to the West Indies after the Revolutionary War, ordered south to secure the Crown's few remaining claims in the Americas. A vanguard detachment was allowed to come ashore unopposed, then set upon by a mob of French-armed and trained Black Carib Indians. The two ships of the expeditionary force were set ablaze in the har-

bor; the landed troops had little choice but to retreat farther and farther up into the hills, establishing themselves finally atop Archer
where they held out for months, slowly dying by attrition in skir-
mishes and then from starvation, awaiting reinforcements that arrived
in time to bury them before dogs and vultures had picked clean the
bones. A cemetery was said to be up here, somewhere on the summit,
marked by a common headstone, but Mitchell had never seen it
though the upper third of the peak had been deforested long ago and
was used now as free-range pasture. Only a surviving handful of
Catherinian Tories and absentee landowners considered the site con-
secrated ground. For the majority of the population it was no more
than a view, the most magnificent within direct reach of Queenstown,
and therefore a natural with sightseers, picnickers, and of course,
lovers. At some point in the past, the colonial government had expropriated what was no more than a shepherd's hut, limed its walls, and
christened it a historical shrine, but Kingsley, the first prime minister
of the associated territory, had its pitiful collection of artifacts carted
down to the new national museum in the botanic gardens, gave the
building to a political crony who gave it the appellation Lookout
House, added a refrigerator and a record player, the former still in
operation after almost twenty years, and promoted it as a bar.
Tourists rarely wandered this far off the track, especially after dark;
the place was as local as callaloo.

A handmade wooden sign, its lettering flaked and unreadable,
marked the turnoff. They parked alongside two other cars, the only
ones there, and got out, Josephine kicking off her heels to walk over
the corrugated ground, holding Mitchell's elbow for support. A short
path led to the bar, which sat out on a rocky hump, jutting prowlike
into space. Reggae thundered from inside its walls, low and heavy on
the bass line, sucking booms, in and out and continuous, like the
stroke of a mighty piston. The slope dropped away to their left into
the sky over the capital; Mitchell had never been here at night, had
never experienced this approximation of divine voyeurism, and he
thought, Whoever doesn't love this needs their soul examined. The
elevation was twenty-five, twenty-eight hundred, something like that.
Capillaries of light spilled down out of the stadium bowl formed by
the southern face of the mountains, a symmetry of peaks horseshoed
eastward and westward. The scattering of lights fattened into electric
arteries that branched into geometric webs, increasing in density
toward the glowing heart of the two-chambered city, Queenstown
and Scuffletown, built along the harbor, outlining the earthly nothingness that was the nighttime sea. Out to the southeast he could see,

with no comments from his conscience, a distant flicker of lonely lights that would have to be Cotton Island, and farther out into the void among the lowest stars, a powdery effluvium that he thought might be the aura of the island of St. Vincent, and were he to see tonight on the farthest horizon the atomic flash that he and his generation had been raised to anticipate, he'd wave good-bye to the world he had come from and keep walking toward the music with the enigmatically glamorous Josephine.

She paused to breathe deeply of the view, tucking herself against his side, remarking on the drop in temperature, the air chilled and aromatic, like a florist's case. Her sexuality closed in on him like a magnetic field—he certainly wasn't finding it cool up here. With her index finger she traced his mustache, then his lower lip, its thinness in marked contrast to the beveled fleshiness of her own. He felt her nail like a blunted knife scoring the circle of his hungry mouth. She wanted him to tell her if he had stayed by black women before. Her voice took it for granted that he had.

In his mind they were already fornicating like cats, clamped together, tumbling down the mountainside. He had to draw his consciousness back out of his cock, gorged with blood and pounding like a second wild heart, before he could order his thoughts and answer. *Staying by* meant *sleeping with*, and he hadn't. The answer was no, but he didn't want to tell her that and thus make his inexperience, which was trifling and irrelevant, suddenly significant. There had been another night, another girl, another booming discotheque, down on the harbor near Scuffletown. Another kiss much like the ones he knew were coming from Josephine standing on the beach in the pitch-black darkness before dawn after the club had closed. She had petted him through the fabric of his pants. Reaching under her tank top, he had touched one of her breasts, she had slapped his hand away, that was that. His impression was that black women had unfortunate breasts: flat, flappy, Tootsie Rolls for paps, sad and overused. On his forays through the countryside, every river had its gang of women, stripped to the waist, bathing. At least along the riverbanks, modesty was not ranked high on the civic code of behavior. Endless nursing might well have been the culprit for the erotic defeat of black breasts but he couldn't say, and he had wondered that night on the beach if, after her strong come-on, he had not dallied but placed his hand between her legs rather than on her tit, what would have happened. He felt he had triggered her self-consciousness, but she was fickle, that was all he really knew, perhaps *there* was the trait he should be focusing on, and the arc of thought circled him back to what George James had warned him about Josephine as they were about to strike out on their own from Howard Bay.

"Yeah," he lied, out of pride, "but I'm no expert."

"Who is, bwoy?" She put him right back on the hook, asking him to tell her the difference between white girls and black girls, and when he resisted, she accused him of being too serious, and then teased him by saying if he were really so serious a man, then she wanted to hear something negative, tell her the bad things about black women.

"I don't think I like this game," he said, the restructuring of desire like a bucket of grimy water dumped on his head. What if he offered an analysis of the difference between North American women and West Indian women, would that pacify her investigative appetite? Josephine said no. She was inexplicably obstinate. Tell her just one thing she wanted to know or walk home. He took one baleful, disbelieving step back away from her before she restrained him. Come on, *bwoy*, she said, full of seductive taunting, he needn't worry, but why couldn't he tell her, tell her to humor a crazy black bitch, tell her as a favor, as a matter of respect. *Respect?* he thought. What she was asking for was sexual suicide, racial self-immolation. Okay, he said, shaking his head, agitated into compliance—what was this, her idea of sadomasochism, did ugliness and conflict turn her on? Here goes: Black women appeared more inclined to style over substance, philosophically they tended to cutesyness, they latched on to the trite, they adored platitudes, they clung to the ankles of a God that clearly couldn't see or hear them, they solicited chauvinism from males, they conspired with men in the continuation of patriarchy, they had yet to get their attachment to slave love and stable breeding behind them, and despite all that they walked around with a chip on their shoulder the size of a banquet platter. *There,* he said in bitter resignation, sick that the evening must end like this. There you have it but the truth is not a foolhardy litany of others' shortcomings or a coerced recitation of stereotype, and what's with you anyway, was this like some ritual scarring, what did she want to hear next, that her uncle was a monkey and swung from trees? He was beginning to believe this was what Catherinians imported white boys for, to pervert them into some sort of intellectual mercenary, targeted against themselves, solidify a role in the world as professional victims.

"Whew, calm youself now," she said. "You are too too serious, Wilson." She was only being mischievous; she knew who she was, she didn't require chivalry from him, she had too much pluck for that.

"Black womahn is in big trouble, I see. And what about we backsides, eh?"

"Yeah, you have big asses. Yours proves to be an exception."

"Um hmm. Ahll right. What else, de final crime?"

"Fine. Black women are fickle."

She thought about it. "So you is tekkin a chance with me, nuh?"

He shrugged—everybody took a chance with everybody else, nobody coupled with the slightest assurance of a guarantee.

"White womens ain fickle?"

"White women are. You didn't demand I eviscerate them in the bargain."

"Carry you ass, bwoy," she chided, but her eyes—effulgent, gleeful, bratty—belied the rebuke. "Carry you white skittery ass." She wanted him to take this black girl inside and get to know her properly, and she gave him a look, trying quite pointedly to read him, to determine what exactly this was that she had captured, and if this was a game, then the time had come for him to be its willing accomplice. She leaned against him to put her heels back on, dropped her head and nipped him in the stomach with enough pressure to make him yelp. Only one impulse registered: *more.* She straightened up, encircling him, and pushed her long tongue into his mouth, purring; hearing the noise in her throat he thought, *more.* Everything in his life had a path to follow except passion, which seemed fated always to be stopped at the border, delayed, made to sit by itself in a waiting room while its credentials and itinerary were placed under indefinite review. *More.* Her blackness shot a bolt of amazement through him; her braids swayed and batted him, the most lenient of flagellations. Her eyes were open with a daring cast—*What will you do if I do this? Or this?* Incredibly, she popped the top button of his shirt, tore it from its threads, to crab her fingers across the muscles of his chest. Her eyes flashed. His lips felt hers ascend into a smile. He felt lifted out of himself and the mountain no longer proffered a competitive view.

Inside, the air reeked of ganja smoke and incense; Josephine's skin turned to licorice under the violet lights. They drank and danced, watched by a row of rastamen sitting along a bench in the back, a dog asleep at their feet, each of them as solemn as members of a palace guard, mourning Haile Selassie, their hair bundled into wool caps towering above their heads like sacks of onions. Josephine made telepathic contact with the bartender, who brought her ice water and scotch and roasted groundnuts without being told. Mitchell smoked some of the dope on hand and found himself wandering in a post-psychedelic neverland. The walls crawled with florescent graffiti, glazed with energy, and Josephine bribed him with the silky hydraulic gestures of temptation to decode himself right off the page of propriety and into a protolanguage of lust, rocking on his feet, his hands on the helm of her hips, absorbed in her sluttishness and his, a diva of blackness, a woman from the circus, from a lost city, from the fables of a continent, from Times Square, from cosmopolitan magazines, from an ivory throne and from the chains of his own history and the darkness of the fictions he constructed about the nature of his own desire. She locked one leg over and behind him and rode his thigh with her face buried in his neck, her breathing labored, the voltage dumbfounding, Josephine chuffing with sexual locomotion to the music, and he could feel the slick scorch of her cunt flat against the top of his thigh, her hipbone mauling him, battering his erection in its own painful seep of fluid, and when she unhooked her leg, gasping, he could feel the stick of wetness on his pants where she had left her imprint. At some point they realized they were performing for the public, took their bows and got outside, sweating profusely. The sky fluttered and split with light and they were greeted with the mercy of a gusting wind, which they inhaled like smelling salts, restoring some small portion of their clarity. Another storm was bearing down on the island and Josephine wanted to hurry down off the mountain because the Deux Chevaux was allergic to rain, leaked miserably and hydroplaned out of control. Thunder rolled from several directions at once, arguing. They flew precipitously down the gullies of Mount Archer toward the last remaining brooch of lights in Queenstown, Mitchell sinking back without pretense into the fantasy of sex, contorting himself so that his head lay cradled in Josephine's lap, his face nuzzling the softness of her stomach with his freest hand jackknifed inside her creamy panties, fingering her while she drove, Josephine murmuring, *You're dangerous*—her voice recommending— *You're a dangerous man*, until finally her thighs began to twitch and quake and she braked radically to a stop, whimpering, to permit herself to come, and then put the car back in gear and continued on as if nothing out of the ordinary had happened, nothing to upset a lady's composure surely. It began to rain. Instantly his legs were soaked and he wrenched himself out from under her arms to crank his window closed and they rolled blindly through the upper neighborhoods, a bubble of steam, the tires fizzing and slipping underneath them, on their way to wherever lust was taking them, which turned out to be a middle-class clapboard house on a densely built street of similarly anonymous houses.

"Dis my home, Wilson."

She wanted him to come in, but if he had reservations, he was free to take Shoovie back to Howard Bay and return it tomorrow, that was no problem, this was no problem either. The rain doubled in intensity, drowning out whatever voice of reason might yet prevent their lovemaking. The string of warning lights were far, far back on the road and he had ignored every one of them. Someone could come throw rocks at his craving and it wouldn't break, not now, not here, not with these horns, not with this black woman named Josephine and her black effluence of heat, the molten dark caramel of her skin, the sensuality of her imperfect beauty, the volcanic wit that made him feel the ground was not entirely safe to walk on. At this deliriously advanced stage of the evening, you'd have to pry him off her with a wrecking bar. They ran through the pelting rain and under the wide eave of the roof. She unlocked the door, they fumbled down a creaky hallway, Josephine said *Shhh; Mitchell, alarmed, said Who's here?* Then he was in her room, standing in the dark, inhaling the aphrodisiac of her private life, thinking contrarily that privacy was white as he wondered, since she hadn't bothered to answer him, who else was there in the house with them. She lit several candles then kissed him with uncharacteristic tenderness, ended it by excusing herself to the bathroom. He couldn't wait himself but unlatched the shutters of a window and pissed out into the rain, then removed his wet shirt and sandals and made a cursory inspection of her furniture and chattels, the bed with its afghan spread and scrolled headboard, an overstuffed chair pinned with doilies, a washstand with its china bowl and pitcher, a bookshelf stacked with romance and mystery, everything quaint and homey except there were piles and piles of magazines stacked up along the walls—back issues of *Glamour, Ebony, Paris Match, Cosmopolitan, Vogue, Der Spiegel*—and a worktable, half of it taken up by a slanted drawing board tacked with curling sketches, sketch after sketch of faceless beauties modeling bold colors, unabashedly predatorial haute couture—jungle elegance, is what someone might name the style—and not a dress pattern in sight. She was indeed good with her hands, not as a seamstress but as a designer, and she'd need an economic revolution and marketing wizardry before her talent ever meant anything on St. Catherine. He had to ask himself again, what was she doing here? The toilet flushed down the hall and a moment later he heard her steps on the floorboards approach the room and then stop, another door creaked open and there was a short hushed conversation between Josephine and a second woman, then she was back in the room, behind him, her face poked over his bare shoulder, her breath smelling of toothpaste, her braids conspicuous by their absence against his skin.

"Come," she said. "Undress me," and he did, turning to see she had banded her hair into a tail and scrubbed the whorish makeup from her face, not by any means transformed into the girl next door but the attempt had been made. He found the zipper, tugged the dress down over her hips, there was something unusual about her bra he couldn't figure out, and it seemed she had left her panties in the bathroom, the thatch of her pubis was a fuzzy ribbon, neat and well trimmed, or, who knows, maybe it grew that way, a goatee ending in the shadowy definition of her labia, and her ass was an absolute plum. A bomb of thunder exploded nearby, making her cringe, and the rain came with torrential force, whipping violently across the roof, the house embroiled in its uproar. The storm aroused Josephine in a peculiar way, animating her with feral urgency, they had to fuck *now*, she said, *quick*, the storm was bad, it was too powerful, maybe it would stop, maybe it would stop, she tackled him down onto the bed, tearing at his belt, Mitchell not equal to this acceleration of pace, still fumbling with her complicated bra, a blockhead determined to solve its logistics. She climbed off him to yank his pants away, scrambled back with an anguished, frustrated cry, spraddling him, the house vibrating with the din of the rain. Mitchell licked the astringency of her perfumed skin, trying to slide himself down to kiss the insides of her thighs, she sank her claws into his scalp to keep him topside, hurting him to do it though he didn't know what she was trying to do, and so he kept edging down, believing she wanted him to feel the pain. The room flared with milky green light. A second later a spear of lightning struck, rattling the windows, the shock wave concussing throughout the house, Josephine cried out and he was wedged between her legs and she was squatting over him, fucking down savagely onto his nose, which snapped him to his senses with a wallop of truly undeniable pain just as the next bolt seemed to hit right on top of them, and in the moment of crackling silence that followed the strike he found himself ejected onto the floor, sprawled out, his chest heaving, finally understanding that the siren gone off in his head was in the house as well and it was a child—her child—screaming. He climbed back on the bed with Josephine, lay facedown next to her, and they waited, confounded, disabled with increasing fatalism, unsexed and thrown out of the garden. They heard footsteps down the hall, someone going into the child's room, the sympathetic rhythm of an older woman's voice, unheeded. He tried to touch Josephine with some suggestion of reverence, to keep the engine of their lovemaking idling, but she tensed, groaning, and told him no, wait a little, be sweet. The child screamed into the rain for his mother, answered by more lightning, three thermonuclear booms, the blasts building one into the other with a ferocity that left even Mitchell rigid and afraid. The street outside crackled with noise. The child screeched for Josephine, who whispered feverishly to Mitchell, Mahn, I have been so good, I have waited so long, nature have no business comin against we like dis. He lay coiled and inert, waiting for more explosions, listening to Josephine's rationalization for not going to the child, but then she sat up, exasperated, went to her dresser for a pair of panties, then pulled a tiger-striped housecoat off the hook on the back of the door, but her aunt was there on the other side with the child, rapping, before she had put it on.

"Comin, Auntie. Comin, comin."

She opened the door only enough for the naked child to be passed through into her arms, shouldered the door closed and turned back into the room, the little boy clinging to her neck, hysterical, bawling his lungs out. You must love this, Wilson, she said with great unhappiness, pacing back and forth, trying to comfort her baby and having no success, secreta bubbling out of his miniature nose and pinched eyes, his spidery body convulsed with misery, his mouth so wide open with yowling you could stuff an orange into it. Josephine wiped the snot from his face with her sleeve and provided a summary answer to the riddle of her brassiere by unfastening one of its cups like a lid and offering her eggplant breast to the boy, who wrenched his head wildly away, wanting nothing to do with it. What now? she groaned. What de hell, mahn, what now? The child hyperventilated.

Good question. *Christ is this weird,* thought Mitchell, an expedition into the domestic wilderness of weirdness here, because he didn't know where he was, or quite how he got there, now that he tried to recall the specifics, and he couldn't exactly pin down whom he was with except that she was some variety of Catherinian Cinderella and abruptly real, having just taken a plunge back into a life in which he was not automatically eager to express an involvement. Propped up with pillows against the headboard, he watched the drama of mother and child with bleary, lidded eyes, but from outside its realm, miles away and high as Franklin's kite in another storm that was also diminishing, his senses overindulged and in a state of mindlessness for which there was no better word than cuntstruck. He hadn't the faintest idea what was expected of him but there he was anyway, established in her bed, following along, not a prince but a mutt, the vapors of her sex still searingly present in each of his inhalations. He closed his eyes and advised himself to snap out of it, yet when he opened them again he had a case of the hiccups and so did the boy, only his, Mitchell's, were infiltrated with distressed giggles, at first mortifying, then irksome, then mortifyingly euphoric as he lost control.

"Wilson, here now, listen, what is so fuckin funny—*hushbaby*," said Josephine, mellowing her tone for the child, as if she were beginning a lullaby, "you mahd, bwoy, *hush cocobum, storm gone now*, Wilson, if you is laughin at me, suck cock, mahn, *hush pretty, hush sweet.*"

He was off the bed, trying his best to be calm and wise, deputized into a provisional role of fatherhood and husbandry, waggling his eyebrows like the clown he seemed to be, raising the top sheet open for Josephine and son. She maneuvered onto the mattress, chagrined but also muttering—*bloody hell, Wilson*—slung with her albatross of child, and this was a shitty shitty joke on love, you know, the sins of the past come home to roost tonight, George James gettin his big revenge now, Wilson, and doan you say a bloody thing to him, and if you is stayin come lie back down, mahn, you enjoyin youself too much, eh?

It made better sense to disappear while she mollified the child, so he took a candle and left the room as she tried again to feed her nipple into the boy's mouth. He headed toward the rear of the house to the kitchen, hot wax spattering his knuckles, and pawed through the uninspiring contents of the refrigerator: tins of Carnation milk, a jar of Ovaltine, glass jars of baby food and bottles of homemade pepper sauce, a bowl of mottled limes, limp vegetables, eggs, some tubes of medicine, juices and jams but no meat in evidence. He had hoped for a chicken leg but settled for a mango and a lone bottle of beer, eating the fruit over the rust-streaked enamel sink, juice running down his hands and chin. But for an occasional gust, the rain had slacked off, the claps of thunder receding out into the harbor. The wall clock read 4:18, a surprise, considering that he now felt giddy and wired with restless energy. With a butter knife, he pried open the bottle of beer and sat drinking it at the kitchen table, a supernatural sense of peace gathering in the candled silence. The feeling that he had been kicked in the groin by a horse dissolved. The floorboards creaked and he looked toward the hallway—there was auntie in her nightgown, a cloud of astonishment, round and gray-haired and wide-eyed.

"Jesus in Bethlehem! Josie get off she high horse and reach home with a fella, and Lahd Ahlmighty, he a white mahn too."

If he didn't mind, she was going to take some treatment, she said. She shuffled wearily into the kitchen, complaining of this ache and that woe, went to a cupboard and sat down at the table with a dark green bottle of ginger wine and two glasses which she filled to the brim, fired hers down in two gulps and took a long but not unkindly look at Mitchell, who was having trouble shaping a response.

"So, you did find youself a bit to eat? We ain keep much on hand, I sorry to tell you," she said, and Mitchell felt touchingly entrapped by this maternal concern. "Nuh! Wait," she commanded, remembering there might still be a piece of pound cake under the plastic dome on the counter. She pushed herself up to cut him a slice, and brought it back to him on a paper napkin, sat down and placed him under observation, satisfied with his appetite.

"Thank you," said Mitchell, finding his voice. It was as if all the night's incongruities were being filtered through Josephine's aunt into a clear pool of acceptance.

"You welcome," she answered, reaching over to pat his hand. "You drinkin daht?" She nodded at the second glass of ginger wine, and when he shook his head, she drank it down, smacking her lips, and made a little whoop. "Baby stop he bawlin, hallelujah." She stood up, wavering but dignified, fixing him with tender scrutiny until Mitchell realized he was being called on a point of etiquette and stood up too.

"You muss come back, hear?" she said. "Good night, mahn."

"Good night, Auntie," said Mitchell, watching her waddle away, leaving behind her bewildering accreditation, an air of warm and absurd harmony, letting him entertain the possibility that maybe he lived there, maybe the house and the lives in it and the island were something ready-made with him in mind. He grabbed the candle and his half-finished beer and returned down the hallway, through the imaginary epicenter of an imaginary life. The kid was still awake but dulcified, curled along his mother's rib cage, his unblinking eyes glued to Mitchell as he crossed the room. Josephine looked exhausted but she smiled timidly and said she wanted him to come lie down. He couldn't begin to say why he felt such supreme ease, such an unburdened willingness to accept this vision of himself as he slid his legs under the sheets, smelling the Vicks Vaporub of his own childhood, the little imp between them sucking his thumb, twisting at his waist to stare in wonderment at the white man in his mother's bed. If she put him back in his crib he'd bawl again, Josephine said. Poor guy, said Mitchell. We can't have that. She asked for a sip of his beer and they talked but Mitchell had trouble paying attention. She wanted to tell him about the business she had started. She had sponsors, backers—George James was one of them, which he thought entitled him to something that it didn't, he should keep his ego in his pants and his mind on Rita, the woman he was with at the bar, a model whom Josephine said she kept on retainer, and on she rambled in her lullaby voice, Wilson, de baby asleep now, you have a womahn?

What? he said. Tranquility had entered his lungs like ether and he was nodding in and out.

It please me daht you stay, you know. Well, it is very fuckin strange, mahn, true? but it please me. You is a funny guy, Wilson, sometimes I watch you and tell meself you are a mahn with a troubled heart, but den I muss tell myself, Oh no, not dis guy, dis one carefree and easy. You fallin asleep? Hello? You have been very patient wit me—sometin muss be wrong wit you, bwoy.

The candles burned down and the shadows stretched closer. He felt downright cozy, hidden away in a side pocket of the future, in residence. Wife, kid, in-laws, a community of one's own. But you could make a principle out of blackness, and never see beyond it, that was the real risk, and where was this baby's father; had she just told him? He was only conscious enough to realize Josephine had reached over to remove the beer bottle from his grip, but that was all until he awoke trickled in sweat, the sheet beneath him saturated, sunlight planing through the cracks in the shutters and the world outside the bedroom operating at high volume, the everyday factory racket of the neighborhood, awoke with what felt like a shove from behind, the contraction of his body into consciousness so sudden that it knocked away Josephine, bent over him to mouth the iron-hard knob of his penis that had worked its way out under the elastic waist of his boxer shorts, arriving midscene straight from a dream which was by no means sweet but seemed, in the rawness of his awakening, to cast a perverse silhouette of eerie significance, brutally and blatantly apropos. A caboose—unmistakably a caboose, barn-red with a crooked stovepipe chimney and the grillwork on its platforms overgrown with vines—had been deposited in a smoky clearing somewhere up in the highlands of a jungle. Monkeys shrieked, exotic birds flitted from branch to branch. In the caboose lived an old white man with crew-cut hair, dressed in rags and skins like Robinson Crusoe, and he was being served a dinner of beans by a rasta-haired black youth, shielded from absolute nakedness by a coarse, burlap loincloth. The old white man wanted . . . *what?* It was unclear, unsaid, but Mitchell had the impression the grizzled old bastard was asking to be entertained while he ate his meal cross-legged on the trash-strewn floor of the caboose. "My dear wild nig," he had begun to say, and then the next thing Mitchell knew he was apologizing to Josephine for conking her in the side of the head with his knee, and she hovered over him, undamaged, neither daylight nor lack of sleep nor sobriety had roughed her up, though her blackness was still a bit of a jolt, as his whiteness must be to her unless she had made white a habit, though he doubted that, and her breasts danced with pendulous gravity toward his lips, beads of milk startling in their whiteness oozed from the tar of her nipples, and it ended like this, they shared a spermy, milky kiss, and a premonition for the awesome novelty of the future, whatever part of it might collapse in on them.

Mitchell had to go. When he closed his eyes he remembered he had a ferry to catch.

Rain check.

It was an instant bad joke between them. She made him promise to see her again, and he would.

On the streets, even walking downhill, he started to sweat inhumanly. It wasn't long before he turned a corner and the view opened up. There was the ferry, halfway out in the becalmed harbor, which was what he expected to see, knowing he had missed it even before he left her house. The commercial flight, a twelve-seater, flew at 4:30, and was never fully booked, so he still counted on making his rendezvous with Johnnie. He was in high spirits, quite pleased with himself, smiling at everybody while he stood in the blaze of sun at the jitney stop. He could hear Isaac say, Bwoy, when it rain pussy it pour jackass. Josephine begged comparison with Johnnie but he'd do better to avoid the impulse, keep them separate—and that meant in his mind, foremost—until he saw how things worked out. However his life-among-women resolved itself, his problems weren't so grandiose and inflated as they had seemed yesterday, they were more like the right sort of opportunities, a source of buoyancy and optimism, at least for the moment. Two blond and blue-eyed Mormon boys bicycled past, their smiles cut and pasted right out of the New Testament, and he raised his hand in a salute—God loves you, gentlemen (it's your line of work He can't stomach)— and then the jitney came, a pickup truck with bench seats and a sun awning stretched over a tube frame, a sweatbox even on cloudy days, and this one was already packed with riders. He squeezed in, glad to be among the people. Josephine mildly disapproved of his intention to take a jitney, a taxi would have been more to her liking. Jitney is fah peasant, Wilson, crush up like sardine with fowl and basket and sack and tree and goat and such. But when he said he enjoyed riding in them, he got to meet and talk with people that way, she rolled her eyes and said, "What you is, anthropologist?" and if it was science he wanted then get ready, she was going to make a study on *him*.

The other passengers responded in kind to his bright mood, We does love de Yankees here, mahn, God bless Kennedy, God bless Carter—*Cah-tuh*—Bless freedom, Bless liberty, Bless Sesame Street, Bless toothpaste, Bless Coca-Cola. At the next stop he was passed a little girl in pigtails and pink organdy and Buster Browns with lacy white ankle socks to hold in his lap, and she told him the names of the flowers along the roadside. They topped the crest of Ooah Mountain, baking in the canvas oven of the awning, their collective smell as rich and pungent as the steamy land. Mitchell jumped out at Augustine to guzzle down a Ju-C; he bought a bag of bread rolls made fresh that morning and stepped across the road to the village beach to where the catboat fishermen sold their catch, coming away with a red snapper to fry for his lunch,. Then he joined the endless pilgrimage of to and fro along the footpath that paralleled the black, blistering pavement, trudging up the grade formed by the shelf of ironrock dividing Augustine from Rosehill and the other beaches quilted south and eastward along the bight. The air shimmered with moist heat along the lush roadside, the grass was vivid and spongy from last night's downpour. Orange puddles sat in foot-shaped depressions. The pasture across the way, home to a herd of dewlapped Brahman bulls, had sprouted a new crop of what the locals called duppie caps—psilocybin mushrooms. It was his nature to walk fast and he did, sweat streaming off his brow, his arms slick with it, on up around the turn where the cliffs plateaued and then dropped again farther past his house to sea level. He sang—nothing with a name to it, just words—because that was how you got from place to place on Saint Cee, singing because mangoes were in season and everybody knew they were sweet as black girls, singing because up around the turn in the road another voice was singing along to a good strong rhythm, and in another dozen steps he recognized the beat, the tennis-playing *thwock* of Mr. Quiddley's chopping arm. When he rounded the turn he saw the tree was already down, Quiddley hacking at its upturned forest of pale branches. Behind the fallen giant of the poinciana, down the slope of the lawn, vermillion flowers scattered like a spray of burning lava, the front door of the cottage stood wide open, and Mitchell Wilson stepped out of the nonsense song that had risen in him, shed himself of the self-romanticizing cosmology he had brought with him to the tropics, the needling American fetish for altruism, forgot what he was doing or supposed to be doing to make the world a better place and blundered through the gate of righteousness into the precursory nightmare that had become 1977, a pathfinder, a trailblazer, paving the way to the personalized ordeals and impacted terrors of the coming decade with what he still believed in his heart were good intentions.

Chapter 23

On the thundery sapphire sea Adrian surprised her by remembering Charybdis, a Classical Lit multiple choice answer—the Homeric god-in-residence in a whirlpool between Sicily and the toe of the Italian boot, a not particularly worrisome malefactor for a corn-fed mid-western girl but now, however, Sally understood. Understood at least why Charybdis was a god, for what else could she be, with such power, and a god's diet of brave hearts? The waves were as sudden and shifting as earthquakes, they plunged and soared. Geysers of spray hung momentarily crystalline at every angle off the bow, like plate glass windows in the lobby of a bank, blowing out. It wasn't a day to be crossing the channel in an open speedboat but here they were, doing it, which was supposed to be fun but, really, they were off the scale of excitement, beyond thrills. Criminally irresponsible bravado was more like it—if this was fun then so was the Normandy invasion.

Doc Travis, with his sadistic grin, set a high standard for macho disregard. His feet braced wide apart against the jolts, he stood post-ed at the steering console in the center of the boat, inscrutable behind his wraparound sunglasses, so filmed with salt Sally doubted he could see. Because he had done his residency in Detroit, Doc preened Motown—the shades, the executive-cut Afro, the jewelry, the urban hipness—but this devil-take-us-all posturing was homegrown. He wrestled the torque of the wheel while sucking on a baby bottle secured to a lanyard around his neck. The plastic bottle of course was filled with rum, the idea being not to spill a drop during nautical maneuvers—the real idea being that he was clever, knew what he was doing, had a long and winning relationship with the ropes and the tricks. In some part of the world other people—terrorists—found full-time employment doing what Doc did for free, without the ruse of ideology. Besides the speedboat, he gave of his time to the National Hospital, the director of surgery, which meant he got to boss around the only other surgeon, an orthopedics specialist, on the staff. Speedboating though was his first love, supplemented by his hobbyist's interest in foreign affairs, an international collection of interchangeable women culled from the nursing and volunteer communities, young darlings afoot in the world, keeping their own count on the coup they took in the bedroom of personalized diplomacy. Saconi was not the complete deterrent she would have hoped to Doc's advances, but the likelihood of her membership in the harem was zed, zero, and lately Doc expended no more energy toward her than that contained in an occasional verbal memo of routine lust: *I could make you feel so good.* Doc's Hippocratic refrain, the best he could do. Sally was less than enthused but she bore him no grudge, other than her willingness to believe in his reputation for professional carelessness, though she also understood he was overworked, like everyone else at the hospital.

Doc hated to waste time on romantic dead-ends, so when they showed up at the dock by noon without Johanna, he fixed on Adrian as the next in line for the unrepentant boasting he mistook for charm, and she, a closet islophile who apparently chose this weekend to go public, only encouraged him along with anything else even remotely *native.* Doc didn't even have to bother to pretend a sudden lack of interest in Johanna, with whom Sally and Adrian had spent a weepy twenty minutes back at Coddy's, who had agreed to let her stay on at his place for a few more days. Sally had begun to think of Johanna as one of those aimless, muddled women, the authenticity of her loneliness and need notwithstanding. Johanna's heartfelt dilemmas always seemed to attenuate into hard-edged clarity, so perhaps her confusion was just another of her ways to manipulate things. What it all boiled down to was silliness—Mitchell had to come get her, she announced. She refused to see other options than this absolute choice, compelling him toward a grand gesture, or irreversible rejection. Poor Mitchell, Sally thought. She couldn't listen to much more of this, these artless and selfish vacillations.

"So you want me to tell him . . . *Come get me or I'll, what?*"

"Leave. I don't know what else I can do, Sally, but don't say it that way, *please.* Don't make it sound like an ultimatum."

What was it then? Sally didn't understand. Adrian came to Johanna's defense to say the rush is she loves him, she knows he loves her but he's freaked, and she has a visa problem not to mention other complications that have to be worked out ASAP, and just fuck!,

I don't know, she's an old-fashioned girl, I guess, Adrian continued, her sarcasm meant to tease and not hurt, though Sally couldn't say for sure. She has a maudlin reality, Adrian said, getting Johanna to finally smile, however nervously. She needs a guy to come running.

"Who said anything about running?" Johanna shot back, as if she just now realized the impression she had made on them and couldn't let them leave with it intact. "I wanted him here yesterday," she joked. "The least he can do is fly." Mirth, belated commiseration, but no outpouring of compassion for those who relied on emotional bribery.

"Dis ain much a'tall," Doc Travis had shouted as they plugged through the cut, their wake scribbled behind them on the sheltered water of the lagoon. "I seen it much worse, you know," he hollered into the wind, but here in midchannel he kept his observations to himself. Saconi kept him company up there, poker-faced, the two of them in their Speedo swimsuits, one butt red and one navy blue, their knees bent in a crouch to absorb the ceaseless sequence of bucking impacts—*boomboomboomboomboom*. She knew cowboys and these were cowboys. At random intervals the boat would smash through the rabid, frothing top of a wave higher than the others and launch into space, and their bodies would levitate for the voiceless heart-stopping second it took to come cannonballing down. Sally would close her eyes but she'd have to open them again to the terrifyingly fascinating horrorscape that the sea had made of itself today. The sun speared in and out of the clouds, like a roving spotlight; dozens of broken rainbows swam in the air around them, near enough to touch but as elusive as hummingbirds. Then a wave would shatter into a blizzard of glass and they'd hold on for dear life. Sally figured Saconi's guitar, still back on Cotton waiting for Johanna to put it on the afternoon flight, was smarter than all of them put together.

Adrian huddled down next to Sally on the seat cushions in the stern. Every five or ten seconds they were drenched anew, the water fire-hosed straight at them, so that they ducked reflexively. Below her cut-off shorts, there was a darkening bruise on Sally's thigh from Adrian's grip on her, her fingers death-locked into Sally's flesh, but still, Adrian continued to surprise. If anyone could be simultaneously green and sanguine, Adrian was. They were being slammed into each other, thrown into the fiberglass hull, made to sit rigidly in place for fear that if they got up they'd be catapulted right out of the boat, and Sally had to give Adrian credit, she wasn't whining, like so many other women—and men—would have. A sissy she was not although, granted, maybe she was too sick and traumatized to open her mouth. Appearances being what they are, Sally was quietly astonished that Adrian could be relied upon to endure something this physical, not to mention homicidal. Adrian's fortitude made Sally gender-proud and she wondered about the hidden reserves of strength in this petite and seemingly overbred woman. Was there a conversion involved?—she had certainly done an about-face in her opinion of the islands. As of yesterday, the islands had become unequivocally fantastic, heavy, gorgeous, replete with unnameable wonders, original personalities, and poignant tableaux.

Which was entirely unexpected, since Sally had written off the weekend as a failure, reduced to the banality of a deceptively simple question: *What was everybody doing here?* Everybody being, quote, a farrago of smelly Eurocentric degenerates and Angloslime, third sons, *nouveau* scruffies and unclaimed daughters, something something trollops in pursuit of sun poisoning, attended by an entire community of chuckleheaded yokels, natural idiots, and obsequious wretches. Who had called it that? Some dreadful ass, someone who fit right in, who wanted her to do a speedball with him. A little fuck-you-up and voilà, Jah loves you.

That first night, Adrian and Johanna, she thought, were lost baggage, hard-core liabilities, and they had deeply upset her. When she returned for them at Coddy's place, there they were, a seclusive pair of needle queens. She had felt bamboozled, her generosity betrayed, and had signed off, they could look after themselves in junkie heaven for all she cared, but she had a man to love and be loved by. If they chose to turn themselves inside out like a chewed mango skin, sleep with the first men they laid eyes on, whatever, that was their business because she wasn't playing mother hen and she was under no further obligation to them. But in the morning, spurred by sisterly guilt and dark curiosity, impulses she could never successfully curb, she left Saconi in bed, where he would sleep till noon, put on her bathing suit under a sundress, and walked down to Coddy's place to assess what damage the girls had inflicted upon themselves. She suspected her appearance might cause a crisis and couldn't predict at what expense she'd play the Pollyannish Voice of Reason, the Saving Hand. But when the three of them were back together, all day yesterday and again last night, she had to reassess her case against the two, based on a more liberal interpretation of the rules of social grace. She had discovered them out on the top step, suited up, munching a breakfast of bananas and gnips someone had dropped by, contrite schoolgirls with pouches under their eyes and morning-after resolutions.

Johanna looked deadly earnest; Adrian had a rash that was probably a reaction to no-see-um bites and said she hadn't slept well
because there was a peeping Tom. Johanna shrugged it off. Sally told
Adrian to keep in mind the islands were a place you were never alone,
though that never once stopped anybody from behaving as they
pleased. The women wanted to impress on her how aware they were
that they had overstepped the bounds, committed improprieties, if
not necessarily in substance then at least in style and etiquette, that
never entirely useless principle. They knew better, but . . . et cetera.
Whatever had transpired during the night was to be labeled a fluke
and consigned to another lifetime. There were no waves of shame,
thank God, and Sally was touched by their considerate regret, enough
to apologize herself, and then they were all giggling about who
ambushed whom, Sally for bringing them to this naked lunch of an
island or Johanna and Adrian for taking advantage of the opportunity
by eating it.

They went out on the beach, tanned and swam, read and gossiped
and joked, enjoying a morning as ordinary and safe as bottled water.
Only when Johanna removed her sunglasses to cool off in the water
did Sally get a glimpse of her sadness, the bruised tenderness in her
hazel eyes unfocused on something far away, and only then Sally
thought with a more measured sense of consequence, *They put needles into their arms, didn't they.* What did they foresee in return that
was worth the risk, and why did that question echo so uncomfortably
in her memory, suggesting the parental caveat against all dangers, real
or imagined? Adrian's culpability, she presumed, was marginal; she
had submitted to a lone temptation, stepped in front of a charging
bull. Johanna's acquiescence to temptation however seemed vastly
more profound, seemed to exist symbiotically with guilt itself.

Addictive personalities—Johanna was, wasn't she?

With the others it wasn't the drug abuse that disturbed Sally as
much as their deep and flagrant lack of moral discipline that, in effect,
made all reflective surfaces, except for crowds and cameras, transparent. Mirrors didn't work anymore. But Johanna *saw* herself, with
Johanna it *was* drugs, self-medicated and self-punished, and Sally
could imagine her saying, My kind of pain is not your kind of pain.
Even if that were true she'd have to be told she was wrong, told that
this long, lost summer of illusion that was the tropics was probably
the wrong place for her to be.

But who had the right and the authority to tell her that, Sally
didn't know. She knew it wasn't her.

By late morning the sun had become a heat lamp and chased

them off the beach, up a stairway carved through terraced coral paddocks to the Norton compound. Saconi was waiting for them to join him for lunch, sitting at a wrought-iron and glass-topped table under a green-and-white striped umbrella, looking splendid in his cricket ducks and jersey, leafing through a back issue of *Rolling Stone.* The patio was imported slate, screened for privacy by bougainvillea, allamanda, and passion-fruit vine trained to lattices, the blue of its seaward view mimicked by a swimming pool. The structure that allowed for all this resembled a neo-Georgian wedding cake, the Princess' very own retreat. Saconi said she called it The Insanatorium. Where was this mythical princess? Adrian asked. Where were the lords and the ladies? Saconi said they rarely visited, their arrivals and departures were liquid and unscheduled, but instead they were represented year-round by their sycophants, who were legion. A servant appeared, pushing a service cart, and they lunched on lobster salad and avocado vinaigrette. Johanna seemed overawed by the milieu of luxury, Adrian critiqued the architecture with scathing wit, Saconi promoted Mitchell and Tillman as honorable men but questionable lovers, since they would permit two such beautiful women to come unescorted to Sodom, and Sally smiled and exclaimed, just plain farm-girl hick-happy with their temporary status in the world. After lunch, Saconi gave them a tour of the house, supplying enough eloquent contempt for the decorating to cover for any effete prince and his eternal absence. While Saconi sauntered off to talk to one of the visiting musicians about recording studios, the women borrowed a mini-moke to circumnavigate the island on its mostly unpaved road, an excursion highlighted by Adrian's glee when they stopped in a weather-beaten, world-forsaken fishing village named Aberdeen for Cokes and contraband scotch. They passed into the cool interior of a one-room concrete bar to be instantly delighted by the eczemic murals decaying on its walls. The artist was sent for and Adrian pronounced him *discovered.* Luther Hendricks was a seventy-year-old Cotton Islander who had painted hundreds of pencil-sketched watercolors of grotesque bellicose fish and what Adrian called Dagons—piscean men—cavorting in a shadowy sea blossomed, so she said, with primitive symbolism. Come the Eighties, Adrian predicted, exotic folkloric would be what everyone wanted. She bought three of Luther's pieces on the spot, promising she was going to arrange a show for him in New York, and Luther committed to the scheme only insofar as to proclaim that a new battery could make an old car go, and that he liked pretty young girls, with or without promises.

Driving back they raced against the stuporous glare of midday and came to the consensus that, before the goat roast, they should either all take naps or kill themselves. The scotch had left Adrian with a headache and she couldn't decide, both alternatives being of equal appeal. Sally dropped them at Coddy's place and then retreated up the coral shelves of land to the Insanatorium, past the volleyball spastics on the lawn and the goat on its spit which looked like a napalmed dog. Saconi anticipated her arrival by keeping bedside, exactly where she wanted him, and then making love to her—the second time that day—with such ardor that their combined output of tangy sweat could be measured in a rain gauge. She plunked immediately into a coma and back up again when she heard Saconi leave at dusk, then showered, dressed in a tangerine shift with orange blossoms like white propellers, and brushed out her hair. Examining herself in the mirror in the guest bathroom, she decided she looked all too healthy and fit to bother with makeup, a private rebuff to the sybarites.

The goat roast came off in an almost civilized fashion, though she noticed for the first time an insidious hierarchic ordering among the locals, the high ground held by a caste of enforcers charged with keeping everybody else out, which was an outrage and just incredibly awful public relations, seeing as how the compound had swallowed a good sixth of the inhabitable part of the island. She tried to manifest her most agreeable grin, her blond Lutheran face befriending and supportive, talking to anybody who would listen about the school or Saconi. All she remembered was the goat was spicy hot and delicious, there were no napkins, most of the people were world-class snobs, she had gotten addled again on rum punches, had met a German boy who only knew English from rock-and-roll lyrics, and Luther Hendricks had arrived on a donkey, which he had ridden across the hump of the island to be there at Adrian's bidding. There was an interlude of sorts in the early evening hours that was actually quite tranquil and lovely, composite groupings slouched on lawn furniture under the clouding sky, chatting and breathing the air, doing impersonations of ordinary people. She saw Doc Travis loitering around Johanna, Adrian yakking nonstop with Luther and thought, *Fine*, though it was not yet the hour for the vampires to be out in force. And when they came, when the bacchanal revved up, they came trailing that question like a barbed tail: *What was everybody doing here?*

Living in the tropics, she had let the visual overload gradually alter her perceptive instincts, born on the blank, stripped prairie and mostly dependent on the give and take of language. Her degree of insight into the world now set forth from a base of images, and she stored away two, at least, from the weekend on Cotton Island for further consideration, not counting the look on Adrian's face when she nearly washed over the side of Doc Travis' speedboat.

Not counting the maggot she tried to strangle, either, a skinhead from one of the London self-mutilation bands currently in vogue. Drunk, coked, whacked, pig-eyed, cretinoid, a psychopathic missionary from a postnuclear, fried shell of a future. Terminally sunburned, he wore unlaced engineer boots, soiled boxer shorts, a sleeveless black tee shirt, his ear lobes festooned with ridiculous safety pins and his phlebitic arms tattooed with insipid swastikas, laughable daggers, and fascist buzz words. His uncircumcised penis wagged in and out of the crease in his shorts. He had crawled out from some crabhole, she hadn't seen him before they had all packed into Lord Norton's outdoor fete house for Saconi's performance. Flambeaus licked the thatch of the ramada's peaked roof with sinister light, light from the voodoo scenes in B movies. It was late, the chemistry in a toxic red zone; worlds split apart into clans and collided in multinational masses simultaneously. Because she identified herself with Saconi she sometimes felt equatorial, a narrow imaginary line of contact between the frictional polarity of hemispheres. (Earlier, she had prevented one set of islanders— security, the chosen ones—from rapping the skulls of another set—the unchosen, harmless goggle-eyed teenagers—who were trying to sneak their way into the festivities. She interceded, they slipped in to stand off to the side, gawking like the tourists they now were.)

Saconi sat on his stool and shook a tamboo he had told her was filled with the bones of a hundred birds. As an experiment in form, he had modeled one of his newest calypsos on the rhythmic phrasings of a Yoruba chant, and this was it. The skinhead stationed himself at arm's length in front of him, wobbling on the twin flames of his legs, his gyroscope broken by all manner of self-abuse and juvenile hatreds. He squinted, puffy and cock-eyed, at Saconi, his fish lips pursed in a sphincter of appraisal. Saconi's voice modulated, like the dipping flight of sparrows, between high and low notes, tenor and baritone.

Whiteman play brains of the world but blackman must play soul, the calypso argued. The title was "Astro-nots," and Sally had never heard the song before. Granted, its melody uplifted, but the lyrics made her uneasy, vaguely resentful—which would of course be Saconi's intention.

Whiteman is the brains, my brother, blackman is the soul, put them all together, my sister, and you still can't make a whole.

The skinhead began to bait Saconi, snarling imbecilic taunts: What language was this the boy sang—Schwarzhili, Mau-Mau, Ma-Ma, Jigaboo fookin' Welsh, is it? Sally narrowed her eyes at him, steaming, knowing something bad was going to happen. He next succumbed to an Englishman's irrepressible urge for the bestowment of titles. Here he is, gents, Our Lad the Nigger Nightingale. Sir Wog the Africoon Troubadour, he brayed, cocking his head left and right, seeking approbation for his mindless bigotry. The blood jumped in Sally's heart and she lunged for the guy's throat, getting her thumbs on his adam's apple before Adrian restrained her from behind and one of the skinhead's own entourage, out of decency or perhaps bloodthirstiness, threw an arm around his shoulder and muscled him outside to the lawn for an airing. Saconi was too married to his song to care; his justice he sang. Sally, shaking with rage, watched the two men out on the edge of darkness, the first jabbing his fist onetwothree into the congenitally lurid mouth, the skinhead laughing, spitting blood, cawing with dementia. Those who loved a sensation applauded.

What was everybody doing there, besides ruining a perfectly good island? There were no princes and princesses, no lords and ladies, only the aptly named Insanatorium. "The global pillage," she had heard someone say. She had this associative image of Elvis Presley nagging away in her mind—a bloated, unctuous white idol of popular decay raiding the tribes, kidnapping the culture for his self-aggrandizement and replacing it with less than thirty dollars' worth of tee shirts, stenciled with the iconography of mass marketeers. *Oops, let's not get carried away, girl,* but the fact remained, these motherfuckers had ridden their own music into the ground and had come a-slaving. She saw how they hankered after Saconi and she was worried for him, he wasn't a found object, and unlike everybody else there, he had come to Cotton because Cotton was his to come to.

It rarely got this out of hand, Saconi assured her, laughing about how swiftly she had clamped down onto the skinhead, fast and fearless, grievous harm intent in her eyes. He had taken a break, would return for three or four more songs. Holding hands, they walked out onto the grounds to be alone. He was so pleased with himself, pleased with her. Saconi satisfied her one unwritten rule about life: Give back. Tend to your karma (thank you, Hindus, for the Judeo-Christian Subversion of the Week). She envisioned high chairs crowned with chubby-cheeked toffee-colored babies with hilarious bows in their hair, and the imaginary snapshot she held in front of her made her hands quiver until it fell away and her delight turned to sadness, the horse back in the barn, because she was afraid to compose their future too precisely. Possibly Saconi was wiser about this than she was.

The paradox was, her days of feeling stranded, anywhere, were over, because the more secure she felt in this part of the world, in no small part thanks to Saconi, the more she felt herself accepting the part she had left behind. If that then was maturity, adulthood wandering in from the wide open space of adolescence, must she concede the converse implication, that her original point of departure, the impulse she had answered to set herself free, was an arbitrary act of immaturity? Saconi's strength of identity, something much deeper than male self-esteem, mystified her. Was identity homegrown, or discovered, researched, dug up and glued, like pottery shards, back together; something *out there*, waiting for you to come gather it? She wasn't the person to ask. She looked at the children warehoused in her school and told herself, The answer is none of the above.

The spree seemed to reconfirm her worst suspicions about the broader culture that insisted on taking responsibility for who she was, but she was being negative and knew she had to watch it, at least for Saconi's sake. He pulled her over to an outcropping of limestone and they sat down, looking out toward the waves turned to lace on the windward barrier reef. Because he knew what she was thinking, he told her that when he was a boy he had a trumpet-playing uncle who one day vanished and then resurfaced playing second horn in a European jazz band, performing on the circuit through all those gray and snowy cities for the next twenty years. Saconi, as he grew up, borrowed the dream. Then the uncle came home. Sally said, I bet I know what happened, and Saconi corrected her. No, the uncle wasn't bitter, was no more racist than sanity allowed, he didn't regret spending the prime of his life communicating through his trumpet to people who were reluctant to find him intelligible when he took the instrument away from his lips. On the contrary. When he came back home, he had been blinded to all but St. Catherine's backwardness, the ignorance of the people, the unsuitability of everything. He left after four months to live permanently in Paris. Saconi took his repudiation personally—he hated his uncle. He thought to himself, Whatever Uncle does have over there, it ain home, you know.

"Sally, you cy-ahn see me jammin wit dem *rock-and-rule* bwoys?" he asked her, snickering at the thought. He was going to go back to the fete house and sing to them "Capitalism Gone Mad."

But he didn't. Instead he climbed back on his stool, propped his guitar across his knees and sang a doleful ballad written by Bob

Marley. The audience pressed in close, standing around like a pack of show dogs remarking upon the hidden potential of a flea-bitten coyote. The crowd had its second wind; some of the visiting celebrities began to overlay harmonies on top of Saconi's voice. Sally heard the beauty in their chorus but she preferred them stoned out of their minds, actually—muffled. Suddenly they wanted to reach down into their hardened hearts and croon, and what was she supposed to do, puke or clap? Guitars were fetched, like homely wives heretofore unclaimed. Saconi segued into a reggae variation on what she took to be a pub song, making Sally choke with laughter, and they went on in this vein, amazing her, these profoundly *tired* men and their scout's singalong, as if this were all they ever really wanted from the music to begin with, this their transiently pure escape from the inexplicable, exiling, addictive burlesque of fame, which had nowhere to take its prisoners but away.

When Doc Travis stopped the boat she thought they had broken down but, nope, the Admiral wanted fresh fish for his supper and he ordered Saconi to break out the gear. Everything was slightly unreal to her from lack of sleep plus a queasy gloss of seasickness and a foolhardy decision like this only heightened the effect. The boat tipped and reeled, wave-slapped; the engines gargled and the world fizzled and hissed and water slurped in a steady flow through the scuppers. Adrian sat up erect but tottering like a drunk, her mouth tense but determined to be a good sport. "Is this battle stations?" she asked.

What this was was frivolous endangerment. Sally thought, Let's just get out of this madness before someone gets hurt. But the Admiral wanted dolphin and Saconi seemed only too happy to play the naked island boy, toting home his string of fish. He rigged a silver lure the size of a butcher knife onto a leader and started to tie it to a ball of trolling line. The waves shoved up and down around them; their immensity made her think of screens in a movie theater, blue and translucent as gemstone. One screen would slide down and another slide up, and sure enough, now that they weren't hurtling through them, she could see fish inside, hovering like creatures trapped in amber, drab brownish-green shapes and elongated streaks of electric radiance, but before Saconi had the chance to feed out the lure into the water a rogue sea, like backwash, cascaded with a soft thunderclap down on the stern, compressing the women into their seats and then lifting them in its swell. When it hit, its power stunned Sally, but she had the presence of mind to grab Adrian's arm and hold on to a cleat. Doc accelerated instantaneously to avoid being swamped but as the boat lurched forward she could feel Adrian's weight pouring over the transom with the slosh. Sally shrieked for Saconi but he already had Adrian's free arm and was dragging her away from the props. Doc sped ahead with no choice but to drain the boat. Adrian bounced on the gunwale, in the water from her breasts down, her legs dancing in a churn of foam. There was a brutally invigorating moment of balance. They had both lost their sunglasses and stared into each other's saucer eyes, Adrian's blanched face written with the knowledge that in the next second or two she might well slip away from them and be gone. Sally would remember the look, and the remarkable fact of Adrian's relative composure, Adrian not saying anything, nothing, not a scream or squeal or just *help!* She never made a sound but just looked at them as if she were prepared to wait all day for a resolution to her fate. Then they succeeded in hauling her back aboard, her clothes nearly torn off by the force of the water.

Sally ranted at Doc above the roar of the twin outboards. *You insane asshole, you silly prick.* He ignored her, or didn't hear. Saconi made the mistake of bending over to tell her to watch her mouth, Doc was sensitive to criticism, so then she was infuriated with Saconi too. Adrian, gasping, looked mauled and overwhelmed but not unhappy, her eyes brilliantly alert, her senses thriving, and certainly she was never more present than this moment, nothing else in the world but this. The water in the boat emptied as they picked up speed, thrusting through the crests, skipping from one to the next like a flat stone flung by a giant until the seas rolled gentle again behind the natural jetty of Pilo Bight, and Doc stopped the boat again so he could pull a pair of water skis and a towline out from their storage hatch and thus enter Howard Bay in heroic fashion, a charioteer slicing through the popular imagination, flying on wings of vanity.

Saconi took the helm with relish and Sally, scowling at his back, had to will herself not to punish him for his misguided defense of the good doctor's ego. It would be a shame and inexcusable to end the weekend mad at him, since she couldn't claim not to know to make herself as little of a target as possible around men like Travis, and more importantly, she had a weekend to preserve, its strange symmetry of fullness and saturation, each sensation captured in that pair of keepsake images, one that glowed, one that disturbed, she was leaving Cotton Island carrying these as yet uncatalogued treasures, and her hope was to one day train herself to get them on record, processed into a form that could express to others what it was like for her to be so far off in the world, and yet never far from meaning. Maybe some day she would learn how to paint or write them, manipulate them onto film, something to say, I was there, very much alive. This is how it was for me.

When the fete had gone on long enough to achieve a second wave of lunacy and then unraveled, Saconi said if she wasn't too knackered he wanted to show her something on the northern point of the island, and didn't know when they'd have another chance. The long arduous effort to enjoy herself among people not of her choosing had left her feeling gorged and dissatisfied, so she told him, "Anything you want that's just us." He grabbed a bottle of champagne from a washtub of melted ice and requisitioned one of the mini-mokes. She could feel the change of weather approaching, on her skin and in the invisible closeness of the sky. Even in the inky darkness before dawn, the landscape was capable of communicating to her its terrarium-like quality, the squat, dusty vegetation, the rockiness, the baking heat that still ticked out from the center of things, like an engine cooling down. Terrain made for reptiles, scorpions, haggard goats. Saconi drove over the washboard road with the bottle of champagne between his knees; his right hand rested reassuringly on her left thigh, and for all the best of reasons they didn't talk but let the night flood away off the land without saying anything to make it human, robbing nature of its pace, as if words had priority over time and a simple exchange of sentences would bring daylight washing down on them.

Which it did eventually but with inordinate stealth, the atmosphere becoming slightly porous, adding fractions of depth, not enough to bring texture but adequate to etch and ridge the earth with a flat, uninterrupted silhouette of shape, blocks of entities, this or that, island or sky being the only differentiation allowed, a hushed brightening but not yet true first light, champion of specificity, with a democratic interest in all things great and small. She wondered if anyone else knew Saconi could be this quiet, because he never was, especially with so sweet a look of gentle resignation, which she understood had nothing to do with her, and she fought back the sentimental explosion that would make her kiss him and weep and confess how completely she cared what happened to him. She wished he had never tried to compartmentalize racial existence with that now expendable word, *soul*.

A pair of wild dogs dashed out from the roadside tangle of palmetto and thorn acacia, a fleeting image of haunted beings. Over the toy-like puttering of the motor she began to notice the birds asking for sunrise, then the distant susurration of heavy surf, like a violent whispering. The antisocial wall of bush thinned out to an equally harsh barrenness of wiry growth and spikes—splattered crusts of blackened rock, red clay crackled like raku, coarse tufts of silvery grass, groves of cactus and Spanish bayonet. Three fourths of the way out the scarred headland that formed the northeast terminus of the island, even the sorry excuse for a road ended and they stopped, sending a warlock's coven of iguanas scrambling for cover.

"Big Sally, you cy-ahn walk wit me a little ways?"

"You'd be surprised how far."

"Ahll right den, darlin. We walkin."

They followed a footpath over the crumbling earth, Saconi in front, carrying the bottle of champagne over his shoulder like a club. A nimbus of seaspray hung over their heads, like dawn itself in colloidal suspension, ready to burst in their faces. The next installment of light showed them the lowness of the paling clouds, the sootiness of their heavenly fabric, loose and ragged, coming unstuffed. Now it was clear they'd be cheated out of a famous sunrise, but if the lighting remained so otherworldly, no one was going to complain. Between the ceiling and the floor, the air swirled with seabirds—gulls, terns, pelicans, boobies, frigates—noisy as parliament, circling in ever-changing patterns. The path disappeared across knuckles of ironrock but Saconi knew where he had to go. They were fifty or sixty feet above sea level, she guessed, the shore itself somewhere out of sight below them though off in the channel between the two islands the ocean was chopped up and frosted with chaos. Shaving a dime of skin off one of her ankles on a burl of ironrock, she tried to step more carefully, taking the precaution of using her hands to steady herself as the rock mounded higher while the path descended. The waves fulminated in sequence, each giving itself a short ovation, and she could feel the tremors under her feet, similar to the inner resonance of her own deferred exhaustion.

Where the land ended, the coast collapsed into a ruined city of rock, fabulous and severe, a phantasmagoric ghetto turned garden rusting into the sea, the skeletal remains of an industrialized center in final breathtaking transition, smelting away, an excrescent stain on the globe, something for the future to step around. It was beautiful, a death progressing peacefully in the midst of its own disordering consequence. Beautiful in the way destruction and decay could sometimes insist on their own beauty, the aesthetics of the opulence of everything that rotted and the magnificence of everything that burned.

It was another geology altogether, too radical to have evolved through the slow accretion of civilized corals. Arched, spindled, hollowed out, the rock contained grottoes and tombs, the vandalized insides of factories, amorphous twisting shapes of worship and agony, ecstatic bodies on the verge of grace, hulks and scooped husks of futility. The craftsman sea would never be satisfied with its work here, fizzing into gaps, slurped through a labyrinth of fissures, scrubbing and polishing, scrubbing and polishing, unable to stop, a mother gone mad. Occasionally a single wave would assert itself and disintegrate vertically, breaking heavily apart in the air like a flock of snow geese startled into rising. It seemed like another type of frontier and Sally greeted the place with joy.

Through sculpted naves and sweeping passages, they climbed down into the liquid gnash and suck of sound, every surface dripping with motion. A plague of tiny crabs the color of charred skin swarmed wherever they looked. They stooped to enter a brief tunnel leading to a chapel that opened again at its far side, a white oculus of light wide enough for them to hoist themselves onto a seaside ledge to gaze down at their feet into a winking eye reflecting their blurred image in the blue smoke of dawn—a perfectly round, sand-carpeted tidal pool inlaid into the tortured rock.

Unhh, said Sally, as if she struggled to unload her burden of disbelief. *Gaa. God. Yes!* the first words spoken. Without discussion Saconi set the bottle down and they removed their clothes, Sally staggered, beguiled, stupefied by the vividness of their bodies in the gloomy light, Saconi so vibrantly black, yet so unlike those first days when his blackness was like a mask she tried to peer behind; she, except for a bikini of alabaster flesh, so healthily golden. They eased themselves into the transparent wine of this rock chalice, revived by its momentary chill, and sat cross-legged on the sugary bottom, heart-deep in the water, Sally's breasts floating between them, bobbing with the surge that fed the pool. Saconi popped the cork on the champagne—more spray, more foam for the universe. They passed the bottle lazily back and forth, no problem imagining what they drank was the essence of the world they found themselves in. Saconi didn't talk and she didn't want him to; he said what he wanted to say and what she needed to know by bringing her here. If she was the latest among other women he had brought, that still didn't make her naive, or Saconi insincere, or the present less real.

The sea heaved. Moments later, after each upswelling, a dying ring of energy would sweep the pool, nudging them, then relax backward and be renewed. She considered the contrast they made to be an ineffable wonder, a piano made of skin and bone, a concrescence of keys, together like this. Sitting up, they knotted themselves into one, her stout legs yoked around his slender waist, Saconi inside her, a bell ringing, first far away but now closer. They didn't move themselves but let the surge lift and lower them on its cushion, the ocean breathing pleasure into them, at first infinitesimal amounts, vaporous, then each increment distinct, each increase warmer and fuller, accepted with gratitude. Given the choice she would stay like this, the sun never rising, the world trapped between night and day, until someone came to tell her she was an old woman, had lived her life and it was over. It took forever, which is what they both seemed to aspire to, but they came in unison and Sally arched her back until her hair spread out across the surface of the water, entwined with the sea anemones that rimmed the basin of the pool, like a wreath of iridescent spider mums, and the wreath became the bowl of a near horizon, her face this other horizon's rising sun, the air the turbulent onslaught of ocean, the firmament a tundra of unfurling clouds. With her head still back and the world inverted, she shut her eyes tight, calling out, some unintelligible noise to say at this moment, this splintering instant in time, she was never so located in the cosmic circulation; thinking, *I don't have to leave,* an involuntary thought, unsolicited, slipping in through the opening the pleasure made and she didn't know what place she meant by it—Kansas or St. Catherine or Cotton Island or the tidal pool or somewhere else. Anywhere, it seemed, would do; that's what she meant, she thought. And then, when the preciousness of life was almost too much to bear, the moment passed, and she raised her head to kiss Saconi.

I don't have to leave. This. Any of it. All.

Did he mind?—she was going to cheer.

Within the hour the image had its counterweight, as if she must be rebuked for wanting too much, and getting it. That she wasn't in the habit of thinking this way seemed moot. There was a woman in the garbage when they returned to the enclave, still early enough for everyone to be asleep but this person on her hands and knees, pawing through a mound of trash the early-rising caretaker had raked to the side of a row of guest cottages. In the grayish, misted light, Sally mistook her at first glance for a dog, and in fact there were three to model herself after, competing with her, scrapping for goat bones. Saconi swerved across the lawn and parked nearby but she didn't look up from her rooting. Her flaxen hair hid her face; she wore a strap tee shirt and silk panties. Sally got out of the mini-moke, mute with horror, to see what could be done to help her. The woman raised herself into a kneeling position. She was young, green-eyed; pretty—but not this morning—and she covered her mouth to hide it, speaking into the cup of her hand to answer Sally's questions. She was semihysterical, speeding, maybe, the words spewing with a mush of consonants into her hand. What happened, she said in a rush, was this: A year ago, more than a year ago, a man raped her, this was in California, and she bit him so hard on the arm she broke her own jaw, then a few months later her teeth began to fall out on the upper left side of her mouth, she had to have a dental plate made but the dentist at the clinic never got the fit right, and her boyfriend still had shrapnel in his back from a land mine in Vietnam and was crazy, and so last night before going to bed she had removed the plate because it hurt, and she put it in an empty cigarette pack on the table, and when her boyfriend came in later he wanted a cigarette, but when he found the empty pack he got mad and threw it outside, at least that's what he thought he did, and somebody had raked up all the trash from the goat roast and fete into this pile and she was praying her teeth were in it.

It began to drizzle. She let her hand fall, sick with embarrassment. One side of her mouth was sunken with damage, withered like a hag's mouth. She was young, but not this morning, and maybe, Sally thought, never again.

She wanted her teeth back. She wanted painkillers. Sally wished she had never seen her, and afterward she told Saconi they couldn't get off Cotton Island fast enough to suit her. She stooped down and tried to help the woman find her teeth in the garbage, already beginning to smell. She picked gingerly through the beer cans and paper plates, the festering fruit skins and greasy remains of goat, thinking this lost and burnt-out child had most likely misplaced the teeth somewhere in her cottage, but then there were the three 5s on the logo of the cigarette pack, and the miracle was, when the woman in the trash had her teeth back in she was beautiful, she was the princess that none of them had believed in, restored to the island of interlopers.

The life was the imagery was the life.

Chapter 24

Perhaps it would not have occurred to Emma Quashie that the boy had paid her such absolute attention, listening and watching, that he would absorb his pair of mothers' sinking universe intact, and drag it behind him into adulthood on a strangulating leash of memory, so that the first time he set foot on Cotton Island, after his resurrection from purgatory by Selwyn Walker, he would come face to face with Erzulie's latest incarnation—Erzulie, the patron saint of the mutilation of his boyhood. Perhaps she would have found it possible to explain her son's bizarre and lethal association with this white woman he saw swimming in the waves at Sandy Bay, when the connection came to light, to destroy him as it had destroyed his mother. But Cotton Island had lost its Emma Quashies and Miss Diedras and even its ability to identify one set of gods from another.

There was no one left to explain such intervention. A place that had not changed in three hundred years had changed overnight.

There was no one left to explain, but Cassius Collymore saw the change and dismissed it for what it was. What could be new in the loa-infested, angel-swarmed, beast-haunted world, of which he had firsthand knowledge? Pure forces and ancient patterns are what they are, eternal, no matter what shape they fancied, year to year. What could be new to a boy chained to the oars of the past, rowing a bloody sea of fables and false hopes and commonplace terrors. What could be new in a life where, regardless of its clumsy trips and stumbles and blank strips of yearning, justice was a measured pace, but so was injustice.

Friday evening, past suppertime, Ibrahim found himself on the Queenstown quay, scuffing his feet along the oil-stained cement, carrying his change of clothes in a canvas handbag, searching for a boat going over. The police launch had been in dry dock for months, busted up, someone had driven it top speed into a reef, so he couldn't just go to them and say, *Tek me down Cotton fah Selwyn,* but had to beg his own way. It was late, but time wasn't bad wind or high seas, and didn't matter to a captain, who sailed when his ship was ready, middle of the night or not.

Who going down? he saluted the men aboard the tied-up boats, and they waved him farther along the quay to the *Lady Luck,* a rusty World War II LST, its open hold stacked with paper bags of cement like neatly packaged troops, its engines hammering the stillness of the lower harbor. The captain was a Vincentian and said, *We ain tek passenger, bwoy,* but shrugged contemptuously and told him, *Come,* the only word he would speak to him, when Ibrahim dug into the pocket of his pants to show the captain his badge, declaring, *NPF business, nuh?—what you goin do now?*

When they arrived at Cotton Island minutes before midnight, Ibrahim felt sluggish, unseeing, slothful—the water could do that to him with its swirling blackness, its dragon's hiss. Underfoot, the pier was funny, not solid, as if it had a sleeping life hidden inside it, causing a gentle shift and roll as he walked down it, half-afraid, to the shore of his hatred. The Green Turtle was closing up for the night but he walked like a man unsure of his step and stopped, there among the tables and the milling, laughing customers, the white people who formed the vaguest, most inarticulate part of his pain. He stood, swaying, as though he were drunk and invisible and where he stood was no place in particular. He closed his eyes and listened to the hum of voices, gnawing at the trance that was his homecoming. He opened his eyes again and no one was looking at him because he was invisible and they were invisible and now he was in control of the situation, and all he must do was pass through. He heard this and heard that but he stopped listening because he knew what to do, where to go, and found himself walking in the center of the blue-white coral road behind the bar, up the rise of the hill, a car crawling by, steering around him: a small boy sucking on a mango pip, on his way to school with his sisters.

The night contained a strong current, an incoming tide of purpose, carrying him along. There is a plan—it is just a plan, has nothing to do with anything else, except he is in it, and he is not powerless. He must see a woman and he must see a man: a two-part plan, one part quiet and one part loud. He could do that. He saw the aura of lights above where the hill flattened, heard streaks of music, like birds let out of cages, and told himself, *I am in it.* Make a story with the woman, to help with a next plan. Come out of nowhere and fuck Marcus. Like so: *Bam!*

At the Norton compound, there was a glossy, painted wall, roaming with flares of light, that hadn't been there before, and a gate with lampposts, and some guys standing by importantly. Ibrahim knew them but he had forgotten their names; he had forgotten everybody's name, he realized, but not their look, which was always both fear and warning. Their eyes sharpened on him and flickered as he approached the gate in a seemingly random, self-absorbed drift, like a stray.

He stepped absently forward, as if to continue on through the stuccoed arch, its flange of wrought-iron doors swept back, but a bony arm swung out in front of him to bar his entry, and, as if he had just become aware of his surroundings, he looked at the guy who challenged him, so the fellow would understand that if he touched Ibrahim, it would be a serious violation. The NPF badge in his pocket burned against his leg, useless under these conditions. The guy squinted at Ibrahim, trying to place him.

"Ain you go away?" he said, turning for confirmation to his two companions. "Ain you disappear, bwoy?"

"Is Collymore, eh?" said another, and they stared at him like an idea they had never cared for, something they would want to wipe off themselves once he had left, the bottom of existence. Ibrahim's eyes flashed, darting between the arrogant cast of their expressions—they were the same, he and they, he had run with them, scuffled with them, schooled with them, obeyed with them, but then one day he wasn't there, and while they ran headlong through the sunny everydayness of their simple boyhoods, he had been sold to the devil for a piece of fish, then indentured to the dull misery of a freedom with no center or meaning, as if vultures had torn the heart from its living flesh, and this was how they knew him, dismissing the dreamworld of their earliest years, as one among them born to badness, as the end of fellowship, a disease to which they could not afford prolonged exposure, a disaster through which they could measure—and applaud— their own secure place in the world as they were given it.

They knew him well enough not to push him, but this was another Collymore, one they had not seen before, a variation on the original.

"You get a new style of rag, eh? Collymore."

"What's up, bwoy? You sellin weed?"

"You ain find cock to suck in St. Cee?"

They tensed and then swelled up, their legs planted in a defensive stance, their chins cocked and their hands instinctively curling into fists, seeing what they had stirred up, the flare of unpredictable intensity in Collymore, the physical contraction—the same as a type of dog—the split-second of withdrawal which was really preparation for an attack. They had known they could not joke with Collymore—now they had a renewed appreciation of how dangerous it could be. There the four of them remained, paralyzed and bristling, in the shell of light from the gate.

But he had discipline now, and kept a list—a list of wrong-thinkers and wrongdoers—to refer back to when everything changed. He thought to himself, *Wait*, though behind the thought he had picked up a rock and cracked it into the head of the fellow who had said what Ibrahim could allow no one to say to him. *Wait*, he advised himself again—waiting was a very important thing. Selwyn didn't have to worry that he could not stay cool.

He was incapable of an ingratiating expression or tone—his manner of speaking was always pressurized, halting, elliptical, or abruptly spilling, as though speech were an accident—but they breathed again and relaxed, exchanging dubious looks, when he told them he had business inside the compound. The one who had blocked him with his arm sniggered at such a notion, but Ibrahim, steady and obstinate, not to be dissuaded from his mission, explained himself—he had a message to deliver to a white woman who had arrived late today on a plane—straining the words stiffly through his clenched jaw.

"Big Sally?"

"No," Ibrahim answered, snapping the sound. "A next one by she."

"Give it to me, I will pass it."

No, he explained further, it was a private message from the woman's husband, a ministry fellow living in Howard Bay, he was instructed to deliver it personally, he must go through the gate.

"She ain reach as yet," said the most easygoing of the three, the one who had asked if he had come to sell marijuana. "She down by Coddy," he revealed disingenuously, earning identical sour looks for this stupidness from his companions, for giving away information so freely to one so strange and untrustworthy as Collymore.

Ibrahim stood at the gate a while longer, disengaged from their presence, staring blindly through the arch at the modern cottages and landscaped walks, in a reverie inspired by the fete, somewhere off behind the cluster of buildings, which he could hear but not see. He remembered the ruins of a small stone church on this land. He remembered goats and thorns, remembered being thirsty. He understood this too had become a place that opposed him, defined him as what was undesirable, what was to be kept out, to be watched carefully, and this understanding seemed to resolve for him an unspoken question he harbored about his own intelligence, about the meaning he put on things and the consistency of the force he found himself against. His right eye twitched. There was a wary, uncertain silence— he knew they were waiting to see what he would do; the confrontation was perpetual, as long as he remained nearby, and for this reason alone he would not deign to move, preferring to rankle them with the fact of his existence, these fellows, who once were meant to be his lifelong friends, and not until a drunken group of white people stumbled out of the dark did they finally ignore him, and then he moved on, then he disappeared, having made himself clear.

He knew the rock track down through the bush to the beach, knew it well, where it dropped steeply and where it turned and branched, but he had not gone twenty paces down its dark channel before he tripped, propelled forward to his hands and knees as though he had been pushed from behind, and, there on the ground, the night suddenly lowered its full weight upon the hump of his back, making a noisy vibration, like an electrical charge. The nerves in his stomach knotted up and Ibrahim prayed. He experienced the same minute heave and sloshing—as if it came from deep within the earth, fading at the surface—that he had felt on the pier. There were things, things to be listened for in the muted clamor of nighttime's unlocking in the bush—things, evils, commands—and if he tried he could name them, he knew them as well as he knew this path, and he prayed to all the spirits that surrounded him not to show themselves, to forgive this trespass, he knew better than to come into the bush after nightfall with an impure mind but citylife had blunted this knowledge, and now he was too afraid to move, to attract the thing that was horror that was the thing always, always stalking him.

He prayed. Angels covered his eyes, lifted him, placed him down noiselessly among the manchineel trees behind Coddy's place, inhaling the thick, stale air at the back of the beach through his open mouth. Here were the white women, the one in the plan and another one, without their clothes, their flesh shiny with oil, their private parts glowing with white radiance in the shape of their bathing suits. It fascinated him, these ghost suits highlighting their womanness. He stepped closer toward the screen and watched them in the dim watery light of a candle, then another step closer in the sand when the candle was extinguished, watching them without thinking, without any sensation or awareness of their reality, as if he were viewing a film, until they climbed into bed together and he pressed his face against the screen, his nervous excitement like a drug that stuns.

He did not know two women could do this with one another, or would, and seeing them with each other, linked up, was like a collision of dreams and nightmares, releasing the fumes of his own filth and shame. His sexual desires had died early—he didn't know when, it was a black spot in his memory—but here they were again, reattached, his own sex rearing up, its aching head burst through the waistband of his trousers.

It was then the other woman, her back arching, her head forced back into a pillow and slinging from side to side, saying *no no no*, saying *uh uh uh*, looked at him, her eyes rolling out of nowhere and stopping, stuck, on the beam of profound discovery that fused him to her. She screamed, but all he did was step backward, not far, just another piece of the night shifting and resetting.

The other woman—his—reared up on her hands and knees, alert and vicious, eyes turned to diamonds, hair thick and scattered, and there was something there in her feral poise that Ibrahim felt he recognized, something he knew from his imagination, something specific from his past, and he could feel his mind slide toward it, traveling toward sanctuary. He thought, *Wait, she is someone* . . . nobody he actually knew, but not a stranger.

Didn't she rise from the bed? Didn't she come to the screen in her nakedness, bewitching? Didn't he smell the cunt on her breath, suddenly, like the smell of a dark, shuttered bedroom? Didn't she look straight at him and whisper, so only he could hear, *Go away*, not vexed, like you might expect, but like this: *This is not the time?*

Didn't he swim away from her through a gyration of fireflies, dragging his balls after him like two bleeding turtles, detached and struggling and exploding with pain?

Didn't the cocks crow, didn't he spiral forward through the night, didn't Marcus answer the door with a gun in his plump hand, saying, *Cashy? Wha de hell, bwoy, how you mekkin it?*, didn't Sergeant's pomaded hair sear his nostrils with the reek of bottomless revulsion, didn't the thump of his weight echo across the floorboards, didn't the cockroaches spin in glinting wheels on the whitewashed walls, didn't Marcus say, *Come . . . you do it . . . come*, and didn't he—Ibrahim— remove the iron bar of his sex from between his aching legs and bring it smashing into the emergent forms of energy, all the grasping demons that life had set upon him, like a red-eyed pack of wolves, until the air became sealed with his many terrible strokes, in a luminescent mist of blood?

And didn't he then break through the mirrored surface of the world to find himself in his father's shanty, waking on the torturous springs of an old car seat, gasping for oxygen, fever-wet with dreams, and hear a dead man breathe again, filling his lungs with desperate life?

Didn't everything stop, and then start again when he followed the woman to Sandy Bay, and saw her in the water, at home in the waves? As he sat on the beach watching her, didn't he come close to the center of the feeling of redemption, where still there were no words, even less, and no name?

He did.

Selwyn had sent him to her, her to him. He had foreseen no less than this encounter when Selwyn Walker ordered him to return to the past, the poisoned island of his marooned birth, but he did not know until he had seen her in the waves to whom he had been sent, that it was her—she who came to him when harm came too near— and that a greater meaning had been added to his secular mission, though he could not say what it was.

There was a plan and he was in it.

The white man came to fetch the woman on Sunday evening, and the three of them returned to St. Catherine on the ferry. Ibrahim was last off, the one passenger remaining in the cabin until everyone had disembarked. He hopped down from the perch he had claimed atop the plywood counter of the ferry's never-operated snack bar, no stranger to the fierce mysteries and hidden powers of the unforgiving sea, and so he scorned his fellow voyagers for their distressed prayers and laments, they who had succumbed to the hardships of the journey before they even thought to resist, trembling in the cellars of their own weakness, the failure of will, not realizing that he was protected and so by extension they were protected too. Their infirmities made him squeamish, now that his feet touched the cabin deck, forced to negotiated their bilious puddles and fermenty splashes, the melon rinds and candy wrappers of their pathetic optimism, the beer cans— *Wanda in Wonderland, Mary in the Mood*—of their cowardice, the groundnut shells and juice boxes and cakes half eaten and half spewed, all of it the regurgitated Sunday faith of Iman Ibrahim's people. No journey guaranteed except for true believers, he had chastised, silently reproaching them throughout the crossing, flinging imprecations over their prostrated bodies, disgusted by their animal fear, berating them in the voice of his father, never speaking a word to anybody but glowering at how little real discomfort they seemed able to endure, until he saw her, an apparition in the underwater light of the exit, saw her again, the mermaid, the woman in the waves, the woman who had reared up from the feast of her own sex, and couldn't restrain himself from calling out, even as the seas calmed as they had entered the harbor and she moved past and was gone, unmanifested:

Yes, look de womahn, Erzulie.

Part III

You can tell the truth by a comparison of the lies.

LEON TROTSKY

No man should be praised for his goodness if he lacks the strength to be bad; in such cases goodness is usually only the effect of indolence or impotence of will.

LA ROCHEFOUCAULD

Chapter 25

It was so much easier to identify an effect, recognize closure, *arrive*, than to ever single out a cause, conception, the subtle or clumsy collisions that composed beginnings. Which meant, he thought, that understanding had no frame to contain it, it multiplied backward through the infinity between one and zero, reversing out of the picture, it diffused responsibility throughout all of history, and that meant when tragedy happened along, guilt could be distributed piecemeal but blame had an altogether different story to tell. Blame had an alibi.

Start . . . where? Throw a dart at the board of existence, however many times, but there was no bull's-eye, no hard red center.

Civilization meant wake up in the morning and go about your business, submerge in the systems. It had always seemed a thick enough surface to hold his weight together with the accumulative weight of society, but somehow it fissured, opening beneath him and he dropped through, not into an abyss but into an unambiguous world that is as it was, where men sat grouped around a campfire, suspended in the wilderness and galvanized by fear, where facts would always be the stunted left hand of myths, the fingers held in a permanent cramp, where truth was not a process, not a song that never finished but simply the singer, the instrument of many songs in a universe of language, so that when it was all over—and it was never over, not for him—it hardly seemed to matter where he started in his attempt to construct a dialectic from the events, he could start on any chord or counterpoint of the sequence of happenstance and complicity, the indifferent countenance of double-faced fate, because wherever he sought the answers it was starting, never at one point but everywhere and nowhere at once, which he thought might mean, contrary to the facts, that in this world there were only middles, never quite extending from a beginning, never fully tapering to an end. A middle, revolving, recycling, interchanging its harmonics; joy, sorrow, beauty, pain; sharp, flat, natural, you could call birth and death whatever you wanted, they were notations of form that had been erased on the score, you didn't need them, you were there regardless, a voice, improvising. Intermezzo, you walked into the middle of things.

It didn't take long for those who wanted answers from him to get irritated with the luxury of his perspective. Where do you get this shit? they wondered, quite literally. Whom did he think he was kidding? He had a lot of explaining to do. For instance, everybody was keen on finding out just who the fuck he was, and they weren't buying bubble-headed musings. They thought he was faking it, someone was kind to suggest post-traumatic stress syndrome. Ultimately, he was made to start somewhere, but again, where? It was a problem. He wasn't trying to dupe anyone, only every beginning seemed freighted with equal significance, which meant perhaps he still hadn't found the one he was looking for.

He could start there on the northern end of the Caribbean island of St. Catherine, where there was an active volcano, Mount Soufrière, dormant since its last eruption in 1902, its massive crater collecting a brown hot lake of tropical rains, though magma had formed the fiery red eye of an island within the lake in a gradual reawakening, not many years before Mitchell Wilson had arrived from the United States, a novitiate in the art of development, to begin his professional career outside of the university. He could start there, certainly, retracing his second and ill-fated climb up the volcano's eastern flank, or he could give in to his greater impulse to understand *forces*, enlarge the aperture and start with St. Catherine, the island itself, the paltry trickle of blood it had contributed to the genocidal enterprise known as the New World, the island named and renamed, owned and disowned many many times before history dumped it into the hands of Edison Banks and his choir of fallen angels, intoning hymns of reformation, men who would eventually engineer a social machine not unlike an internal combustion engine, mounting it over an axle of senseless change, measured in meaningless revolutions per minute.

No, he told himself. In the beginning was neglect, it all starts with neglect, the ruin of a rag-draped old man shuffling toward you with his hand outstretched.

No, not that either. In the beginning was love—but they would only let him take this thought so far, and then laughed ruefully, as if that would have made them happy, cleared things up.

Starting with Johnnie of course was a disaster. He could blame everything on Johnnie or he could ex her out of each scenario entirely, and both ways the result was the same. What happened was, for the most part, with a few Johnniesque flourishes, going to happen anyway, with or without her, she was born to the periphery, though it would be years before he would ever concede, however partially, to this truth. He couldn't start with Johnnie because he had loved her, and that skewed the methodology.

Preoccupation was the end of life. He had stopped living, began to think of where he was as a welcome refuge from life. He stood in a cell below the battlements of Fort Gregory, his face in the barred window opening onto the courtyard where they had hanged Iman Ibrahim. The exposure was northern; he didn't appreciate the irony, or the lack of sunlight, but he would stare at the courtyard—it was usually empty, it had its rush hours—until a panic came over him, stare and stare, repeating his mistakes, carrying them back and forth in his memory, the terrible seductive comfort of repetition, the deadness of it, he could go all day and night like this, the panic would only come when he stopped, when in his nowhereness he could feel the outward punch of life within, and that would terrorize him, then he'd be right in the middle of the sloppy work they did with Ibrahim, Collymore, who refused to march across the courtyard to his death, who kicked and screamed and flailed in the grip of his escort like a fish in a net. Even with his wrists bound behind him he was beyond control. The guards beat the daylight out of him with their bootoos, they beat on him stupidly, without expertise, and they knocked him unconscious, which enabled them to drag his limp body up the scaffolding and loop the noose around his neck but prevented them from hanging him, because it was not cricket to execute a man unless he was alive and aware, in the fullness of his blood and breath, standing on his own doomed feet, in the shoes that would point him, momentarily, toward the grave. There was a policy, a protocol, to follow, very colonial. They had been required to wait while the medical officer in attendance went in search of smelling salts.

Here was what you could call an end.

Once it started it was always starting, and once it finished it was always finishing but in fact he knew it was only a story about a short time in his life and the lives of some people he knew, set far off on an island in the middle of the sea, a small place of little apparent consequence to the world, inhabited by a people no one ever thought about except, with a covetous twinge of yearning, as the smiling images beneath the palm trees in travel brochures, and in fact he always started with the day he returned to Howard Bay, having spent a strangely prefatory night in the house of a black woman named Josephine. He remembered a hot, happy walk. He thought of weeding his kitchen garden, which the rains had made mad with growth. He thought of a swim and then a shower, afterward he would fry his fish and eat it reading on the veranda and by then it would be time to find a ride to the airport. After the night with Josephine, he felt well rehearsed for Johnnie: now he had an image restored of how it could be.

Quiddley had brought down the tree. It was wrong, it broke his heart, but it was done. Quiddley rushed to explain the second he saw him at the top of the drive, nodding convincingly, wanting to be believed—he didn't do it, he had found it this way; a rapid stream of language—not about the poinciana but about the house. There was a boy inside, Quiddley revealed, ask him. Whatever anger he might have felt about the loss of the tree rode on the coattails of a greater dismay, finding the cottage trashed. The boy sat sprawled and asleep in one of the plastic-cushioned chairs in the front room, a toylike birdgun leveled across his knees, his hands clutching the barrel and stock. It started this way because Mitchell was one hundred percent sure Davidius had gotten into his house and gone berserk. Robbery was not the point, from what he could tell. Things were smashed and thrown down and scatterkicked and pulled from drawers and half busted, but the little there that had any value still remained. The radio, his bicycle, the liquor, Johnnie's jewelry, cheap as it was, and most tellingly, the small amount of cash, about twenty dollars' worth, on his dresser and in the pocket of the pants he had worn to work on Thursday, flung out of his wardrobe with everything else. Like someone couldn't take it a second longer, the way his life looked from outside. Perhaps going mad needed no more motive than that. In the bathroom the shower gurgled, drooling, and he turned it all the way off. His wristwatch was where he had left it, on the back of the sink, and when he turned around he saw that the metal eye of the hook had been torn from the wood frame of the door.

The boy didn't know anything about it. Sometime in the middle of the night before the storm hit Tillman came to his pallet in the gardener's shed, shook him awake and told him, Go guard the white man's house down on the road to Augustine. He didn't see or hear a soul until Mr. Quiddley arrived early to take down the tree and scrape his coal pits. The evidence in the kitchen was that Captain Pat had indeed fried and eaten his hamburger. A fan of bread slices lay on the floor like playing cards. A jar of mayonnaise had been chucked through the window of the door leading from the kitchen to an outside set of steps on the side of the house, but the door itself remained deadbolted. Nobody in Augustine was outfitted for glass repair, but the boy thought Grampa Hell the gardener could handle the job. Wilson gave him some money for his trouble and sent him off, first to the Augustine police station. He went outside and sat on the stoop, watching Mr. Quiddley reducing the enormity of the tree into bundles, and waited. Everything had become a shade worse than bothersome. His private world was in the process of being dismantled, rearranged off center. Even the beautiful trees weren't immune to whatever nameless, nibbling force was at play against him. Its agents however were not anonymous. Johnnie was certainly part of it, the general tendency toward subversiveness, but could be turned. Out or in. *In* meaning what? he thought. Mr. Quiddley, loyal servant of faraway voices. Creeps like Davidius. It was up to him to assert himself, be clear and firm, fight wrong with right. The cops contradicted their standard reputation by not taking all day to move their ass. There were two of them, an inspector and a private, big shot and flunky. They arrived not in a police car but something civilian, a Japanese compact dripping wet, as though it had just been washed, and their innocuous amateurity bumped Mitchell forward into a minor epiphany, realizing that in all the time he had lived on St. Catherine he had never once heard a siren, seen an ambulance. Any crisis was disguised in the normal flow of things. Even the two police checkpoints midpoint on the windward and leeward highways were unremarkably routine, details in the landscape, if you chose to see them clearly.

The inspector carried a composition notebook and pencil and proceeded to take Mitchell's statement, crafting his script at an excruciating pace, three or four words to a measure. However many sentences gushed from Wilson's mouth, the inspector made him stop and repeat himself, over and over, nodding his receptivity with the unhurried concentration of a woodcarver. As an authority figure he was comic, tall and lanky, his regulation-issue shorts so baggy they looked like culottes ballooned over the poles of his legs. The private inhabited a planet of his own, staring dully inside the house, screwing a blunt finger into his enlarged nose.

Mitchell felt gratified when the inspector seemed to agree with him about Davidius. The fellow who skulk in the bush around discotheque and such, making a damn nuisance of heself with the women. That's the guy, said Mitchell. We does call him Bushwhacker, the inspector said, permitting himself a thin smile.

That's him, said Mitchell. You know him. Great.

They stepped inside and toured the disarray and when they came out again into the sunshine, the boy was up along the road, kicking a soccer ball of paper trash ahead of him, just now passing back on his way from Augustine. The cops being cops wouldn't have thought to give him a lift up the hill. Mitchell called out to him, offering him a ride. "Okay?" he said, looking at the inspector, who grunted unfavorably, but with the police anything less than outright no was consent.

The boy slowed, his shoulders sinking, as if he were being made to obey. They were all up on the road now, standing by the car, waiting for him. "Come on," Mitchell said. "We'll drop you down by the Beach Bar." He walked back reluctantly, sullen; he had a problem with this. His head hung and he seemed to be studying the length of his feet. Evidently something had happened to him—he was rifleless for one thing. Mitchell asked him about the gun. *Dem tek it,* he mumbled, careful not to look at the police who, ignoring him, got into the car. Mitchell opened the rear door and motioned for the boy to get in first. "Who took it?" he asked. "These guys?" The boy began to answer but thought better of it, cops and white men equals keep your mouth closed almost anywhere in the world.

"We confiscatin firearms," said the inspector to the windscreen.

"Since when?"

"Since—I believe it come de way of some emergency decree."

Mitchell asked what was the emergency and the inspector said he didn't know. Some damn thing. He'd buy him a new one, Mitchell told the boy, feeling responsible for sending the boy to the station.

"Sah, best not," the inspector warned, friendly advice. He stopped to let the boy out at Rosehill's entrance, taking his servant's pay in the form of a gratuitous reprimand.

"Ease it," he barked, finding fault with the way the boy had closed the car door. "Ease it, mahn. Dese dyamn bwoys."

They parked down at the anchorage several hundred yards past the Beach Bar, next to an outfitter's shed and the kiosk for charters and rentals, and went out on the dinghy dock to hail Captain Pat and the woman but only five sailboats lazed on slack lines out in the postcard of Howard Bay—four sloops and a two-masted schooner. They asked around and learned the ketch had pulled anchor shortly after sunrise and motored out the channel. Terror, guilt, or slaves to a schedule? Mitchell wondered, more hurt and disappointed by discourtesy than this rather effective denial of confirmation from eyewitnesses. Case closed, he thought, but the inspector didn't seem to regard this as a setback. He intended to carry on, swing by the shanty where Davidius made a crude home for himself, out on Pilo Bight.

"You don't need me anymore, do you?" The thought of confronting so depraved a personality as Davidius produced in Mitchell a small cautionary surge of adrenaline.

No, they didn't need him anymore, he'd be kept informed. Off went the police, happy to be involved. At the Beach Bar, a new relief bartender explained he was in the dark about white people on a sailboat, but Winston would be back for the evening shift. He walked the long drive up the steepening land to Rosehill, feeling the need for a nap. The gardener was out on the grounds chopping something up, said he'd go down directly to measure for new glass. Mitchell tracked down Tillman catching up on paperwork in his cluttered, airless office behind the registration desk. He was hunched over his desk, bare-chested, wearing a bathing suit and reading glasses, a pot of tea at his elbow. An overhead fan stirred the atmosphere like oatmeal. He knew next to nothing about last night, except that ransack and plunder appeared to be a theme. One of his own guests had been robbed at gunpoint, somebody came at him out of the bushes as he walked down the drive to the bar. Two night watchmen had been added to the payroll this morning to supplement the worthless one who had been thrown into the deal with the original purchase. As for Mitchell's situation, Tillman said he wasn't one to lecture but what was he thinking of, giving the key to perfect strangers and then bugging out?

According to Winston, the boat people returned to the bar sometime shortly after midnight, arguing loudly and insensibly among themselves. The captain had a shiner half closing one of his eyes. He bellowed for a drink, bellowed for Mitchell, cursed black demons, cursed womankind. Winston calmed him down, got the key back, the captain implied there'd been trouble up at the house but he wasn't in what you'd want to call a coherent state of mind. Heading back out to the anchorage in their Zodiac, he tottered overboard just ten feet out from shore, pulled himself back in and continued on. Later, when Tillman had finished talking with the police about the assault on his guest, he came down the hill to help the staff close and got the story from Winston, decided to drive over to Mitchell's place for a look, saw what had happened, the breakage popular with juveniles and psychotics. Didn't look like a robbery as much as a rampage. It seemed like a good idea to have the gardener's boy sit by until Mitchell returned, get everything sorted out in the morning.

"They hauled their fucking anchor and cut out," said Mitchell.

"Ah, well that explains it. Dragged out to sea on a guilty conscience."

"Does it? Maybe they thought that was the best way to protect themselves from more trouble. Maybe they thought they were vulnerable, maybe they thought let's get the hell out of here."

"Maybe they thought, Hoist sails, party ho!" Tillman paused, tapping his ballpoint pen on the desk. "Vulnerable to what, exactly?"

"That son of a bitch Davidius." Mitchell explained the scenario he believed had occurred, but Tillman was not as persuaded as he would have liked. Davidius offended with style, his transgressions were masturbatory, but who knows, conceded Tillman, maybe another screw came loose in the guy.

Tillman invited Mitchell to stay for lunch, grouper sandwiches, fried plantain, tall cold glasses of lime rickey, which they ate on the front veranda, gazing like crows down on the majesty of Howard Bay and its ocher dollops of reef. Tillman was smitten with his new cook, Vera, she was big, in resolve as much as weight, wore a blue watch cap over her knotty hair and smoked bush cigars and defied anyone, dead or alive, to cross her path.

"The dead have too much power here."

"They just don't die as fully as they do up north."

"Which reminds me, have you heard from Isaac?"

"I imagine he'll have quite a headache by the time we track him down."

He would do anything for this Vera, she was a master of procurement, had wooed the Augustine fishermen and ordered a cousin to lead a chubby pair of beef cattle up the hill, where yesterday he had slaughtered and butchered them for a fair price, and here was an island miracle for you, the meat was not so rangy it couldn't be grilled. So he felt good, Tillman declared, there was every reason for optimism, things were going well, he could finally say, and let's see last night's crime spree as an aberration, not what's becoming fashionable, though God knows the gods are hoarse from clamoring for my downfall. It would be better if Davidius weren't implicated, so he wouldn't have to crack down on the minority of riffraff that had found a Friday night home at the Beach Bar, but you do, he said cheerily, what you have to do, and playing master was part of it, as long as you recognized when to stop.

The boy came by—Calvin was his name, Mitchell had been too distracted to ask before at the house, a bad sign, namelessness being next to soullessness. He reported that Abel had been down the road and back, for measurements, but glass won't reach till Monday day. Meaning Mitchell would have to board up the hole until then. Calvin shambled off, swinging his machete at gnats.

"I forgot to mention, I owe him a rifle. They took his away from him."

"Who did?"

"The police. They're confiscating firearms."

"That's the first I've heard of it. Why, do you know?"

"I don't, I couldn't even guess. Every farmer keeps a little twenty-two or shotgun to hunt monkeys and manicou. They're the only ones with guns. They'll be the ones affected. No more pigeon fricassee for the peasants."

"Someone in the government's paranoid."

"*Everyone* in the government's paranoid. The coalition can't survive another six months, no way. Banks will have to call a new election."

"There's an original idea. Then what?"

"And then there'll be a new coalition, I guess."

"Here an oink, there an oink. They should just hold a fucking Cold War raffle."

"That's flattery. No one's beating down the door to get in."

"You're going to hurt people's feelings, talking that way. What about Edison Banks? Doesn't he know a place like this can't exist except in the back pocket of a superpower?"

"No, that's wrong. I believe in him. He's the one I think who has the will and the vision. We'll see."

"Crippled imaginations galore. Dark inspirations. It's what we do now instead of war. Good night, Vietnam."

"Just what are you predicting?"

"Never a dull moment in this world."

"Listen to us. We sound like whitemen in control. Smug and self-amusing."

"We can't help it. We're good at it—the sound, I mean. The confident tonalities, the morally superior inflections. We have a noble tradition to mimic. At least we know better than to take ourselves seriously."

"I'm not sure about that. What kind of flowering tree is that you've planted over there?"

"Scarlet datura from Peru. It seems to like it here. As long as you've changed the subject, I'm not your mother but where were you last night, and what do you suggest we do to keep our womenfolk happy, now that they've tasted of the sins of Cotton Island? Can we compete with aging rock stars? Must we?"

"And that one over there?"

"Blood-red trumpet. Mexican. It climbs. What about Adrian and Johnnie? If you want to talk about those who take themselves seriously, what about Josephine?"

"You know about her? *Already?* Jesus."

"We're a brotherhood of cocksmen, here at Rosehill. Winston noticed you left the bar with her last night. She's strictly a no-touch item, all work, no play. She's obsessed with being the island version of Coco Chanel, if I'm thinking of the right person. Are you now an investor?"

"I'm now an admirer, that's all."

It was easier to debate the lesser crises, break-ins and politics, than to think about the women. They demanded a deeper understanding, self-knowledge and a high level of emotional acuity, all of which he felt were irregular qualities. The adjustment produced a dullness of mind, incipient depression.

"Do you love Adrian?"

Tillman grinned: the question was queer. "Am I supposed to?" Hotel guests drifted by, complaints replaced with dreamy, sun-drunk smiles, coming and going to the beach.

"I'm supposed to love Johnnie. That's what I've been made to feel."

"Extortion."

"No, heartwashing. That should be a word. And a statutory offense."

"Wilson, I have to say, you look and act like a man in love."

"Maybe I am. But I shouldn't have to feel obligated, that it's do or die for her if I'm not. She's gotten herself into some kind of trouble, needs me, and can't afford to leave love to chance. Love should be left to chance."

"Trouble?"

"Drugs, I think. She probably got busted and skipped town."

"The islands are overrun with America's drug fugitives."

"There's also the matter of a husband somewhere, whom she doesn't seem to want anymore. She hasn't elaborated. In fact, she hasn't said a thing. I suspect he sees things differently. I can't trust this girl."

"You can only love her?"

It ruled him in a way that begged understanding. "What type of tree is that?" he said, pointing. They agreed an excursion up one of the coasts was in order, contingent upon Mitchell's ability to borrow a Rover from the ministry's motor pool, since Tillman's wagon and his own Rover couldn't be relied upon for the distance. They left it at that.

A trail of sucked-out halves of orange guided him home. He was in a mood, knew he would spend the day inactive and inert. The sun stung like an astringent on the skin of his face, the beer he drank after lunch made him drowsy. In the yard, there was Mr. Quiddley, termite erectus, triumphant in denuding the giant of its limbs, stacking cords of branches in his double pits. Mitchell, implacable, ignored him, unwilling to make peace.

Inside the cottage, he felt the wantonness of the violation set upon him, heard its war cry, which only unlocked the door of his depression and instead of cleaning up the place first thing, he lay down to a nap in the sweatbox of his shuttered room, waking hours later in the same false night he had fallen into, cloudy-eyed and clueless, thinking he had missed something but what could it be. Johnnie was there, tangible in his napheaded lust but he failed to make the connection and rolled over in the agony of his sweat, the bedsheet tangled between his legs like a coolie's dhoti, to fall reaching toward erotic chimeras, burying his face in the feverish images of desire that were outside of him but relenting, welcoming him back to the release of sleep. He awoke a second time in Saturday's true nightfall, breathing a haze of smoky incense, mosquitoes stuck to his cheeks and forearms, realizing he had missed the plane to Cotton but there was nothing he could do about it now. He showered and dressed, then thumbtacked his bath towel over the shattered glass in the kitchen door. Outside, fragrant curls of smoke rose like wraiths from within Mr. Quiddley's coal pit number one, which resembled a burial mound, its dead smoldering as if hell had found them.

Down at the beach, there was no salvation in Winston's account, only a single answer that Mitchell dreaded hearing. The sailor and his woman had made no mention of housebreak, they were spatting between themselves, Winston said, remembering the man was drunk and angry, the woman's hair and clothes were wet, maybe she hit him, maybe him walk into a tree. Trouble at the house he understood to mean lovers' quarrel. Captain said tell the owner sorry about the window, which he had to stop cussing the woman to say. And here now, Wilson, that kunkle-face pussy mad bwoy Davidius dance up a frog-storm on the patio, I have to tell you in truth, the whole time the whitepeople up the road in the house, I am not saying so to protect a scamp such as he, right, and when he leave off he follow home a whore from the Bight he does fancy, and this is what I know. Here, mahn. Here. Fire a next rum. The police lock him up in the station, you know.

There was a moment before him where self-assurance seemed to collapse inward and he was confronted with the speciousness of his own certainty. The music was as dissonant as shopwork, harrying. He declined the rum, rum was not the leap to clarity he must depend on to judge this mistake that did not quite feel like a mistake. He left, goaded by an unclean touch of responsibility back over the hump in the road, and at the Augustine station they told him to go home and come in Monday morning, the inspector was off duty until then, only he could answer Mitchell's queries, don't worry yourself, Davidius was staying by them till Monday when an official statement would be required and the magistrate would see to this confusion. To argue otherwise against the villainous mutability of events was futile. He didn't try.

At the cottage he finally committed himself to straightening up the mess, taking the broom to the knocked-over plants in their pots and coffee tins, relined his collection of books on the dining room shelves, righted the furniture, wiped the ejaculatory spray of mayonnaise off the kitchen door, washed the frying pan where Captain Pat had cooked and devoured his hospitality and even threw out the panties and gold hoop earrings the seawitch had left behind in the haste of her alleged violence, then he changed the sheets on the bed and returned clothes neatly to their hangers, firm in his opinion that perhaps some but not all of what he repaired was the result of what lovers might dare to call a quarrel. He discovered his briefcase open, its contents—reports and documents—rifled though complete. No blackmarket for statistics? he said out loud to an invisible thief, a lingering presence he couldn't seem to clean away. When he had done what he could do, he went back to the kitchen to cook himself the fish he had intended for lunch. Watching it brown in the pan, he realized what the thief or thieves had taken, though he checked again throughout the house, because it was too hard to believe that their greed could be so stupidly appeased, that all they wanted out of all they could have had, seeing only what wasn't there instead of what was, was the daypack he had prepared the night before to carry on his endlessly delayed trip of goodwill to Cotton Island.

Out on the veranda, he sat on his packing crate eating his dinner, hunkered over the plate, pondering the charmed life he had led, never robbed or assaulted or knocked down, never cornered into bargaining with his own mortality, never doubting the future or his modest place in it. The offense he suffered now was slight, inconsequential, in the scheme of greater wrongs that surrounded him a superfluity but it nevertheless aroused a dormant appetite for reprisal. It sullied the view, stained the canvas of wonder. How many uplifting evenings had he spent mesmerized on this veranda, at rest with the bay, the channel, the running sea and its flaming sunsets, the darkening sky and brightening ensemble of stars, inhaling the garden perfumes of unlimited promise, those essences that seeped from the center of desire that was the inescapable truth of the tropic world?

He had been wrong about Davidius, and the slander seemed both justified and self-corrupting, which is where he would start in the long narrative of absolution he would compose, throughout the years ahead, for himself. Not with Isaac and *Miss Defy* on Ooah Mountain, not with Johnnie descending out of the self-perpetuating blue that would always be her life, not with Isaac being swallowed whole by the mythical dragon of change that had awakened on the island nor with the dream-snarled imbroglio of politics and reform but with the swaggering refuse named Davidius, the pathetic cock-brained troll who seemed the very embodiment of an underlying force threading the smell of decay along the inseam of the beauty-struck, sun-blessed egalitarian pleasures of the island; Davidius, who served a nature fundamentally wrong in the island's ambition for itself. Davidius was the pig-slop garbage piled along the roadside, the buckets of filth from the abattoir swirling in the harbor, the peeling facades of the colonial buildings, the pus-rimmed eyes of the pariah dogs, the rags and rickets and herniated navels of the peasant children, their illiteracy and their hunger, the wasted gonorrheal seed of St. Catherine, and *he was innocent.*

Mitchell could not bring himself to hoist the terrible, wearying weight of remorse—that part of him held itself in reserve. Waiting. Ambivalent. Davidius in jail for the weekend was no crime against humanity; what did it matter if one's punishment was out of sync and off-schedule with one's offense? It isn't kosher but it *is* karma, right? he argued with himself, diluting his already watery guilt. Retrospect would always deal harsh and seemingly unfair blows to men like Davidius, but who would want to say they didn't have it coming?

Chapter 26

The STOL De Havilland remained below the ceiling of clouds, battered along by crosswinds, not hurtling through the space of a Sunday afternoon but slowly advancing, like a bumblebee, in lurching arabesques. He watched the channel as it whipped itself into endless whitecaps, his last obstacle on the unexpectedly straightforward path of his life that was turning out to be a path back to her. To return where you started without circling or retreat was a damn good trick if you could pull it off, seeing as how death was the only commonly accepted solution to that brainteaser. At Christmastime one of the interisland boats put into service for the holidays had gone down somewhere beneath him, overloaded with homeward-bound passengers. There were women on the Queenstown quay, waiting for the husbands who had hired on to construction teams, taking advantage of Cotton's building boom, and when the news came in, the women tore the hair from their scalps, bloody uprooted clumps of it, in unquenchable grief. He couldn't remember why he had been on the docks then, but now it seemed as if he had been there explicitly *to see*—he had not known sorrow could be so violent, that loss could be so communal, that anything like the women's explosion of anguish had existed anywhere on the face of the earth. He had never led a life that had taken him there.

He stared through and past the image of the women, ordering his thoughts returned from this unwelcome morbidity. In the cockpit the co-pilot balanced a pizza in its flat white box on his lap, special delivery for one of the mucky-mucks on Cotton Island; God knows where it came from, with the nearest pizzeria over the rainbow. His fellow passenger, the only other, was a scrawny old man in a rumpled suit and neck brace—didn't pay attention where I was going, he explained inadequately—flying home from medical treatment in Barbados.

Mitchell was sure about this: Going for Johnnie was good; accordingly, Johnnie compelling him to act was proper—he wanted to act, make the definitive statement of action, carry her back, get beyond this wringing of hands, his soliloquy to vacillation. Let the fever run its course or kill him—what was so complicated about that? Don't waver, he coached himself, walking off the plane. Don't waste time.

Sally, more rubicund than ever when she had stopped by Howard Bay to tell him, not quite knowing how to tell him, where Johnnie was, had worried that she had somehow failed him, by not returning Johnnie back where she had found her. It was not an issue, he had explained, watching her cringe, uncharacteristically. Sally was one of the very few people he could say he knew whom he trusted to improve upon the world. So Johnnie's still over there, I'm not surprised, he had said, trying to match the famously embracing outwardness of Sally's smile, and what about Isaac, did he stay too?

"Oh! . . . Isaac! Jesus Christ. Isn't it strange?" Actually, she'd forgotten to ask Saconi but Isaac wasn't over there or she'd have seen him, Cotton Island wasn't a place you could vanish into.

And Johnnie, it seemed, wasn't even going to try, because, well, well, there she was, more less on cue, a responsible woman waiting with Saconi's guitar among the queue of departing passengers, dutifully installed under the tin roof of the rain shelter that served as the airstrip's sole facility. When her face tensed, seeing him step off the plane, he had to think she anticipated the worst from him—but went ahead and did it anyway. He felt mildly wronged, nothing he couldn't wave off but still, he hadn't rushed here to scale defenses, and how habituated was she to being struck, anyway, since halfway to her across the hard marl of the runway she had yet to rid herself of the expression of a woman prepared to weather an attack.

But what was he smoldering on about? He realized he owed it to her to soften his mouth, *finally*—Good God—and manage a clarifying though sore-hearted smile. She was getting what she asked for when she first sought him out, he was allowing her back in, welcoming the runaway home; he had reacquired the taste. The result was immediate: she laid down the guitar, jumped to greet him with a slippery kiss, and breathed her breathless thanks into his ear. He sensed her tension in his arms, but when they separated from their embrace, he saw that she had gone so far as to adopt a coyness toward him, as charming as it was disingenuous.

There's not much time, he said, and they traded practical explanations. He couldn't spend the night, he had business to attend to on the big island in the morning. The hour was five now and the ferry set sail at half past—the airline left him no choice, able to get him over to Cotton but then he was on his own, all return seats booked solid for the next two days. The party was over, the rats abandoning ship, someone had called in the exterminator, but then who was he to talk. Even the charter pilots were off somewhere in the yonder. The weather's bad, he said; she should begin to accustom herself to the likelihood of getting wet. She tried to hide her disappointment as they ensured that Saconi's guitar would be taken high and dry onto the plane, as she had promised him. She liked Cotton, there was a mile-long beach with nobody on it right where she was staying, she had imagined the two of them alone on the sand; earlier that afternoon she had ventured to the windward side and discovered a terrific cove, barred with steep-sided waves, perfect for body-surfing. An aloof batch of the white hiptocracy, famous behind sunglasses and hangovers, loaded up and the De Havilland taxied toward the austere border of the airfield. This place, she tried not to say outright, would be better for them.

Why, he wanted to know, sending dour looks toward a second group of casualties who waited for a charter from the south. They had monopolized the charters too, making themselves beloved by spreading cash like fruit off a tamarind tree. When he had asked if they could possibly squeeze the two of them aboard, they told him they were headed directly for Barbados, which he didn't think was a legal routing.

"Why?"

"Don't you think it's purer here, more innocent?"

Once upon a time, with a big *maybe* attached. He couldn't believe she thought that. I want you back on St. Catherine with me, he felt obligated to say; she threw her arms around him again with a degree more passion and told him, Anything, name it, you got it. They walked a short distance to the main road and flagged down a minimoke driven by Desmond, one of Lord Norton's retainers—I am de come-talk-wit-me-nobody-get-hurt-mahn, he said with a swell of hubris, taking them to Coddy's without further utterance, as if it were a regular part of his job, then came in with them to swipe a beer from Coddy, who had swiped them from the compound, but daht's de style we livin here now, bruddah, and Mitchell couldn't tell if he meant it was a privilege, or a tragedy easily swallowed. No problem, he announced, watching Johnnie dash around, throwing clothes and cosmetics into her shoulder bag: the ferry had been delayed.

Desmond dropped them at the Green Turtle, among the highborn and the lowborn and the ones born off the map, to have a drink and wait while the stevedores hand-loaded hundreds of cases of empty bottles into the hold of the *Carolanne,* an interisland workboat, licensed by the government to carry as many passengers as it could issue life jackets to should the occasion require—said to be forty, though no one responsible would care to put that number to a test, and it was not uncommon for the *Carolanne* to ferry twice or, during holidays and weekends, three times that many citizens between the main island and its Sleeping Beauty little sister, now money-kissed. Alcohol was probably a mistake, in light of the voyage ahead of them, but they ordered rum and tonics from the bar and sat at one of the bench-and-plank tables, shooing off a pair of shameless grackles.

"Even the birds beg."

She seemed to think of one thing and say another. Not all the doors were open, he cautioned himself; he hadn't expected this— could he call it a rescue?—to automatically fill every void.

"I'm counting on you."

"For what?" she asked warily, unrelaxed.

"To be happy now."

"Oh. Boy. So am I." She shredded the fibers of a plastic swizzle stick. "Don't get the wrong idea." He didn't listen to her words but watched her, the language of her body, her blushing grammar of doubt and pause, the awkward submissive punctuation of her eyes. She noticed how he read her and, with frantic exclamation, worried that he was picking out messages that weren't there, but still she had trouble governing her tendency to question her success, his willingness. Stop waiting for the punchline, he wanted to say, but instead placed his hand over hers until she spread open her fingers and his own filled the gaps: I'm here, aren't I? We're together—must everything be too little, or too much?

"Tell me about your weekend. Does it bear scrutiny?"

"I didn't sleep with anybody, if that's what you mean."

"No, no," he smiled. "I'm not asking that."

She sipped her drink and exhaled laughing, shaking her head. "I keep treating this as a departure from reality," she confessed. "When I saw you get off the plane I thought, Ohhh, *fuck,* what have I done, he's going to kill me."

He truly didn't care what she had left behind, he wasn't going to waste time considering the eventuality of its pursuit, as long as she herself didn't flirt with the notion of it catching up with her, summoning it forward, as she had him.

"Did you have fun, that's what I want to know. Get any autographs?"

"Mitch, I missed you. I thought about you."

He addressed a nonexistent audience. "She's in love."

"I dreamed you were with me."

"I dreamed the same thing."

"Why didn't you come? Why did you make me make you?"

"Does it matter, since I'm here now? One standard for you, another for me?"

"Yes it matters. But no, you're right."

Accepting her contradictory concession, he talked about the increasingly perplexing demands of his work, how they had prevented him—he wasn't lying, only omitting certain things—from coming sooner, and told her about the break-in and its odd act of burglary, which made her freeze.

"What about my map?" she asked. A puzzling moment of anxiety. She closed her eyes. "Did they take it?"

"What map?" he said, screwing up his face at another of Johnnie's mysteries. "The South American thing?" he continued, remembering. "No, it's still there. Why?"

He watched her become agitated, then resolved to challenge him.

"There's twenty thousand dollars taped to the back of it."

"Oh." He whistled, low and short—what else were you supposed to do?

"Oh, *nothing*," she cried, as in *That won't do*, opened her mouth and shut it. "Okay," she said finally. "Mitch, before I get on that ferry, before we really do this, let's settle things."

He merely widened his eyes and she went on, asserting his right to know what happened, back in Hawaii.

"It's not the big deal you think it is, Johnnie," he said. "I already know."

At first she fixed him with a dubious stare, as if what he had said was just another way he had found to be combative, but her poise faltered, and panic began to spread in her eyes.

"You're making me incredibly paranoid."

"I don't understand."

"Please try. You can't possibly know. It's impossible. You can't. What do you know?"

"You've suffered the fate of enterprising frat boys and old hippies who haven't woken up to the fact that these are the Seventies, almost the Eighties, and nobody gives a fuck about drugs anymore. You got busted." He was conscious of making his voice a mellow stream of neutrality, not because he cared one way or the other about drugs, but she was jumpy enough already, sitting there pop-eyed, and he didn't want to scare her. "Although, I doubt on mere possession, or you wouldn't be here." How many thousands did she say she had pasted to her map? At least she wasn't insolvent. "Unless we're talking tons. Are we talking tons? Count on me being impressed by your ambition, if we are."

Relief, like a weak light, made a pass over her face and was gone, replaced by a look so forlorn, he hesitated.

"Am I wrong? You're telling me that's not it?"

She gave a garrulous nod and said, "You're acting so superior, Mitch."

A herd of goats burst out of the few blocks of residential shops that composed the town behind the dock, bleating and gamboling, funneled toward the *Carolanne* by young boys with switches. A bucket brigade of sweaty laborers were passing lumpy burlap sacks of who knows what from dockside wheelbarrows up to the roof of the wheelhouse. Why hadn't all this been done earlier in the day, Mitchell wondered, as if the delay were an aberration and not business as usual, as he knew it was. Your life could change, its context made foreign, but it took forever to change the basics of the way you thought.

"I find that difficult to believe," he said. "Some people here in the government seem to know about you. They have a list and you're on it. High-up people. Like the man I work for, for instance, he thought it worth his while to suggest to me that your presence on his island might be impolitic, if I understood him correctly."

"Oh my God, Mitch, what are you saying!" Her aggrieved eyes went blank; she became instantly pale, her voice dull. "Oh my God. There's no point to this anymore. I'm as good as dead."

"The point," he said stubbornly, "is the same as before. Isn't it?"

She snapped back, executing a radical leap away from the edge of whatever doomsday she imagined for herself, actually swallowing hard before reaffirming that yes, the point remained, intact and unaltered, and was, still, love. For Mitchell, the idea of any relationship, and any mistakes that relationship might engender, being high-risk, not emotionally but physically, was surreal, cinematic in the most ludicrous sense. Perhaps his reaction was irrational and self-deceiving, but her apocalyptic rhetoric—the hyperbole of a not-so-unusual life, when you got right down to it, in a generation once teeming with

Johnnies—made him feel peculiarly affectionate. From the ferry a deep, bullish vowel of noise reverberated throughout the lagoon. He stood, grinning, took her hand and pulled her to her feet, wanting to cheer her up though all he could offer her at the moment was an hour and a half's toss across a nine-mile swath of misery. He'd done it before, on the government's tab, under similar bleakness of conditions, down to deliver an unacceptable verdict to the island's ever-dwindling community of farmers, that the way to the future was actually a loop road into the past, that the crop—sea island cotton— that was their namesake offered a steady market and net profits that were nothing to sneer at, but sneer they did, opting for their tomatoes and melons, those undemanding mainstays of subsistence, their goats and sheep, the cattle of impoverishment. *Daht cotton slave wuk, mahn.* Fine. No arguing with that. Toodleloo.

"We've got to go. Come on." She strapped her bag over her shoulder and they fell in among the last glum-faced stragglers, the only other whites in the bunch, three of them, Latin America on five dollars a day types, engaged in a match of gallows humor, their legs wooden with second thoughts, the farther they ventured down the dock toward the confidence-flaunting hulk of the *Carolanne.* A chill had descended through the late afternoon air, and a purplish, graying autumnal light that seemed to have sagged down the globe from the great north obviously found its equal in Johnnie's melancholy.

"Say good-bye to the beau monde," he teased. "It's back to our hovel among the coal pits. Hey, come on"—he squeezed her waist— "everything will be all right."

"That's what you think," she said. "For one thing, what about my fucking visa. That's first."

"They have better things to worry about these days, believe me. No one's really going to care."

"Easy for you to say, Mitch. With me they might care."

"See that drunk man praying, up by the mast. That's the captain."

"Get off it."

"Honest to God. He never sets out sober, and never without asking for a blessing. Damn good policy. Anyone not on the boat when he crosses himself—you know, Father, Son, Holy Ghost—gets left behind. You have to walk faster."

"*Mitchell.*" She whined his name, tugging his arm backward. "My visa. I want to stay here."

"You *are* paranoid." A crew member hunkered over a capstan, unwrapping the bowline; the gangway plank was dragged on deck. She tried to stop but he rushed her along. "Okay, look, someone knows about you, but there's nothing in it for them to give you the boot. That's all they care about. If someone wants to make an issue out of the visa, we'll deal with it, we'll fix it. With the government here, there are two sides to everything; whatever one side does, there's someone on the other side to undo it. Okay? *Okay?*"

"Oh brother."

He hopped the space between the dock and the boat and reached back for her hand. "Jump on."

"Mitch, you still don't understand."

"Great. Fuck it. Jump aboard."

And here she came, with a look of such woeful, piteous resignation it was if she had agreed to the inevitable ruination of her life.

"By the way," he said, light of heart, filled with an upsurge of self-renewal; he was going to be the person he was before Johnnie dared to come here to him, that calm and reliable self that knew what to do about her, without withering, without overwrought interpretations, "how do you do on boats?"

"I do fine anywhere," she said peevishly, answering his question, and, it seemed, more.

The gate in the rail was closed and bolted, the unhitched lines flung aboard to the crew. The exhaust pipe sneezed a ball of black smoke into the Catherinian tricolor—red sandwiched by green and blue—fluttering above the wheelhouse, where below the captain reversed engines into the lagoon and swung the ferry seaward toward the miasmic haze of the channel. Mitchell said hello to three or four people he knew.

"What, no deck chairs?" Johnnie cracked, it having dawned on her what sort of voyage she had committed herself to, the sloop-rigged *Carolanne* built on Bequia decades ago by the last of the master shipwrights, when such locally made cargo boats were the proud lifeblood of the Caribbean, not the grease-soaked, worm-eaten, paint-blistered floating junkyards they had become. With any less maintenance than the minimum provided, she'd rot and sink to the bottom in a month. Scarred, splintered, black with crud from the mean freight she carried day in day out, the *Carolanne's* deck seemed part flea market, part squatters' camp, hoard, town dump, and barnyard. Up in the bow, goats and black-bellied sheep shat in a chorus of unanimous fear. Behind the mast, men sprawled on top a loaf-shaped mass of cargo, secured and covered with a ragged tarp. Empty oil drums from the power plant were lashed up and down the gunwale rails. Families crouched in whatever available space they could find, eating their communal dinner from sooty cookpots. Mitchell stood at the rail, looking over the side, seduced by the lagoon's cerulean perfection, daydreaming of diving and old emotions, watching the reef like treetops pass underneath, until Johnnie pressed herself into him, wanting a reply to the reasonable question of where they could sit. Somewhere safe and private, she added, which was *not* reasonable.

"There's a passenger cabin behind the wheelhouse, but I don't think you'll like it. Not in weather like this."

They watched together as the crew raised a massive but low-hung sail, blocking the western sky with a lung of rust-stained fabric; a deckhand tied the boom down for a straight shot across.

"Not much glory left in that old sheet, is there?"

"Some," said Mitchell. The men strained on the lines, the ship heeled obediently and picked up speed. He felt a boyish thrill, hearing the sibilance of the water peeling off the hull in the boat's steady, brave charge toward the channel and its howl of wind.

She needed a bathroom (he corrected her jargon: *head; Oh, I know,* she said) and he led her to the ship's one toilet, in a closet in the passageway between wheelhouse and cabin, and left her there to scout what sort of seating he could arrange on the stern. Just to be sure, first he poked his head inside what he once overheard a matronly commonwealth tourist refer to as *the lounge*—the pestilential cabin to where invariably the majority of the *Carolanne's* passengers removed themselves, fair weather or foul, as if it were not only demanded of them but a rule of civilized travel, undissuaded by its formidable stench and its claustrophobic crush of humanity, partying, puking, and praying. With the channel as bad as it was today, riding on the benches of the airless cabin would be not unlike flipping through a picture book of pandemonium, page one of which he now observed, glancing around at the bodies huddled on the floor and jammed on the benches, reeking humiliation as well as dread, the first trombone groans of seasickness rehearsing in the baby-wailing, radio-blasted din, and this trip even the rare assault of malice as one of the passengers, a young islander with vaguely oriental eyes, fixed him with a silent, murderous snarl, as if Mitchell were about to trespass on property the fellow had sworn to defend to death. *Hey, it's all yours, every last godforsaken cubic inch of it,* Mitchell telegraphed as he withdrew, shambling back toward the stern, the deck beginning to roll and shove, out of rhythm, with hydraulic force and counterforce. On the aft deck, horseshoe-shaped like a bandstand or orchestra pit, there were four benches, spaced by scuppers, stapled into the planking in a half circle along the rail, all but one of them empty, a white couple, husband and wife, whom he recognized from the devo community (as in development or develoflict), fully prepared to tough it out in their exposed position, dressed in hooded slickers and drinking from a cooler of Heineken on ice at their feet. "Cheers," they toasted, and handed him a beer.

He twisted around, surveying the deck, at a loss. They could sit for a while at one of the other benches, but once they were out from behind Cotton Island and in open water, they'd be creamed. There was a three-tiered stack of crates of some sort, tarped and secured with a webbing of line, against the rear wall of the passenger cabin which, upon closer inspection, could be heard emitting a frantic per-colation—*buck?buck?buck?*—and he lifted a corner of the oilcloth.

Chickens.

Crammed like balled-up Kleenex into lath coops. On the port end of the stack the third tier was missing, forming a high seat out of the bottom two rows, and he sat down gingerly, testing the strength of the slating, and decided it might hold one but two was pushing their luck, and he scoured around up in the bow until he found a length of one-by-six to lay atop the frame in order to distribute their combined weight more evenly, and thought with this improvement they could give it a try.

Happily nursing his bottle of beer, he sat on the chickens as if he had cooped his conflicting selves and there they would stay, clucking harmlessly in their cages. Who had a chicken project going on Cotton, he wondered? The particulars tripped a switch and off went his mind: co-op or private? underwritten by? profit margin? over-head? return on investment over five years? free range or? Were these leghorns? Where were they going, and how soon could he eat one? The wind started to blow like it meant business, snaring Johnnie and bringing her to him, *there you are, I've been looking all over.* She had, evidently, doctored herself, tied a white scarf kerchief-style around her head, put on her sunglasses; arms, legs, and cheeks sleek with spray, her movement tense with coiled energy from having dipped into her glassine envelope of fearlessness.

"I see what you mean about the cabin," she said.

"I know that expressionless mouth from somewhere, the facial structure, those perfect lobes." He patted the nook between his body and the wall, inviting her to sit. "You're that actress in that Fifties movie, what's her name? what's its name?" He was terrible with Hollywood trivia.

"To begin with, I'm married."

"Well . . . right." So much for levity. "I know. Mrs. Fernandez, sit down."

Pinched eyebrows. Parted mouth. Speechlessness. Then, *YOU ABSOLUTE BASTARD,* she shrieked, nailing a spike of frustration into his chest with the side of her clenched fist, enraged at Mitchell for having thwarted the sublime pleasure of confessing one's greatest secrets and sins. She flung herself down next to him, creating a bow in their loveseat above the chickens, speaking through clenched teeth, the muscles in her lovely jaw twitching.

"*Damnit.* You! You think you know everything."

"Come on, I looked at your passport."

She folded her arms across her chest, nodding angrily, *I should have known.* They swayed together like co-stars in a Broadway musical to the rock of the ever-more-real boat. Straight out in front of them, at eye level on the western horizon, a tangerine disk of sun fell from the ash of clouds and a road of hammered bronze appeared on the surface of the sea. Mitchell thought, thanks but no thanks, we're not taking omens today, and, in seconds, both the sun and the road to it disappeared.

"You let me. Admit it. You left it lying around."

The possibility was left unconceded; she insisted he empty his bag of revelations, but Mitchell professed innocence.

"That's it," he swore, his arm around her shoulder. "You've cornered the market. Anybody wants a secret, they come see you."

She granted him this and attempted to make amends, but on terms that still seemed to require him to play the courtier, the seducer, to her shy and hesitant ingenue. She asking him to ask, he telling her to tell, until he relented, but not by giving up.

"Why do you have a rosary?"

Highly strange he should mention it, her mystified look told him; then, annoyed, she wiggled a symbolic distance between them on the board.

"You've really combed through my belongings, haven't you?" she said, her lips turned down, this indignity of the sort that sours its victims. "The rosary isn't mine, it's Katherine's. Well, I suppose it's mine now. Next question."

That was easy. "Who's Katherine?"

An abrupt and violent shift made her grab his arm; the boat seemed to jump a yard sideways, as if they'd been broadsided; cargo shifted with crashing, crunching noises, the boat's timbers shivered through their flesh, and inside the tuba blasts of wind and the engine's drumming, they could just hear the thousands of empty bottles chattering in the hold.

"The channel. We're into it now."

They looked out upon a mountainous field of intersecting waves, tasseled with spume. Sheets of soapy-looking water, warmer than air, came rinsing down the deck and he removed and stowed his shoes behind him, hoping to keep them dry. In the failing light the sea was so much bluer, the color glowing deep within its awesome shapes. Spray rained down on the yellow-headed couple planted on the bench, their whoops of pleasure barely audible in the chaos. Impervious to these unsubtle changes in the world, Johnnie concentrated on her mission of unburdening herself for a new life, dumping the heaviest ballast.

"Let's start again. First, I'm married, okay? Bobby Fernandez, a worthless piece of shit but at any rate I married him. God's punishment for stupid women. He's evil and insane."

"God?"

"I hope somebody shoots him. I hope somebody already has."

"I take it you're not getting along."

"Man, this is really funny, isn't it, Mitch?"

"So go ahead. Tell me about the guy."

"No. As of right now, you should just listen and not say anything or ask anything. That privilege has been revoked, denied, canceled. The accused will be available to take your questions after she makes her statement."

"If I want to know."

"Yeah."

"Second thoughts are my second nature, but go on."

She was about to when a goat came skiing back to them in the slosh, bleating like a burglar alarm, and went down, kicking in front of the beer drinkers, who, helping it stagger to its feet, now had an exotic pet. At the same time, Mitchell heard a muffled flapping above his head and looked up at a bevy of storm-driven land birds—sparrows he thought—alighting one by one on the upper crates to huddle under the narrow eave of the cabin. This was beginning to be like Noah's ark, he told himself, and as if to humor him, drops of rain splattered down. He looked to the west again to see in the distance a trio of rain squalls, and just then the sun took an encore bow for its very moody performance, sinking from sight between golden columns of liquid fire pouring from the ruptured sky. The coops flexed precariously underneath them, and it was all rather exhilarating, really, the angry engulfing beauty of it sweeping them along. The overhead rain stopped for the time being, but Mitchell set his fingers worrying at the knots fastened to the section of tarp they sat on. Either to shake him or steady herself, Johnnie clutched the bicep of his right arm with both hands, speaking to his ear.

"*Second*, was I busted? *You* think so but the answer is no. Not to my knowledge, anyway. Okay? Number three, are we talking about a few lids of Maui Wowie, college kid capers? Wrong. I wish we were. Fourth, did I love the son of a bitch? The answer is no, never. Got that? We were living together, housemates, there was an attraction, I'll be honest about that but it was a dark, dark thing, and the marriage—this will sound horrible but I'll explain—was like a business decision." When she paused he glanced up from the square knot his fingers picked at to see the color draining from her face. "Mitch, you know what, I think I might be sick."

"If we go to the cabin I can virtually guarantee it, but if you want, we can try."

Groaning, determined to finish what she had begun, she shook her head no; then afterward, she said, he could do her the great favor of tossing her overboard, for all she cared, if she kept feeling this punk. And maybe he would, he thought, for the sole purpose of saving her. A ritual to stand, retroactively, for the whole.

With darkness falling, the *Carolanne's* running lights came on; a red bulb on a pole above the cabin globed the stern in its dim theatrical aura. An empty oil drum rolled down the deck and the unflappable daredevil couple out on the bench somehow managed to field it and gave it the heave-ho, like a depth charge, off the stern. The ship's flags cracked like pistols in the wind. He and Johnnie were getting drenched; whether from rain or twisting spume was impossible to tell. He plucked loose the last knot on the corner of tarping and they succeeded, after they had pulled the board out from underneath them and replaced it directly atop the crates, in raising the skirt of heavy cloth and pulling it over their heads, drawing their legs up inside, a shroud of red-tinted, clucking darkness, the sea a beast eating through the door, never in their lives more alone with one another than this. Johnnie shivered into his side, opening her shoulder bag, he thought for a dry shirt but that was wrong, she wanted the cocaine, offered him a share and, when he declined, licked the last of it from the envelope with her eager tongue. That's better, she announced. I'm feeling a little better now.

The chickens pecked his fingers.

＊   ＊   ＊

Though she spoke with reckless, feverish candor, the plausibility of the life she described for herself nagged at him: he could not easily suffer Johnnie's reality, no matter how recognizable he found its form. Drugs were a great mischief, which speaks for itself, but also part and parcel of a generational warp in the culture—his generation and his culture—which he accepted. Fine and well, but where do you go from there? Stories like Johnnie's were infected with a perverse popularity, propelled by universal acclamation into the gloating, self-congratulatory counterfeit glamor of the myths the culture feasted upon, the romance of moonshine, the rumrunner's antiheroics, the wild-hearted music of defiance seeping out from behind locked and guarded doors, bathtubs filled to the brim with illicit pleasure. What was it there in the puritan heart that so idolized corruption; or was it capitalism, the New England slave traders, exchanging syrup for souls, for more syrup and more souls, in an unabashed triangle of profit between continents. What was the polemic here, which ethos and ethic? Would Johnnie argue, when you try to legislate human nature, what do you expect? Dare you suggest in America that its citizens can't trust themselves to know what's best for them but can of course trust the state, you awaken the sleeping minuteman, the recumbent individualist, in the breast of the populace, and what you *should* expect is a many-layered response of rebellion, variously enacted by ideological wholesalers to true-believers, jump-aboards, apolitical middlemen, street-corner entrepreneurs, ringmasters, prophets, impresarios, and anybody else inclined to retail the liberty de jour to the vast majority of bourgeoisie who prefer to digest their rebellion symbolically, as entertainment. Was she saying, let's shipwreck ourselves and start over? What was she telling him, describing a life contained in actions but offering few insights as to how she saw her actions in a larger context, or even what that larger context might be? People stand in line to get fucked up and who cares what the government says about it? Who cares what the government says about anything, period? You lose a few who were lost to begin with, c'est la vie.

How callous was he going to be was a fair question. He could hear the flattery of voices from her future, where she lay pillowed in a more conventional existence, *Fucking Christ, what a terrific movie they could make out of your life; honey, you should write a book,* and could he, or could he not, see her brandishing a complicitous smile, sending for a ghostwriter to supply the publishers and producers, the libraries and theaters, with a fresh dose, to fill the never-ending demand, of bullshit. Sooner or later, the only heroes would be self-anesthetized losers and the only stories would be stories about failure and greed, and either this was what Vietnam had done to everybody, or else America's vaunted, cherished antiheroes had always been frauds, clever fabrications, the titillating fantasies of future Republicans, the system's method of jacking off. What in the devil was this malaise the president kept talking about, causing people to scratch their psychic heads and cry out, *There's something wrong with me, with us,* and what, finally, was the question to the answer that was drugs.

Johnnie didn't pretend, perhaps to her credit, to provide either question or context, although she hinted, obliquely and unreliably, in that direction. He had known her for what now felt, in his blood, like a long time. Knew her when. Knew her as an intoxicated teenager shedding her springtime dresses, the ruffles and Peter Pan collars of exalted girlhood, watched her learn how to dance: innocence slurred, pubescence conquered. Knew her as a schoolgirl in tights and blue-jean jackets stenciled with red fists of freedom, college-bound, smelling of sandalwood, letting the soldiers ringing the Pentagon see her unsucked tits, trading Rod McKuen for Richard Brautigan, Disney for dope. But then there was a gap, an unscheduled intermission, the curtain dropping midscene, from which she reemerged outfitted in the brooding, shapeless winter wools of inwardness and alienation, and then, like the Rimbaud he doubted she ever read, disappeared.

Nobody could make themselves up to be what she said she was, hers was a role that followed fate unwittingly, like a deer. It was all pent-up inside her and came spilling out, the distance she had traveled in her life as a consequence of what she called this dark attraction that was not love to Bobby Fernandez, Cuban-born Miami-raised Nam vet North Shore kamikaze surfer with a club card to every VIP transit lounge in every airport from Bangkok to Beirut.

God I'm sick I have to lie down, she groaned but only slumped against him and kept talking, a rave in the hushed tone of the confessional box, burning the excess of energy she had ingested, *the first time I went out with him the son of a bitch took me across the international dateline for dinner, Hong Kong, turn your fucking head, right? that floating restaurant you see in all the advertisements, he knew the guy who ran it, he knew somebody anyway, I was living in a rabbit hutch behind Diamond Head—Mitch, I was living in a rabbit hutch, thirty dollars a month—I thought, like, drugs for sure, Thai sticks, I was absolutely ready for that, silly wayward me, we stayed in this famous white hotel, each room came with a limousine for your private use, he said we had to go back in the morning, quick trip, right, can you do me a favor, and what do you think I was going to say to him but name it, man, he said can you carry these pearls through Customs, I said* pearls, shit, *what are you talking about, but that's how straight and show-offy it was to begin with, he was starting over from scratch, not with the pearls I mean but with a network, something had gone wrong with the old system and routes, it had something I think to do with Cambodia, are you listening to me, I have to tell you this now that you've come for me, this guy's a motherfucker, he's a crazy person, the pearls were like a trial run, just to see how I handled myself, he saw right away I was no angel, not so hard to figure out, is it, but I could look and act the all-American girl, never gave her parents a day of trouble, he would never let me leave the hotels, he had buddies all over Southeast Asia, well, that's not the half of it, he's got friends like you wouldn't believe, if you ask me I think he works for the government, Mitch, maybe more than one, it's a gut feeling, he worms his way out of too much trouble, he has a Cuban passport besides his regular one, he doesn't know but I've seen it so who am I to get mad at you, oh Jesus I'm going to throw up.*

She leaned away from him, bending over at the waist, her head between her knees, gagging helplessly and without relief, nothing inside, it seemed, to come out. He was experiencing a trace of sea-sickness himself, like low-grade flu, but it, like the crossing, had to be endured, survived, there was no on/off switch to make it all go away. Johnnie hadn't taken off her sunglasses, even in the dark tent of the tarp: they slipped from her face to the deck and were dragged away in the swirl. Mitchell ducked out into the air to retrieve them, and did, before they washed out through the scuppers. More goats had surfed back to the stern and seemed to plead, when they saw him, their devil-slit eyes red and popping in the bloody globe of light from above, which had attracted a flurry of birds, hundreds of them, he guessed, keening like harpies in the banshee winds, making the music of nightmares. The couple on the bench was gone. The boat lurched severely down the slope of a wave that suddenly loomed up around him in the light, drooling and slathering with foam, and he reeled back under the tarp and wrapped his fingers through the slats of the coop to anchor himself. Johnnie straightened herself, tilted her fore-head on his shoulder and continue her whispery speaking, impossible for her to stop, *he's the kind who when he's drunk will say things like he knows who killed Kennedy, that's who I married, a freak like that— he probably does too—he says he's friends with the general in Panama with the Australian hat but I don't know how that can be because he hasn't even been to fucking Panama, not yet or I'd know, and listen, Israelis once came to our house, you should have seen it, it was no rabbit hutch, that's for damn sure, and you know what Bobby did, he sold those assholes four keys of China White, like, don't they have enough smack in the fucking Mideast, what are they doing scoring in Hawaii, we never even dealt in Hawaii, strictly transshipment, we weren't even shooting it, I was forbidden to so I should have known better, right, when that bastard said he wanted to get Katherine and me high, but look, it all went with couriers on private planes to San Francisco and Seattle, sometimes L.A. but that meant turf wars with some very ugly people, but I was saying, I only muled from Hong Kong and Manila to Honolulu, six months was the limit, one flight a month, beyond that people you don't want to talk to start getting nosy, we never took the same flights back, we got married I think to make a Filipino desk clerk happy, don't look for anything to explain it all, Mitch, it's not there, it was the stupidest thing I've ever done but Bobby was obsessed with me, out of his mind, he was handsome, I'll say that for him, that Latin lover shit is true if you like being caged and knocked around, he wanted me to get pregnant, you know why, because pregnant women and old people in wheelchairs are the only ones who get cut any slack at Customs, but there was no way, Bobby could be smooth, so charming and generous sometimes you'd think, here's the nicest guy on earth, but he was deranged, the guy was a monster, I got fat instead, for six months I just pigged out, you can't fake it with pillows and ace bandages, the women know, they spot it right away, but you can put on a muumuu and stick out your belly and start waddling flat-footed and saying Oh my God, I'm never going to get knocked up again unless I can stay in bed with my feet up, you would not believe how polite everybody gets, yes ma'am, move to the front, let her through, folks, what do you want, boy or girl? Bobby loved it when I got fat. I think what he really wanted was for me to get so big I couldn't fit through the door, Cuban men have this thing for huge asses, I've noticed, you wouldn't . . . you wouldn't believe all the crap I ate. I became like this garbage disposal. If. If you've never tasted poi. Don't. Excuse me, I want to die, I'm going to be sick again.*

Doubling over, she convulsed, straining, a dry silent scream; I hope to God that's it, he thought, dizzied by her exorcism, the sea's turbulent collaboration. She had developed an outrageously high threshold for mortification, hadn't she? Johnnie reeled back up, a thread of spittle icicled from her lower lip, and he wiped it off, sorrowed by her cadaverous, embalmed look, the sunken shadows of her eyes and cheeks. There was more, she murmured weakly, she had to tell him the worst of it, about Katherine, but he put a finger to her waxy lips, *shhh,* returning the compassion she had showed him that night on the beach below Rosehill, saying lay your head in my lap and take it easy, think of solid ground, the worst is almost over and we'll be across sooner than you know, and in another minute he felt her weight deaden as she skated out of consciousness into shallow, whimpering sleep. In this other silence she left him with, for the first time he was aware of the caterwauling of the passengers, garbled through the cabin wall.

Throughout this manic autobiography of Johnnie's he had not let slip his mask of imperturbability but it was, after all, much more than he had ever asked for or needed to hear, and now he wondered how, exactly, to grasp what she had told him. As a shell in his palm, to sail back into the deep? He wasn't jealous of the past per se but of the absences it contained, the persisting shapes of what he had missed; Bobby Fernandez was of no more significance to him than a finished bottle of wine, left on a table in an empty banquet hall. The only question of any value, the only answer he was interested in, was where do we go from here. Johnnie had a story, one of millions, and nothing new. Better to leave it where it was, open-ended, out here in the roaring serpent hisses of the sea, and make room for a newer story, for lost time, for better lives to come, for a denouement that would allow a finer sense of things. There was a fallibility to the two of them that was perhaps permanent, but they had given themselves fair warning. If he required a more perfect and noble Johnnie than this one who had come to him, then now was the time to let go—but he didn't. If he was to stand accused, let it be for callowness, not callousness.

A lesser but no less determined force of nature disengaged them: he had to free himself from her to use the head; he took her shoulder bag from behind her legs and slipped it under her head and, despite her groggy protests, let him bind her firmly in place with his belt and one of the loose ends of rope from the tarping. Out on deck, he kneed his way through a multiplication of goats, lunging from handhold to handhold forward up the portside passageway to the WC. Its door yawned open and shut, beckoning the damned to come see its unenterable filth, and he simply braced himself at its threshold, since no one else was about or likely to be, and urinated down at his feet. Whites, he thought gratuitously; it was they who had stumbled this far, the only ones who cared to hide their messes. Vomit in a bag, die in a hospital, appear as if you deserve the world since, no matter what anybody said, it was yours anyway. He should have known just to piss off the stern, spare himself the infernal vision of this, and the writhing specters in the ghoulish green light of the cabin. Like a guillotine, a window on the side of the wheelhouse clanged down in its metal frame. A crew member stuck his grizzled head out into the driving wind.

"How many goat we lose bahck dere, skip?"

"None, far as I could tell." He didn't know, had no idea.

"Oh ho!" He relayed the news inside to the echo of shouts and victorious whoops. Mitchell approached, peering in through the lowered window for a look at these foolhardy pirates—captain, helmsman and mates—the bulge of forearms, the blazing eyes, how they swaggered in place, the bottle making its rounds, the sea flying up like bombs off the bow, the island appearing and disappearing in front of them as if its very existence had yet to be fully resolved, and they were loving it, they were living like men, skip, and he realized that however much she contrived her story and however much was true, Johnnie had enjoyed its telling, Johnnie liked her life and the story it made, the dangers it skirted, *this much.*

They were, he judged, about a mile out from the harbor mouth and rebirth. He could see the pole below the navigational beacon atop Fort Gregory, car lights snaking along the headlands road, the land taking on dimension, landmarks materializing out of the hostile ether. The *Carolanne* wallowed across a visible line of current, bordered by flotsam and a floating salad of orangish sargasso weed, an instantaneous transition, salvation happening always with a suddenness. The seas sat down, dropping their edges and then their height, carrying them along on a roll of friendly shoulders. On the stern he threw back the tarp to uncover Johnnie flailing against the restraints he had fashioned for her safety, tears in her eyes, struggling to free herself. Her blind effort had only tightened the knots and it took him a while to untie her. "Why did you leave me?" she asked without a hint of irony. She was afraid, he had frightened her, she thought he wasn't coming back. He sat her up, consoling her; she recomposed herself out of her bag, momentarily barebreasted while she rid herself of her channel-ruined peasant blouse and shimmied a wheat-colored shift over her head, rising to step out of her shorts, sitting back down to fish for her compact case, fumbling it open for no other reason than to hypnotize herself with its mirror, Mitchell observing her behold herself, a goddess learning to accept the fact that her immortality had begun to rust, and this too, perhaps this alone, made it possible to love her again. He told her they'd be docking soon, they should move up front, and as they moved past the doorless entrance to the passenger cabin, she seemed confused and made to go in and then recoiled, pulling back, shuddering.

"My God, it's like a slave ship in there."

Deckhands rounded up the wandering goats and made token attempts to drag loose cargo out from underfoot. Passengers began to emerge from their quarters like zombies out of a grave. The sail crumpled and dropped down the mast; for some reason the sight of it collapsing resembled, in Mitchell's video bank of images, a man in front of a firing squad, life cut away from its support. Hawsers whipped through the air, the engines reversed, and they were firmly attached to the world again, filing ashore, pressing through a swarm of men and boys, a sinister gleam of faces under the solitary cone of light, daunted by the shouts and grabbing, unsure of their legs, empty of stomach and head, the travelers shoving to escape the stink and leavings of their misery.

Beyond the waterfront, Queenstown seemed unusually deserted, shabbily lit and advanced in age. Christian curfew—city streets could be depressing, he thought, on Sunday nights, the feeling that everybody cowered behind locked doors. He liked it like this though, having it all to themselves; Johnnie was still woozy but growing chipper with every step. On a side street near the post office they found an open kitchen, a workingman's restaurant no wider than a hallway wedged into a row of merchants, without customers until they sat down at one of the tables along the stone wall. The cook was in the back on a stool, reading out loud a verse from a Bible in her hands, the words mixing in with Kingsley on the radio, ranting about Edison Banks, what else was new, good children and bad children, madmen running Jamaica, stirring it all together in one associative mess. The cook finished her page and came to tell them curried conch and rice, no fish, the men couldn't get out. She was stocky and had calm eyes.

Johnnie was reanimated, transformed, the dread gone from her eyes, the anxiety off her face, nothing quite like a harrowing experience to make the old tensions paltry and tedious, quick with mirthful smiles now that the rules had changed, the probation over with and done. If he was stealing her, if that's what they were leaving unspoken, fine; that kind of larceny seemed entirely justified and had its own inner logic, bittersweet: he was stealing her *back*. Love wanted to mitigate every damn thing, let nothing obstruct. She had the sense not to attempt again to bring him up to speed on her vita; stories like the one she had told him on the boat he wanted left behind with jungle warfare, peace signs, Nixon. No borrowing this sort of toxic glamor from their own cloying past.

She put her bag in her lap and began taking things out with ceremonial enthusiasm, covering the table with a potpourri of talismanic scavengings.

"Hey, look what you found."

Enough feathers for a headdress, delicate variegated blades, and shells of course—a mingling of cowries, augers, limpets, tiny peppermint-colored wafers and angel wings, a spidery fighting whelk, transparent gold bangles that he had forgotten the name of. There was an anchor-embossed brass button filmed in verdigris, an edgeless medallion of violet glass frosted by the surf, an assortment of odd seeds and pods and finally, the last to be shown, the pièce de résistance, the burgundy-colored clay head of a tiny animal, a bat-faced adorno with pointy ears, upturned snout, and slightly grinning diabolic triangular mouth, undoubtedly off the rim of a pre-Columbian pot or bowl.

Johnnie rhapsodized. "Isn't it wonderful?"

He turned it over in his hand, noticing the two holes drilled through the snout, these, he had read, for snorting jimsonweed and other hallucinogens during religious rituals. "The Indians thought bats were spirits," he said.

"It gives off vibrations, doesn't it. Whenever I hold it in my hand, there's something there."

The cook brought their food on a tray, two bottles of beer, waited for them to clear a space.

"Where did you find it? Wherever there's a freshwater source along the coasts, you're going to find artifacts."

"Mmm!" Johnnie's eyes said *wait*. Her mouth was full and the conch seemed to require a rigorous chew. She had something important to say. Impatience showed on her face from the delay in swallowing.

"I just remembered. I have a message for you. From your missing friend, Isaac."

"What?" His fork stopped in midair. "Do you really?"

"Oh, yeah," she nodded, gulping. "God, that's tough. He says to tell you he's been cooling out. That there's a good reason he hasn't been around lately but can't say what it is right now. Also, to tell you he'll be in contact soon, and not to worry. Do you think they serve salad here?"

"Isaac told you that? You talked to him?"

"No, not to him. He's supposed to be up north, in the mountains,

I think. One of his friends over there. What happened was"—but she was off and running again, bursting with words, too fast for any lingering wiles to keep apace, she wasn't crazy about being in seawater that gave you the same experience you could get from a bathtub or swimming pool, Makapuu Point, east of Honolulu, on the other side of Diamond Head, was her favorite beach, two or three times a week she'd take her swim fins and head down there, one of the premier body-surfing spots *in the world*, right, she was a powerful swimmer, did he remember from their weekends at Virginia Beach and Rehoboth, Makapuu's waves were long blue chutes of pure joyous ecstasy, they centered your existence, sectioning off behind you like a giant white fist slamming down, she became addicted to the sliding weightless free-fall during which you gradually mastered control, the sudden elevation and the hurling down through seamless crystal tunnels alive with curling energy, the single-minded triumph of escaping disaster, the gripping force rippling over her breasts and stomach, down through her legs and out the soles of her feet, exploding. The ultimate convergence of motions. She became expert at it and could hotdog, do tricks, rolls and tucks, windmills, backward entries, a maneuver called Scream in the Cathedral, it all became so effortless she began to look for the wrong places, make deliberate mistakes, it was something she had profound thoughts about, late takeoffs on waves too big to finesse, edging closer to the known danger zones, the shallow or rocky spots, she felt bare, stripped down to her finest essence, Here I am and I'm strong enough to risk this, rather than a fear of flying an unqualified devotion to it in its liquid form. I wanted to see how much there was to learn, she said, what it felt like to be at the very core of a toppling universe, push and push the limits because, I don't know, that's the way we grew up, isn't it, everybody let us go farther and farther, as if their warnings were not sincere, as if they couldn't wait to see just what we'd do next.

He was amazed by what she was telling him, how much, the dance of truth in her sentences. Her excitement got the better of her and she had to stop to light a cigarette.

"Then," she went on, *"bang!"* She got what she asked for, not just a muscle sprain or sand burns but an honest to God fight for her life, claimed by a mammoth swell that she tried to back out of but got sucked over the falls, the devastating contraction, the inescapability of it, the only way out something of a paradox, submit without surrendering, here was a power that didn't look kindly upon flirtation, it was an avalanche and she was only another one of its boiling molecules, down in its depths, somersaulting along the bottom, registering blows, seeing stars, black flames, when she began to lose consciousness she thought, Now it will release me and let me go, but it didn't, not before she had swallowed gallons, was missing a chunk out of her leg, and had to be rescued by two of the guys in the water and helped to shore. Her eyes bulged, the recollection ended. She stubbed out her cigarette and looked at him apologetically.

"I completely forgot what I was going to tell you. Where was I?"

"Isaac's friend."

"Oh, right. Sorry. You know me, when I get going. Anyway, the lesson was not lost on me, that's why I'm here, but I'll never see the point of getting in the water to just sit there, as if the ocean were a lake and you're three years old. It's boring, it's for fat girls, lazy-minded people. The beach in front of Coddy's place was no good if you got restless." On Saturday, she had taken a drive with Adrian and Sally. Not far along the windward coast she spotted a cove that made her think of Makapuu and wanted to stop but the others didn't. After everybody left she had the urge to do something invigorating, not just stick around the bungalow feeling sorry for herself while people lacquered in happiness traipsed in and out, wanting to get high. Her mood did not match. She put her suit back on under her shorts and shirt and walked up to the paved road, started hitchhiking, on Cotton Island everybody pulls over for you, it seemed, and she was there before she knew it, the waves all to herself, perfect and regular as clockwork, like they were being pumped out of a machine, ghosts of milky sand rising halfway up within the blue walls, the bottom visible in the flat light so there'd be no surprises, the swells just big enough to be head-clearing, make her blood race. After a while she felt a strange feeling, a premonition she guessed he could call it, and she emerged from inside a wave to see someone sitting on the beach, a local guy, watching her, he came out of nowhere. She didn't think much of it though she decided to stay in the water until he left, just to be on the safe side, but he didn't move and she was worried about the time, keeping her promise to Saconi to put his guitar on the plane. Finally she pointed herself straight ahead and went the distance, the wave expiring underneath her in the shallows, she on her stomach in a deposit of foam. The cove was absolutely secluded, the coast dropped off about ten feet from land to sea level, so that you couldn't see most of the beach from the road. She realized then that he was waiting for her, he wanted something, and she had to stand up. When she came closer, she started feeling afraid, he had what seemed a bright-eyed menace to his features and she wasn't about to do anything to encourage him, not even say hello, just get her towel and clothes and go, but the thing was, he gave her a shock—he knew her name, he knew Mitchell's. She was nonplussed, something was wrong with him, it was hard to describe, the menace she thought she had identified was really more like a trance, he didn't move his head right when he spoke, and when she responded she felt she had to speak to him as if to a small child. He seemed so absorbed by her, so pathetic, and yet so latent with threat, she found herself feeling a sort of reflexive sympathy and wanted him to see it. He was horrifically scarred on an arm and leg.

"He touched my scar, I mean, no, what am I saying, what does all this have to do with anything, he didn't touch it but I knew that's what he wanted to do, he looked at it in a way that felt like he did, his fingers tracing it. Okay, that doesn't make sense. I mean his eyes. He wasn't at all talkative after he said what Isaac said. I promised I'd pass the word along. I didn't ask questions, like what if Mitchell needs to talk to Isaac tomorrow, what does he do? I toweled off and put my tee shirt back on and said I had to be somewhere and thanks, but he followed me up the path and, to finally answer your question, that's where I found the bat thing, poking out of the clay in the bank next to the path, the next good rain would have dislodged it, probably, it was just hanging there, waiting for me to come along. The guy had a moped parked up on the road—you know, he never told me his name so I can't tell you if you know him or not. He offered me a ride but honestly, he was way too spooky. I said no thanks, I'm out for a walk, and he drove away. If you can eat that," she said, pointing her fork at his mouth, "I guess I can too."

Kingsley's inflammatory drivel poured out of the radio. Mitchell watched her chewing the rubbery conch, trying to read the unforeseeable future in her face. Her bottom lip was cracked and he wondered if it was like that before and he hadn't noticed. It was a detail he'd have to keep in mind, later on, back at the house. Both stories, this one and the one aboard the *Carolanne*, communicated an opening up, an aggrandizement of spirit in their infectious, inflated intensity. She was switching on lights, implicating herself; he was elated to hear her talk so freely, without calculation.

He had not missed the message she carried to him: Isaac was okay, he'd be in touch. It brought genuine relief, a lifting of impending responsibility, like the silencing of a noise on the other side of the wall that was getting too loud, interfering.

Johnnie had an appetite, he was glad to see. He wanted to get her home.

"Did I tell you," she said, laughing at the image that came into her head, "that Sally tried to strangle some jerk who said she wanted to be black."

In another minute or two, he saw—because there it was, already flowing forward into its shapes, ribboning across the border of consciousness—he would fall asleep to taste the unrefined sugar of love's sweetest dream. Once they were in the house she immediately wanted to check the map, touch her money. He looked at the green bills in rows and his first thought was they didn't make sense, arranged the way they were, like pop art—something about meaninglessness, another statement. Profits, his professional bailiwick, why people sought him out for advice; talking about profits was how he made his own living but now there was nothing to say, no theories to apply, no statistics to overcome the loneliness of this money. They took showers, Johnnie first. He organized his briefcase for the morning, waiting for her to come out. The house was quiet, filled with a gauzy haze of perfumed smoke, like a temple. "All yours," she said into the hall, meaning the bathroom. The salt washed away like greasy ointment, uncovering a hard bark of skin, and it fascinated him, placing a forearm against his hipbone, to rediscover how brown the sun had made him. Wrapping a gritty towel around his waist, he opened the door to let in a draft while he shaved, which he preferred to do at night instead of the foggy dash of morning. Johnnie had gone to her own bed to read a magazine, deferring this last decision to him, careful not to risk assumptions, wearing only panties but nevertheless demure, and he was touched by the gesture that her recession was meant to be. He leaned against her doorway, grinning uncomfortably, not quite finding the very simple words that would move her from here to there, bringing her to his own bed.

"You're all right, aren't you?" Artless, or so he felt. The best he could do. He was deferring back, letting her take care of it. Was she still having her period?—he didn't ask, and she didn't say.

She closed the magazine and put it aside, propping herself up on her elbows to nod. "If you hold me I'll be better."

"There's actually a room for that, with a real bed."

Candlelight, a saxophone on the radio, played in another world and the notes blown in from the sea. He loved what a candle did, how it transformed the values of the colors in the house—leather and autumn rubies, golds and ambery varnish, so old it cracked like snakeskin. The air was cool enough for them to pull the topsheet over them like a vow, or blessing. His touch was speculative—he hoped wise. Every time he gazed at the twin flames locked in her eyes time was backward, forward. He was a little shaky; for his body's own reason adrenaline had escaped into his blood, a beating heart. She rolled and fastened herself to him, he was holding his breath, clinging to the tautness of her, reading the riddle of her face, the poets who first linked sex and death weren't joking, there was a spreading, escalating moan that he listened to and then reproduced, submerging in the fiery current that was them, and then was them dissolving. She was changing him again, somebody else would have to say how.

He couldn't help himself then. The simplicity of it all was profound. He became silly, daffy, giddy, trite, a self only a woman would ever see in just this way.

"Back into the Woods," he said.

She gurgled, falling asleep, her warm mouth a wetness on his shoulder, mumbling that she figured he'd say something like that, a revision of an old joke.

"Don't go into the Woods alone."

"Shhh," and then she was snoring, soft, erratic slurps; for a brief time she twitched, a snap of volts flashing through her body into his. Outside, a motorcycle went by on the road toward Augustine and he seemed to go with it and its zippering noise, not yet asleep but sealed into the dream,

and what it is, this dream of dreams, is only an embrace but it is final, the last exchanged on the road that was their lives, though the physical bodies of the man and the woman he sees are not old and withered but youthful and whole. Like a bare stage, there is no setting or background but darkness; he and Johnnie sit unclothed at its center, cross-legged, facing one another, their knees almost touching, their arms so tense and static with movement the action they are about to perform already exists in the mind of the viewer, and the light that makes them visible does not shine down upon them, does not enhance or dull their skin, but is simply there, a natural condition. He feels intense sympathy for the dream characters, and protective of their sentimentality—after all, their lives are at a close, they are composing an image of farewell. It is what they have, perhaps the world has no need for it but they do, it forms the welcoming place where they might rest momentarily and take account, strive against forgetting and the nonexistence that is imminent, the silence they will fall back into when they let each other go. Their arms lift and encircle, their cheeks press together, warm and smooth and powerfully comforting. Their heads lower onto respective shoulders, tears cornered in their closed eyes. There is a relieved sense of tenderness fulfilled. He wants to open his mouth but cannot, knows he will choke. If their feelings for each other have meant anything, she will have to interpret that meaning from the way he holds her. She will have to look back at the distance they've come and the separate spans of their isolation and find a way to measure the value of the journey against whatever standard time would hold them to at this second of grace that is their reunion. They are naked, in blackness, and now their flesh is incandescent. What extraordinary kindness destiny was capable of, if it could remember love so well, if it could bring them together at such a moment so that they might have the opportunity to know the worth of all the days behind them, to see each other finally in whatever completeness they have managed, to know with certainty that they have truly survived the worst, have survived indifference and betrayal and the scattering force of passion into inertia. They have made their own small, unheralded, and soon-to-be-lost history of love, survived its airless depths and tended it enduringly in times of barrenness, and now, completed, justified, they could defer once more to the separateness of travel, where death was no more or less than the necessary absence of the other, the absence they knew as well as anything else, the serene absence that did not prohibit or restrict, the absence they could not regret, the absence that never caused despair, because it changed nothing. All he wanted to do finally was to thank her for coming here, for the embrace, to express the gratitude that was never so profound or real as in this chapter of dream, and when he awoke it was still night and he was crying noiselessly, knowing that the vision of the dream, everything it contained, the exultant faith of it, was unobtainable, was a perjury, and could not be appealed. Sometimes it would feel like the only dream he had ever been allowed, but it was nevertheless a dream, it overstepped reality by miles, its truth had no language and no world. It was too brave for mortal beings. Immanent in its sweetness was a whiff of decay. There was no chance they might ever conjure its delicate substance.

It was terribly, terribly cruel.

We have to give up everything of love, he remembered reading, the first time she left. *Even the ghost.*

Chapter 27

Now it was over, the government had quietly issued an order for his deportation: Today, tomorrow, *soon*. It seemed like years since he had been arrested, since the friends of golf had come and gone, since the trial of the person who called himself Iman Ibrahim.

Falling darkness throughout the underworld of prison. The pungent, rotting heat of July. The privations and humiliations of being locked up infinitely more tolerable than the culture of infernal noise.

Start where?—when all that ever really begins is the end.

Start where?—because he hadn't known where to start in order to do the right thing. Save a friend. Save *anyone*.

He wasn't a victim. All manner of treachery and bad luck had come his way, as it might in any life, and he had dealt with it, and he was willing to be held accountable for his own actions. He hadn't, to his knowledge, fucked up; there was no subjective moral dilemma but rather an evaluation of his culpability within the objective whole. Which is to say he felt contaminated; being locked up then was like detox, quarantine. To be honest he'd have to conclude that the shrinking of one's affairs and the enforced passivity were not without their small virtues. Incarceration made alienation, for instance, utterly permissible, a normal condition, despair too if you'd like, help yourself, take all you want. And a cell, at least a solitary one such as his, offered its occupant a monastic invitation to grandiose soul-searching, perhaps impossible to decline given the fact of one's material and sensory deprivations, and seemed the only correct environment for the conscience to fester uninterrupted in the garbage of aborted possibilities, and then (the penitent could always hope) clear.

He knew what freedom meant—perhaps this was what was wrong with him.

Start with the alphabet then, the evolution of *E* to *R*, a sleight of

403

hand that produced, had hoped to produce, a revolutionary government? For that matter he could start with what had been called the *Cuban disease*. That was easy enough—he could stand at his casement window and look down upon an olive-green APR parked on the cobblestones of the prison courtyard, a timely gift from Havana. He could start at the Cuban embassy in Mexico City, the day Bobby Fernandez was told by one of the political attachés, *Maricon*, I just speak with this guy on the telephone: Did you misplace a wife? Johnnie had tried to put as much distance between herself and Bobby Fernandez as she could, understandably, but she got no farther than this, St. Catherine, to the illusionary haven of a man who reluctantly approached love in such a way as to make it always and forever include her, the primary source and reference, in its working definition. He could just start with Cuba, couldn't he: the guerrillas in the Sierra Maestra, the Triumph, the apparent gut-shot wounding of imperialism, the heroes, so many of them—Fidel, Raul, Vilma, Che, the list ran on and on—their successful ascent up the Everest of all political endeavor. Start with Che perhaps, for his unearthly idealism, his doctor's kit stocked with the hallucinatory medicines of violence.

What were you doing with the wife of Bobby Fernandez? they asked him. Why was Fernandez in Mexico City, what was he doing in Panama? They asked him . . . and then they unasked him. They had answers, he didn't. Of course. The only answer he wanted from them was whether or not Johnnie's husband had made a surprise visit to St. Catherine, as she seemed to be convinced he had. The only answer they were truly interested in from Mitchell Wilson was to the question, Who is Mitchell Wilson? They couldn't decide. Finally someone settled on a neat bureaucratic catchphrase: an uncontrollable element in the field. It became his official definition.

He called them the friends of golf. They dressed like that, as though they had just strolled in off the links.

They found it difficult, these friends, to be very upbeat about 1977, where forces obliquely historic had set them all down. The year was turning out to be a riddle they were itching to solve, St. Catherine and Mitchell Wilson the latest installment of clues. They weren't convinced Wilson was sincere about the future. His convictions were suspect—convictions were no longer something Americans shared, wouldn't you say that's true, Wilson? The president had pardoned the draft evaders, was going to give back the Canal to a gang of greaser narcotraffickers and, even as they spoke, was conducting formal negotiations with Havana for the first time since the Bay of Pigs. You see what we mean? wondered the friends of golf.

Human rights were on the agenda; whatever that meant, it raised possibilities. The president had appointed a very dangerous man from Atlanta to be the nation's apologist at the UN. Lists were made, allies lectured. Lists were unmade. America's friends are nervous, said the friends of golf.

When he was with them, he invoked his status as a fellow Virginian, started there with a quote from Henry Adams: "It's always the good people who do the most harm in the world." Adams had said that about Robert E. Lee. Wasn't that a first-rate motto for the century that had been assigned for safekeeping to America? They could engrave it in Roman lettering, bold-edged serifs, over the entrance to their agency. We're not the people you think we are, they said. And isn't it funny, Wilson said, that I'm not whoever you think I am either. Now what did this mean? Why were they having this tea party? What was their point, what did they care about, they had no feeling one way or another about St. Catherine, a nigger among nations, an obscure place, strategically nullified and invisible to their eyes, so what were they after? St. Catherine!? they scoffed—Guy, the Army Corps of Engineers keeps grader blades *in stock* big enough to scrape pissants right off the map, no more trouble than bread crumbs off a tablecloth. They hadn't rushed down here when it was all about Sally—they came for him alone, this *shit,* an uncontrollable element, and only after Archibol raised a stink about him on the floor of the UN.

When he asked his own questions they said, *interesting, worth some thought.*

"What are good intentions, and how much do they count?"

Another one, just as sticky, was, "What were my intentions?" Like asking if wishes were fishes.

He had a pet set of answers too, he kept them to himself; the questions they might have fit seemed separated and lost:

Liberté, égalité, fraternité (revolution's Holy Trinity, the best of all possible answers, countless applications, reusable, universally appreciated, came with a money-back guarantee).

Us v. *Us* (an anagogicist's wet dream). They thought he was a charlatan, they thought he was real, they thought he was a mastermind, they thought he was a dope.

Drugs as electrochemical poetry, the cantos of the metabolism (handy tools of the metaphysic for the New Man and New Woman).

Drugs as revolutionary discipline, as war. To tell the truth, he knew the question to this answer. Bobby Fernandez was in Panama to arrange the transshipment of eight kilos of heroin to New York. Small beginnings, a shift in operations from one hemisphere to another. Let the colossus die a happy death.

Tell us again, they said, who are you? Mitchell was confused about this. They had the resources, the networks, they seemed to know a considerable amount more about who he was than he did. He wanted to master the data, the process, the logic, the inferences, but he had been converted to their point of view without knowing it, and then he wanted everything to be smaller, less complex, filed.

What happened? the friends of golf kept asking. *You can tell us, really.* They didn't browbeat, that wasn't their style. They were his friends, the occasion called for cooperation. Sometimes they would say, Let's be straight with one another; sometimes they would ignite with exclamatory curses, but not often. He felt listless under the officious sincerity of their interrogation. (Business first, with due and solemn respect for the seriousness of the matter, but afterward, casual talk, a mutual exchange of insights and ideas, et cetera. We're here to talk freely, the linksmen emphasized.) He was without defense, neither the person he wanted to be nor the one they seemed to require.

He was twenty-six years old, an agricultural economist serving in an advisory capacity to an agrarian reform program on an island named St. Catherine in the Lesser Antilles. His answers were circular, he had no clear idea how you got from point A to point B or C, how you started out assuming the shape of a lost self and ended up being that agent of a conspiracy that didn't exist, the co-instigator, with a phantom, of a phantom uprising. When an army fights, he told them, it's given the name of one man, and when a make-believe army fights, it's still given the name of one man. Isaac Knowles, Jack Nasty, whatever, what's the difference?

What did you want to happen? they asked, not meaning to antagonize him. They wanted him to be more ingratiating, perhaps, in support of his gullibility. Did he have fantasies of power, was he glory-grubbing, hunting for a place in history? But those were roles given to kings and assassins; the rest of us were the pages history wrote upon. We were the blank pages of history, waiting to be inscribed, invented, only we never were. What happened was he couldn't forgive, requital had assumed that shape of the lost self, he had interceded on his own behalf. Meaning, this was not an ideology at work. It was only a human heart, fallible and bleeding.

They were fascinated by his relationship with Johanna Woods Fernandez and thought they could make something out of it. *Did you love her?* they persisted. *Do you love her?*

It was hot in the room where they had talked; the painkillers he was taking had made his head swim. There was always another *her* popping in and out of the dialogues, *her,* the one he had forsaken, and he sometimes confused the two, thinking the her they were asking about, the one he might love, was America. They said Johnnie and he thought they meant America.

Cocktails in hand, they had sat down on the veranda right at sunset: a soapy talc of pinks and plums, a sudden sneeze of scarlet and then gone. Tillman asked to hear the story on Davidius; was it true that Mitchell would be covering the fellow's bar tab until further notice. Sore subject, not much of a story either, but Mitchell told. They were releasing Davidius by the time he got down to the station, yesterday morning. No hearing had been scheduled before the magistrate after all. Apparently the inspector regarded both apologies and explanations as superfluities, and didn't bother with them. The attitude was outlandish but what do you do. The incident was a bewildering embarrassment, not to mention accident and mistake of justice. He had hurried back out the door after Davidius, calling his name to no avail. Davidius' only reaction was to cast a brief, glazed look over his shoulder that even in its brevity erased any claim this white man was making on his affairs. Mitchell had steeled himself for resentment but not apathy. Have it your way, he thought, throwing out his hands in frustration and walking back to the jitney stop to join the queue into town.

"I don't think he actually made the connection. He didn't know who I was."

"You'd have to be female, I think."

"I feel lousy about it but in a sense we were both victims of the police."

"Look at it this way—ultimately it has nothing to do with you."

He told Tillman don't let on at the bar. Let Davidius think, lucky stars. He didn't know what else to do. False arrest was not a concept in places like St. Catherine.

Johnnie had called them to the table for appetizers—conch seviche, white marlin fritters with a garlicky cilantro, tomato and onion sauce, a vegetable pâté from a tin with soda crackers that were not stale—unaccustomed joy for stoic palates. In response to praise she protested it was easier than they imagined, once you hunted down ingredients. She'd probably get fat again, she fretted, living here, and Adrian said, Liar, you were never fat and won't be, the way you burn through things. There was a shine in Johnnie's butternut eyes, she had ascended the ladder of her happiness. She excused herself and came back carrying the fish, a cookie sheet for a platter layered with a bed of steamed banana leaves, the glistening beast garnished with a halo of hibiscus flowers arranged red white red white, its jaws and tail overhanging the ends. *Beautiful, beautiful, beautiful,* Tillman hailed. Johnnie's face had beamed, this was everybody's idea of a triumph, and Mitchell deboned the monster with a butter knife and spatula, its fragrance lifting into his face, startlingly familiar, redolent of warming fires. Everyone held out their plates and let the first bite sit revered in their mouths before swallowing.

Let's stop for a minute and savor this, Tillman had said, how lovely it all is.

There were side dishes of blanched chard sprinkled with fruit vinegar and a bowl of black beans. Johnnie was transported, flush, saying Eat the flowers too, they're good for you. The cottage being without an oven, they had badgered her to reveal her secret—it was simple, so obvious, but undeniably clever. Mr. Quiddley's coal pits had reminded her of luaus; when she first saw them she told herself, *heat source.* The old fart grumbled she'd "bust his science" but they put their heads together and figured out how to do it without damaging the draft. They ate like well-behaved hogs, annihilating the fish, then Johnnie knocked them senseless with dessert, pomegranate seeds marinated in orange liqueur, served in teacups swimming in ruby light. A fresh breeze slipped in silkily through the veranda windows; around the room shadows crawled out from shadows and everyone said, *God!* and *Goddamn!,* and Mitchell had thought, someone has to be blessed and tonight it looks like us.

Candlelight and lovelight are the same, aren't they? said Adrian. She had picked up a horrible rash from something on Cotton Island but was being more than brave about it. Johnnie had placed four votive candles laced with citronella in saucers and their illumination reflected up with a rich brush of sensuality, here in the latitudes of play. Tillman had brought along a joint so not only were they boozy, well advanced through a bottle of French brandy after two of chardonnay, but now they were stoned too, getting cross-eyed, loony, waggishly upping the erotic ante with bawdy teasing, already considerable given who they were and where they were, the Epicurean remains of a massive kingfish, picked over and its bones sucked, centered on the table. The radio was tuned to a Christian superstation in

St. Kitts—it was C & W hour, they were playing Marty Robbins' "Rosa's Cantina," and the girls began to sing along.

The felicitous intimacy heated up, became Rabelaisian, how they got just this far no one could reconstruct, but now the most appropriate brandy-inspired next step seemed to be for Tillman to dare the women to expose their breasts. Up flashed Johnnie's tee shirt, Adrian's blouse, *oho!* now you see 'em, now you don't.

"Would you look at how bloody proud they are."

Next Johnnie dared the men to stand up straight like gentlemen and show their rear ends—no moons, no groaty assholes, just prime beef—and the fellows rose solemnly if not soberly, stood paired like brothers, rotated so their backs were turned and thereupon dropped their shorts. Adrian, they found out, could whistle like a doorman for a cab. They reordered themselves, sat down, then Mitchell double-dared, we want to see yours, the doctor here and me, and Adrian said, deadpan, No way, Jasper, the butt stops here, *here* escaping from her mouth with a soblike shriek of laughter and all four of them howled in unison, falling figuratively out of their chairs but dabbing literal tears from their eyes, and that set a timely brake on one of the evening's more dangerous trends.

"You can't count on the sexual revolution anymore, these days of the MBA."

"Hasn't begun. Just getting started."

"It snuck right by."

"You should have been on Cotton Island."

"We know better than to ask."

"We know better than to tell."

"Sin is a nutrient. Isn't there a daily recommended requirement?"

"Allowance. Recommended allowance."

"All revolutions are passé."

"The Khmer Rouge?"

"Africa."

"Rhodesia. The so-called Marxist-dominated minority."

"But they're killing everybody."

"Right. The shits. Let's wipe 'em out."

"Exterminate the brutes."

"All in favor say aye."

"Everybody says time's speeded up but I think it's stuck."

"I do too. What if our kids—"

"Who's having children?"

"What if the kids ten years from now still smoke ganj and listen to Bob Dylan and Mick Jagger?"

"Peter, Paul, and Mary."

"Revert to Sinatra and martinis."

"Marley rules. He's a living god. Possibly Christ."

"Rock and roll will never die."

"Isn't it time we made the backward leap to Rossini?"

"It's dead as a crapaud in the road. White tedium. Somebody bury it please."

"Johnnie," said Tillman, doing something odd with his face in an approximation of sincerity, "why don't you come up the ancestral hill and work for me?"

"Now?" she said innocently. Wine sloshed from her jar glass.

"He needs a new slave since I didn't work out."

"Mitchell?"

"Great idea. Depends on you."

"Pay stinks but there go your visa problems."

"When?"

"Whenever you want. Next week. Start by toadying to my new cook. Then lay your magic fingers on my menu."

"Or his throat."

"This meal tonight. You must have taken classes."

"Mitchell," said Adrian, "can we decide about the volcano?"

"We're back to the weaker sex issue."

"You wouldn't be saying that, Tillman, if you took the time to know me better."

Adrian had been scanning her guidebook that morning and discovered Mount Soufrière. She read the paragraph of description and decided a volcano fit her requirement for a last unique adventure before she flew away; also, the location was right to accommodate Sally, who needed a lift up north to a windward village, but Sally wasn't free until Saturday, and in Mitchell's view the logistics were problematic.

"I don't think you realize what you're getting yourself into," he said to her, repeating his earlier objection, to which Johnnie had remarked, Don't underestimate us girls, and then rhapsodized about a hike she had taken up Mauna Kea. You should never bypass something like this, was her argument—volcanoes providing a climber with such a mighty picture of Planet Earth as unfinished business.

"The path is rugged and steep and very, very long." Mitchell tried to make her see. "It's going to push hard on your limits."

From Adrian, a confident, resolute murmur: All the better.

"We're not into parasols and picnic baskets," agreed Johnnie. "That's not us."

Volcanoes shouldn't be much of a problem for her, Tillman offered tartly, since Adrian had only just encountered poverty too and look how well she was doing with that. Meaning, let's give her what she wants and see how much she likes it. Adrian silenced him with a battle-ready look and then sighed indulgently. From all appearances tonight they seemed to be getting along fine, but occasionally there were these small flaring tensions, and she had changed her flight reservations, moved them up three days to Sunday. Still, Tillman had relented to a rare social foray off Rosehill property, and the evening had flowed seamlessly forward, more or less perfectly.

What Adrian wanted wasn't technically an alteration in plans; neither Mitchell nor Tillman had yet to spell out what they had in mind for their promised excursion, but in fact Mitchell, without telling anybody, had already gone ahead and requisitioned a Land Rover from the ministry's motor pool—five o'clock Thursday to five o'clock Friday—and then had stood in line at National Police Headquarters to experience the government's most recent brainstorm of bureaucratic harassment: the issuance of travel passes to all vehicles journeying to North Leeward and North Windward destinations. Noncommercial vehicles, except commuters, required individual permits for each trip, an infuriating and pointless inconvenience, especially as nobody took the stated reason for the passes—to halt the transport of illegal weapons—the least bit seriously. It was harassment, pure and simple, and one more way to strip revenues out of pockets already empty and threadbare.

Mitchell had heard that Adrian was lending a hand down at Sally's school; she'd taken slumming to heart, he had thought unkindly, but then kicked himself for his cynicism about someone who, for whatever intent or purpose, seemed to be making an effort. Girls from NYC usually deserved any prejudice you cared to have. He told her okay, he'd see if he could work it out, if she was at school with Sally tomorrow he'd swing by before noon and let them know. Tillman said it was time to go, touching Adrian's arm as he said it, a gesture of peacemaking. They got up from the table together, the four of them, exchanging kisses between couples. Dinner was fucking fabulous, Adrian told Johnnie; to Mitchell she stage-whispered dryly, with comic hauteur, Whatever you have her on, darling, increase the dosage.

"That would be Mandrax and Durophet," cracked Tillman. Slow, fast; the two gears of the merry metabolism. Everybody laughed, and of course he was right.

"I wish Sally and Saconi could have come," Johnnie said. She and

Mitchell went and stood at the door, waved their guests good-bye. "I wish Adrian wasn't going away."

"By God, we've entertained," Mitchell crowed, finding something new in life to celebrate. "We received company. We treated them well. Nobody got hurt. Our genteel reputation will spread."

"We tried."

He grabbed her shoulders. "It was a great, great evening."

"Don't act so shocked. I come with a set of wholesome instincts and traditional values." She stuck her tongue out at him. "Some, anyway."

He said Go relax, he'd do the cleaning up. She suggested he leave it till morning but he insisted, the cockroaches relied on him for this, a clarity of relationship, consistency of message. Johnnie, affectionately, said Yack yack yack, sometimes he really got himself going on the silliest things, and took her glass, refilled it with wine, and went out on the veranda.

Our Lady of the Forage, Mitchell was calling her, in his bliss. Yesterday Johnnie had met him for lunch in town; he had handed her back her passport, its visa stamped with a three-month extension, and it was like, Stand back, I'm nesting. Already she'd found a woman to bring cut flowers to the house, once a week—anthuriums, lilies, stalks of ginger, orchid sprays—two dollars an armload. When he opened the front door this morning, there was a whiskey bottle of fresh milk waiting on the stoop. She'd met this farmer and they'd be getting a bottle every other day for as long as the cow held up, and no charge for delivery. Mitchell was amazed. To his chagrin she had even been able to locate a source for chickens and eggs, and someone who sold rabbits (pre-butchered, or else she wanted nothing to do with them), and someone else who sold ducks, and somewhere in town she had wandered into a shop that stocked, among its illogical array of mundanities, imported Parma cheeses and Swiss chocolates. Her talent for hustling, he was forced to admit, was rather highly developed; here was a firsthand demonstration of her wage-earning skills, and as long as she did nothing more with drugs than place a certain amount of them into her bloodstream, he would have to step out of the life he had led so far, and the culture that had given it to him, to find something to actually, and righteously, complain about.

She went splashing into this instant, better life, craving its surface of convention, the subtle payback of ordinary pleasures, anxious to wallow in a hurry-up version of domesticity, be a honey bee busily luxuriating in the routine of little chores, a pollen she collected and added up to a golden purpose threaded from one end of the day to the other. She cooked, he was happy to report, like nobody's business; the cupboards were crowded with jams, fruit preserves, a virtually inedible batch of fiery chutney, all of which she had made that afternoon. She washed laundry, by hand, in a galvanized tub with a bar of lye soap and a washboard, wringing the clothes to drape over the bushes in the yard like the local wives. He hadn't asked her to do any of this, her motivation was her own. The most enterprising hags at the market suddenly knew Johnnie by name, bent their graying heads to hers, cackling old women, making deals with their prize missy, bargains, special offers. Mitchell would come back to Howard Bay, she'd meet him at the door saying, Look what I got, and he'd want to see. She stated her intention to add aubergine, green beans, capsicums and red bell peppers, lemon grass and a spice rack of other herbs to the kitchen garden, plant the walk up to the road with purple heart, make a wind chime for the veranda if she couldn't find one to buy she liked. She was slowly taming the cat, who now came puling from the bush, twice a day for kibble, answering to the name she gave it, Pelé. For the soccer player, he asked? She said No, the god.

He blew out her candles and began clearing the table, taking the plates out the kitchen door to scrape into a slops pail for his neighbor Mrs. Fetchalub's pig. He put the dishes in the sink to soak for a minute while he shook the crumbs off another of Johnnie's purchases—grass placemats plaited in the shape of angelfish—and wiped up the leavings with a rag. Eternal life sprang forth from the radio again, a low Baptist drawl of a voice meting out salvation to lonely sinners with their ears to the air waves. He spun the dial searching for music, caught a fragment of GIS propaganda regarding *activities*—like *festivities*, the announcer's enthusiasm would have you believe—at unspecified locations in the northern districts. Nonsense, trustworthy people had told him, including Ballantyne, someone who would know. Ananci stories. Bullshit, eh? Drifting down from Martinique came a Creole station, uttering strange and pretty words like incantation, unintelligible, but music all the same, and he stopped the dial there. He rinsed the dishes and silverware, stacked them on a towel, covered the leftovers in foil. Johnnie was saying his name softly, seductively, saying, That's enough.

He went out to the veranda, looking beyond at the night, asking, So where's the moon, was it rising or gone? Johnnie was bent at the waist, a right angle attached to the rail, her skirt fluted around her legs, and he came up from behind and fitted himself naturally against her body, reaching to massage where her shoulders bunched into her neck. No question she broadcast readiness and heat. There was something wrong with the word *loins* because he had never said it, even to himself. Under her breath she talked to him, a husky passionate *grr;* he asked her twice, What? and she groped behind her for one of his arms and brought his hand forth to cup it to her breast, ripe with gravity, which was also a way of pulling him down. Her hair curtained her face and when he lowered his ear to it she thrust her pelvis backward into the pressure of him, and behind the shield of her hair she was saying fuck me like this, just like this, words swift and fierce and narcotic, an injection of words, pure thrill of words, and he stifled a nervous, imbecilic urge to laugh, emit a goat's bleat of laughter, for surely if he opened his mouth even the gentlest sound he chanced would betray him to himself, his greenness and hunger, his need, which he could never accept in the way he accepted hers. The energy-build of lust was like being crushed out of himself. Like this, she said, a burning whisper. Just like you are—words inside a furnace, inside a church. I want to watch the ocean while you fuck me. You fuck me. He stepped away and back into himself to raise the gray stripes of her skirt, she had made it easy, had already removed her underwear, and there, the rictus like an inverted exclamation mark, he was greeted by the dark invitation of her holes, slashed into the flesh between her legs, the one mystery that was not unapproachable, and he thought, despite himself, God did this. Servitude of flesh. He locked his hands on her hips, looking out over her head to the horizon, which offered him a strangely congruent epiphany, a transitory feeling of navigation, steering by stars. He rolled her shirt up to reveal the close-knit chain of islands that formed her spine, gliding his fingers along her skin, wanting his hands, especially his hands, to be loving, to bring solace. Somewhere in the middle he fell forward across her ribs and used the rail to brace himself, placing his hands beside her crooked elbows, and she turned her head in the cradle of her arms and began to bite him, hard, her teeth above his right wrist, grinding the past and future between her jaws, and what his body seemed to want to know was what could make her shove so violently, back against him. He ripped away his arm and straightened up, staring down, mesmerized, at himself, at her, linked by the spike of his erection, the ineffability of this act, this invasion, sticking her, sticking in, the crude enchantment, the ceaseless fascinating beauty of its essential savagery. He became aware of his panting, Johnnie began a stammering cry that sounded like—

> sounded like she was being fucked
> like she was being fucked or beaten

and he balked, it wasn't clear if he was hurting her, if he should stop, he didn't want to hurt anybody, most of all a woman, most of all her, not this way, not with love, he'd stop but her cries were translated by his own flesh into a firmness of motion and made to gallop, her high sharp language not really like an animal's but somewhere in the range for Mrs. Fetchalub's dogs to hear the call and respond with a wild, eerie singing, later in their lives they might have laughed, the hair on the back of Mitchell's neck and arms bristled and he clamped his hand over Johnnie's mouth so the dogs would stop, but they didn't stop, they never stopped, they yipped even at the moment he made her leave, so that even then as she walked away he could not tell their cries from hers, his mind let go and the dogs took over and bwoy these dogs goin mek one everlastin racket in you head fah true. I love it, Johnnie gasped, I love it. What's it like with the ocean, the dogs wanted to know, and he answered by buckling at the knees, poured through a stream of words drowning his brain, the dogs,

> *Who knows what we might do*
> *There is no telling what we'll do*
> *In our fierce drive to come together*

Under her skin, throughout the plane of muscles along her spine, down into her thighs, the last flicker of whatever it was passion chased through the course of the body.

(When your head is underwater any puddle is a flood.)

He'd never get rid of the dogs; they were going to be a part of this, always, always proposing their midnight coda to the duet:

I wish my soul were larger than it is.

Love you, Johnnie said. In fucking credible. I love you. *Te amo.*

"Tonight's been an education," Tillman had said at dinner. He was the oldest of them. Twenty-seven.

Chapter 28

He told the necessary lie to make a weekend sign-out of a Land Rover permissible (a lie he would hear repeated, more than once, in the mouths of his accusers). At National Police Headquarters, someone listened to his request for a new pass and then made him wait a good part of the morning before telling him *No problem,* those black magic words that never meant the same thing twice, but this time the police wanted a passenger manifest, passport numbers of all non-nationals, destination, time of arrival, time of departure, reason for trip, and in this circumstance he found it politic to tell the truth. I've got everything but the passport numbers, he told them. They made him wait another half hour and said okay.

He walked back through town toward Sally's school, enjoying its bustle, its mix of high and low, buying a snow cone from a bare-chested vendor who shaved the ice from its dripping block, poured on cherry syrup from a bottle swarmed with honey bees, then dribbled sweetened condensed milk over the top from a can of Carnation. Tourists would no sooner lick the streets; still, one day Mitchell had followed a pushcart back to the icehouse, a happy place to work in the tropics. He met the owner, a good businessman who promoted science, hygiene, pragmatism, fifteen percent net profit, and an honorable reputation.

The harbor front bounced with harsh light, sweaty workmen. The arched doors of the warehouses swung open to darkened, cavernous interiors, the economy's stomach filling with sacks of cement, rice, flour, meal, beans, sugar, fertilizers—all imports, the wealth of other nations, not its own. He had made a good faith effort to climb back into the harness of his work, only to see that the ministry had dropped the reins. Against a sudden and irrational xenophobic rise in rhetoric, pointedly anti-Yank, he felt himself contract and withdraw,

become a wallflower. Not *you* we is fightin, various ministry personalities, like Morrison, assured him. It's the imperial octopus, it's the
lackeys, but you is behavin youself, Wilson, you will make out okay
for a white mahn if you keep your distance from devils like Kingsley.
The new CAO called an unscheduled staff meeting: out of the blue
Jack Dawes would be converted back to cane production; a new
refinery and deep water port would be constructed on the central leeward coast. Which was the same as saying, for nostalgia's sake, we've
all decided to be slaves again. Mitchell stated his protests, to no
effect. Sugar makes them demented, doesn't it, one of the foreign service Brits clucked. They can't seem to get beyond it, psychologically
or politically. We should admit they are addicts to how the crop structures societies like St. Catherine's. Sugar's communal narrative: master and chattel. All the same, isn't it.

If the government proved incapable of organizing the estates in
any sensible way, then land for the landless had to be where the line
was drawn, but Kingsley, refusing to attend a cabinet meeting scheduled on Tuesday, stayed up leeward in his home parish, manipulating
his manipulators, he and Banks engaged in a round of musical chairs
with the peasants, trucking them on and off the estates, stirring the
nest, creating a pervasive mood of belligerence on the island. This
then, was Kingsley's strategy unfolding—allow Banks to alienate the
peasantry while he, Kingsley, vowed to restore to them a less oppressive version of the good old days. From Kingsley's point of view,
sugar was economically achromatic, its power symbolic, a source of
votes rather than a source of foreign exchange. Something to promise
Joe Pittance: *we does give you wuk, mahn. Plenty!* Kingsley didn't
have to explain it to them. For Mitchell the question became whether
to repudiate the land reform program as it was being presently distorted and exploited or hold his peace and wait for the tide to go back
out. The ministry rang with a dissonance that made him think, get
out of here, go to Johnnie, and he did, hungering for the commerce
between bodies and souls.

He crossed the cobbled street, paved with the ballast of a dead
empire's ships, and passed along a high wooden fence, its old boards
blackened with weather and exhaust but newly painted with graffiti,
many PEPs and PIPs—the People's Independence Party, Kingsley's
crowd—a dominant (its letters were four feet tall) but heretofore
unheard of party, the PRP, easy enough to guess what the acronym
stood for, and a solitary NJM—this would be the hand of an exile,
someone from Grenada, a New Jewel Movement cadre member—
plenty of references to Zion, Yah-weh, Jah, Babylon, The Lion,

Marcus Garvey, Michael Manley, Marley, five-spired marijuana leaves, and the latest slogans anthologized, *Banks is Bankrupt* and *Revo, Now* prominent among them; *U.S. out of ST. C.* Meaning, Mitchell reckoned, himself, though he could not make a visceral connection with the demand. Someone would have to come up and tap him on the shoulder and say *You.*

Where the fence abutted a bricked, windowless wall fronting the street, there was a door that he opened and went through, entering a narrow courtyard fenced on three sides and on the fourth side, Sally's school. A tin-covered walkway hugged the back of the fence, turning down the face of the onion warehouse to its center doors, thrown open, as were the shutters of its casement windows. Under the rain-proofed walk the school had fashioned a makeshift kitchen and storage area, there were hooks anchored into the wall for umbrellas and caps, vegetable seedlings sprouting in waxed cartons and a concrete planter crammed with traveler's palm. Behind the sheaf of fronds he found Adrian, presiding over the most marvelous sight, a bright row of dollish children, no more than three and four years old, dresses up or shorts down, each small pair of ankles cuffed in underpants, each cherubic bottom settled upon an enamel chamberpot, like upturned bowler hats, Adrian encouraging them to all make weewee. Their faces, however, so lovely, were universally raised in wonderment, as if in the newness of their minds they had seen Mitchell and said to themselves, Hey. There's God. Fathers, Sally had told him, steered clear of the school.

"Concentrate," urged Adrian. "One two three: weewee."

"This seems like a flawless crop," said Mitchell. "What's wrong with them?"

Not a thing—Sally had felt driven to do something about the community's lack of structured care for preschoolers, so she'd devised a pilot program, and Adrian had volunteered to staff it for a week. Otherwise, the tots were mixed in with the regular students, Sally's theory being that despite the chronological differences between them, developmentally they were all more or less the same age, and the mix helped socialize the weirder kids.

"They are so cute I can't stand it," confessed Adrian. "Weewee, ladies. Weewee, guys." She dropped her voice so that two women making sandwiches in the kitchen wouldn't hear. "If my father were here he'd say, 'Right, Adrian, cute as pups, too bad they grow up to be curs.' And you know what, Mitchell, every year that son of a bitch writes out a check to the NAACP. Here," she said, slapping a roll of toilet paper in his hands. "Make a contribution. Start at that end, check everybody to see what they did, and, you know, give them a wipe where necessary."

"I'm untrained," he said, not the least enthusiastic. "I'm not a member of the union."

"Go on. It's easy."

Because they were boys, the first two were, but the third was a girl, her face smooth as a chestnut, with pigtails like ganglia and no front teeth. She stared at him with the most cheerful expectation, and he made an absurd stab at etiquette by asking her name as he swiped a pad of tissue between her legs. He stood her on her feet and pulled up her drawers, and the next one was a girl too, pretty as Easter morning. She laughed heartily when he lifted her off the pot and saw she had left an unfeminine loaf-sized turd for Mitchell to praise. "Caca," she chuckled. Jesus. He really wasn't ready for this and set her back down, leaving the roll of toilet paper in her lap as he went to tell Adrian that it looked as if Saturday was going to work out. Great, she said from where she stooped, wrenching her head up, and he could see the obsession foremost in her eyes.

"You know, he won't say nigger," she went on, "he's too liberal for that so he says cur. That's the point. You see what I have to overcome?"

"Join the club. Sally's inside, isn't she?"

The school, by no means a sane and ordered world despite its effort to manufacture just such an illusion, was nevertheless not the madhouse he had at first anticipated either, but an asylum in the original sense of the word, dedicated to the habits the outside world took for granted but had denied these children, thereby denying their humanity, and it took less getting used to than Mitchell had imagined, once he began seeing the nation itself as an abused, misshapen child. On the back wall Sally had hung a banner, heralding the coalition's motto in big block letters: *We all is one.* There was a poster-board listing school rules, devised by a committee of her more competent students:

1. Keep hands and feet to yourself
2. 1 person talks at a time
3. Don't bite teachers
4. Good manners
5. Listen
6. Walk

A narrative pictureboard explained A Visit to the Zoo; maps illus-
trated a display showing Here's Where We Are. Any reader could
learn that

The Day is *Wednesday, the sixth.*

The Month is *April.*

The Year is *1977.*

Today is *Mona*'s Birthday.

Her Birth Sign is *Aries.*
Everything was labeled with red letters: chair, window, door,
broom, table, cup, books, shelf, clock, light switch, light. The children were divided in three circles on the floor, a fourth group preparing for lunch at a long folding table—these the kids needing to be
strapped in their seats in order to sit upright, otherwise they'd topple
over, slide out. In one of the circles it was story time, the teacher
reading from a book, letting everyone see the pictures. In the second,
all girls, they were painting each other's nails—fingers and toes and
anything in the way—and in Sally's group they were raucously dis-
mantling a box of already mashed up toys, Sally refereeing disputes
over property rights. Noticing Mitchell, a boy in her circle stood up
with a cold, sparkling smile and shot him, silently and repeatedly,
with his hand made into a gun, recoil and all, blowing the smoke
from the tip of his index finger when he had finished. Jerome, sit
your fanny back down, Sally said in a normal tone, and when he hesitated, testing her, she barked *Now!* and Sally's authority sent a shiver
down Mitchell's spine; he had to ignore the impulse to sit himself.
Sally got up and came over, happy to see him.

"They're so into violence," she said cheerily, as if this were not as
bad as it sounded. "Jerome always shoots you with his finger when he
doesn't like something you do."

"What'd I do?"

"Who knows." Sally cut her eyes back at Jerome, checking on him,
and made an amused grimace and snort. "Usually it's touch touch
touch, hit hit hit. 'Me goin stick this in you.' They grab their crotch,
boys and girls both. We're into the great passions here. Violence and
sex. Have you had your lunch? We're on first shift. You'd be crazy to
pass up fried corn mush and Spam sandwiches. Come on, sit down
with us for a minute, I don't see that much of you, and Hyacinth
could use the help."

They dragged over two more chairs to the lunch table, Sally positioning hers to keep watch on her circle. Mitchell found himself next to a godling, this folded-in elfin boy of East Indian descent, his bobbing head transformed by a dreamy smile, a miniature Krishna. Mitchell looked down the table at the other children, cow-faced, water-headed, roamy-eyed, their expressions emblazoned with awe, which he could not help but return, confronted by the staggering inscrutability of biology and birth. At Sally's prodding, Mitchell picked up a spoon and began feeding the boy, who hummed the melody from a toothpaste commercial as he chewed. Sally asked how were things at the ministry, and when he told her, she said the whole fiasco reminded her of this big crisis that took place while she was working toward her teaching certificate in Kansas, a conflict between the university's lab school and the College of Education, both squabbling about who was responsible for what, with the staff at the lab school vying for a greater measure of autonomy. The dean of arts and science stepped in to arbitrate the imbroglio, ordering the College of Education to back off and sanctioning the two people most intimately involved in the daily operation of the school to co-author new job definitions, top to bottom, for everybody who had a role to play, and whatever the co-authors came up with would be law, the last word, end of crisis. The two women dispatched their assignment with the utmost commitment, fair-mindedness, common sense, sensitivity, and fellowship. By mutual agreement, they clarified the lines of authorities, meticulously defined each staff member's obligations, reconceptualized the college's oversight function, and developed a power-sharing arrangement in which they were co-equals. Only, for administrative purposes, co-author A was first among equals, in charge of managing personnel and budget, while responsibility for curriculum, methodology, and vision fell upon the able shoulders of co-author B. They submitted their hard work to the dean, who congratulated them for a superb effort and sent them back to the lab school where, to everyone's dismay, co-author A's first official act was . . . can you guess?

"She fired co-author B?"

"Exactly."

Mitchell ventured a moral to the tale: Power corrupts. But Sally made a thoughtful frown and said, No, she didn't think so, this wasn't a story about corruption. Spooning fried mush between the boy's lips he had the sense he was feeding a sacred bird. What's the story about then? he asked.

"I don't know. I think it's just about relationships."

"I wonder if that's strictly a female's perspective. What's wrong with this kid, by the way?"

"Shiva? I don't know that either. He has a freakish muscular dysfunction that nobody on this island is qualified to diagnose."

"What's going to happen to him?"

"I don't know. Also he's blind. Eat your sandwich too, Shiva. Mitchell, give him his sandwich."

"Fuck all. Is he really?"

"Don't bring pity into here. This isn't Calcutta. We're doing just fine here, although, Mitchell, look, I want milk for these kids."

The ministry ran a small dairy farm, its purpose to provide milk exclusively to Queenstown schools, though that in fact *was* a story about corruption. Sally said there hadn't been a delivery in weeks and he promised to look into it. Then she told him about Jolene, who had gone up north to her home village for a weekend visit and hadn't returned to her uncle's in Scuffletown, where she was employed in his upholstery shop. Into the story came an ill child and the child's angry, ashamed father—both, Sally suspected, belonging to Jolene. The uncle had described the child's symptoms and Sally figured it was cerebral palsy. Four years old and had never been outside his paternal grandmother's shanty. There's a real person trapped inside the disease, she told Mitchell. Someone has to reach in there and pull him out. He asked did she want to be dropped off or would she come up the mountain with them, he had to know because of timing, and she said it depends, let's wait and see, if it was no trouble.

"Juice," said Shiva, and Sally was all over him with praise, because he never talked.

Adrian began herding her pygmies in for lunch, and Mitchell asked what was with her anyway, what was this Mother Teresa act, and he wished he hadn't asked it quite that way because Sally became prickly, defending her, saying Adrian was one of those people waiting all their lives to help, but need to be asked, and no one ever asked before, she'd only been asked to make money, look out for herself, be a success. So now she was spending mornings at the school and afternoons scouring Queenstown and environs for local Michelangelos, the latest being a guy who was into a ceremonial sacrifice motif, obeah, working with house paint on pieces of Masonite. She was wild about him, Sally said.

Children monkeyed up to climb into his lap, touch his face, his mustache, poking their greasy fingers into his mouth. Hey, open this, said a kid with a groggy voice, and threw a juice box at him. The surface of the table was pooled with spillage and scrap; the teacher's

assistant, Hyacinth, was untying children from their chairs and setting them along the wall like statues of Buddha, brushing mush from
laps, out of Brillo pads of hair. I knew it was too good to be true,
Sally muttered, when a fight broke out in her untended circle. A girl
battered the skull of a bigger but seemingly helpless boy with a plastic car. *Jerusha, stop that right now,* Sally thundered. The girl named
Jerusha obeyed by redirecting her violence back upon herself, slamming the toy into her own face, something religious in the image she
made, the mechanical dimension of the act, holding the toy in both
hands, something frighteningly holy in her masochism, how she
bowed her forehead into the blows. When Sally grabbed her she went
berserk. Sally had to fight back and Mitchell had to help.

He would always wonder afterward about Sally's prescience, enlist-
ing Adrian into the school. If you knew Adrian better, Sally had
assured him, you wouldn't be surprised she's here.

"Guilt?"

"Maybe a little of that," Sally had conceded, "but I would say
heart. She's looking for it," and Mitchell had replied, Aren't we all.

This was the week that didn't exist because he had given it to Johnnie
and when she left, he closed his eyes and ears, sheathed his heart in
ashes, and made sure she took these days of respite with her too, days
of what he would not afterward say, which was happiness. He sur-
faced randomly in his other life, observing his participation in everything outside of Johnnie swiftly erode. He felt his awareness of the
sea broaden, wherever he happened to be he was conscious of its
ceaseless calling forth, and thought, for an island to open up it need
only be a mirror to its audience, if not of paradise then perhaps of
love, if not of love then perhaps of imagination, if not of imagination
then perhaps of history and if not of history then perhaps only of the
blinding, narcissistic reflection of the present, an environment
secured and isolated between looking forward and remembering,
somewhere at last where stars shine unencumbered by longing which
is not paradise, not love, not imagination, not history, not here and
not now but all of them together which is, Mitchell believed he
learned, *self,* and its paradox, which he supposed must be called
fusion. But in five days you can learn everything, and then lose it in
an instant.

Important things happened but he didn't know it, he would have
to wait for time to awake and point its finger—Look there, see what
you missed. The rain held off or stalled respectfully until the middle
of the night to rouse them with its rich significance of drumming,

and an unchanging pattern of imperial white cumulus frescoed the brilliant blue canopy of the daytime skies. Mitchell felt the island undergoing a charmed resurgence of vitality and light that had everything to do with his purpose there; some bedrock-deep antidote, tropic and marvelously real, in the works against the proliferation of tension and controversy. The trade winds lofted flowers into the roads, always evocative of falling embers. He and Johnnie took twilight swims together, nosing out side by side into the vastness of the darkening sea. They took postprandial walks, tromping off toward Augustine or the Bight, raiding Rosehill's dusty library, making love and then reading to each other in bed at night.

Johnnie, from the classic *A High Wind in Jamaica:* "Emily was still so saturated in earthquake as to be dumb. She ate earthquake and slept earthquake: her fingers and legs were earthquake."

Mitchell, from *A Historie of Barbadoes,* penned in 1650: "They [the skins of women] are so sweaty and clammy, as the hand cannot passe over, without being glued or cemented in the passage or motion; and by that means, little pleasure is given to, or received, by the agent or patient," and they both snickered, Johnnie saying what the author needed was an Emily, someone to cement him into sultriness as a concept, as a state of being.

Oldest story in the world.

He observed Johnnie's quotidian relationship with drugs and wondered about the nature of its competition with him. The question wasn't settled, and perhaps never would be, since the genie was out of the bottle, there was no such thing as a drug-free America, or a drug-free world, and wouldn't be, ever again. The chance for that was zero, and he shared America's ambivalence for its endowment of narcotics, recognizing in the background of his coming of age, and hers, that drugs had underlined every rite of passage, drugs were a best-selling way of knowledge, drugs stopped war, beckoned the divine sentience out from a tree, a mountain, a field of flashing corn, pointing to a secret life concealed within the inanimate; brought the inner travel of music into the space age, fed the culture's growing need for anti-heroes, did everything that love could never do; or do, but not sustain. And yet drugs could not sustain it either. He had been there; saw and did. Put the ups in your left pocket, put the downs in your right pocket. Don't get them confused. Every kid knows that. This one you take at breakfast in the morning, this one you take when you come home at night. There was never a dark pull; always and inevitably, he had been brought back to his point of departure, leaving not so much as a scruff mark on society, though he knew others who did: from a distance he had known friends to die and had thought there's going to be winners and losers, no matter what, but he could not look at Johnnie and see, as others might, a wreck in process, despite whatever trouble she had gotten herself into in Hawaii. Did he love her? Yes, but with the knowledge that it's dangerous to measure an element as unstable and volatile as love, and so he chose to give their coupling every benefit of the doubt. Which is why he lied, and then only spoke of it obliquely, when they were frightened awake in the middle of the night by Johnnie's past, nailed gruesomely to the front door. It happened Friday morning around four, four-thirty, he and Johnnie asleep in his bed. Like all ghost stories and tales of horror, they were awakened by three rapid, hammering strokes on the front door, the sort of archetypical pounding events have conditioned us to associate with facism, terror, death squads. What you never wanted to hear in the middle of the night without the following voice of a friend behind it; what only the parts of you that are most interior and unknown imagine opening up to.

He told Johnnie to stay where she was and grabbed the machete he kept behind the headboard, flicking on lights, hitting the switch to the outside bulb above the stoop, peering through the cracks in the shutters, calling out in a voice disquieting in its bearishness, *who is it?* He placed his ear to the door as if it were a sternum, to listen for breathing on the other side. In a high-pitched voice Johnnie asked what it was from the bedroom. Just someone's idea of a prank, nothing, he told her to go back to sleep. He unlocked the door and stepped back, crouching, hating this moment with heart and soul, prepared to defend himself. The door swung open into the room, the dead cat pinned there on it with a sixteen-penny nail driven through its throat. The damn cat, he heard himself whisper. He braced for a charge, for someone to say boo. No one though was there and after a minute he stood up, looked outside for a good long time. He wrenched the nail back and forth until it came out of the wood, telling himself he told her not to feed the fucking cat, then walked to the side yard and heaved Johnnie's newly adopted Pelé far into the bushes, where it had always belonged. Not everything had a home or needed one.

He urinated on one of Quiddley's coal pits, fed up with being wrapped in their smoke, and then went back to bed. Johnnie was wide awake, staring straight up at the roof beams, her body rigid. Her voice was barely audible. What was it? she asked. Nothing I could find, he told her. Probably some drunk. He wanted to think about it before he told her. He didn't want to ruin things.

For the first time he had experienced true panic, a wild animal leashed to the most remote part of one's humanity, breaking its restraint and clawing its way out, and he struggled to master it, hearing his own response echo so many others he had read in newspapers and books, without a glimmer of the horror behind the words: *Who could do such a thing?* But he knew the answer and the answer was, *anyone.* Thinking back on it, he would gag with angst at the fiction that had become his life, rot people read on airplanes, the trash ever in demand by lives untouched by evil. There was nothing highbrow about violence except of course its most successful instigators, throughout the centuries, and guns, however beautifully they were manufactured, were the ultimate vulgarity, which is not what he thought, crouching to the side of the opened door that night, a machete trembling in his hand, his short, gulping breaths ragged with fright, one eye on the impaled cat crucified to the door, one eye outside on the threatening darkness, willing himself to stop shaking, willing himself to calm down, cursing the rise of panic in his throat. What he thought then about guns was that he wanted one, not because he wanted to shoot somebody, his desire had nothing whatsoever to do with the destructive power of guns, but now he had been twice violated, tasted the indignity of his own terror, and this alone suggested the validity of firearms, to protect him from this poisonous taste. Because he hated this vision of himself, crouched in panic, more than he hated the invisible malefactor. Because these violations clarified some sense of his own Americanness, because to be helpless was not American, that was something he saw now was in his grain.

It was then for the most personal and deeply private, almost shameful reason that he went to Scuffletown Friday morning in search of a gun, looking for the youth who had come too close with his hissing the week before, the boy with the Barbeques dancing in his head. By the time he was on the road Mitchell wasn't talking to himself anymore about why he was doing this, and in the light of day guns were again the abstractions to him they always had been. Guns were pistols—he knew a few legendary names but couldn't type on sight and in fact had never even held one in his hand, though he had shot a friend's .22 rifle at cans and bottles, growing up. He knew what a shotgun was, knew the names AK-47 and Uzi because he read newspapers. Caliber he assumed meant bullet size but he wouldn't swear to it. Violence was mythic, historical, and he was mere flesh, made of the suburbs, not even drawn to it as a fiction, making love and not war in his fantasies, shunning the blood sports, bored by firepower's lethal technology; he had always perceived in the function of guns an innate cowardice, which now struck him as ironic since he was aware that behind this ostensible quest for protection, his truest motive for owning a gun was it would inoculate him against just that—cowardice. More than anything else it was a state of mind that he went looking for, there in Scuffletown.

Given how the government was behaving recently, there were no longer legitimate options for anyone wishing to purchase a gun. He stopped off at the ministry first, to see if Ballantyne was around, because earlier in the week the forest ranger had agreed to sell him a bird rifle, to replace the one the police in Augustine had confiscated from Calvin, the gardener's assistant at Rosehill. There, he heard a piece of disturbing news from one of the front-office secretaries, which only seemed to underscore the rightness of his decision about going to Scuffletown: during the night someone had broken into the home of Morrison, from the veterinary department, and beaten him badly; he was in the hospital. No one had any idea what it was all about.

Ballantyne was out in the field, he was told, and so instead he went by the motor pool, to see if it was possible to sign out the Land Rover early, and the supervisor said come back in two hours, at noon, and it would be okay. Then he took a slow, hot walk down into Scuffletown, avoiding the Knowles' house, because when he had gone to see Isaac's mother and brothers on Monday, to pass along the word about Isaac being up north, they had acted oddly, seeming to know more than they were willing to say, which only reinforced Mitchell's sense that Isaac was around and all right but for reasons he was keeping to himself had withdrawn, didn't want to see anybody and didn't want to talk.

Everyone in Scuffletown was burning coconut husks, to keep off mosquitoes that had come with the rains. He stepped around scummy puddles in the rutted lane, headed for the open-air barbershop out on the beach, and from there tracking down the fellow he was looking for was less trouble than he had expected. He paid the asking price—one hundred U.S.—without further discussion, zipped the pistol inside his new daypack, and left. That was that—no etiquette required. Bullets were not included, the guy simply didn't have any, but Mitchell shrugged off this detail, unless something else happened ammunition wasn't critical, wasn't nearly as important as the look and feel of the gun, the weight of it in his hand, the threat it so unmistakably carried when raised—which more often than not, he reasoned, seemed to do the job—and when the time came, Ballantyne would know about bullets, would even be able to tell him what the seller could not. What the gun was; its name, what it was called.

He walked back up to the ministry imagining he had taken the right step to clarify himself and preserve his nerves from paralysis. That someone might actually seek to hurt him didn't have the impact on his thoughts or emotions as did the image of himself succumbing to hysteria, squealing like an animal, quaking with fear, and now he knew that would not happen, he would never let it, he had passed over that abyss in the soul, vaccinated by the first prick of terror.

Checking his mail, he found two envelopes—one letter-sized, the other the size of an unfolded page, set on his desk. The smaller one was addressed to Mrs. J. Fernandez and he opened it first. The note inside was typewritten on government stationary. It said, *Te amo, bollo.* Two of its three words reverberated. He knew what *te amo* meant, had heard it before.

Okay, okay, okay, he said to himself. The guy knew where she was. So, apparently, did everyone else, anyone interested. This meant . . . no telling what this meant. This meant be glad you own a gun.

He slit open the second envelope and removed its contents. There was a cover letter from George James down at the *Crier,* attached to a second and third envelope, both sealed: *You fellows at the ministry frightening us, you know, Wilson. Stop over re: an interview, when you have the time. Josephine asked that I pass this note along to you. Also, someone (never seen the fellow before) stop by to say he heard you were headed up north windward and asked that you pass a message along to a fellow up there by the name of Isaac Knowles. I don't know why he come to me with it, you know, he can't seem to say, but here it is (enclosed).*

He read the note from Josephine: *Dear Mitchell, I hear you have a woman staying by you but you know that is not important to me, please don't forget me because you are a nice man and I am your friend. Love, Jo,* crumpled it, threw it in his wastebasket, put everything else in his backpack, and left.

He was given the keys to the Rover and off he went, back to Howard Bay, where he found Johnnie on her knees in the front yard, busting out of her cut-off shorts, her face hidden underneath a haystack of hair. Mr. Quiddley was standing over her and the two of them were chattering away like parrots while Johnnie planted a scalloped border of pink and white impatiens on each side of the stoop. When he saw Mitchell, the old man began to back away, instinctively, after a lifetime of backing away only to come round again from another direction, saying he'd just stopped by to check on the coal pits, dem finish coalin up, and he planned to crack them open in the morning. Good, said Mitchell, not trying to be unfriendly, but he missed the tree, its flamboyant springtime blaze of flowers, missed it each and every time he walked out the door. I've eaten just about all the smoke I can take, he said, and Johnnie got up, brushing off dirt, and asked if he'd like a grilled cheese sandwich. Inside the house, he put the daypack with the gun and letters in the bottom of his armoire and forgot about it, went into the kitchen where Johnnie was washing her hands at the sink, became curious about what was boiling in a soup kettle on the back burner, a black unappetizing mess. What was it, he asked, but, asking, knew, as soon as the words were out of his mouth, that she was making psilocybin tea.

"Hey," she said excitedly, drying her hands, waltzing over to him. "You didn't tell me about the mushrooms."

"If this is for the volcano," he said, reluctant to play the spoilsport, "go easy on it, would you. It's a very difficult hike. Don't get too fucked up."

"Mitch," she said blithely, "do I ever get too fucked up," and he let it go at that.

After lunch, he took her in the Rover a short distance up the windward coast, turning off on a coral track leading to a somnambulant fishing village behind a ridge of dunes, and from there they walked over a ridge another twenty minutes to a two-mile-long beach, utterly deserted, end to end, washed by sets of lazy combers that broke far out on a bar and churned in foamy rows over a shallow, sandy bottom. Johnnie wanted to strip all the way but he told her to leave her suit on.

"Even here?" she pouted.

"Even here."

"Jesus, what a prig," she teased, and he chased her into the surf, whooping; they rode the waves for hours, rushed headlong on flying carpets of forgiving energy, each ride ending in a tumble of celebration, though Johnnie was just a little disappointed that the swells lacked symmetry and shape, denying the rider the cannonshot burst from a perfect locus of power, and yet still there was enough force to them to do what he had prohibited, so the joke was on Mitchell, Johnnie said, because although the waves disrobed her again and again, it was he who ended up losing his trunks.

On the way home, Johnnie asked what was that up on the hill, meaning the ruins of a colonial church, destroyed by a hurricane in the Sixties. Can we stop and walk up, she asked, and Mitchell said sure, why not, it was a pretty place, with an always breezy view of one of the roughest stretches of coastline on the island. He parked off the road and they followed a goat path up the knoll, Mitchell scanning the land, wondering where the old plantation had been, and who had walked before them up this hill to worship. Johnnie began stopping to pluck shards of Indian pottery out of the furrow of the path, pocketing the fragments that held a design. The church was roofless and had not been used in many years, but as they came up the rise they began to hear singing, and when they approached the chapel entrance and peered in beyond the threshold, they saw a nun with her back turned to them, a group of children who sat on the larger stones in a pile of rubble, the sister leading them in hymn as the sun lowered behind the mountains and the last full light of the day to reach inside the church lifted off their faces. It was one of the most peaceful, cohering scenes he had ever chanced to witness, so infused with timelessness and serenity that it allayed, finally, something inside of him he sensed but could not reach, a deep disturbance at his core that he could not name or describe or associate with anything happening around him, not even Johnnie. "Let's leave them alone," he whispered to her; she nodded, kissing the side of his face, whispering back to him if he thought God was still here in the desecrated church, and if not who were the children singing to. The memory of God? They moved away from the entrance, down the bricked portico, and when they passed the vestry, the only part of the ruin still roofed, bats flew out, small flapping blurs of being, scattering into the onset of dusk. For a moment they stood and watched the eastern rim of the ocean cool and harden, and then went back to Howard Bay, and from there to town for dinner, making good use of the Rover, eating in a centuries-old yellowstone building that had once housed the offices of the West Indian Trading Company, the dining room divided by stonework arches, the heaviness of the past mellowed by linen tablecloths, underlighting, good bread and wine, a clientele who appreciated subtleties enough to pay for them, a kitchen that served French Creole. They both ordered lobster, split down the middle and grilled. At many of the tables, Mitchell recognized familiar personalities from the government, and for a while he eavesdropped on a pair of couples sitting nearby, where the evening's specialty seemed to be contempt, dished out cold upon the reputations of the island's growing corps of soothsayers predicting a civil war. "And who de hell goin fight it?" one man said to the other. They chupsed in unison. They chupsed and chupsed and chupsed, ridiculing the very notion of Catherinians caring enough about anything to kill one another in an organized fashion. They would all choke to death on the smoke first.

Mitchell warned they had to make it an early night, but after dinner he went ahead and took Johnnie up above the city, not spelling it out to himself what he had in mind until they were all the way atop Mount Archer and he was pulling off the road to park at the toolshed disco that Josephine had taken him to the week before. Johnnie said she didn't know he liked places like this, so raw and proletarian and funky, and he had to say, proletarian? are you kidding? Holding onto one another, they drank rum, smoked the reefer being thumbed around, and danced. Mitchell got bombed, higher than he intended, and they stayed longer than they should have, sweating through their clothes, pressed into each other, rocking to the music without moving their feet, eyes half-lidded, spinning. He couldn't explain this, his timing, why he did it, but, nuzzling her, he mumbled a phrase that suddenly resurfaced in his mind. *Te amo.*

"What?" Johnnie said, jerking awake in his arms. "What did you just say?"

"*Te amo.* You were saying it the other night, out on the veranda."

"I don't remember." Her eyes were steely, she looked at him as if to say, what are you trying to do? Underneath his hands he could feel her muscles twitching. Not with alarm though. She wasn't alarmed. It was more like she was all there, all at once, full-sized, every part of her, every desire, every danger, every strength and weakness, all that must be reckoned with.

"What does it mean?"

"I love you. My husband used to say it, the only time he spoke Spanish to me. It's unsettling, to say the least, hearing it come from your mouth."

"You ripped him off, didn't you?"

Her eyes were locked on his, unnerving in their concentration, but also shining; if this was a game it intrigued her, it stimulated. "What do you think," she said. "I tried to tell you on the ferry but you stopped me."

"What did he do about it? Is he after you?"

"I don't know. I don't think so. In a very evil way it pleased him, what I did. He didn't punish me directly, he punished someone close to me, as if to say, every time you fuck me over, you're hurting the ones you love. I'll talk about it if you want but I don't want to. I want to go home. I want you to make love to me." Her voice dropped to its lowest register. "I want you to do whatever you want to me."

She was changing him: he was beginning to see how. It attracted a devil in him, for them to be in this place, having this conversation, about these things, in this tone, to see her lit up by both her ability to survive and her compulsion to self-destruct. What did it mean, when a woman told you, you can do whatever you want to me? What was she talking about? There's less, he thought, to total control than meets the eye, and for one moment he accepted the pleasure this knowledge brought. Meaning, for one moment, until he shook himself out of the spell, *he* was Bobby Fernandez. It was, if he had stopped to understand it, the most incriminating moment of his life.

Saturday at dawn, he argued with her about footgear—she intended to wear her sandals, he insisted she take along her tennis shoes—and the last thing she did before they left the house was to fill a bowl with kibble, leaving it, despite his mutterings to forget the cat, out on the front stoop for Pelé.

Chapter 29

He had been "detained," as they called it in the GIS press release, on Saturday, April 16—found up north in the jungle and taken into custody. His name never appeared on any list, there was no need for that. Too much attention could breed its own emptiness and anonymity and seem as bad as too little, though not as bad as none at all.

The friends of golf were on the island by the following Monday, a day and a half later, that's all the time it took once they had been attracted by the novelty of Mitchell Wilson. There were four of them, then three, then only two, not counting on the first day legal counsel and the PC-CD, standing for country director, Sally's administrator who also happened to be Archibol's brother-in-law, and from the start, everybody wanted to make it clear they were his friends. Plus the consul, flown in from the regional embassy in Barbados, whom he saw and spoke with only once during the three days the friends convened—the time it took for the consul to exhaust his efforts to secure Wilson's immediate (albeit conditional) release. Failing then to reach an arrangement, the consul lobbied for some semblance of due process, charges quietly filed somewhere other than on the streets and in the government-controlled press and given the chance to be appropriately addressed.

But no one, including the embassy, unofficially of course, wanted to see Mitchell Wilson anywhere but where he was, for the time being. Which he accepted, so far. He was outside the process, but nobody could actually say he wasn't cooperating—all he was doing was seeing past their questions to other questions, the ones nobody asked, and they thought perhaps he was hiding things.

Being an embarrassment though to either government was no embarrassment at all, nor was he moved by the accusation that he was, absurdly, an enemy of the people. He had become everything to everybody, equally useful to opposing points of view, the infant split down the middle by arrogance. Off the record, the embassy scrambled to come up with a position on him they could best adapt to their own interests, once they had identified what those were. St. Catherine was a surprise—what had they missed, where was the flea collar on this dog? Wilson was a crash course in what was going on. There was no consensus about which side they were on; these days you couldn't really depend on one. There were interests within interests, so it was no small chore figuring out whether to sacrifice or defend him or simply pretend he wasn't there, so that policy might be furthered, and perhaps one or another principles upheld.

Who did they *want* him to be was just another one of those questions. The embassy would neither confirm nor deny who he was, who he wasn't, who he was supposed to be—and that was for the record.

His first morning among the friends was pro forma. Perhaps because of the cast on his right wrist, no one offered to shake his hand, not that he took it personally. They met in a closed room, around two long blond wooden tables placed end to end, somewhere inside the administrative wing of Fort Gregory. His guards had led him down vaulted underground passageways, then up four right-turning flights of steps, the stones worn smooth in the center from many generations of boots. The guards—now everybody on the police force was wearing camouflage fatigues, though the color of berets differed, depending on loyalties—remained outside the door. He'd been through this Q&A again and again with the National Police, two different sets, one antagonistic, one solicitous and patronizing. Then the factions switched roles after he was brought down out of the mountains where he had been looking for Isaac, and jailed.

There was a free-standing, old-fashioned fan that no one could make work. An earthy smell of mortar and dankness from the walls. The view out the windows was back down toward the harbor and town, spectacular, making Mitchell think Fort Gregory had a viable future as a resort. Except for the lawyer—barrister—and Grambling, Archibol's slouching brother-in-law, they introduced themselves namelessly. Bill Smith, Jim Grey, what's the difference? He stopped listening and named them himself. Ben, Jack, Arnold, Sam. Sam, like the barrister and country director, was black. The back channels were becoming equal opportunity; maybe in other circumstances he'd regard this as progress. The white men in the room had what his mother would call nice hair.

He sat down opposite them. He had no plans, he was hostage to somebody else's, at this point. They offered him cigarettes and that was how he started smoking again. If he put his nose to his cast he could smell the rancidness inside like a dead animal. Legal counsel had gold fillings and a Bajan accent; he was the only one wearing a necktie, something Ivy League, burgundy, with tiny sailboats. He asked if Mitchell was being mistreated, or required medical attention. Mitchell smiled tightly and shook his head. The cigarette had made him high.

"What we wish to do this morning," the lawyer said, opening his briefcase and holding up a folder bound with a dark blue strip of ribbon, "is have you verify this statement you made to the National Police on—" He removed a clip of papers, recited date and place, pushed a three-page handwritten document across the table toward Mitchell, blotting up the sweat from the glass of water placed there beforehand. Ink ran like black smoke out of the bottom line of words.

"Then we'd like to depose you—"

He must have made a face.

"—take your deposition, that is, have you elaborate certain areas of interest, ask you some questions for the record. The Collymore trial is all I'm concerned with, at present. These other gentlemen I believe have questions of their own."

"All right."

"So if you could, sir, reread the statement and confirm that it is true and accurate of the facts. To the best of your knowledge."

"All right."

His fingers were flat on the table, the pages in between. They looked at him, their eyes serious, waiting for him to drop his head and begin.

"Is this a problem? You're not going to have trouble doing this, are you?"

"No."

"Take your time. We understand."

He shrugged, rubbing a dry corner of the coarse, blue-ruled paper between his fingers. Each of his sentences had been given its own line or lines, as if he had recited an epic poem to the police.

"Out loud, if you don't mind. So it will be fresh for all of us."

He drank half the glass of water and started.

Shortly after dawn Saturday April ninth I left my house in Howard Bay.

I was driving a government Land Rover and I was accompanied by my house guest, Johanna Woods, who has since left the island.

We went to Rosehill Plantation to pick up three friends— Tillman Hyde, Adrian Roberts, and Sally Jorgensen—who planned to hike with us to the top of Mount Soufrière.

Sally Jorgensen had also asked me to make a short detour to the village of Retreat for the purpose of visiting a woman with a child who could possibly benefit from enrollment in Sally's school.

We stopped at the checkpoint outside of the town of Camell where our travel pass was inspected by the officer on duty.

I don't remember his name.

He refused to return the pass to me but said we could go on.

He gave us no advice or warning about any danger of any type reported in the North Windward District, or of any law enforcement operations in process in the vicinity of Mount Soufrière.

Around 9:15 we arrived in Retreat and asked someone where we could find a woman named Jolene, who was either the aunt or mother of the child.

We were given directions to a house where Jolene was and went there.

Sally went inside while the rest of us remained in the vehicle.

We heard a loud argument, then Sally screamed my name.

Tillman and I went inside to help Sally.

The child's father was pointing a rifle at Sally.

I told him to calm down, nobody was going to take his child away.

He said he was going to kill Jolene and the child.

I put my arm around Sally and said This is my wife, there's been a mistake.

He accepted my explanation and we left.

Sally was worried for the woman's safety and so we went to find a policeman.

We had to go to Belair, the next village, and drive him back with us to Jolene's.

The husband had run away and Sally convinced Jolene to go back to Queenstown with her baby.

Her mother-in-law who had been taking care of the child refused to leave and cursed Sally and Jolene.

Jolene and her son sat in the carry-all space in the back of the Rover.

We took the policeman back to Belair who said he would talk to Jolene's husband.

We then discussed among ourselves whether to continue with our plan to hike Soufrière or go directly back to Queenstown.

We decided not to change our plans since Adrian Roberts was sched-

uled to leave the island the next afternoon and this was her only chance to see Soufrière.

Sally especially insisted we do this and said she preferred to keep the woman and child company while we were on the mountain.

We drove back south several miles to the turnoff and then to the end of the track to the trailhead.

There were three other Land Rovers already parked at the turnaround.

I recognized one as the vehicle assigned to the forest ranger Godfred Ballantyne.

The other two Rovers had no markings but bore NPF license tags.

I did not think anything of this since the police force has a youth program with organized outings, or off-duty personnel might have come with their families.

I had no reason to believe otherwise.

We were looking forward to our expedition.

Since we were getting a late start I suggested we hike at a fast pace if we were to reach the summit and come back down before nightfall.

Jolene got out of the Rover with the child and she strongly insisted Sally walk up Soufrière with her friends or she would be very unhappy for ruining Sally's holiday.

Jolene sat down in the grass and began making a palm frond doll for her child and refused to speak or look at Sally.

I saw how Jolene looked at us and thought she had changed her mind about Queenstown and I was right because when we came back down off the mountain Jolene and the child were gone.

Sally reluctantly agreed to come with us after making Jolene promise she would stay by the Rover.

We started up the path which was a little muddy.

I was in the lead.

After twenty minutes I stopped to wait for the others at a fork in the trail.

Tillman Hyde and Adrian Roberts came first, then Sally Jorgensen and Johanna Woods a few minutes behind.

I told them they should try to keep up and we started out again.

An hour later I halted at the waterfall which is about one third of the way up to the crater.

Somebody was camping there in a small canvas tent but they didn't seem to be around.

Tillman and Adrian were in sight below me on the trail.

We waited about ten minutes for Sally and Johanna and finally I called out for them.

I heard Sally answer that they were coming and then I saw her on the trail below.

I yelled down to her where was Johnnie and she said Johnnie was right behind her and told us to go on and they'd catch up.

I said they should pick up their pace if they could or they'd never make the summit in time.

Also it was less sunny and I worried about the cloud coverage.

We continued on.

After another hour or so we were above the thickest jungle and the forest began to thin out.

Tillman and Adrian were close behind me, in sight, but I had not seen Sally and Johanna since the waterfall.

We walked for another half hour coming up to the altitude where the mountain is banded in high grasses and scrub, cut through by many old lava flows that have made twisting gullies and deep channels, like a maze, and there are many large basalt boulders scattered around.

In this area it's very hard to keep your companions in sight and the going is slow.

About halfway through this terrain there is a high lava shelf and the path enters the bottom of a steep gully through which you can ascend to the top of the rock by climbing footholds that have been cut in the side.

When you reach the top you come out into a rock gallery and it was there I encountered the four policemen, two of them standing to watch me come up, two of them resting against the rocks, and on the ground between them sat three men who were not policemen, by the looks of them, but ordinary peasants.

I was surprised by this unexpected sight.

The two policemen standing held rifles and the other two, pistols in holsters.

I stepped up on a nearby rock and had a view of the slope all the way back to the trees.

I called out to make Tillman and Adrian look up and they saw me and waved back.

One of the officers on the rocks stood up and called me over.

This was Captain Eddins.

When he asked for identification I showed him my driver's license.

He asked where I had come from and then he wanted to see my travel pass.

I told him the guard at the Camell checkpoint had kept it and told me to go on.

It is not true that I was never issued a travel pass.

We had been granted permission by the proper authorities to go to Soufrière, and at no time did anyone warn us against going there, or try to prevent us.

I asked Captain Eddins if anything was wrong and he answered by asking how many people were with me.

Tillman and Adrian emerged from the gully onto the top of the shelf.

Captain Eddins asked to see identification which they then provided.

Eddins then asked Tillman Hyde why we were there.

Tillman replied he was escorting tourists from his hotel on an excursion to the summit of the volcano.

Eddins then informed him there were antigovernment mercenaries in the area and advised him to be careful and also said he would provide Tillman and Adrian with an armed escort up to the rim.

Tillman declined the offer but Eddins insisted or ordered he and Adrian go on to see what they had come so far to see, and that the others—myself, Sally, and Johanna—would be along shortly.

Tillman protested but Eddins threatened him with arrest if he refused to obey and so he and Adrian continued on toward the cone, followed by one of the lower-ranking policemen with a rifle.

Mitchell stopped, only to finish the glass of water, and even as he drank he never raised his eyes from the words, didn't want to see their faces, however they might look at him. Everybody knew what was ahead.

I looked down the slope and could see Sally coming through the high grass.

She disappeared momentarily into one of the lava gullies and then reappeared.

I shouted and waved so she would look up and see us.

When she arrived on the shelf, Captain Eddins asked to see her identification.

She told him her name, that she was a volunteer and had founded a school in Queenstown, that she had lived on St. Catherine for eighteen months and everybody knew who she was, that she never carried identification with her because no one had told her it was required and no one had ever asked to see it except at the airport and at the bank, and they didn't even ask at the bank anymore.

Eddins asked where the other woman was and Sally said Johanna had been not far behind her.

Captain Eddins then instructed Sally to wait with me for Johanna.

The three of us stood on the edge of the shelf, looking down the slope for Johanna, while the others stayed where they were in the rocks.

439

We couldn't see Johanna.

A little while later, perhaps ten minutes, there was a shot, a gunshot.

It was possible to hear the bullet go by in the air above our heads.

We turned to look toward the treeline in the direction the shot had come from, down to our right, and just then there was a second shot.

Sally stumbled backward into me and I grabbed her knapsack to keep her from falling.

I was not immediately aware that the bullet had hit her.

There was a third shot and I looked down the slope again and could see a man standing at the edge of the forest with a pistol raised in his hand pointing up at us.

I saw him turn and run at the same time Captain Eddins and the two policemen in the rocks opened fire on him but he vanished into the trees.

Captain Eddins said a name like Abraham and I believe he was referring to the man we had seen below us with the gun.

Eddins then ran back down through the grasses toward the forest.

During the confusion the three men who had been sitting on the ground also ran away without anyone trying to stop them.

I couldn't see Tillman and Adrian above us but I yelled for them to come back.

Sally was bleeding and in pain but conscious.

The bullet had struck the bottom side of her right breast.

I examined her and there seemed to be an exit wound at the top of her breast, near the breastbone.

The two remaining policemen seemed confused about whether to follow Captain Eddins or help me with Sally.

I convinced them to help me carry Sally down off the mountain so she could be taken to a hospital.

We started down the path holding up Sally however we could.

Before we reached the trees the fourth policeman caught up with us and I asked him where Tillman and Adrian were but he didn't answer.

Corporal Gonsalves ordered him to run ahead to assist Captain Eddins.

We hurried on and entered the forest.

A few minutes later we heard a shot in the distance below us and then around a bend we found Johanna sitting a few yards off the trail in some rocks.

She was upset because she hadn't been able to keep up and thought she had lost us and then she had heard the shots.

She said she hadn't seen anybody but a policeman running down the path, and then another policeman, shortly before we had found her.

She became hysterical when she saw Sally had been hurt.

She seemed to go into shock and wouldn't move and I had to leave her behind.

I continued down with the two policemen who were helping me with Sally, who had lost consciousness.

I heard Tillman calling to us far back up the trail but we kept going.

Sometime later we saw Captain Eddins lying down in the path below us.

When we got up to him I saw that he too had been shot and I checked his breathing and pulse and determined he was dead.

The fourth policeman was nowhere in sight.

The two policemen with me called for him and then became frightened and ran away down the mountain.

I put Sally over my shoulder and carried her but this was very difficult.

A while later I heard people above me on the trail.

This was Tillman and the two women.

Tillman had a blanket in his backpack and we used it like a sling to carry Sally between us.

It began to rain and the path became slippery and slowed us down.

Just before we reached the waterfall I heard someone running down the trail behind us and this was the forest ranger Ballantyne who said he had been up at the crater collecting scientific data.

With him helping us carry Sally we were able to move faster and we reached the trailhead as it was turning dark.

One of the vehicles with police tags was gone but the other one was still there.

Our own vehicle had bullet holes in the doors and windscreen.

Sally was conscious again but in much pain.

We laid her on the back seat of our Rover and followed Ballantyne back out to the road and south to St. Andrews where he said there was a doctor.

The clinic was closed but Dr. Betancourt was at his house next door.

He told us that only the hospital in Queenstown was equipped to deal with a gunshot wound such as Sally's and that he thought the bullet might have entered her lung though I doubted this because there was no blood coming from her mouth or nose and her breathing was not noticeably labored.

He gave her a shot of morphine and agreed to come along with us to administer a blood transfusion. We drove immediately back to the main road with Ballantyne following us in his vehicle.

It was still raining though not very hard and the road was dark and slick.

I drove at top speed.

About a mile south of Ashton Park there were cattle in the road and one swung out unexpectedly in front of me and when I hit it I was unable to stop the Land Rover from going off the road into the drainage ditch.

This was when my wrist was broken.

During the accident, Adrian and Tillman who were crouched on the floor between the back and front seats were able to prevent Sally from being tossed around.

It was necessary to transfer ourselves to Ballantyne's vehicle.

There was no room for Dr. Betancourt so we left him there.

I don't know how much later it was we arrived at the National Hospital and took Sally inside.

The pain and fear and the wrenching, riveting horror seemed so expendable when all was said and done. He was awed by how sanitary everything had become, how quick it happened. The statement was like reading a newspaper, it had its own recognizable air of fantasy that seemed perfectly adapted to the way he saw the present moment. This was a new reality and he didn't know where it would lead or what might stop it. He felt a tightness in his chest, his throat and hands; his wrist throbbed within its decaying shell as if it were being baked with radiation. Archibol's brother-in-law, the Peace Corps County Director for St. Catherine, looked vexed and anxious to speak but nobody else so much as batted an eye at this bonanza of mayhem, catastrophe, ill-fate, cursed luck and cursed lives. The Bajan lawyer was scribbling on a legal pad. What Wilson had told them must happen every day and for them stories like this were like blood to doctors. This would never be a mystery for them, no matter what went unanswered. Nothing was primitive, all events could be institutionalized, violence wasn't even legendary anymore, not after two world wars and the indelible surrealism of the last war. What the government did, Mitchell realized belatedly, he could not prevent himself from also doing, which was to objectify suffering, to place a higher value on the concept of truth rather than truth itself.

The friends pursed their lips, waiting in ambiguous silence, the token respect you might give to a competitor up on the tee. He had the childish and self-destructive impulse to keep going, I should just keep going, he said to himself, but when he opened his mouth it was to say, Yes, the statement was correct, to the best of his knowledge.

"Mister Wilson, now I'd like—" began the legal counsel the

embassy had sent but he was interrupted by Archibol's brother-in-law.

"Perhaps you will now put to rest these ugly rumors, mahn, these shameless rumors—"

"Why don't you tell us where these goddamn rumors are coming from, okay?"

It was Mitchell's turn to interrupt, rising to his feet to fling his acid-bottle of words at the man who was there to represent Sally and protect her interests, out of control, wound up tight and let go, losing it for the first time since the torment of the ordeal with Sally. "Why don't you just tell Edison Banks and your brother-in-law and Lloyd Peters and everybody else to shut their fucking mouths and stop spreading lies about Sally and assassinating her character after all the good work she did for the children of this fucking country, and while you're at it why don't you leave Adrian Roberts alone and stop trying to screw her and why don't you just tell us what you know that we're not supposed to about all this bullshit, all this entrapment, and why don't you tell me why I'm here locked up in this fucking place, and what I'm guilty of, and I'm tired of this, I'm tired of men like you, I'm tired of opportunists, I'm tired of people who use the rhetoric of justice and then act like savages, I'm tired of this eternal fucking shit where innocent people pay the cost, this fucking shit, this shit."

He had been banging the cadence of his voice on the table with his plaster wrist and didn't even know it, Archibol's brother-in-law looked on smugly, off the hook, because clearly here was a loose cannon, a man whose emotions got the better of him, and Mitchell contracted back into his seat, trying to stay outraged for as long as he could to fight off the deep, deep lethargy that threatened to swell up from his stomach and absorb him.

The legal counsel cleared his throat to attract Mitchell's attention.

"As long as the issue has been raised by Mister Grambling, can you tell us what Miss Jorgensen was carrying in her knapsack that day on the mountain. If you know."

"Sandwiches, fruit, a water bottle, a camera, a rain poncho."

"And you know this, how?"

"I looked in it, trying to find something, I don't know what, to stop the bleeding."

"And there was nothing inside to compromise Miss Jorgensen, if you understand me?"

"Absolutely not," he had lied.

Archibol's brother-in-law was nodding, deeply satisfied by the line of questioning and the crispness of the response.

"And did you throw the knapsack into the bushes or try to hide it in any way?"

"Absolutely not. It was left on the trail. Let the soldiers who were up there on Soufrière come forward and testify otherwise."

"The police."

"I stand corrected."

He noticed one of the friends of golf giving him a roguish smile and he wanted to rip it off his face, he didn't want that sort of camaraderie with these men, he only wanted to make them know that there is no secret to who Sally was, you know the Sallys finally and always by their goodness alone, by the luminous simplicity of their gift.

He didn't think he was going to get past his problem with Grambling, the veneer of competence that was going to keep him in his job, his vindication in front of men important to him. He wanted Archibol's brother-in-law disgraced—let the taxpayers pay for *that*. The Bajan lawyer started back up the mountain, step by step, sifting for details, and Mitchell felt himself losing it again.

I have mean thoughts, he said to himself. I have hot thoughts.

"If you want atrocity, let's talk about the butcher." His left eye flinched in spasms and his jaw was grinding madly. "Let's talk about Grambling just standing by and letting them do it. They bring this guy up from the fucking abattoir with his fucking hacksaw. Let's talk about that."

Instead they broke for lunch.

Mitchell requested he be allowed to remain in the conference room and the friends spoke to his keepers on his behalf. One of the guards went to talk to his superior and the deal was, okay, but no food. Which he had no appetite for anyway but then for whatever reason one of the mess hall cooks noticed he was missing and took up his cause, personally bringing him a bowl of stew and a glass of lemonade, and he ate after all, because it wasn't half bad. When the lawyer and foursome of friends returned, without Archibol's brother-in-law, he was standing at the windows, smoking one of Sam's or Jack's cigarettes, his eyes roaming the slums of Scuffletown, trying to identify the house, seriously wondering if there had ever really been anyone named Isaac Knowles. Now he existed in the newspapers, on the radio, in PRP briefings, strategy sessions. The phantom raider of the north. The invisible force set against the legitimate government of St.

Catherine. Jack Nasty and his bad children. Isaac. The dream of aggression come true.

He was given a present—a carton of Marlboros. *See?* . . . friends. They all sweated copiously and smelled like garlic and remarked how the restaurants were ridiculously cheap and good. Everyone sat in the same arrangement as before, minus Grambling.

"Mister Wilson, we've got to nail this guy and want you to know how much we appreciate your help." This was Arnold and he meant Collymore. Arnold was name-brand synthetic knit sportswear and the deceptively boyish smile of a Southern Baptist. His concern for Sally was disingenuous.

"They want to make you happy with Collymore," Mitchell said. "Believe me. This is very important to them."

They went back up the mountain again, like Calvary, like the stations of the cross, then back down again, Sally bleeding all over him, and then they jumped ahead to the morning he identified Iman Ibrahim who was Cassius Collymore in a police lineup in the village of Scarborough, and got that over with and done. The room was hot and they kept asking for water. He had an insomniac's need for an afternoon nap and a tingling in his neck and back. There was a mood shift that he just barely caught, and then they were asking if he was a Marxist, or a Marxist-Leninist, or had leanings. The police were in possession of some texts, his name appeared on the flyleaves and his handwriting on the page margins.

Which police? he asked. Which side? The police up there or the police down here? PIP or PRP? If they would tell him he could figure out what this meant. And if this was a deposition why wasn't counsel taking it down? He had not committed himself to Utopia, all right? Paradise frightened him, the concept had that lockjaw feel. With reasoned disclaimers and certain reservations and bearing in mind a world of helpless lives, he believed in common markets, he believed in producing, in orderly production and orderly consumption. Ideology, he was beginning to think, was the source of excess. Excessive loss or excessive gain. Perhaps he was just another of your average bourgeois individualists, although that seemed oxymoronic. Whatever revolutionary sentimentality he had carried out of the Sixties had been replaced with a flat pain. Nationality was not useful in a religion of markets. Rather, not especially relevant, not like culture or even race. St. Catherine had everything it needed for a cultural exhibition but otherwise it was just camping out, it had very little of what it needed to be a modern nation. Any type of nation.

He no longer believed in self-sufficiency but interdependence and self-efficiency. He believed that the individual impulse to exploit must be balanced with the collective impulse to share. He believed in the tension between the two.

He didn't know what the world would look like ten years into the future, or who would win the Cold War, but suspected that for orphans like St. Catherine it couldn't possibly matter.

Did he have a mission? Yes. To possibly save one person. A friend or a stranger, it didn't matter.

Had he failed? he asked rhetorically, and answered himself.

Unequivocally.

They should tell him which police—here at the fort or down at headquarters. The national force had divided and was growing into two separate and opposing militias. Hang around, he said, and see for yourself. The friends' indulgence gave them amiable, relaxed smiles. Why were they asking about communism if what they wanted to know about was Sally and Collymore? Right.

They gently changed the subject to Johnnie and he blew it big time by automatically reversing direction, exposing his one genuine weakness by rambling on about Roberto Fernandez. They danced around Fernandez for a few minutes and then of course the door was wide open on Johanna Fernandez née Woods.

Talking about Johnnie made him sore and defensive. He wanted to emphasize she didn't represent the answers they seemed to think she did, not in the context they were working with here, trying to establish a scaffolding of facts around a monolith of as yet unveiled truth and so on, he blundered, at least that was his opinion. Johnnie was a red herring. She was a drug dealer. Like, who the fuck cares? Their interest in her was misplaced. She was sidelines, bleacher seats, pure audience, and this was a discussion about actors, or about victimizers and victims was another way to see it, but whatever Johnnie did she did to herself. Used drugs and sold drugs and so what, where's the angle? Drug dealers are sensitive people, if they're smart and no more greedy than your standard-issue Wall Street vampire. They get out of the way fast. She got out of the way. Came for a vacation, shit happened, and she hightailed out of here. What more was there to talk about. She enjoyed herself the last week she was here and one thing about happiness is that it's not often that it's memorable. Ask the people who publish newspapers. Maybe in your old age.

That was enough, a good day's work, they thought he did well. One of the major aspects of this, they said, was that they could see him in his own right as a hero, the thing no one's supposed to try to be. The word cut, as much an insult—*more*—as accolade.

Back in his cell for the night he learned how energy was his real enemy. Out in the interior courtyard he could hear the ticking heels and practiced laughter of the whores being let in for the night. One of the guards sold him a soda bottle of homemade rum and its taste and effect were unsparing, slamming his head into a soft flaming wall of grief. Rustling sounds came out of the spaces where the light didn't fall. The butcher's name was Mr. Madlock. He was very fat and wore a woman's style of sunglasses. What was so terrible was that he had on a yellow tee shirt from a casino in Antigua, there was an image of a white woman stenciled on the front, a cartoon, her mouth was saying *wow* and she was waving a fistful of money, and beneath the image was the slogan *We make the night better.* This alone could never be forgiven. His pants drooped, showing red nylon underwear and the crack in his ass. He was the postmortem "cutter," kept on retainer by the hospital for weekend emergencies, when the coroner was off duty. He smoked constantly and the ash kept tumbling off into Sally's chest cavity. This is what brought his heart to its knees, this was why he had decided to hate when everything froze up in the jungle when he was with the woodcutters, because at least the hatred presented itself as a way out.

Every morning it was the same, biscuits and tea, prayerlessness. Noise, a debilitating cultural noise factor. Everybody shouting. Guards having conversations in shouts to be able to hear each other at opposite ends of the galleries. Inmates shouting for the same reason, hands like a row of snakes extended through the barred windows in the wooden doors, and the radios like electronic Babylon. Prisoners in military formation in the yard, sweating through their rags, calling off exercises, push-ups, knee-bends, slogging in place. Occasionally a lovely baritone voice climbed up and up in song and he remembered an old proverb he had heard somewhere: *When danger approaches, sing to it.* A trip to the sewer of a washroom for a supervised shower and shave. He was not a prisoner but a detainee, though the difference was hard to appreciate. When he came back from the washroom someone had pinched his carton of Marlboros and he realized that was bound to happen when you had too much of something.

Chapter 30

As he had been trained by Ballantyne, he went up and up and up, single-mindedly and with angry exhilaration, leaving the world below. He set a brisk pace going up, rising through a sea of cellulose and chlorophyll toward a brilliant surface, a phototropic entity, brushing through a stand of dripping fern trees, light streaming down through the canopy overhead. The others were somewhere behind him. He wasn't teacher, wasn't going to be. Soufrière was.

The journey to the mountain had been strange, unpleasant, subdued with tension, and, eventually, almost disastrous, certainly nothing to laugh about. It had been a late night for everyone; no one had much to say, except Johnnie. She awoke grouchy, then on the road she was manic, affectated; she babbled. Just like on the ferry, her Pacific escapades, *we had to get up and back before dark too, flick your Bic every two feet if the sun set before you were down, by then your pickup was probably sitting at a bar in Lahaina, I'm talking about Maui, now, we'd be dropped off at dawn with backpacks full of keikis—you know, starts, young plants—keikis means children in Hawaiian, also we'd carry fifteen pounds of powdered Angelica root and fertilizer, the Angelica minimized plant shock, once you transplanted you sprinkled it around the keikis, we'd run way the fuck up Kipuhulu Gap, where Charles Lindbergh is buried, you know, down at the bottom, and we'd go way up, past Seven Sacred Pools, you have to get down on your hands and knees and crawl through the hau tree roots, and the staghorn ferns were as big as houses, it was like we were hobbits or something, we'd stamp them down in the center and plant the keikis, our world-famous keikis.*

Tillman dozed. Mitchell felt like telling her to pipe down but took a mental step backward, away from her, instead, and concentrated on driving. Adrian finally complained about Johnnie's cigarettes and she put them away in Mitchell's daypack and became quiet and edgy. It was just too damn early for good sense and grace.

The road north was twisty and potholed, abundant with hazard; after an hour they felt carsick and stopped in Missionary for sodas to settle their stomachs. Johnnie and Adrian had been nipping on her water bottle of black tea, which only made it worse for them. The two women had a stop-go relationship that he realized he wasn't understanding. Only Sally seemed cleanly awake and pleased to be doing this, and even the good-naturedness of her mood was subject to the influence of Saconi, his last-minute decision, made the night before, not to come along. She relayed his list of negatives: wrong season; the jungle was a shitty place; the northern peasants depressed him with their fierce, subhuman backwardness. He was weary of counting their afflictions, their patriarchal clamoring. A peasant is someone who likes to salute, he had said, which sounded too much like a change of heart, coming from Saconi. Worst of all, from Sally's point of view, he disapproved of what she was going to do, made an accusation of meddling and took the side of the child's father. Sally blew up at him, said aren't you being a hypocrite, heard what came from his mouth as an anathema, and his words weighed heavily on her now, as well they might, considering she had almost gotten herself killed.

It was too much to deal with, too much sadness and too much fear and too much ignorance, the poor son of a bitch and his kid. The father was handsome as a Belafonte too, straight-backed with virility and the will to endure, but his son lay crumpled on a pile of crocus sacking, fluttering with spasticity, face rimed with mucous and his limbs neurologically havocked, like a burnt insect's, and however hopeless this was, Sally was right, because the boy's eyes telegraphed a desperate intelligence, the eyes were alive within his cage of flesh.

Mitchell didn't know why he wasn't afraid entering the shack, backed by Tillman. Adrian said sangfroid, which was at least better than having to hear this stuff about macho. He simply thought reason would prevail, face to face, in the light of day. The fellow had the rifle leveled at Sally, the barrel inches from her abdomen; Jolene and her mother-in-law were in a corner, blubbering; the little boy's eyes darted from adult to adult and his father raved—*M'pé, nap boulé*—his English boiling with Creole, virtually unintelligible but Mitchell had interviewed enough northerners to catch the gist of it: God created the monkey and then the white man came and took away the monkey and put him in the zoo (*behind the fence,* was how the man expressed it in Creole).

There was the dilemma.

It reminded Mitchell of a folk proverb one of the politicians— Banks or Kingsley, he couldn't remember which one—was fond of using: When the black man takes, he take one; when the white man takes, he take all. Something along those lines. They must have been about the same age, he and the father. He began talking to him as he might without the rifle there, in a conversational tone, not pacing his words, he didn't think the wretch was deaf or stupid, saying to him, This is my wife. The barrel of the gun swung on him then. The words came automatically—survival had its muse. She's a doctor, he said calmly. *Oh God no!* Jolene shrieked. *Is a doctor he blame!*

This is my wife, Mitchell repeated, meeting the man's inchoate eyes. You know like me there are good doctors and bad doctors. This is my wife, she loves children, she helps children get well, she would sooner hurt herself than hurt your son or take him away from you. I swear she doesn't want to take him away. He put his arm around Sally's shoulder and began to slowly sidestep toward the door. This is my wife. She helps sick children. Do you want us to leave? I think it would be better if we left.

The barrel of the gun divined Tillman in utmost circumspection, then circled away to the far side of the humble room, coming to rest on the child. Shuddering, the child's father began to weep. Mitchell, believing the father was going to settle the child's fate this way and kill him, pulled Sally toward the door, Tillman slipping out ahead of them into the dirt yard with its spindly crotons. Any second he expected the boom.

"*Mitchell!*"

"There's not a thing you can do, Sally. What do you think you can do?"

The distinction between mercy-killing and murder was not a discussion she was going to have with him. They went on a scavenger hunt for a cop, anybody with authority would do, if he came with a gun.

Given the choice between phototropic and psychotropic, he was going up, not in, unable to reconcile his two selves and their separate cures. Of the many things love could not provide, one was such a thing as a mountain. He passed through an abandoned cocoa grove, the fruit pods stunted, its wood rusty with molds. The heat was like something inside a steam lodge. He removed his long-sleeved outer shirt, so helpful in protecting a climber's arms from the incessant cat-scratchings of the jungle. He wiped a spiderweb from his face and kept on going. His body cleansed itself, reeking a skunky stench not unlike the jungle's own smell, though not as rich and not as curious.

Only Johnnie would take a tenuous morning like the one they had and turn it around into a referendum on the counterculture of cow-shit. Was this a penchant being expressed for trivialization or enhancement, was the question, and he couldn't decide. The question was new—suggesting that raising it was part of the answer. Everyone went along because everyone went along. He fretted that they weren't taking the mountain seriously, that he hadn't convinced them. Or that he had, and made them lazy with the challenge. There had seemed to be, however, a collective need to switch gears, throw themselves forward into a fantastic day, away from the day they were so far having. He had certainly felt it, the strong desire to put some distance between himself and the Jolenes of the world, the central characters of pathos. The world blamed good wombs that bore bad children, or so it often seemed. Between mother and child and the mountain stood Sally, torn, agonizing whether they should get back down to Queenstown before something else happened, but Jolene was adamant, she would walk out to the coast road and home if Miss Big Sally sacrificed for her. Miss Sally's "holiday" was all-important, something Jolene wanted to believe in. What Jolene was doing was pretty blatant and finally Mitchell told Sally, Leave them and come on, they'd be all right. Sally wasn't being given the choice of remaining behind. She must have known, because she wrenched a promise to wait out of Jolene, and Jolene promised, halfheartedly, her head bent over the palm frond doll she was weaving for the child.

Ten yards up the trail, Sally stopped and pleaded with them. "What do you think, you all? Tell me to go back and stay with her."

"I think she's going to bolt for the guy," said Mitchell.

Johnnie kept her own counsel, but both Tillman and Adrian agreed. I think you're going to have to let it be, Tillman told her, until she comes to you. Use the mountain to get used to the fact that at this juncture you're the problem not the solution. The phrase "use the mountain" stuck in Mitchell's thoughts.

Mitchell had become very insistent, saying we have *got* to move. He was also giving Johnnie a hard time about her zorries again. She said come on, just relax. She didn't have a knapsack of her own and wanted to transfer her bottle of tea and sneakers from Mitchell's pack to Sally's. Johnnie and Adrian were already round-eyed from the mushrooms. The bottle was passed around, Sally taking a good slug like it was bourbon. Don't drink too much or you'll just want to sit down and let the mountain come to you, which it won't, Mitchell said.

"Which it just might," Johnnie countered, with a bogus air of enlightenment, squandering spirituality. Mitchell thought the less he communicated with her today the better. All morning he had felt out of rhythm with her, her capriciousness. Selfish and pious, he wanted to say. As if there was her way and his way and neither was wrong because all ways were equal and one shouldn't seek to dominate or oppress the other. This exasperating stubbornness of hers about shoes. These are native feet, she kept asserting, wanting him to run his hand over her calluses, but he knew perfectly well how thick they were. Mitch, you don't know, she kept telling him. She knew how to walk in the goddamn jungle. Why was this an issue? He should remove his own boots and feel the mud as it was meant to be felt. Look, she knew what she was doing. It was time for him to shut up and let her do it her way. She weeded the kitchen garden by yanking off the tops and leaving the roots and he couldn't talk with her about that either. He supposed he should be grateful they weren't in an airplane, co-pilots, quibbling over how to fly, or by now they would have crashed and burned. Like flight, the mountain came with its own rules. If they still wanted to swim in the crater's lake, it was imperative they stop dicking around, they had to *go*, haul ass; Let's haul ass, he told them. Otherwise, have a nice day. That's fine, said Johnnie, stop acting like we can't take care of ourselves. Go ahead, said Tillman. We're right behind you. They'd save him a mouthful of tea for the summit. They would make of the mountain what they would. No problem.

Man, look at this, he heard Johnnie say, before he had taken three steps. Who knows what it was she was nickering about. A child's enchantment. He didn't stop, he didn't turn around. He was now a guide to somewhere else, not well marked on the map.

His body was cleansing itself and so was his mind. The Indians had called the mushrooms flesh of the gods. Ascend clearheaded. They should have waited till they reached the top, taken a look at the fiery red pupil of the crater, make an informed decision about how close they wanted to get to such things with sulfurous eyes.

The ferns gave way to a forest of hardwoods. The density opened and closed like a fist. His boots sucked obscenely in the skin of black mud. Ahead he heard what sounded like a laugh track, weird peals of artificial hilarity, which he mistook for monkeys but on up the trail was a cluster of calabash trees, heavy with globular fruit, gourds like great green tits suspended from the branches populated by a flock of crows, maybe a dozen of them, eerie with mirth. Haw haw haw—real comedians. When he did finally see monkeys, feeding high up in a sapodilla tree, he wouldn't have known they were there if not for the sound of fruit scraps raining down through the leaves. They were vervets, he was pretty sure; at maturity about three feet tall. Catherinians called them apes and ate them.

The thing about the mushrooms was, he had done them before, and now was afraid of them, didn't want to lose control. The monkeys were fine, just the way they were, and what could be more surreal than the jungle, just as it was, slapping into your face. He trotted through an immense echoing hush of exalted space, like the interiors of cathedrals, here composed by towering colonnades of silk cotton trees. The path steepened and when it leveled off again he was in an airless thicket of huge bamboo, its girth about the same as his upper thigh. The dead trunks interspersed among the live stalks had a glow like goldenrod, precise stripes of light that punctured deep into the shadows. The room of the jungle darkened and he listened to a rain shower farther up the mountainside, scraping through the canopy. It clattered southward and away from him like a flight of locusts. He had purposely shortened his stride, checking the reflexive leaps and stretches he would have made under other circumstances to enjoy the precarious dance of footing.

As he crossed a shallow stream, he heard, faint at first, what was easily imagined as an electric razor—then on the opposite bank was a dead black snake, its head crushed, swarmed with horseflies. The first sign of their human company, today on Soufrière, since the trailhead. Here the foliage became so thick it was impossible to step off the path, even to urinate, without being slashed and swallowed.

Tillman was making an effort to keep Adrian moving; she was beginning to feel the punishing rate in her legs. Sally and Johnnie were on their own schedule, which he acquiesced to more than he thought he should, because of Sally, whom today he regarded as The Innocent. Meaning, she really hadn't expected to be spending her day on the volcano, tripping. By default, he was the one responsible, had to hold himself back, not run for the sheer joyous punishment of the challenge, and he resented that, and resented that he had been sucked into the drama back in Retreat, which had preempted his intention to ask around about Isaac. The ugliness of his voice bludgeoned the peace of the mountainside, trespassed on its integrity, and so he gave up hollering back down the trail for his companions, and at the waterfall he removed his pack, deciding he had better wait for everybody, stop using the mountain this way, against Johnnie, as though it were proof the time had arrived for her to tone up. Objective evidence—something's wrong with your life, something in the way you see things is slowing me down. He'd deliver one last pep talk and then push on, every man for himself. Private parties.

The waterfall, more accurately a short cascade of small waterfalls, spilled over humps of gray boulders into a pool of cool clear water distilled from the slopes of the volcano, a mercy to parched throats and safer to drink than what sputtered out of the tap in Howard Bay. He lay on his stomach on a flat rock baking in a circle of sun and lowered his whole face into the pool, feeling its wonderful sting of cold. With his eyes closed, he drank until he felt rehydrated and then lifted out his head refreshed, watching a crayfish angling along the gravel of the bottom, but when he saw where it headed he jumped up, revolted, wanting to spit the water back out. The crayfish joined a ring of other crayfish, feeding on the white threads of flesh at the severed wrist of a puny black hand, its long fingers curled toward the surface.

He found a dead branch and raked the thing out, saw its fur and realized what it was, a monkey's paw. With the stick he flung it back into the bush, where it was meant to be and made a better secret of itself. A wave of nausea passed through him and then everything was back to normal. He stood up on a point of rock to sight back down the trail, visible in three framed openings before it hooked deep and vanished into the plush green mass. From this new vantage he saw what he hadn't noticed before, a tent pitched on the perimeter of the glade behind the boulders, two surplus canvas half shelters, buttoned together ineffectively at the peak. He called out but no one responded or seemed to be around, so he went over to explore. There was a fire ring containing a meal's worth of blackened bones, the hideously fanged skull of an infant devil, its cranium smashed open to get at its delicacy of brains. That was enough to put him off but there was something more, another monkey's paw, this one dangling from a low branch above the tent, a strip of sisal cord threaded through its palm, the paw shriveled and glossy, apparently smoke-cured, dried out as a fetish or grisly trophy. The tent was empty, not even a ground cover inside to sleep on, and Mitchell stood up from its entrance, saying *Fucking defects.*

He went back to where he had dropped his pack and sat down in the sun, removed his rank tee shirt and spread it out for a few minutes to dry while he ate a banana and took a swig of iced passion-fruit juice from his thermos. Before long, here came Tillman and Adrian, emerging into the clearing, the first two of his bad children, sweat-drenched, each with a wet triangle down the front of their shirts and half-moons under their arms, puffing with adulation for the sleeping beast Soufrière. Elation fixed on their dumbstruck faces. Tillman's mouth gasped like a fish's but words were not forthcoming through the flux of stimuli. Adrian broke the silence, testifying never did she think she would see and feel what she was seeing and feeling. Don't ask her to name it, please, she said. Everybody knew the name and it was the name of something, a place, that wasn't real. Back in the city, she had deluded herself into believing the half was a whole. Tillman set his pack down and found his voice.

"Fantastic!" He repeated the superlative several times. "I'd forgotten what I was doing here, living on this island. It's all right here."

You have to love them, Mitchell told himself. Don't grumble. "It's, like, *pulsating,*" Adrian said. "The beauty." It was so visceral and potent she said she could feel the volcano vibrating under her feet like the subway or something.

You ain't seen nothing yet, Mitchell told them. Save your amazement. Adrian asked where was the top and he explained they were less than halfway.

"It changes," Mitchell said. "It becomes a wasteland. Unless the weather changes we'll be going into the clouds." And then. . . well, they'd see for themselves. They'd connect.

"I'm so fucking connected already," Adrian laughed, "I'm the one who's going to erupt." She looked around in slow delight.

"We have it all to ourselves, that's what I can't get over. I'm not used to that. It's spooky, in a way."

Not exactly to ourselves, cautioned Mitchell, lifting his chin in the direction of the tent. There was a hunter's camp. Also, somewhere up ahead was a forest ranger. And either a youth group or possibly a family.

"Don't be surprised to see other people on top."

"Extraordinary," said Tillman, his hands outstretched, as if he were blessing the pool. Without saying why, Mitchell warned him not to drink the water. They saw Sally's yellow hair bobbing below them on the trail.

"Are you two all right?" Mitchell called down to her.

"The parrot," she yelled up ecstatically. "Did you see the parrot?"

"That's good luck," he shouted back. The indigenous parrots were virtually extinct. It was rare to spot one. Where was Johnnie? "She's right behind me. Hear her singing? Whew!"

"Tell her to put on her shoes," he hollered.

"She has them on. Did you see the begonias? God!"

"You have to keep up better. It's almost noon."

"Go on," Sally said. "We're doing fine. Don't worry about us. We'll catch up. Go on."

"We'll wait for you where the lava starts."

"All right. Go on."

Johnnie's head appeared in the lowest frame. "Don't drink the water up here," he called down to Sally, and then they were climbing again, going up.

Chapter 31

Sally soaked her feet in the pool below the largest cascade, massaging the cramp in her calf muscle, which didn't hurt the way she knew a cramp was supposed to hurt. She was aware of the lump in the muscle and the tugging, inside, but her body wasn't there in the regular sense, her head and her body weren't properly engaged, her head seemed to have taken over, all the body's energy and sensation channeled into it. There was a fascinating but also scary feeling of overload. Blisters had erupted on the backs of her heels too, big whitish domes, ready to burst, but she hadn't even known they were there until she took off her boots and socks.

"I don't feel it," said Johnnie with a lopsided grin and a lopsided look. Sally didn't know if she was talking about the pain or the thorn itself in the ball of her left foot, slivered into the callus, which she was trying to tweeze out with her fingernails. There was blood in Johnnie's shoe. "I just looked at my foot, not doing what it was supposed to, and knew something was wrong."

Sally was just about to say let me do it when Johnnie raised her head with a strange expression of alertness, as if she had heard an unusual noise.

"There's something here," she said meaningfully.

"What?"

"Like in Hawaii. The forbidden places. Spirits."

They both saw him simultaneously and stared. Someone had appeared on the rocks at the top of the waterfall and was looking down at them. A small man with slanted eyes, deformed by intensity.

It's him, Johnnie whispered. I know who he is.

Sally thought, forest ogre? volcano goblin? loup-garou? what? Is that a real person? she asked Johnnie. Neither of them could take their eyes off the creature; his own were welded to Johnnie. He is so

457

ugly, Sally said to herself. *Ugly.* Something made him heinous and ugly. She was amazed.

Where is Wilson? the man said. He had a mumbly voice. Johnnie seemed mesmerized by him. Sally tried to pull herself away from the mushrooms to answer.

He went up.

Him say to meet here, by de hole.

Who?

To give de bundle.

I don't know what you're talking about.

Where is Wilson? the man asked again.

Sally said if he ran he could catch him. Or wait for him to come back down in a couple hours. The guy was looking at Johnnie like, There she is, girl of my dreams. We're rape bait, Sally thought, feeling the threat of him tingle in her fingers. He definitely was making her nervous.

Him say to meet here.

Who are you talking about? Mitchell?

She couldn't tell you how many conversations she'd had like this on the island, as though a segment of the population had learned their verbal patterns off broken records. Is this guy really real? she hissed at Johnnie. This was going to be the last time she ever took psilocybin. The day was fated to be spoiled, the mushrooms were telling her now, one way or another, and now here was a visit, if she could trust what she saw written on his face, from madness. Everything had become difficult to understand. She started putting her boots back on, thinking, almost as if it were a riddle: The only way down is up.

Let's keep going, she said to Johnnie, who finally spoke herself, saying to the man on the rocks, Come down.

Don't encourage him, Sally protested.

It's all right, said Johnnie. He knows something. He's a messenger.

Johanna is so goddamn weird sometimes, Sally told herself. So deliberate.

Johnnie was saying, Do you feel it? Something's here.

Maybe he knows about the Indians, Johnnie said.

He's some kind of priest I think, said Johnnie. He might have magical powers.

On the trail Johnnie had put orchids in their hair, behind their ears. Sally took hers out now, tossing it into the pool, so as not to seem invitingly foolish.

He disappeared from the rocks above and then reappeared almost instantaneously, next to them, squatting on his heels, holding a parcel about the size of a shoebox, wrapped in newspaper and tied with a cross of cord.

Iman Ibrahim climbed down the rocks to where Erzulie was, telling himself he was no jungle bwoy, telling himself there were ape beasts, there were spirits he had knowledge of, there was an old language that echoed back to the incantatory songs of his earliest boyhood. Also, a type of serpent man, and a type of dog man, out in the darkness, watching him, last night while he hugged the campfire, waiting for first light, then waiting for Captain Eddins and his men to pass on the trail. He had not slept, had not come up against the desire to sleep. One thing he didn't like about the jungle was you could not see very far, you always had to listen carefully. He had posted signs, one in a tree and one in the water, warning *Stay back.* Telling himself, there were men and anti-men, spirits good and bad together—tricksters. Everything had a dense, heavy, perilous, glutinous presence, which he knew was the mountain. He shot an ape beast with Sergeant's pistol and ate it, trying to get close to the power. You are eating a boy, he had said out loud, after the fire had burned the hair off the beast.

Telling himself, Here is the woman in the waves and she welcomes me. That is something.

Selwyn had said tell the white man the fellow by the name of Isaac waited for him, up Soufrière; tell the white man pass the bundle to Isaac, it was important, then go down to the road, take a jitney to Queenstown, never say what happened—that was the plan but now he knew he didn't like this plan, he wasn't telling himself why.

She said, Do you know about the Indians?

He said, Yes.

She said, Are they the people who live here?

He said, Yes.

She said, Do you know their name?

He said, Yes. Jumbies.

Jumbies?

Yes. Loas.

The big woman said, Put on your shoe and let's go.

Wait, he said. Wait.

The big woman said, No, we have to go now.

She said, Come with us and tell me about the Indians.

The big woman said, No, you stay here. We're going.

Wait, he said. He tried to think of a good reason to tell her.

Why?

The bundle. It must go to the white man.

Why?

It is his.

Do you want some of our mushroom tea? she said.

He said, Yes.

The big woman said, Don't give him any of that. Are you crazy?

She said, Do you know what it is?

He didn't but he said, Yes.

She said, Do you want to see the Indians?

He didn't but he said, Yes.

When she took the plastic bottle out of the big woman's pack, the big woman said, This is really stupid, you know. I'm going ahead. You can put the bundle in my pack and I'll take it to Mitchell. Iman looked at her, puzzling over this, knowing she shouldn't have it, but then he gave it to her and she left.

In the bottle was black shit turned liquid. She drank from it and he drank from it and then it was empty. Don't worry, she called up the path, we are right behind you.

She started walking and he followed after her saying, Wait, wait, wait, wait.

She said, Tell me if you can see them.

He said, Yes, I see them.

The face of his mother blinked into his mind.

He said, Wait. He said, It is not safe for us. I am here to protect you, he said. There was a plan and they were in it but it was not the same plan as before. Then he could move but he couldn't speak. The jungle swarmed with moths of light and began to fly apart.

Chapter 32

It was less sunny and Mitchell began to worry about the clouds, congealed in a tissuey mass around the summit. The jungle was opening up, broken more frequently by sky. They passed a rank of spiky gru-gru palms, sylvan terrorists, the bayonet-like thorns hung with a gauzy lace of webs.

The deciduous highlands were trimly grassed, the landscaped order of its trees and sun-dappled hollows reminiscent of a city park. Here at its interface of green and gold, the mountain began to tease the climbers with its true identity. Catspaws of cooler breeze evaporated the sweat on their faces. Mitchell's pace was unrelenting: Tillman and Adrian fell behind.

The ground became crusty and porous and he came to the labyrinthine gouge of trails, the main branch clearly evident, entering the girdle of tall brown grasses that thrived below the upper cone. He could hear the sweep of the wind, the crystal tinkle and patter of cinders loosened by his advance, the interrogatory piping of an unfamiliar bird. He looked down the island's backbone at the surrounding peaks, wonderfully Euclidian, the classical proportion of their spatial properties like a textbook illustration.

Ten or twelve stories above him, there was a fault in the plane of the slope, as if the land had sighed, creating a long rampart of rock which from Mitchell's position made a false horizon, obstructing the view of the summit. At places, the trail cut deep into the surface, as if he were tunneling his way up. There were notches and footholds in the rock ledge. He climbed to the top, pausing to fill his lungs with bracing air.

When he saw the police patrol he thought, This cannot be right. One of the officers wore an olive-colored kepi; the other a beret. They waved but he surmised they were waving him away, so he kept going, and they yelled for him to come back. They had prisoners, or so it appeared, three riffraff hunkered in the dirt. He was breathing hard from the deliberateness of the ascent he had made, thinking this was how he liked his blood to feel, pounding in circulation, fat with oxygen.

What's up? he asked. The officer who spoke to him wore a pair of field binoculars around his neck; there were captain's chevrons on the sleeve of his blouse. All four had shaved heads, muddied boots. Their countenance was unconcerned but their intention was obscure.

The questions came with a sobering and fatalistic, familiar rhythm. Captain Eddins told him to remove his pack and open it for inspection. For no apparent reason, Eddins withdrew the envelope George James had given him to forward to Isaac, and slid it into his back pocket. Why are you taking my letter? Mitchell demanded. Evidence, said Captain Eddins, without further explanation. His heart rate leveled off to its routine. Eddins ordered one of the privates to frisk him and he thought, Oh shit. The breeze was cold and he clamped his jaws shut to prevent his teeth from chattering.

Tillman and Adrian came up, their faces rapt with discovery. What's wrong? Adrian said, unable to do anything about her grin. She had a photocopy of her passport folded in her back pocket. Tillman mentioned all the right names, invoking the Tourist Board and the Chamber of Commerce. Bandits, said Eddins. Ruffians. He cocked his eyebrows and smiled, as if they were sharing a practical joke. With apologies, their haversacks were searched. Eddins jutted his chin toward the men on the ground. You see? he said. Bad men. This was for their own protection.

How so? asked Tillman, achieving the vastly undesirable result of being assigned an escort and exiled with Adrian into the clouds.

Mitchell started to protest but thought better of it. This event was wholly artificial, he could feel it. An exercise in power. He calmly sat down on the ledge to wait for Sally and Johnnie and ate one of the tuna sandwiches Johnnie had made for them and drank most of the juice remaining in his thermos. He looked out at the sea which was dressed in light—foxfire and jewels. It did not occur to him this was anything more than harassment. Which leader? he thought, which philosophy today? The two officers were not on friendly terms with one another.

He saw Sally then, entering the maze of lava and grass. Rising to his feet, he waved and shouted her name, wanting her to look up, see whom he was with, figure it out and compose herself for trouble.

Turn back, perhaps, though that would be a shame. Eddins told him to stop signaling.

This is the signal for hello, Mitchell said.

When she reached the point where the trail wedged into the wall of the shelf, he said he was going to give her a hand up and nobody made an objection. Her face was flushed and disconcerted, her hair dark and wet on her forehead. She wanted to know what was happening and he told her he wasn't sure.

Where's Johnnie? he asked. Sally popped up beside him with a balletic leap.

Were you to meet someone back at the waterfall? Sally said. He shook his head and frowned. She looked puzzled by this and began to say there was a man back there, but then Eddins interrupted, calling her over. I'm too stoned to be dealing with the police, she whispered as she obeyed Eddins, yet the next second she was engaged in a battle of wills over her identification and Mitchell was astounded by her contentiousness, her fearless lack of cooperation.

Eddins wanted to look in her knapsack; Sally made a brazen claim about her rights. For some reason, Eddins backed off from the demand and asked where the other woman was and Sally answered Johanna was not far behind.

Eddins said they would wait for her and he allowed Sally and Mitchell to sit on the ledge to rest their legs after the climb. Sally lowered her voice and said somebody's going to a lot of trouble here. The jungle riffled below their feet, like choppy water, as the wind came up and they perused the treeline, waiting for their lost fifth to emerge.

Where is she? he asked.

She drank more tea. She gave some to the lunatic who didn't know what it was. Mitchell, Sally said, look, I can't get my thoughts to cohere but there's a problem. Let's stand up and go, she didn't think the police would do anything to try to stop them.

This is so stupid, she said loudly for Eddins' benefit. Really really stupid.

Mitchell was flabbergasted by her behavior. What the fuck is going on? he snapped, grappling with his temper, and Sally whispered as she unknotted her legs to stand that down by the waterfall she had put something into her knapsack that evidently shouldn't be there. Don't ask me what it is, she said angrily, ask Johanna and that psychopath she's with. I can't think straight, This is some kind of a setup, I think, Mitchell, she said. Let's go back. Right now, let's start walking down.

Mitchell had stood up with her and together they confronted the end of Captain Eddins' patience. We have to go back down and find our friend, Sally told him. She might be in trouble.

Johanna Fernandez, said Eddins, stepping toward Sally, unbuckling the holster on his belt. Mitchell wasn't certain if he was referring to Johnnie herself, naming her, or if he had come to the conclusion that Sally was not who she claimed to be. This has gone too far, Mitchell said, and he instinctively placed himself between the two of them. Eddins reached to shove him aside, but Mitchell wrenched himself free of his grip. When he heard the first shot, Mitchell thought, *And now the bastards are shooting.* Eddins himself looked bewildered by the gunfire, scanning down the slope like the rest of them. Mitchell felt a spontaneous detachment from the present danger—what made it easy to kill with a gun also made it easy to stand there while someone far away shot at you. The second shot came, whether from the same direction or not he couldn't tell. With a sharp intake of breath, Sally stumbled back into his arms. After the third shot he and Eddins both located Collymore at the edge of the trees, his pistol raised straight up into the air. Run, he heard one of the cops say, and thought for sure he was telling this to the men on the ground. Two of them scrambled off into the high grass; the third remained sitting right where he was, peering down the slope and yelling, What the fuck is this nonsense, Eddins? who is down there shooting at we?

He remembered looking at the ocean, its cold sparkle, wisps of precipitation licking out from the clouds and evaporating before they fell to the surface, and then he was engulfed by the devastating task of saving her. It was not a time for revelation, and she said only what she might be expected to say, that she was sorry for the mortal burden she had just become and that what she wanted was to live.

Her unopened pack was left behind, there on the ledge. As far as Mitchell was willing to say, that was the last anybody ever saw of it.

When they found Johnnie on the trail she was hysterical, screaming and sobbing, screaming *What happened to Sally? What happened to her? He was trying to protect us!* but he passed by without attempting to deal with her, consumed by the totality of his labor. When they passed by Eddins facedown on the trail, the cop who was helping him with Sally put her down, and before Mitchell took her up again, without even thinking he bent over Eddins' body with its bloody insignia and removed the envelope from the captain's back pocket, tucking it into his own. Somewhere on the periphery of the terrible rush to the trailhead, Tillman and Adrian tripped and faltered, pale ghosts, clumsy with horror, and then Ballantyne was there like an answered prayer and Mitchell, groaning with hope, was saying, Where have you been? Man, where were you?

He remembered reading Jolene's note, tied with a rib of frond to the steering wheel, holding it in front of him while he drove. *Miss: Him does love dis mash-up child more than me. We gone back. I am sorry for dis trouble.*

At the clinic in Scarborough, every breath he took threatened to strangle him with fumes of desperation. There was a pernicious argument whether or not to transfuse Sally. She could speak but couldn't say what her blood type was. It can go very nicely or it can go very badly, Betancourt explained. If they make it they make it, if they seize up they seize up, but she had lost too much already, he believed, not to risk it, and so he rode along with them, squeezing a plastic container of fresh whole blood into her arm. Almost an hour passed before Betancourt said quietly, There's a reaction. Sally became combative and then, shivering feverishly, went into shock. Mitchell was only marginally aware of slamming into the long-horned Brahman bull, careening into the ditch, the renewed flow of blood, this time Tillman's, his forehead shattering the windshield. The cowherd blocked Ballantyne's Land Rover with his body, demanding compensation, being a silly bastard; under ordinary circumstances killing a cow was a serious affair. Ballantyne wasted time reasoning with the man until Adrian, shrieking at him to go, hitched her leg over the transmission housing and stomped down on the accelerator, sending the cowherd windmilling into the darkness. In his mindlessness, he welcomed the pain in his wrist, which worked on him like a stimulant, a transfixing point of clarity in the void, and on that part of the ride Mitchell was back on the mountain again, Sally over his shoulder, soaking him with warm, slippery blood, the rain pelting them, depth and texture draining out of the jungle until it became two-dimensional, a black on black intaglio; the palpable foreknowledge of death, his muscles quaking under the sad weight of the future she would not attend as he carried her off the mountain. He kept smelling the bay rum smell of Captain Eddins, and Johnnie was tripping, totally freaked, blindly keening in the downpour, what happened? what happened? over and over again, until the violence he felt against her was incommunicable, and an unforgiving mantra ran through his head like a vicious jingle: You are stupid, you've been stupid all your life, this should be you, *I wish it were you.*

As they lifted Sally into the vestibule of the hospital, she grasped his right hand, shooting a blast of flame up through his arm. He drooped to his knees, trying to ease her leverage on his broken wrist, which brought his face down next to hers. *Let go*, he was forced to beg her, *please, please let go.* Her eyes were upturned to his, her forehead creased as if she were considering how to refuse him, and he listened to her shallow inhalations, waiting, wondering that after all she'd been through, how Sally found the strength for this, but she wouldn't release him and he had no choice but to peel back her fingers one by one. He curled up on the wooden floor, spasmed with pain, while the attendants and nurses placed Sally on a gurney and wheeled her away, Adrian by her side, offering Sally a better hand than his.

Tillman and a nurse helped Mitchell to his feet and then he turned on Johnnie, excoriating her, bellowing, a maniac. That she didn't understand what had happened only further indicted her in his eyes, he had reversed and replayed the mental video of all of them on the volcano, editing her out of the frames, *and guess what*, he was saying, *without you there nothing bad happens.* He pointed down the dark corridor where they had taken Sally. *That should have been you*, he seethed. *Not Sally, you*, he thundered brutally. Johnnie went blank and he asked Tillman to take her back to Howard Bay and said in parting that he wanted her off the island, tomorrow wouldn't be soon enough. What he was saying was already inside of him, had been there all along.

Blood had made the fabric of his shirt stiff and waxy; the nurses assumed he'd been shot as well and cut it off him, searching for the wound while he stood sagging in the vestibule, suddenly disoriented after his rage, and then they pulled him into a room, making him lay down on a cot, and banged him with morphine and he remembered thinking as he swirled lovingly away into the drug's vortex, *so this is where she goes.*

The remainder of the night he had to reconstruct later. Off-hours emergency service at the National Hospital amounted to a nurse ringing up staff at their homes, rousing them from bed. It took several hours just to get the X-ray technician there. The surgeon arrived, but he was an orthopedic man and, after examining the X-rays, seeing how the bullet had spent itself, fragmenting right against one of Sally's ribs near her sternum and had caused no respiratory distress, determined that the wound was not life-threatening, ordered more blood, and somehow tracked down Doc Travis on Cotton Island, who said he would come back across the channel within the hour. They had his wrist on ice to take down the swelling; his arm was off away from him, a second self. He watched them entomb it in starchy white plaster and had the feeling he could get up and walk out and leave them to their business, and then a nurse with a moon face and vaguely nunnish dress came in and used the word expired, talking about Sally, and he didn't register it, he had no idea what she meant. They finished with the cast and left him there. He was conscious of the plaster tightening, growing hard around the core of an immense throb, and he remembered getting up, going to find Adrian and Sally, walking down the creaky wooden hallways in some sort of misty suspension created by the fatiguing light of dawn, calling their names, opening doors, a shirtless white man zombie roaming the hospital. Then he was in a room with them. Adrian was sitting in a chair, unrecognizable, her eyes dead as dead and her face puffed grotesquely with sorrow. She was inconsolable, she didn't want to be touched or held. I forbid anyone to ever see me dead, she whispered, and that was all she said. She had kept vigil with Sally and now was watching them wash the body. The window was open and birds outside in a mango tree were singing. He had never seen a corpse before and now here was Sally on a rubber sheet, a syrupy knob of blood capping the bullet's vivid hole, her head and breasts lolling, her arms and legs flopping with unspeakable submission as the nurses rolled her, and he thought, what will ever happen to this ache, when would he ever have a heart again, and if there was one world, if we all is one, if there was a human universal mocking borders and nations, transcending the divisions, it was and only could be grief. It was all that anyone would ever have in common. It wrote the book on love. It put everything in its place.

A minister came in saying Christ has risen. Mitchell had forgotten it was Easter and the pathetic irony sickened him. Attendants came to take Sally over to the morgue and Adrian in a voice that no one dared trifle with said, we're staying with her, and with supernatural weariness he followed along in the procession.

The bureaucratic horror show began. They laid Sally out on a steel table in the middle of a windowless cinderblock room, not bothering to cover her until Adrian insisted they must. Within minutes there was a crowd of officials and police. An argument ensued about who was supposed to be on duty back at the station on this holiday. They wrote contradictory reports that Mitchell and Adrian refused to sign. Doc Travis finally arrived in a bathing suit and windbreaker. Someone raised the issue of autopsy, which the law demanded in cases of violent death. Grambling, the Peace Corps' man, concurred. The hospital's coroner and cutter were sent for. In death, Sally was hypnotic; Mitchell's disbelieving eyes kept returning to her inert shape; he kept thinking, *dead*, the most rivetingly exotic of states. She definitely did not look like any moment she'd get up and walk away, nor did she look angelic, beatific, or at rest in peace; she looked horribly, everlastingly lifeless and dead. The coroner couldn't be found. Doc Travis said *shitass* and grudgingly agreed to conduct the postmortem examination. The house cutter wanted triple overtime for work on Easter Sunday and a hospital administrator refused to allow it and a Mr. Madlock was sent for instead. Saconi came and got in a tussle with one of the cops when they wouldn't let him enter. They took him away before Mitchell could get outside to speak to him even though he didn't know what he would have said. There was too much hubbub, too much yelling and disagreement, too many questions and too many questioners and Mitchell stopped talking, his mind vacant and his emotions battered and anesthetized. His wrist seemed to be the only alive part of him. Doc Travis left, saying he would have his breakfast and be back. Madlock walked in with a cleaver and hacksaw and Adrian lost control with an arm-swinging ferocity that paralyzed the scene. She succeeded in making everybody get out but Grambling, Mitchell, a nurse, and Madlock. Her authority was uncontestable, her voice resonating with near-hysterical command. Madlock went to work. Tell him to stop, she shrieked at Grambling, look at what he's doing to her, tell him to stop. Her eyes bulged, wild and terrified. Doc Travis returned and said, Christ Almighty, look the fuckin mess this man make. He declared it out of the question to determine cause of death. Adrian finally broke, standing in the corner with her face to the wall, wracked with howling sobs, saying Sally, I'm sorry. I'm sorry sorry sorry they're doing this to you. There were two women, PCVs, waiting outside, and when Mitchell told Adrian they were waiting for her to go with them to Sally's house to pick out clothes to dress the body properly, she became calm and lucid again and agreed to go with them after making Mitchell promise he'd stay. He didn't want to anymore but said he would. Fancy up the corpse, was how Madlock put it, once Adrian was out of range.

Afterward, it was out of their hands; Grambling insisted on offering condolence in the form of alcohol and took them in his car down to a waterfront bar. Mitchell wore a surgeon's blouse but the rest of him looked as though he had been dragged through carnage and could use a good hosing off. Oblivious to their suffering, Grambling drank two double vodkas while Adrian sat staring insensate out at the street and Mitchell felt that any moment he was going to black out. He mumbled his response to Grambling's questions about what had happened up north on the mountain, then Grambling turned his attention to Adrian, seeming to make a pass at her, an irrelevant contribution to the larger unreality. Adrian looked right through him, then stood up and left without a word. Mitchell wanted to react but failed to move himself out from underneath the stupefying crush of Sally, and when he finally got to his feet and out the door, Adrian was gone and he didn't know where. Grambling waddled out after him on his flat feet, only to say it was time to notify the embassy in Barbados, getting in his car and driving off without offering Mitchell a lift.

He took a taxi out to Howard Bay, floating in a cold-blooded dream. News of this atrocity was now on the radio. He went straight for the shower, past the closed door of Johnnie's bedroom. Keeping the cast dry proved too much of a task and he didn't bother. The water failed to grant him a new life and, after toweling off, he opened up the medicine cabinet and swallowed one of Johnnie's amphetamines. He put on fresh clothes and then went to her room, through the door without knocking, without looking or seeing, took her map down from the wall and made her poorer by a thousand dollars, then left without speaking or hearing but with an image in his head of Johnnie curled on the mattress in a fetal position, her eyes red and bleary, her jaw quivering as she sucked like an infant on her three middle fingers, and by the time he reached the front room the image had lodged in his chest, imitating a heart, which thawed him only enough to double back, find his briefcase, remove the envelope addressed to Johnnie. There's your mail, he said numbly, placing it on the pillow in front of her face. He gritted his teeth and told her Sally had died, no one knew quite why. The tears rolled but she didn't move or respond, and he left, unchained his bike and took it up to the road, pounding the pedals all the way up Ooah Mountain and down to the airport, disciplining the rising chorus of Furies in his head to sing in one voice, against her, one shrill song of negation. In the airport bar he found the charter pilot he wanted to see. It was of course only a question of money, in advance. First flight out in the morning, the pilot said. He'd be prepared to leave at daybreak, a flight plan filed for Cotton Island, she could board right where the road crossed the runway, he'd be there waiting, they'd do a stop-and-go on Cotton, then on to Barbados. No problem other than the exit tax, he said winking. Illegal routes were expensive. You look bad, brother, said the pilot, taking the money. I shouldn't ask, eh?

Then he was standing out in front of the terminal, straddling his bike, lost in the glare of midafternoon, his blood thumping explosively. What he didn't want was to start second-guessing himself, reflecting upon the myriad implications of what had taken place on

Soufrière, because he didn't understand the implications, he didn't understand how the island had become a beast that had turned on him, that ever since he had come into this house his destiny had been bound to the beast, and that one day the beast would rear up on its hind legs and serpent's tail and have them all dancing in flames, until their flesh circled their bones in a swirl of flakes, and their hearts cooked into bricks of charcoal. He didn't even know the name of this beast but he knew this: that Johnnie had betrayed him. That there was nothing complicated, clandestine, or conspiratorial about her betrayal; that its consequence was coincidental. That she had betrayed him by being who she was: it was as simple as shoes; it was as simple as—not drugs, but what the drugs meant to her, a way to make the world more than it was. Drugs were Johnnie's democracy. Drugs were her good intentions, her foreign policy, the happy face she wanted to paint on the world.

An Avro took off behind him and he suddenly realized Adrian had a seat booked on the flight. He turned the bike toward Queenstown and rode to Sally's house on Ballycieux Lane, he didn't know quite why until he got there and found Sally's stoop deep in flowers, the yard filled with neighborhood women bawling, and when he went inside it was crowded with volunteers, teachers from the school, the minister of education was there, and so were Saconi and Adrian, packing up Sally's things, Mitchell and Saconi sat down at the kitchen table with a bottle of rum between them and by the time it was empty it was dark outside and Tillman was there and the three of them had told Saconi all they knew, and Saconi told him, what the hell is wrong with you, Mitchell, you ain't so savvy, you know, you can't see this is a police state now and we gunning the people down, that boy Iman Ibrahim is police. We can't go to massa so is weself we try to kill.

What massa? Who massa? said Mitchell, wired, on the precipice of self-exit, some sort of out-of-bodyness.

You massa, said Saconi, himself drunk.

You mean Sally?

No, mahn, you know what the fuck I am saying, said Saconi. He gripped Mitchell's left hand in his, put his head on the table, and wept.

Adrian was steely and composed. How is it possible to fly away from this? she said. What sort of person would I be when I got off the plane at Kennedy? She was staying overnight in Sally's house, going down to the school in the morning; she wanted Tillman to bring her bags there and wouldn't hear his soft-spoken objections to remain at Rosehill, at least for another day or two. Sometime after midnight, they put Mitchell's bicycle in the back of Tillman's station wagon and the two of them went back out to Howard Bay. They stopped at Mitchell's cottage; Tillman remained in the car while Mitchell staggered in, pawing his way through the darkness to the bathroom to take another Durophet to keep him on his feet, finally turning on the light in the hallway to go into Johnnie's room to stand over her mattress, gathering into himself all the malignant ugliness he could summon, everything he would have seen in the bathroom mirror if he had turned the light on and stood for a long time looking. Johnnie hadn't moved, hadn't taken her fingers out of her mouth, hadn't stopped whimpering. He hovered over her for a moment before he realized she was talking to him, whispering to him in a broken, adolescent voice, and he had to squat down to be able to hear. *Bobby did this,* she kept repeating. *Bobby did this.* What does *bollo* mean? he asked gruffly. He had to ask several times before she told him, in a voice so low he had to put his ear close to her lips. *Cunt,* she said. It means *cunt.* I see, he said, giddy, taunting her. You are Bobby's cunt. He was pleased to hear the damning power of the word. I'll be back for you, he said. You're on a flight at six.

Then he left her again and went with Tillman up to Rosehill. They sat in the kitchen for a while. Tillman opened two cans of beef consommé and they drank them down. The second hit of speed roared through his veins, bringing a ragged, jerky, resurrective surge and no hint whatsoever of redemption. Tillman surrendered to bed, leaving Mitchell the keys to the station wagon and access to the bar. His mind was a static, wordless hum and he preferred it that way, nursing a bottle of beer until five when he got in the car and went down the road for Johnnie. She was sitting in darkness in the front room, smoking a cigarette, dressed in the clothes she had first arrived in, wearing sunglasses, her hair pulled back in a ponytail and her sun visor on, her bags at her feet. "This isn't right," she said. "I didn't do anything to deserve this."

"What did you give Sally on the mountain?"

"I didn't give her anything, Mitch. This guy who came out of the jungle did. He had a package. He said it was for you."

"What was in it?"

"I don't know," she said coolly. "He wouldn't let me come up with her. He was paranoid, he was seeing things. I shouldn't have let him drink the tea."

"We're not going to discuss this."

"Just tell me this. What am I guilty of?"

"Of being here."

He carried her things out to the car, not to help her but to force her to move, and the two of them climbed in. Another dawn was breaking as they crested Ooah Mountain. The silence in the car was hellish and evil and he accepted that this hell was his own, it came from him, it was him. She asked him to stop at the top of the last foothill overlooking Brandon Vale and the airport. The De Havilland was out on the airstrip already, waiting for her, glistening in the pale blue advent of dawn. She lit a final cigarette and whipped the match down on the floormat, stamping on it, changed her mind about her anger and turned to look at him with a matter-of-fact expression.

"Mitch, what are you doing in this fucking place? You don't belong here either, especially now." She put a hand carefully atop his trembling knee. "Come with me," she said. "I know how to make money."

"What are you saying to me? What?" He started to cry, push her. "Get the fuck out. *Get the fuck out!*"

"You're sending me back to him," she said with urgency, pleading. "Don't, please, God, please don't."

"I know exactly where I'm sending you," he rasped, and that was all he needed to say.

She wouldn't let him take her any further but sprang open the door and jumped out, leaving behind everything but one of her straw bags. He turned off the engine and watched her walk away under the streetlamps of the village, through splashes of light and shadow, down the hill past a cluster of houses where the dogs came out into the street to harry her, the sounds he heard drifting up the slope came from her as well, an anguished chorus of sobs and yelps, and she continued trudging onward to the bottom of the mountain, passing by the stripped hulk of *Miss Defy* in the cane field, to the plane.

"We're here to talk freely," the friends of golf said, after the original foursome became a threesome then finally a twosome, teeing up on Johnnie as if she were a particularly problematic par five. "Why did she leave? If you know."

She didn't simply leave, Mitchell told them. She didn't leave. He had sent her away.

"Oh," they said, flashing one another looks—here was something new; you didn't get anything from this guy except Hamlet, if you didn't ask the right questions. "That doesn't look good, does it?"

"No," he had to agree. "It probably doesn't."

✳   ✳   ✳

He slept for a day and a half, and would have slept more, but they made such a noise at his door that he had no choice but to get up before they broke it down. He opened up to an NPF team, six of them altogether, traveling in two vehicles, three to a faction. Get dressed, they said. Although the police who had been on Soufrière had said they were unable to corroborate Mitchell's statement, that same Saturday, early in the morning, a forest ranger had spotted someone whom he knew as Iman Ibrahim camped at a waterfall on the path up the volcano, and this fellow fit Mitchell Wilson's description. What description? Mitchell thought. His brain was foggy. All he remembered telling them was a guy in a khaki tee shirt and blue jeans.

Come, the police at his door said. They were taking him up north to Scarborough, where they were holding Iman Ibrahim, after capturing him in the mountains.

The villagers had assembled themselves around the small station that still bore the seal of the queen above its door. The banana plantations stretched up the mountainsides and out of sight into a dust of clouds, where the Rastamen lived off mangoes thieved from government-owned trees. Beautiful children, naked or in hand-me-down rags, ran forward laughing and yelling as the cars stopped and Mitchell and the policemen climbed out. He put on his sunglasses to close his eyes off to the crowd.

The sounds of excitement faded. The children slowed their wild dance and backed away, wide-eyed and suddenly shy from the wonder of a man so different so near. *Ahll dis wickedness, bwoy.* He looked around at the subdued young women making babies and fat matrons in bright-colored dresses, the schoolgirls in spotless blue and white uniforms, country girls with hard new breasts pushing out blouses hand-sewn from flour sacks, all pressed in for a view of him as the afternoon gathered the golden accents of twilight. A mongrel dog ran through the lot and a boy whacked it, *tek daht!,* with the broad side of the cutlass he carried to open waternuts. He felt cold, disjoined, elevated out of his own humanity, knowing his color was still the color of their fate and hope for mercy. Where are all the men? he wondered.

The police escorted him into the station, lifting their knees high in their black cotton pants or leopard fatigues. The officer at the desk in the unpainted front room swung his arm out and back revealing a sweat-soaked armpit and they followed his direction down a passageway of gray concrete to a rear exit and stepped out into the sunlight again.

The inspector in charge of the case, known to be a Kingsley loyalist, was waiting, dressed in street clothes and black leather shoes without socks. Mitchell remained on the doorstep, looking at the white dust in the creases of the man's ankle, thinking the same dirt would show up black on his own skin. The collar of the inspector's blue-striped shirt was open, the top buttons unfastened to exhibit the gum-pink shine of a starburst scar on his chest, no clearer badge of authority necessary. Strong, arrogant, and he would not die. The small dirt square smelled of urine and decay and the musky fertility of the lowlands. An occasional ribbon of breeze carried the sweet rotting odor of bitte into the village from an arrowroot-processing factory farther up the small river that flowed alongside the road. The private who had escorted Mitchell snapped his heels together in response to a nod from the inspector and took one step back away from him.

"Yes, well, come down, mahn," said the inspector. He turned to survey his arrangement and Mitchell continued looking at the back of the inspector's head rather than the line of men awaiting him.

"Here now," said the inspector, swinging his arm toward the twelve, their hard and scornful faces waiting for Mitchell to acknowledge their presence. The inspector's arm remained in the air and he spoke to the space between Mitchell and the men. Look closely at these men here, the inspector was saying, and if you see the man who fired upon you on Mount Soufrière, identify the fellow by walking up and touching him.

The cast on Mitchell's hand and forearm was unbearably hot and sticky, nightmarishly tight, as though his arm was half stuck in the bone-ringed gullet of a large and powerful snake. He showed no intention of moving. He felt a whimsical desire to live on horseback, to walk home to his family's house in Virginia like a Confederate parolee. The inspector bent his knees slightly, impatient, and pressed his body up to its full height, imploring his cooperation.

"Yes, please. Step up, mahn. Walk down the line and tap the fella if you see him."

He glanced briefly at the row of faces but could not overcome the inertia holding him fast in place. Some of the men watched the ground, some looked straight ahead with more apathy than interest and some eyed him disdainfully, anticipating judgment. Who are these men and are they being paid for their time? he thought; then their faces blurred but still he stared ahead as if reviewing them, not comprehending how he was to fulfill his purpose here. Saturday remained fragmented, shattered into pieces, moments so slow as to be endless, but the whole eluded him and the danger never had a face to it.

A man grabbed a running child by the shoulder and set him down roughly at his feet. It was nearing suppertime. The inspector spoke again, his voice harsh, intimidating.

"Come, mahn, come. Step up to the men."

He didn't want to touch anyone, that was the problem. It would be an obscene and juvenile gesture, resonant with vindictiveness. There would be no need. He knew from the general movement in the crowd behind him people were beginning to feel cheated by his inability to act, and he wanted to scatter them back to their own affairs.

"Go on, please. Positive identification is the law."

He took a step closer and stopped, scrutinizing them for the first time. First man too young. Second man looked vaguely like someone he knew. Third man too big. Fourth man too ugly to say even, yes, you are part of this. Fifth man dressed too rich and stylish. Six the same as the first five, black men with no reason to tolerate the humiliation of his indecision. Seven was a smiling student he recognized, enrolled at the Teacher's College. He raised his eyebrows and nodded: *Hey.* The eighth man lodged his face into his shoulder and Mitchell stared, empty-headed, and continued on to those remaining. The third man in line called for the inspector to dismiss them, but instead the policeman took Mitchell by the arm and drew him forward, walking him down the line.

They came back to the eighth man, the fellow shaking like a cold, wet dog, his head still buried tight in his shoulder in a posture of such classical guilt Mitchell thought, Get me away from him. Bits of grass and leaves adhered to his natty hair, as though he had spent a night in the bush, and he rocked from foot to foot, bent in shame. Mitchell noted the high cheekbones and long shallow cheeks, the darting set of slanting eyes and crest of hair on his forehead, asking himself could he identify this man they meant for him to identify. He looked so much like nobody. Then he was doing it, he lifted his broken hand, touching the arm of the fellow with his swollen fingers, thinking Here is the death you gave my friend. Vicious. Violent. Unworthy of us all. A man he didn't know whom he could perhaps kill without remorse and he told himself, You don't know who he is and you must not feel this way.

The inspector exhaled satisfaction, digging into his pocket to pay the men who had volunteered their innocence.

"Wilson," said the inspector, "why you hesitate so?"

But even before they deposited him back at Howard Bay, the car radio was broadcasting a contradictory allegation, the Government Information Service reporting that the American woman Sally Jorgensen had been murdered by a pro-PIP bandit at large in the mountains, the ringleader of a counterrevolutionary movement, a former Scuffletown youth, son of the infamous henchman and dirty-worker Crissy Knowles.

Chapter 33

On the second day there was Ben, Jack, Sam. The barrister was gone and so was Arnold, who seemed flabby and off his game anyway. Three was a number he could actually see. Jack had a chiseled, military crudeness to him, like he was out of uniform, like there was a time in his life when he had been redeemed by a uniform. Ben had the classic imperturbable self-regard of money and Yale. And Sam, who now seemed to be the designated giver of cigarettes, was black and couldn't be but a few years older than he was. He felt the least animosity toward Sam and thought about why. Sam held himself well, he was no nigger-for-hire like Grambling nor overly concerned that he *do* white, like the Bajan lawyer. He was secure in his negritude and Wilson defined this aspect of his character as Isaacness. Sam was thoughtful, the one you'd have to say was the theoretician, though he lacked the bad eyes behind wire-rimmed spectacles to complete the picture. Hearing the slight lilt in Sam's voice, he had asked him where he was born and he said Jamaica but his parents moved to the States the same year. The other two seemed to acknowledge that if he was going to let anybody in it was going to be Sam.

But Sam wore a thousand-dollar watch on his wrist, so there was that too. It wasn't like he was kidding himself about Sam.

They began with easy questions and right away Mitchell felt himself backsliding into his obsession with Bobby Fernandez. Jack started to respond with surprising candor—*what were you doing with Fernandez's wife, Mister Wilson? why was Fernandez in Mexico City?*—but Ben and Sam held up their hands and said wait a minute, we should have gotten this straight before we started. They went over to the windows and whispered out. Mitchell thought *Aha!* they know, someone did their homework. This appeared to be an organizational problem, compartmentalization, the right hand not aware what the left hand, et cetera. They settled the issue and sat back down. Fernandez, overnight, became taboo. Which meant they went round and round and round until Mitchell was addled and ranting about the filth-strewn floor of the morgue, the mop full of blood, flies and cockroaches and dogs, and they quit for lunch.

Sam wondered if Mitchell minded if he kept him company. He said okay but he wanted to look out the windows. There was a big white Cunard ocean liner in the harbor, and something that looked like a tiny battleship. He asked Sam if he knew what it was and he said Venezuelan navy out on maneuvers. The Cubans will be next, Mitchell muttered, an afterthought. Why do you say that? Sam asked but he didn't answer, he was trying to find Isaac's house again, down in the scrap heap of Scuffletown.

"It must be tough."

"It's not tough, man. I'm not dead. I'm not missing."

"Is there anything you need that we can get you? Books or something? Phone your family back home?"

"Yeah, a coat hanger." The itch inside the plaster cast was getting to him. He was digging into it with a pencil, plucking out tufts of cotton wool, but he needed something like a coat hanger to go deeper. The door opened and there was the cook's jolly face, the food she left no match for her kindness—a bowl of jaundiced sweet potatoes atop a rank scoop of Guyanese rice, stinking like the breath of death. Mitchell set it on the table and walked back to the windows.

"Soul food. You can eat it."

Sam bent over the bowl, sniffing, his nostrils scrolled.

"Uh huh, right," he said, and came back to the window to light a cigarette, shake one out for Mitchell. "Man, you want to talk?"

"I've been doing that. Just wind me up."

"What about Edison Banks?"

Sam leaned back from the waist, a little startled by Mitchell's sudden surge of passion.

"The man suffers, he's suffering for his people. He'll bleed for them if he has to."

"I didn't expect to hear this, coming from you."

"Look, I still believe in him, maybe more than ever. He's a well-intentioned man. His heart's pure. He's suffering for his people. He'll bleed for them if he has to. At the moment he's getting lousy advice. These bad elements, they've gotten too close to him. He needs other points of view."

"Whose side should we be on here? Or does it matter?"

"What the hell do you mean, *does it matter?* You could be a moderating influence. He wants moderating influences. He knows he's got a tiger by the tail."

"We might disagree about which tiger. Or maybe we don't. Tell me about Joshua Kingsley."

"Kingsley's very very happy you're here, poking around. If he was here right now he'd probably kiss me. The more of you the merrier for the PIP. He's jumping for joy. He's convinced you're going to save him . . ."

"And?"

"And that would be a mistake."

"Because of his ideology?"

"Because of corruption, because of his disregard for the welfare of his people. You can achieve justice without ideology, you're not going to change my mind about that."

"What about this Selwyn Walker?"

"Selwyn Walker's why I'm here. This is the way his mind works. His idea of nation-building."

"And you know this because . . . ?"

"I know."

"Chances for armed conflict?"

"I would imagine that depends on you. What about this Bobby Fernandez?"

Sam grimaced and lowered his voice unnecessarily, almost causing Mitchell to snort at his pretense of secrecy. "We're still working that out. There may be a problem there. I can tell you a few things. Walker telephoned a contact of his at the Cuban embassy in Mexico City, inquiring about Fernandez. This was an indiscretion on Walker's part. The Cubans made it clear that certain things should only be discussed in person, not by phone or cable. Certain sensitive issues require face-to-face meetings, of course. They dispatched someone to the island, we have reason to believe."

"Fernandez."

"We don't think so. No."

"He was here, wasn't he?" He told Sam about the cat on the door, the note, *Te amo.*

"Maybe he arranged something," conceded Sam. A *recuerdo de amor.* Something to jog her memory, to let her know he still cared. "We don't know much about Fernandez, we're still learning. What about Fernandez's wife? Was she in touch with him?"

"Fuck if I know."

"They were quite a pair. He seems to be responsible for the death of her girlfriend in Hawaii. Did you know that?"

"I don't know."

"Why did you send her off so quickly? What was going on there?"

"I don't know. I can't explain it." Finally, here they were. Mitchell didn't think he was going to be able to handle this much longer, the weariness was bone-deep, soul-deep. He held firm to Sally's death, unwilling to barter for anything of unequal value.

"Oh," Sam said quietly. After a pause he said, "Look, let's not talk about this in front of Jack, okay. He's excitable. He'll overreact. Jack'll be gone tomorrow."

They talked about Julius Nyerere until the other two returned. They talked about who was teaching what at the University of Chicago School of Economics.

They wanted to know if he loved her, how much. Enough to lie? His relationship with Johnnie was embarking on a separate, secret life of its own, being given a new identity. No one really liked saying the word *love* and he was beginning to appreciate how it stuck in the mouth, then dropped out like an egg and you had no idea what was inside the shell.

There are so many ways to see this problem, Ben was saying. Between you and me, he told Mitchell, if you're lying it doesn't matter. Not to us, not among friends. Let's put it behind us and move on.

What matters, Ben was saying, it that you've fucked with the magnetic field around here. We rather wish you hadn't. At least some of us. My estimable colleague here at my side says he believes he smells a trend, he's afraid there's been a shift in how people imagine things in this part of the world. I tell him not to worry but he says it's in his job description. We're the only people in government who believe wholeheartedly in the power of the imagination. Think of us as a praetorian guard of the imagination, guarding the very limited ways in which the world must imagine itself. A civilized world. We find the theories very interesting, but we're concerned about individuals too. For instance, did someone imagine you, or did you imagine yourself? You understand what I'm saying. What brought you into being, my friend? That's all we care about, to be honest with you, and we realize this is not a simple question, answers to these questions are always complicated.

We don't like anyone imagining they're *us*, that's part of it. It gives us pause. *Are* they us? we are compelled to ask ourselves, and the answer's not always as clear as we'd like. You see the quandary it puts us in, Ben was saying.

"I am you," Mitchell said. "That's the problem." A sentiment for which he was rebuked.

"No, Mister Wilson, you are not us," said Jack. "You are not me. You are not me because if you were, you would never have gone up into the mountains, looking for trouble. You are not me because if you were, you would have at least loaded your goddamn gun, first."

Jack is our logician, Sam said grinning. Ben you could say is one of our poets.

Jack began to regard him, it seemed, as a personal affront to his world view. He began calling Mitchell *Professor*, changing the topic back to Soufrière.

"Professor, what do you think happened up there with this man Collymore?"

"He lost his mind, supposedly. He began seeing things."

"Now, why, do you suppose?"

"How could I know."

"Professor, what would you say caused him to go stone crazy like that, start shooting people?"

"How the fuck would I know, Jack?"

"He shot that girl, Professor. A good, decent person."

She was nobody, he said, raising his voice. All he meant by that was Sally was innocent, completely, tragically, out of the picture the friends of golf were painting. Once Sally had died, he saw no way out of it for himself, everything that had happened became his responsibility, even Johnnie became his responsibility, he wasn't Sally's avenging angel as some had said but simply the custodian of her memory, because far more than in her life, in death Sally needed someone to protect her from harm, though he couldn't say even now if he had accomplished that, if it were possible. Sally and Isaac, he couldn't help them after all and, what made it worse, that very impulse had contributed to his failure.

He spent the late afternoon and early evening composing what he hoped would be a letter of placation, for Sam to carry back to the States with him and mail to his parents. Because it felt as if his intestines were beginning to disintegrate, he refused his dinner of watery stew, admitting he was making himself sick, he was going to have to get someone to start bringing him food—family members were allowed to deliver meals, or you could pay somebody. After lights out, a card game commenced in one of the communal cells; the dissent among the players filled the block and kept him awake throughout the night. Not that it mattered, not that it really interfered in his more central habitat—the vortex of mosquitoes, the rotting of his right forearm, the mind's enormously nonproductive restlessness.

Lack of sleep notwithstanding, the morning of his third and last day with the friends of golf, he greeted the team's two holdouts in good spirits, old comrades-in-arms.

"So it's good-bye, Jack. Sayonara, Jack."

"Actually, Jack's out scouting around today," Sam said, offering to light Mitchell's cigarette for him, because of his cast. "Making new friends."

"With who?"

"Everybody. It makes more sense nowadays."

They had arranged a little farewell celebration of sorts, gotten permission from the warden to have their chat out in the fresh air, brought Mitchell a modest package of gifts—a copy of *Time International,* candy bars, a thermos of good coffee, a cablegram from his parents in Virginia saying they had lit a fire under Senator so-and-so's rear end, had high hopes, were praying for him and so on. They were up on the southern-facing battlement of Fort Gregory, strolling back and forth between two squat bastions where guards, discreet with laziness, were posted. Occasionally they would pause to gaze over the parapet, looking off in the blueness toward a continent that filled the distance in their thoughts, but generally Mitchell preferred the exercise, and would be the first to break the spell and get them walking again. Like any other citizen he could make his Hollywood-educated guess, but he still didn't know who these men were, not really, the government's men of course, but then he was one himself or close enough. *Close enough* was an answer Ben and Sam found quite admissible. They both wore gold wedding bands, had wives and maybe kids somewhere in the suburbs, as if to advertise the mundanity of their lives and free themselves from the imbecilic fantasies of the popular imagination. They weren't making myths or movies: this was business, Patriots Anonymous, an American Civ pop quiz, metapolitics, Roman Catholic confession, and apparently, Mitchell thought by the end of it, something near to being a job interview as well.

There was a sailing ship, a windjammer with crossbars and square sails, out on the sea midpoint between them and the horizon, running downwind toward Grenada. Sam asked, Is that what you call a frigate? but none of them knew.

"You didn't care much for our Jack, did you?" said Ben.

"I found him lacking in empathy."

"He doesn't understand someone like you," said Ben. "He doesn't get it. Frankly, it's not easy to get. He says, 'Fuck this kid, throw him off the roof, we got better things to do.' Jack's worried there's a flu going around down here. He doesn't want the island to catch cold. You know what I mean, the Cuban disease. He doesn't want anyone coming up to him a year or two from now whining about Who lost St. Catherine. Hah-hah. Of course that's his hang-up. Jack's a little bit of an alarmist, isn't he? It's not easy to convince him of the truth, that places like this never really amount to diplomatic disaster. Give him credit though, he feels very bad about the girl. It's eating him up. He has a daughter about her age. That's Jack."

He had not forgotten how quickly the tropic sun seared, like a thin veneer of pain swabbed across your forehead and lips, around the back of your neck. They were all beginning to sweat, and the scum inside his cast was coming alive. The guards weren't allowing him to have the coat hanger Sam had brought; he looked around, preoccupied, until finally Sam gave him his ballpoint pen.

"That thing is nasty. You should have them crack it off and give you a new one."

"This is already the second one."

The nature of his longing seemed to be centered there, trapped in plaster, inaccessible, degrading and infernal. Void.

"On the other hand," said Ben, walking with his own hands folded behind him, "Sam here shares your admiration for the honorable Mr. Edison Banks. A moderate and a populist, says Sam. What happened he thinks has just been a question of unfortunate experimentation. Does that feel right to you? Some misguided individual sitting around asking himself, What will happen if I push this button? Oops. Dead girl. Perhaps you recognize the impulse yourself."

Mitchell said things: I am not the agent provocateur. For every contrivance, a contradiction. No one can imagine.

"Wrong," said Sam, "this is exactly what everyone can imagine and there's a deep, deep problem inherent in that."

"What you are," said Ben, "is St. Catherine's very own attempt at a self-fulfilling prophecy."

He chain-smoked and wanted to debate his soul but he was no match for the two of them, teaming up like the Founding Fathers. He didn't know whom or what he should be striving to appease, or why, or to what moral authority he might appeal his actions.

"Are you a religious man?" Ben asked in a benign tone. "Have you by chance read Paul's writings? Romans? seven-eighteen?" He looked at Mitchell with his head cocked, eyebrows lifted, the blueness of his eyes, the aquilinity of his nose, the fine, thin flax of his balding hair all saying let us know ourselves by our country's traditions, and out came the quote like a gentleman's silk handkerchief of commiseration. "'To will is present with me, but how to perform that good I find not. For the good that I would, I do not; but the evil which I would not, that I do.' Does that help? Words of an apostle, keep in mind. "

Mitchell squinted back into the sun at Ben, feeling only callousness toward such ministering, saying no it didn't help but he imagined Ben had gotten good mileage out of it on his own political trek toward nobility.

"I see you as a man in transition between contexts," said Ben. "I see you as a rider galloping hellbent from his father's house to the border, trying to stay in the saddle until the rules change or all is forgiven. Would you like the key to the code? Here it is, no conversion necessary: The rules don't change. All can be forgiven."

"I grant you this is a bad state of affairs," Sam offered, "but not a hopeless case. Cut yourself some slack on this."

"Sam will only meet me halfway on this," Ben said ruefully, "but ideologies are not always reliable. And political decisions based on moral arguments are not always a good bargain. Think of fairness. It's the perfect template, the ideal standard of conduct. It precludes the need for justice. But who plays fair?"

"Let's turn the corner on this," said Sam. "You relied on yourself and the goodness of your intentions. It was the best you could do. We applaud that effort."

"You don't like the banality of being railroaded," said Ben. "You don't appreciate the simplicity of it. There was no old white bwana up there in the mountains running the show, was there? There was only you."

"Moral dandyism," said Sam. "Moral vanity. That's where Ben and I agree. The folly of sentimental commitment."

"The world preys on naïveté. It's not much of an insight, is it? Priced too fucking high, for one thing. But you learned something, didn't you?"

"About gamesmanship. You have to play. You can't not play."

"Well wait, it ain't that goddamn simple," said Ben. "You have to play *well*. Let's put the emphasis where it belongs. And, man, you didn't do that, did you," he said with a cryptic smile, showing teeth too perfect not to be caps. "Not even with alacrity, not even for the fuck of it. You're here running around taking drugs with the wife of a bigtime shithead, you purchased a weapon illegally, you go tramping around the jungle with a gun in an area that had been placed under martial law, telling yourself you're making the world a better place. I'm afraid I side with Jack on this. People like you give me the creeps."

They reached the western limit of their walk, there was the guard with his sinister curiosity, Ben grabbed Mitchell's arm only to swing him around, because it appeared he was about to keep on going. He was just too tired, his brain circuitry signaling emergency sleep, to protest. Ben kept his arm, marshaling him forward.

"Do you want an explanation or not?" Mitchell said.

Ben stopped and so they all stopped to watch him spit over the parapet, watching like boys must watch anything fall as the white dot of phlegm sailed out down to the rocks and placid sea.

"You know," said Ben, "Sam's right. Your case is not hopeless. I think you've been getting better at this. I think you're at like the fifth-grade level of a formative political and spiritual experience, which means you are now as smart as any ten-year-old who realizes that lies solve problems, especially when nobody, for reasons that are not often admirable but sometimes unavoidable, is able or willing to listen to the truth."

"Maybe Ben's saying he's worried your explanation will bore him," said Sam.

"Bore us," Ben corrected him.

"Maybe he's concerned it won't be of use to anybody, especially to your own situation."

"Let me be clear," said Ben. "I want to hear a really first-rate lie, something that inspires me, something that works for us all. I don't think I'm asking too much, am I? We came all this way. I don't think this is going to strain your creative resources, is it? It would just ruin my little vacation here in paradise to have to listen to some weak-minded explanation."

"Or maybe," suggested Sam, "the particular truth we seek from Wilson is so delectable, he's saying to himself, Why lie at all?"

"Maybe," Ben allowed, skeptical.

"Another thing," said Sam. "A free man blames nobody but himself."

"What do you think about that, Mister Wilson?" chuckled Ben. "There's something to think about. Once they let you out."

That was it. No more friends. He was on his own, knowing that he, in history, must assume the blame for Sally, but someone would have to rub his face in it hard, harder than this, before he'd live with the guilt.

Don't be insolent. Don't set precedents. Final advice from the friends of golf. It's better to believe the lies, they said. In a case like this.

They were off to brief the ambassador for the Windward Islands, who had just arrived from Barbados. The ambassador would be talking with Edison Banks that afternoon. He was going to lecture Banks about cozying up to Cuba. He would also be announcing a new aid package for the island: a five-thousand-dollar shipment of school supplies.

By the end of the week, Mitchell had a higher understanding, a supreme understanding, of his naïveté. He had underestimated them, the friends of golf. He had of course underestimated everybody. Kingsley got on the radio to electrify the island with his demagoguery, laying out a sequence of astounding accusations. Yes, it was true, he harangued, as the new People's Revolutionary Party alleged, that a paramilitary force existed in the northern mountains. Yes, it was true, as the PRP alleged, that a young man named Isaac Knowles was the leader of this international conspiracy. Yes, it was true, as the PRP alleged, that there were foreign agents involved—one of them sitting right now in a cell in Fort Gregory. But, *it is not true*, Kingsley countercharged, that these were his bad children. This allegation was a Machiavellian lie, another of the PEP/PRP's falsehoods, because, in fact, these people he was talking about were the enemies of the PIP and the enemies of democracy. He could prove it, he railed, he had gathered the evidence, and it was damning. Let us go to the courts, he challenged. Let us have two trials, three trials, many. Let us go to the ballot box and divine the truth.

When Mitchell heard the news, his mind leapt to Johnnie, and he felt as though Kingsley had just married them, bonded them forever together. Some things you can't get behind you no matter what, he thought: an amendment to the extraordinary power of Johnnie's imagination, which had convinced her to reappear in his life, to come back aboard, as if it were a beautiful white ship under beautiful blue skies, and away they'd sail.

You're so mine, she had said, and it was proving true.

The St. Catherine Crier

June 9, 1977

Low & Behold
by Epictetus

Eppy: Well, gents, the politicians have us stumped again, I can see by the hard put look on your faces. Let me make my little speech and then have at it: Things either are what they appear to be; or they neither are, nor appear to be; or they are, and do not appear to be; or they are not, and yet appear to be. Now I am willing to gamble I speak for many Catherinians when I ask, *What in God's name is going on???* Anything reasonable will be supported.

Sir Cease-All: Murder and Mayhem, sir, Wickedness and Undo-itness, and not a lick of it in God's name. The signatures I read at the bottom of the page are Joe Stalin, Mr. Castro, and the Prince of Darkness. Now add to that rogue's gallery a most unexpected lackey, this poor misguided fellow from the great USA who has grabbed the spotlight in our High Court follies.

Beau of the Bawl: Grabbed? Why not pushed, kicked, shoved, and booted into it?

Joe Pittance: Murder it is, and mayhem too, fellers, but Sir C has stood the perpetration on its head, to accommodate his favorite view, arse-backwards topsy-turvy. Why, it wasn't so very long ago Sir C was screaming bloody hell in this scamp Wilson's defense, no surprise a'tall from an enthusiastic admirer of James Bond fantasy, the Vietnam War, the ruling class, the gilded class, the House of Lords, the Shah of Iran, men on the moon, Princess Margaret, the flim *Lawrence of Arabia* and, last and most, His Majesty Joshua Kingsley.

Beau: I see gallows humor is the coming rage. He left out Jesus Christ, Will Shakespeare, and the kitchen sink.

Joe: And after such spirited support for Mr. Kingsley's Yankee agent—er, I mean economist, that is what they are calling saboteurs these days at the Ministry of Agriculture—Sir C and his disloyaltists gall us with their cry, *About-Face, Abracadabra!* and poof, come look, their Innocent Boy Scout is the Second Coming of Che Guevara. Even our obeahmen wouldn't dare try that brand of black magic.

Sir C: Funny you should mention the name of this feller's mentor, Joe, who is also the matinee idol of your man Edison Banks and his bloodthirsty band of schoolboys. There is no depth low enough, including Flames of Hell, that these so-called Revolutionaries won't scrape and bow to, to disgrace us. The only magic to be had is the stuff supplied by the two magicians Fidel sent PRP to entertain at rallies and witch-hunts, not to mention the Cuban teachers who are pushing our own out of the classroom. Next we'll see the Russian bear dancing at carnival. As if Communist basketball coaches and Soviet-trained dentists weren't bad enough, now we have Cuban ships pulling into the harbor, and when the lights go out at night, I don't have to tell you what comes ashore and is hidden in depots around the island. This is not scandal, Joe, we must call it what it is—Treason. We demand new elections, as I for one have no desire to conduct my business in the language of Spain. Failing that, let me once more issue a plea to those guardians of liberty in Washington: *Come save us.*

Beau: I'm flummoxed, fellers. You have me playing eenie meenie minie mo. My plea goes out to our spook-in-residence, this boy we hear so much about, Isaac Knowles, to come down out of the mountains, if he is truly there, and answer Eppy's question. Is it as Banks says—like father like son—or Kingsley says—monkey see monkey do? Who was it firing the shot killing that poor woman up in the wilds of Soufrière, isn't that the question? Bandits, we hear from PRP. Cassius Iman Colly-ibra-more-him or whatever this unfortunate is calling himself, we hear from PIP. Well, which is it, eh? This fellow Wilson seems uncertain, and now he is discredited by these new allegations.

Sir C: Not allegations, fellers. Evidence. The books in this man's library were printed in the Kremlin. He purchased firearms illegally, for what purpose I shudder to imagine. And his mistress is the moll of a notorious renegade and drug peddler, of Cuban extraction, who takes his orders from cigar-smokers in Havana. Seriously, Joe, this Wilson is not the type you'll likely find conspiring with a man of Kingsley's principles.

Joe: The principles of a gangster, no less.

Beau: Well, that fixes it, boys. No longer am I flummoxed—now I'm bewildered as well.

Eppy: Gents, am I mistaken or is it not Mr. Wilson on trial in our courts, though prosecution and defense seem to think otherwise, but this pitiful tongue-tied orphan from Cotton Island, the youth Cassius Collymore. Mr. Wilson should be allowed to testify without disruption or further accusation and sent home. Difficulties are things that show what men are, and he has conducted himself with dignity. By the way, life goes on despite our crab antics and current turmoil. Family Planning will hold a fair this Saturday on the esplanade, with balloons, games, and free food for the kids.

Until next week then, *Clarior E Tenebris.*

Chapter 34

After the trip to Scarborough, he went home then to Howard Bay for the sole purpose of knocking himself out flat and senseless, washing down codeine from the hospital with numerous rum and tonics and after a while, still awake but floundering, hurrying unconsciousness along with one of the Mandrax Johnnie had so considerately left behind. He passed out in the hammock on the veranda and woke up at dawn with a brain seriously fogged and every joint aching, wondering how close he had come to killing himself, which was not as far as he knew what he had in mind.

He showered cold and began to dress, only to stop himself in the middle of slipping on his pants to sit on the edge of the bed, lost in a void, fighting back the desire to vomit which made him break out in a sweat. He was not well, he was not going to be well anytime soon, but he had things to do, only he couldn't put his finger on what they were, all he could remember was that he had forgotten something, and was forced to sit there sweating and wanting to puke while his thoughts, sluggish and blind, grabbed at whatever it was, until he had regained enough presence of mind to notice, there on the floor, kicked into a corner of the room, the pair of pants he had worn up Soufrière, streaked and splotched with stains that were Sally's blood, and he thought, *Get rid of those.* He sat there for a few more minutes, unsatisfied, and then of course remembered the letter he had retrieved from the body of Captain Eddins. He buttoned his pants and stood up.

It was exactly what he now knew it would be—evidence, a crudely drawn map of a camp in the mountains behind the volcano—not the sort of thing you should be carrying in your pocket up Soufrière, in this day and time.

Addressed to nobody, signed by nobody, all-incriminating. He

ripped it up and poked the pieces down into the fly-blown slop bucket on the side stoop—more garbage for Mrs. Fetchalub's pig. Mr.
Quiddley was in the yard, cracking open the second pit. Removing
his hat, he stood up straight and offered condolence.

"I am sorry to hear of dis sahd news of you lady friend."

"You should never have done this," Mitchell shouted irrationally.
"Never. Never," and he went back inside to finish dressing, packed
his knapsack with bread and cheese, a water bottle, gym shorts and a
change of underwear, his rain poncho and envelope of codeine and
the handgun he had bought in Scuffletown wrapped in a tee shirt,
walked down to Augustine and took a jitney loaded with merry
schoolchildren into Queenstown, saw as they passed toward Brandon
Vale that the red letters PRP had been splash-painted on the roof of
Miss Defy, soon to be invisible in a sea of cane. He went to the ministry which was still locked up though he was taken aback to see the
vet's assistant Morrison standing in the door of his dispensary, a clean
bandage around his head and both eyes puffy, reading a government
broadside. They does get you too, eh bwoy? Morrison smiled, curling
his upper lip into a sneer. Morrison told him Kingsley was still up leeward side, playing the fool, but the time was coming to kick his ass,
Wilson, we will have some fun with these fuckers, we will revenge the
girl, nuh?

Walking down to the esplanade, the morning light was blinding
and seemed to shine right down on his witlessness, and he queued up
with a workforce of laborers at a line of lorries ferrying the men leeward, wondering what he was doing, an explanation of sorts bursting
through like madness, telling himself, But Isaac was up north in the
mountains with Jack Nasty and the old white patriarch he had
dreamed of at Josephine's and the bandits and the mercenaries and
the forest gods that had migrated with the slaves from Guinea, the
lost spirits of the Arawaks and now Sally and all the other phantoms
that were gathering to consummate the destiny of the island in this
day and in this time. So there was that, the mountains like a parallel
universe, a land outside of the world where he might begin to look
for the truth.

Asking himself, But does this make sense? and when the lorry
came and the men started climbing onto the bed he stepped out of
line, confused and homeless—both the ministry and the cottage in
Howard Bay had been rendered uninhabitable—swallowed a codeine
pill dry to soften the rising pulse in his wrist, and started walking,
thinking, whoever his enemies were, all they had to do was let him be
himself and eventually, as if it were a law of nature, he'd find a way to

fit their bill, he'd end up being whatever it was they needed him to be. It was easy work if you could get it.

In Scuffletown he stood in Mrs. Knowles' front-room apothecary, breathing the tannic aromas of her bush medicines, confronted by the armor of her hard and unpitying dignity, until finally she acquiesced to tell him what it would do him no good to know, that old friends still high-up had whispered to her of Isaac's incarceration on an unspecified charge, which these high-ups were not even aware of until someone had whispered to them about his release, or perhaps his escape, it wasn't clear to them and it wasn't clear to her. They say my Isaac gone to hide, she said without emotion, they say him start a *movement*. Tell me, Mistah Wilson, what kind of movement that bwoy goin start except the mind-you-own-business kind, the Keep-to-Youself Party. Eh? Eh? She sucked her teeth, chupsing, and said, Now I suppose you goin join up, nuh? She rebuked him, sucking her teeth angrily: You and my first son who is not a'tall like his poor dead father, you and he and the king of duppies, and you with all the woe you need since crazy men take to shootin good white people here on we St. Catherine of sorrow, and when she had spoken her mind she told him, Wait, left the room and came back to slip a juju around his neck, a tiny hand-stitched leather pouch attached to a strip of rawhide, to keep him safe from evil, from all the many evils.

As long as he was in Scuffletown he thought he would try again to find some bullets and stepped into several of the rougher bars—the Black Cat, Our Place, Hughes Alley—only to learn the police were arresting people on ammunition charges—he was unconcerned, there was nothing left to explain to himself about firearms and such—but until one of the men throwing back his rum in the daytime darkness of Our Place asked, he had forgotten that he still had no idea of the caliber of bullet he required. He fired a rum himself, washing down a codeine, while the fellow examined the gun in his pack and concluded he couldn't help him.

From Scuffletown, he dreamwalked to National Police Headquarters where he suddenly woke up into a disruption that was himself demanding to see the front desk logbook of two weeks past, learning just how big of a fuss was enough to convert the duty officer to the cult of possibility, and there on the log's blue-lined copybook pages, like a schoolboy's homework, was *Miss Defy*'s accident report, a statement given in person by Renata Archibol, but no entry attesting to Isaac's presence at the station, and no record of arrest. From there he flagged a cab which took him through the lower slums and up the hills to Hubbard Heights, the ruling-class neighborhood preferred by elite businessmen and those of ministerial rank, regardless of party affiliation, they lived in peace together in the Heights but not in parliament, the driver cruised the walled yards, the modern airy homes with their gardens and guard dogs, the grillwork on the windows and doors, families of domestic staff housed on the property, until finally he asked where exactly was it he wished to go, and Mitchell didn't know the address so they pulled over to where two yardmen were "mowing" a perfect zoysia lawn with machetes, stooped over like the old men the job would soon make of them, snicking the errant blades of grass, and the miracle of the day was that the two of them agreed immediately about the location of Archibol's house and were of the same mind as to the best and quickest way to get there. The minister was not home but the Missus was; she was not disinclined to speak with him but on the contrary gave Mitchell a warm reception, made him sit with her for a cup of tea, and answered his questions with cautious but unfailing courtesy, saying all she remembered was going to the station with her husband and a drunk boy who had banged up her import. She then paid effusive and heartfelt tribute to Sally, saying What I would like to know is this, did anyone ever say thanks to this young woman who gave these frequently despised youngsters friendship and understanding? That was all she could say except would you like another cup of tea, something stronger? we are a warm people, despite we troubles. He asked if she had any painkillers and he left with a handful of Darvon, walking aimlessly down the slope and then across it until the houses no longer boasted their affluence and he knew where he was without a conscious understanding of what he was doing there.

It was lunchtime, Josephine's Shoovie wasn't in the drive, so he didn't even bother knocking but sat down on the stoop to wait. He wondered, for the first time, and not with confidence, if this was a revolution, if that's why things were even more fucked up than ever.

He thought, the liberation of zero commitment would be at least one way to describe Johnnie.

He took a Darvon. There were steamy wraiths of self-condemnation in his head. Josephine came home, took him inside, and made him lie down.

"I don't know why I'm here," he mumbled apologetically. "I wasn't sure. I didn't know. Where else really."

She sat on the edge of her bed, where she had put him, stroking his unshaven cheek. She understood, she said, she understood everything, she was sad, for the dead girl but for him too. Her hair was trussed in a kerchief, the braids extruding under a triangle of calico at the back of her neck. She looked fresh and youthful but still urbane, sleek in her designer jeans and remarkably white tee shirt, almost gaunt with seductiveness though both of them knew his coming here, and her accepting him, wasn't about sex, and couldn't be, naturally, until . . . but neither of them could say. She acknowledged his depression, made a halfhearted attempt to be plucky and cheering—*But you does know why you come here, mahn,* she said with affectionate sarcasm, *ain dis what black women do, eh? tek in hand white bwoys? eh? eh?*—then brushed her lips across his and let him be, shuttering the room and then retreating to her work desk where she sat on a stool in the shadows, sketching, while he stared, unseeing, listening to the gliding scratch of her pencil. Mourning, he had heard, can be a very selfish act, but what was he to do? Sometime later he was aware of her leaving the room, he heard Josephine talking to her aunt, heard her scolding and then playing with her child, smelled cooking, she came back after a while to ask him if he wanted to eat but he wasn't hungry, then she came back to tell him she had to go out for a while to meet some people, he watched her change into a dress, shyly turning her back to him, then she was leaving, telling him not to bother himself with anything, he could stay by her as long as he wished, he was to think of her house as his, and then she had returned, smelling of cigarette smoke and sweat and perfume, candles guttered in the stale air of the room, and she was beside him in bed, holding him sleepily and telling him she had heard that tomorrow there would be a memorial service for Sally at her school on the waterfront, in the morning, wiping the tears on his face, whispering, *but it hurts me to see you grieve so, Wilson,* whispering, *okay, okay, mahn, okay,* but in the morning he only got out of bed to use the bathroom, he watched her prepare to leave the house and then woke up when she came back in at noon, he asked for a glass of water to help swallow his pills, and she told him the island was losing its mind, everybody making speeches and calling for strikes, there was a way in which he was at the center of it but in truth it had nothing to do with him at all, it was nothing more than PEP versus PIP, there were many speeches by both sides, new security measures, Kingsley's men were in parliament demanding a vote of no-confidence in the prime minister, it was all a mess, he had no understanding of his political position, there seemed to be a growing mood of belligerence among the people, someone she knew wanted to pass by to see him this afternoon and wanted to know if he would be received.

There was nobody he wanted to see, he tried to tell her, but she said he was an important person, a good man, and Mitchell acqui-

esced without bothering to ask why, or who it was, because what difference did it make, everything he had to say and anything anybody
had to say to him, all of it came from a very lean and common script,
and what did it matter who read the lines, and no one came anyway, it
was just he and Josephine alone in the house, she working quite con-
tentedly at her desk on designs for a show she had been contracted to
put on at one of the better hotels, he remained supine on her bed,
wearing only his gym shorts and sweating unhealthily, listening to the
alarm clock of pain in his lower right arm, unable to move, his mind
recycling an impoverished array of thoughts, asking himself how do
you match up the moments and the answer was, you can't.

When the aunt returned with the boy Josephine set aside her pens
and colored pencils and went into the other part of the house to be
with them. He heard the child pestering her, he heard her husky
laughter. At suppertime she marched back into the bedroom, head-
strong and feisty, to tell him he didn't have a say-so in the matter, he
must get up and come eat a bite of Auntie's chicken-back and
dumplings, don't bother dressing just come, and so he followed after
her down the hall, shirtless and barefooted, and took his seat with the
family at the kitchen table, Auntie gracious and solicitous, the boy in
his high chair, enthralled again by Mitchell, absently smearing his bits
of fruit and dumpling on the board in front of him, Josephine popping morsels into his mouth when she could get his attention,
Mitchell practiced holding a spoon in his left hand but ate sparingly,
unable to find his appetite, Auntie said if he would eat a little more
she would bring him a rum, and then she got up and brought him the
rum and put a plate of sweet biscuits in the center of the table. They
talked, careful not to say anything that might plug the trickle of his
forgetting.

After a second rum, he found himself entertaining the idea that
this now was his life.

He watched the women clear and wash the dishes, comforted by
the mock indignation of their gossip, uncensored and unsweetened,
about a neighborhood romance between a too-old man and a too-
young but slutty girl. Josephine took a washcloth and wiped off the
boy and his high chair, saying to Mitchell, Come, we will let him look
at a show and then it is his bedtime. They adjourned to the front parlor, Josephine going ahead to turn on the television, and sat down,
the boy cross-legged in front of the screen, Josephine on a plaid settee, Mitchell adhering himself to the surface of a red vinyl-covered
chair, like the type commonly seen in doctors' offices in another
country. Auntie followed a minute later, lowering herself into a rock-

ing chair. The TV was old, a big wooden box with its own legs, covered with a large doily and a vase of plastic roses, and it projected an ethereal blue light throughout the room after Josephine had flicked off the overhead. Television was still a novelty on St. Catherine and there was only one station, the bulk of its programming transmitted from Barbados, frequently jolted by static interference. They were all immobilized by a commercial for the Royal Bank of Canada and then, to his dismay, on came "The Dick Van Dyke Show," a rerun from the early Sixties, the unearthly blue light in the air, emanated from the characters, was like a clear, odorless exhaust of mortality, at the sound of the first laugh track he got up and went to the kitchen, poured himself a third rum, and came back to the parlor and sat down, his eyes wandered over the chromoliths of Jesus and Virgin Mother and Child and another of St. Catherine being unpinned from her wheel by the bridegroom Christ, then back to the screen, Dick Van Dyke tripping over an ottoman as he entered a room, it was the wrong thing to be watching, it made being here with Josephine and her aunt and son seem promiscuous and far too unreal, it was a starburst of decomposing nostalgia and he felt it thrusting him back to a boyhood he no longer claimed or wanted for himself. He knew the only thing to do was get back up and get back inside the sanctuary of her bedroom but first there was the television's own awful attraction to overcome, he could also just stay there and bathe in its soporific light, but then it was Josephine, not Mitchell, getting up, stepping behind the set to pull aside the lace curtains drawn across the open window and look out onto the street, where he too had heard someone stop in front of the house, a car door clicked open and then slammed close.

Eddy has come, Josephine said, walking back through the parlor and out into the hallway to answer the soft rap at the door, and then she was back in the room with Edison Banks, Banks was nodding at him with a sheepish grin, soon disposed of, saying, Stay put, mahn, don't disturb yourself, but Mitchell was frozen with embarrassment anyway, humiliated to be discovered in the awkward and counterfeit position of bare-chested domesticity, and then the prime minister had taken a seat on the settee, next to Josephine, who by way of explanation was saying, Wilson, Eddy is an old friend of the family, you know. Banks ignored him, though not with any blatancy, catching up on family news with Josephine and her aunt, and Mitchell slipped away to put on a shirt and came back to his chair, stricken by curiosity, the boy was being admired by Banks, bounced on his knee, and Mitchell could not help but gaze overtly upon this man who had made himself the hope incarnate of his people, by appearance alone he succeeded as the model citizen, a well-shaped symbol of the new St. Catherine, he had the physical charisma granted to slim, self-assured men and seemed to be made absolutely solid and unbreakable by the understated but prideful arrogance that honed a razor-edge of glamour to the sword of power, and yet watching Edison Banks with Josephine's son he could easily believe that not all the innocence had gone from the world, that still there were dreams that were more than the illusions of powerless men. His mind shifted toward gratitude and kinship, he felt a transcendent sense of relief foreshadowing the healing that he imagined, wrongly, was the purpose of this visit.

Edison Banks asked permission from the women to speak with Mister Wilson alone, and when Josephine had scooped up the child and they had withdrawn from the room, he asked permission of Mitchell to speak informally as well as frankly and with confidentiality, and then he turned his attention full upon him, his eyes seemed suddenly hounded, the cinnamon hue of his skin bleached by the light of the television. There was no exchange of pleasantries, no attempt to explain how it was he had come to be there, other than the fact that he had expected to see Mitchell at the memorial service for the teacher, where he had hoped to take him aside and ask him what he was asking now, without any other consideration but a respect for the truth, was there anything that had happened on Mount Soufrière that he thought it best not to entrust to the police, for political or personal reasons?

Mitchell received the question as his first and perhaps only opportunity to tell the truth, as he knew it, and it was the only time he ever did, unburdening himself to Edison Banks, whose expression hardened as he listened to the story, the tulip-shaped scar disfiguring one of his eyebrows glowed white on his high forehead, and he leaned out on the edge of the settee to prop his elbows on his knees, his elegant hands cupped over his meticulous beard, and asked for a brief moment of clarification.

"What was in the woman's pack?"

Mitchell didn't know and he refused to speculate.

"Is it possible that she lied to you? Is it possible that she and the other woman, your friend—"

Mitchell cut him off. "Absolutely not."

Looking slighted by the curt tone of the denial, Banks held up a hand in concession to the point, sighing heavily with regret, sorry he had found it necessary to even suggest such a possibility, he was after all an apostle of infinite faith, the woman's death was a mystery that perhaps would remain a mystery, or perhaps it was not so big a mystery at all, but Wilson, Banks said emphatically, do you understand, we forgive each other our sins, we act with this future of forgiveness in our hearts, in order to move on. We have no days of real glory here, no heroic structures, no history of dignity. We have only fools and forgiveness and the rest, the balance, we must invent.

You have lived among us, Banks said, you have been a student of our souls, you know this is how we let our histories pass, unrecorded except in the ruin of hearts, in the dust and bones of our ancestors, in the violent spilling of their blood, in the changeless faces of children who wrap themselves in newspaper and fall asleep on the street . . . Edison Banks paused, his eyes locked upon Mitchell's, his lips bending in irony and he shook his head, self-amused, ridiculed by the television and then he continued, less fervently, saying he did not come to make a speech, he had come to make a request. Few people understood the powerlessness of being powerful. He was powerless, for instance, to interfere in the filing of a criminal charge, powerless to interfere in the jurisdiction of the courts, he was powerless to prevent political opponents from manufacturing lies and fabricating illusions and so he was asking Mitchell Wilson to reconsider his accusation against Corporal Cassius Collymore of the PDF.

"Why?"

Because, Banks said with resignation in his voice, a confessional sag to his frame, it could only bring disruption and harm to his nation and his nation's struggle. Because, Banks said, raising his head and tilting it backward away from Mitchell, his eyes imperious, finishing with him, because the whole sense of the act of the woman's murder suggested another murderer than Cassius Collymore, truth to tell, mahn, I don't know who killed the woman, it has yet to be determined, but perhaps this man was innocent, examine your memory and examine your conscience, and if you say so then it is so but then that will be an occasion when you will need my help and I will be powerless to help, and the dead woman will need *your* help, Wilson, and *you* will be powerless to help her, you see.

Both men nodded bitterly at one another. Mitchell made a cold demand to be told about Isaac Knowles and was flabbergasted by what he heard.

"I am not convinced of this," said Edison Banks. "I know much less about all this than you might suspect. These tales of this fellow Isaac, perhaps they are only another ananci story"—he paused, diverting his gaze toward the television which anointed their discussion with laughter—"but you know, Wilson, whatever you might say about the other woman, the woman who has left the island, eh? the woman who might know more than either of us about this affair, perhaps that would be ananci story too."

"Isaac Knowles is my friend."

"But you are serious?" said Banks, taken aback. "But this the first I hear of it."

"This bandit stuff," Mitchell said, frustrated, impulsively pointing at the program. "Where are you getting this from, the TV? This is horseshit."

"But you are serious, really?" Banks repeated, incredulous, coming to his feet, saying, in that case, as a personal favor, he would ask Wilson to leave this island, he would ask him to stay away until they straightened these matters out among themselves.

Mitchell remained slumped in his chair, listening to the driver of the prime minister's car start its engine at the same moment that Banks opened the front door to go out of the house. He was too pent up, the encounter had left him overcharged with useless energy and he went back through the dimness of the house to the kitchen to fire back another rum, desperate to tame his aimless urge to action, pouring a second one when Josephine came to collect what was left of him.

"Wha happen, bwoy?"

She was in her nightgown, sleepy-eyed. It was as if he had come home blasted in the middle of the night to tell his wife he had just been laid off, cut from the payroll that made it possible for them to be together.

"I think I've just been deported."

She brought him by his good hand to bed, saying only this, *you cyahn trust Eddy, Mitchell, he out of all dem fellas is de only one,* and then she harbored him within the flesh of her compassion, this night she made her love wordless and melting for him, a tender respite from his impotence, and in the early light of morning when he dressed and left her house, fearing her remonstrations he didn't tell her where he was going, only that he was coming back to her. Don't wait on him, he said, hoisting his daypack over his shoulders, but he'd most likely be home for supper.

Again he walked down to the esplanade, again the light was blinding and seemed to shine right down on his nerves and witlessness, and he queued up a second time with a workforce of laborers at a line of lorries ferrying men to leeward, wondering when he had done this before, he couldn't remember, and he climbed onto the back of a slat-bedded truck, crowding in with the rest of them when they were told to hop aboard, someone making room for him to sit down on one of the benches, saying Sah, we is very very deep-sad about the girl Big Sally. Along the road he saw the familiar posting of old billboards, erected by the coalition during the final days of the campaign against the tyrant Pepper, political relics, the didactic murals—heroic peasants with uplifted eyes and hoes slung over their shoulders; children thankfully learning their ABC's—were beginning to flake and peel and their identical slogans—*Stop the Oppression; We All is One*—fade, but someone with a bucket of red paint had altered their attribution, the formula for change and unity—*PEP + PIP = PEAS*—had lost all but its first three letters, and its *E* had scaled the alphabet to become a crude, splattered *R*, as if to suggest to the population that the PEP had never quite been able to switch gears away from its former function and was still capable of rebelling against the status quo, regardless of their role in its construction. The *R* of course expressed evolutionary logic, survival of the fittest, and stood for Revolution, though he knew of no announcement from the party to this effect. Farther up the road, past a brown swamp of mangrove and near the junction with the leeward highway, they slowed and moved as far to the left as the asphalt allowed, to let pass a caravan of twelve lorries, similar to their own, transporting hundreds of peasants south to the capital where, it was said among the men on the truck, they were to demonstrate against the PLDP (Mitchell later heard that during the rally, three dispossessed squatters, to dramatize their plight, allowed themselves to be symbolically crucified on makeshift crosses and paraded through the streets by several thousand outraged supporters; in the process, shop windows were broken and tear gas, making its debut on the island, was fired, and it could reasonably be said that this was the day the nebulous slow burn of opposition on the island combusted into bright blue flames).

In the hour of barnyard jostling and sweat and black tobacco smoke it took to reach the police checkpoint, they were entertained by a PEP man and a PIP man engaged in an argument remarkable for the beauty of its oratory applied to the ridiculous nonsense of their mirror-image demands, each of them wanting their workers' union to strike against different halves of the same government. Is like de mahn refuse to bring home food, said one of the onlookers, and de womahn say she ain goin cook, and so who goin sit hungry but we children, nuh? Tell me Catherinians is not lunatics, bwoy. It seemed Kingsley supporters among the police commanded the leeward checkpoint, and there the PIP fellow loudly denounced his PEP counterpart, who was then ordered down off the truck and left standing in the middle of the road, no one paying him the least attention, his arms flung out from his sides and saying, JesusfuckinChrist, what I do? what I do? And then, when the lorry was almost but not yet out of sight and anyone who looked could see, one of the officers stepped over and struck the man with his ferule, the driver downshifted up the mountainside and the scene closed with the drymouthed aftertaste of brutality. Mitchell hopped off himself when the truck turned inland toward one of the cocoa estates and continued on up the glorious coast, its ridges cradling fertile savannas dotted with idyllic farms and groves, hitchhiking to Kingsley's home village and then walking the last quarter mile to Poppi's house. The yard was filled with peasants, standing around, not much given to talk, as if they were waiting to be hired, or addressed. Mitchell said his good mornings and they nodded back expressionlessly. When he knocked on the door the maid answered and grunted, Wait. His wrist, which had been quiet all morning, started to pulse again, like a small engine, and he wasn't thinking properly about what it was he was doing here, come to see the ancient parasitic hulk of a vampire, but here was Kingsley at the door, just who he was, a pea-hearted cunning maniac, frog-eyed and corpulent but still the man he once was, a man of lean and youthful lusts, who had once swallowed three gold coins and then pulled down his pants to shit them out in front of a crowd of cheering workers at a rally of the Mental and Manual Worker's Union, back in the old days, when he was their leader, a flea up the skirts of Britannia and Her Majesty the Queen. Rumors sifted down and filled Kingsley's mad and venal world, and now they had him dabbling in obeah, offering blood sacrifices to monkey gods and holding séances and all manner of foolishness. They made him out to be larger than life when really all he was was a dangerous infant, empowered with urgent infant needs, a full-bodied human shape with unformed, ungerminated but voraciously needy interiors squalling *me, me, me*, not a dreamer like Edison Banks but a burning bottomless hole in a people's culture of existence. He was wearing the same glossy black suit he favored, his collar unbuttoned and his necktie loosened, his swollen feet poked into bedroom slippers, and he was drunk, at least that was the impression he gave.

"You are of no use to me, Mistah Wilson." Mitchell turned his face down and to the side, embarrassed for himself and intimidated by the inhuman authority, the terrorizing force of it, Kingsley so effortlessly communicated with his gaze, and Mitchell's own eyes came to rest on the row of vehicles parked down behind the kitchen, quite a collection of them meaning the house must be full, he had interrupted what didn't take much imagination to think of as a war council, and of the three Rovers on the lot Ballantyne's was among them, he knew its plate numbers by now, but now the numbers clicked in defining revelation and he realized what he should have known all along, that it could only be Ballantyne who picked up and disposed of Sally's daypack off the slopes of Mount Soufrière. Tillman hadn't, Adrian hadn't, nor had he seen it being carried off by any of the cops.

"I have lost patience with you, you see, Mistah Wilson. What I tell you to heed me about de womahn, eh, to get she gone? The bitch fuck you up, bwoy."

Mitchell found the courage to speak, he thought he was going to ask what's happening around here, why are these things happening, what is the fucking point, why is the price so high with the stakes so low, but what came out of his mouth was a question he doubted Kingsley could answer, who had killed the Peace Corps girl?

"That is fah you to say, and you have said, true?"

"Then one last question. Where's your godson, Isaac Knowles?"

"We is a young nation, Mistah Wilson. We are finding our way through darkness."

"Isaac."

"Why you come so long a ways to ask such questions as you youself must answer? *Isaac is wherever you are.* Now, go home to you house and stay," and so he walked back to the coastal road, having now learned that power had its lethal metaphysics, and its treacherous poetry, inviting bloody explication.

He kept on to the north, following the enigma of his instincts. They rumbled through the village of Petit Santé, the village of Coragill, last and least the hamlet of Youlou, end of the road, where the pickup truck he had flagged a ride with backed down to the stony shore and its crew jumped out and began filling the cargo bed with round, wave-polished paving stones. He walked ahead to the cluster of clapboard shanties raised on stilts, built around a packed-dirt common ground centered with a statue of the Virgin Mary to keep off hurricanes, this prevention her local specialty. After Kingsley, he went quickly back to the Darvon-codeine mix, because the pain was greedy, would take the day for itself, and was unique in the way that it boasted its own clear cause, which he knew to be seductive. Behind the houses was a real beach, or the photographic negative of one, with black sand and colorless water, six or seven catboats hauled up beyond the reach of the tide and salt-burnished fishermen cleaning and selling their catch. The glare off the water made him queasy, he walked and felt as though he were bundled up in many layers of clothes. A man stood crotch-deep in the ocean, a style of cap like Robin Hood's on his head, and he wore trousers and a white perma-press shirt in fair shape, as if up here high on the leeward coast people took to the sea whenever the whim so moved them. Mitchell stared amiably at two naked grave-faced boys, one a mulatto with straight hair and an incipient swarthiness there in his Latin or probably mesti-zo blood, both of them had bung navels like grotesque joke penises sticking out from their round bellies, this was the first time in months and months that he wished he had a camera with him to cap-ture this, the boys each supporting one end of reedlike stick and between them, suspended like storybook creatures, a flat-nosed clown-faced parrot fish too blue to be real, and a red hogfish with its cowlick crimson plume arched in gorgeous extravagance from its dor-sal spine. The grace of it nagged him—boys with their fish. Women laughed and moved their hips unconsciously, there were children wanting gum and men at work. There was beauty and peace and way of life and Mitchell found himself experiencing a weird and helpless sense of belonging, he slipped in among the women with their bas-kets and the men with their machetes and began talking to the fisher-men, collecting their data, saying, If we could get you a Honda generator and a freezer box, how many cubic centimeters do you think? suppose a refrigerated truck came once every week? why have none of you taken advantage of the loan program for outboard motors? and he stopped just as abruptly as he had started, turned on his heels and went back to the hamlet's sweetdrink shop and drank a Ju-C, and then another one, and still a third, unable to stop his sud-den thirst, and the proprietor came out from behind the rough-hewn counter of his livelihood to point his visiting dignitary of a white man up into the surrounding peaks and their gravitational pull. Off he marched, sanguine, heedless, across the threshold of the outside world, authoring his own transgressions.

He inhaled the luxuriant sweet fetidness of the humid bush, like smelling one's private attars of putrefaction, an unwholesomely plea-surable question mark here extrapolated into the ecosystem, magni-fied into realm, the not so missing and not so secret ingredient of the nothing-is-replaceable side of life. Time that had been so clumsy and listless now whistled, he forgot about its torturous second hand implanted in his wrist, he quickly passed the last traces and signs of cultivation, the last cassava patch, the last tannia clump and cocoa tree, thinking now here we have an island that's free, no pretension of progress necessary, give me a fucking frontier, however paltry, and a hand-drawn map and watch me go. There was a network of paths and at each junction he chose whatever branch seemed less traveled, saying *at your service* though he had no idea what he meant by that and the land itself was clearly superior to whatever thoughts loped inanely into his head. Within the hour he was smeared in pungent sweat and mud of his own making, he stopped to eat an orange, took another codeine tablet just to be sure he wouldn't have to start talking to his pain, and removed most of his clothes, changing from his chinos into the pair of gym shorts. The path turned straight up, where he thought for some reason it was too soon to go, but in the absence of turnoffs he had no choice and out of the increased difficulty came exhilaration like a fever breaking. Shortly before sundown he walked into a corona of light that was a clearing. A blue wraith of smoke danced above a small cookfire. At your service, he said out loud, now that he had someone to say it to, not that it had any more meaning than before. Three Rastafarians, the local version, were homesteading the meadowy patch, doing what Rastamen do in the wild mountains of their vision, tend a garden of squash and beans and husband a straight-rowed micro-forest of sensamilla, bushy as Christmas trees. All they wore was jockey briefs and looked like bogeymen, like African warriors, like lion men, like personifications of trees, and the piercing sagacity of their bleary unblinking eyes fell one volt short of blessed delusion. They fingered the juju strung around his neck and said welcome, gave him a rusted tin can containing a sharp-smelling herbal grease to rub on his face and body to keep off mosquitoes and jiggers. Darkness herded them together around the campfire, they fed it more fuel and it blazed up beautifully around their cookpot and he sat with them on footstools that were concave blocks of Catherinian mahogany and smoked their ganj with them until the black jungle began to flash with rips and tears and sudden renderings of energy and his brain resonated with the same dynamo throbbing hum of all the countless insects in the world. They shared a bag of coco plums with him and he ate stewed vegetables from a clay bowl, staring at them while they stared back in some telepathic exchange of poor human striving for expansion or dilation into the godly purities. Mitchell felt himself receding back into a cave of disembodiment and far up at the cave's entrance he heard himself say in a low voice, I'm looking for my brother Isaac, and received the answer, He is not among we people, and after that he was vaguely aware of crawling off like a feral dog to one of their thatched lean-tos where he fell asleep to a universe of buck-dancing and saw-boning, drumming and song.

In the morning he awoke to the tympanic thundering of a storm somewhere over the mountains and a headache of such crushing intensity it bowed him with nausea, the pain jetting right out of his wrist into his eyes, he wanted to chew off his odiferous cast, he could feel the break in the metacarpal bone suspended in its egg of fire, see his hand flap lifelessly, something that wasn't his anymore. He took two Darvon and a codeine, choked them down with a swig of water from his bottle, ate a banana to buffer his stomach, and then lay back on his bed of burlap sacking until the torment eased its prohibition against moving on, downgraded to a dull insistent warning addressed to the madness of his resolve. When he rolled out finally under the sky it was misty and gray, early, though he couldn't tell if the sun was up or not, the three Rastas each lay stretched facedown under their lean-tos, their hair in great animal mounds, as if they were big game trophies, beasts taken on safari, waiting to be dressed and mounted. With his left hand he cupped cool water into his face from a galvanized pail, hoisted his pack back onto his shoulders, and continued walking. More than ever he wondered now if he was all right, mentally, if he was still among the sane. Only a few hundred yards ahead was the summit of the mountain and when he stood on it, the wet wind chilling his skin, it was possible to see Soufrière, the verdant trapezoid of her hips dominating the southern vista, her peak hidden in a wrath of purpled scouring clouds, and out before him from the ship's prow of the rock where he was, the view of the interior had a deceptive magnitude, the surrounding mountains of the north stacked undulant one after another, higher and higher until they disappeared, like runaway slaves, into an ancestral homeland of clouds. He began his descent, the jungle more welcoming then ever, puckered and pleated with refracted light, like a descent toward the bottom of a suffocatingly green, green sea. He talked to himself, nothing he ever would have wanted anyone to overhear, asking himself where had the strength come from, the earth-moving force at his center that made it possible to carry Sally down off the mountain, the transforming blast of lucidity that mastered his panic, silencing the sudden writhing ball of gibberish that choked his throat—this was the miserable consolation of Sally's dying—he had known exactly what he had to do, in a split second he had known everything of significance about himself, the world ruptured and then by his own act of will sealed back together again in perfect order, Here is your trial, here is what you do, this is how you save her, carry her, talk to her, tell her it's all right because it is all right, tell her when she says she doesn't want to die that she isn't dying, because she isn't dying, he had focused with such fine and determined precision on life and living, he had performed with all possible expediency, everything he had done had made profound sense, and she shouldn't have died, as long as they remained connected by such clarity of purpose, clarity all but divine for the strength it gave him, she was the only one in the world and he was carrying her to safety until he wrecked the Land Rover which splintered his concentration into a thousand hopeless pieces and it was like dropping her, she was vulnerable then and he could not pick her back up and then it was out of his hands, the clarity went from positive to negative, and its new subject was Johnnie, within whom danger and desire were inseparable.

He lost his footing on a slick moss-covered rock and somersaulted into the soft dirt of the trail, his cast landing in a reddish sludge.

He asked himself, How many times did this Collymore fire?

He asked himself, What was he wearing? Okay then, what colors, name a color. You don't know the first thing about it, he told himself, and then he told himself, The hell you don't.

He took the opportunity to eat more painkillers and then picked himself up and continued on, almost down, the land bottoming out into a clotted valley, he came to a stream running fast with milky water, took off his shorts and socks and boots and lay down in the flesh-gripping shock of the flow, his right arm in the air like a salute to folly, making up a melody to sing something Johnnie had read him from the Richard Hughes book, something about the bouncing limerick jazz of the lines attracting him so that he committed them to memory the following morning as he drank his basil tea:

> *Quacko Sam*
> *Him bery fine man:*
> *Him dance all de dances dat de darkies can:*
> *Him dance de schottische, him dance de Cod Reel:*
> *Him dance ebery kind of dance till him foot-bottom peel.*

Now he knew a song.

Keep going, he told himself, and put what little he was wearing back on, no point in waiting around to dry off. The trees here ran a carnival of monkeys and birds, once he saw a manicou waddling into the underbrush ahead of him, there were wild boars back in this part of the island, hound-slashing tusks and a blood-curdling charge, or so he had heard; he wanted to see one, he wanted to see something big and awe-inspiring, an elephant would be asking too much but something at least the size of a horse.

He thought, I am here up the bumhole of nowhere because I think if I was anywhere else what I'd want to do to feel better is to kill somebody, he could see how that can come to be the one and only right thing to do, and that was the current rationale for being here and not there. Try as he might—and he was giving up on it—he could not make Sally's death meaningful or transcendent, couldn't offer it anything but pointlessness or deliver it unto a place of rest, so, *good-bye, Sally. Sally, good-bye*, but if ghosts were this facilely excisable from the emotional vocabulary and identity of the living then a forgotten ex-colony of drifting wretches like St. Catherine would be a fucking St. Tropez, and either you were a tinderbox of murderous rages or a clutter of empty flesh grazing complacently upon the resources or you were submerged in sorrow and mourning and bereavement and too bad for you. Whatever it was he was leaving out he had lost hold of, maybe only temporarily, maybe forever, but he had not lost a sense of its importance.

The steamy heat and subsurface closeness of air and his own sick blood were making him weak in the knees but the trail here through level terrain was embanked with dense and matted vegetation, doorless, you could cut a niche into it but to what purpose, he could sit down in the middle of the path with his butt in the muck or just take five on his feet, but he kept on going, some minutes later he thought or imagined he heard drumming in the distance and the animating force of its rhythm cheered him, it brought hope, he remembered the bloodstained map and expected to come upon a camp meeting, a ceremony, he wanted to dance and beat the drums himself, be baptized into any religion that would encourage him to lose control, have a clan of elders assign him the procreative duty of a wife, he wanted to be initiated into the mysteries of manhood, paint his body with the colors of virtue and bravery, and live proudly among human beings.

Because the smell of the jungle was one thing, a single sluggish atmosphere, it readily communicated all adulteration—he smelled wood smoke long before he arrived at its source but not before the drums, real or otherwise, muffled into silence, as if they were being carried off into the spongy distance, and he began hearing instead a sound like a bat hitting a ball, a solid authoritative recurring slap—*thock . . . thock . . . thock . . . thock*—and he kept walking toward the sharp, familiar beat of these home runs through the sinking green darkness until the jungle towered again and gave the illusion of opening up, an organic cathedral, many-chambered, the mosaic of its ceilings excessively pillared, halled with expansive naves and pocketed with alcoves, echoless chapels, a maze of overgrown aisles. Then he heard a second, fuller, more complete rhythm, a soft wheezing respiration, lulling, lispy with succulence, the forest itself breathing out its life, and he followed the sibilant rise and fall of this unexpected engine, the pungency of incense increasing as he tramped ahead, through one bower after another, until under a soaring dome of foliation he found himself among the woodcutters.

They were a crew of six, divided into teams of two; one team alternating strokes, bringing down a column; the second team straddling a fallen giant, their torsos rocking over its girth, a lyre-shaped handsaw between them, their synchronized motion like a swaying prayer. The last team was housed in a bamboo construction, like a sketched diagram of a cube, the joints lashed with hemp, one man atop the scaffolding, one man down within its box, up to his waist in a pit, and on a diagonal between them, hoisted and secured, a massive log, one side sliced flat to reveal a pink face, and each man held with both hands the wooden pin of a handle at opposite ends of a long rusty blade of saw, the fangs of its crosscut teeth wheezing out another rough-cut board as one man's limbs extended while the other's contracted, heave and ho, see and saw. The clearing was flaked and powdered with fresh wood, coconut husks burned like smoldering bombs to ward off mosquitoes, and at the back end of the grove the crew had fashioned themselves a makeshift open-sided quarters with bamboo, their hand-hewn planks, and a squalid wrap of plastic sheeting. As if someone had pulled the plug on the scene, they froze in concert and in position when they became aware of the fact that Mitchell had penetrated the immense and isolated sufficiency of their world.

You're Ballantyne's men, he said with a strange smile of enthusiasm. They nodded, grunted, daht's right, yes sah, this was all the protocol they required to justify a white man's appearance among them. For a moment more they watched him to see what needs he might present them with, and with none forthcoming, each pair of men reanimated, back to work, solemn and methodic and with the graceful dignity of men who labor honestly and skillfully against the hardships brought by life. He was no imposition, his requirements were not an issue, he thought he had never in his life heard a sound more soothing and intimate than the snoring push and pull of their saws. No one objected when he sat down on a stump to overtly admire their industry. The stalwartness of their bodies and their strength made him glad. Veins wrapped around the muscles in their arms like garter snakes. He applauded the flex and nimble accuracy of their strokes. The greenness darkened further and it began to rain, or so their ears told them, but it did not rain like it rained in the outside world, instead it leaked and seeped and dripped, silvery globules rolled, caromed, zigzagged leaf to leaf, down through the foliage, fattening themselves. The worst of downpours seemed like water fissuring down through the decks, catastrophic squirts and sprays, into the bilge of a mighty vessel, but this was not such a rain and the woodcutters kept on working. Mitchell groaned and a man responded Sah? and that was the end of the exchange, but he took the last of the Darvon and with loving but near-hallucinatory conviction addressed the economic integrity of their efforts and how they might best achieve the maximum benefits from their enterprise. Ballantyne does see to it, one of the choppers answered, and for some reason that soured him on further consultation. He gave them a chain saw and then took it away before they mashed it up. He gave them a chain saw and watched them reduce the forest to Death Valley. He made them wealthy men and—he censored himself, which for the moment seemed to be the one defining difference between himself and God.

He was peppered with bites and stings but the medication inured him to the torture that a clearer mind would know. From the elbow down, his right arm was another life he once led, now dead and decomposing in its awful coffin. At dusk they retired to the shelter, built a fire, sat on logs, and drank strong rum. They sang songs and told tales and Mitchell tried without success to commit what they sang and said to memory. They baked sweet potatoes in the flames and cracked them open like pies and wolfed them down, burning their tongues. He asked where was Isaac and they said, *Not here.* They didn't know who he was talking about. Before they all passed out a demon runner stumbled huffing and breathless into camp, a messenger sent by the forest ranger Ballantyne. *Get out, Get out,* he shouted into the face of Mitchell's stupefaction. *Go, Go.* All Mitchell could think was, Where the fuck did he come from, what's this stunt? The man sat down, his lungs heaving, slugging from the plastic jug of rum, waiting for Mitchell to move, his eyes flickering with the firelight of righteous determination. It seemed that soldiers were coming up the trail and the fellow didn't want the white man there when they arrived. He stood up and shook Mitchell by the shoulders, with no effect, walked out of the light and then came back with a cutlass and before anyone knew what was happening, whacked him along the collarbone with the flat of the blade, and then again, and then once more, and finally Mitchell grabbed his pack off the dirt and sprang to his feet, bolting in the direction where he hoped he would find the trail onward into roadless, unmapped heart of the north but in a few minutes he was hopelessly ensnared in a shredding tangle of darkness, the only light a form of heat lightning that was his fear, he could not see any part of himself, not even the pale plaster worm slowly consuming him, the night so implacably, intractably black, and he a most integral part of its blackness, its darkest spirit, his eyes opened the same as his eyes closed, and there he remained in the clutch of nonexistence until first light, when he unraveled himself from hell and found the eastward trail and ran, running through the mists of morning, if he hadn't appreciated the danger why was there the pure dread weight of a pistol clapping the center of his back with every footfall, running like Ballantyne ran from danger though forever monitoring it, running but simultaneously crashing forward toward it, uncertain of the distinction between danger and desire, running and running, and Isaac in his head and heart advising, when danger approaches sing to it, but Kingsley was correct, now he understood, Isaac would be found wherever Mitchell was, not on any map but somewhere within a moral atlas, his very existence had diffused back into the wild land, Mitchell saw the sense of that now and snapped wide awake from his storybook dream of rescue, and then, trudging around a bend in the trail the forest opened up to a grassy clearing where two paths intersected and there was Godfred Ballantyne, sweated through his khaki work clothes, posed on a rock and waiting for him, having dashed up from the windward side to avoid the sudden troublesome increase of traffic on the leeward route.

"Come," said Ballantyne, the man who trained for such days as this. He hopped away from his perch, his muscles bulging, and started walking toward the northward branch of the intersecting trail, confident the white man would follow him to the safety he was there to provide, but Mitchell dragged his heavy feet and stopped and, with no other choice, Ballantyne stopped too and turned with a questioning look of impatience, putting his hands on his hips: he would listen, but then they must hurry.

"Where's the path go?"

"It come down beside Retreat."

"And this way?" Mitchell wondered, pointing to its steep traverse south.

"Up Soufrière."

He wanted to know how far it was from Retreat to the cone of Soufrière and Ballantyne's carved lips formed a trace of smile. It came out about the same, he answered cryptically. About the same. Meaning, the same distance as from the trailhead at the windward access with which Mitchell was familiar.

"So somebody can run up from Retreat in the same time it takes to get up from windward."

Ballantyne feigned a look of introspection. "Maybe."

"But maybe not, right?"

"Maybe not," he agreed, and clapped his hands to end the game. "Come, Wilson, lehwe go."

Mitchell shifted his feet indecisively, thinking to himself, Ballantyne is not decent, something he should have figured out before now, and instead of following him he went over to the same rock Ballantyne had vacated and sat down on its lichened cusp, easing his knapsack off his shoulders to hold in his lap. He wasn't angry, he was only downhearted and solitary, and when he asked Ballantyne to tell him what had been in Sally's backpack that was so inexcusable it had cost her life, he softened the words with regret, he asked as if he knew he was asking too much, and Ballantyne seemed to accept the legitimacy of the question, but he would not deign to answer it, not, at any rate, forthrightly.

"You tell me," he said, planting his legs as if to brace himself for what they were now going to say or do to one another.

"It would have to be drugs," said Mitchell. He moved his head slowly, straining, trying to work out a crick in his neck. "It would have to be money. Drugs and money, drugs or money. Right?"

"Dis drug dem does cy-all cocaine," Ballantyne agreed, his black eyes expressionless and his face a mask. "Some money as well."

"To finance I don't know who. Ghosts." He grinned with pain, grievously amused. "I'm supposed to be what, CIA or something? This is pretty fucking wild, Ballantyne, for a guy like me."

"Lehwe mek dem fail twice, Wilson. Come, mahn," he cajoled, his temper shortening. He gestured back over his shoulder. "Down de trail."

With a clumsy motion Mitchell unzipped his pack, offering Ballantyne an orange but Ballantyne refused to respond, and Mitchell kept his left hand inside the pack, wrapped around the worthless gun, feeling the adrenaline jet through his veins. His thoughts raced out of control—what was this trick with the orange? what was he trying to pull?—and he trembled, watching Ballantyne watch him change, Ballantyne narrowing his eyes, swelling alert. The sun broke out momentarily, causing Mitchell to blink white flashes, crimson and crystal birds, depositing a kind of flat pain in his head, eroding down through his arms.

"Get up, mahn."

"Did you kill her?" He heard himself grunt the unreal words between his teeth, his jaw clenched to prevent their chattering. He heard a peal of artificial laughter escaping his throat.

Ballantyne turned supercilious, he stood there sizing Mitchell up, saying he was going to tell him the truth, "If I shoot somebody, nuh? it is you—*you, Wilson*—I shoot," people like that woman get killed, he said, because of people like *you.*

"All right. All right. I get it." His voice was panicky but he was shouting, he had been shivering but now he had the gun out and it was steady in his hand, he had at least the satisfaction of Ballantyne's dumbstruck look, at least he knew he could take it this far if there was no other recourse. He wanted Ballantyne to drop his haversack on the ground and step away from it and when Ballantyne hesitated Mitchell said he was sorry but do it now or he would shoot him in the fucking face. Ballantyne shrugged with scorn and did it. Mitchell squatted and picked up the frayed leather case by its strap, he had gotten this far and he was not afraid but he still could not span the psychic distance between his empty pistol and the loaded one Ballantyne never was without in his haversack, he wasn't prepared to go that far, to be honest he wasn't even prepared to go as far as he had already, and he didn't know where it would end but it was not going to end here, with one of them on the ground, dying.

"How good of a shot are you anyway? Pretty good, huh?"

"Not so bahd," Ballantyne said. He made a mean smile and shook his head with disbelief.

"You wouldn't miss, would you?" he asked, and when Ballantyne would not admit this, Mitchell asked again, who killed the woman.

"Daht mahd bwoy." That mad boy. The mad boy. Mad.

Mitchell looked down at his gun, turning it side to side, marveling, it could have been a fish, something absurd, any alien object in its strangeness, and he wondered how in the world he was ever going to get it out of his hand.

"I think this guy Ibrahim only fired once . . ." he said, but without conviction and his voice trailed, his memory not helping him out on this. "I don't know. The sound was different, man. Something was different."

"Once is enough," said Ballantyne.

He had more questions, he would always have more questions, but the world spun in both directions, here on the island of contradiction, both directions at once, backward and forward, self-opposed and irreconcilable and, finally, irrecoverable. Gunfire crackled in a businesslike volley through the distance from the camp he had left behind and he said to Ballantyne, Those are your men, aren't they? but Ballantyne sucked his teeth and answered, No, mahn, no no no, Wilson, how you so foolish, bwoy, *those men are yours,* and with that he spun away, he would have nothing more to do with Mitchell Wilson, he could do as he pleased, he could go stand beside the bodies of the Rastamen, festooned with belts of ammunition, and have his picture taken, he could go sit in a cell in Fort Gregory and tell any story that came to mind but he, Ballantyne, was moving off down the trail to Retreat, he was getting in his Rover and going home and firing back a strong rum, he'd listen to the story of Mitchell's capture on the radio but this would not be the end of it for either of them, he vowed, and though Mitchell took a step to follow Godfred Ballantyne, he stopped to consider where he was, which was also as far as he could ever go, a jack spanier flew into his mouth and stung its way out, laying a lava-hot track of pain on his tongue, he lowered the gun and watched the forest ranger swallowed up in the bush, and then he pitched it deep into the jungle, and went back, to finally rendezvous with his missing friend Isaac, but Isaac wasn't there, and Mitchell Wilson was.

The course of fate runs strong and straight through most of history. At the beginning of every tragedy, the elements are all in place; they only need time to combine into disaster or chaos or stalemate, or all three. But add good intentions, and fate gets more imaginative.

JULIAN EVANS

Tomorrow, the new government assured him, and this time they meant it. He had been given clemency, he would be their first official act of mercy, bestowed in the aura of their triumph. Something worked out back channel; his story wasn't even reported in the *Herald*.

The beleaguered Kingsley and the PIP had appealed to both the hemispheric and traditional guardians of democracy, citing certain obvious and hair-raising threats to liberty, and the guardians success-fully pressured the coalition government of St. Catherine, led by Edison Banks, to call for new elections. Even Fidel Castro thought it was a good idea, convinced that, in this historic instance, a popular vote would validate the wave of revolution washing over the island, as it recently had, though less conclusively, in Jamaica. After vehement resistance to the idea, Banks and his People's Revolutionary Party, nearsighted with hubris and perhaps, it could be argued, myopic with ideals, agreed. The ensuing campaigns were lively, impassioned, both sides unrestrained in their public displays of nationalism, blood was shed, but not excessively. Thanks to the ill-considered gerrymander-ing conducted during the spring by the former PEP, which dispersed their opponents' seed in a wider radius than seemed possible at the time, the PIP won, the Honorable Joshua Kingsley was named, for a second time, prime minister; the formerly discredited Pepper was recalled from New York and given the agricultural portfolio, Castro learned a memorable lesson about encouraging elections in the region, and Maurice Bishop and the New Jewel Movement of Grenada issued a statement declaring they had closely followed the downturn of events in St. Catherine and were forced to conclude that the PEAS was a failed experiment at sensible governance, and as such the NJM would forgo coalition-building—this two-headed beast—in favor of one-party rule, to be installed commensurate with the over-throw of the madman Sir Eric Gairy.

Not exactly front-page headlines in the United States or Britain, but news nevertheless. Of Edison Banks, it would always be said that he had meant well.

Throughout the months it took for Kingsley and the PIP to orchestrate its victory, Mitchell Wilson would wake in his cell, asking himself where he was, asking himself, had he been a child all this time, out there? They refused to allow him visitors until they discovered him crippled with dysentery, spraying blood out of his rectum into the bucket in his cell. After that, it was Josephine who brought him food, who kept him connected (although once he entertained a local group called the Volunteers for Human Rights, who hinted at an immediate end to his misfortune if he would sign, not a confession, but an apology).

Josephine was the most loyal and objective of messengers, bearing the news she knew would most inform him.

Your friend Tillman tried to see you, ya know, before he left, she said. Rosehill close down. He say, find him in Cambridge. He is there studying an MBA.

Josephine told him, Saconi gone to England.

She arrived flustered one day, set down her basket of bread and fried fish, and told him, Adrian does tell me to tell you something.

Adrian tell me tell you, this woman Johnnie you living with? she in Panama, nuh? Well, Mitch, she is pregnant, Adrian does hear from a letter that reach, I believe she having an abortion.

From Josephine he learned the news that Ballantyne had been murdered, in his own bed, but first his testicles had been cut off and shoved down the throat of his wife, whose mouth was held shut by her husband's assassins, until she swallowed them.

One day, before Adrian had been replaced by a Cuban volunteer and sent home, Josephine said, Adrian tell me not to forget: a girl named Jolene stop by the school, saying her husband gone away, she carrying a sick sick child in she arms and she leave him by Adrian, bawling, Take him, help him. She take him, nuh? Mitch, one more child to save.

That was one thing about expats, he remembered a friend of golf telling him, *the journalists, the volunteers, the specialists, the careerists, the opportunists, even the wandering jews: Everybody found a kid they wanted to help.* This had been Ben talking, an inference he was making about decency, the complications thereof. Ben, the poet.

That, said Ben, *was how it started.*

Acknowledgments

The act of writing a novel, no matter how solitary the process seems, is simultaneously the act of creating communities—one fictional, of course, but another quite real. The act of finishing a book, this book, is also a long-awaited opportunity to say thanks to the leading citizens of that vital, blessedly real group, the extended family of *Swimming in the Volcano:*

First, always, to Miss F.

To Gail Hochman and Barbara Grossman.

To Alice Turner, Theresa Grosch, Bruce Weber, Tom Jenks, Diane Roberts, Nan Graham.

To Jack Leggett, Tay Maltsberger, Dave Smith, Brian Dyson, Gary and Cindy Rich, Carol Ann Koch-Weser, Bob, Brian, Lynette, and Robert Antoni, Barbara Davis, Joy Smith, Marianne Merola, John and Cheryl Andrews, Helen and Shack, Michael Malone, Don Hendrie, Jr., Maxine and Jerry Stern, Connie Nelson, John Parker, Kathy Bradt, Pete Ripley, Bill Vinyard, Ross Anderson, Pat Mitchell, Bill Armstrong, Barry Hannah, Bill Peden, Charlie and Tammy Oberbeck, and Steve Brumfield.

To two of the language's finest poets, Andrew Hudgins and Heather McHugh, of whose work a half-dozen lines appear in this text. And to Richard Powers, one of the best novelists of my generation, who coined the phrase *global pillage.*

To Maurice Bishop, a man of good intentions.